THE
FOUNDATION TRILOGY

Three Classics of Science Fiction

By ISAAC ASIMOV

FOUNDATION
FOUNDATION AND EMPIRE
SECOND FOUNDATION

AVON
PUBLISHERS OF BARD, CAMELOT, DISCUS AND FLARE BOOKS

AVON BOOKS
A division of
The Hearst Corporation
959 Eighth Avenue
New York, New York 10019

First Avon Printing, November, 1974

FOUNDATION

To My Mother

Of Whose Authentic Gray Hairs
Not a Few Were Caused by Myself

Contents

PART I   *THE PSYCHOHISTORIANS*   1

PART II   *THE ENCYCLOPEDISTS*   37

PART III   *THE MAYORS*   77

PART IV   *THE TRADERS*   133

PART V   *THE MERCHANT PRINCES*   157

PART I

THE PSYCHOHISTORIANS

1.

HARI SELDON—... born in the 11,988th year of the Galactic Era; died 12,069. The dates are more commonly given in terms of the current Foundational Era as –79 to the year 1 F.E. Born to middle-class parents on Helicon, Arcturus sector (where his father, in a legend of doubtful authenticity, was a tobacco grower in the hydroponic plants of the planet), he early showed amazing ability in mathematics. Anecdotes concerning his ability are innumerable, and some are contradictory. At the age of two, he is said to have ...

... Undoubtedly his greatest contributions were in the field of psychohistory. Seldon found the field little more than a set of vague axioms; he left it a profound statistical science. ...

... The best existing authority we have for the details of his life is the biography written by Gaal Dornick who, as a young man, met Seldon two years before the great mathematician's death. The story of the meeting ...

ENCYCLOPEDIA GALACTICA[*]

His name was Gaal Dornick and he was just a country boy who had never seen Trantor before. That is, not in real life. He *had* seen it many times on the hyper-video, and occasionally in tremendous three-dimensional newscasts covering an Imperial Coronation or the opening of a Galactic Council. Even though he had lived all his life on the world of Synnax, which circled a star at the edges of the Blue Drift, he was not cut off from civilization, you see. At that time, no place in the Galaxy was.

There were nearly twenty-five million inhabited planets

* All quotations from the Encyclopedia Galactica here reproduced are taken from the 116th Edition published in 1020 F.E. by the Encyclopedia Galactica Publishing Co., Terminus, with permission of the publishers.

in the Galaxy then, and not one but owed allegiance to the Empire whose seat was on Trantor. It was the last half-century in which that could be said.

To Gaal, this trip was the undoubted climax of his young, scholarly life. He had been in space before so that the trip, as a voyage and nothing more, meant little to him. To be sure, he had travelled previously only as far as Synnax's only satellite in order to get the data on the mechanics of meteor driftage which he needed for his dissertation, but space-travel was all one whether one travelled half a million miles, or as many light years.

He had steeled himself just a little for the Jump through hyper-space, a phenomenon one did not experience in simple interplanetary trips. The Jump remained, and would probably remain forever, the only practical method of travelling between the stars. Travel through ordinary space could proceed at no rate more rapid than that of ordinary light, (a bit of scientific knowledge that belonged among the few items known since the forgotten dawn of human history), and that would have meant years of travel between even the nearest of inhabited systems. Through hyper-space, that unimaginable region that was neither space nor time, matter nor energy, something nor nothing, one could traverse the length of the Galaxy in the interval between two neighboring instants of time.

Gaal had waited for the first of those Jumps with a little dread curled gently in his stomach, and it ended in nothing more than a trifling jar, a little internal kick which ceased an instant before he could be sure he had felt it. That was all.

And after that, there was only the ship, large and glistening; the cool production of 12,000 years of Imperial progress; and himself, with his doctorate in mathematics freshly obtained and an invitation from the great Hari Seldon to come to Trantor and join the vast and somewhat mysterious Seldon Project.

What Gaal was waiting for after the disappointment of the Jump was that first sight of Trantor. He haunted the View-room. The steel shutter-lids were rolled back at announced times and he was always there, watching the hard brilliance of the stars, enjoying the incredible hazy swarm of a star cluster, like a giant conglomeration of fire-flies caught in mid-motion and stilled forever. At one time there was the cold, blue-white smoke of a gaseous nebula within five light years of the ship, spreading over the window like distant milk, filling the room with an icy tinge, and disappearing out of sight two hours later, after another Jump.

The first sight of Trantor's sun was that of a hard, white speck all but lost in a myriad such, and recognizable only because it was pointed out by the ship's guide. The stars were thick here at the Galactic center. But with each Jump, it shone more brightly, drowning out the rest, paling them and thinning them out.

An officer came through and said, "View-room will be closed for the remainder of the trip. Prepare for landing."

Gaal had followed after, clutching at the sleeve of the white uniform with the Spaceship-and-Sun of the Empire on it.

He said, "Would it be possible to let me stay? I would like to see Trantor."

The officer smiled and Gaal flushed a bit. It occurred to him that he spoke with a provincial accent.

The officer said, "We'll be landing on Trantor by morning."

"I mean I want to see it from Space."

"Oh. Sorry, my boy. If this were a space-yacht we might manage it. But we're spinning down, sunside. You wouldn't want to be blinded, burnt, and radiation-scarred all at the same time, would you?"

Gaal started to walk away.

The officer called after him, "Trantor would only be gray blur anyway, Kid. Why don't you take a space-tour once you hit Trantor. They're cheap."

Gaal looked back, "Thank you very much."

It was childish to feel disappointed, but childishness comes almost as naturally to a man as to a child, and there was a lump in Gaal's throat. He had never seen Trantor spread out in all its incredibility, as large as life, and he hadn't expected to have to wait longer.

2.

The ship landed in a medley of noises. There was the far-off hiss of the atmosphere cutting and sliding past the metal of the ship. There was the steady drone of the conditioners fighting the heat of friction, and the slower rumble of the engines enforcing deceleration. There was the human sound of men and women gathering in the debarkation rooms and the grind of the hoists lifting baggage, mail, and freight to the long axis of the ship, from which they would be later moved along to the unloading platform.

Gaal felt the slight jar that indicated the ship no longer had an independent motion of its own. Ship's gravity had been giving way to planetary gravity for hours. Thousands of passengers had been sitting patiently in the debarkation rooms which swung easily on yielding force-fields to accommodate its orientation to the changing direction of the gravitational forces. Now they were crawling down curving ramps to the large, yawning locks.

Gaal's baggage was minor. He stood at a desk, as it was quickly and expertly taken apart and put together again. His visa was inspected and stamped. He himself paid no attention.

This was Trantor! The air seemed a little thicker here, the gravity a bit greater, than on his home planet of Synnax, but he would get used to that. He wondered if he would get used to immensity.

Debarkation Building was tremendous. The roof was almost lost in the heights. Gaal could almost imagine that clouds could form beneath its immensity. He could see no opposite wall; just men and desks and converging floor till it faded out in haze.

The man at the desk was speaking again. He sounded annoyed. He said, "Move on, Dornick." He had to open the visa, look again, before he remembered the name.

Gaal said, "Where—where—"

The man at the desk jerked a thumb, "Taxis to the right and third left."

Gaal moved, seeing the glowing twists of air suspended high in nothingness and reading, "TAXIS TO ALL POINTS."

A figure detached itself from anonymity and stopped at the desk, as Gaal left. The man at the desk looked up and nodded briefly. The figure nodded in return and followed the young immigrant.

He was in time to hear Gaal's destination.

Gaal found himself hard against a railing.

The small sign said, "Supervisor." The man to whom the sign referred did not look up. He said, "Where to?"

Gaal wasn't sure, but even a few seconds hesitation meant men queuing in line behind him.

The Supervisor looked up, "Where to?"

Gaal's funds were low, but there was only this one night and then he would have a job. He tried to sound nonchalant, "A good hotel, please."

The Supervisor was unimpressed, "They're all good. Name one."

Gaal said, desperately, "The nearest one, please."

The Supervisor touched a button. A thin line of light formed along the floor, twisting among others which brightened and dimmed in different colors and shades. A ticket was shoved into Gaal's hands. It glowed faintly.

The Supervisor said, "One point twelve."

Gaal fumbled for the coins. He said, "Where do I go?"

"Follow the light. The ticket will keep glowing as long
as you're pointed in the right direction."

Gaal looked up and began walking. There were hundreds
creeping across the vast floor, following their individual trails,
sifting and straining themselves through intersection points
to arrive at their respective destinations.

His own trail ended. A man in glaring blue and yellow
uniform, shining and new in unstainable plasto-textile,
reached for his two bags.

"Direct line to the Luxor," he said.

The man who followed Gaal heard that. He also heard
Gaal say, "Fine," and watched him enter the blunt-nosed
vehicle.

The taxi lifted straight up. Gaal stared out the curved,
transparent window, marvelling at the sensation of airflight
within an enclosed structure and clutching instinctively at
the back of the driver's seat. The vastness contracted and
the people became ants in random distribution. The scene
contracted further and began to slide backward.

There was a wall ahead. It began high in the air and extended upward out of sight. It was riddled with holes that
were the mouths of tunnels. Gaal's taxi moved toward one
then plunged into it. For a moment, Gaal wondered idly how
his driver could pick out one among so many.

There was now only blackness, with nothing but the past-
flashing of a colored signal light to relieve the gloom. The
air was full of a rushing sound.

Gaal leaned forward against deceleration then and the
taxi popped out of the tunnel and descended to ground-level
once more.

"The Luxor Hotel," said the driver, unnecessarily. He
helped Gaal with his baggage, accepted a tenth-credit tip
with a businesslike air, picked up a waiting passenger, and
was rising again.

In all this, from the moment of debarkation, there had
been no glimpse of sky.

3

TRANTOR— . . . At the beginning of the thirteenth millennium, this tendency reached its climax. As the center of the Imperial Government for unbroken hundreds of generations and located, as it was, in the central regions of the Galaxy among the most densely populated and industrially advanced worlds of the system, it could scarcely help being the densest and richest clot of humanity the Race had ever seen.

Its urbanization, progressing steadily, had finally reached the ultimate. All the land surface of Trantor, 75,000,000 square miles in extent, was a single city. The population, at its height, was well in excess of forty billions. This enormous population was devoted almost entirely to the administrative necessities of Empire, and found themselves all too few for the complications of the task. (It is to be remembered that the impossibility of proper administration of the Galactic Empire under the uninspired leadership of the later Emperors was a considerable factor in the Fall.) Daily, fleets of ships in the tens of thousands brought the produce of twenty agricultural worlds to the dinner tables of Trantor. . . .

Its dependence upon the outer worlds for food and, indeed, for all necessities of life, made Trantor increasingly vulnerable to conquest by siege. In the last millennium of the Empire, the monotonously numerous revolts made Emperor after Emperor conscious of this, and Imperial policy became little more than the protection of Trantor's delicate jugular vein. . . .

ENCYCLOPEDIA GALACTICA

Gaal was not certain whether the sun shone, or, for that matter, whether it was day or night. He was ashamed to ask. All the planet seemed to live beneath metal. The meal of which he had just partaken had been labelled luncheon, but there were many planets which lived a standard time-scale that took no account of the perhaps inconvenient alternation of day and night. The rate of planetary turnings differed, and he did not know that of Trantor.

At first, he had eagerly followed the signs to the "Sun Room" and found it but a chamber for basking in artificial radiation. He lingered a moment or two, then returned to the Luxor's main lobby.

He said to the room clerk, "Where can I buy a ticket for a planetary tour?"

"Right here."

"When will it start?"

"You just missed it. Another one tomorrow. Buy a ticket now and we'll reserve a place for you."

"Oh." Tomorrow would be too late. He would have to be at the University tomorrow. He said, "There wouldn't be an observation tower—or something? I mean, in the open air."

"Sure! Sell you a ticket for that, if you want. Better let me check if it's raining or not." He closed a contact at his elbow and read the flowing letters that raced across a frosted screen. Gaal read with him.

The room clerk said, "Good weather. Come to think of it, I do believe it's the dry season now." He added, conversationally, "I don't bother with the outside myself. The last time I was in the open was three years ago. You see it once, you know and that's all there is to it. —Here's your ticket. Special elevator in the rear. It's marked 'To the Tower.' Just take it."

The elevator was of the new sort that ran by gravitic repulsion. Gaal entered and others flowed in behind him. The operator closed a contact. For a moment, Gaal felt suspended in space as gravity switched to zero, and then he had weight again in small measure as the elevator accelerated upward. Deceleration followed and his feet left the floor. He squawked against his will.

The operator called out, "Tuck your feet under the railing. Can't you read the sign?"

The others had done so. They were smiling at him as he madly and vainly tried to clamber back down the wall. Their shoes pressed upward against the chromium of the railings that stretched across the floor in parallels set two feet apart. He had noticed those railings on entering and had ignored them.

Then a hand reached out and pulled him down.

He gasped his thanks as the elevator came to a halt.

He stepped out upon an open terrace bathed in a white brilliance that hurt his eyes. The man, whose helping hand he had just now been the recipient of, was immediately behind him.

The man said, kindly, "Plenty of seats."

Gaal closed his mouth; he had been gaping; and said, "It certainly seems so." He started for them automatically, then stopped.

He said, "If you don't mind, I'll just stop a moment at the railing. I—I want to look a bit."

The man waved him on, good-naturedly, and Gaal leaned out over the shoulder-high railing and bathed himself in all the panorama.

He could not see the ground. It was lost in the ever increasing complexities of man-made structures. He could see no horizon other than that of metal against sky, stretching out to almost uniform grayness, and he knew it was so over all the land-surface of the planet. There was scarcely any motion to be seen—a few pleasure-craft lazed against the sky —but all the busy traffic of billions of men were going on, he knew, beneath the metal skin of the world.

There was no green to be seen; no green, no soil, no life other than man. Somewhere on the world, he realized vaguely, was the Emperor's palace, set amid one hundred square miles of natural soil, green with trees, rainbowed with flowers. It was a small island amid an ocean of steel, but it wasn't visible from where he stood. It might be ten thousand miles away. He did not know.

Before very long, he must have his tour!

He sighed noisily, and realized finally that he was on Trantor at last; on the planet which was the center of all the Galaxy and the kernel of the human race. He saw none of its weaknesses. He saw no ships of food landing. He was not aware of a jugular vein delicately connecting the forty billion of Trantor with the rest of the Galaxy. He was conscious only of the mightiest deed of man; the complete and almost contemptuously final conquest of a world.

He came away a little blank-eyed. His friend of the elevator was indicating a seat next to himself and Gaal took it.

The man smiled, "My name is Jerril. First time on Trantor?"

"Yes, Mr. Jerril."

"Thought so. Jerril's my first name. Trantor gets you if you've got the poetic temperament. Trantorians never come up here, though. They don't like it. Gives them nerves."

"Nerves!—My name's Gaal, by the way. Why should it give them nerves? It's glorious."

"Subjective matter of opinion, Gaal. If you're born in a cubicle and grow up in a corridor, and work in a cell, and vacation in a crowded sun-room, then coming up into the open with nothing but sky over you might just give you a nervous breakdown. They make the children come up here once a year, after they're five. I don't know if it does any good. They don't get enough of it, really, and the first few times they scream themselves into hysteria. They ought to start as soon as they're weaned and have the trip once a week."

He went on, "Of course, it doesn't really matter. What if they never come out at all? They're happy down there and they run the Empire. How high up do you think we are?"

He said, "Half a mile?" and wondered if that sounded naive.

It must have, for Jerril chuckled a little. He said, "No. Just five hundred feet."

"What? But the elevator took about—"

"I know. But most of the time it was just getting up to ground level. Trantor is tunneled over a mile down. It's like an iceberg. Nine-tenths of it is out of sight. It even works itself out a few miles into what was once the sub-ocean soil at the shorelines. In fact, we're down so low that we can make use of the temperature difference between ground level and a couple of miles under to supply us with all the energy we need. Did you know that?"

"No, I thought you used atomic generators."

"Did once. But this is cheaper."

"I imagine so."

"What do you think of it all?" For a moment, the man's good nature evaporated into shrewdness. He looked almost sly.

Gaal fumbled. "Glorious," he said, again.

"Here on vacation? Traveling? Sight-seeing?"

"Not exactly. —At least, I've always wanted to visit Trantor but I came here primarily for a job."

"Oh?"

Gaal felt obliged to explain further, "With Dr. Seldon's project at the University of Trantor."

"Raven Seldon?"

"Why, no. The one I mean is Hari Seldon. —The psychohistorian Seldon. I don't know of any Raven Seldon."

"Hari's the one I mean. They call him Raven. Slang, you know. He keeps predicting disaster."

"He does?" Gaal was genuinely astonished.

"Surely, you must know." Jerril was not smiling. "You're coming to work for him, aren't you?"

"Well, yes, I'm a mathematician. Why does he predict disaster? What kind of disaster?"

"What kind would you think?"

"I'm afraid I wouldn't have the least idea. I've read the

papers Dr. Seldon and his group have published. They're on mathematical theory."

"Yes, the ones they publish."

Gaal felt annoyed. He said, "I think I'll go to my room now. Very pleased to have met you."

Jerril waved his arm indifferently in farewell.

Gaal found a man waiting for him in his room. For a moment, he was too startled to put into words the inevitable, "What are you doing here?" that came to his lips.

The man rose. He was old and almost bald and he walked with a limp, but his eyes were very bright and blue.

He said, "I am Hari Seldon," an instant before Gaal's befuddled brain placed the face alongside the memory of the many times he had seen it in pictures.

4.

PSYCHOHISTORY— . . . Gaal Dornick, using nonmathematical concepts, has defined psychohistory to be that branch of mathematics which deals with the reactions of human conglomerates to fixed social and economic stimuli. . . .

. . . Implicit in all these definitions is the assumption that the human conglomerate being dealt with is sufficiently large for valid statistical treatment. The necessary size of such a conglomerate may be determined by Seldon's First Theorem which . . . A further necessary assumption is that the human conglomerate be itself unaware of psychohistoric analysis in order that its reactions be truly random. . . .

The basis of all valid psychohistory lies in the development of the Seldon Functions which exhibit properties congruent to those of such social and economic forces as . . .

ENCYCLOPEDIA GALACTICA

"Good afternoon, sir," said Gaal. "I—I—"

"You didn't think we were to meet before tomorrow?

Ordinarily, we would not have. It is just that if we are to use your services, we must work quickly. It grows continually more difficult to obtain recruits."

"I don't understand, sir."

"You were talking to a man on the observation tower, were you not?"

"Yes. His first name is Jerril. I know no more about him."

"His name is nothing. He is an agent of the Commission of Public Safety. He followed you from the space-port."

"But why? I am afraid I am very confused."

"Did the man on the tower say nothing about me?"

Gaal hesitated, "He referred to you as Raven Seldon."

"Did he say why?"

"He said you predict disaster."

"I do. —What does Trantor mean to you?"

Everyone seemed to be asking his opinion of Trantor. Gaal felt incapable of response beyond the bare word, "Glorious."

"You say that without thinking. What of psychohistory?"

"I haven't thought of applying it to the problem."

"Before you are done with me, young man, you will learn to apply psychohistory to all problems as a matter of course. —Observe." Seldon removed his calculator pad from the pouch at his belt. Men said he kept one beneath his pillow for use in moments of wakefulness. Its gray, glossy finish was slightly worn by use. Seldon's nimble fingers, spotted now with age, played along the hard plastic that rimmed it. Red symbols glowed out from the gray.

He said, "That represents the condition of the Empire at present."

He waited.

Gaal said finally, "Surely that is not a complete representation."

"No, not complete," said Seldon. "I am glad you do not accept my word blindly. However, this is an approximation which will serve to demonstrate the proposition. Will you accept that?"

"Subject to my later verification of the derivation of the function, yes." Gaal was carefully avoiding a possible trap.

"Good. Add to this the known probability of Imperial assassination, viceregal revolt, the contemporary recurrence of periods of economic depression, the declining rate of planetary explorations, the . . ."

He proceeded. As each item was mentioned, new symbols sprang to life at his touch, and melted into the basic function which expanded and changed.

Gaal stopped him only once, "I don't see the validity of that set-transformation."

Seldon repeated it more slowly.

Gaal said, "But that is done by way of a forbidden socio-operation."

"Good. You are quick, but not yet quick enough. It is not forbidden in this connection. Let me do it by expansions."

The procedure was much longer and at its end, Gaal said, humbly, "Yes, I see now."

Finally, Seldon stopped. "This is Trantor five centuries from now. How do you interpret that? Eh?" He put his head to one side and waited.

Gaal said, unbelievingly, "Total destruction! But—but that is impossible. Trantor has never been—"

Seldon was filled with the intense excitement of a man whose body only had grown old, "Come, come. You saw how the result was arrived at. Put it into words. Forget the symbolism for a moment."

Gaal said, "As Trantor becomes more specialized, it becomes more vulnerable, less able to defend itself. Further, as it becomes more and more the administrative center of Empire, it becomes a greater prize. As the Imperial succession becomes more and more uncertain, and the feuds among the great families more rampant, social responsibility disappears."

"Enough. And what of the numerical probability of total destruction within five centuries?"

"I couldn't tell."

"Surely you can perform a field-differentiation?"

Gaal felt himself under pressure. He was not offered the calculator pad. It was held a foot from his eyes. He calculated furiously and felt his forehead grow slick with sweat.

He said, "About 85%?"

"Not bad," said Seldon, thrusting out a lower lip, "but not good. The actual figure is 92.5%."

Gaal said, "And so you are called Raven Seldon? I have seen none of this in the journals."

"But of course not. This is unprintable. Do you suppose the Imperium could expose its shakiness in this manner. That is a very simple demonstration in psychohistory. But some of our results have leaked out among the aristocracy."

"That's bad."

"Not necessarily. All is taken into account."

"But is that why I'm being investigated?"

"Yes. Everything about my project is being investigated."

"Are you in danger, sir?"

"Oh, yes. There is probability of 1.7% that I will be executed, but of course that will not stop the project. We have taken that into account as well. Well, never mind. You will meet me, I suppose, at the University tomorrow?"

"I will," said Gaal.

5.

COMMISSION OF PUBLIC SAFETY— . . . The aristocratic coterie rose to power after the assassination of Cleon I, last of the Entuns. In the main, they formed an element of order during the centuries of instability and uncertainty in the Imperium. Usually under the control of the great families of the Chens and the Divarts, it degenerated eventually into a blind instrument for maintenance of the status quo. . . . They were not completely removed as a power in the state until after the accession of the last strong Emperor, Cleon II. The first Chief Commissioner. . . .

*. . . In a way, the beginning of the Commission's decline
can be traced to the trial of Hari Seldon two years before
the beginning of the Foundational Era. That trial is described in Gaal Dornick's biography of Hari Seldon. . . .*

ENCYCLOPEDIA GALACTICA

Gaal did not carry out his promise. He was awakened the
next morning by a muted buzzer. He answered it, and the
voice of the desk clerk, as muted, polite and deprecating as
it well might be, informed him that he was under detention
at the orders of the Commission of Public Safety.

Gaal sprang to the door and found it would no longer
open. He could only dress and wait.

They came for him and took him elsewhere, but it was
still detention. They asked him questions most politely. It
was all very civilized. He explained that he was a provincial of Synnax; that he had attended such and such schools
and obtained a Doctor of Mathematics degree on such and
such a date. He had applied for a position on Dr. Seldon's
staff and had been accepted. Over and over again, he gave
these details; and over and over again, they returned to the
question of his joining the Seldon Project. How had he heard
of it; what were to be his duties; what secret instructions
had he received; what was it all about?

He answered that he did not know. He had no secret instructions. He was a scholar and a mathematician. He had
no interest in politics.

And finally the gentle inquisitor asked, "When will Trantor
be destroyed?"

Gaal faltered, "I could not say of my own knowledge."

"Could you say of anyone's?"

"How could I speak for another?" He felt warm; over-
warm.

The inquisitor said, "Has anyone told you of such destruction; set a date?" And, as the young man hesitated, he
went on, "You have been followed, doctor. We were at the
airport when you arrived; on the observation tower when

you waited for your appointment; and, of course, we were able to overhear your conversation with Dr. Seldon."

Gaal said, "Then you know his views on the matter."

"Perhaps. But we would like to hear them from you."

"He is of the opinion that Trantor would be destroyed within five centuries."

"He proved it,—uh—mathematically?"

"Yes, he did,"—defiantly.

"You maintain the—uh—mathematics to be valid, I suppose."

"If Dr. Seldon vouches for it, it is valid."

"Then we will return."

"Wait. I have a right to a lawyer. I demand my rights as an Imperial citizen."

"You shall have them."

And he did.

It was a tall man that eventually entered, a man whose face seemed all vertical lines and so thin that one could wonder whether there was room for a smile.

Gaal looked up. He felt disheveled and wilted. So much had happened, yet he had been on Trantor not more than thirty hours.

The man said, "I am Lors Avakim. Dr. Seldon has directed me to represent you."

"Is that so? Well, then, look here. I demand an instant appeal to the Emperor. I'm being held without cause. I'm innocent of anything. Of *anything*." He slashed his hands outward, palms down, "You've got to arrange a hearing with the Emperor, instantly."

Avakim was carefully emptying the contents of a flat folder onto the floor. If Gaal had had the stomach for it, he might have recognized Cellomet legal forms, metal thin and tapelike, adapted for insertion within the smallness of a personal capsule. He might also have recognized a pocket recorder.

Avakim, paying no attention to Gaal's outburst, finally

looked up. He said, "The Commission will, of course, have a spy beam on our conversation. This is against the law, but they will use one nevertheless."

Gaal ground his teeth.

"However," and Avakim seated himself deliberately, "the recorder I have on the table,—which is a perfectly ordinary recorder to all appearances and performs it duties well—has the additional property of completely blanketing the spy beam. This is something they will not find out at once."

"Then I can speak."

"Of course."

"Then I want a hearing with the Emperor."

Avakim smiled frostily, and it turned out that there was room for it on his thin face after all. His cheeks wrinkled to make the room. He said, "You are from the provinces."

"I am none the less an Imperial citizen. As good a one as you or as any of this Commission of Public Safety."

"No doubt; no doubt. It is merely that, as a provincial, you do not understand life on Trantor as it is. There are no hearings before the Emperor."

"To whom else would one appeal from this Commission? Is there other procedure?"

"None. There is no recourse in a practical sense. Legalistically, you may appeal to the Emperor, but you would get no hearing. The Emperor today is not the Emperor of an Entun dynasty, you know. Trantor, I am afraid is in the hands of the aristocratic families, members of which compose the Commission of Public Safety. This is a development which is well predicted by psychohistory."

Gaal said, "Indeed? In that case, if Dr. Seldon can predict the history of Trantor five hundred years into the future—"

"He can predict it fifteen hundred years into the future."

"Let it be fifteen thousand. Why couldn't he yesterday have predicted the events of this morning and warned me. —No, I'm sorry." Gaal sat down and rested his head in one sweating palm, "I quite understand that psychohistory is a statistical science and cannot predict the future of a single man with any accuracy. You'll understand that I'm upset."

"But you are wrong. Dr. Seldon was of the opinion that you would be arrested this morning."

"What!"

"It is unfortunate, but true. The Commission has been more and more hostile to his activities. New members joining the group have been interfered with to an increasing extent. The graphs showed that for our purposes, matters might best be brought to a climax now. The Commission of itself was moving somewhat slowly so Dr. Seldon visited you yesterday for the purpose of forcing their hand. No other reason."

Gaal caught his breath, "I resent—"

"Please. It was necessary. You were not picked for any personal reasons. You must realize that Dr. Seldon's plans, which are laid out with the developed mathematics of over eighteen years include all eventualities with significant probabilities. This is one of them. I've been sent here for no other purpose than to assure you that you need not fear. It will end well; almost certainly so for the project; and with reasonable probability for you."

"What are the figures?" demanded Gaal.

"For the project, over 99.9%."

"And for myself?"

"I am instructed that this probability is 77.2%."

"Then I've got better than one chance in five of being sentenced to prison or to death."

"The last is under one per cent."

"Indeed. Calculations upon one man mean nothing. You send Dr. Seldon to me."

"Unfortunately, I cannot. Dr. Seldon is himself arrested."

The door was thrown open before the rising Gaal could do more than utter the beginning of a cry. A guard entered, walked to the table, picked up the recorder, looked upon all sides of it and put it in his pocket.

Avakim said quietly, "I will need that instrument."

"We will supply you with one, Counsellor, that does not cast a static field."

"My interview is done, in that case."

Gaal watched him leave and was alone.

6.

The trial (Gaal supposed it to be one, though it bore little resemblance legalistically to the elaborate trial techniques Gaal had read of) had not lasted long. It was in its third day. Yet already, Gaal could no longer stretch his memory back far enough to embrace its beginning.

He himself had been but little pecked at. The heavy guns were trained on Dr. Seldon himself. Hari Seldon, however, sat there unperturbed. To Gaal, he was the only spot of stability remaining in the world.

The audience was small and drawn exclusively from among the Barons of the Empire. Press and public were excluded and it was doubtful that any significant number of outsiders even knew that a trial of Seldon was being conducted. The atmosphere was one of unrelieved hostility toward the defendants.

Five of the Commission of Public Safety sat behind the raised desk. They wore scarlet and gold uniforms and the shining, close-fitting plastic caps that were the sign of their judicial function. In the center was the Chief Commissioner Linge Chen. Gaal had never before seen so great a Lord and he watched him with fascination. Chen, throughout the trial, rarely said a word. He made it quite clear that much speech was beneath his dignity.

The Commission's Advocate consulted his notes and the examination continued, with Seldon still on the stand:

Q. Let us see, Dr. Seldon. How many men are now engaged in the project of which you are head?

A. Fifty mathematicians.

Q. Including Dr. Gaal Dornick?

A. Dr. Dornick is the fifty-first.

Q. Oh, we have fifty-one then? Search your memory, Dr. Seldon. Perhaps there are fifty-two or fifty-three? Or perhaps even more?

A. Dr. Dornick has not yet formally joined my organization. When he does, the membership will be fifty-one. It is now fifty, as I have said.

Q. Not perhaps nearly a hundred thousand?

A. Mathematicians? No.

Q. I did not say mathematicians. Are there a hundred thousand in all capacities?

A. In all capacities, your figure may be correct.

Q. *May* be? I say it *is*. I say that the men in your project number ninety-eight thousand, five hundred and seventy-two.

A. I believe you are counting women and children.

Q. (raising his voice) Ninety eight thousand five hundred and seventy-two individuals is the intent of my statement. There is no need to quibble.

A. I accept the figures.

Q. (referring to his notes) Let us drop that for the moment, then, and take up another matter which we have already discussed at some length. Would you repeat, Dr. Seldon, your thoughts concerning the future of Trantor?

A. I have said, and I say again, that Trantor will lie in ruins within the next five centuries.

Q. You do not consider your statement a disloyal one?

A. No, sir. Scientific truth is beyond loyalty and disloyalty.

Q. You are sure that your statement represents scientific truth?

A. I am.

Q. On what basis?

A. On the basis of the mathematics of psychohistory.

Q. Can you prove that this mathematics is valid?

A. Only to another mathematician.

Q. (with a smile) Your claim then, is that your truth is of so esoteric a nature that it is beyond the understanding of a plain man. It seems to me that truth should be clearer than that, less mysterious, more open to the mind.

A. It presents no difficulties to some minds. The physics of energy transfer, which we know as thermodynamics, has been clear and true through all the history of man since the mythical ages, yet there may be people present who would find it impossible to design a power engine. People of high intelligence, too. I doubt if the learned Commissioners—

At this point, one of the Commissioners leaned toward the Advocate. His words were not heard but the hissing of the voice carried a certain asperity. The Advocate flushed and interrupted Seldon.

Q. We are not here to listen to speeches, Dr. Seldon. Let us assume that you have made your point. Let me suggest to you that your predictions of disaster might be intended to destroy public confidence in the Imperial Government for purposes of your own.

A. That is not so.

Q. Let me suggest that you intend to claim that a period of time preceding the so-called ruin of Trantor will be filled with unrest of various types.

A. That is correct.

Q. And that by the mere prediction thereof, you hope to bring it about, and to have then an army of a hundred thousand available.

A. In the first place, that is not so. And if it were, investigation will show you that barely ten thousand are men of military age, and none of these has training in arms.

Q. Are you acting as an agent for another?

A. I am not in the pay of any man, Mr. Advocate.

Q. You are entirely disinterested? You are serving science?

A. I am.

Q. Then let us see how. Can the future be changed, Dr. Seldon?

A. Obviously. This courtroom may explode in the next few hours, or it may not. If it did, the future would undoubtedly be changed in some minor respects.

Q. You quibble, Dr. Seldon. Can the overall history of the human race be changed?

A. Yes.

Q. Easily?

A. No. With great difficulty.

Q. Why?

A. The psychohistoric trend of a planet-full of people contains a huge inertia. To be changed it must be met with something possessing a similar inertia. Either as many people must be concerned, or if the number of people be relatively small, enormous time for change must be allowed. Do you understand?

Q. I think I do. Trantor need not be ruined, if a great many people decide to act so that it will not.

A. That is right.

Q. As many as a hundred thousand people?

A. No, sir. That is far too few.

Q. You are sure?

A. Consider that Trantor has a population of over forty billions. Consider further that the trend leading to ruin does not belong to Trantor alone but to the Empire as a whole and the Empire contains nearly a quintillion human beings.

Q. I see. Then perhaps a hundred thousand people can change the trend, if they and their descendants labor for five hundred years.

A. I'm afraid not. Five hundred years is too short a time.

Q. Ah! In that case, Dr. Seldon, we are left with this deduction to be made from your statements. You have gathered one hundred thousand people within the confines of your project. These are insufficient to change the history of Trantor within five hundred years. In other words, they cannot prevent the destruction of Trantor no matter what they do.

A. You are unfortunately correct.

Q. And on the other hand, your hundred thousand are intended for no illegal purpose.

A. Exactly.

Q. (slowly and with satisfaction) In that case, Dr. Seldon— Now attend, sir, most carefully, for we want a considered answer. What is the purpose of your hundred thousand?

The Advocate's voice had grown strident. He had sprung his trap; backed Seldon into a corner; driven him astutely from any possibility of answering.

There was a rising buzz of conversation at that which swept the ranks of the peers in the audience and invaded even the row of Commissioners. They swayed toward one another in their scarlet and gold, only the Chief remaining uncorrupted.

Hari Seldon remained unmoved. He waited for the babble to evaporate.

A. To minimize the effects of that destruction.

Q. And exactly what do you mean by that?

A. The explanation is simple. The coming destruction of Trantor is not an event in itself, isolated in the scheme of human development. It will be the climax to an intricate drama which was begun centuries ago and which is accelerating in pace continuously. I refer, gentlemen, to the developing decline and fall of the Galactic Empire.

The buzz now became a dull roar. The Advocate, unheeded, was yelling, "You are openly declaring that—" and stopped because the cries of "Treason" from the audience showed that the point had been made without any hammering.

Slowly, the Chief Commissioner raised his gavel once and

let it drop. The sound was that of a mellow gong. When the reverberations ceased, the gabble of the audience also did. The Advocate took a deep breath.

Q. (theatrically) Do you realize, Dr. Seldon, that you are speaking of an Empire that has stood for twelve thousand years, through all the vicissitudes of the generations, and which has behind it the good wishes and love of a quadrillion human beings?

A. I am aware both of the present status and the past history of the Empire. Without disrespect, I must claim a far better knowledge of it than any in this room.

Q. And you predict its ruin?

A. It is a prediction which is made by mathematics. I pass no moral judgements. Personally, I regret the prospect. Even if the Empire were admitted to be a bad thing (an admission I do not make), the state of anarchy which would follow its fall would be worse. It is that state of anarchy which my project is pledged to fight. The fall of Empire, gentlemen, is a massive thing, however, and not easily fought. It is dictated by a rising bureaucracy, a receding initiative, a freezing of caste, a damming of curiosity—a hundred other factors. It has been going on, as I have said, for centuries, and it is too majestic and massive a movement to stop.

Q. Is it not obvious to anyone that the Empire is as strong as it ever was?

A. The appearance of strength is all about you. It would seem to last forever. However, Mr. Advocate, the rotten tree-trunk, until the very moment when the storm-blast breaks it in two, has all the appearance of might it ever had. The storm-blast whistles through the branches of the Empire even now. Listen with the ears of psychohistory, and you will hear the creaking.

Q. (uncertainly) We are not here, Dr. Seldon, to lis—

A. (firmly) The Empire will vanish and all its good with it. Its accumulated knowledge will decay and the order it has imposed will vanish. Interstellar wars will be endless; interstellar trade will decay; population will decline; worlds will lose touch with the main body of the Galaxy. —And so matters will remain.

Q. (a small voice in the middle of a vast silence) Forever?

A. Psychohistory, which can predict the fall, can make statements concerning the succeeding dark ages. The Empire, gentlemen, as has just been said, has stood twelve thousand years. The dark ages to come will endure not twelve, but *thirty* thousand years. A Second Empire will rise, but between it and our civilization will be one thousand generations of suffering humanity. We must fight that.

Q. (recovering somewhat) You contradict yourself. You said earlier that you could not prevent the destruction of Trantor; hence, presumably, the fall;—the *so-called* fall of the Empire.

A. I do not say now that we can prevent the fall. But it is not yet too late to shorten the interregnum which will follow. It is possible, gentlemen, to reduce the duration of anarchy to a single millennium, if my group is allowed to act now. We are at a delicate moment in history. The huge, onrushing mass of events must be deflected just a little,— just a little— It cannot be much, but it may be enough to remove twenty-nine thousand years of misery from human history.

Q. How do you propose to do this?

A. By saving the knowledge of the race. The sum of human knowing is beyond any one man; any thousand men. With the destruction of our social fabric, science will be broken into a million pieces. Individuals will know much of exceedingly tiny facets of what there is to know. They will be helpless and useless by themselves. The bits of lore, meaningless, will not be passed on. They will be lost through the generations. *But,* if we now prepare a giant summary of *all* knowledge, it will never be lost. Coming generations will build on it, and will not have to rediscover if for themselves. One millennium will do the work of thirty thousand.

Q. All this—

A. All my project; my thirty thousand men with their wives and children, are devoting themselves to the preparation of an "Encyclopedia Galactica." They will not complete it in their lifetimes. I will not even live to see it fairly begun. But by the time Trantor falls, it will be complete and copies will exist in every major library in the Galaxy.

The Chief Commissioner's gavel rose and fell. Hari Seldon left the stand and quietly took his seat next to Gaal.

He smiled and said, "How did you like the show?"

Gaal said, "You stole it. But what will happen now?"

"They'll adjourn the trial and try to come to a private agreement with me."

"How do you know?"

Seldon said, "I'll be honest. I don't know. It depends on the Chief Commissioner. I have studied him for years. I have tried to analyze his workings, but you know how risky it is to introduce the vagaries of an individual in the psychohistoric equations. Yet I have hopes."

7.

Avakim approached, nodded to Gaal, leaned over to whisper to Seldon. The cry of adjournment rang out, and guards separated them. Gaal was led away.

The next day's hearings were entirely different. Hari Seldon and Gaal Dornick were alone with the Commission. They were seated at a table together, with scarcely a separation between the five judges and the two accused. They were even offered cigars from a box of iridescent plastic which had the appearance of water, endlessly flowing. The eyes were fooled into seeing the motion although the fingers reported it to be hard and dry.

Seldon accepted one; Gaal refused.

Seldon said, "My lawyer is not present."

A Commissioner replied, "This is no longer a trial, Dr. Seldon. We are here to discuss the safety of the State."

Linge Chen said, "*I* will speak," and the other Commissioners sat back in their chairs, prepared to listen. A silence formed about Chen into which he might drop his words.

Gaal held his breath. Chen, lean and hard, older in looks than in fact, was the actual Emperor of all the Galaxy. The child who bore the title itself was only a symbol manufactured by Chen, and not the first such, either.

Chen said, "Dr. Seldon, you disturb the peace of the Emperor's realm. None of the quadrillions living now among all the stars of the Galaxy will be living a century from now. Why, then, should we concern ourselves with events of five centuries distance?"

"I shall not be alive half a decade hence," said Seldon, "and yet it is of overpowering concern to me. Call it idealism. Call it an identification of myself with that mystical generalization to which we refer by the term, 'man.'"

"I do not wish to take the trouble to understand mysticism. Can you tell me why I may not rid myself of yourself and of an uncomfortable and unnecessary five-century future which I will never see by having you executed tonight?"

"A week ago," said Seldon, lightly, "you might have done so and perhaps retained a one in ten probability of yourself remaining alive at year's end. Today, the one in ten probability is scarcely one in ten thousand."

There were expired breaths in the gathering and uneasy stirrings. Gaal felt the short hairs prickle on the back of his neck. Chen's upper eyelids dropped a little.

"How so?" he said.

"The fall of Trantor," said Seldon, "cannot be stopped by any conceivable effort. It can be hastened easily, however. The tale of my interrupted trial will spread through the Galaxy. Frustration of my plans to lighten the disaster will convince people that the future holds no promise to them.

Already they recall the lives of their grandfathers with envy. They will see that political revolutions and trade stagnations will increase. The feeling will pervade the Galaxy that only what a man can grasp for himself at that moment will be of any account. Ambitious men will not wait and unscrupulous men will not hang back. By their every action they will hasten the decay of the worlds. Have me killed and Trantor will fall not within five centuries but within fifty years and you, yourself, within a single year."

Chen said, "These are words to frighten children, and yet your death is not the only answer which will satisfy us."

He lifted his slender hand from the papers on which it rested, so that only two fingers touched lightly upon the topmost sheet.

"Tell me," he said, "will your only activity be that of preparing this encyclopedia you speak of?"

"It will."

"And need that be done on Trantor?"

"Trantor, my lord, possesses the Imperial Library, as well as the scholarly resources of the University of Trantor."

"And yet if you were located elsewhere; let us say upon a planet where the hurry and distractions of a metropolis will not interfere with scholastic musings; where your men may devote themselves entirely and single-mindedly to their work;—might not that have advantages?"

"Minor ones, perhaps."

"Such a world has been chosen, then. You may work, doctor, at your leisure, with your hundred thousand about you. The Galaxy will know that you are working and fighting the Fall. They will even be told that you will prevent the Fall." He smiled, "Since I do not believe in so many things, it is not difficult for me to disbelieve in the Fall as well, so that I am entirely convinced I will be telling the truth to the people. And meanwhile, doctor, you will not trouble Trantor and there will be no disturbance of the Emperor's peace.

"The alternative is death for yourself and for as many of

your followers as will seem necessary. Your earlier threats I disregard. The opportunity for choosing between death and exile is given you over a time period stretching from this moment to one five minutes hence."

"Which is the world chosen, my lord?" said Seldon.

"It is called, I believe, Terminus," said Chen. Negligently, he turned the papers upon his desk with his fingertips so that they faced Seldon. "It is uninhabited, but quite habitable, and can be molded to suit the necessities of scholars. It is somewhat secluded—"

Seldon interrupted, "It is at the edge of the Galaxy, sir."

"As I have said, somewhat secluded. It will suit your needs for concentration. Come, you have two minutes left."

Seldon said, "We will need time to arrange such a trip. There are twenty thousand families involved."

"You will be given time."

Seldon thought a moment, and the last minute began to die. He said, "I accept exile."

Gaal's heart skipped a beat at the words. For the most part, he was filled with a tremendous joy for who would not be, to escape death. Yet in all his vast relief, he found space for a little regret that Seldon had been defeated.

8.

For a long while, they sat silently as the taxi whined through the hundreds of miles of worm-like tunnels toward the University. And then Gaal stirred. He said:

"Was what you told the Commissioner true? Would your execution have really hastened the Fall?"

Seldon said, "I never lie about psychohistoric findings. Nor would it have availed me in this case. Chen knew I spoke the truth. He is a very clever politician and politicians by the very nature of their work must have an instinctive feeling for the truths of psychohistory."

"Then need you have accepted exile," Gaal wondered, but Seldon did not answer.

When they burst out upon the University grounds, Gaal's muscles took action of their own; or rather, inaction. He had to be carried, almost, out of the taxi.

All the University was a blaze of light. Gaal had almost forgotten that a sun could exist. Nor was the University in the open. Its buildings were covered by a monstrous dome of glass-and-yet-not-glass. It was polarized; so that Gaal could look directly upon the blazing star above. Yet its light was undimmed and it glanced off the metal buildings as far as the eye could see.

The University structures themselves lacked the hard steel-gray of the rest of Trantor. They were silvery, rather. The metallic luster was almost ivory in color.

Seldon said, "Soldiers, it seems."

"What?" Gaal brought his eyes to the prosaic ground and found a sentinel ahead of them.

They stopped before him, and a soft-spoken captain materialized from a near-by doorway.

He said, "Dr. Seldon?"

"Yes."

"We have been waiting for you. You and your men will be under martial law henceforth. I have been instructed to inform you that six months will be allowed you for preparations to leave for Terminus."

"Six months!" began Gaal, but Seldon's fingers were upon his elbow with gentle pressure.

"These are my instructions," repeated the captain.

He was gone, and Gaal turned to Seldon, "Why, what can be done in six months? This is but slower murder."

"Quietly. Quietly. Let us reach my office."

It was not a large office, but it was quite spy-proof and quite undetectably so. Spy-beams trained upon it received neither a suspicious silence nor an even more suspicious static. They received, rather, a conversation constructed at random out of a vast stock of innocuous phrases in various tones and voices.

"Now," said Seldon, at his ease, "six months will be enough."

"I don't see how."

"Because, my boy, in a plan such as ours, the actions of others are bent to our needs. Have I not said to you already that Chen's temperamental makeup has been subjected to greater scrutiny than that of any other single man in history. The trial was not allowed to begin until the time and circumstances were right for the ending of our own choosing."

"But could you have arranged—"

"—to be exiled to Terminus? Why not?" He put his fingers on a certain spot on his desk and a small section of the wall behind him slid aside. Only his own fingers could have done so, since only his particular print-pattern could have activated the scanner beneath.

"You will find several microfilms inside," said Seldon. "Take the one marked with the letter, T."

Gaal did so and waited while Seldon fixed it within the projector and handed the young man a pair of eyepieces. Gaal adjusted them, and watched the film unroll before his eyes.

He said, "But then—"

Seldon said, "What surprises you?"

"Have you been preparing to leave for two years?"

"Two and a half. Of course, we could not be certain that it would be Terminus he would choose, but we hoped it might be and we acted upon that assumption—"

"But why, Dr. Seldon? If you arranged the exile, why? Could not events be far better controlled here on Trantor?"

"Why, there are some reasons. Working on Terminus, we will have Imperial support without ever rousing fears that we would endanger Imperial safety."

Gaal said, "But you aroused those fears only to force exile. I still do not understand."

"Twenty thousand families would not travel to the end of the Galaxy of their own will perhaps."

"But why should they be forced there?" Gaal paused, "May I not know?"

Seldon said, "Not yet. It is enough for the moment that you know that a scientific refuge will be established on Terminus. And another will be established at the other end of the Galaxy, let us say," and he smiled, "at Star's End. And as for the rest, I will die soon, and you will see more than I. —No, no. Spare me your shock and good wishes. My doctors tell me that I cannot live longer than a year or two. But then, I have accomplished in life what I have intended and under what circumstances may one better die."

"And after you die, sir?"

"Why, there will be successors—perhaps even yourself. And these successors will be able to apply the final touch in the scheme and instigate the revolt on Anacreon at the right time and in the right manner. Thereafter, events may roll unheeded."

"I do not understand."

"You will." Seldon's lined face grew peaceful and tired, both at once, "Most will leave for Terminus, but some will stay. It will be easy to arrange. —But as for me," and he concluded in a whisper, so that Gaal could scarcely hear him, "I am finished."

PART II
THE ENCYCLOPEDISTS

1

TERMINUS—. . . . Its location (see map) was an odd one for the role it was called upon to play in Galactic history, and yet as many writers have never tired of pointing out, an inevitable one. Located on the very fringe of the Galactic spiral, an only planet of an isolated sun, poor in resources and negligible in economic value, it was never settled in the five centuries after its discovery, until the landing of the Encyclopedists. . . .

It was inevitable that as a new generation grew, Terminus would become something more than an appendage of the psychohistorians of Trantor. With the Anacreonian revolt and the rise to power of Salvor Hardin, first of the great line of. . . .

ENCYCLOPEDIA GALACTICA

Lewis Pirenne was busily engaged at his desk in the one well-lit corner of the room. Work had to be co-ordinated. Effort had to be organized. Threads had to be woven into a pattern.

Fifty years now; fifty years to establish themselves and set up Encyclopedia Foundation Number One into a smoothly working unit. Fifty years to gather the raw material. Fifty years to prepare.

It had been done. Five more years would see the publication of the first volume of the most monumental work the Galaxy had ever conceived. And then at ten-year intervals—regularly—like clockwork—volume after volume. And with them there would be supplements; special articles on events of current interest, until—

Pirenne stirred uneasily, as the muted buzzer upon his desk muttered peevishly. He had almost forgotten the appointment. He shoved the door release and out of an abstracted corner of one eye saw the door open and the broad figure of Salvor Hardin enter. Pirenne did not look up.

Hardin smiled to himself. He was in a hurry, but he knew better than to take offense at Pirenne's cavalier treatment of anything or anyone that disturbed him at his work. He buried himself in the chair on the other side of the desk and waited.

Pirenne's stylus made the faintest scraping sound as it raced across paper. Otherwise, neither motion nor sound. And then Hardin withdrew a two-credit coin from his vest pocket. He flipped it and its stainless-steel surface caught flitters of light as it tumbled through the air. He caught it and flipped it again, watching the flashing reflections lazily. Stainless steel made good medium of exchange on a planet where all metal had to be imported.

Pirenne looked up and blinked. "Stop that!" he said querulously.

"Eh?"

"That infernal coin tossing. Stop it."

"Oh." Hardin pocketed the metal disk. "Tell me when you're ready, will you? I promised to be back at the City Council meeting before the new aqueduct project is put to a vote."

Pirenne sighed and shoved himself away from the desk. "I'm ready. But I hope you aren't going to bother me with city affairs. Take care of that yourself, please. The Encyclopedia takes up all my time."

"Have you heard the news?" questioned Hardin, phlegmatically.

"What news?"

"The news that the Terminus City ultrawave set received two hours ago. The Royal Governor of the Prefect of Anacreon has assumed the title of king."

"Well? What of it?"

"It means," responded Hardin, "that we're cut off from the inner regions of the Empire. We've been expecting it but that doesn't make it any more comfortable. Anacreon stands square across what was our last remaining trade route to Santanni and to Trantor and to Vega itself. Where is our metal to come from? We haven't managed to get a steel or aluminum shipment through in six months and now we won't be able to get any at all, except by grace of the King of Anacreon."

Pirenne tch-tched impatiently. "Get them through him, then."

"But can we? Listen, Pirenne, according to the charter which established this Foundation, the Board of Trustees of the Encyclopedia Committee has been given full administrative powers. I, as Mayor of Terminus City, have just enough power to blow my own nose and perhaps to sneeze if you countersign an order giving me permission. It's up to you and your Board then. I'm asking you in the name of the City, whose prosperity depends upon uninterrupted commerce with the Galaxy, to call an emergency meeting—"

"Stop! A campaign speech is out of order. Now, Hardin, the Board of Trustees has not barred the establishment of a municipal government on Terminus. We understand one to be necessary because of the increase in population since the Foundation was established fifty years ago, and because of the increasing number of people involved in non-Encyclopedia affairs. *But* that does not mean that the first and *only* aim of the Foundation is no longer to publish the definitive Encyclopedia of all human knowledge. We are a State-supported, scientific institution, Hardin. We cannot—must not—*will* not interfere in local politics."

"Local politics! By the Emperor's left big toe, Pirenne, this is a matter of life and death. The planet, Terminus, by itself cannot support a mechanized civilization. It lacks metals. You know that. It hasn't a trace of iron, copper, or aluminum in the surface rocks, and precious little of anything else. What do you think will happen to the Encyclopedia if this watchmacallum King of Anacreon clamps down on us?"

"On *us?* Are you forgetting that we are under the direct control of the Emperor himself? We are not part of the Prefect of Anacreon or of any other prefect. Memorize that! We are part of the Emperor's personal domain, and no one touches us. The Empire can protect its own."

"Then why didn't it prevent the Royal Governor of Anacreon from kicking over the traces? And only Anacreon? At least twenty of the outermost prefects of the Galaxy, the entire Periphery as a matter of fact, have begun steering things their own way. I tell you I feel darned uncertain of the Empire and its ability to protect us."

"Hokum! Royal Governors, Kings—what's the difference? The Empire is always shot through with a certain amount of politics and with different men pulling this way and that. Governors have rebelled, and, for that matter, Emperors have been deposed, or assassinated before this. But what has that to do with the Empire itself? Forget it, Hardin. It's none of our business. We are first of all and last of all—scientists. And our concern is the Encyclopedia. Oh, yes, I'd almost forgotten. Hardin!"

"Well?"

"Do something about that paper of yours!" Pirenne's voice was angry.

"The Terminus City *Journal*? It isn't mine; it's privately owned. What's it been doing?"

"For weeks now it has been recommending that the fiftieth anniversary of the establishment of the Foundation be made the occasion for public holidays and quite inappropriate celebrations."

"And why not? The radium clock will open the First Vault in three months. I would call this a big occasion, wouldn't you?"

"Not for silly pageantry, Hardin. The First Vault and its opening concern the Board of Trustees alone. Anything of importance will be communicated to the people. That is final and please make it plain to the *Journal*."

"I'm sorry, Pirenne, but the City Charter guarantees a certain minor matter known as freedom of the press."

"It may. But the Board of Trustees does not. I am the Emperor's representative on Terminus, Hardin, and have full powers in this respect."

Hardin's expression became that of a man counting to ten, mentally. He said, grimly: "In connection with your status as Emperor's representative, then, I have a final piece of news to give you."

"About Anacreon?" Pirenne's lips tightened. He felt annoyed.

"Yes. A special envoy will be sent to us from Anacreon. In two weeks."

"An envoy? Here? From Anacreon?" Pirenne chewed that. "What for?"

Hardin stood up, and shoved his chair back up against the desk. "I give you one guess."

And he left—quite unceremoniously.

2.

Anselm haut Rodric—"haut" itself signifying noble blood —Sub-prefect of Pluema and Envoy Extraordinary of his Highness of Anacreon—plus half a dozen other titles—was met by Salvor Hardin at the spaceport with all the imposing ritual of a state occasion.

With a tight smile and a low bow, the sub-prefect had flipped his blaster from its holster and presented it to Hardin butt first. Hardin returned the compliment with a blaster specifically borrowed for the occasion. Friendship and good will were thus established, and if Hardin noted the barest bulge at Haut Rodric's shoulder, he prudently said nothing.

The ground car that received them then—preceded, flanked, and followed by the suitable cloud of minor functionaries—proceeded in a slow, ceremonious manner to Cyclopedia Square, cheered on its way by a properly enthusiastic crowd.

Sub-prefect Anselm received the cheers with the complaisant indifference of a soldier and a nobleman.

He said to Hardin, "And this city is all your world?"

Hardin raised his voice to be heard above the clamor. "We are a young world, your eminence. In our short history we have had but few members of the higher nobility visiting our poor planet. Hence, our enthusiasm."

It is certain that "higher nobility" did not recognize irony when he heard it.

He said thoughtfully: "Founded fifty years ago. Hm-m-m! You have a great deal of unexploited land here, mayor. You have never considered dividing it into estates?"

"There is no necessity as yet. We're extremely centralized; we have to be, because of the Encyclopedia. Some day, perhaps, when our population has grown—"

"A strange world! You have no peasantry?"

Hardin reflected that it didn't require a great deal of acumen to tell that his eminence was indulging in a bit of fairly clumsy pumping. He replied casually, "No—nor nobility."

Haut Rodric's eyebrows lifted. "And your leader—the man I am to meet?"

"You mean Dr. Pirenne? Yes! He is the Chairman of the Board of Trustees—and a personal representative of the Emperor."

"*Doctor?* No other title? A *scholar?* And he rates above the civil authority?"

"Why, certainly," replied Hardin, amiably. "We're all scholars more or less. After all, we're not so much a world as a scientific foundation—under the direct control of the Emperor."

There was a faint emphasis upon the last phrase that seemed to disconcert the sub-prefect. He remained thoughtfully silent during the rest of the slow way to Cyclopedia Square.

If Hardin found himself bored by the afternoon and evening that followed, he had at least the satisfaction of realizing that Pirenne and Haut Rodric—having met with loud and mutual protestations of esteem and regard—were detesting each other's company a good deal more.

Haut Rodric had attended with glazed eye to Pirenne's lecture during the "inspection tour" of the Encyclopedia Building. With polite and vacant smile, he had listened to the latter's rapid patter as they passed through the vast storehouses of reference films and the numerous projection rooms.

It was only after he had gone down level by level into and through the composing departments, editing departments, publishing departments, and filming departments that he made the first comprehensive statement.

"This is all very interesting," he said, "but it seems a strange occupation for grown men. What good is it?"

It was a remark, Hardin noted, for which Pirenne found no answer, though the expression of his face was most eloquent.

The dinner that evening was much the mirror image of the events of that afternoon, for Haut Rodric monopolized the conversation by describing—in minute technical detail and with incredible zest—his own exploits as battalion head during the recent war between Anacreon and the neighboring newly proclaimed Kingdom of Smyrno.

The details of the sub-prefect's account were not completed until dinner was over and one by one the minor officials had drifted away. The last bit of triumphant description of mangled spaceships came when he had accompanied Pirenne and Hardin onto the balcony and relaxed in the warm air of the summer evening.

"And now," he said, with a heavy joviality, "to serious matters."

"By all means," murmured Hardin, lighting a long cigar of Vegan tobacco—not many left, he reflected—and teetering his chair back on two legs.

The Galaxy was high in the sky and its misty lens shape stretched lazily from horizon to horizon. The few stars here at the very edge of the universe were insignificant twinkles in comparison.

"Of course," said the sub-prefect, "all the formal discussions—the paper signing and such dull technicalities, that is—will take place before the— What is it you call your Council?"

"The Board of Trustees," replied Pirenne, coldly.

"Queer name! Anyway, that's for tomorrow. We might as well clear away some of the underbrush, man to man, right now, though. Hey?"

"And this means—" prodded Hardin.

"Just this. There's been a certain change in the situation out here in the Periphery and the status of your planet has become a trifle uncertain. It would be very convenient if we succeeded in coming to an understanding as to how the matter stands. By the way, mayor, have you another one of those cigars?"

Hardin started and produced one reluctantly.

Anselm haut Rodric sniffed at it and emitted a clucking sound of pleasure. "Vegan tobacco! Where did you get it?"

"We received some last shipment. There's hardly any left. Space knows when we'll get more—if ever."

Pirenne scowled. He didn't smoke—and, for that matter, detested the odor. "Let me understand this, your eminence. Your mission is merely one of clarification?"

Haut Rodric nodded through the smoke of his first lusty puffs.

"In that case, it is soon over. The situation with respect to Encyclopedia Foundation Number One is what it always has been."

"Ah! And what is it that it always has been?"

"Just this: A State-supported scientific institution and part of the personal domain of his august majesty, the Emperor."

The sub-prefect seemed unimpressed. He blew smoke rings. "That's a nice theory, Dr. Pirenne. I imagine you've got charters with the Imperial Seal upon it—but what's the actual situation? How do you stand with respect to Smyrno? You're not fifty parsecs from Smyrno's capital, you know. And what about Konom and Daribow?"

Pirenne said: "We have nothing to do with any prefect. As part of the Emperor's—"

"They're not prefects," reminded Haut Rodric; "they're kingdoms now."

"Kingdoms then. We have nothing to do with them. As a scientific institution—"

"Science be dashed!" swore the other, via a bouncing soldierly oath that ionized the atmosphere. "What the devil has that got to do with the fact that we're liable to see Terminus taken over by Smyrno at any time?"

"And the Emperor? He would just sit by?"

Haut Rodric calmed down and said: "Well, now, Dr. Pirenne, you respect the Emperor's property and so does Anacreon, but Smyrno might not. Remember, we've just signed a treaty with the Emperor—I'll present a copy to that Board of yours tomorrow—which places upon us the responsibility of maintaining order within the borders of the old Prefect of Anacreon on behalf of the Emperor. Our duty is clear, then, isn't it?"

"Certainly. But Terminus is not part of the Prefect of Anacreon."

"And Smyrno—"

"Nor is it part of the Prefect of Smyrno. It's not part of any prefect."

"Does Smyrno know that?"

"I don't care what it knows."

"*We* do. We've just finished a war with her and she still holds two stellar systems that are ours. Terminus occupies an extremely strategic spot, between the two nations."

Hardin felt weary. He broke in: "What is your proposition, your eminence?"

The sub-prefect seemed quite ready to stop fencing in favor of more direct statements. He said briskly: "It seems perfectly obvious that, since Terminus cannot defend itself, Anacreon must take over the job for its own sake. You understand we have no desire to interfere with internal administration—"

"Uh-huh," grunted Hardin dryly.

"—but we believe that it would be best for all concerned to have Anacreon establish a military base upon the planet."

"And that is all you would want—a military base in some of the vast unoccupied territory—and let it go at that?"

"Well, of course, there would be the matter of supporting the protecting forces."

Hardin's chair came down on all four, and his elbows went forward on his knees. "Now we're getting to the nub. Let's put it into language. Terminus is to be a protectorate and to pay tribute."

"Not tribute. Taxes. We're protecting you. You pay for it."

Pirenne banged his hand on the chair with sudden violence. "Let me speak, Hardin. Your eminence, I don't care a rusty half-credit coin for Anacreon, Smyrno, or all your local politics and petty wars. I tell you this is a State-supported tax-free institution."

"State-supported? But *we* are the State, Dr. Pirenne, and we're not supporting."

Pirenne rose angrily. "Your eminence, I am the direct representative of—"

"—his august majesty, the Emperor," chorused Anselm haut Rodric sourly, "And I am the direct representative of the King of Anacreon. Anacreon is a lot nearer, Dr. Pirenne."

"Let's get back to business," urged Hardin. "How would you take these so-called taxes, your eminence? Would you take them in kind: wheat, potatoes, vegetables, cattle?"

The sub-prefect stared. "What the devil? What do we need with those? We've got hefty surpluses. Gold, of course. Chromium or vanadium would be even better, incidentally, if you have it in quantity."

Hardin laughed. "Quantity! We haven't even got iron in

quantity. Gold! Here, take a look at our currency." He tossed a coin to the envoy.

Haut Rodric bounced it and stared. "What is it? Steel?"

"That's right."

"I don't understand."

"Terminus is a planet practically without metals. We import it all. Consequently, we have no gold, and nothing to pay unless you want a few thousand bushels of potatoes."

"Well—manufactured goods."

"Without metal? What do we make our machines out of?"

There was a pause and Pirenne tried again. "This whole discussion is wide of the point. Terminus is not a planet, but a scientific foundation preparing a great encyclopedia. Space, man, have you no respect for science?"

"Encyclopedias don't win wars." Haut Rodric's brows furrowed. "A completely unproductive world, then—and practically unoccupied at that. Well, you might pay with land."

"What do you mean?" asked Pirenne.

"This world is just about empty and the unoccupied land is probably fertile. There are many of the nobility on Anacreon that would like an addition to their estates."

"You can't propose any such—"

"There's no necessity of looking so alarmed, Dr. Pirenne. There's plenty for all of us. If it comes to what it comes, and you co-operate, we could probably arrange it so that you lose nothing. Titles can be conferred and estates granted. You understand me, I think."

Pirenne sneered, "Thanks!"

And then Hardin said ingenuously: "Could Anacreon supply us with adequate quantities of plutonium for our atomic-power plant? We've only a few years' supply left."

There was a gasp from Pirenne and then a dead silence for minutes. When Haut Rodric spoke it was in a voice quite different from what it had been till then:

"You have atomic power?"

"Certainly. What's unusual in that? I imagine atomic power

is fifty thousand years old now. Why shouldn't we have it? Except that it's a little difficult to get plutonium."

"Yes . . . yes." The envoy paused and added uncomfortably: "Well, gentlemen, we'll pursue the subject tomorrow. You'll excuse me—"

Pirenne looked after him and gritted through his teeth: "That insufferable, dull-witted donkey! That—"

Hardin broke in: "Not at all. He's merely the product of his environment. He doesn't understand much except that 'I got a gun and you ain't.'"

Pirenne whirled on him in exasperation. "What in space did you mean by the talk about military bases and tribute? Are you crazy?"

"No. I merely gave him rope and let him talk. You'll notice that he managed to stumble out with Anacreon's real intentions—that is, the parceling up of Terminus into landed estates. Of course, I don't intend to let that happen."

"*You* don't intend. *You* don't. And who are you? And may I ask what you meant by blowing off your mouth about our atomic-power plant? Why, it's just the thing that would make us a military target."

"Yes," grinned Hardin. "A military target to stay away from. Isn't it obvious why I brought the subject up? It happened to confirm a very strong suspicion I had had."

"And that was what?"

"That Anacreon no longer has an atomic-power economy. If they had, our friend would undoubtedly have realized that plutonium, except in ancient tradition is not used in power plants. And therefore it follows that the rest of the Periphery no longer has atomic power either. Certainly Smyrno hasn't, or Anacreon wouldn't have won most of the battles in their recent war. Interesting, wouldn't you say?"

"Bah!" Pirenne left in fiendish humor, and Hardin smiled gently.

He threw his cigar away and looked up at the outstretched Galaxy. "Back to oil and coal, are they?" he murmured—and what the rest of his thoughts were he kept to himself.

When Hardin denied owning the *Journal*, he was perhaps technically correct, but no more. Hardin had been the leading spirit in the drive to incorporate Terminus into an autonomous municipality—he had been elected its first mayor—so it was not surprising that, though not a single share of *Journal* stock was in his name, some sixty percent was controlled by him in more devious fashions.

There were ways.

Consequently, when Hardin began suggesting to Pirenne that he be allowed to attend meetings of the Board of Trustees, it was not quite coincidence that the *Journal* began a similar campaign. And the first mass meeting in the history of the Foundation was held, demanding representation of the City in the "national" government.

And, eventually, Pirenne capitulated with ill grace.

Hardin, as he sat at the foot of the table, speculated idly as to just what it was that made physical scientists such poor administrators. It might be merely that they were too used to inflexible fact and far too unused to pliable people.

In any case, there was Tomaz Sutt and Jord Fara on his left; Lundin Crast and Yate Fulham on his right; with Pirenne, himself, presiding. He knew them all, of course, but they seemed to have put on an extra-special bit of pomposity for the occasion.

Hardin half dozed through the initial formalities and then perked up when Pirenne sipped at the glass of water before him by way of preparation and said:

"I find it very gratifying to be able to inform the Board that since our last meeting, I have received word that Lord Dorwin, Chancellor of the Empire, will arrive at Terminus in two weeks. It may be taken for granted that our relations with Anacreon will be smoothed out to our complete satisfaction as soon as the Emperor is informed of the situation."

He smiled and addressed Hardin across the length of the

table. "Information to this effect has been given the *Journal*."

Hardin snickered below his breath. It seemed evident that Pirenne's desire to strut this information before him had been one reason for his admission into the sacrosanctum.

He said evenly: "Leaving vague expressions out of account, what do you expect Lord Dorwin to do?"

Tomaz Sutt replied. He had a bad habit of addressing one in the third person when in his more stately moods.

"It is quite evident," he observed, "that Mayor Hardin is a professional cynic. He can scarcely fail to realize that the Emperor would be most unlikely to allow his personal rights to be infringed."

"Why? What would he do in case they were?"

There was an annoyed stir. Pirenne said, "You are out of order," and, as an afterthought, "and are making what are near-treasonable statements, besides."

"Am I to consider myself answered?"

"Yes! If you have nothing further to say—"

"Don't jump to conclusions. I'd like to ask a question. Besides this stroke of diplomacy—which may or may not prove to mean anything—has anything concrete been done to meet the Anacreonic menace?"

Yate Fulham drew one hand along his ferocious red mustache. "You see a menace there, do you?"

"Don't you?"

"Scarcely"—this with indulgence. "The Emperor—"

"Great space!" Hardin felt annoyed. "What is this? Every once in a while someone mentions 'Emperor' or 'Empire' as if it were a magic word. The Emperor is fifty thousand parsecs away, and I doubt whether he gives a damn about us. And if he does, what can he do? What there was of the imperial navy in these regions is in the hands of the four kingdoms now and Anacreon has its share. Listen, we have to fight with guns, not with words.

"Now, get this. We've had two months' grace so far, mainly because we've given Anacreon the idea that we've got atomic weapons. Well, we all know that that's a little white lie. We've got atomic power, but only for commercial uses, and darn little at that. They're going to find that out soon, and if you think they're going to enjoy being jollied along, you're mistaken."

"My dear sir—"

"Hold on: I'm not finished." Hardin was warming up. He liked this. "It's all very well to drag chancellors into this, but it would be much nicer to drag a few great big siege guns fitted for beautiful atomic bombs into it. We've lost two months, gentlemen, and we may not have another two months to lose. What do you propose to do?"

Said Lundin Crast, his long nose wrinkling angrily: "If you're proposing the militarization of the Foundation, I won't hear a word of it. It would mark our open entrance into the field of politics. We, Mr. Mayor, are a scientific foundation and nothing else."

Added Sutt: "He does not realize, moreover, that building armaments would mean withdrawing men—valuable men —from the Encyclopedia. That cannot be done, come what may."

"Very true," agreed Pirenne. "The Encyclopedia first— always."

Hardin groaned in spirit. The Board seemed to suffer violently from Encyclopedia on the brain.

He said icily: "Has it ever occurred to this Board that it is barely possible that Terminus may have interests other than the Encyclopedia?"

Pirenne replied: "I do not conceive, Hardin, that the Foundation can have *any* interest other than the Encyclopedia."

"I didn't say the Foundation; I said *Terminus*. I'm afraid you don't understand the situation. There's a good million of us here on Terminus, and not more than a hundred and fifty thousand are working directly on the Encyclopedia. To the rest of us, this is *home*. We were born here. We're living here. Compared with our farms and our homes and our factories, the Encyclopedia means little to us. We want them protected—"

He was shouted down.

"The Encyclopedia first," ground out Crast. "We have a mission to fulfill."

"Mission, hell," shouted Hardin. "That might have been true fifty years ago. But this is a new generation."

"That has nothing to do with it," replied Pirenne. "We are scientists."

And Hardin leaped through the opening. "Are you, though? That's a nice hallucination, isn't it? Your bunch here is a perfect example of what's been wrong with the entire Galaxy for thousands of years. What kind of science is it to be stuck out here for centuries classifying the work of scientists of the last millennium? Have you ever thought of working onward, extending their knowledge and improving upon it? No! You're quite happy to stagnate. The whole Galaxy is, and has been for space knows how long. That's why the Periphery is revolting; that's why communications are breaking down; that's why petty wars are becoming eternal; that's why whole systems are losing atomic power and going back to barbarous techniques of chemical power.

"If you ask me," he cried, *"the Galaxy is going to pot!"*

He paused and dropped into his chair to catch his breath, paying no attention to the two or three that were attempting simultaneously to answer him.

Crast got the floor. "I don't know what you're trying to gain by your hysterical statements, Mr. Mayor. Certainly, you are adding nothing constructive to the discussion. I move, Mr. Chairman, that the speaker's remarks be placed out of order and the discussion be resumed from the point where it was interrupted."

Jord Fara bestirred himself for the first time. Up to this point Fara had taken no part in the argument even at its hottest. But now his ponderous voice, every bit as ponderous as his three-hundred-pound body, burst its bass way out.

"Haven't we forgotten something, gentlemen?"

"What?" asked Pirenne, peevishly.

"That in a month we celebrate our fiftieth anniversary." Fara had a trick of uttering the most obvious platitudes with great profundity.

"What of it?"

"And on that anniversary," continued Fara, placidly, "Hari Seldon's Vault will open. Have you ever considered what might be in the Vault?"

"I don't know. Routine matters. A stock speech of congratulations, perhaps. I don't think any significance need be placed on the Vault—though the *Journal*"—and he glared at Hardin, who grinned back—"did try to make an issue of it. I put a stop to that."

"Ah," said Fara, "but perhaps you are wrong. Doesn't it strike you"—he paused and put a finger to his round little nose—"that the Vault is opening at a very convenient time?"

"Very *in*convenient time, you mean," muttered Fulham. "We've got some other things to worry about."

"Other things more important than a message from Hari Seldon? I think not." Fara was growing more pontifical than ever, and Hardin eyed him thoughtfully. What was he getting at?

"In fact," said Fara, happily, "you all seem to forget that Seldon was the greatest psychologist of our time and that he was the founder of our Foundation. It seems reasonable to assume that he used his science to determine the probable course of the history of the immediate future. If he did, as seems likely, I repeat, he would certainly have managed to find a way to warn us of danger and, perhaps, to point out a solution. The Encyclopedia was very dear to his heart, you know."

An aura of puzzled doubt prevailed. Pirenne hemmed. "Well, now, I don't know. Psychology is a great science, but—there are no psychologists among us at the moment, I believe. It seems to me we're on uncertain ground."

Fara turned to Hardin. "Didn't you study psychology under Alurin?"

Hardin answered, half in reverie: "Yes, I never completed my studies, though. I got tired of theory. I wanted to be a psychological engineer, but we lacked the facilities, so I did the next best thing—I went into politics. It's practically the same thing."

"Well, what do you think of the Vault?"

And Hardin replied cautiously, "I don't know."

He did not say a word for the remainder of the meeting —even though it got back to the subject of the Chancellor of the Empire.

In fact, he didn't even listen. He'd been put on a new track and things were falling into place—just a little. Little angles were fitting together—one or two.

And psychology was the key. He was sure of that.

He was trying desperately to remember the psychological theory he had once learned—and from it he got one thing right at the start.

A great psychologist such as Seldon could unravel human emotions and human reactions sufficiently to be able to predict broadly the historical sweep of the future.

And that meant—hm-m-m!

4.

Lord Dorwin took snuff. He also had long hair, curled intricately and, quite obviously, artificially, to which were added a pair of fluffy, blond sideburns, which he fondled affectionately. Then, too, he spoke in overprecise statements and left out all the r's.

At the moment, Hardin had no time to think of more of the reasons for the instant detestation in which he had held the noble chancellor. Oh, yes, the elegant gestures of one hand with which he accompanied his remarks and the studied condescension with which he accompanied even a simple affirmative.

But, at any rate, the problem now was to locate him. He had disappeared with Pirenne half an hour before—passed clean out of sight, blast him.

Hardin was quite sure that his own absence during the preliminary discussions would quite suit Pirenne.

But Pirenne had been seen in this wing and on this floor. It was simply a matter of trying every door. Halfway down, he said, "Ah!" and stepped into the darkened room. The profile of Lord Dorwin's intricate hair-do was unmistakable against the lighted screen.

Lord Dorwin looked up and said: "Ah, Hahdin. You ah looking foah us, no doubt?" He held out his snuffbox—over-adorned and poor workmanship at that, noted Hardin—and was politely refused whereat he helped himself to a pinch and smiled graciously.

Pirenne scowled and Hardin met that with an expression of blank indifference.

The only sound to break the short silence that followed was the clicking of the lid of Lord Dorwin's snuffbox. And then he put it away and said:

"A gweat achievement, this Encyclopedia of yoahs, Hahdin. A feat, indeed, to rank with the most majestic accomplishments of all time."

"Most of us think so, milord. It's an accomplishment not quite accomplished as yet, however."

"Fwom the little I have seen of the efficiency of yoah Foundation, I have no feahs on that scoah." And he nodded to Pirenne, who responded with a delighted bow.

Quite a love feast, thought Hardin. "I wasn't complaining about the lack of efficiency, milord, as much as of the definite excess of efficiency on the part of the Anacreonians —though in another and more destructive direction."

"Ah, yes, Anacweon." A negligent wave of the hand. "I have just come from theah. Most bahbawous planet. It is thowoughly inconceivable that human beings could live heah in the Pewiphewy. The lack of the most elementawy wequiah-ments of a cultuahed gentleman; the absence of the most fundamental necessities foah comfoht and convenience—the uttah desuetude into which they—"

Hardin interrupted dryly: "The Anacreonians, unfortu-nately, have all the elementary requirements for warfare and all the fundamental necessities for destruction."

"Quite, quite." Lord Dorwin seemed annoyed, perhaps at being stopped midway in his sentence. "But we ahn't to discuss business now, y'know. Weally, I'm othahwise con-cuhned. Doctah Piwenne, ahn't you going to show me the second volume? Do, please."

The lights clicked out and for the next half-hour Hardin might as well have been on Anacreon for all the attention they paid him. The book upon the screen made little sense to him, nor did he trouble to make the attempt to follow, but Lord Dorwin became quite humanly excited at times. Hardin noticed that during these moments of excitement the chancellor pronounced his r's.

When the lights went on again, Lord Dorwin said: "Mahvelous. Twuly mahvelous. You ah not, by chance, in-tewested in ahchaeology, ah you, Hahdin?"

"Eh?" Hardin shook himself out of an abstracted reverie. "No, milord, can't say I am. I'm a psychologist by original intention and a politician by final decision."

"Ah! No doubt intewesting studies. I, myself, y'know"—he helped himself to a giant pinch of snuff—"dabble in ahchaeology."

"Indeed?"

"His lordship," interrupted Pirenne, "is most thoroughly acquainted with the field."

"Well, p'haps I am, p'haps I am," said his lordship com-placently. "I *have* done an awful amount of wuhk in the science. Extwemely well-read, in fact. I've gone thwough all of Jawdun, Obijasi, Kwomwill . . . oh, all of them, y'know."

"I've heard of them, of course," said Hardin, "but I've never read them."

"You should some day, my deah fellow. It would amply repay you. Why, I cutainly considah it well wuhth the twip heah to the Pewiphewy to see this copy of Lameth. Would you believe it, my libwawy totally lacks a copy. By the way, Doctah Piwenne, you have not fohgotten yoah pwomise to twansdevelop a copy foah me befoah I leave?"

"Only too pleased."

"Lameth, you must know," continued the chancellor, pontifically, "pwesents a new and most intwesting addition to my pwevious knowledge of the 'Owigin Question.'"

"Which question?" asked Hardin.

"The 'Owigin Question.' The place of the owigin of the human species, y'know. Suahly you must know that it is thought that owiginally the human wace occupied only one planetawy system."

"Well, yes, I know that."

"Of cohse, no one knows exactly which system it is—lost in the mists of antiquity. Theah ah theawies, howevah. Siwius, some say. Othahs insist on Alpha Centauwi, oah on Sol, oah on 61 Cygni—all in the Siwius sectah, you see."

"And what does Lameth say?"

"Well, he goes off along a new twail completely. He twies to show that ahchaeological wemains on the thuhd planet of the Ahctuwian System show that humanity existed theah befoah theah wah any indications of space-twavel."

"And that means it was humanity's birth planet?"

"P'haps. I must wead it closely and wigh the evidence befoah I can say foah cuhtain. One must see just how weliable his obsuhvations ah."

Hardin remained silent for a short while. Then he said, "When did Lameth write his book?"

"Oh—I should say about eight hundwed yeahs ago. Of cohse, he has based it lahgely on the pwevious wuhk of Gleen."

"Then why rely on him? Why not go to Arcturus and study the remains for yourself?"

Lord Dorwin raised his eyebrows and took a pinch of

snuff hurriedly. "Why, whatevah foah, my deah fellow?"

"To get the information firsthand, of course."

"But wheah's the necessity? It seems an uncommonly woundabout and hopelessly wigmawolish method of getting anywheahs. Look heah, now, I've got the wuhks of all the old mastahs—the gweat ahchaeologists of the past. I wigh them against each othah—balance the disagweements—analyze the conflicting statements—decide which is pwobably cowwect—and come to a conclusion. That is the scientific method. At least"—patronizingly—"as *I* see it. How insuffewably cwude it would be to go to Ahctuwus, oah to Sol, foah instance, and blundah about, when the old mastahs have covahed the gwound so much moah effectually than we could possibly hope to do."

Hardin murmured politely, "I see."

Scientific method, hell! No wonder the Galaxy was going to pot.

"Come, milord," said Pirenne, "think we had better be returning."

"Ah, yes. P'haps we had."

As they left the room, Hardin said suddenly, "Milord, may I ask a question?"

Lord Dorwin smiled blandly and emphasized his answer with a gracious flutter of the hand. "Cuhtainly, my deah fellow. Only too happy to be of suhvice. If I can help you in any way fwom my pooah stoah of knowledge—"

"It isn't exactly about archaeology, milord."

"No?"

"No. It's this: Last year we received news here in Terminus about the explosion of a power plant on Planet V of Gamma Andromeda. We got the barest outline of the accident—no details at all. I wonder if you could tell me exactly what happened."

Pirenne's mouth twisted. "I wonder you annoy his lordship with questions on totally irrelevant subjects."

"Not at all, Doctah Piwenne," interceded the chancellor. "It is quite all wight. Theah isn't much to say concuhning it in any case. The powah plant did explode and it was quite a catastwophe, y'know. I believe sevewal million people wah killed and at least half the planet was simply laid in wuins. Weally, the govuhnment is sewiously considewing placing seveah westwictions upon the indiscwiminate use of atomic powah—though that is not a thing for genewal publication, y'know."

"I understand," said Hardin. "But what was wrong with the plant?"

"Well, weally," replied Lord Dorwin indifferently, "who knows? It had bwoken down some yeahs pweviously and it is thought that the weplacements and wepaiah wuhk wuh most infewiah. It is *so* difficult these days to find men who *weally* undahstand the moah technical details of ouah powah systems." And he took a sorrowful pinch of snuff.

"You realize," said Hardin, "that the independent kingdoms of the Periphery had lost atomic power altogether?"

"Have they? I'm not at all suhpwised. Bahbawous planets— Oh, but my deah fellow, don't call them independent. They ahn't, y'know. The tweaties we've made with them ah pwoof positive of that. They acknowledge the soveweignty of the Empewah. They'd have to, of cohse, oah we wouldn't tweat with them."

"That may be so, but they have considerable freedom of action."

"Yes, I suppose so. Considewable. But that scahcely mattahs. The Empiah is fah bettah off, with the Pewiphewy thwown upon its own wesoahces—as it is, moah oah less. They ahn't any good to us, y'know. *Most* bahbawous planets. Scahcely civilized."

"They were civilized in the past. Anacreon was one of the richest of the outlying provinces. I understand it compared favorably with Vega itself."

"Oh, but, Hahdin, that was centuwies ago. You can scahcely dwaw conclusion fwom that. Things wah diffewent in the old gweat days. We ahn't the men we used to be, y'know. But, Hahdin, come, you ah a most puhsistent chap. I've told you I simply won't discuss business today. Doctah Piwenne did pwepayah me foah you. He told me you would twy to badgah me, but I'm fah too old a hand foah that. Leave it foah next day."

And that was that.

5.

This was the second meeting of the Board that Hardin had attended, if one were to exclude the informal talks the Board members had had with the now-departed Lord Dorwin. Yet the mayor had a perfectly definite idea that at least one other, and possibly two or three, had been held, to which he had somehow never received an invitation.

Nor, it seemed to him, would he have received notification of this one had it not been for the ultimatum.

At least, it amounted to an ultimatum, though a superficial reading of the visigraphed document would lead one to suppose that it was a friendly interchange of greetings between two potentates.

Hardin fingered it gingerly. It started off floridly with a salutation from "His Puissant Majesty, the King of Anacreon, to his friend and brother, Dr. Lewis Pirenne, Chairman of the Board of Trustees, of the Encyclopedia Foundation Number One," and it ended even more lavishly with a gigantic, multicolored seal of the most involved symbolism.

But it was an ultimatum just the same.

Hardin said: "It turned out that we didn't have much time after all—only three months. But little as it was, we threw it away unused. This thing here gives us a week. What do we do now?"

Pirenne frowned worriedly. "There must be a loophole. It is absolutely unbelievable that they would push matters to extremities in the face of what Lord Dorwin has assured us regarding the attitude of the Emperor and the Empire."

Hardin perked up. "I see. You have informed the King of Anacreon of this alleged attitude?"

"I did—after having placed the proposal to the Board for a vote and having received unanimous consent."

"And when did this vote take place?"

Pirenne climbed onto his dignity. "I do not believe I am answerable to you in any way, Mayor Hardin."

"All right. I'm not that vitally interested. It's just my opinion that it was your diplomatic transmission of Lord Dorwin's valuable contribution to the situation"—he lifted the corner of his mouth in a sour half-smile—"that was the direct cause of this friendly little note. They might have delayed longer otherwise—though I don't think the additional time would have helped Terminus any, considering the attitude of the Board."

Said Yate Fulham: "And just how do you arrive at that remarkable conclusion, Mr. Mayor?"

"In a rather simple way. It merely required the use of that much-neglected commodity—common sense. You see, there is a branch of human knowledge known as symbolic logic, which can be used to prune away all sorts of clogging deadwood that clutters up human language."

"What about it?" said Fulham.

"I applied it. Among other things, I applied it to this document here. I didn't really need to for myself because I knew what it was all about, but I think I can explain it more easily to five physical scientists by symbols rather than by words."

Hardin removed a few sheets of paper from the pad under his arm and spread them out. "I didn't do this myself, by the way," he said. "Muller Holk of the Division of Logic has his name signed to the analyses, as you can see."

Pirenne leaned over the table to get a better view and Hardin continued: "The message from Anacreon was a simple problem, naturally, for the men who wrote it were men of action rather than men of words. It boils down easily and straightforwardly to the unqualified statement, when in symbols is what you see, and which in words, roughly translated, is, 'You give us what we want in a week, or we beat the hell out of you and take it anyway.'"

There was silence as the five members of the Board ran down the line of symbols, and then Pirenne sat down and coughed uneasily.

Hardin said, "No loophole, is there, Dr. Pirenne?"

"Doesn't seem to be."

"All right." Hardin replaced the sheets. "Before you now you see a copy of the treaty between the Empire and Anacreon—a treaty, incidentally, which is signed on the Emperor's behalf by the same Lord Dorwin who was here last week—and with it a symbolic analysis."

The treaty ran through five pages of fine print and the analysis was scrawled out in just under half a page.

"As you see, gentlemen, something like ninety percent of the treaty boiled right out of the analysis as being meaningless, and what we end up with can be described in the following interesting manner:

"Obligations of Anacreon to the Empire: *None!*

"Powers of the Empire over Anacreon: *None!*"

Again the five followed the reasoning anxiously, checking carefully back to the treaty, and when they were finished, Pirenne said in a worried fashion, "That seems to be correct."

"You admit, then, that the treaty is nothing but a declaration of total independence on the part of Anacreon and a recognition of that status by the Empire?"

"It seems so."

"And do you suppose that Anacreon doesn't realize that, and is not anxious to emphasize the position of independence—so that it would naturally tend to resent any appearance of threats from the Empire? Particularly when it is evident that the Empire is powerless to fulfill any such threats, or it would never have allowed independence."

"But then," interposed Sutt, "how would Mayor Hardin account for Lord Dorwin's assurances of Empire support?

They seemed—" He shrugged. "Well, they seemed satisfactory."

Hardin threw himself back in the chair. "You know, that's the most interesting part of the whole business. I'll admit I had thought his Lordship a most consummate donkey when I first met him—but it turned out that he was actually an accomplished diplomat and a most clever man. I took the liberty of recording all his statements."

There was a flurry, and Pirenne opened his mouth in horror.

"What of it?" demanded Hardin. "I realize it was a gross breach of hospitality and a thing no so-called gentleman would do. Also, that if his lordship had caught on, things might have been unpleasant; but he didn't, and I have the record, and that's that. I took that record, had it copied out and sent that to Holk for analysis, also."

Lundin Crast said, "And where is the analysis?"

"That," replied Hardin, "is the interesting thing. The analysis was the most difficult of the three by all odds. When Holk, after two days of steady work, succeeded in eliminating meaningless statements, vague gibberish, useless qualifications—in short, all the goo and dribble—he found he had nothing left. Everything canceled out."

"Lord Dorwin, gentlemen, in five days of discussion *didn't* say one *damned thing*, and said it so you never noticed. *There* are the assurances you had from your precious Empire."

Hardin might have placed an actively working stench bomb on the table and created no more confusion than existed after his last statement. He waited, with weary patience, for it to die down.

"So," he concluded, "when you sent threats—and that's what they were—concerning Empire action to Anacreon, you merely irritated a monarch who knew better. Naturally, his ego would demand immediate action, and the ultimatum is the result—which brings me to my original statement. We have one week left and what do we do now?"

"It seems," said Sutt, "that we have no choice but to allow Anacreon to establish military bases on Terminus."

"I agree with you there," replied Hardin, "but what do we do toward kicking them off again at the first opportunity?"

Yate Fulham's mustache twitched. "That sounds as if you have made up your mind that violence must be used against them."

"Violence," came the retort, "is the last refuge of the incompetent. But I certainly don't intend to lay down the welcome mat and brush off the best furniture for their use."

"I still don't like the way you put that," insisted Fulham. "It is a dangerous attitude; the more dangerous because we have noticed lately that a sizable section of the populace seems to respond to all your suggestions just so. I might as well tell you, Mayor Hardin, that the board is not quite blind to your recent activities."

He paused and there was general agreement. Hardin shrugged.

Fulham went on: "If you were to inflame the City into an act of violence, you would achieve elaborate suicide—and we don't intend to allow that. Our policy has but one cardinal principle, and that is the Encyclopedia. Whatever we decide to do or not to do will be so decided because it will be the measure required to keep that Encyclopedia safe."

"Then," said Hardin, "you come to the conclusion that we must continue our intensive campaign of doing nothing."

Pirenne said bitterly: "You have yourself demonstrated that the Empire cannot help us; though how and why it can be so, I don't understand. If compromise is necessary—"

Hardin had the nightmarelike sensation of running at top speed and getting nowhere. "There *is* no compromise! Don't you realize that this bosh about military bases is a particularly inferior grade of drivel? Haut Rodric told us what Anacreon was after—outright annexation and imposition of its own feudal system of landed estates and peasant-aristocracy economy upon us. What is left of our bluff of atomic power may force them to move slowly, but they will move nonetheless."

He had risen indignantly, and the rest rose with him—except for Jord Fara.

And then Jord Fara spoke. "Everyone will please sit down. We've gone quite far enough, I think. Come, there's no use looking so furious, Mayor Hardin; none of us have been committing treason."

"You'll have to convince me of that!"

Fara smiled gently. "You know you don't mean that. Let me speak!"

His little shrewd eyes were half closed, and the perspiration gleamed on the smooth expanse of his chin. "There seems no point in concealing that the Board has come to the decision that the real solution to the Anacreonian problem lies in what is to be revealed to us when the Vault opens six days from now."

"Is that your contribution to the matter?"

"Yes."

"We are to do nothing, is that right, except to wait in quiet serenity and utter faith for the *deus ex machina* to pop out of the Vault?"

"Stripped of your emotional phraseology, that's the idea."

"Such unsubtle escapism! Really, Dr. Fara, such folly smacks of genius. A lesser mind would be incapable of it."

Fara smiled indulgently. "Your taste in epigrams is amusing, Hardin, but out of place. As a matter of fact, I think you remember my line of argument concerning the Vault about three weeks ago."

"Yes, I remember it. I don't deny that it was anything but a stupid idea from the standpoint of deductive logic alone. You said—stop me when I make a mistake—that Hari Seldon was the greatest psychologist in the System; that, hence, he could foresee the right and uncomfortable spot we're in now; that, hence, he established the Vault as a method of telling us the way out."

"You've got the essence of the idea."

"Would it surprise you to hear that I've given considerable thought to the matter these last weeks?"

"Very flattering. With what result?"

"With the result that pure deduction is found wanting. Again what is needed is a little sprinkling of common sense."

"For instance?"

"For instance, if he foresaw the Anacreonian mess, why not have placed us on some other planet nearer the Galactic centers? It's well known that Seldon maneuvered the Commissioners on Trantor into ordering the Foundation established on Terminus. But why should he have done so? Why put us out here at all if he could see in advance the break in communication lines, our isolation from the Galaxy, the threat of our neighbors—and our helplessness because of the lack of metals on Terminus? That above all! Or if he foresaw all this, why not have warned the original settlers in advance that they might have had time to prepare, rather than wait, as he is doing, until one foot is over the cliff, before doing so?

"And don't forget this. Even though he could foresee the problem *then*, we can see it equally well *now*. Therefore, if he could foresee the solution *then*, we should be able to see it *now*. After all, Seldon was not a magician. There are no trick methods of escaping from a dilemma that he can see and we can't."

"But, Hardin," reminded Fara, "we can't!"

"But you haven't *tried*. You haven't tried once. First, you refused to admit that there was a menace at all! Then you reposed an absolutely blind faith in the Emperor! Now you've shifted it to Hari Seldon. Throughout you have invariably relied on authority or on the past—never on yourselves."

His fists balled spasmodically. "It amounts to a diseased attitude—a conditioned reflex that shunts aside the independence of your minds whenever it is a question of opposing authority. There seems no doubt ever in your minds that the Emperor is more powerful than you are, or Hari Seldon wiser. And that's wrong, don't you see?"

For some reason, no one cared to answer him.

Hardin continued: "It isn't just you. It's the whole Galaxy. Pirenne heard Lord Dorwin's idea of scientific research. Lord Dorwin thought the way to be a good archaeologist was to read all the books on the subject—written by men who were dead for centuries. He thought that the way to solve archaeological puzzles was to weigh the opposing authorities. And Pirenne listened and made no objections. Don't you see that there's something wrong with that?"

Again the note of near-pleading in his voice. Again no answer.

He went on: "And you men and half of Terminus as well are just as bad. We sit here, considering the Encyclopedia the all-in-all. We consider the greatest end of science is the classification of past data. It is important, but is there no further work to be done? We're receding and forgetting, don't you see? Here in the Periphery they've lost atomic power. In Gamma Andromeda, a power plant has blown up because of poor repairs, and the Chancellor of the Empire complains that atomic technicians are scarce. And the solution? To train new ones? Never! Instead they're to restrict atomic power."

And for the third time: "Don't you see? It's Galaxywide. It's a worship of the past. It's a deterioration—a *stagnation!*"

He stared from one to the other and they gazed fixedly at him.

Fara was the first to recover. "Well, mystical philosophy isn't going to help us here. Let us be concrete. Do you deny that Hari Seldon could easily have worked out historical trends of the future by simple psychological technique?"

"No, of course not," cried Hardin. "But we can't rely on him for a solution. At best, he might indicate the problem, but if ever there is to be a solution, we must work it out ourselves. He can't do it for us."

Fulham spoke suddenly. "What do you mean—'indicate the problem'? We *know* the problem."

Hardin whirled on him. "You think you do? You think Anacreon is all Hari Seldon is likely to be worried about. I disagree! I tell you, gentlemen, that as yet none of you has the faintest conception of what is really going on."

"And you do?" questioned Pirenne, hostilely.

"I think so!" Hardin jumped up and pushed his chair away. His eyes were cold and hard. "If there's one thing that's definite, it is that there's something smelly about the whole situation; something that is bigger than anything we've talked about yet. Just ask yourself this question: Why was it that among the original population of the Foundation not one first-class psychologist was included, except Bor Alurin? And *he* carefully refrained from training his pupils in more than the fundamentals."

A short silence and Fara said: "All right. Why?"

"Perhaps because a psychologist might have caught on to what this was all about—and too soon to suit Hari Seldon. As it is, we've been stumbling about, getting misty glimpses of the truth and no more. And that is what Hari Seldon wanted."

He laughed harshly. "Good day, gentlemen!"

He stalked out of the room.

6.

Mayor Hardin chewed at the end of his cigar. It had gone out but he was past noticing that. He hadn't slept the night before and he had a good idea that he wouldn't sleep this coming night. His eyes showed it.

He said wearily, "And that covers it?"

"I think so." Yohan Lee put a hand to his chin. "How does it sound?"

"Not too bad. It's got to be done, you understand, with impudence. That is, there is to be no hesitation; no time to allow them to grasp the situation. Once we are in a position to give orders, why, give them as though you were born to do so, and they'll obey out of habit. That's the essence of a coup."

"If the Board remains irresolute for even—"

"The Board? Count them out. After tomorrow, their importance as a factor in Terminus affairs won't matter a rusty half-credit."

Lee nodded slowly. "Yet it is strange that they've done nothing to stop us so far. You say they weren't entirely in the dark."

"Fara stumbles at the edges of the problem. Sometimes he makes me nervous. And Pirenne's been suspicious of me since I was elected. But, you see, they never had the capacity of really understanding what was up. Their whole training has been authoritarian. They are sure that the Emperor, just because he is the Emperor, is all-powerful. And they are sure that the Board of Trustees, simply because it is the Board of Trustees acting in the name of the Emperor, cannot be in a position where it does not give the orders. That incapacity to recognize the possibility of revolt is our best ally."

He heaved out of his chair and went to the water cooler. "They're not bad fellows, Lee, when they stick to their Encyclopedia—and we'll see that that's where they stick in the future. They're hopelessly incompetent when it comes to ruling Terminus. Go away now and start things rolling. I want to be alone."

He sat down on the corner of his desk and stared at the cup of water.

Space! If only he were as confident as he pretended! The Anacreonians were landing in two days and what had he to go on but a set of notions and half-guesses as to what Hari Seldon had been driving at these past fifty years? He wasn't even a real, honest-to-goodness psychologist—just a fumbler with a little training trying to outguess the greatest mind of the age.

If Fara were right; if Anacreon were all the problem Hari Seldon had foreseen; if the Encyclopedia were all he was interested in preserving—then what price *coup d'état?*

He shrugged and drank his water.

7

The Vault was furnished with considerably more than six chairs, as though a larger company had been expected. Hardin noted that thoughtfully and seated himself wearily in a corner just as far from the other five as possible.

The Board members did not seem to object to that arrangement. They spoke among themselves in whispers, which fell off into sibilant monosyllables, and then into nothing at all. Of them all, only Jord Fara seemed even reasonably calm. He had produced a watch and was staring at it somberly.

Hardin glanced at his own watch and then at the glass cubicle—absolutely empty—that dominated half the room. It was the only unusual feature of the room, for aside from that there was no indication that somewhere a speck of radium was wasting away toward that precise moment when a tumbler would fall, a connection be made and—

The lights went dim!

They didn't go out, but merely yellowed and sank with a suddenness that made Hardin jump. He had lifted his eyes to the ceiling lights in startled fashion, and when he brought them down the glass cubicle was no longer empty.

A figure occupied it—a figure in a wheel chair!

It said nothing for a few moments, but it closed the book upon its lap and fingered it idly. And then it smiled, and the face seemed all alive.

It said, "I am Hari Seldon." The voice was old and soft.

Hardin almost rose to acknowledge the introduction and stopped himself in the act.

The voice continued conversationally: "As you see, I am confined to this chair and cannot rise to greet you. Your grandparents left for Terminus a few months back in my time and since then I have suffered a rather inconvenient paralysis. I can't see you, you know, so I can't greet you properly. I don't even know how many of you there are, so all this must be conducted informally. If any of you are standing, please sit down; and if you care to smoke, I wouldn't mind." There was a light chuckle. "Why should I? I'm not really here."

Hardin fumbled for a cigar almost automatically, but thought better of it.

Hari Seldon put away his book—as if laying it upon a desk at his side—and when his fingers let go, it disappeared.

He said: "It is fifty years now since this Foundation was established—fifty years in which the members of the Foundation have been ignorant of what it was they were working toward. It was necessary that they be ignorant, but now the necessity is gone.

"The Encyclopedia Foundation, to begin with, is a fraud, and always has been!"

There was a sound of a scramble behind Hardin and one or two muffled exclamations, but he did not turn around.

Hari Seldon was, of course, undisturbed. He went on: "It is a fraud in the sense that neither I nor my colleagues care at all whether a single volume of the Encyclopedia is ever published. It has served its purpose, since by it we extracted an imperial charter from the Emperor, by it we attracted the hundred thousand humans necessary for our scheme, and by it we managed to keep them preoccupied while events shaped themselves, until it was too late for any of them to draw back.

"In the fifty years that you have worked on this fraudulent project—there is no use in softening phrases—your retreat has been cut off, and you have now no choice but to proceed on the infinitely more important project that was, and is, our real plan.

"To that end we have placed you on such a planet and at such a time that in fifty years you were maneuvered to the point where you no longer have freedom of action. From now on, and into the centuries, the path you must take is inevitable. You will be faced with a series of crises, as you are now faced with the first, and in each case your freedom of action will become similarly circumscribed so that you will be forced along one, and only one, path.

"It is that path which our psychology has worked out—and for a reason.

"For centuries Galactic civilization has stagnated and declined, though only a few ever realized that. But now, at last, the Periphery is breaking away and the political unity of the Empire is shattered. Somewhere in the fifty years just past is where the historians of the future will place an arbitrary line and say: 'This marks the Fall of the Galactic Empire.'

"And they will be right, though scarcely any will recognize that Fall for additional centuries.

"And after the Fall will come inevitable barbarism, a period which, our psychohistory tells us, should, under ordinary circumstances, last for thirty thousand years. We cannot stop the Fall. We do not wish to; for Empire culture has lost whatever virility and worth it once had. But we can shorten the period of Barbarism that must follow—down to a single thousand of years.

"The ins and outs of that shortening, we cannot tell you; just as we could not tell you the truth about the Foundation fifty years ago. Were you to discover those ins and outs, our plan might fail; as it would have, had you penetrated the fraud of the Encyclopedia earlier; for then, by knowledge, your freedom of action would be expanded and the number of additional variables introduced would become greater than our psychology could handle.

"But you won't, for there are no psychologists on Terminus, and never were, but for Alurin—and he was one of us.

"But this I can tell you: Terminus and its companion Foundation at the other end of the Galaxy are the seeds of the Renascence and the future founders of the Second Galactic Empire. And it is the present crisis that is starting Terminus off to that climax.

"This, by the way, is a rather straightforward crisis, much simpler than many of those that are ahead. To reduce it to its fundamentals, it is this: You are a planet suddenly cut off from the still-civilized centers of the Galaxy, and threatened by your stronger neighbors. You are a small world of scientists surrounded by vast and rapidly expanding reaches of barbarism. You are an island of atomic power in a growing ocean of more primitive energy; but are helpless despite that, because of your lack of metals.

"You see, then, that you are faced by hard necessity, and that action is forced on you. The nature of that action—that is, the solution to your dilemma—is, of course, obvious!"

The image of Hari Seldon reached into open air and the book once more appeared in his hand. He opened it and said:

"But whatever devious course your future history may take, impress it always upon your descendants that the path has been marked out, and that at its end is new and greater Empire!"

And as his eyes bent to his book, he flicked into nothingness, and the lights brightened once more.

Hardin looked up to see Pirenne facing him, eyes tragic and lips trembling.

The chairman's voice was firm but toneless. "You were right, it seems. If you will see us tonight at six, the Board will consult with you as to the next move."

They shook his hand, each one, and left; and Hardin smiled to himself. They were fundamentally sound at that; for they were scientists enough to admit that they were wrong—but for them, it was too late.

He looked at his watch. By this time, it was all over. Lee's men were in control and the Board was giving orders no longer.

The Anacreonians were landing their first spaceships tomorrow, but that was all right, too. In six months, *they* would be giving orders no longer.

In fact, as Hari Seldon had said, and as Salvor Hardin had guessed since the day that Anselm haut Rodric had first revealed to him Anacreon's lack of atomic power—the solution to this first crisis was obvious.

Obvious as all hell!

PART III
THE MAYORS

1

THE FOUR KINGDOMS—The name given to those portions of the Province of Anacreon which broke away from the First Empire in the early years of the Foundational Era to form independent and short-lived kingdoms. The largest and most powerful of these was Anacreon itself which in area . . .

. . . Undoubtedly the most interesting aspect of the history of the Four Kingdoms involves the strange society forced temporarily upon it during the administration of Salvor Hardin. . . .

ENCYCLOPEDIA GALACTICA

A deputation!

That Salvor Hardin had seen it coming made it none the more pleasant. On the contrary, he found anticipation distinctly annoying.

Yohan Lee advocated extreme measures. "I don't see, Hardin," he said, "that we need waste any time. They can't do anything till next election—legally, anyway—and that gives us a year. Give them the brush-off."

Hardin pursed his lips. "Lee, you'll never learn. In the forty years I've known you, you've never once learned the gentle art of sneaking up from behind."

"It's not my way of fighting," grumbled Lee.

"Yes, I know that. I suppose that's why you're the one man I trust." He paused and reached for a cigar. "We've come a long way, Lee, since we engineered our coup against the Encyclopedists way back. I'm getting old. Sixty-two. Do you ever think how fast those thirty years went?"

Lee snorted. "I don't feel old, and I'm sixty-six."

"Yes, but I haven't your digestion." Hardin sucked lazily at his cigar. He had long since stopped wishing for the mild Vegan tobacco of his youth. Those days when the planet,

Terminus, had trafficked with every part of the Galactic Empire belonged in the limbo to which all Good Old Days go. Toward the same limbo where the Galactic Empire was heading. He wondered who the new emperor was—or if there was a new emperor at all—or any Empire. Space! For thirty years now, since the breakup of communications here at the edge of the Galaxy, the whole universe of Terminus had consisted of itself and the four surrounding kingdoms.

How the mighty had fallen! *Kingdoms!* They were prefects in the old days, all part of the same province, which in turn had been part of a sector, which in turn had been part of a quadrant, which in turn had been part of the all-embracing Galactic Empire. And now that the Empire had lost control over the farther reaches of the Galaxy, these little splinter groups of planets became kingdoms—with comic-opera kings and nobles, and petty, meaningless wars, and a life that went on pathetically among the ruins.

A civilization falling. Atomic power forgotten. Science fading to mythology—until the Foundation had stepped in. The Foundation that Hari Seldon had established for just that purpose here on Terminus.

Lee was at the window and his voice broke in on Hardin's reverie. "They've come," he said, "in a last-model ground car, the young pups." He took a few uncertain steps toward the door and then looked at Hardin.

Hardin smiled, and waved him back. "I've given orders to have them brought up here."

"Here! What for? You're making them too important."

"Why go through all the ceremonies of an official mayor's audience? I'm getting too old for red tape. Besides which, flattery is useful when dealing with youngsters—particularly when it doesn't commit you to anything." He winked. "Sit down, Lee, and give me your moral backing. I'll need it with this young Sermak."

"That fellow, Sermak," said Lee, heavily, "is dangerous. He's got a following, Hardin, so don't underestimate him."

"Have I ever underestimated anybody?"

"Well, then, arrest him. You can accuse him of something or other afterward."

Hardin ignored that last bit of advice. "There they are, Lee." In response to the signal, he stepped on the pedal beneath his desk, and the door slid aside.

They filed in, the four that composed the deputation, and Hardin waved them gently to the armchairs that faced his desk in a semicircle. They bowed and waited for the mayor to speak first.

Hardin flicked open the curiously carved silver lid of the cigar box that had once belonged to Jord Fara of the old Board of Trustees in the long-dead days of the Encyclopedists. It was a genuine Empire product from Santanni, though the cigars it now contained were home-grown. One by one, with grave solemnity, the four of the deputation accepted cigars and lit up in ritualistic fashion.

Sef Sermak was second from the right, the youngest of the young group—and the most interesting with his bristly yellow mustache trimmed precisely, and his sunken eyes of uncertain color. The other three Hardin dismissed almost immediately; they were rank and file on the face of them. It was on Sermak that he concentrated, the Sermak who had already, in his first term in the City Council, turned that sedate body topsy-turvy more than once, and it was to Sermak that he said:

"I've been particularly anxious to see you, Councilman, ever since your very excellent speech last month. Your attack on the foreign policy of this government was a most capable one."

Sermak's eyes smoldered. "Your interest honors me. The attack may or may not have been capable, but it was certainly justified."

"Perhaps! Your opinions are yours, of course. Still you are rather young."

Dryly. "It is a fault that most people are guilty of at some period of their life. You became mayor of the city when you were two years younger than I am now."

Hardin smiled to himself. The yearling was a cool customer. He said, "I take it now that you have come to see me concerning this same foreign policy that annoys you so greatly in the Council Chamber. Are you speaking for your three colleagues, or must I listen to each of you separately?"

There were quick mutual glances among the four young men, a slight flickering of eyelids.

Sermak said grimly, "I speak for the people of Terminus—a people who are not now truly represented in the rubber-stamp body they call the Council."

"I see. Go ahead, then!"

"It comes to this, Mr. Mayor. We are dissatisfied—"

"By 'we' you mean 'the people,' don't you?"

Sermak stared hostilely, sensing a trap, and replied coldly, "I believe that my views reflect those of the majority of the voters of Terminus. Does that suit you?"

"Well, a statement like that is all the better for proof, but go on, anyway. You are dissatisfied."

"Yes, dissatisfied with the policy which for thirty years has been stripping Terminus defenseless against the inevitable attack from outside."

"I see. And therefore? Go on, go on."

"It's nice of you to anticipate. And therefore we are forming a new political party; one that will stand for the immediate needs of Terminus and not for a mystic 'manifest destiny' of future Empire. We are going to throw you and your lick-spittle clique of appeasers out of City Hall—and that soon."

"Unless? There's always an 'unless,' you know."

"Not much of one in this case: Unless you resign now. I'm not asking you to change your policies—I wouldn't trust you that far. Your promises are worth nothing. An outright resignation is all we'll take."

"I see." Hardin crossed his legs and teetered his chair back on two legs. "That's your ultimatum. Nice of you to give me warning. But, you see, I rather think I'll ignore it."

"Don't think it was a warning, Mr. Mayor. It was an announcement of principles and of action. The new party has already been formed, and it will begin its official activities tomorrow. There is neither room nor desire for compromise, and, frankly, it was only our recognition of your services to the City that induced us to offer the easy way out. I didn't think you'd take it, but my conscience is clear. The next election will be a more forcible and quite irresistible reminder that resignation is necessary."

He rose and motioned the rest up.

Hardin lifted his arm. "Hold on! Sit down!"

Sef Sermak seated himself once more with just a shade too much alacrity and Hardin smiled behind a straight face. In spite of his words, he was waiting for an offer—an offer.

Hardin said, "In exactly what way do you want our foreign policy changed? Do you want us to attack the Four Kingdoms, now, at once, and all four simultaneously?"

"I make no such suggestion, Mr. Mayor. It is our simple proposition that all appeasement cease immediately. Throughout your administration, you have carried out a policy of scientific aid to the Kingdoms. You have given them atomic power. You have helped rebuild power plants on their territories. You have established medical clinics, chemical laboratories and factories."

"Well? And your objection?"

"You have done this in order to keep them from attacking us. With these as bribes, you have been playing the fool in a colossal game of blackmail, in which you have allowed Terminus to be sucked dry—with the result that now we are at the mercy of these barbarians."

"In what way?"

"Because you have given them power, given them weapons, actually serviced the ships of their navies, they are infinitely stronger than they were three decades ago. Their demands are increasing, and with their new weapons, they will eventually satisfy all their demands at once by violent annexation of Terminus. Isn't that the way blackmail usually ends?"

"And your remedy?"

"Stop the bribes immediately and while you can. Spend your effort in strengthening Terminus itself—and attack first!"

Hardin watched the young fellow's little blond mustache with an almost morbid interest. Sermak felt sure of himself or he wouldn't talk so much. There was no doubt that his remarks were the reflection of a pretty huge segment of the population, pretty huge.

His voice did not betray the slightly perturbed current of his thoughts. It was almost negligent. "Are you finished?"

"For the moment."

"Well, then, do you notice the framed statement I have on the wall behind me? Read it, if you will!"

Sermak's lips twitched. "It says: 'Violence is the last refuge of the incompetent.' That's an old man's doctrine, Mr. Mayor."

"I applied it as a young man, Mr. Councilman—and successfully. You were busily being born when it happened, but perhaps you may have read something of it in school."

He eyed Sermak closely and continued in measured tones, "When Hari Seldon established the Foundation here, it was for the ostensible purpose of producing a great Encyclopedia, and for fifty years we followed that will-of-the-wisp, before discovering what he was really after. By that time, it was almost too late. When communications with the central regions of the old Empire broke down, we found ourselves a world of scientists concentrated in a single city, possessing no industries, and surrounded by newly created kingdoms, hostile and largely barbarous. We were a tiny island of atomic power in this ocean of barbarism, and an infinitely valuable prize.

"Anacreon, then as now, the most powerful of the Four Kingdoms, demanded and actually established a military base upon Terminus, and the then rulers of the City, the Encyclopedists, knew very well that this was only a preliminary to taking over the entire planet. That is how matters stood when I . . . uh . . . assumed actual government. What would you have done?"

Sermak shrugged his shoulders. "That's an academic question. Of course, I know what *you* did."

"I'll repeat it, anyway. Perhaps you don't get the point. The temptation was great to muster what force we could and put up a fight. It's the easiest way out, and the most satisfactory to self-respect—but, nearly invariably, the stupidest. *You* would have done it; you and your talk of 'attack first.' What I did, instead, was to visit the three other kingdoms, one by one; point out to each that to allow the secret of atomic power to fall into the hands of Anacreon was the quickest way of cutting their own throats; and suggest gently that they do the obvious thing. That was all. One month after the Anacreonian force had landed on Terminus, their king received a joint ultimatum from his three neighbors. In seven days, the last Anacreonian was off Terminus.

"Now tell me, where was the need for violence?"

The young councilman regarded his cigar stub thoughtfully and tossed it into the incinerator chute. "I fail to see the analogy. Insulin will bring a diabetic to normal without the faintest need of a knife, but appendicitis needs an operation. You can't help that. When other courses have failed, what is left but, as you put it, the last refuge? It's your fault that we're driven to it."

"I? Oh, yes, again my policy of appeasement. You still seem to lack grasp of the fundamental necessities of our position. Our problem wasn't over with the departure of the Anacreonians. They had just begun. The Four Kingdoms were more our enemies than ever, for each wanted atomic power—and each was kept off our throats only for fear of the other three. We are balanced on the point of a very sharp sword, and the slightest sway in any direction— If, for instance, one kingdom becomes too strong; or if two form a coalition— You understand?"

"Certainly. That was the time to begin all-out preparations for war."

"On the contrary. That was the time to begin all-out prevention of war. I played them one against the other. I helped each in turn. I offered them science, trade, education, scientific medicine. I made Terminus of more value to them as a flourishing world than as a military prize. It worked for thirty years."

"Yes, but you were forced to surround these scientific gifts with the most outrageous mummery. You've made half religion, half balderdash out of it. You've erected a hierarchy of priests and complicated, meaningless ritual."

Hardin frowned. "What of that? I don't see that it has anything to do with the argument at all. I started that way at first because the barbarians looked upon our science as a sort of magical sorcery, and it was easiest to get them to accept it on that basis. The priesthood built itself and if we help it along we are only following the line of least resistance. It is a minor matter."

"But these priests are in charge of the power plants. That is *not* a minor matter."

"True, but *we* have trained them. Their knowledge of their tools is purely empirical; and they have a firm belief in the mummery that surrounds them."

"And if one pierces through the mummery, and has the genius to brush aside empiricism, what is to prevent him from learning actual techniques, and selling out to the most satisfactory bidder? What price our value to the kingdoms, then?"

"Little chance of that, Sermak. You are being superficial. The best men on the planets of the kingdoms are sent here to the Foundation each year and educated into the priesthood. And the best of these remain here as research students. If you think that those who are left, with practically no knowledge of the elementals of science, or worse, still, with the distorted knowledge the priests receive, can penetrate at a bound to atomic power, to electronics, to the theory of the hyperwarp—you have a very romantic and very foolish idea of science. It takes lifetimes of training and an excellent brain to get that far."

Yohan Lee had risen abruptly during the foregoing speech and left the room. He had returned now and when Hardin finished speaking, he bent to his superior's ear. A whisper was exchanged and then a leaden cylinder. Then, with one short hostile look at the deputation, Lee resumed his chair.

Hardin turned the cylinder end for end in his hands, watching the deputation through his lashes. And then he opened it with a hard, sudden twist and only Sermak had the sense not to throw a rapid look at the rolled paper that fell out.

"In short, gentlemen," he said, "the Government is of the opinion that it knows what it is doing."

He read as he spoke. There were the lines of intricate, meaningless code that covered the page and the three penciled words scrawled in one corner that carried the message. He took it in at a glance and tossed it casually into the incinerator shaft.

"That," Hardin then said, "ends the interview, I'm afraid. Glad to have met you all. Thank you for coming." He shook hands with each in perfunctory fashion, and they filed out.

Hardin had almost gotten out of the habit of laughing, but after Sermak and his three silent partners were well out of earshot, he indulged in a dry chuckle and bent an amused look on Lee.

"How did you like that battle of bluffs, Lee?"

Lee snorted grumpily. "I'm not sure that *he* was bluffing. Treat him with kid gloves and he's quite liable to win the next election, just as he says."

"Oh, quite likely, quite likely—if nothing happens first."

"Make sure they don't happen in the wrong direction this time, Hardin. I tell you this Sermak has a following. What if he doesn't wait till the next election? There was a time when you and I put things through violently, in spite of your slogan about what violence is."

Hardin cocked an eyebrow. "You *are* pessimistic today, Lee. And singularly contrary, too, or you wouldn't speak of violence. Our own little putsch was carried through without loss of life, you remember. It was a necessary measure put through at the proper moment, and went over smoothly, painlessly, and all but effortlessly. As for Sermak, he's up against a different proposition. You and I, Lee, aren't the Encyclopedists. *We* stand prepared. Sick your men onto these youngsters in a nice way, old fellow. Don't let them know they're being watched—but eyes open, you understand."

Lee laughed in sour amusement. "I'd be a fine one to wait for your orders, wouldn't I, Hardin? Sermak and his men have been under surveillance for a month now."

The mayor chuckled. "Got in first, did you? All right. By the way," he observed, and added softly, "Ambassador Verisof is returning to Terminus. Temporarily, I hope."

There was a short silence, faintly horrified, and then Lee said, "Was that the message? Are things breaking already?"

"Don't know. I can't tell till I hear what Verisof has to say. They may be, though. After all, they *have* to before election. But what are you looking so dead about?"

"Because I don't know how it's going to turn out. You're too deep, Hardin, and you're playing the game too close to your chest."

"Thou, too, Brutus," murmured Hardin. And aloud, "Does that mean you're going to join Sermak's new party?"

Lee smiled against his will. "All right. You win. How about lunch now?"

2.

There are many epigrams attributed to Hardin—a confirmed epigrammatist—a good many of which are probably apocryphal. Nevertheless, it is reported that on a certain occasion, he said:

"It pays to be obvious, especially if you have a reputation for subtlety."

Poly Verisof had had occasion to act on that advice more

than once for he was now in the fourteenth year of his double status on Anacreon—a double status the upkeep of which reminded him often and unpleasantly of a dance performed barefoot on hot metal.

To the people of Anacreon he was high priest, representative of that Foundation which, to those "barbarians," was the acme of mystery and the physical center of this religion they had created—with Hardin's help—in the last three decades. As such, he received a homage that had become horribly wearying, for from his soul he despised the ritual of which he was the center.

But to the King of Anacreon—the old one that had been, and the young grandson that was now on the throne—he was simply the ambassador of a power at once feared and coveted.

On the whole, it was an uncomfortable job, and his first trip to the Foundation in three years, despite the disturbing incident that had made it necessary, was something in the nature of a holiday.

And since it was not the first time he had had to travel in absolute secrecy, he again made use of Hardin's epigram on the uses of the obvious.

He changed into his civilian clothes—a holiday in itself—and boarded a passenger liner to the Foundation, second class. Once at Terminus, he threaded his way through the crowd at the spaceport and called up City Hall at a public visiphone.

He said, "My name is Jan Smite. I have an appointment with the mayor this afternoon."

The dead-voiced but efficient young lady at the other end made a second connection and exchanged a few rapid words, then said to Verisof in dry, mechanical tone, "Mayor Hardin will see you in half an hour, sir," and the screen went blank.

Whereupon the ambassador to Anacreon bought the latest edition of the Terminus City *Journal*, sauntered casually to City Hall Park and, sitting down on the first empty bench he came to, read the editorial page, sport section and comic sheet while waiting. At the end of half an hour, he tucked the paper under his arm, entered City Hall and presented himself in the anteroom.

In doing all this he remained safely and thoroughly unrecognized, for since he was so entirely obvious, no one gave him a second look.

Hardin looked up at him and grinned. "Have a cigar! How was the trip?"

Verisof helped himself. "Interesting. There was a priest in the next cabin on his way here to take a special course in the preparation of radioactive synthetics—for the treatment of cancer, you know—"

"Surely, he didn't call it radioactive synthetics, now?"

"I guess *not!* It was the Holy Food to him."

The mayor smiled. "Go on."

"He inveigled me into a theological discussion and did his level best to elevate me out of sordid materialism."

"And never recognized his own high priest?"

"Without my crimson robe? Besides, he was a Smyrnian. It was an interesting experience, though. It *is* remarkable, Hardin, how the religion of science has grabbed hold. I've written an essay on the subject—entirely for my own amusement; it wouldn't do to have it published. Treating the problem sociologically, it would seem that when the old Empire began to rot at the fringes, it could be considered that science, as science, had failed the outer worlds. To be reaccepted it would have to present itself in another guise—and it has done just that. It works out beautifully when you use symbolic logic to help out."

"Interesting!" The mayor placed his arms behind his neck and said suddenly, "Start talking about the situation at Anacreon!"

The ambassador frowned and withdrew the cigar from his mouth. He looked at it distastefully and put it down. "Well, it's pretty bad."

"You wouldn't be here, otherwise."

"Scarcely. Here's the position. The key man at Anacreon

is the Prince Regent, Wienis. He's King Lepold's uncle."

"I know. But Lepold is coming of age next year, isn't he? I believe he'll be sixteen in February."

"Yes." Pause, and then a wry addition. "*If* he lives. The king's father died under suspicious circumstances. A needle bullet through the chest during a hunt. It was called an accident."

"Hmph. I seem to remember Wienis the time I was on Anacreon, when we kicked them off Terminus. It was before your time. Let's see now. If I remember, he was a dark young fellow, black hair and a squint in his right eye. He had a funny hook in his nose."

"Same fellow. The hook and the squint are still there, but his hair's gray now. He plays the game dirty. Luckily, he's the most egregious fool on the planet. Fancies himself as a shrewd devil, too, which makes his folly the more transparent."

"That's usually the way."

"His notion of cracking an egg is to shoot an atomic blast at it. Witness the tax on Temple property he tried to impose just after the old king died two years ago. Remember?"

Hardin nodded thoughtfully, then smiled. "The priests raised a howl."

"They raised one you could hear way out to Lucreza. He's shown more caution in dealing with the priesthood since, but he still manages to do things the hard way. In a way, it's unfortunate for us; he has unlimited self-confidence."

"Probably an over-compensated inferiority complex. Younger sons of royalty get that way, you know."

"But it amounts to the same thing. He's foaming at the mouth with eagerness to attack the Foundation. He scarcely troubles to conceal it. And he's in a position to do it, too, from the standpoint of armament. The old king built up a magnificent navy, and Wienis hasn't been sleeping the last two years. In fact, the tax on Temple property was originally intended for further armament, and when that fell through he increased the income tax twice."

"Any grumbling at that?"

"None of serious importance. Obedience to appointed authority was the text of every sermon in the kingdom for weeks. Not that Wienis showed any gratitude."

"All right. I've got the background. Now what's happened?"

"Two weeks ago an Anacreonian merchant ship came across a derelict battle cruiser of the old Imperial Navy. It must have been drifting in space for at least three centuries."

Interest flickered in Hardin's eyes. He sat up. "Yes, I've heard of that. The Board of Navigation has sent me a petition asking me to obtain the ship for purposes of study. It is in good condition, I understand."

"In entirely too good condition," responded Verisof, dryly. "When Wienis received your suggestion last week that he turn the ship over to the Foundation, he almost had convulsions."

"He hasn't answered yet."

"He won't—except with guns, or so he thinks. You see, he came to me on the day I left Anacreon and requested that the Foundation put this battle cruiser into fighting order and turn it over to the Anacreonian navy. He had the infernal gall to say that your note of last week indicated a plan of the Foundation's to attack Anacreon. He said that refusal to repair the battle cruiser would confirm his suspicions; and indicated that measures for the self-defense of Anacreon would be forced upon him. Those are his words. Forced upon him! And that's why I'm here."

Hardin laughed gently.

Verisof smiled and continued, "Of course, he expects a refusal, and it would be a perfect excuse—in his eyes—for immediate attack."

"I see that, Verisof. Well, we have at least six months to spare, so have the ship fixed up and present it with my compliments. Have it renamed the Wienis as a mark of our esteem and affection."

He laughed again.

And again Verisof responded with the faintest trace of a smile, "I suppose it's the logical step, Hardin—but I'm worried."

"What about?"

"It's a *ship!* They could *build* in those days. Its cubic capacity is half again that of the entire Anacreonian navy. It's got atomic blasts capable of blowing up a planet, and a shield that could take a Q-beam without working up radiation. Too much of a good thing, Hardin—"

"Superficial, Verisof, superficial. You and I both know that the armament he now has could defeat Terminus handily, long before we could repair the cruiser for our own use. What does it matter, then, if we give him the cruiser as well? You know it won't ever come to actual war."

"I suppose so. Yes." The ambassador looked up. "But Hardin—"

"Well? Why do you stop? Go ahead."

"Look. This isn't my province. But I've been reading the paper." He placed the *Journal* on the desk and indicated the front page. "What's this all about?"

Hardin dropped a casual glance. "'A group of Councilmen are forming a new political party.'"

"That's what it says." Verisof fidgeted. "I know you're in better touch with internal matters than I am, but they're attacking you with everything short of physical violence. How strong are they?"

"Damned strong. They'll probably control the Council after next election."

"Not before?" Verisof looked at the mayor obliquely. "There are ways of gaining control besides elections."

"Do you take me for Wienis?"

"No. But repairing the ship will take months and an attack after that is certain. Our yielding will be taken as a sign of appalling weakness and the addition of the Imperial Cruiser will just about double the strength of Wienis' navy.

He'll attack as sure as I'm a high priest. Why take chances? Do one of two things. Either reveal the plan of campaign to the Council, or force the issue with Anacreon now!"

Hardin frowned. "Force the issue now? Before the crisis comes? It's the one thing I mustn't do. There's Hari Seldon and the Plan, you know."

Verisof hesitated, then muttered, "You're absolutely sure, then, that there is a Plan?"

"There can scarcely be any doubt," came the stiff reply. "I was present at the opening of the Time Vault and Seldon's recording revealed it then."

"I didn't mean that, Hardin. I just don't see how it could be possible to chart history for a thousand years ahead. Maybe Seldon overestimated himself." He shriveled a bit at Hardin's ironical smile, and added, "Well, I'm no psychologist."

"Exactly. None of us are. But I did receive some elementary training in my youth—enough to know what psychology is capable of, even if I can't exploit its capabilities myself. There's no doubt but that Seldon did exactly what he claims to have done. The Foundation, as he says, was established as a scientific refuge—the means by which the science and culture of the dying Empire was to be preserved through the centuries of barbarism that have begun, to be rekindled in the end into a second Empire."

Verisof nodded, a trifle doubtfully. "Everyone knows that's the way things are *supposed* to go. But can we afford to take chances? Can we risk the present for the sake of a nebulous future?"

"We must—because the future isn't nebulous. It's been calculated out by Seldon and charted. Each successive crisis in our history is mapped and each depends in a measure on the successful conclusion of the ones previous. This is only the second crisis and Space knows what effect even a trifling deviation would have in the end."

"That's rather empty speculation."

"*No!* Hari Seldon said in the Time Vault, that at each crisis our freedom of action would become circumscribed to the point where only one course of action was possible."

"So as to keep us on the straight and narrow?"

"So as to keep us from deviating, yes. But, conversely, as long as *more* than one course of action is possible, the crisis has not been reached. We *must* let things drift so long as we possibly can, and by space, that's what I intend doing."

Verisof didn't answer. He chewed his lower lip in a grudging silence. It had only been the year before that Hardin had first discussed the problem with him—the real problem; the problem of countering Anacreon's hostile preparations. And then only because he, Verisof, had balked at further appeasement.

Hardin seemed to follow his ambassador's thoughts. "I would much rather never to have told you anything about this."

"What makes you say that?" cried Verisof, in surprise.

"Because there are six people now—you and I, the other three ambassadors and Yohan Lee—who have a fair notion of what's ahead; and I'm damned afraid that it was Seldon's idea to have no one know."

"Why so?"

"Because even Seldon's advanced psychology was limited. It could not handle too many independent variables. He couldn't work with individuals over any length of time; any more than you could apply the kinetic theory of gases to single molecules. He worked with mobs, populations of whole planets, and only *blind* mobs who do not possess foreknowledge of the results of their own actions."

"That's not plain."

"I can't help it. I'm not psychologist enough to explain it scientifically. But this you know. There are no trained psychologists on Terminus and no mathematical texts on the science. It is plain that he wanted no one on Terminus capable of working out the future in advance. Seldon wanted us to proceed blindly—and therefore correctly—according to the law of mob psychology. As I once told you, I never knew where we were heading when I first drove out the Anacreonians. My idea had been to maintain balance of power, no more than that. It was only afterward that I thought I saw a pattern in events; but I've done my level best not to act on that knowledge. Interference due to foresight would have knocked the Plan out of kilter."

Verisof nodded thoughtfully. "I've heard arguments almost as complicated in the Temples back on Anacreon. How do you expect to spot the right moment of action?"

"It's spotted already. You admit that once we repair the battle cruiser nothing will stop Wienis from attacking us. There will no longer be any alternative in that respect."

"Yes."

"All right. That accounts for the external aspect. Meanwhile, you'll further admit that the next election will see a new and hostile Council that will force action against Anacreon. There is no alternative there."

"Yes."

"And as soon as all the alternatives disappear, the crisis has come. Just the same—I get worried."

He paused, and Verisof waited. Slowly, almost reluctantly, Hardin continued, "I've got the idea—just a notion—that the external and internal pressures were planned to come to a head simultaneously. As it is, there's a few months difference. Wienis will probably attack before spring, and elections are still a year off."

"That doesn't sound important."

"I don't know. It may be due merely to unavoidable errors of calculation, or it might be due to the fact that I knew too much. I tried never to let my foresight influence my action, but how can I tell? And what effect will the discrepancy have? Anyway," he looked up, "there's one thing I've decided."

"And what's that?"

"When the crisis does begin to break, I'm going to Anacreon. I want to be on the spot . . . Oh, that's enough, Verisof. It's getting late. Let's go out and make a night of it. I want some relaxation."

"Then get it right here," said Verisof. "I don't want to be recognized, or you know what this new party your precious Councilmen are forming would say. Call for the brandy."

And Hardin did—but not for too much.

3·

In the ancient days when the Galactic Empire had embraced the Galaxy, and Anacreon had been the richest of the prefects of the Periphery, more than one emperor had visited the Viceregal Palace in state. And not one had left without at least one effort to pit his skill with air speedster and needle gun against the feathered flying fortress they call the Nyakbird.

The fame of Anacreon had withered to nothing with the decay of the times. The Viceregal Palace was a drafty mass of ruins except for the wing that Foundation workmen had restored. And no Emperor had been seen in Anacreon for two hundred years.

But Nyak hunting was still the royal sport and a good eye with the needle gun still the first requirement of Anacreon's kings.

Lepold I, King of Anacreon and—as was invariably, but untruthfully added—Lord of the Outer Dominions, though not yet sixteen had already proved his skill many times over. He had brought down his first Nyak when scarcely thirteen; had brought down his tenth the week after his accession to the throne; and was returning now from his forty-sixth.

"Fifty before I come of age," he had exulted. "Who'll take the wager?"

But Courtiers don't take wagers against the king's skill. There is the deadly danger of winning. So no one did, and the king left to change his clothes in high spirits.

"Lepold!"

The king stopped mid-step at the one voice that could cause him to do so. He turned sulkily.

Wienis stood upon the threshold of his chambers and bee-tled at his young nephew.

"Send them away," he motioned impatiently. "Get rid of them."

The king nodded curtly and the two chamberlains bowed and backed down the stairs. Lepold entered his uncle's room.

Wienis stared at the king's hunting suit morosely. "You'll have more important things to tend to than Nyak hunting soon enough."

He turned his back and stumped to his desk. Since he had grown too old for the rush of air, the perilous dive within wing-beat of the Nyak, the roll and climb of the speedster at the motion of a foot, he had soured upon the whole sport.

Lepold appreciated his uncle's sour-grapes attitude and it was not without malice that he began enthusiastically, "But you should have been with us today, uncle. We flushed one in the wilds of Samia that was a monster. And game as they come. We had it out for two hours over at least seventy square miles of ground. And then I got to Sunwards"—he was motioning graphically, as though he were once more in his speedster—"and dived torque-wise. Caught him on the rise just under the left wing at quarters. It maddened him and he canted athwart. I took his dare and veered a-left, waiting for the plummet. Sure enough, down he came. He was within wing-beat before I moved and then—"

"Lepold!"

"Well!—I got him."

"I'm sure you did. Now *will* you attend?"

The king shrugged and gravitated to the end table where he nibbled at a Lera nut in quite an unregal sulk. He did not dare to meet his uncle's eyes.

Wienis said, by way of preamble, "I've been to the ship today."

"What ship?"

"There is only one ship. *The* ship. The one the Foundation is repairing for the navy. The old Imperial cruiser. Do I make myself sufficiently plain?"

"That one? You see, I told you the Foundation would repair it if we asked them to. It's all poppycock, you know, that story of yours about their wanting to attack us. Because if they did, why would they fix the ship? It doesn't make sense, you know."

"Lepold, you're a fool!"

The king, who had just discarded the shell of the Lera nut and was lifting another to his lips, flushed.

"Well now, look here," he said, with anger that scarcely rose above peevishness, "I don't think you ought to call me that. You forget yourself. I'll be of age in two months, you know."

"Yes, and you're in a fine position to assume regal responsibilities. If you spent half the time on public affairs that you do on Nyak hunting, I'd resign the regency directly with a clear conscience."

"I don't care. That has nothing to do with the case, you know. The fact is that even if you are the regent and my uncle, I'm still king and you're still my subject. You oughtn't to call me a fool and you oughtn't to sit in my presence, anyway. You haven't asked my permission. I think you ought to be careful, or I might do something about it—pretty soon."

Wienis' gaze was cold. "May I refer to you as 'your majesty'?"

"Yes."

"Very well! You are a fool, your majesty!"

His dark eyes blazed from beneath his grizzled brows and the young king sat down slowly. For a moment, there was sardonic satisfaction in the regent's face, but it faded quickly. His thick lips parted in a smile and one hand fell upon the king's shoulder.

"Never mind, Lepold. I should not have spoken harshly to you. It is difficult sometimes to behave with true propriety when the pressure of events is such as— You understand?" But if the words were conciliatory, there was something in his eyes that had not softened.

Lepold said uncertainly, "Yes. Affairs of State are deuced

difficult, you know." He wondered, not without apprehension, whether he were not in for a dull siege of meaningless details on the year's trade with Smyrno and the long, wrangling dispute over the sparsely settled worlds on the Red Corridor.

Wienis was speaking again. "My boy, I had thought to speak of this to you earlier, and perhaps I should have, but I know that your youthful spirits are impatient of the dry detail of statecraft."

Lepold nodded. "Well, that's all right—"

His uncle broke in firmly and continued, "However, you will come of age in two months. Moreover, in the difficult times that are coming, you will have to take a full and active part. You will be *king* henceforward, Lepold."

Again Lepold nodded, but his expression was quite blank.

"There will be war, Lepold."

"War! But there's been truce with Smyrno—"

"Not Smyrno. The Foundation itself."

"But, uncle, they've agreed to repair the ship. You said—"

His voice choked off at the twist of his uncle's lip.

"Lepold"—some of the friendliness had gone—"we are to talk man to man. There is to be war with the Foundation, whether the ship is repaired or not; all the sooner, in fact, since it is being repaired. The Foundation is the source of power and might. All the greatness of Anacreon; all its ships and its cities and its people and its commerce depend on the dribbles and leavings of power that the Foundation have given us grudgingly. I remember the time—I, myself—when the cities of Anacreon were warmed by the burning of coal and oil. But never mind that; you would have no conception of it."

"It seems," suggested the king, timidly, "that we ought to be grateful—"

"Grateful?" roared Wienis. "Grateful that they begrudge us the merest dregs, while keeping space knows what for themselves—and keeping it with what purpose in mind? Why, only that they may some day rule the Galaxy."

His hand came down on his nephew's knee, and his eyes narrowed. "Lepold, you are king of Anacreon. Your children and your children's children may be kings of the universe— if you have the power that the Foundation is keeping from us!"

"There's something in that." Lepold's eyes gained a sparkle and his back straightened. "After all, what right have they to keep it to themselves? Not fair, you know. Anacreon counts for something, too."

"You see, you're beginning to understand. And now, my boy, what if Smyrno decides to attack the Foundation for its own part and thus gains all that power? How long do you suppose we could escape becoming a vassal power? How long would you hold your throne?"

Lepold grew excited. "Space, yes. You're absolutely right, you know. We must strike first. It's simply self-defense."

Wienis' smile broadened slightly. "Furthermore, once, at the very beginning of the reign of your grandfather, Anacreon actually established a military base on the Foundation's planet, Terminus—a base vitally needed for national defense. We were forced to abandon that base as a result of the machinations of the leader of that Foundation, a sly cur, a scholar, with not a drop of noble blood in his veins. You understand, Lepold? Your grandfather was humiliated by this commoner. I remember him! He was scarcely older than myself when he came to Anacreon with his devil's smile and devil's brain— and the power of the other three kingdoms behind him, combined in cowardly union against the greatness of Anacreon."

Lepold flushed and the sparkle in his eyes blazed. "By Seldon, if I had been my grandfather, I would have fought even so."

"No, Lepold. We decided to wait—to wipe out the insult at a fitter time. It had been your father's hope, before his untimely death, that he might be the one to— Well, well!" Wienis turned away for a moment. Then, as if stifling emotion, "He was my brother. And yet, if his son were—"

"Yes, uncle, I'll not fail him. I have decided. It seems only proper that Anacreon wipe out this nest of troublemakers, and that immediately."

"No, not immediately. First, we must wait for the repairs of the battle cruiser to be completed. The mere fact that they are willing to undertake these repairs proves that they fear us. The fools attempt to placate us, but we are not to be turned from our path, are we?"

And Lepold's fist slammed against his cupped palm. "Not while I am king in Anacreon."

Wienis' lip twitched sardonically. "Besides which we must wait for Salvor Hardin to arrive."

"Salvor Hardin!" The king grew suddenly round-eyed, and the youthful contour of his beardless face lost the almost hard lines into which they had been compressed.

"Yes, Lepold, the leader of the Foundation himself is coming to Anacreon on your birthday—probably to soothe us with buttered words. But it won't help him."

"Salvor Hardin!" It was the merest murmur.

Wienis frowned. "Are you afraid of the name? It is the same Salvor Hardin, who on his previous visit, ground our noses into the dust. You're not forgetting that deadly insult to the royal house? And from a commoner. The dregs of the gutter."

"No. I guess not. No, I won't. I won't! We'll pay him back —but . . . but—I'm afraid—a little."

The regent rose. "Afraid? Of what? Of what, you young—" He choked off.

"It would be . . . uh . . . sort of blasphemous, you know, to attack the Foundation. I mean—" He paused.

"Go on."

Lepold said confusedly, "I mean, if there were *really* a Galactic Spirit, he . . . uh . . . it mightn't like it. Don't you think?"

"No, I don't," was the hard answer. Wienis sat down again and his lips twisted in a queer smile. "And so you really bother your head a great deal over the Galactic Spirit, do you? That's what comes of letting you run wild. You've been listening to Verisof quite a bit, I take it."

"He's explained a great deal—"

"About the Galactic Spirit?"

"Yes."

"Why, you unweaned cub, he believes in that mummery a good deal less than I do, and I don't believe in it at all. How many times have you been told that all this talk is nonsense?"

"Well, I know that. But Verisof says—"

"Damnation to Verisof. It's nonsense."

There was a short, rebellious silence, and then Lepold said, "Everyone believes it just the same. I mean all this talk about the Prophet Hari Seldon and how he appointed the Foundation to carry on his commandments that there might some day be a return of the Earthly Paradise: and how anyone who disobeys his commandments will be destroyed for eternity. They believe it. I've presided at festivals, and I'm sure they do."

"Yes, *they* do; but we don't. And you may be thankful it's so, for according to this foolishness, you are king by divine right—and are semi-divine yourself. Very handy. It eliminates all possibilities of revolts and insures absolute obedience in everything. And that is why, Lepold, you must take an active part in ordering the war against the Foundation. I am only regent, and quite human. You are king, and more than half a god—to them."

"But I suppose I'm not really," said the king, reflectively.

"No, not really," came the ironic response, "but you are to everyone but the people of the Foundation. Get that? To everyone but those of the Foundation. Once they are removed there will be no one to deny you the godhead. Think of that!"

"And after that we will ourselves be able to operate the power boxes of the temples and the ships that fly without men and the holy food that cures cancer and all the rest? Verisof said only those blessed with the Galactic Spirit could—"

"Yes, Verisof said! Verisof, next to Salvor Hardin, is your greatest enemy. Stay with me, Lepold, and don't worry about them. Together we will recreate an empire—not just the kingdom of Anacreon—but one comprising every one of the billions of suns of the Galaxy. Is that better than a wordy 'Earthly Paradise'?"

"Ye-es."

"Can Verisof promise more?"

"No."

"Very well." His voice became peremptory. "I suppose we may consider the matter settled." He waited for no answer. "Get along. I'll be down later. And just one thing, Lepold."

The young king turned on the threshold.

Wienis was smiling with all but his eyes. "Be careful on these Nyak hunts, my boy. Since the unfortunate accident to your father, I have had the strangest presentiments concerning you, at times. In the confusion, with needle guns thickening the air with darts, one can never tell. You *will* be careful, I hope. And you'll do as I say about the Foundation, won't you?"

Lepold's eyes widened and dropped away from those of his uncle. "Yes—certainly."

"Good!" He stared after his departing nephew, expressionlessly, and returned to his desk.

And Lepold's thoughts as he left were somber and not unfearful. Perhaps it *would* be best to defeat the Foundation and gain the power Wienis spoke of. But afterward, when the war was over and he was secure on his throne— He became acutely conscious of the fact that Wienis and his two arrogant sons were at present next in line to the throne.

But he was king. And kings could order people shot.

Even uncles and cousins.

4.

Next to Sermak himself, Lewis Bort was most active in rallying those dissident elements which had fused into the now-vociferous Action Party. Yet he had not been one of the deputation that had called on Salvor Hardin almost half a year previously. That this was so was not due to any lack of recognition of his efforts; quite the contrary. He was absent for the very good reason that he was on Anacreon's capital world at the time.

He visited it as a private citizen. He saw no official and he did nothing of importance. He merely watched the obscure corners of the busy planet and poked his stubby nose into dusty crannies.

He arrived home toward the end of a short winter day that had started with clouds and was finishing with snow and within an hour was seated at the octagonal table in Sermak's home.

His first words were not calculated to improve the atmosphere of a gathering already considerably depressed by the deepening snow-filled twilight outside.

"I'm afraid," he said, "that our position is what is usually termed, in melodramatic phraseology, a 'Lost Cause.'"

"You think so?" said Sermak, gloomily.

"It's gone past thought, Sermak. There's no room for any other opinion."

"Armaments—" began Dokor Walto, somewhat officiously, but Bort broke in at once.

"Forget that. That's an old story." His eyes traveled round the circle. "I'm referring to the people. I admit that it was my idea originally that we attempt to foster a palace rebellion of some sort to install as king someone more favorable to the Foundation. It was a good idea. It still is. The only trifling flaw about it is that it is impossible. The great Salvor Hardin saw to that."

Sermak said sourly, "If you'd give us the details, Bort—"

"Details! There aren't any! It isn't as simple as that. It's the whole damned situation on Anacreon. It's this religion the Foundation has established. It works!"

"Well!"

"You've got to *see* it work to appreciate it. All you see here is that we have a large school devoted to the training of priests, and that occasionally a special show is put on in some obscure corner of the city for the benefit of pilgrims—and that's all. The whole business hardly affects us as a general thing. But on Anacreon—"

Lem Tarki smoothed his prim little Vandyke with one finger, and cleared his throat. "What kind of a religion is it? Hardin's always said that it was just a fluffy flummery to get them to accept our science without question. You remember, Sermak, he told us that day—"

"Hardin's explanations," reminded Sermak, "don't often mean much at face value. But what kind of a religion is it, Bort?"

Bort considered. "Ethically, it's fine. It scarcely varies from the various philosophies of the old Empire. High moral standards and all that. There's nothing to complain about from that viewpoint. Religion is one of the great civilizing influences of history and in that respect, it's fulfilling—"

"We know that," interrupted Sermak, impatiently. "Get to the point."

"Here it is." Bort was a trifle disconcerted, but didn't show it. "The religion—which the Foundation has fostered and encouraged, mind you—is built on strictly authoritarian lines. The priesthood has sole control of the instruments of science we have given Anacreon, but they've learned to handle these tools only empirically. They believe in this religion entirely, and in the . . . uh . . . spiritual value of the power they handle. For instance, two months ago some fool tampered with the power plant in the Thessalekian Temple—one of the large ones. He blew up five city blocks, of course. It was considered divine vengeance by everyone, including the priests."

"I remember. The papers had some garbled version of the story at the time. I don't see what you're driving at."

"Then, listen," said Bort, stiffly. "The priesthood forms a hierarchy at the apex of which is the king, who is regarded as a sort of minor god. He's an absolute monarch by divine right, and the people believe it, thoroughly, and the priests, too. You can't overthrow a king like that. *Now* do you get the point?"

"Hold on," said Walto, at this point. "What did you mean when you said Hardin's done all this? How does he come in?"

Bort glanced at his questioner bitterly. "The Foundation has fostered this delusion assiduously. We've put all our scientific backing behind the hoax. There isn't a festival at which the king does not preside surrounded by a radioactive aura shining forth all over his body and raising itself like a coronet above his head. Anyone touching him is severely burned. He can move from place to place through the air at crucial moments, supposedly by inspiration of divine spirit. He fills the temple with a pearly, internal light at a gesture. There is no end to these quite simple tricks that we perform for his benefit; but even the priests believe them, while working them personally."

"Bad!" said Sermak, biting his lip.

"I could cry—like the fountain in City Hall Park," said Bort, earnestly, "when I think of the chance we muffed. Take the situation thirty years ago, when Hardin saved the Foundation from Anacreon— At that time, the Anacreonian people had no real conception of the fact that the Empire was running down. They had been more or less running their own affairs since the Zeonian revolt, but even after communications broke down and Lepold's pirate of a grandfather made himself king, they never quite realized the Empire had gone kaput.

"If the Emperor had had the nerve to try, he could have taken over again with two cruisers and with the help of the internal revolt that would have certainly sprung to life. And we, *we* could have done the same; but no, Hardin established monarch worship. Personally, I don't understand it. Why? Why? Why?"

"What," demanded Jaim Orsy, suddenly, "does Verisof do? There was a day when he was an advanced Actionist. What's he doing there? Is he blind, too?"

"I don't know," said Bort, curtly. "He's high priest to them.

As far as I know, he does nothing but act as adviser to the priesthood on technical details. Figurehead, blast him, figurehead!"

There was silence all round and all eyes turned to Sermak. The young party leader was biting a fingernail nervously, and then said loudly, "No good. It's fishy!"

He looked around him, and added more energetically, "Is Hardin then such a fool?"

"Seems to be," shrugged Bort.

"Never! There's something wrong. To cut our own throats so thoroughly and so hopelessly would require colossal stupidity. More than Hardin could possibly have even if he were a fool, which I deny. On the one hand, to establish a religion that would wipe out all chance of internal troubles. On the other hand, to arm Anacreon with all weapons of warfare. I don't see it."

"The matter *is* a little obscure, I admit," said Bort, "but the facts are there. What else can we think?"

Walto said, jerkily, "Outright treason. He's in their pay."

But Sermak shook his head impatiently. "I don't see that, either. The whole affair is as insane and meaningless— Tell me, Bort, have you heard anything about a battle cruiser that the Foundation is supposed to have put into shape for use in the Anacreon navy?"

"Battle cruiser?"

"An old Imperial cruiser—"

"No, I haven't. But that doesn't mean much. The navy yards are religious sanctuaries completely inviolate on the part of the lay public. No one ever hears anything about the fleet."

"Well, rumors have leaked out. Some of the Party have brought the matter up in Council. Hardin never denied it, you know. His spokesmen denounced rumor mongers and let it go at that. It might have significance."

"It's of a piece with the rest," said Bort. "If true, it's absolutely crazy. But it wouldn't be worse than the rest."

"I suppose," said Orsy, "Hardin hasn't any secret weapon waiting. That might—"

"Yes," said Sermak, viciously, "a huge jack-in-the-box that will jump out at the psychological moment and scare old Wienis into fits. The Foundation may as well blow itself out of existence and save itself the agony of suspense if it has to depend on any secret weapon."

"Well," said Orsy, changing the subject hurriedly, "the question comes down to this: How much time have we left? Eh, Bort?"

"All right. It is the question. But don't look at me; I don't know. The Anacreonian press never mentions the Foundation at all. Right now, it's full of the approaching celebrations and nothing else. Lepold is coming of age next week, you know."

"We have months then." Walto smiled for the first time that evening. "That gives us time—"

"That gives us time, my foot," ground out Bort, impatiently. "The king's a god, I tell you. Do you suppose he has to carry on a campaign of propaganda to get his people into fighting spirit? Do you suppose he has to accuse us of aggression and pull out all stops on cheap emotionalism? When the time comes to strike, Lepold gives the order and the people fight. Just like that. That's the damnedness of the system. You don't question a god. He may give the order tomorrow for all I know; and you can wrap tobacco round that and smoke it."

Everyone tried to talk at once and Sermak was slamming the table for silence, when the front door opened and Levi Norast stamped in. He bounded up the stairs, overcoat on, trailing snow.

"Look at that!" he cried, tossing a cold, snow-speckled newspaper onto the table. "The visicasters are full of it, too."

The newspaper was unfolded and five heads bent over it. Sermak said, in a hushed voice, "Great Space, he's going to Anacreon! *Going to Anacreon!*"

"It *is* treason," squeaked Tarki, in sudden excitement. "I'll be damned if Walto isn't right. He's sold us out and now he's going there to collect his wage."

Sermak had risen. "We've no choice now. I'm going to ask the Council tomorrow that Hardin be impeached. And if *that* fails—"

5.

The snow had ceased, but it caked the ground deeply now and the sleek ground car advanced through the deserted streets with lumbering effort. The murky gray light of incipient dawn was cold not only in the poetical sense but also in a very literal way—and even in the then turbulent state of the Foundation's politics, no one, whether Actionist or pro-Hardin found his spirits sufficiently ardent to begin street activity that early.

Yohan Lee did not like that and his grumblings grew audible. "It's going to look bad, Hardin. They're going to say you sneaked away."

"Let them say it if they wish. I've got to get to Anacreon and I want to do it without trouble. Now that's enough, Lee."

Hardin leaned back into the cushioned seat and shivered slightly. It wasn't cold inside the well-heated car, but there was something frigid about a snow-covered world, even through glass, that annoyed him.

He said, reflectively, "Some day when we get around to it we ought to weather-condition Terminus. It could be done."

"I," replied Lee, "would like to see a few other things done first. For instance, what about weather-conditioning Sermak? A nice, dry cell fitted for twenty-five centigrade all year round would be just right."

"And then I'd really *need* bodyguards," said Hardin, "and not just those two." He indicated two of Lee's bully-boys sitting up front with the driver, hard eyes on the empty streets, ready hands at their atom blasts. "You evidently want to stir up civil war."

"*I* do? There are other sticks in the fire and it won't require much stirring, I can tell you." He counted off on blunt fingers, "One: Sermak raised hell yesterday in the City Council and called for an impeachment."

"He had a perfect right to do so," responded Hardin, coolly. "Besides which, his motion was defeated 206 to 184."

"Certainly. A majority of twenty-two when we had counted on sixty as a minimum. Don't deny it; you know you did."

"It was close," admitted Hardin.

"All right. And two; after the vote, the fifty-nine members of the Actionist Party reared upon their hind legs and stamped out of the Council Chambers."

Hardin was silent, and Lee continued, "And three: Before leaving, Sermak howled that you were a traitor, that you were going to Anacreon to collect your thirty pieces of silver, that the Chamber majority in refusing to vote impeachment had participated in the treason, and that the name of their party was not 'Actionist' for nothing. What does *that* sound like?"

"Trouble, I suppose."

"And now you're chasing off at daybreak, like a criminal. You ought to face them, Hardin—and if you have to, declare martial law, by space!"

"Violence is the last refuge—"

"—Of the incompetent. Nuts!"

"All right. We'll see. Now listen to me carefully, Lee. Thirty years ago, the Time Vault opened, and on the fiftieth anniversary of the beginning of the Foundation, there appeared a Hari Seldon recording to give us our first idea of what was really going on."

"I remember," Lee nodded reminiscently, with a half smile. "It was the day we took over the government."

"That's right. It was the time of our first major crisis. This is our second—and three weeks from date will be the eightieth anniversary of the beginning of the Foundation. Does that strike you as in any way significant?"

"You mean he's coming again?"

"I'm not finished. Seldon never said anything about returning, you understand, but that's of a piece with his whole plan. He's always done his best to keep all foreknowledge from us. Nor is there any way of telling whether the radium lock is set for further openings short of dismantling the Vault —and it's probably set to destroy itself if we were to try that. I've been there every anniversary since the first appearance, just on the chance. He's never shown up, but this is the first time since then that there's really been a crisis."

"Then he'll come."

"Maybe. I don't know. However, this is the point. At today's session of the Council, just after you announce that I have left for Anacreon, you will further announce, officially, that on March 14th next, there will be another Hari Seldon recording, containing a message of the utmost importance regarding the recent successfully concluded crisis. That's very important, Lee. Don't add anything more no matter how many questions are asked."

Lee stared. "Will they believe it?"

"That doesn't matter. It will confuse them, which is all I want. Between wondering whether it is true and what I mean by it if it isn't—they'll decide to postpone action till after March 14th. I'll be back considerably before then."

Lee looked uncertain. "But that 'successfully concluded.' That's bull!"

"Highly confusing bull. Here's the airport!"

The waiting spaceship bulked somberly in the dimness. Hardin stamped through the snow toward it and at the open air lock turned about with outstretched hand.

"Good-by, Lee. I hate to leave you in the frying pan like this, but there's not another I can trust. Now please keep out of the fire."

"Don't worry. The frying pan is hot enough. I'll follow orders." He stepped back, and the air lock closed.

Salvor Hardin did not travel to the planet Anacreon—from which planet the kingdom derived its name—immediately. It was only on the day before the coronation that he arrived, after having made flying visits to eight of the larger stellar systems of the kingdom, stopping only long enough to confer with the local representatives of the Foundation.

The trip left him with an oppressive realization of the vastness of the kingdom. It was a little splinter, an insignificant fly speck compared to the inconceivable reaches of the Galactic Empire of which it had once formed so distinguished a part; but to one whose habits of thought had been built around a single planet, and a sparsely settled one at that, Anacreon's size in area and population was staggering.

Following closely the boundaries of the old Prefect of Anacreon, it embraced twenty-five stellar systems, six of which included more than one habitable world. The population of nineteen billion, though still far less than it had been in the Empire's heyday was rising rapidly with the increasing scientific development fostered by the Foundation.

And it was only now that Hardin found himself floored by the magnitude of *that* task. Even in thirty years, only the capital world had been powered. The outer provinces still possessed immense stretches where atomic power had not yet been re-introduced. Even the progress that had been made might have been impossible had it not been for the still workable relics left over by the ebbing tide of Empire.

When Hardin did arrive at the capital world, it was to find all normal business at an absolute standstill. In the outer provinces there had been and still were celebrations; but here on the planet Anacreon, not a person but took feverish part in the hectic religious pageantry that heralded the coming-of-age of their god-king, Lepold.

Hardin had been able to snatch only half an hour from a haggard and harried Verisof before his ambassador was forced to rush off to supervise still another temple festival But the half-hour was a most profitable one, and Hardin prepared himself for the night's fireworks well satisfied.

In all, he acted as an observer, for he had no stomach for the religious tasks he would undoubtedly have had to undertake if his identity became known. So, when the palace's ballroom filled itself with a glittering horde of the kingdom's very highest and most exalted nobility, he found himself hugging the wall, little noticed or totally ignored.

He had been introduced to Lepold as one of a long line of introducees, and from a safe distance, for the king stood apart in lonely and impressive grandeur, surrounded by his deadly blaze of radioactive aura. And in less than an hour this same king would take his seat upon the massive throne of rhodium-iridium alloy with jewel-set gold chasings, and then, throne and all would rise majestically into the air, skim the ground slowly to hover before the great window from which the great crowds of common folk could see their king and shout themselves into near apoplexy. The throne would not have been so massive, of course, if it had not had an atomic motor built into it.

It was past eleven. Hardin fidgeted and stood on his toes to better his view. He resisted an impulse to stand on a chair. And then he saw Wienis threading through the crowd toward him and he relaxed.

Wienis' progress was slow. At almost every step, he had to pass a kindly sentence with some revered noble whose grandfather had helped Lepold's grandfather brigandize the kingdom and had received a dukedom therefor.

And then he disentangled himself from the last uniformed peer and reached Hardin. His smile crooked itself into a smirk and his black eyes peered from under grizzled brows with glints of satisfaction in them.

"My dear Hardin," he said, in a low voice, "you must expect to be bored, when you refuse to announce your identity."

"I am not bored, your highness. This is all extremely interesting. We have no comparable spectacles on Terminus, you know."

"No doubt. But would you care to step into my private chambers, where we can speak at greater length and with considerably more privacy?"

"Certainly."

With arms linked, the two ascended the staircase, and more than one dowager duchess raised her lorgnette in surprise and wonder at the identity of this insignificantly dressed and uninteresting-looking stranger on whom such signal honor was being conferred by the prince regent.

In Wienis' chambers, Hardin relaxed in perfect comfort and accepted with a murmur of gratitude the glass of liquor that had been poured out by the regent's own hand.

"Locris wine, Hardin," said Wienis, "from the royal cellars. The real thing—two centuries in age. It was laid down ten years before the Zeonian Rebellion."

"A really royal drink," agreed Hardin, politely. "To Lepold I, King of Anacreon."

They drank, and Wienis added blandly, at the pause, "And soon to be Emperor of the Periphery, and further, who knows? The Galaxy may some day be reunited."

"Undoubtedly. By Anacreon?"

"Why not? With the help of the Foundation, our scientific superiority over the rest of the Periphery would be undisputable."

Hardin set his empty glass down and said, "Well, yes, except that, of course, the Foundation is bound to help any nation that requests scientific aid of it. Due to the high idealism of our government and the great moral purpose of our founder, Hari Seldon, we are unable to play favorites. That can't be helped, your highness."

Wienis' smile broadened. "The Galactic Spirit, to use the popular cant, helps those who help themselves. I quite understand that, left to itself, the Foundation would never cooperate."

"I wouldn't say that. We repaired the Imperial cruiser for

you, though my board of navigation wished it for themselves for research purposes."

The regent repeated the last words ironically. "Research purposes! Yes! Yet you would not have repaired it, had I not threatened war."

Hardin made a deprecatory gesture. "I don't know."

"*I* do. And that threat always stood."

"And still stands now?"

"Now it is rather too late to speak of threats." Wienis had cast a rapid glance at the clock on his desk. "Look here, Hardin, you were on Anacreon once before. You were young then; we were both young. But even then we had entirely different ways of looking at things. You're what they call a man of peace, aren't you?"

"I suppose I am. At least, I consider violence an uneconomical way of attaining an end. There are always better substitutes, though they may sometimes be a little less direct."

"Yes. I've heard of your famous remark: 'Violence is the last refuge of the incompetent.' And yet"—the regent scratched one ear gently in affected abstraction—"I wouldn't call myself exactly incompetent."

Hardin nodded politely and said nothing.

"And in spite of that," Wienis continued, "I have always believed in direct action. I have believed in carving a straight path to my objective and following that path. I have accomplished much that way, and fully expect to accomplish still more."

"I know," interrupted Hardin. "I believe you are carving a path such as you describe for yourself and your children that leads directly to the throne, considering the late unfortunate death of the king's father—your elder brother—and the king's own precarious state of health. He *is* in a precarious state of health, is he not?"

Wienis frowned at the shot, and his voice grew harder. "You might find it advisable, Hardin, to avoid certain subjects. You may consider yourself privileged as mayor of

Terminus to make . . . uh . . . injudicious remarks, but if you do, please disabuse yourself of the notion. I am not one to be frightened at words. It has been my philosophy of life that difficulties vanish when faced boldly, and I have never turned my back upon one yet."

"I don't doubt that. What particular difficulty are you refusing to turn your back upon at the present moment?"

"The difficulty, Hardin, of persuading the Foundation to co-operate. Your policy of peace, you see, has led you into making several very serious mistakes, simply because you underestimated the boldness of your adversary. Not everyone is as afraid of direct action as you are."

"For instance?" suggested Hardin.

"For instance, you came to Anacreon alone and accompanied me to my chambers alone."

Hardin looked about him. "And what is wrong with that?"

"Nothing," said the regent, "except that outside this room are five police guards, well armed and ready to shoot. I don't think you can leave, Hardin."

The mayor's eyebrows lifted, "I have no immediate desire to leave. Do you then fear me so much?"

"I don't fear you at all. But this may serve to impress you with my determination. Shall we call it a gesture?"

"Call it what you please," said Hardin, indifferently. "I shall not discommode myself over the incident, whatever you choose to call it."

"I'm sure that attitude will change with time. But you have made another error, Hardin, a more serious one. It seems that the planet Terminus is almost wholly undefended."

"Naturally. What have we to fear? We threaten no one's interest and serve all alike."

"And while remaining helpless," Wienis went on, "you kindly helped us to arm ourselves, aiding us particularly in the development of a navy of our own, a great navy. In fact, a navy which, since your donation of the Imperial cruiser, is quite irresistible."

"Your highness, you are wasting time." Hardin made as if

to rise from his seat. "If you mean to declare war, and are informing me of the fact, you will allow me to communicate with my government at once."

"Sit down, Hardin. I am not declaring war, and you are not communicating with your government at all. When the war is fought—not declared, Hardin, *fought*—the Foundation will be informed of it in due time by the atom blasts of the Anacreonian navy under the lead of my own son upon the flagship, Wienis, once a cruiser of the Imperial navy."

Hardin frowned. "When will all this happen?"

"If you're really interested, the ships of the fleet left Anacreon exactly fifty minutes ago, at eleven, and the first shot will be fired as soon as they sight Terminus, which should be at noon tomorrow. You may consider yourself a prisoner of war."

"That's exactly what I do consider myself, your highness," said Hardin, still frowning. "But I'm disappointed."

Wienis chuckled contemptuously. "Is that all?"

"Yes. I had thought that the moment of coronation—midnight, you know—would be the logical time to set the fleet in motion. Evidently, you wanted to start the war while you were still regent. It would have been more dramatic the other way."

The regent stared. "What in Space are you talking about?"

"Don't you understand?" said Hardin, softly. "I had set my counterstroke for midnight."

Wienis started from his chair. "You are not bluffing me. There is no counterstroke. If you are counting on the support of the other kingdoms, forget it. Their navies, combined, are no match for ours."

"I know that. I don't intend firing a shot. It is simply that the word went out a week ago that at midnight tonight, the planet Anacreon goes under the interdict."

"The interdict?"

"Yes. If you don't understand, I might explain that every priest in Anacreon is going on strike, unless I countermand the order. But I can't while I'm being held incommunicado; nor do I wish to even if I weren't!" He leaned forward and added, with sudden animation, "Do you realize, your highness, that an attack on the Foundation is nothing short of sacrilege of the highest order?"

Wienis was groping visibly for self-control. "Give me none of that, Hardin. Save it for the mob."

"My dear Wienis, whoever do you think I *am* saving it for? I imagine that for the last half hour every temple on Anacreon has been the center of a mob listening to a priest exhorting them upon that very subject. There's not a man or woman on Anacreon that doesn't know that their government has launched a vicious, unprovoked attack upon the center of their religion. But it lacks only four minutes of midnight now. You'd better go down to the ballroom to watch events. I'll be safe here with five guards outside the door." He leaned back in his chair, helped himself to another glass of Locris wine, and gazed at the ceiling with perfect indifference.

Wienis blistered the air with a muffled oath and rushed out of the room.

A hush had fallen over the elite in the ballroom, as a broad path was cleared for the throne. Lepold sat on it now, hands solidly on its arms, head high, face frozen. The huge chandeliers had dimmed and in the diffused multi-colored light from the tiny Atomo bulbs that bespangled the vaulted ceiling, the royal aura shone out bravely, lifting high above his head to form a blazing coronet.

Wienis paused on the stairway. No one saw him; all eyes were on the throne. He clenched his fists and remained where he was; Hardin would *not* bluff him into silly action.

And then the throne stirred. Noiselessly, it lifted upward— and drifted. Off the dais, slowly down the steps, and then horizontally, six inches off the floor, it worked itself toward the huge, open window.

At the sound of the deep-toned bell that signified midnight, it stopped before the window—and the king's aura died.

For a frozen split second, the king did not move, face twisted in surprise, without an aura, merely human; and then the throne wobbled and fell the six inches to the floor with a crashing thump, just as every light in the palace went out.

Through the shrieking din and confusion, Wienis' bull voice sounded. "Get the flares! Get the flares!"

He buffeted right and left through the crowd and forced his way to the door. From without, palace guards had streamed into the darkness.

Somehow the flares were brought back to the ballroom; flares that were to have been used in the gigantic torchlight procession through the streets of the city after the coronation.

Back to the ballroom guardsmen swarmed with torches—blue, green, and red; where the strange light lit up frightened, confused faces.

"There is no harm done," shouted Wienis. "Keep your places. Power will return in a moment."

He turned to the captain of the guard who stood stiffly at attention. "What is it, Captain?"

"Your highness," was the instant response, "the palace is surrounded by the people of the city."

"What do they want?" snarled Wienis.

"A priest is at the head. He has been identified as High Priest Poly Verisof. He demands the immediate release of Mayor Salvor Hardin and cessation of the war against the Foundation." The report was made in the expressionless tones of an officer, but his eyes shifted uneasily.

Wienis cried, "If any of the rabble attempt to pass the palace gates, blast them out of existence. For the moment, nothing more. Let them howl! There will be an accounting tomorrow."

The torches had been distributed now, and the ballroom was again alight. Wienis rushed to the throne, still standing by the window, and dragged the stricken, wax-faced Lepold to his feet.

"Come with me." He cast one look out of the window. The

city was pitch-black. From below there were the hoarse confused cries of the mob. Only toward the right, where the Argolid Temple stood was there illumination. He swore angrily, and dragged the king away.

Wienis burst into his chambers, the five guardsmen at his heels. Lepold followed, wide-eyed, scared speechless.

"Hardin," said Wienis, huskily, "you are playing with forces too great for you."

The mayor ignored the speaker. In the pearly light of the pocket Atomo bulb at his side, he remained quietly seated, a slightly ironic smile on his face.

"Good morning, your majesty," he said to Lepold. "I congratulate you on your coronation."

"Hardin," cried Wienis again, "order your priests back to their jobs."

Hardin looked up coolly. "Order them yourself, Wienis, and see who is playing with forces too great for whom. Right now, there's not a wheel turning in Anacreon. There's not a light burning, except in the temples. There's not a drop of water running, except in the temples. On the wintry half of the planet, there's not a calorie of heat, except in the temples. The hospitals are taking in no more patients. The power plants have shut down. All ships are grounded. If you don't like it, Wienis, *you* can order the priests back to their jobs. *I* don't wish to."

"By Space, Hardin, I will. If it's to be a showdown, so be it. We'll see if your priests can withstand the army. Tonight, every temple on the planet will be put under army supervision."

"Very good, but how are you going to give the orders? Every line of communication on the planet is shut down. You'll find that radio won't work and the televisors won't work and the ultrawave won't work. In fact, the only communicator of the planet that will work—outside of the temples, of course—is the televisor right here in this room, and I've fitted it only for reception."

Wienis struggled vainly for breath, and Hardin continued,

"If you wish you can order your army into the Argolid Temple just outside the palace and then use the ultrawave sets there to contact other portions of the planet. But if you do that, I'm afraid the army contingent will be cut to pieces by the mob, and then what will protect your palace, Wienis? And your *lives*, Wienis?"

Wienis said thickly, "We can hold out, devil. We'll last the day. Let the mob howl and let the power die, but we'll hold out. And when the news comes back that the Foundation has been taken, your precious mob will find upon what vacuum their religion has been built, and they'll desert your priests and turn against them. I give you until noon tomorrow, Hardin, because you can stop the power on Anacreon but *you can't stop my fleet*." His voice croaked exultantly. "They're on their way, Hardin, with the great cruiser you yourself ordered repaired, at the head."

Hardin replied lightly. "Yes, the cruiser I myself ordered repaired—but in my own way. Tell me, Wienis, have you ever heard of an ultrawave relay? No, I see you haven't. Well, in about two minutes you'll find out what one can do."

The televisor flashed to life as he spoke, and he amended, "No, in two seconds. Sit down, Wienis, and listen."

7.

Theo Aporat was one of the very highest ranking priests of Anacreon. From the standpoint of precedence alone, he deserved his appointment as head priest—attendant upon the flagship *Wienis*.

But it was not only rank or precedence. He knew the ship. He had worked directly under the holy men from the Foundation itself in repairing the ship. He had gone over the motors under their orders. He had rewired the 'visors; revamped the communications system; replated the punctured hull; reinforced the beams. He had even been permitted to help while the wise men of the Foundation had installed a device so holy it had never been placed in any previous ship, but had been reserved only for this magnificent colossus of a vessel—the ultrawave relay.

It was no wonder that he felt heartsick over the purposes to which the glorious ship was perverted. He had never wanted to believe what Verisof had told him—that the ship was to be used for appalling wickedness; that its guns were to be turned on the great Foundation. Turned on that Foundation, where he had been trained as a youth, from which all blessedness was derived.

Yet he could not doubt now, after what the admiral had told him.

How could the king, divinely blessed, allow this abominable act? Or was it the king? Was it not, perhaps, an action of the accursed regent, Wienis, without the knowledge of the king at all. And it was the son of this same Wienis that was the admiral who five minutes before had told him:

"Attend to your souls and your blessings, priest. *I* will attend to my ship."

Aporat smiled crookedly. He would attend to his souls and his blessings—and also to his cursings; and Prince Lefkin would whine soon enough.

He had entered the general communications room now. His acolyte preceded him and the two officers in charge made no move to interfere. The head priest-attendant had the right of free entry anywhere on the ship.

"Close the door," Aporat ordered, and looked at the chronometer. It lacked five minutes of twelve. He had timed it well.

With quick practiced motions, he moved the little levers that opened all communications, so that every part of the two-mile-long ship was within reach of his voice and his image.

"Soldiers of the royal flagship *Wienis,* attend! It is your priest-attendant that speaks!" The sound of his voice reverberated, he knew, from the stern atom blast in the extreme rear to the navigation tables in the prow.

"Your ship," he cried, "is engaged in sacrilege. Without your knowledge, it is performing such an act as will doom the soul of every man among you to the eternal frigidity of space! Listen! It is the intention of your commander to take this ship to the Foundation and there to bombard that source of all blessings into submission to his sinful will. And since that is his intention, I, in the name of the Galactic Spirit, remove him from his command, for there is no command where the blessing of the Galactic Spirit has been withdrawn. The divine king himself may not maintain his kingship without the consent of the Spirit."

His voice took on a deeper tone, while the acolyte listened with veneration and the two soldiers with mounting fear. "And because this ship is upon such a devil's errand, the blessing of the Spirit is removed from it as well."

He lifted his arms solemnly, and before a thousand televisors throughout the ship, soldiers cowered, as the stately image of their priest-attendant spoke:

"In the name of the Galactic Spirit and of his prophet, Hari Seldon, and of his interpreters, the holy men of the Foundation, I curse this ship. Let the televisors of this ship, which are its eyes, become blind. Let its grapples, which are its arms, be paralyzed. Let the atom blasts, which are its fists, lose their function. Let the motors, which are its heart, cease to beat. Let the communications, which are its voice, become dumb. Let its ventilations, which are its breath, fade. Let its lights, which are its soul, shrivel into nothing. In the name of the Galactic Spirit, I so curse this ship."

And with his last word, at the stroke of midnight, a hand, light-years distant in the Argolid Temple, opened an ultrawave relay, which at the instantaneous speed of the ultrawave, opened another on the flagship *Wienis*.

And the ship died!

For it is the chief characteristic of the religion of science, that it works, and that such curses as that of Aporat's are really deadly.

Aporat saw the darkness close down on the ship and heard

the sudden ceasing of the soft, distant purring of the hy-peratomic motors. He exulted and from the pocket of his long robe withdrew a self-powered Atomo bulb that filled the room with pearly light.

He looked down at the two soldiers who, brave men though they undoubtedly were, writhed on their knees in the last extremity of mortal terror. "Save our souls, your reverence. We are poor men, ignorant of the crimes of our leaders," one whimpered.

"Follow," said Aporat, sternly. "Your soul is not yet lost."

The ship was a turmoil of darkness in which fear was so thick and palpable, it was all but a miasmic smell. Soldiers crowded close wherever Aporat and his circle of light passed, striving to touch the hem of his robe, pleading for the tiniest scrap of mercy.

And always his answer was, "Follow me!"

He found Prince Lefkin, groping his way through the of-ficers' quarters, cursing loudly for lights. The admiral stared at the priest-attendant with hating eyes.

"There you are!" Lefkin inherited his blue eyes from his mother, but there was that about the hook in his nose and the squint in his eye that marked him as the son of Wienis. "What is the meaning of your treasonable actions? Return the power to the ship. I am commander here."

"No longer," said Aporat, somberly.

Lefkin looked about wildly. "Seize that man. Arrest him, or by Space, I will send every man within reach of my voice out the air lock in the nude." He paused, and then shrieked, "It is your admiral that orders. Arrest him."

Then, as he lost his head entirely, "Are you allowing your-selves to be fooled by this mountebank, this harlequin? Do you cringe before a religion compounded of clouds and moonbeams? This man is an impostor and the Galactic Spirit he speaks of a fraud of the imagination devised to—"

Aporat interrupted furiously. "Seize the blasphemer. You listen to him at the peril of your souls."

And promptly, the noble admiral went down under the clutching hands of a score of soldiers.

"Take him with you and follow me."

Aporat turned, and with Lefkin dragged along after him, and the corridors behind black with soldiery, he returned to the communications room. There, he ordered the ex-commander before the one televisor that worked.

"Order the rest of the fleet to cease course and to prepare for the return to Anacreon."

The disheveled Lefkin, bleeding, beaten, and half stunned, did so.

"And now," continued Aporat, grimly, "we are in contact with Anacreon on the ultrawave beam. Speak as I order you."

Lefkin made a gesture of negation, and the mob in the room and the others crowding the corridor beyond, growled fearfully.

"Speak!" said Aporat. "Begin: The Anacreonian navy—"

Lefkin began.

8.

There was absolute silence in Wienis' chambers when the image of Prince Lefkin appeared at the televisor. There had been one startled gasp from the regent at the haggard face and shredded uniform of his son, and then he collapsed into a chair, face contorted with surprise and apprehension.

Hardin listened stolidly, hands clasped lightly in his lap, while the just-crowned King Lepold sat shriveled in the most shadowy corner, biting spasmodically at his gold-braided sleeve. Even the soldiers had lost the emotionless stare that is the prerogative of the military, and, from where they lined up against the door, atom blasts ready, peered furtively at the figure upon the televisor.

Lefkin spoke, reluctantly, with a tired voice that paused at intervals as though he were being prompted—and not gently:

"The Anacreonian navy . . . aware of the nature of its mission . . . and refusing to be a party . . . to abominable sacrilege . . . is returning to Anacreon . . . with the following ultimatum issued . . . to those blaspheming sinners . . . who would dare to use profane force . . . against the Foundation . . . source of all blessings . . . and against the Galactic Spirit. Cease at once all war against . . . the true faith . . . and guarantee in a manner suiting us of the navy . . . as represented by our . . . priest-attendant, Theo Aporat . . . that such war will never in the future . . . be resumed, and that"—here a long pause, and then continuing—"and that the one-time prince regent, Wienis . . . be imprisoned . . . and tried before an ecclesiastical court . . . for his crimes. Otherwise the royal navy . . . upon returning to Anacreon . . . will blast the palace to the ground . . . and take whatever other measures . . . are necessary . . . to destroy the nest of sinners . . . and the den of destroyers . . . of men's souls that now prevail."

The voice ended with half a sob and the screen went blank.

Hardin's fingers passed rapidly over the Atomo bulb and its light faded until in the dimness, the hitherto regent, the king, and the soldiers were hazy-edged shadows; and for the first time it could be seen that an aura encompassed Hardin.

It was not the blazing light that was the prerogative of kings, but one less spectacular, less impressive, and yet one more effective in its own way, and more useful.

Hardin's voice was softly ironic as he addressed the same Wienis who had one hour earlier declared him a prisoner of war and Terminus on the point of destruction, and who now was a huddled shadow, broken and silent.

"There is an old fable," said Hardin, "as old perhaps as humanity, for the oldest records containing it are merely copies of other records still older, that might interest you. It runs as follows:

"A horse having a wolf as a powerful and dangerous enemy lived in constant fear of his life. Being driven to desperation, it occurred to him to seek a strong ally. Whereupon he approached a man, and offered an alliance, pointing out that the wolf was likewise an enemy of the man. The man accepted the partnership at once and offered to kill the wolf immediately, if his new partner would only co-operate by placing his greater speed at the man's disposal. The horse was willing, and allowed the man to place bridle and saddle upon him. The man mounted, hunted down the wolf, and killed him.

"The horse, joyful and relieved, thanked the man, and said: 'Now that our enemy is dead, remove your bridle and saddle and restore my freedom.'

"Whereupon the man laughed loudly and replied, 'The hell you say. Giddy-ap, Dobbin,' and applied the spurs with a will."

Silence still. The shadow that was Wienis did not stir.

Hardin continued quietly, "You see the analogy, I hope. In their anxiety to cement forever total domination over their own people, the kings of the Four Kingdoms accepted the religion of science that made them divine; and that same religion of science was their bridle and saddle, for it placed the life blood of atomic power in the hands of the priesthood —who took their orders from us, be it noted, and not from you. You killed the wolf, but could not get rid of the m—"

Wienis sprang to his feet and in the shadows, his eyes were maddened hollows. His voice was thick, incoherent. "And yet I'll get you. You won't escape. You'll rot. Let them blow us up. Let them blow everything up. You'll rot! I'll get you!

"Soldiers!" he thundered, hysterically. "Shoot me down that devil. Blast him! Blast him!"

Hardin turned about in his chair to face the soldiers and smiled. One aimed his atom blast and then lowered it. The others never budged. Salvor Hardin, mayor of Terminus, surrounded by that soft aura, smiling so confidently, and before whom all the power of Anacreon had crumbled to powder was too much for them, despite the orders of the shrieking maniac just beyond.

Wienis screamed a curse and staggered to the nearest soldier. Wildly, he wrested the atom blast from the man's hand—aimed it at Hardin, who didn't stir, shoved the lever and held it contacted.

The pale continuous beam impinged upon the force-field that surrounded the mayor of Terminus and was sucked harmlessly to neutralization. Wienis pressed harder and laughed tearingly.

Hardin still smiled and his force-field aura scarcely brightened as it absorbed the energies of the atom blast. From his corner Lepold covered his eyes and moaned.

And, with a yell of despair, Wienis changed his aim and shot again—and toppled to the floor with his head blown into nothingness.

Hardin winced at the sight and muttered, "A man of 'direct action' to the end. The last refuge!"

9.

The Time Vault was filled; filled far beyond the available seating capacity, and men lined the back of the room, three deep.

Salvor Hardin compared this large company with the few men attending the first appearance of Hari Seldon, thirty years earlier. There had only been six, then; the five old Encyclopedists—all dead now—and himself, the young figurehead of a mayor. It had been on that day, that he, with Yohan Lee's assistance had removed the "figurehead" stigma from his office.

It was quite different now; different in every respect. Every man of the City Council was awaiting Seldon's appearance. He, himself, was still mayor, but all-powerful now; and since the utter rout of Anacreon, all-popular. When he had returned from Anacreon with the news of the death of Wienis, and the new treaty signed with the trembling Lepold, he was greeted with a vote of confidence of shrieking unanimity. When this was followed in rapid order, by similar treaties signed with each of the other three kingdoms—treaties that gave the Foundation powers such as would forever prevent any attempts at attack similar to that of Anacreon's —torchlight processions had been held in every city street of Terminus. Not even Hari Seldon's name had been more loudly cheered.

Hardin's lips twitched. Such popularity had been his after the first crisis also.

Across the room, Sef Sermak and Lewis Bort were engaged in animated discussion, and recent events seemed to have put them out not at all. They had joined in the vote of confidence; made speeches in which they publicly admitted that they had been in the wrong, apologized handsomely for the use of certain phrases in earlier debates, excused themselves delicately by declaring they had merely followed the dictates of their judgement and their conscience—and immediately launched a new Actionist campaign.

Yohan Lee touched Hardin's sleeve and pointed significantly to his watch.

Hardin looked up. "Hello there, Lee. Are you still sour? What's wrong now?"

"He's due in five minutes, isn't he?"

"I presume so. He appeared at noon last time."

"What if he doesn't?"

"Are you going to wear me down with your worries all your life? If he doesn't, he won't."

Lee frowned and shook his head slowly. "If this thing flops, we're in another mess. Without Seldon's backing for what we've done, Sermak will be free to start all over. He wants outright annexation of the Four Kingdoms, and immediate expansion of the Foundation—by force, if necessary. He's begun his campaign, already."

"I know. A fire eater must eat fire even if he has to kindle it himself. And you, Lee, have got to worry even if you must kill yourself to invent something to worry about."

Lee would have answered, but he lost his breath at just

that moment—as the lights yellowed and went dim. He raised his arm to point to the glass cubicle that dominated half the room and then collapsed into a chair with a windy sigh.

Hardin himself straightened at the sight of the figure that now filled the cubicle—a figure in a wheel chair! He alone, of all those present could remember the day, decades ago, when that figure had appeared first. He had been young then, and the figure old. Since then, the figure had not aged a day, but he himself had in turn grown old.

The figure stared straight ahead, hands fingering a book in its lap.

It said, "I am Hari Seldon!" The voice was old and soft.

There was a breathless silence in the room and Hari Seldon continued conversationally, "This is the second time I've been here. Of course, I don't know if any of you were here the first time. In fact, I have no way of telling, by sense perception, that there is anyone here at all, but that doesn't matter. If the second crisis has been overcome safely, you are bound to be here; there is no way out. If you are not here, then the second crisis has been too much for you."

He smiled engagingly. "I doubt *that*, however, for my figures show a ninety-eight point four percent probability there is to be no significant deviation from the Plan in the first eighty years.

"According to our calculations, you have now reached domination of the barbarian kingdoms immediately surrounding the Foundation. Just as in the first crisis you held them off by the use of the Balance of Power, so in the second, you gained mastery by use of the Spiritual Power as against the Temporal.

"However, I might warn you here against overconfidence. It is not my way to grant you any foreknowledge in these recordings, but it would be safe to indicate that what you have now achieved is merely a new balance—though one in which your position is considerably better. The Spiritual Power, while sufficient to ward off attacks of the Temporal is *not* sufficient to attack in turn. Because of the invariable growth of the counteracting force known as Regionalism, or Nationalism, the Spiritual Power cannot prevail. I am telling you nothing new, I'm sure.

"You must pardon me, by the way, for speaking to you in this vague way. The terms I use are at best mere approximations, but none of you is qualified to understand the true symbology of psychohistory, and so I must do the best I can.

"In this case, the Foundation is only at the start of the path that leads to New Empire. The neighboring kingdoms, in manpower and resources are still overwhelmingly powerful as compared to yourselves. Outside them lies the vast tangled jungle of barbarism that extends around the entire breadth of the Galaxy. Within that rim there is still what is left of the Galactic Empire—and that, weakened and decaying though it is, is still incomparably mighty."

At this point, Hari Seldon lifted his book and opened it. His face grew solemn. "And never forget there was *another* Foundation established eighty years ago; a Foundation at the other end of the Galaxy, at Star's End. They will always be there for consideration. Gentlemen, nine hundred and twenty years of the Plan stretch ahead of you. The problem is yours! Go to it!"

He dropped his eyes to his book and flicked out of existence, while the lights brightened to fullness. In the babble that followed, Lee leaned over to Hardin's ear. "He didn't say when he'd be back."

Hardin replied, "I know—but I trust that he won't return until you and I are safely and cozily dead!"

PART IV

THE TRADERS

1

TRADERS— . . . and constantly in advance of the political hegemony of the Foundation were the Traders, reaching out tenuous fingerholds through the tremendous distances of the Periphery. Months or years might pass between landings on Terminus; their ships were often nothing more than patchquilts of home-made repairs and improvisations; their honesty was none of the highest; their daring . . .

Through it all they forged an empire more enduring than the pseudo-religious despotism of the Four Kingdoms. . . .

Tales without end are told of these massive, lonely figures who bore half-seriously, half-mockingly a motto adopted from one of Salvor Hardin's epigrams, "Never let your sense of morals prevent you from doing what is right!" It is difficult now to tell which tales are real and which apocryphal. There are none probably that have not suffered some exaggeration. . . .

ENCYCLOPEDIA GALACTICA

Limmar Ponyets was completely a-lather when the call reached his receiver—which proves that the old bromide about telemessages and the bathtub holds true even in the dark, hard space of the Galactic Periphery.

Luckily that part of a free-lance trade ship which is not given over to miscellaneous merchandise is extremely snug. So much so, that the shower, hot water included, is located in a two-by-four cubby, ten feet from the control panels. Ponyets heard the staccato rattle of the receiver quite plainly.

Dripping suds and a curse, he stepped out to adjust the vocal, and three hours later a second trade ship was alongside, and a grinning youngster entered through the air tube between the ships.

Ponyets rattled his best chair forward and perched himself on the pilot-swivel.

"What've you been doing, Gorm?" he asked, darkly. "Chasing me all the way from the Foundation?"

Les Gorm broke out a cigarette, and shook his head definitely, "Me? Not a chance. I'm just the sucker who happened to land on Glyptal IV the day after the mail. So they sent me out after you with this."

The tiny, gleaming sphere changed hands, and Gorm added, "It's confidential. Super-secret. Can't be trusted to the sub-ether and all that. Or so I gather. At least, it's a Personal Capsule, and won't open for anyone but you."

Ponyets regarded the capsule distastefully, "I can see that. And I never knew one of these to hold good news, either."

It opened in his hand and the thin, transparent tape unrolled stiffly. His eyes swept the message quickly, for when the last of the tape had emerged, the first was already brown and crinkled. In a minute and a half it had turned black and, molecule by molecule, fallen apart.

Ponyets grunted hollowly, "Oh, *Galaxy!*"

Les Gorm said quietly, "Can I help somehow? Or is it too secret?"

"It will bear telling, since you're of the Guild. I've got to go to Askone."

"That place? How come?"

"They've imprisoned a trader. But keep it to yourself."

Gorm's expression jolted into anger, "Imprisoned! That's against the Convention."

"So is interference with local politics."

"Oh! Is that what he did?" Gorm meditated. "Who's the trader? Anyone I know?"

"No!" said Ponyets sharply, and Gorm accepted the implication and asked no further questions.

Ponyets was up and staring darkly out the visiplate. He mumbled strong expressions at that part of the misty lens-form that was the body of the Galaxy, then said loudly, "Damnedest mess! I'm way behind quota."

Light broke on Gorm's intellect, "Hey, friend, Askone is a closed area."

"That's right. You can't sell as much as a penknife on Askone. They won't buy atomic gadgets of *any* sort. With my quota dead on its feet, it's murder to go there."

"Can't get out of it?"

Ponyets shook his head absently, "I know the fellow involved. Can't walk out on a friend. What of it? I am in the hands of the Galactic Spirit and walk cheerfully in the way he points out."

Gorm said blankly, "Huh?"

Ponyets looked at him, and laughed shortly, "I forgot. You never read the 'Book of the Spirit,' did you?"

"Never heard of it," said Gorm, curtly.

"Well, you would if *you'd* had a religious training."

"Religious training? For the *priesthood?*" Gorm was profoundly shocked.

"Afraid so. It's my dark shame and secret. I was too much for the Revered Fathers, though. They expelled me, for reasons sufficient to promote me to a secular education under the Foundation. Well, look, I'd better push off. How's your quota this year?"

Gorm crushed out his cigarette and adjusted his cap, "I've got my last cargo going now. I'll make it."

"Lucky fellow," gloomed Ponyets, and for many minutes after Les Gorm left, he sat in motionless reverie.

So Eskel Gorov was on Askone—and in prison as well!

That was bad! In fact, considerably worse than it might appear. It was one thing to tell a curious youngster a diluted version of the business to throw him off and send him about his own. It was a thing of a different sort to face the truth.

For Limmar Ponyets was one of the few people who happened to know that Master Trader Eskel Gorov was not a trader at all; but that entirely different thing, an agent of the Foundation!

Two weeks gone! Two weeks wasted.

One week to reach Askone, at the extreme borders of which the vigilant warships speared out to meet him in converging numbers. Whatever their detection system was, it worked—and well.

They sidled him in slowly, without a signal, maintaining their cold distance, and pointing him harshly towards the central sun of Askone.

Ponyets could have handled them at a pinch. Those ships were holdovers from the dead-and-gone Galactic Empire —but they were sports cruisers, not warships; and without atomic weapons, they were so many picturesque and impotent ellipsoids. But Eskel Gorov was a prisoner in their hands, and Gorov was not a hostage to lose. The Askonians must know that.

And then another week—a week to wind a weary way through the clouds of minor officials that formed the buffer between the Grand Master and the outer world. Each little sub-secretary required soothing and conciliation. Each required careful and nauseating milking for the flourishing signature that was the pathway to the next official one higher up.

For the first time, Ponyets found his trader's identification papers useless.

Now, at last, the Grand Master was on the other side of the Guard-flanked gilded door—and two weeks had gone.

Gorov was still a prisoner and Ponyets' cargo rotted useless in the holds of his ship.

The Grand Master was a small man; a small man with a balding head and very wrinkled face, whose body seemed weighed down to motionlessness by the huge, glossy fur collar about his neck.

His fingers moved on either side, and the line of armed

men backed away to form a passage, along which Ponyets strode to the foot of the Chair of State.

"Don't speak," snapped the Grand Master, and Ponyets' opening lips closed tightly.

"That's right," the Askonian ruler relaxed visibly, "I can't endure useless chatter. You cannot threaten and I won't abide flattery. Nor is there room for injured complaints. I have lost count of the times you wanderers have been warned that your devil's machines are not wanted anywhere in Askone."

"Sir," said Ponyets, quietly, "there is no attempt to justify the trader in question. It is not the policy of traders to intrude where they are not wanted. But the Galaxy is great, and it has happened before that a boundary has been trespassed unwittingly. It was a deplorable mistake."

"Deplorable, certainly," squeaked the Grand Master. "But mistake? Your people on Glyptal IV have been bombarding me with pleas for negotiation since two hours after the sacrilegious wretch was seized. I have been warned by them of your own coming many times over. It seems a well-organized rescue campaign. Much seems to have been anticipated—a little too much for mistakes, deplorable or otherwise."

The Askonian's black eyes were scornful. He raced on, "And are you traders, flitting from world to world like mad little butterflies, so mad in your own right that you can land on Askone's largest world, in the center of its system, and consider it an unwitting boundary mixup? Come, surely not."

Ponyets winced without showing it. He said, doggedly, "If the attempt to trade was deliberate, your Veneration, it was most injudicious and contrary to the strictest regulations of our Guild."

"Injudicious, yes," said the Askonian, curtly. "So much so, that your comrade is likely to lose life in payment."

Ponyets' stomach knotted. There was no irresolution there. He said, "Death, your Veneration, is so absolute and irrevocable a phenomenon that certainly there must be some alternative."

There was a pause before the guarded answer came, "I have heard that the Foundation is rich."

"Rich? Certainly. But our riches are that which you refuse to take. Our atomic goods are worth—"

"Your goods are worthless in that they lack the ancestral blessing. Your goods are wicked and accursed in that they lie under the ancestral interdict." The sentences were intoned; the recitation of a formula.

The Grand Master's eyelids dropped, and he said with meaning, "You have nothing else of value?"

The meaning was lost on the trader, "I don't understand. What is it you want?"

The Askonian's hands spread apart, "You ask me to trade places with you, and make known to you *my* wants. I think not. Your colleague, it seems, must suffer the punishment set for sacrilege by the Askonian code. Death by gas. We are a just people. The poorest peasant, in like case, would suffer no more. I, myself, would suffer no less."

Ponyets mumbled hopelessly, "Your Veneration, would it be permitted that I speak to the prisoner?"

"Askonian law," said the Grand Master coldly, "allows no communication with a condemned man."

Mentally, Ponyets held his breath, "Your Veneration, I ask you to be merciful towards a man's soul, in the hour when his body stands forfeit. He has been separated from spiritual consolation in all the time that his life has been in danger. Even now, he faces the prospect of going unprepared to the bosom of the Spirit that rules all."

The Grand Master said slowly and suspiciously, "You are a Tender of the Soul?"

Ponyets dropped a humble head, "I have been so trained. In the empty expanses of space, the wandering traders need men like myself to care for the spiritual side of a life so given over to commerce and worldly pursuits."

The Askonian ruler sucked thoughtfully at his lower lip. "Every man should prepare his soul for his journey to his ancestral spirits. Yet I had never thought you traders to be believers."

3·

Eskel Gorov stirred on his couch and opened one eye as Limmar Ponyets entered the heavily reinforced door. It boomed shut behind him. Gorov sputtered and came to his feet.

"Ponyets! They sent you?"

"Pure chance," said Ponyets, bitterly, "or the work of my own personal malevolent demon. Item one, you get into a mess on Askone. Item two, my sales route, as known to the Board of Trade, carries me within fifty parsecs of the system at just the time of item one. Item three, we've worked together before and the Board knows it. Isn't that a sweet, inevitable set-up? The answer just pops out of a slot."

"Be careful," said Gorov, tautly. "There'll be someone listening. Are you wearing a Field Distorter?"

Ponyets indicated the ornamented bracelet that hugged his wrist and Gorov relaxed.

Ponyets looked about him. The cell was bare, but large. It was well-lit and it lacked offensive odors. He said, "Not bad. They're treating you with kid gloves."

Gorov brushed the remark aside, "Listen, how did you get down here? I've been in strict solitary for almost two weeks."

"Ever since I came, huh? Well, it seems the old bird who's boss here has his weak points. He leans toward pious speeches, so I took a chance that worked. I'm here in the capacity of your spiritual adviser. There's something about a pious man such as he. He will cheerfully cut your throat if it suits him, but he will hesitate to endanger the welfare of your immaterial and problematical soul. It's just a piece of empirical psychology. A trader has to know a little of everything."

Gorov's smile was sardonic, "And you've been to theological school as well. You're all right, Ponyets. I'm glad they sent you. But the Grand Master doesn't love my soul exclusively. Has he mentioned a ransom?"

The trader's eyes narrowed, "He hinted—barely. And he also threatened death by gas. I played safe, and dodged; it might easily have been a trap. So it's extortion, is it? What is it he wants?"

"Gold."

"Gold!" Ponyets frowned. "The metal itself? What for?"

"It's their medium of exchange."

"Is it? And where do I get gold from?"

"Wherever you can. Listen to me; this is important. Nothing will happen to me as long as the Grand Master has the scent of gold in his nose. Promise it to him; as much as he asks for. Then go back to the Foundation, if necessary, to get it. When I'm free, we'll be escorted out of the system, and then we part company."

Ponyets stared disapprovingly, "And then you'll come back and try again."

"It's my assignment to sell atomics to Askone."

"They'll get you before you've gone a parsec in space. You know that, I suppose."

"I don't," said Gorov. "And if I did, it wouldn't affect things."

"They'll kill you the second time."

Gorov shrugged.

Ponyets said quietly, "If I'm going to negotiate with the Grand Master again, I want to know the whole story. So far, I've been working it too blind. As it was, the few mild remarks I did make almost threw his Veneration into fits."

"It's simple enough," said Gorov. "The only way we can increase the security of the Foundation here in the Periphery is to form a religion-controlled commercial empire. We're still too weak to be able to force political control. It's all we can do to hold the Four Kingdoms."

Ponyets was nodding, "This I realize. And any system that doesn't accept atomic gadgets can never be placed under our religious control—"

"And can therefore become a focal point for independence and hostility. Yes."

"All right, then," said Ponyets, "so much for theory. Now what exactly prevents the sale. Religion? The Grand Master implied as much."

"It's a form of ancestor worship. Their traditions tell of an evil past from which they were saved by the simple and virtuous heroes of the past generations. It amounts to a distortion of the anarchic period a century ago, when the imperial troops were driven out and an independent government was set up. Advanced science and atomic power in particular became identified with the old imperial regime they remember with horror."

"That so? But they have nice little ships which spotted me very handily two parsecs away. That smells of atomics to me."

Gorov shrugged. "Those ships are holdovers of the Empire, no doubt. Probably with atomic drive. What they have, they keep. The point is that they will not innovate and their internal economy is entirely nonatomic. That is what we must change."

"How were you going to do it?"

"By breaking the resistance at one point. To put it simply, if I could sell a penknife with a force-field blade to a nobleman, it would be to his interest to force laws that would allow him to use it. Put that baldly, it sounds silly, but it is sound, psychologically. To make strategic sales, at strategic points, would be to create a pro-atomics faction at court."

"And they send *you* for that purpose, while I'm only here to ransom you and leave, while you keep on trying? Isn't that sort of tail-backward?"

"In what way?" said Gorov, guardedly.

"Listen," Ponyets was suddenly exasperated, "you're a diplomat, not a trader, and calling you a trader won't make you one. This case is for one who's made a business of selling—and I'm here with a full cargo stinking into uselessness, and a quota that won't ever be met, it looks like."

"You mean you're going to risk your life on something that isn't your business?" Gorov smiled thinly.

Ponyets said, "You mean that this is a matter of patriotism and traders aren't patriotic?"

"Notoriously not. Pioneers never are."

"All right. I'll grant that. I don't scoot about space to save the Foundation or anything like that. But I'm out to make money, and this is my chance. If it helps the Foundation at the same time, all the better. And I've risked my life on slimmer chances."

Ponyets rose, and Gorov rose with him, "What are you going to do?"

The trader smiled, "Gorov, I don't know—not yet. But if the crux of the matter is to make a sale, then I'm your man. I'm not a boaster as a general thing, but there's one thing I'll always back up. I've never *ended up* below quota yet."

The door to the cell opened almost instantly when he knocked, and two guards fell in on either side.

4.

"A show!" said the Grand Master, grimly. He settled himself well into his furs, and one thin hand grasped the iron cudgel he used as a cane.

"And gold, your Veneration."

"*And* gold," agreed the Grand Master, carelessly.

Ponyets set the box down and opened it with as fine an appearance of confidence as he could manage. He felt alone in the face of universal hostility; the way he had felt out in space his first year. The semicircle of bearded councilors who faced him down, stared unpleasantly. Among them was

Pherl, the thin-faced favorite who sat next to the Grand Master in stiff hostility. Ponyets had met him once already and marked him immediately as prime enemy, and, as a consequence, prime victim.

Outside the hall, a small army awaited events. Ponyets was effectively isolated from his ship; he lacked any weapon, but his attempted bribe; and Gorov was still a hostage.

He made the final adjustments on the clumsy monstrosity that had cost him a week of ingenuity, and prayed once again that the lead-lined quartz would stand the strain.

"What is it?" asked the Grand Master.

"This," said Ponyets, stepping back, "is a small device I have constructed myself."

"That is obvious, but it is not the information I want. Is it one of the black-magic abominations of your world?"

"It is atomic in nature," admitted Ponyets, gravely, "but none of you need touch it, or have anything to do with it. It is for myself alone, and if it contains abominations, I take the foulness of it upon myself."

The Grand Master had raised his iron cane at the machine in a threatening gesture and his lips moved rapidly and silently in a purifying invocation. The thin-faced councilor at his right leaned towards him and his straggled red mustache approached the Grand Master's ear. The ancient Askonian petulantly shrugged himself free.

"And what is the connection of your instrument of evil and the gold that may save your countryman's life?"

"With this machine," began Ponyets, as his hand dropped softly onto the central chamber and caressed its hard, round flanks, "I can turn the iron you discard into gold of the finest quality. It is the only device known to man that will take iron—the ugly iron, your Veneration, that props up the chair you sit in and the walls of this building—and change it to shining, heavy, yellow gold."

Ponyets felt himself botching it. His usual sales talk was smooth, facile and plausible; but this limped like a shot-up space wagon. But it was the content, not the form, that interested the Grand Master.

"So? Transmutation? There have been fools who have claimed the ability. They have paid for their prying sacrilege."

"Had they succeeded?"

"No." The Grand Master seemed coldly amused. "Success at producing gold would have been a crime that carried its own antidote. It is the attempt plus the failure that is fatal. Here, what can you do with my staff?" He pounded the floor with it.

"Your Veneration will excuse me. My device is a small model, prepared by myself, and your staff is too long."

The Grand Master's small shining eye wandered and stopped, "Randel, your buckles. Come, man, they shall be replaced double if need be."

The buckles passed down the line, hand to hand. The Grand Master weighed them thoughtfully.

"Here," he said, and threw them to the floor.

Ponyets picked them up. He tugged hard before the cylinder opened, and his eyes blinked and squinted with effort as he centered the buckles carefully on the anode screen. Later, it would be easier but there must be no failures the first time.

The homemade transmuter crackled malevolently for ten minutes while the odor of ozone became faintly present. The Askonians backed away, muttering, and again Pherl whispered urgently into his ruler's ear. The Grand Master's expression was stony. He did not budge.

And the buckles were gold.

Ponyets held them out to the Grand Master with a murmured, "Your Veneration!" but the old man hesitated, then gestured them away. His stare lingered upon the transmuter.

Ponyets said rapidly, "Gentlemen, this is gold. Gold through and through. You may subject it to every known physical and chemical test, if you wish to prove the point. It cannot be identified from naturally-occurring gold in any way. Any iron can be so treated. Rust will not interfere, nor will a moderate amount of alloying metals—"

But Ponyets spoke only to fill a vacuum. He let the buckles remain in his outstretched hand, and it was the gold that argued for him.

The Grand Master stretched out a slow hand at last, and the thin-faced Pherl was roused to open speech. "Your Veneration, the gold is from a poisoned source."

And Ponyets countered, "A rose can grow from the mud, your Veneration. In your dealings with your neighbors, you buy material of all imaginable variety, without inquiring as to where they get it, whether from an orthodox machine blessed by your benign ancestors or from some space-spawned outrage. Come, I don't offer the machine. I offer the gold."

"Your Veneration," said Pherl, "you are not responsible for the sins of foreigners who work neither with your consent nor knowledge. But to accept this strange pseudo-gold made sinfully from iron in your presence and with your consent is an affront to the living spirits of our holy ancestors."

"Yet gold is gold," said the Grand Master, doubtfully, "and is but an exchange for the heathen person of a convicted felon. Pherl, you are too critical." But he withdrew his hand.

Ponyets said, "You are wisdom, itself, your Veneration. Consider—to give up a heathen is to lose nothing for your ancestors, whereas with the gold you get in exchange you can ornament the shrines of their holy spirits. And surely, were gold evil in itself, if such a thing could be, the evil would depart of necessity once the metal were put to such pious use."

"Now by the bones of my grandfather," said the Grand Master with surprising vehemence. His lips separated in a shrill laugh, "Pherl, what do you say of this young man? The statement is valid. It is as valid as the words of my ancestors."

Pherl said gloomily, "So it would seem. Grant that the validity does not turn out to be a device of the Malignant Spirit."

"I'll make it even better," said Ponyets, suddenly. "Hold the gold in hostage. Place it on the altars of your ancestors as an offering and hold me for thirty days. If at the end of that time, there is no evidence of displeasure—if no disasters occur—surely, it would be proof that the offering was accepted. What more can be offered?"

And when the Grand Master rose to his feet to search out disapproval, not a man in the council failed to signal his agreement. Even Pherl chewed the ragged end of his mustache and nodded curtly.

Ponyets smiled and meditated on the uses of a religious education.

5.

Another week rubbed away before the meeting with Pherl was arranged. Ponyets felt the tension, but he was used to the feeling of physical helplessness now. He had left city limits under guard. He was in Pherl's suburban villa under guard. There was nothing to do but accept it without even looking over his shoulder.

Pherl was taller and younger outside the circle of Elders. In nonformal costume, he seemed no Elder at all.

He said abruptly, "You're a peculiar man." His close-set eyes seemed to quiver. "You've done nothing this last week, and particularly these last two hours, but imply that I need gold. It seems useless labor, for who does not? Why not advance one step?"

"It is not simply gold," said Ponyets, discreetly. "Not *simply* gold. Not merely a coin or two. It is rather all that lies behind gold."

"Now what can lie behind gold?" prodded Pherl, with a down-curved smile. "Certainly this is not the preliminary of another clumsy demonstration."

"Clumsy?" Ponyets frowned slightly.

"Oh, definitely." Pherl folded his hands and nudged them

gently with his chin. "I don't criticize you. The clumsiness was on purpose, I am sure. I might have warned his Veneration of *that*, had I been certain of the motive. Now had I been you, I would have produced the gold upon my ship, and offered it alone. The show you offered us and the antagonism you aroused would have been dispensed with."

"True," Ponyets admitted, "but since I was myself, I accepted the antagonism for the sake of attracting your attention."

"Is that it? Simply that?" Pherl made no effort to hide his contemptuous amusement. "And I imagine you suggested the thirty-day purification period that you might assure yourself time to turn the attraction into something a bit more substantial. But what if the gold turns out to be impure?"

Ponyets allowed himself a dark humor in return, "When the judgement of that impurity depends upon those who are most interested in finding it pure?"

Pherl lifted his eyes and stared narrowly at the trader. He seemed at once surprised and satisfied.

"A sensible point. Now tell me why you wished to attract me."

"This I will do. In the short time I have been here, I have observed useful facts that concern you and interest me. For instance, you are young—very young for a member of the council, and even of a relatively young family."

"You criticize my family?"

"Not at all. Your ancestors are great and holy; all will admit that. But there are those that say you are not a member of one of the Five Tribes."

Pherl leaned back, "With all respect to those involved," and he did not hide his venom, "the Five Tribes have impoverished loins and thin blood. Not fifty members of the Tribes are alive."

"Yet there are those who say the nation would not be willing to see any man outside the Tribes as Grand Master. And so young and newly-advanced a favorite of the Grand Master is bound to make powerful enemies among the great ones of the State—it is said. His Veneration is aging and his protection will not last past his death, when it is an enemy of yours who will undoubtedly be the one to interpret the words of his Spirit."

Pherl scowled, "For a foreigner you hear much. Such ears are made for cropping."

"That may be decided later."

"Let me anticipate." Pherl stirred impatiently in his seat. "You're going to offer me wealth and power in terms of those evil little machines you carry in your ship. Well?"

"Suppose it so. What would be your objection? Simply your standard of good and evil?"

Pherl shook his head. "Not at all. Look, my Outlander, your opinion of us in your heathen agnosticism is what it is—but I am not the entire slave of our mythology, though I may appear so. I am an educated man, sir, and, I hope, an enlightened one. The full depth of our religious customs, in the ritualistic rather than the ethical sense, is for the masses."

"Your objection, then?" pressed Ponyets, gently.

"Just that. The masses. *I* might be willing to deal with you, but your little machines must be used to be useful. How might riches come to me, if I had to use—what is it you sell?—well, a razor, for instance, only in the strictest, trembling secrecy. Even if my chin were more simply and more cleanly shaven, how would I become rich? And how would I avoid death by gas chamber or mob frightfulness if I were ever once caught using it?"

Ponyets shrugged, "You are correct. I might point out that the remedy would be to educate your own people into the use of atomics for their convenience and your own substantial profit. It would be a gigantic piece of work; I don't deny it; but the returns would be still more gigantic. Still that is your concern, and, at the moment, not mine at all. For I offer neither razor, knife, nor mechanical garbage disposer."

"What do you offer?"

"Gold itself. Directly. You may have the machine I demonstrated last week."

And now Pherl stiffened and the skin on his forehead moved jerkily. "The transmuter?"

"Exactly. Your supply of gold will equal your supply of iron. That, I imagine, is sufficient for all needs. Sufficient for the Grand Mastership itself, despite youth and enemies. And it is safe."

"In what way?"

"In that secrecy is the essence of its use; that same secrecy you described as the only safety with regard to atomics. You may bury the transmuter in the deepest dungeon of the strongest fortress on your furthest estate, and it will still bring you instant wealth. It is the *gold* you buy, not the machine, and that gold bears no trace of its manufacture, for it cannot be told from the natural creation."

"And who is to operate the machine?"

"Yourself. Five minutes teaching is all you will require. I'll set it up for you wherever you wish."

"And in return?"

"Well," Ponyets grew cautious. "I ask a price and a handsome one. It is my living. Let us say,—for it is a valuable machine—the equivalent of a cubic foot of gold in wrought iron."

Pherl laughed, and Ponyets grew red. "I point out, sir," he added, stiffly, "that you can get your price back in two hours."

"True, and in one hour, you might be gone, and my machine might suddenly turn out to be useless. I'll need a guarantee."

"You have my word."

"A very good one," Pherl bowed sardonically, "but your presence would be an even better assurance. I'll give you *my* word to pay you one week after delivery in working order."

"Impossible."

"Impossible? When you've already incurred the death penalty very handily by even offering to sell me anything.

The only alternative is my word that you'll get the gas chamber tomorrow otherwise."

Ponyets' face was expressionless, but his eyes might have flickered. He said, "It is an unfair advantage. You will at least put your promise in writing?"

"And also become liable for execution? No, sir!" Pherl smiled a broad satisfaction. "No, sir! Only one of us is a fool."

The trader said in a small voice, "It is agreed, then."

6.

Gorov was released on the thirtieth day, and five hundred pounds of the yellowest gold took his place. And with him was released the quarantined and untouched abomination that was his ship.

Then, as on the journey into the Askonian system, so on the journey out, the cylinder of sleek little ships ushered them on their way.

Ponyets watched the dimly sun-lit speck that was Gorov's ship while Gorov's voice pierced through to him, clear and thin on the tight, distortion-bounded ether-beam.

He was saying, "But it isn't what's wanted, Ponyets. A transmuter won't do. Where did you get one, anyway?"

"I didn't," Ponyets answer was patient. "I juiced it up out of a food irradiation chamber. It isn't any good, really. The power consumption is prohibitive on any large scale or the Foundation would use transmutation instead of chasing all over the Galaxy for heavy metals. It's one of the standard tricks every trader uses, except that I never saw an iron-to-gold one before. But it's impressive, and it works—very temporarily."

"All right. But that particular trick is no good."

"It got you out of a nasty spot."

"That is very far from the point. Especially since I've got to go back, once we shake our solicitous escort."

"Why?"

"You yourself explained it to this politician of yours," Gorov's voice was on edge. "Your entire sales-point rested on the fact that the transmuter was a means to an end, but of no value in itself; that he was buying the gold, not the machine. It was good psychology, since it worked, but—"

"But?" Ponyets urged blandly and obtusely.

The voice from the receiver grew shriller, "But we want to sell them a machine of value in itself; something they would want to use openly; something that would tend to force them out in favor of atomic techniques as a matter of self-interest."

"I understand all that," said Ponyets, gently. "You once explained it. But look at what follows from my sale, will you? As long as that transmuter lasts, Pherl will coin gold; and it will last long enough to buy him the next election. The present Grand Master won't last long."

"You count on gratitude?" asked Gorov, coldly.

"No—on intelligent self-interest. The transmuter gets him an election; other mechanisms—"

"No! No! Your premise is twisted. It's not the transmuter, he'll credit—it'll be the good, old-fashioned gold. That's what I'm trying to tell you."

Ponyets grinned and shifted into a more comfortable position. All right. He'd baited the poor fellow sufficiently. Gorov was beginning to sound wild.

The trader said, "Not so fast, Gorov. I haven't finished. There are other gadgets already involved."

There was a short silence. Then, Gorov's voice sounded cautiously, "What other gadgets?"

Ponyets gestured automatically and uselessly, "You see that escort?"

"I do," said Gorov shortly. "Tell me about those gadgets."

"I will,—if you'll listen. That's Pherl's private navy escorting us; a special honor to him from the Grand Master. He managed to squeeze that out."

"So?"

"And where do you think he's taking us? To his mining

estates on the outskirts of Askone, that's where. Listen!"
Ponyets was suddenly fiery, "I told you I was in this to make
money, not to save worlds. All right. I sold that transmuter
for nothing. Nothing except the risk of the gas chamber and
that doesn't count towards the quota."

"Get back to the mining estates, Ponyets. Where do they
come in?"

"With the profits. We're stacking up on tin, Gorov. Tin
to fill every last cubic foot this old scow can scrape up, and
then some more for yours. I'm going down with Pherl to
collect, old man, and you're going to cover me from upstairs
with every gun you've got—just in case Pherl isn't as sporting
about the matter as he lets on to be. That tin's my profit."

"For the transmuter?"

"*For my entire cargo of atomics.* At double price, plus
a bonus." He shrugged, almost apologetically. "I admit I
gouged him, but I've got to make quota, don't I?"

Gorov was evidently lost. He said, weakly, "Do you mind
explaining?"

"What's there to explain? It's obvious, Gorov. Look, the
clever dog thought he had me in a foolproof trap, because
his word was worth more than mine to the Grand Master.
He took the transmuter. That was a capital crime in Askone.
But at any time he could say that he had lured me on into
a trap with the purest of patriotic motives, and denounce
me as a seller of forbidden things."

"*That* was obvious."

"Sure, but word against simple word wasn't all there was
to it. You see, Pherl had never heard nor conceived of a
microfilm-recorder."

Gorov laughed suddenly.

"That's right," said Ponyets. "He had the upper hand. I
was properly chastened. But when I set up the transmuter
for him in my whipped-dog fashion, I incorporated the recorder into the device and removed it in the next day's
overhaul. I had a perfect record of his sanctum sanctorum,
his holy-of-holies, with he himself, poor Pherl, operating the

transmuter for all the ergs it had and crowing over his first piece of gold as if it were an egg he had just laid."

"You showed him the results?"

"Two days later. The poor sap had never seen three-dimensional color-sound images in his life. He claims he isn't superstitious, but if I ever saw an adult look as scared as he did then, call me rookie. When I told him I had a recorder planted in the city square, set to go off at midday with a million fanatical Askonians to watch, and to tear him to pieces subsequently, he was gibbering at my knees in half a second. He was ready to make any deal I wanted."

"Did you?" Gorov's voice was suppressing laughter. "I mean, have one planted in the city square."

"No, but that didn't matter. He made the deal. He bought every gadget I had, and every one you had for as much tin as we could carry. At that moment, he believed me capable of anything. The agreement is in writing and you'll have a copy before I go down with him, just as another precaution."

"But you've damaged his ego," said Gorov. "Will he use the gadgets?"

"Why not? It's his only way of recouping his losses, and if he makes money out of it, he'll salve his pride. And he *will* be the next Grand Master—and the best man we could have in our favor."

"Yes," said Gorov, "it was a good sale. Yet you've certainly got an uncomfortable sales technique. No wonder you were kicked out of a seminary. Have you no sense of morals?"

"What are the odds?" said Ponyets, indifferently. "You know what Salvor Hardin said about a sense of morals."

PART V

THE MERCHANT PRINCES

1

TRADERS— . . . With psychohistoric inevitability, economic control of the Foundation grew. The traders grew rich; and with riches came power. . . .

It is sometimes forgotten that Hober Mallow began life as an ordinary trader. It is never forgotten that he ended it as the first of the Merchant Princes. . . .

ENCYCLOPEDIA GALACTICA

Jorane Sutt put the tips of carefully-manicured fingers together and said, "It's something of a puzzle. In fact—and this is in the strictest confidence—it may be another one of Hari Seldon's crises."

The man opposite felt in the pocket of his short Smyrnian jacket for a cigarette. "Don't know about that, Sutt. As a general rule, politicians start shouting 'Seldon crisis' at every mayoralty campaign."

Sutt smiled very faintly, "I'm not campaigning, Mallow. We're facing atomic weapons, and we don't know where they're coming from."

Hober Mallow of Smyrno, Master Trader, smoked quietly, almost indifferently. "Go on. If you have more to say, get it out." Mallow never made the mistake of being overpolite to a Foundation man. He might be an Outlander, but a man's a man for a' that.

Sutt indicated the trimensional star-map on the table. He adjusted the controls and a cluster of some half-dozen stellar systems blazed red.

"That," he said quietly, "is the Korellian Republic."

The trader nodded, "I've been there. Stinking rathole! I suppose you can call it a republic but it's always someone out of the Argo family that gets elected Commdor each time. And if you ever don't like it—*things* happen to you." He twisted his lip and repeated, "I've been there."

"But you've come back, which hasn't always happened. Three trade ships, inviolate under the Conventions, have disappeared within the territory of the Republic in the last year. And those ships were armed with all the usual nuclear explosives and force-field defenses."

"What was the last word heard from the ships?"

"Routine reports. Nothing else."

"What did Korell say?"

Sutt's eyes gleamed sardonically, "There was no way of asking. The Foundation's greatest asset throughout the Periphery is its reputation of power. Do you think we can lose three ships and *ask* for them?"

"Well, then, suppose you tell me what you want with *me*."

Jorane Sutt did not waste his time in the luxury of annoyance. As secretary to the mayor, he had held off opposition councilmen, jobseekers, reformers, and crackpots who claimed to have solved in its entirety the course of future history as worked out by Hari Seldon. With training like that, it took a good deal to disturb him.

He said methodically, "In a moment. You see, three ships lost in the same sector in the same year can't be accident, and atomic power can be conquered only by more atomic power. The question automatically arises: if Korell has atomic weapons, where is it getting them?"

"And where does it?"

"Two alternatives. Either the Korellians have constructed them themselves—"

"Far-fetched!"

"Very! But the other possibility is that we are being afflicted with a case of treason."

"You think so?" Mallow's voice was cold.

The secretary said calmly, "There's nothing miraculous about the possibility. Since the Four Kingdoms accepted the Foundation Convention, we have had to deal with considerable groups of dissident populations in each nation. Each former kingdom has its pretenders and its former noblemen, who can't very well pretend to love the Foundation. Some of them are becoming active, perhaps."

Mallow was a dull red. "I see. Is there anything you want to say to *me*? I'm a Smyrnian."

"I know. You're a Smyrnian—born in Smyrno, one of the former Four Kingdoms. You're a Foundation man by education only. By birth, you're an Outlander and a foreigner. No doubt your grandfather was a baron at the time of the wars with Anacreon and Loris, and no doubt your family estates were taken away when Sef Sermak redistributed the land."

"No, by Black Space, no! My grandfather was a blood-poor son-of-a-spacer who died heaving coal at starving wages before the Foundation. I owe nothing to the old regime. But I was born in Smyrno, and I'm not ashamed of either Smyrno or Smyrnians, by the Galaxy. Your sly little hints of treason aren't going to panic me into licking Foundation spittle. And now you can either give your orders or make your accusations. I don't care which."

"My good Master Trader, I don't care an electron whether your grandfather was King of Smyrno or the greatest pauper on the planet. I recited that rigmarole about your birth and ancestry to show you that I'm not interested in them. Evidently, you missed the point. Let's go back now. You're a Smyrnian. You know the Outlanders. Also, you're a trader and one of the best. You've been to Korell and you know the Korellians. That's where you've got to go."

Mallow breathed deeply, "As a spy?"

"Not at all. As a trader—but with your eyes open. If you can find out where the power is coming from— I might remind you, since you're a Smyrnian, that two of those lost trade ships had Smyrnian crews."

"When do I start?"

"When will your ship be ready?"

"In six days."

"Then that's when you start. You'll have all the details at the Admiralty."

"Right!" The trader rose, shook hands roughly, and strode out.

Sutt waited, spreading his fingers gingerly and rubbing out the pressure; then shrugged his shoulders and stepped into the mayor's office.

The mayor deadened the visiplate and leaned back. "What do *you* make of it, Sutt?"

"He could be a good actor," said Sutt, and stared thoughtfully ahead.

2.

It was evening of the same day, and in Jorane Sutt's bachelor apartment on the twenty-first floor of the Hardin Building, Publis Manlio was sipping wine slowly.

It was Publis Manlio in whose slight, aging body were fulfilled two great offices of the Foundation. He was Foreign Secretary in the mayor's cabinet, and to all the outer suns, barring only the Foundation itself, he was, in addition, Primate of the Church, Purveyor of the Holy Food, Master of the Temples, and so forth almost indefinitely in confusing but sonorous syllables.

He was saying, "But he agreed to let you send out that trader. It is a point."

"But such a small one," said Sutt. "It gets us nothing immediately. The whole business is the crudest sort of stratagem, since we have no way of foreseeing it to the end. It is a mere paying out of rope on the chance that somewhere along the length of it will be a noose."

"True. And this Mallow is a capable man. What if he is not an easy prey to dupery?"

"That is a chance that must be run. If there is treachery, it is the capable men that are implicated. If not, we need a capable man to detect the truth. And Mallow will be guarded. Your glass is empty."

"No, thanks. I've had enough."

Sutt filled his own glass and patiently endured the other's uneasy reverie.

Of whatever the reverie consisted, it ended indecisively, for the primate said suddenly, almost explosively, "Sutt, what's on your mind?"

"I'll tell you, Manlio." His thin lips parted, "We're in the middle of a Seldon crisis."

Manlio stared, then said softly, "How do you know? Has Seldon appeared in the Time Vault again?"

"That much, my friend, is not necessary. Look, reason it out. Since the Galactic Empire abandoned the Periphery, and threw us on our own, we have never had an opponent who possessed atomic power. Now, for the first time, we have one. That seems significant even if it stood by itself. And it doesn't. For the first time in over seventy years, we are facing a major domestic political crisis. I should think the synchronization of the two crises, inner and outer, puts it beyond all doubt."

Manlio's eyes narrowed, "If that's all, it's not enough. There have been two Seldon crises so far, and both times the Foundation was in danger of extermination. Nothing can be a third crisis till that danger returns."

Sutt never showed impatience, "That danger is coming. Any fool can tell a crisis when it arrives. The real service to the state is to detect it in embryo. Look, Manlio, we're proceeding along a planned history. We *know* that Hari Seldon worked out the historical probabilities of the future. We *know* that some day we're to rebuild the Galactic Empire. We *know* that it will take a thousand years or thereabouts. And we *know* that in that interval we will face certain definite crises.

"Now the first crisis came fifty years after the establishment of the Foundation, and the second, thirty years later than that. Almost seventy-five years have gone since. It's time, Manlio, it's time."

Manlio rubbed his nose uncertainly, "And you've made your plans to meet this crisis?"

Sutt nodded.

"And I," continued Manlio, "am to play a part in it?"

Sutt nodded again, "Before we can meet the foreign threat of atomic power, we've got to put our own house in order. These traders—"

"Ah!" The primate stiffened, and his eyes grew sharp.

"That's right. These traders. They are useful, but they are too strong—and too uncontrolled. They are Outlanders, educated apart from religion. On the one hand, we put knowledge into their hands, and on the other, we remove our strongest hold upon them."

"If we can prove treachery?"

"If we could, direct action would be simple and sufficient. But that doesn't signify in the least. Even if treason among them did not exist, they would form an uncertain element in our society. They wouldn't be bound to us by patriotism or common descent, or even by religious awe. Under their secular leadership, the outer provinces, which, since Hardin's time, look to us as the Holy Planet, might break away."

"I see all that, but the cure—"

"The cure must come quickly, before the Seldon Crisis becomes acute. If atomic weapons are without and disaffection within, the odds might be too great." Sutt put down the empty glass he had been fingering, "This is obviously your job."

"Mine?"

"*I* can't do it. My office is appointive and has no legislative standing."

"The mayor—"

"Impossible. His personality is entirely negative. He is energetic only in evading responsibility. But if an independent party arose that might endanger re-election, he might allow himself to be led."

"But, Sutt, I lack the aptitude for practical politics."

"Leave that to me. Who knows, Manlio? Since Salvor Hardin's time, the primacy and the mayoralty have never been combined in a single person. But it might happen now —if your job were well done."

3

And at the other end of town, in homelier surroundings, Hober Mallow kept a second appointment. He had listened long, and now he said cautiously, "Yes, I've heard of your campaigns to get direct trader representation in the council. But why *me*, Twer?"

Jaim Twer, who would remind you any time, asked or unasked, that he was in the first group of Outlanders to receive a lay education at the Foundation, beamed.

"I know what I'm doing," he said. "Remember when I met you first, last year."

"At the Traders' Convention."

"Right. You ran that meeting. You had those red-necked oxen planted in their seats, then put them in your shirt-pocket and walked off with them. And you're all right with the Foundation masses, too. You've got *glamor*—or, at any rate, solid adventure-publicity, which is the same thing."

"Very good," said Mallow, dryly. "But why now?"

"Because now's our chance. Do you know that the Secretary of Education has handed in his resignation? It's not out in the open yet, but it will be."

"How do *you* know?"

"That—never mind—" He waved a disgusted hand. "It's so. The Actionist party is splitting wide open, and we can murder it right now on a straight question of equal rights for traders; or, rather, democracy, pro- and anti-."

Mallow lounged back in his chair and stared at his thick fingers, "Uh-uh. Sorry, Twer. I'm leaving next week on business. You'll have to get someone else."

Twer stared, "Business? What kind of business?"

"Very super-secret. Triple-A priority. All that, you know. Had a talk with the mayor's own secretary."

"Snake Sutt?" Jaim Twer grew excited. "A trick. The son-of-a-spacer is getting rid of you. Mallow—"

"Hold on!" Mallow's hand fell on the other's balled fist.

"Don't go into a blaze. If it's a trick, I'll be back some day for the reckoning. If it isn't, your snake, Sutt, *is* playing into our hands. Listen, there's a Seldon crisis coming up."

Mallow waited for a reaction but it never came. Twer merely stared. "What's a Seldon crisis?"

"Galaxy!" Mallow exploded angrily at the anticlimax. "What the blue blazes did you do when you went to school? What do you mean anyway by a fool question like that?"

The elder man frowned, "If you'll explain—"

There was a long pause, then, "I'll explain." Mallow's eyebrows lowered, and he spoke slowly. "When the Galactic Empire began to die at the edges, and when the ends of the Galaxy reverted to barbarism and dropped away, Hari Seldon and his band of psychologists planted a colony, the Foundation, out here in the middle of the mess, so that we could incubate art, science, and technology, and form the nucleus of the Second Empire."

"Oh, yes, yes—"

"I'm not finished," said the trader, coldly. "The future course of the Foundation was plotted according to the science of psychohistory, then highly developed, and conditions arranged so as to bring about a series of crises that will force us most rapidly along the route to future Empire. Each crisis, each *Seldon* crisis, marks an epoch in our history. We're approaching one now—our third."

"Of course!" Twer shrugged, "I should have remembered. But I've been out of school a long time—longer than you."

"I suppose so. Forget it. What matters is that I'm being sent out into the middle of the development of this crisis. There's no telling what I'll have when I come back, and there is a council election every year."

Twer looked up, "Are you on the track of anything?"

"No."

"You have definite plans?"

"Not the faintest inkling of one."

"Well—"

"Well, nothing. Hardin once said: 'To succeed, planning

alone is insufficient. One must improvise as well.' I'll improvise."

Twer shook his head uncertainly, and they stood, looking at each other.

Mallow said, quite suddenly, but quite matter-of-factly, "I tell you what, how about coming with me? Don't stare, man. You've been a trader before you decided there was more excitement in politics. Or so I've heard."

"Where are you going? Tell me that."

"Towards the Whassallian Rift. I can't be more specific till we're out in space. What do you say?"

"Suppose Sutt decides he wants me where he can see me."

"Not likely. If he's anxious to get rid of me, why not of you as well? Besides which, no trader would hit space if he couldn't pick his own crew. I take whom I please."

There was a queer glint in the older man's eyes, "All right. I'll go." He held out his hand, "It'll be my first trip in three years."

Mallow grasped and shook the other's hand, "Good! All fired good! And now I've got to round up the boys. You know where the *Far Star* docks, don't you? Then show up tomorrow. Good-by."

4.

Korell is that frequent phenomenon in history: the republic whose ruler has every attribute of the absolute monarch but the name. It therefore enjoyed the usual despotism unrestrained even by those two moderating influences in the legitimate monarchies: regal "honor" and court etiquette.

Materially, its prosperity was low. The day of the Galactic Empire had departed, with nothing but silent memorials and broken structures to testify to it. The day of the Foundation had not yet come—and in the fierce determination of its ruler, the Commdor Asper Argo, with his strict regulation of

the traders and his stricter prohibition of the missionaries, it
was never coming.

The spaceport itself was decrepit and decayed, and the
crew of the *Far Star* were drearily aware of that. The moldering hangars made for a moldering atmosphere and Jaim
Twer itched and fretted over a game of solitaire.

Hober Mallow said thoughtfully, "Good trading material
here." He was staring quietly out the viewport. So far, there
was little else to be said about Korell. The trip here
was uneventful. The squadron of Korellian ships that had
shot out to intercept the *Far Star* had been tiny, limping
relics of ancient glory or battered, clumsy hulks. They had
maintained their distance fearfully, and still maintained it,
and for a week now, Mallow's requests for an audience with
the local government had been unanswered.

Mallow repeated, "Good trading here. You might call
this virgin territory."

Jaim Twer looked up impatiently, and threw his cards
aside, "What the devil do you intend doing, Mallow? The
crew's grumbling, the officers are worried, and I'm wondering—"

"Wondering? About what?"

"About the situation. And about you. What are we doing?"

"Waiting."

The old trader snorted and grew red. He growled, "You're
going it blind, Mallow. There's a guard around the field and
there are ships overhead. Suppose they're getting ready to
blow us into a hole in the ground."

"They've had a week."

"Maybe they're waiting for reinforcements." Twer's eyes
were sharp and hard.

Mallow sat down abruptly, "Yes, I'd thought of that. You
see, it poses a pretty problem. First, we got here without
trouble. That may mean nothing, however, for only three
ships out of better than three hundred went a-glimmer last
year. The percentage is low. But that may mean also that
the number of their ships equipped with atomic power is

small, and that they dare not expose them needlessly, until that number grows.

"But it could mean, on the other hand, that they haven't atomic power after all. Or maybe they have and are keeping undercover, for fear we know something. It's one thing, after all, to piratize blundering, light-armed merchant ships. It's another to fool around with an accredited envoy of the Foundation when the mere fact of his presence may mean the Foundation is growing suspicious.

"Combine this—"

"Hold on, Mallow, hold on." Twer raised his hands. "You're just about drowning me with talk. What're you getting at? Never mind the in-betweens."

"You've *got* to have the in-betweens, or you won't understand, Twer. We're both waiting. They don't know what I'm doing here and I don't know what they've got here. But I'm in the weaker position because I'm one and they're an entire world—maybe with atomic power. I can't afford to be the one to weaken. Sure it's dangerous. Sure there may be a hole in the ground waiting for us. But we knew that from the start. What else is there to do?"

"I don't— Who's that, now?"

Mallow looked up patiently, and tuned the receiver. The visiplate glowed into the craggy face of the watch sergeant.

"Speak, sergeant."

The sergeant said, "Pardon, sir. The men have given entry to a Foundation missionary."

"A *what?*" Mallow's face grew livid.

"A missionary, sir. He's in need of hospitalization, sir—"

"There'll be more than one in need of that, sergeant, for this piece of work. Order the men to battle stations."

Crew's lounge was almost empty. Five minutes after the order, even the men on the off-shift were at their guns. It was speed that was the great virtue in the anarchic regions of the interstellar space of the Periphery, and it was in speed above all that the crew of a master trader excelled.

Mallow entered slowly, and stared the missionary up and down and around. His eye slid to Lieutenant Tinter, who shifted uneasily to one side and to Watch-Sergeant Demen, whose blank face and stolid figure flanked the other.

The Master Trader turned to Twer and paused thoughtfully, "Well, then, Twer, get the officers here quietly, except for the co-ordinators and the trajectorian. The men are to remain at stations till further orders."

There was a five-minute hiatus, in which Mallow kicked open the doors to the lavatories, looked behind the bar, pulled the draperies across the thick windows. For half a minute he left the room altogether, and when he returned he was humming abstractedly.

Men filed in. Twer followed, and closed the door silently.

Mallow said quietly, "First, who let this man in without orders from me?"

The watch sergeant stepped forward. Every eye shifted. "Pardon, sir. It was no definite person. It was a sort of mutual agreement. He was one of us, you might say, and these foreigners here—"

Mallow cut him short, "I sympathize with your feelings, sergeant, and understand them. These men, were they under your command?"

"Yes, sir."

"When this is over, they're to be confined to individual quarters for a week. You yourself are relieved of all supervisory duties for a similar period. Understood?"

The sergeant's face never changed, but there was the slightest droop to his shoulders. He said, crisply, "Yes, sir."

"You may leave. Get to your gun-station."

The door closed behind him and the babble rose.

Twer broke in, "Why the punishment, Mallow? You know that these Korellians kill captured missionaries."

"An action against my orders is bad in itself whatever other reasons there may be in its favor. No one was to leave or enter the ship without permission."

Lieutenant Tinter murmured rebelliously, "Seven days without action. You can't maintain discipline that way."

Mallow said icily, "I can. There's no merit in discipline under ideal circumstances. I'll have it in the face of death, or it's useless. Where's this missionary? Get him here in front of me."

The trader sat down, while the scarlet-cloaked figure was carefully brought forward.

"What's your name, reverend?"

"Eh?" The scarlet-robed figure wheeled towards Mallow, the whole body turning as a unit. His eyes were blankly open and there was a bruise on one temple. He had not spoken, nor, as far as Mallow could tell, moved during all the previous interval.

"Your name, revered one?"

The missionary started to sudden feverish life. His arms went out in an embracing gesture. "My son—my children. May you always be in the protecting arms of the Galactic Spirit."

Twer stepped forward, eyes troubled, voice husky, "The man's sick. Take him to bed, somebody. Order him to bed, Mallow, and have him seen to. He's badly hurt."

Mallow's great arm shoved him back, "Don't interfere, Twer, or I'll have you out of the room. Your name, revered one?"

The missionary's hands clasped in sudden supplication, "As you are enlightened men, save me from the heathen." The words tumbled out, "Save me from these brutes and darkened ones who raven after me and would afflict the Galactic Spirit with their crimes. I am Jord Parma, of the Anacreonian worlds. Educated at the Foundation; the Foundation itself, my children. I am a Priest of the Spirit educated into all the mysteries, who have come here where the inner voice called me." He was gasping, "I have suffered at the hands of the unenlightened. As you are Children of the Spirit; and in the name of that Spirit, protect me from them."

A voice broke in upon them, as the emergency alarm box clamored metallically:

"Enemy units in sight! Instruction desired!"

Every eye shot mechanically upward to the speaker.

Mallow swore violently. He clicked open the reverse and yelled, "Maintain vigil! That is all!" and turned it off.

He made his way to the thick drapes that rustled aside at a touch and stared grimly out.

Enemy units! Several thousands of them in the persons of the individual members of a Korellian mob. The rolling rabble encompassed the port from extreme end to extreme end, and in the cold, hard light of magnesium flares the foremost straggled closer.

"Tinter!" The trader never turned, but the back of his neck was red. "Get the outer speaker working and find out what they want. Ask if they have a representative of the law with them. Make no promises and no threats, or I'll kill you."

Tinter turned and left.

Mallow felt a rough hand on his shoulder and he struck it aside. It was Twer. His voice was an angry hiss in his ear, "Mallow, you're bound to hold onto this man. There's no way of maintaining decency and honor otherwise. He's of the Foundation and, after all, he—*is* a priest. These savages outside— Do you hear me?"

"I hear you, Twer." Mallow's voice was incisive. "I've got more to do here than guard missionaries. I'll do, sir, what I please, and, by Seldon and all the Galaxy, if you try to stop me, I'll tear out your stinking windpipe. Don't get in my way, Twer, or it will be the last of you."

He turned and strode past. "You! Revered Parma! Did you know that, by convention, no Foundation missionaries may enter the Korellian territory?"

The missionary was trembling, "I can but go where the Spirit leads, my son. If the darkened ones refuse enlightenment, is it not the greater sign of their need for it?"

"That's outside the question, revered one. You are here

against the law of both Korell and the Foundation. I cannot in law protect you."

The missionary's hands were raised again. His earlier bewilderment was gone. There was the raucous clamor of the ship's outer communication system in action, and the faint, undulating gabble of the angry horde in response. The sound made his eyes wild.

"You hear them? Why do you talk of law to me, of a law made by men? There are higher laws. Was it not the Galactic Spirit that said: Thou shalt not stand idly by to the hurt of thy fellowman. And has he not said: Even as thou dealest with the humble and defenseless, thus shalt thou be dealt with.

"Have you not guns? Have you not a ship? And behind you is there not the Foundation? And above and all about you is there not the Spirit that rules the universe?" He paused for breath.

And then the great outer voice of the *Far Star* ceased and Lieutenant Tinter was back, troubled.

"Speak!" said Mallow, shortly.

"Sir, they demand the person of Jord Parma."

"If not?"

"There are various threats, sir. It is difficult to make much out. There are so many—and they seem quite mad. There is someone who says he governs the district and has police powers, but he is quite evidently not his own master."

"Master or not," shrugged Mallow, "he is the law. Tell them that if this governor, or policeman, or whatever he is, approaches the ship alone, he can have the Revered Jord Parma."

And there was suddenly a gun in his hand. He added, "I don't know what insubordination is. I have never had any experience with it. But if there's anyone here who thinks he can teach me, I'd like to teach him my antidote in return."

The gun swiveled slowly, and rested on Twer. With an effort, the old trader's face untwisted and his hands unclenched and lowered. His breath was a harsh rasp in his nostrils.

Tinter left, and in five minutes a puny figure detached itself from the crowd. It approached slowly and hesitantly, plainly drenched in fear and apprehension. Twice it turned back, and twice the patently obvious threats of the many-headed monster urged him on.

"All right," Mallow gestured with the hand-blaster, which remained unsheathed. "Grun and Upshur, take him out."

The missionary screeched. He raised his arms and rigid fingers speared upward as the voluminous sleeves fell away to reveal the thin, veined arms. There was a momentary, tiny flash of light that came and went in a breath. Mallow blinked and gestured again, contemptuously.

The missionary's voice poured out as he struggled in the two-fold grasp, "Cursed be the traitor who abandons his fellowman to evil and to death. Deafened be the ears that are deaf to the pleadings of the helpless. Blind be the eyes that are blind to innocence. Blackened forever be the soul that consorts with blackness—"

Twer clamped his hands tightly over his ears.

Mallow flipped his blaster and put it away. "Disperse," he said, evenly, "to respective stations. Maintain full vigil for six hours after dispersion of crowd. Double stations for forty-eight hours thereafter. Further instructions at that time. Twer, come with me."

They were alone in Mallow's private quarters. Mallow indicated a chair and Twer sat down. His stocky figure looked shrunken.

Mallow stared him down, sardonically. "Twer," he said, "I'm disappointed. Your three years in politics seem to have gotten you out of trader habits. Remember, I may be a democrat back at the Foundation, but there's nothing short of tyranny that can run my ship the way I want it run. I never had to pull a blaster on my men before, and I wouldn't have had to now, if you hadn't gone out of line.

"Twer, you have no official position, but you're here on

my invitation, and I'll extend you every courtesy—in private. However, from now on, in the presence of my officers or men, I'm 'sir,' and not 'Mallow.' And when I give an order, you'll jump faster than a third-class recruit just for luck, or I'll have you ironed in the sub-level even faster. Understand?"

The party-leader swallowed dryly. He said, reluctantly, "My apologies."

"Accepted! Will you shake?"

Twer's limp fingers were swallowed in Mallow's huge palm. Twer said, "My motives were good. It's difficult to send a man out to be lynched. That wobbly-kneed governor or whatever-he-was can't save him. It's murder."

"I can't help that. Frankly, the incident smelled too bad. Didn't you notice?"

"Notice what?"

"This spaceport is deep in the middle of a sleepy far section. Suddenly a missionary escapes. Where from? He comes here. Coincidence? A huge crowd gathers. From where? The nearest city of any size must be at least a hundred miles away. But they arrive in half an hour. How?"

"How?" echoed Twer.

"Well, what if the missionary were brought here and released as bait. Our friend, Revered Parma, was considerably confused. He seemed at no time to be in complete possession of his wits."

"Hard usage—" murmured Twer bitterly.

"Maybe! And maybe the idea was to have us go all chivalrous and gallant, into a stupid defense of the man. He was here against the laws of Korell and the Foundation. If I withhold him, it is an act of war against Korell, and the Foundation would have no legal right to defend *us*."

"That—that's pretty far-fetched."

The speaker blared and forestalled Mallow's answer: "Sir, official communication received."

"Submit immediately!"

The gleaming cylinder arrived in its slot with a click. Mallow opened it and shook out the silver-impregnated sheet it held. He rubbed it appreciatively between thumb and finger and said, "Teleported direct from the capital. Commdor's own stationery."

He read it in a glance and laughed shortly, "So my idea was far-fetched, was it?"

He tossed it to Twer, and added, "Half an hour after we hand back the missionary, we finally get a very polite invitation to the Commdor's august presence—after seven days of previous waiting. *I* think we passed a test."

5.

Commdor Asper was a man of the people, by self-acclamation. His remaining back-fringe of gray hair drooped limply to his shoulders, his shirt needed laundering, and he spoke with a snuffle.

"There is no ostentation here, Trader Mallow," he said. "No false show. In me, you see merely the first citizen of the state. That's what Commdor means, and that's the only title I have."

He seemed inordinately pleased with it all, "In fact, I consider that fact one of the strongest bonds between Korell and your nation. I understand you people enjoy the republican blessings we do."

"Exactly, Commdor," said Mallow gravely, taking mental exception to the comparison, "an argument which I consider strongly in favor of continued peace and friendship between our governments."

"Peace! Ah!" The Commdor's sparse gray beard twitched to the sentimental grimaces of his face. "I don't think there is anyone in the Periphery who has so next to his heart the ideal of Peace, as I have. I can truthfully say that since I succeeded my illustrious father to the leadership of the state, the reign of Peace has never been broken. Perhaps I shouldn't say it"—he coughed gently—"but I *have* been told that my people, my fellow-citizens rather, know me as Asper, the Well-Beloved."

Mallow's eyes wandered over the well-kept garden. Perhaps the tall men and the strangely-designed but openly-vicious weapons they carried just happened to be lurking in odd corners as a precaution against himself. That would be understandable. But the lofty, steel-girdered walls that circled the place had quite obviously been recently strengthened—an unfitting occupation for such a Well-Beloved Asper.

He said, "It is fortunate that I have you to deal with then, Commdor. The despots and monarchs of surrounding worlds, which haven't the benefit of enlightened administration, often lack the qualities that would make a ruler well-beloved."

"Such as?" There was a cautious note in the Commdor's voice.

"Such as their concern for the best interests of their people. You, on the other hand, would understand."

The Commdor kept his eyes on the gravel path as they walked leisurely. His hands caressed each other behind his back.

Mallow went on smoothly, "Up to now, trade between our two nations has suffered because of the restrictions placed upon our traders by your government. Surely, it has long been evident to you that unlimited trade—"

"Free Trade!" mumbled the Commdor.

"Free Trade, then. You must see that it would be of benefit to both of us. There are things you have that we want, and things we have that you want. It asks only an exchange to bring increased prosperity. An enlightened ruler such as yourself, a friend of the people—I might say, a *member* of the people—needs no elaboration on that theme. I won't insult your intelligence by offering any."

"True! I have seen this. But what would you?" His voice was a plaintive whine. "Your people have always been so unreasonable. I am in favor of all the trade our economy can support, but not on your terms. I am not sole master here." His voice rose, "I am only the servant of public opinion. My people will not take commerce which sparked in crimson and gold."

Mallow drew himself up, "A compulsory religion?"

"So it has always been in effect. Surely you remember the case of Askone twenty years ago. First they were sold some of your goods and then your people asked for complete freedom of missionary effort in order that the goods might be run properly; that Temples of Health be set up. There was then the establishment of religious schools; autonomous rights for all officers of the religion and with what result? Askone is now an integral member of the Foundation's system and the Grand Master cannot call his underwear his own. Oh, no! Oh, no! The dignity of an independent people could never suffer it."

"None of what you speak is at all what I suggest," interposed Mallow.

"No?"

"No. I'm a Master Trader. Money is *my* religion. All this mysticism and hocus-pocus of the missionaries annoy me, and I'm glad you refuse to countenance it. It makes you more my type of man."

The Commdor's laugh was high-pitched and jerky, "Well said! The Foundation should have sent a man of your caliber before this."

He laid a friendly hand upon the trader's bulking shoulder, "But man, you have told me only half. You have told me what the catch is *not*. Now tell me what it *is*."

"The only catch, Commdor, is that you're going to be burdened with an immense quantity of riches."

"Indeed?" he snuffled. "But what could I want with riches? The true wealth is the love of one's people. I have that."

"You can have both, for it is possible to gather gold with one hand and love with the other."

"Now that, my young man, would be an interesting phenomenon, if it were possible. How would you go about it?"

"Oh, in a number of ways. The difficulty is choosing among them. Let's see. Well, luxury items, for instance. This object here, now—"

Mallow drew gently out of an inner pocket a flat, linked chain of polished metal. "This, for instance."

"What is it?"

"That's got to be demonstrated. Can you get a girl? Any young female will do. *And* a mirror, full length."

"Hm-m-m. Let's get indoors, then."

The Commdor referred to his dwelling place as a house. The populace undoubtedly would call it a palace. To Mallow's straightforward eyes, it looked uncommonly like a fortress. It was built on an eminence that overlooked the capital. Its walls were thick and reinforced. Its approaches were guarded, and its architecture was shaped for defense. Just the type of dwelling, Mallow thought sourly, for Asper, the Well-Beloved.

A young girl was before them. She bent low to the Commdor, who said, "This is one of the Commdora's girls. Will she do?"

"Perfectly!"

The Commdor watched carefully while Mallow snapped the chain about the girl's waist, and stepped back.

The Commdor snuffled, "Well. Is that all?"

"Will you draw the curtain, Commdor. Young lady, there's a little knob just near the snap. Will you move it upward, please? Go ahead, it won't hurt you."

The girl did so, drew a sharp breath, looked at her hands, and gasped, "Oh!"

From her waist as a source she was drowned in a pale, streaming luminescence of shifting color that drew itself over her head in a flashing coronet of liquid fire. It was as if someone had torn the aurora borealis out of the sky and molded it into a cloak.

The girl stepped to the mirror and stared, fascinated.

"Here, take this." Mallow handed her a necklace of dull pebbles. "Put it around your neck."

The girl did so, and each pebble, as it entered the luminescent field became an individual flame that leaped and sparkled in crimson and gold.

"What do you think of it?" Mallow asked her. The girl didn't answer but there was adoration in her eyes. The Commdor gestured and reluctantly, she pushed the knob down, and the glory died. She left—with a memory.

"It's yours, Commdor," said Mallow, "for the Commdora. Consider it a small gift from the Foundation."

"Hm-m-m." The Commdor turned the belt and necklace over in his hand as though calculating the weight. "How is it done?"

Mallow shrugged, "That's a question for our technical experts. But it will work for you without—mark you, *without*—priestly help."

"Well, it's only feminine frippery after all. What could you do with it? Where would the money come in?"

"You have balls, receptions, banquets—that sort of thing?"

"Oh, yes."

"Do you realize what women will pay for that sort of jewelry? Ten thousand credits, at least."

The Commdor seemed struck in a heap, "Ah!"

"And since the power unit of this particular item will not last longer than six months, there will be the necessity of frequent replacements. Now we can sell as many of these as you want for the equivalent in wrought iron of one thousand credits. There's nine hundred percent profit for you."

The Commdor plucked at his beard and seemed engaged in awesome mental calculations, "Galaxy, how the dowagers will fight for them. I'll keep the supply small and let them bid. Of course, it wouldn't do to let them know that I personally—"

Mallow said, "We can explain the workings of dummy corporations, if you would like. —Then, working further at random, take our complete line of household gadgets. We have collapsible stoves that will roast the toughest meats to the desired tenderness in two minutes. We've got knives that won't require sharpening. We've got the equivalent of a complete laundry that can be packed in a small closet and will work entirely automatically. Ditto dish-washers. Ditto-ditto floor-scrubbers, furniture polishers, dust-precipitators, lighting fixtures—oh, anything you like. Think of your increased popularity, *if* you make them available to the public. Think of your increased quantity of, uh, worldly goods, if they're available as a government monopoly at nine hundred percent profit. It will be worth many times the money to them, and they needn't know what *you* pay for it. And, mind you, none of it will require priestly supervision. Everybody will be happy."

"Except you, it seems. What do *you* get out of it?"

"Just what every trader gets by Foundation law. My men and I will collect half of whatever profits we take in. Just you buy all I want to sell you, and we'll both make out quite well. *Quite* well."

The Commdor was enjoying his thoughts, "What did you say you wanted to be paid with? Iron?"

"That, and coal, and bauxite. Also tobacco, pepper, magnesium, hardwood. Nothing you haven't got enough of."

"It sounds well."

"I think so. Oh, and still another item at random, Commdor. I could retool your factories."

"Eh? How's that?"

"Well, take your steel foundries. I have handy little gadgets that could do tricks with steel that would cut production costs to one percent of previous marks. You could cut prices by half, and still split extremely fat profits with the manufacturers. I tell you, I could show you exactly what I mean, if you allowed me a demonstration. Do you have a steel foundry in this city? It wouldn't take long."

"It could be arranged, Trader Mallow. But tomorrow, tomorrow. Would you dine with us tonight?"

"My men—" began Mallow.

"Let them all come," said the Commdor, expansively. "A

symbolic friendly union of our nations. It will give us a chance for further friendly discussion. But one thing," his face lengthened and grew stern, "none of your religion. Don't think that all this is an entering wedge for the missionaries."

"Commdor," said Mallow, dryly, "I give you my word that religion would cut my profits."

"Then that will do for now. You'll be escorted back to your ship."

6.

The Commdora was much younger than her husband. Her face was pale and coldly formed and her black hair was drawn smoothly and tightly back.

Her voice was tart. "You are quite finished, my gracious and noble husband? Quite, *quite* finished? I suppose I may even enter the garden if I wish, now."

"There is no need for dramatics, Licia, my dear," said the Commdor, mildly. "The young man will attend at dinner tonight, and you can speak with him all you wish and even amuse yourself by listening to all I say. Room will have to be arranged for his men somewhere about the place. The stars grant that they be few in numbers."

"Most likely they'll be great hogs of eaters who will eat meat by the quarter-animal and wine by the hogshead. And you will groan for two nights when you calculate the expense."

"Well now, perhaps I won't. Despite your opinion, the dinner is to be on the most lavish scale."

"Oh, I see." She stared at him contemptuously. "You are very friendly with these barbarians. Perhaps that is why I was not to be permitted to attend your conversation. Perhaps your little weazened soul is plotting to turn against my father."

"Not at all."

"Yes, I'd be likely to believe you, wouldn't I? If ever a poor woman was sacrificed for policy to an unsavory marriage, it was myself. I could have picked a more proper man from the alleys and mudheaps of my native world."

"Well, now, I'll tell you what, my lady. Perhaps you would enjoy returning to your native world. Only to retain as a souvenir that portion of you with which I am best acquainted, I could have your tongue cut out first. And," he lolled his head, calculatingly, to one side, "as a final improving touch to your beauty, your ears and the tip of your nose as well."

"You wouldn't dare, you little pug-dog. My father would pulverize your toy nation to meteoric dust. In fact, he might do it in any case, if I told him you were treating with these barbarians."

"Hm-m-m. Well, there's no need for threats. You are free to question the man yourself tonight. Meanwhile, madam, keep your wagging tongue still."

"At your orders?"

"Here, take this, then, and keep still."

The band was about her waist and the necklace around her neck. He pushed the knob himself and stepped back.

The Commdora drew in her breath and held out her hands stiffly. She fingered the necklace gingerly, and gasped again.

The Commdor rubbed his hands with satisfaction and said, "You may wear it tonight—and I'll get you more. *Now* keep still."

The Commdora kept still.

7.

Jaim Twer fidgeted and shuffled his feet. He said, "What's twisting *your* face?"

Hober Mallow lifted out of his brooding, "Is my face twisted? It's not meant so."

"Something must have happened yesterday,—I mean, besides that feast." With sudden conviction, "Mallow, there's trouble, isn't there?"

"Trouble? No. Quite opposite. In fact, I'm in the position of throwing my full weight against a door and finding it ajar at the time. We're getting into this steel foundry too easily."

"You suspect a trap?"

"Oh, for Seldon's sake, don't be melodramatic." Mallow swallowed his impatience and added conversationally, "It's just that the easy entrance means there will be nothing to see."

"Atomic power, huh?" Twer ruminated. "I'll tell you. There's just about no evidence of any atomic power economy here in Korell. And it would be pretty hard to mask all signs of the widespread effects a fundamental technology such as atomics would have on everything."

"Not if it was just starting up, Twer, and being applied to a war economy. You'd find it in the shipyards and the steel foundries only."

"So if we don't find it, then—"

"Then they haven't got it—or they're not showing it. Toss a coin or take a guess."

Twer shook his head, "I wish I'd been with you yesterday."

"I wish you had, too," said Mallow stonily. "I have no objection to moral support. Unfortunately, it was the Commdor who set the terms of the meeting, and not myself. And *that* outside there would seem to be the royal ground-car to escort us to the foundry. Have you got the gadgets?"

"All of them."

8.

The foundry was large, and bore the odor of decay which no amount of superficial repairs could quite erase. It was empty now and in quite an unnatural state of quiet, as it played unaccustomed host to the Commdor and his court.

Mallow had swung the steel sheet onto the two supports

with a careless heave. He had taken the instrument held out to him by Twer and was gripping the leather handle inside its leaden sheath.

"The instrument," he said, "is dangerous, but so is a buzz saw. You just have to keep your fingers away."

And as he spoke, he drew the muzzle-slit swiftly down the length of the steel sheet, which quietly and instantly fell in two.

There was a unanimous jump, and Mallow laughed. He picked up one of the halves and propped it against his knee, "You can adjust the cutting-length accurately to a hundredth of an inch, and a two-inch sheet will slit down the middle as easily as this thing did. If you've got the thickness exactly judged, you can place steel on a wooden table, and split the metal without scratching the wood."

And at each phrase, the atomic shear moved and a gouged chunk of steel flew across the room.

"That," he said, "is whittling—with steel."

He passed back the shear. "Or else you have the plane. Do you want to decrease the thickness of a sheet, smooth out an irregularity, remove corrosion? Watch!"

Thin, transparent foil flew off the other half of the original sheet in six-inch swarths, then eight-inch, then twelve.

"Or drills? It's all the same principle."

They were crowded around now. It might have been a sleight-of-hand show, a corner magician, a vaudeville act made into high-pressure salesmanship. Commdor Asper fingered scraps of steel. High officials of the government tiptoed over each other's shoulders, and whispered, while Mallow punched clean, beautiful round holes through an inch of hard steel at every touch of his atomic drill.

"Just one more demonstration. Bring two short lengths of pipe, somebody."

An Honorable Chamberlain of something-or-other sprang to obedience in the general excitement and thought-absorption, and stained his hands like any laborer.

Mallow stood them upright and shaved the ends off with

a single stroke of the shear, and then joined the pipes, fresh cut to fresh cut.

And there was a single pipe! The new ends, with even atomic irregularities missing, formed one piece upon joining. Johannison blocks, at a stroke.

Then Mallow looked up at his audience, stumbled at his first word and stopped. There was the keen stirring of excitement in his chest, and the base of his stomach went tingly and cold.

The Commdor's own bodyguard, in the confusion, had struggled to the front line, and Mallow, for the first time, was near enough to see their unfamiliar hand-weapons in detail.

They were atomic! There was no mistaking it; an explosive projectile weapon with a barrel like that was impossible. But that wasn't the big point. That wasn't the point at all.

The butts of those weapons had, deeply etched upon them, in worn gold plating, the Spaceship-and-Sun!

The same Spaceship-and-Sun that was stamped on every one of the great volumes of the original Encyclopedia that the Foundation had begun and not yet finished. *The same Spaceship-and-Sun that had blazoned the banner of the Galactic Empire through millennia.*

Mallow talked through and around his thoughts, "Test that pipe! It's one piece. Not perfect; naturally, the joining shouldn't be done by hand."

There was no need of further legerdemain. It had gone over. Mallow was through. He had what he wanted. There was only one thing in his mind. The golden globe with its conventionalized rays, and the oblique cigar shape that was a space vessel.

The Spaceship-and-Sun of the Empire!

The Empire! The words drilled! A century and a half had passed but there was still the Empire, somewhere deeper in the Galaxy. And it was emerging again, out into the Periphery.

Mallow smiled!

9

The *Far Star* was two days out in space, when Hober Mallow, in his private quarters with Senior Lieutenant Drawt, handed him an envelope, a roll of microfilm, and a silvery spheroid.

"As of an hour from now, Lieutenant, you're Acting Captain of the *Far Star,* until I return,—or forever."

Drawt made a motion of standing but Mallow waved him down imperiously.

"Quiet, and listen. The envelope contains the exact location of the planet to which you're to proceed. There you will wait for me for two months. If, before the two months are up, the Foundation locates you, the microfilm is my report of the trip.

"If, however," and his voice was somber, "I do *not* return at the end of two months, and Foundation vessels do not locate you, proceed to the planet, Terminus, and hand in the Time Capsule as the report. Do you understand that?"

"Yes, sir."

"At no time are you, or any of the men, to amplify in any single instance, my official report."

"If we are questioned, sir?"

"Then you know nothing."

"Yes, sir."

The interview ended, and fifty minutes later, a lifeboat kicked lightly off the side of the *Far Star.*

10.

Onum Barr was an old man, too old to be afraid. Since the last disturbances, he had lived alone on the fringes of the land with what books he had saved from the ruins. He had nothing he feared losing, least of all the worn remnant of his life, and so he faced the intruder without cringing.

"Your door was open," the stranger explained.

His accent was clipped and harsh, and Barr did not fail to notice the strange blue-steel hand-weapon at his hip. In the half-gloom of the small room, Barr saw the glow of a force-shield surrounding the man.

He said, wearily, "There is no reason to keep it closed. Do you wish anything of me?"

"Yes." The stranger remained standing in the center of the room. He was large, both in height and bulk. "Yours is the only house about here."

"It is a desolate place," agreed Barr, "but there is a town to the east. I can show you the way."

"In a while. May I sit?"

"If the chairs will hold you," said the old man, gravely. They were old, too. Relics of a better youth.

The stranger said, "My name is Hober Mallow. I come from a far province."

Barr nodded and smiled, "Your tongue convicted you of that long ago. I am Onum Barr of Siwenna—and once Patrician of the Empire."

"Then this *is* Siwenna. I had only old maps to guide me."

"They would have to be old, indeed, for star-positions to be misplaced."

Barr sat quite still, while the other's eyes drifted away into a reverie. He noticed that the atomic force-shield had vanished from about the man and admitted dryly to himself that his person no longer seemed formidable to strangers —or even, for good or for evil, to his enemies.

He said, "My house is poor and my resources few. You may share what I have if your stomach can endure black bread and dried corn."

Mallow shook his head, "No, I have eaten, and I can't stay. All I need are the directions to the center of government."

"That is easily enough done, and poor though I am, deprives me of nothing. Do you mean the capital of the planet, or of the Imperial Sector?"

The younger man's eyes narrowed, "Aren't the two identical? Isn't this Siwenna?"

The old patrician nodded slowly, "Siwenna, yes. But Siwenna is no longer capital of the Normannic Sector. Your old map has misled you after all. The stars may not change even in centuries, but political boundaries are all too fluid."

"That's too bad. In fact, that's very bad. Is the new capital far off?"

"It's on Orsha II. Twenty parsecs off. Your map will direct you. How old is it?"

"A hundred and fifty years."

"That old?" The old man sighed. "History has been crowded since. Do you know any of it?"

Mallow shook his head slowly.

Barr said, "You're fortunate. It has been an evil time for the provinces, but for the reign of Stannell VI, and he died fifty years ago. Since that time, rebellion and ruin, ruin and rebellion." Barr wondered if he were growing garrulous. It was a lonely life out here, and he had so little chance to talk to men.

Mallow said with sudden sharpness, "Ruin, eh? You sound as if the province were impoverished."

"Perhaps not on an absolute scale. The physical resources of twenty-five first-rank planets take a long time to use up. Compared to the wealth of the last century, though, we have gone a long way downhill—and there is no sign of turning, not yet. Why are you so interested in all this, young man? You are all alive and your eyes shine!"

The trader came near enough to blushing, as the faded eyes seemed to look too deep into his and smile at what they saw.

He said, "Now look here. I'm a trader out there—out toward the rim of the Galaxy. I've located some old maps, and I'm out to open new markets. Naturally, talk of impoverished provinces disturbs me. You can't get money out of a world unless money's there to be got. Now how's Siwenna, for instance?"

The old man leaned forward, "I cannot say. It will do even yet, perhaps. But *you* a trader? You look more like a fighting man. You hold your hand near your gun and there is a scar on your jawbone."

Mallow jerked his head, "There isn't much law out there where I come from. Fighting and scars are part of a trader's overhead. But fighting is only useful when there's money at the end, and if I can get it without, so much the sweeter. Now will I find enough money here to make it worth the fighting? I take it I can find the fighting easily enough."

"Easily enough," agreed Barr. "You could join Wiscard's remnants in the Red Stars. I don't know, though, if you'd call that fighting or piracy. Or you could join our present gracious viceroy—gracious by right of murder, pillage, rapine, and the word of a boy Emperor, since rightfully assassinated." The patrician's thin cheeks reddened. His eyes closed and then opened, bird-bright.

"You don't sound very friendly to the viceroy, Patrician Barr," said Mallow. "What if I'm one of his spies?"

"What if you are?" said Barr, bitterly. "What can you take?" He gestured a withered arm at the bare interior of the decaying mansion.

"Your life."

"It would leave me easily enough. It has been with me five years too long. But you are *not* one of the viceroy's men. If you were, perhaps even now instinctive self-preservation would keep my mouth closed."

"How do you know?"

The old man laughed, "You seem suspicious. Come, I'll wager you think I'm trying to trap you into denouncing the government. No, no. I am past politics."

"Past politics? Is a man ever past that? The words you used to describe the viceroy—what were they? Murder, pillage, all that. You didn't sound objective. Not exactly. Not as if you were past politics."

The old man shrugged, "Memories sting when they come suddenly. Listen! Judge for yourself! When Siwenna was the provincial capital, I was a patrician and a member of the provincial senate. My family was an old and honored one. One of my great-grandfathers had been— No, never mind that. Past glories are poor feeding."

"I take it," said Mallow, "there was a civil war, or a revolution."

Barr's face darkened, "Civil wars are chronic in these degenerate days, but Siwenna had kept apart. Under Stannell VI, it had almost achieved its ancient prosperity. But weak emperors followed, and weak emperors mean strong viceroys, and our last viceroy—the same Wiscard, whose remnants still prey on the commerce among the Red Stars —aimed at the Imperial Purple. He wasn't the first to aim. And if he had succeeded, he wouldn't have been the first to succeed.

"But he failed. For when the Emperor's Admiral approached the province at the head of a fleet, Siwenna itself rebelled against its rebel viceroy." He stopped, sadly.

Mallow found himself tense on the edge of his seat, and relaxed slowly, "Please continue, sir."

"Thank you," said Barr, wearily. "It's kind of you to humor an old man. They rebelled; or I should say, *we* rebelled, for I was one of the minor leaders. Wiscard left Siwenna, barely ahead of us, and the planet, and with it the province, were thrown open to the admiral with every gesture of loyalty to the Emperor. Why we did this, I'm not sure. Maybe we felt loyal to the symbol, if not to the person, of the Emperor,— a cruel and vicious child. Maybe we feared the horrors of a siege."

"Well?" urged Mallow, gently.

"Well," came the grim retort, "that didn't suit the admiral. He wanted the glory of conquering a rebellious province and his men wanted the loot such conquest would involve. So while the people were still gathered in every large city, cheering the Emperor and his admiral, he occupied all armed centers, and then ordered the population put to the atom-blast."

"On what pretext?"

"On the pretext that they had rebelled against their viceroy, the Emperor's anointed. And the admiral became the new viceroy, by virtue of one month of massacre, pillage and complete horror. I had six sons. Five died—variously. I had a daughter. I *hope* she died, eventually. *I* escaped because I was old. I came here, too old to cause even our viceroy worry." He bent his gray head, "They left me nothing, because I had helped drive out a rebellious governor and deprived an admiral of his glory."

Mallow sat silent, and waited. Then, "What of your sixth son?" he asked softly.

"Eh?" Barr smiled acidly. "He is safe, for he has joined the admiral as a common soldier under an assumed name. He is a gunner in the viceroy's personal fleet. Oh, no, I see your eyes. He is not an unnatural son. He visits me when he can and gives me what he can. He keeps me alive. And some day, our great and glorious viceroy will grovel to his death, and it will be my son who will be his executioner."

"And you tell this to a stranger? You endanger your son."

"No. I help him, by introducing a new enemy. And were I a friend of the viceroy, as I am his enemy, I would tell him to string outer space with ships, clear to the rim of the Galaxy."

"There are no ships there?"

"Did you find any? Did any space-guards question your entry? With ships few enough, and the bordering provinces filled with their share of intrigue and iniquity, none can be spared to guard the barbarian outer suns. No danger ever threatened us from the broken edge of the Galaxy,—until *you* came."

"I? I'm no danger."

"There will be more after you."

Mallow shook his head slowly, "I'm not sure I understand you."

"Listen!" There was a feverish edge to the old man's

voice. "I knew you when you entered. You have a force-shield about your body, or had when I first saw you."

Doubtful silence, then, "Yes,—I had."

"Good. That was a flaw, but you didn't know that. There are some things I know. It's out of fashion in these decaying times to be a scholar. Events race and flash past and who cannot fight the tide with atom-blast in hand is swept away, as I was. But I was a scholar, and I know that in all the history of atomics, no portable force-shield was ever invented. We have force-shields—huge, lumbering powerhouses that will protect a city, or even a ship, but not one, single man."

"Ah?" Mallow's underlip thrust out. "And what do you deduce from that?"

"There have been stories percolating through space. They travel strange paths and become distorted with every parsec, —but when I was young there was a small ship of strange men, who did not know our customs and could not tell where they came from. They talked of magicians at the edge of the Galaxy; magicians who glowed in the darkness, who flew unaided through the air, and whom weapons would not touch.

"We laughed. I laughed, too. I forgot it till today. But you glow in the darkness, and I don't think my blaster, if I had one, would hurt you. Tell me, can you fly through air as you sit there now?"

Mallow said calmly, "I can make nothing of all this."

Barr smiled, "I'm content with the answer. I do not examine my guests. But if there are magicians; if *you* are one of them; there may some day be a great influx of them, or you. Perhaps that would be well. Maybe we need new blood." He muttered soundlessly to himself, then, slowly, "But it works the other way, too. Our new viceroy also dreams, as did our old Wiscard."

"Also after the Emperor's crown?"

Barr nodded, "My son hears tales. In the viceroy's personal entourage, one could scarcely help it. And he tells me of them. Our new viceroy would not refuse the Crown if offered, but he guards his line of retreat. There are stories that, failing Imperial heights, he plans to carve out a new Empire in the Barbarian hinterland. It is said, but I don't vouch for this, that he has already given one of his daughters as wife to a Kinglet somewhere in the uncharted Periphery."

"If one listened to every story—"

"I know. There are many more. I'm old and I babble nonsense. But what do you say?" And those sharp, old eyes peered deep.

The trader considered, "I say nothing. But I'd like to ask something. Does Siwenna have atomic power? Now, wait, I know that it possesses the knowledge of atomics. I mean, do they have power generators intact, or did the recent sack destroy them?"

"Destroy them? Oh, no. Half a planet would be wiped out before the smallest power station would be touched. They are irreplaceable and the suppliers of the strength of the fleet." Almost proudly, "We have the largest and best on this side of Trantor itself."

"Then what would I do first if I wanted to see these generators?"

"Nothing!" replied Barr, decisively. "You couldn't approach any military center without being shot down instantly. Neither could anyone. Siwenna is still deprived of civic rights."

"You mean all the power stations are under the military?"

"No. There are the small city stations, the ones supplying power for heating and lighting homes, powering vehicles and so forth. Those are almost as bad. They're controlled by the tech-men."

"Who are they?"

"A specialized group which supervises the power plants. The honor is hereditary, the young ones being brought up in the profession as apprentices. Strict sense of duty, honor, and all that. No one but a tech-man could enter a station."

"I see."

"I don't say, though," added Barr, "that there aren't cases where tech-men haven't been bribed. In days when we have nine emperors in fifty years and seven of these are assassinated,—when every space-captain aspires to the usurpation of a viceroyship, and every viceroy to the Imperium, I suppose even a tech-man can fall prey to money. But it would require a good deal, and I have none. Have you?"

"Money? No. But does one always bribe with money?"

"What else, when money buys all else."

"There is quite enough that money won't buy. And now if you'll tell me the nearest city with one of the stations, and how best to get there, I'll thank you."

"Wait!" Barr held out his thin hands. "Where do you rush? You come here, but I ask no questions. In the city, where the inhabitants are still called rebels, you would be challenged by the first soldier or guard who heard your accent and saw your clothes."

He rose and from an obscure corner of an old chest brought out a booklet. "My passport,—forged. I escaped with it."

He placed it in Mallow's hand and folded the fingers over it. "The description doesn't fit, but if you flourish it, the chances are many to one they will not look closely."

"But you. You'll be left without one."

The old exile shrugged cynically, "What of it? And a further caution. Curb your tongue! Your accent is barbarous, your idioms peculiar, and every once in a while you deliver yourself of the most astounding archaisms. The less you speak, the less suspicion you will draw upon yourself. Now I'll tell you how to get to the city—"

Five minutes later, Mallow was gone.

He returned but once, for a moment, to the old patrician's house, before leaving it entirely, however. And when Onum Barr stepped into his little garden early the next morning, he found a box at his feet. It contained provisions, concentrated provisions such as one would find aboard ship, and alien in taste and preparation.

But they were good, and lasted long.

The tech-man was short, and his skin glistened with well-kept plumpness. His hair was a fringe and his skull shone through pinkly. The rings on his fingers were thick and heavy, his clothes were scented, and he was the first man Mallow had met on the planet who hadn't looked hungry.

The tech-man's lips pursed peevishly, "Now, my man, quickly. I have things of great importance waiting for me. You seem a stranger—" He seemed to evaluate Mallow's definitely un-Siwennese costume and his eyelids were heavy with suspicion.

"I am not of the neighborhood," said Mallow, calmly, "but the matter is irrelevant. I have had the honor to send you a little gift yesterday—"

The tech-man's nose lifted, "I received it. An interesting gewgaw. I may have use for it on occasion."

"I have other and more interesting gifts. Quite out of the gewgaw stage."

"Oh-h?" The tech-man's voice lingered thoughtfully over the monosyllable. "I think I already see the course of the interview; it has happened before. You are going to give me some trifle or other. A few credits, perhaps a cloak, second-rate jewelry; anything your little soul may think sufficient to corrupt a tech-man." His lower lip puffed out belligerently, "And I know what you wish in exchange. There have been others to suffice with the same bright idea. You wish to be adopted into our clan. You wish to be taught the mysteries of atomics and the care of the machines. You think because you dogs of Siwenna—and probably your strangerhood is assumed for safety's sake—are being daily punished for your rebellion that you can escape what you deserve by throwing over yourselves the privileges and protections of the tech-man's guild."

Mallow would have spoken, but the tech-man raised himself into a sudden roar. "And now leave before I report your name to the Protector of the City. Do you think that I would betray the trust? The Siwennese traitors that preceded me, —perhaps! But you deal with a different breed now. Why, Galaxy, I marvel that I do not kill you myself at this moment with my bare hands."

Mallow smiled to himself. The entire speech was patently artificial in tone and content, so that all the dignified indignation degenerated into uninspired farce.

The trader glanced humorously at the two flabby hands that had been named as his possible executioners then and there, and said, "Your Wisdom, you are wrong on three counts. First, I am not a creature of the viceroy come to test your loyalty. Second, my gift is something the Emperor himself in all his splendor does not and will never possess. Third, what I wish in return is very little; a nothing; a mere breath."

"So you say!" He descended into heavy sarcasm. "Come, what is this imperial donation that your godlike power wishes to bestow upon me? Something the Emperor doesn't have, eh?" He broke into a sharp squawk of derision.

Mallow rose and pushed the chair aside, "I have waited three days to see you, Your Wisdom, but the display will take only three seconds. If you will just draw that blaster whose butt I see very near your hand—"

"Eh?"

"And shoot me, I will be obliged."

"*What?*"

"If I am killed, you can tell the police I tried to bribe you into betraying guild secrets. You'll receive high praise. If I am not killed, you may have my shield."

For the first time, the tech-man became aware of the dimly-white illumination that hovered closely about his visitor, as though he had been dipped in pearl-dust. His blaster raised to the level and with eyes a-squint in wonder and suspicion, he closed contact.

The molecules of air caught in the sudden surge of atomic disruption, tore into glowing, burning ions, and marked out the blinding thin line that struck at Mallow's heart—and splashed!

While Mallow's look of patience never changed, the atomic forces that tore at him consumed themselves against that fragile, pearly illumination, and crashed back to die in mid-air.

The tech-man's blaster dropped to the floor with an unnoticed crash.

Mallow said, "Does the Emperor have a personal force-shield? *You* can have one."

The tech-man stuttered, "Are you a tech-man?"

"No."

"Then—then where did you get that?"

"What do you care?" Mallow was coolly contemptuous. "Do you want it?" A thin, knobbed chain fell upon the desk, "There it is."

The tech-man snatched it up and fingered it nervously, "Is this complete?"

"Complete."

"Where's the power?"

Mallow's finger fell upon the largest knob, dull in its leaden case.

The tech-man looked up, and his face was congested with blood, "Sir, I am a tech-man, senior grade. I have twenty years behind me as supervisor and I studied under the great Bler at the University of Trantor. If you have the infernal charlatanry to tell me that a small container the size of a —of a walnut, blast it, holds an atomic generator, I'll have you before the Protector in three seconds."

"Explain it yourself then, if you can. I say it's complete."

The tech-man's flush faded slowly as he bound the chain about his waist, and, following Mallow's gesture, pushed the knob. The radiance that surrounded him shone into dim relief. His blaster lifted, then hesitated. Slowly, he adjusted it to an almost burnless minimum.

And then, convulsively, he closed circuit and the atomic fire dashed against his hand, harmlessly.

He whirled, "And what if I shoot you now, and keep the shield."

"Try!" said Mallow. "Do you think I gave you my only sample?" And he, too, was solidly incased in light.

The tech-man giggled nervously. The blaster clattered onto the desk. He said, "And what is this mere nothing, this breath, that you wish in return?"

"I want to see your generators."

"You realize that that is forbidden. It would mean ejection into space for both of us—"

"I don't want to touch them or have anything to do with them. I want to *see* them—from a distance."

"If not?"

"If not, you have your shield, but I have other things. For one thing, a blaster especially designed to pierce that shield."

"Hm-m-m." The tech-man's eyes shifted. "Come with me."

12.

The tech-man's home was a small two-story affair on the outskirts of the huge, cubiform, windowless affair that dominated the center of the city. Mallow passed from one to the other through an underground passage, and found himself in the silent, ozone-tinged atmosphere of the powerhouse.

For fifteen minutes, he followed his guide and said nothing. His eyes missed nothing. His fingers touched nothing. And then, the tech-man said in strangled tones, "Have you had enough? I couldn't trust my underlings in *this* case."

"Could you ever?" asked Mallow, ironically. "I've had enough."

They were back in the office and Mallow said, thoughtfully, "And all those generators are in your hands?"

"Every one," said the tech-man, with more than a touch of complacency.

"And you keep them running and in order?"

"Right!"

"And if they break down?"

The tech-man shook his head indignantly, "They don't break down. They never break down. They were built for eternity."

"Eternity is a long time. Just suppose—"

"It is unscientific to suppose meaningless cases."

"All right. Suppose I were to blast a vital part into nothingness? I suppose the machines aren't immune to atomic forces? Suppose I fuse a vital connection, or smash a quartz D-tube?"

"Well, then," shouted the tech-man, furiously, "you would be killed."

"Yes, I know that," Mallow was shouting, too, "but what about the generator? Could you repair it?"

"Sir," the tech-man howled his words, "you have had a fair return. You've had what you asked for. Now get out! I owe you nothing more!"

Mallow bowed with a satiric respect and left.

Two days later he was back at the base where the *Far Star* waited to return with him to the planet, Terminus.

And two days later, the tech-man's shield went dead, and for all his puzzling and cursing never glowed again.

13.

Mallow relaxed for almost the first time in six months. He was on his back in the sunroom of his new house, stripped to the skin. His great, brown arms were thrown up and out, and the muscles tautened into a stretch, then faded into repose.

The man beside him placed a cigar between Mallow's teeth and lit it. He champed on one of his own and said, "You must be overworked. Maybe you need a long rest."

"Maybe I do, Jael, but I'd rather rest in a council seat. Because I'm going to have that seat, and you're going to help me."

Ankor Jael raised his eyebrows and said, "How did I get into this?"

"You got in obviously. Firstly, you're an old dog of a politico. Secondly, you were booted out of your cabinet seat by Jorane Sutt, the same fellow who'd rather lose an eyeball than see me in the council. You don't think much of my chances, do you?"

"Not much," agreed the ex-Minister of Education. "You're a Smyrnian."

"That's no legal bar. I've had a lay education."

"Well, come now. Since when does prejudice follow any law but its own. Now, how about your own man—this Jaim Twer? What does *he* say?"

"He spoke about running me for council almost a year ago," replied Mallow easily, "but I've outgrown him. He couldn't have pulled it off in any case. Not enough depth. He's loud and forceful—but that's only an expression of nuisance value. I'm off to put over a real coup. I need *you*."

"Jorane Sutt is the cleverest politician on the planet and he'll be against you. I don't claim to be able to outsmart him. And don't think he doesn't fight hard, and dirty."

"I've got money."

"That helps. But it takes a lot to buy off prejudice,—you dirty Smyrnian."

"I'll have a lot."

"Well, I'll look into the matter. But don't ever you crawl up on your hind legs and bleat that I encouraged you in the matter. Who's that?"

Mallow pulled the corners of his mouth down, and said, "Jorane Sutt himself, I think. He's early, and I can understand it. I've been dodging him for a month. Look, Jael, get into the next room, and turn the speaker on low. I want you to listen."

He helped the council member out of the room with a shove of his bare foot, then scrambled up and into a silk robe. The synthetic sunlight faded to normal power.

The secretary to the mayor entered stiffly, while the solemn major-domo tiptoed the door shut behind him.

Mallow fastened his belt and said, "Take your choice of chairs, Sutt."

Sutt barely cracked a flicking smile. The chair he chose was comfortable but he did not relax into it. From its edge, he said, "If you'll state your terms to begin with, we'll get down to business."

"What terms?"

"You wish to be coaxed? Well, then, what, for instance, did you do at Korell? Your report was incomplete."

"I gave it to you months ago. You were satisfied then."

"Yes," Sutt rubbed his forehead thoughtfully with one finger, "but since then your activities have been significant. We know a good deal of what you're doing, Mallow. We know, exactly, how many factories you're putting up; in what a hurry you're doing it; and how much it's costing you. And there's this palace you have," he gazed about him with a cold lack of appreciation, "which set you back considerably more than my annual salary; and a swathe you've been cutting— a very considerable and expensive swathe—through the upper layers of Foundation society."

"So? Beyond proving that you employ capable spies, what does it show?"

"It shows you have money you didn't have a year ago. And that can show anything—for instance, that a good deal went on at Korell that we know nothing of. Where are you getting your money?"

"My dear Sutt, you can't really expect me to tell you."

"I don't."

"I didn't think you did. That's why I'm going to tell you. It's straight from the treasure-chests of the Commdor of Korell."

Sutt blinked.

Mallow smiled and continued, "Unfortunately for you, the money is quite legitimate. I'm a Master Trader and the money I received was a quantity of wrought iron and chromite in exchange for a number of trinkets I was able to supply him with. Fifty per cent of the profit is mine by hidebound contract with the Foundation. The other half goes to the government at the end of the year when all good citizens pay their income tax."

"There was no mention of any trade agreement in your report."

"Nor was there any mention of what I had for breakfast that day, or the name of my current mistress, or any other irrelevant detail." Mallow's smile was fading into a sneer. "I was sent—to quote yourself—to keep my eyes open. They were never shut. You wanted to find out what happened to the captured Foundation merchant ships. I never saw or heard of them. You wanted to find out if Korell had atomic power. My report tells of atomic blasters in the possession of the Commdor's private bodyguard. I saw no other signs. And the blasters I did see are relics of the old Empire, and may be show-pieces that do not work, for all my knowledge.

"So far, I followed orders, but beyond that I was, and still am, a free agent. According to the laws of the Foundation, a Master Trader may open whatever new markets he can, and receive therefrom his due half of the profits. What are your objections? I don't see them."

Sutt bent his eyes carefully towards the wall and spoke with a difficult lack of anger, "It is the general custom of all traders to advance the religion with their trade."

"I adhere to law, and not to custom."

"There are times when custom can be the higher law."

"Then appeal to the courts."

Sutt raised somber eyes which seemed to retreat into their sockets. "You're a Smyrnian after all. It seems naturalization and education can't wipe out the taint in the blood. Listen, and try to understand, just the same.

"This goes beyond money, or markets. We have the science of the great Hari Seldon to prove that upon us depends the future empire of the Galaxy, and from the course that leads to that Imperium we cannot turn. The religion we have is our all-important instrument towards that end. With it we have brought the Four Kingdoms under our control, even at the moment when they would have crushed us. It is the most potent device known with which to control men and worlds.

"The primary reason for the development of trade and traders was to introduce and spread this religion more quickly, and to insure that the introduction of new techniques and a new economy would be subject to our thorough and intimate control."

He paused for breath, and Mallow interjected quietly, "I know the theory. I understand it entirely."

"Do you? It is more than I expected. Then you see, of course, that your attempt at trade for its own sake; at mass production of worthless gadgets, which can only affect a world's economy superficially; at the subversion of interstellar policy to the god of profits; at the divorce of atomic power from our controlling religion—can only end with the overthrow and complete negation of the policy that has worked successfully for a century."

"And time enough, too," said Mallow, indifferently, "for a policy outdated, dangerous and impossible. However well your religion has succeeded in the Four Kingdoms, scarcely another world in the Periphery has accepted it. At the time we seized control of the Kingdoms, there were a sufficient number of exiles, Galaxy knows, to spread the story of how Salvor Hardin used the priesthood and the superstition of the people to overthrow the independence and power of the secular monarchs. And if that wasn't enough, the case of Askone two decades back made it plain enough. There isn't a ruler in the Periphery now that wouldn't sooner cut his own throat than let a priest of the Foundation enter the territory.

"I don't propose to force Korell or any other world to accept something I know they don't want. No, Sutt. If atomic power makes them dangerous, a sincere friendship through trade will be many times better than an insecure overlordship, based on the hated supremacy of a foreign spiritual power, which, once it weakens ever so slightly, can only fall entirely and leave nothing substantial behind except an immortal fear and hate."

Sutt said cynically, "Very nicely put. So, to get back to the original point of discussion, what are your terms? What do you require to exchange your ideas for mine?"

"You think my convictions are for sale?"

"Why not?" came the cold response. "Isn't that your business, buying and selling?"

"Only at a profit," said Mallow, unoffended. "Can you offer me more than I'm getting as is?"

"You could have three-quarters of your trade profits, rather than half."

Mallow laughed shortly, "A fine offer. The whole of the trade on your terms would fall far below a tenth share on mine. Try harder than that."

"You could have a council seat."

"I'll have that anyway, without and despite you."

With a sudden movement, Sutt clenched his fist, "You could also save yourself a prison term. Of twenty years, if I have my way. Count the profit in that."

"No profit at all, unless you can fulfill such a threat."

"It's trial for murder."

"Whose murder?" asked Mallow, contemptuously.

Sutt's voice was harsh now, though no louder than before, "The murder of an Anacreonian priest, in the service of the Foundation."

"Is that so now? And what's your evidence?"

The secretary to the mayor leaned forward, "Mallow, I'm not bluffing. The preliminaries are over. I have only to sign one final paper and the case of the Foundation versus Hober Mallow, Master Trader, is begun. You abandoned a subject of the Foundation to torture and death at the hands of an alien mob, Mallow, and you have only five seconds to prevent the punishment due you. For myself, I'd rather you decided to bluff it out. You'd be safer as a destroyed enemy, than as a doubtfully-converted friend."

Mallow said solemnly, "You have your wish."

"Good!" and the secretary smiled savagely. "It was the mayor who wished the preliminary attempt at compromise, not I. Witness that I did not try too hard."

The door opened before him, and he left.

Mallow looked up as Ankor Jael re-entered the room.

Mallow said, "Did you hear him?"

The politician flopped to the floor. "I never heard him as angry as that, since I've known the snake."

"All right. What do you make of it?"

"Well, I'll tell you. A foreign policy of domination through spiritual means is his *idee fixe*, but it's my notion that his ultimate aims aren't spiritual. I was fired out of the Cabinet for arguing on the same issue, as I needn't tell you."

"You needn't. And what are those unspiritual aims according to your notion?"

Jael grew serious, "Well, he's not stupid, so he must see the bankruptcy of our religious policy, which has hardly made a single conquest for us in seventy years. He's obviously using it for purposes of his own.

"Now *any* dogma, primarily based on faith and emotionalism, is a dangerous weapon to use on others, since it is almost impossible to guarantee that the weapon will never be turned on the user. For a hundred years now, we've supported a ritual and mythology that is becoming more and more venerable, traditional—and immovable. In some ways, it isn't under our control any more."

"In what ways?" demanded Mallow. "Don't stop. I want your thoughts."

"Well, suppose one man, one ambitious man, uses the force of religion against us, rather than for us."

"You mean Sutt—"

"You're right. I mean Sutt. Listen, man, if he could mobilize the various hierarchies on the subject planets against the Foundation in the name of orthodoxy, what chance would we stand? By planting himself at the head of the standards of the pious, he could make war on heresy, as represented by you, for instance, and make himself king eventually. After all, it was Hardin who said: 'An atom-blaster is a good weapon, but it can point both ways.'"

Mallow slapped his bare thigh, "All right, Jael, then get me in that council, and I'll fight him."

Jael paused, then said significantly, "Maybe not. What was all that about having a priest lynched? It isn't true, is it?"

"It's true enough," Mallow said, carelessly.

Jael whistled, "Has he definite proof?"

"He should have." Mallow hesitated, then added, "Jaim Twer was his man from the beginning, though neither of them knew that I knew that. And Jaim Twer was an eye-witness."

Jael shook his head. "Uh-uh. That's bad."

"Bad? What's bad about it? That priest was illegally upon the planet by the Foundation's own laws. He was obviously used by the Korellian government as a bait, whether involuntary or not. By all the laws of common-sense, I had no choice but one action—and that action was strictly within the law. If he brings me to trial, he'll do nothing but make a prime fool of himself."

And Jael shook his head again, "No, Mallow, you've missed it. I told you he played dirty. He's not out to convict you; he knows he can't do that. But he *is* out to ruin your standing with the people. You heard what he said. Custom *is* higher than law, at times. You could walk out of the trial scot-free, but if the people think you threw a priest to the dogs, your popularity is gone.

"They'll admit you did the legal thing, even the sensible thing. But just the same you'll have been, in their eyes, a cowardly dog, an unfeeling brute, a hard-hearted monster. *And* you would never get elected to the council. You might even lose your rating as Master Trader by having your citizenship voted away from you. You're not native born, you know. What more do you think Sutt can want?"

Mallow frowned stubbornly, "So!"

"My boy," said Jael. "I'll stand by you, but *I* can't help. You're on the spot,—dead center."

14.

The council chamber was full in a very literal sense on the fourth day of the trial of Hober Mallow, Master Trader. The only councilman absent was feebly cursing the fractured skull that had bedridden him. The galleries were filled to the aisleways and ceilings with those few of the crowd who by influence, wealth, or sheer diabolic perseverance had managed to get in. The rest filled the square outside, in swarming knots about the open-air trimensional 'visors.

Ankor Jael made his way into the chamber with the near-futile aid and exertions of the police department, and then through the scarcely smaller confusion within to Hober Mallow's seat.

Mallow turned with relief, "By Seldon, you cut it thin. Have you got it?"

"Here, take it," said Jael. "It's everything you asked for."

"Good. How are they taking it outside?"

"They're wild clear through." Jael stirred uneasily, "You should never have allowed public hearings. You could have stopped them."

"I didn't want to."

"There's lynch talk. And Publis Manlio's men on the outer planets—"

"I wanted to ask you about that, Jael. He's stirring up the Hierarchy against me, is he?"

"*Is* he? It's the sweetest setup you every saw. As Foreign Secretary, he handles the prosecution in a case of interstellar law. As High Priest and Primate of the Church, he rouses the fanatic hordes—"

"Well, forget it. Do you remember that Hardin quotation you threw at me last month? We'll show them that the atom-blaster can point both ways."

The mayor was taking his seat now and the council members were rising in respect.

Mallow whispered, "It's my turn today. Sit here and watch the fun."

The day's proceedings began and fifteen minutes later, Hober Mallow stepped through a hostile whisper to the empty space before the mayor's bench. A lone beam of light centered upon him and in the public 'visors of the city, as well as on the myriads of private 'visors in almost every home of the Foundation's planets, the lonely giant figure of a man stared out defiantly.

He began easily and quietly, "To save time, I will admit the truth of every point made against me by the prosecution. The story of the priest and the mob as related by them is perfectly accurate in every detail."

There was a stirring in the chamber and a triumphant mass-snarl from the gallery. He waited patiently for silence.

"However, the picture they presented fell short of completion. I ask the privilege of supplying the completion in my own fashion. My story may seem irrelevant at first. I ask your indulgence for that."

Mallow made no reference to the notes before him:

"I begin at the same time as the prosecution did; the day of my meetings with Jorane Sutt and Jaim Twer. What went on at those meetings you know. The conversations have been described, and to that description I have nothing to add—except my own thoughts of that day.

"They were suspicious thoughts, for the events of that day were queer. Consider. Two people, neither of whom I knew more than casually, make unnatural and somewhat unbelievable propositions to me. One, the secretary to the mayor, asks me to play the part of intelligence agent to the government in a highly confidential matter, the nature and importance of which has already been explained to you. The other, self-styled leader of a political party, asks me to run for a council seat.

"Naturally I looked for the ulterior motive. Sutt's seemed evident. He didn't trust me. Perhaps he thought I was selling atomic power to enemies and plotting rebellion. And perhaps he was forcing the issue, or thought he was. In that case, he would need a man of his own near me on my proposed mission, as a spy. The last thought, however, did not occur to me until later on, when Jaim Twer came on the scene.

"Consider again: Twer presents himself as a trader, retired into politics, yet I know of no details of his trading career, although my knowledge of the field is immense. And further, although Twer boasted of a lay education, *he had never heard of a Seldon crisis.*"

Hober Mallow waited to let the significance sink in and was rewarded with the first silence he had yet encountered, as the gallery caught its collective breath. That was for the inhabitants of Terminus itself. The men of the Outer Planets could hear only censored versions that would suit the requirements of religion. They would hear nothing of Seldon crises. But there would be further strokes they would not miss.

Mallow continued:

"Who here can honestly state that *any* man with a lay education can possibly be ignorant of the nature of a Seldon crisis? There is only one type of education upon the Foundation that excludes all mention of the planned history of Seldon and deals only with the man himself as a semi-mythical wizard—

"I knew at that instant that Jaim Twer had never been a trader. I knew then that he was in holy orders and perhaps a full-fledged priest; and, doubtless, that for the three years he had pretended to head a political party of the traders, *he had been a bought man of Jorane Sutt.*

"At the moment, I struck in the dark. I did not know Sutt's purposes with regard to myself, but since he seemed to be feeding me rope liberally, I handed him a few fathoms of my own. My notion was that Twer was to be with me on my voyage as unofficial guardian on behalf of Jorane Sutt. Well, if he didn't get on, I knew well there'd be other devices waiting—and those others I might not catch in time. A known enemy is relatively safe. I invited Twer to come with me. He accepted.

"That, gentlemen of the council, explains two things. First, it tells you that Twer is not a friend of mine testifying against me reluctantly and for conscience' sake, as the prosecution would have you believe. He is a spy, performing his paid job. Secondly, it explains a certain action of mine on the occasion of the first appearance of the priest whom I am accused of having murdered—an action as yet unmentioned, because unknown."

Now there was a disturbed whispering in the council. Mallow cleared his throat theatrically, and continued:

"I hate to describe my feelings when I first heard that we had a refugee missionary on board. I even hate to remember them. Essentially, they consisted of wild uncertainty. The event struck me at the moment as a move by Sutt, and passed beyond my comprehension or calculation. I was at sea—and completely.

"There was one thing I could do. I got rid of Twer for five minutes by sending him after my officers. In his absence, I set up a Visual Record receiver, so that whatever happened might be preserved for future study. This was in the hope, the wild but earnest hope, that what confused me at the time might become plain upon review.

"I have gone over that Visual Record some fifty times since. I have it here with me now, and will repeat the job a fifty-first time in your presence right now."

The mayor pounded monotonously for order, as the chamber lost its equilibrium and the gallery roared. In five million homes on Terminus, excited observers crowded their receiving sets more closely, and at the prosecutor's own bench,

Jorane Sutt shook his head coldly at the nervous high priest, while his eyes blazed fixedly on Mallow's face.

The center of the chamber was cleared, and the lights burnt low. Ankor Jael, from his bench on the left, made the adjustments, and with a preliminary click, a scene sprang to view; in color, in three-dimensions, in every attribute of life but life itself.

There was the missionary, confused and battered, standing between the lieutenant and the sergeant. Mallow's image waited silently, and then men filed in, Twer bringing up the rear.

The conversation played itself out, word for word. The sergeant was disciplined, and the missionary was questioned. The mob appeared, their growl could be heard, and the Revered Jord Parma made his wild appeal. Mallow drew his gun, and the missionary, as he was dragged away, lifted his arms in a mad, final curse and a tiny flash of light came and went.

The scene ended, with the officers frozen at the horror of the situation, while Twer clamped shaking hands over his ears, and Mallow calmly put his gun away.

The lights were on again; the empty space in the center of the floor was no longer even apparently full. Mallow, the real Mallow of the present, took up the burden of his narration:

"The incident, you see, is exactly as the prosecution has presented it—on the surface. I'll explain that shortly. Jaim Twer's emotions through the whole business shows clearly a priestly education, by the way.

"It was on that same day that I pointed out certain incongruities in the episode to Twer. I asked him where the missionary came from in the midst of the near-desolate tract we occupied at the time. I asked further where the gigantic mob had come from with the nearest sizable town a hundred miles away. The prosecution has paid no attention to such problems.

"Or to other points; for instance, the curious point of Jord

Parma's blatant conspicuousness. A missionary on Korell, risking his life in defiance of both Korellian and Foundation law, parades about in a very new and very distinctive priestly costume. There's something wrong there. At the time, I suggested that the missionary was an unwitting accomplice of the Commdor, who was using him in an attempt to force us into an act of wildly illegal aggression, to justify, *in law,* his subsequent destruction of our ship and of us.

"The prosecution has anticipated this justification of my actions. They have expected me to explain that the safety of my ship, my crew, my mission itself were at stake and could not be sacrificed for one man, when that man would, in any case, have been destroyed, with us or without us. They reply by muttering about the Foundation's 'honor' and the necessity of upholding our 'dignity' in order to maintain our ascendancy.

"For some strange reason, however, the prosecution has neglected Jord Parma himself,—as an individual. They brought out no details concerning him; neither his birthplace, nor his education, nor any detail of previous history. The explanation of this will also explain the incongruities I have pointed out in the Visual Record you have just seen. The two are connected.

"The prosecution has advanced no details concerning Jord Parma because it *cannot.* That scene you saw by Visual Record seemed phoney because Jord Parma was phoney. There never *was* a Jord Parma. *This whole trial is the biggest farce ever cooked up over an issue that never existed.*"

Once more he had to wait for the babble to die down. He said, slowly:

"I'm going to show you the enlargement of a single still from the Visual Record. It will speak for itself. Lights again, Jael."

The chamber dimmed, and the empty air filled again with frozen figures in ghostly, waxen illusion. The officers of the *Far Star* struck their stiff, impossible attitudes. A gun pointed from Mallow's rigid hand. At his left, the Revered

Jord Parma, caught in mid-shriek, stretched his claws upward, while the falling sleeves hung halfway.

And from the missionary's hand there was that little gleam that in the previous showing had flashed and gone. It was a permanent glow now.

"Keep your eye on that light on his hand," called Mallow from the shadows. "Enlarge that scene, Jael!"

The tableau bloated—quickly. Outer portions fell away as the missionary drew towards the center and became a giant. Then there was only a head and an arm, and then only a hand, which filled everything and remained there in immense, hazy tautness.

The light had become a set of fuzzy, glowing letters: K S P.

"That," Mallow's voice boomed out, "is a sample of tattooing, gentlemen. Under ordinary light it is invisible, but under ultraviolet light—with which I flooded the room in taking this Visual Record, it stands out in high relief. I'll admit it is a naive method of secret identification, but it works on Korell, where UV light is not to be found on street corners. Even in our ship, detection was accidental.

"Perhaps some of you have already guessed what K S P stands for. Jord Parma knew his priestly lingo well and did his job magnificently. Where he had learned it, and how, I cannot say, but K S P stands for 'Korellian Secret Police.'"

Mallow shouted over the tumult, roaring against the noise, "I have collateral proof in the form of documents brought from Korell, which I can present to the council, if required.

"And where is now the prosecution's case? They have already made and re-made the monstrous suggestion that I should have fought for the missionary in defiance of the law, and sacrificed my mission, my ship, and myself to the 'honor' of the Foundation.

"But to do it for an impostor?

"Should I have done it then for a Korellian secret agent tricked out in the robes and verbal gymnastics probably bor-

rowed of an Anacreonian exile? Would Jorane Sutt and Publis Manlio have had me fall into a stupid, odious trap—"

His hoarsened voice faded into the featureless background
of a shouting mob. He was being lifted onto shoulders, and
carried to the mayor's bench. Out the windows, he could see
a torrent of madmen swarming into the square to add to the
thousands there already.

Mallow looked about for Ankor Jael, but it was impossible
to find any single face in the incoherence of the mass. Slowly
he became aware of a rhythmic, repeated shout, that was
spreading from a small beginning, and pulsing into insan-
ity:

"Long live Mallow—long live Mallow—long live Mallow—"

15.

Ankor Jael blinked at Mallow out of a haggard face. The
last two days had been mad, sleepless ones.

"Mallow, you've put on a beautiful show, so don't spoil it
by jumping too high. You can't seriously consider running
for mayor. Mob enthusiasm is a powerful thing, but it's
notoriously fickle."

"Exactly!" said Mallow, grimly, "so we must coddle it, and
the best way to do that is to continue the show."

"Now what?"

"You're to have Publis Manlio and Jorane Sutt arrested—"

"What!"

"Just what you hear. Have the mayor arrest them! I don't
care what threats you use. I control the mob,—for today, at
any rate. He won't dare face them."

"But on what charge, man?"

"On the obvious one. They've been inciting the priesthood
of the outer planets to take sides in the factional quarrels
of the Foundation. That's illegal, by Seldon. Charge them
with 'endangering the state.' And I don't care about a con-

viction any more than they did in my case. Just get them out of circulation until I'm mayor."

"It's half a year till election."

"Not too long!" Mallow was on his feet, and his sudden grip of Jael's arm was tight. "Listen, I'd seize the government by force if I had to—the way Salvor Hardin did a hundred years ago. There's still that Seldon crisis coming up, and when it comes I have to be mayor *and* high priest. Both!"

Jael's brow furrowed. He said, quietly, "What's it going to be? Korell, after all?"

Mallow nodded, "Of course. They'll declare war, eventually, though I'm betting it'll take another pair of years."

"With atomic ships?"

"What do you think? Those three merchant ships we lost in their space sector weren't knocked over with compressed-air pistols. Jael, they're getting ships from the Empire itself. Don't open your mouth like a fool. I said the Empire! It's still there, you know. It may be gone here in the Periphery but in the Galactic center it's still very much alive. And one false move means that it, itself, may be on our neck. That's why I must be mayor and high priest. I'm the only man who knows how to fight the crisis."

Jael swallowed dryly, "How? What are you going to do?"

"Nothing."

Jael smiled uncertainly, "Really! All of that!"

But Mallow's answer was incisive, "When I'm boss of this Foundation, I'm going to do nothing. One hundred percent of nothing, and that is the secret of this crisis."

16.

Asper Argo, the Well-Beloved, Commdor of the Korellian Republic greeted his wife's entry by a hangdog lowering of his scanty eyebrows. To her at least, his self-adopted epithet did not apply. Even he knew that.

She said, in a voice as sleek as her hair and as cold as her eyes, "My gracious lord, I understand, has finally come to a decision upon the fate of the Foundation upstarts."

"Indeed?" said the Commdor, sourly. "And what more does your versatile understanding embrace?"

"Enough, my very noble husband. You had another of your vacillating consultations with your councilors. Fine advisors." With infinite scorn, "A herd of palsied purblind idiots hugging their sterile profits close to their sunken chests in the face of my father's displeasure."

"And who, my dear," was the mild response, "is the excellent source from which your understanding understands all this?"

The Commdora laughed shortly, "If I told you, my source would be more corpse than source."

"Well, you'll have your own way, as always." The Commdor shrugged and turned away. "And as for your father's displeasure: I much fear me it extends to a niggardly refusal to supply more ships."

"More ships!" She blazed away, hotly, "And haven't you five? Don't deny it. I *know* you have five; and a sixth is promised."

"Promised for the last year."

"But one—just one—can blast that Foundation into stinking rubble. Just one! One, to sweep their little pygmy boats out of space."

"I couldn't attack their planet, even with a dozen."

"And how long would their planet hold out with their trade ruined, and their cargoes of toys and trash destroyed?"

"Those toys and trash mean money," he sighed. "A good deal of money."

"But if you had the Foundation itself, would you not have all it contained? And if you had my father's respect and gratitude, would you not have more than ever the Foundation could give you? It's been three years—more—since that barbarian came with his magic sideshow. It's long enough."

"My dear!" The Commdor turned and faced her. "I am growing old. I am weary. I lack the resilience to withstand your rattling mouth. You say you know that I have decided. Well, I have. It is over, and there is war between Korell and the Foundation."

"Well!" The Commdora's figure expanded and her eyes sparkled, "You learned wisdom at last, though in your dotage. And now when you are master of this hinterland, you may be sufficiently respectable to be of some weight and importance in the Empire. For one thing, we might leave this barbarous world and attend the viceroy's court. Indeed we might."

She swept out, with a smile, and a hand on her hip. Her hair gleamed in the light.

The Commdor waited, and then said to the closed door, with malignance and hate, "And when I am master of what you call the hinterland, I may be sufficiently respectable to do without your father's arrogance and his daughter's tongue. Completely—without!"

17.

The senior lieutenant of the *Dark Nebula* stared in horror at the visiplate.

"Great Galloping Galaxies!" It should have been a howl, but it was a whisper instead, "What's that?"

It was a ship, but a whale to the *Dark Nebula's* minnow; and on its side was the Spaceship-and-Sun of the Empire. Every alarm on the ship yammered hysterically.

The orders went out, and the *Dark Nebula* prepared to run if it could, and fight if it must,—while down in the ultrawave room, a message stormed its way through hyperspace to the Foundation.

Over and over again! Partly a plea for help, but mainly a warning of danger.

Hober Mallow shuffled his feet wearily as he leafed through the reports. Two years of the mayoralty had made him a bit more housebroken, a bit softer, a bit more patient, —but it had not made him learn to like government reports and the mind-breaking officialese in which they were written.

"How many ships did they get?" asked Jael.

"Four trapped on the ground. Two unreported. All others accounted for and safe." Mallow grunted, "We should have done better, but it's just a scratch."

There was no answer and Mallow looked up, "Does anything worry you?"

"I wish Sutt would get here," was the almost irrelevant answer.

"Ah, yes, and now we'll hear another lecture on the home front."

"No, we won't," snapped Jael, "but you're stubborn, Mallow. You may have worked out the foreign situation to the last detail but you've never given a care about what goes on here on the home planet."

"Well, that's your job, isn't it? What did I make you Minister of Education and Propaganda for?"

"Obviously to send me to an early and miserable grave, for all the co-operation you give me. For the last year, I've been deafening you with the rising danger of Sutt and his Religionists. What good will your plans be, if Sutt forces a special election and has you thrown out?"

"None, I admit."

"And your speech last night just about handed the election to Sutt with a smile and a pat. Was there any necessity for being so frank?"

"Isn't there such a thing as stealing Sutt's thunder?"

"No," said Jael, violently, "not the way you did it. You claim to have foreseen everything, and don't explain why you traded with Korell to their exclusive benefit for three years. Your only plan of battle is to retire without a battle. You abandon all trade with the sectors of space near Korell. You openly proclaim a stalemate. You promise no offensive, even in the future. Galaxy, Mallow, what am I supposed to do with such a mess?"

"It lacks glamor?"

"It lacks mob emotion-appeal."

"Same thing."

"Mallow, wake up. You have two alternatives. Either you present the people with a dynamic foreign policy, whatever your private plans are, or you make some sort of compromise with Sutt."

Mallow said, "All right, if I've failed the first, let's try the second. Sutt's just arrived."

Sutt and Mallow had not met personally since the day of the trial, two years back. Neither detected any change in the other, except for that subtle atmosphere about each which made it quite evident that the roles of ruler and defier had changed.

Sutt took his seat without shaking hands.

Mallow offered a cigar and said, "Mind if Jael stays? He wants a compromise earnestly. He can act as mediator if tempers rise."

Sutt shrugged, "A compromise will be well for you. Upon another occasion I once asked you to state your terms. I presume the positions are reversed now."

"You presume correctly."

"Then these are my terms. You must abandon your blundering policy of economic bribery and trade in gadgetry, and return to the tested foreign policy of our fathers."

"You mean conquest by missionary?"

"Exactly."

"No compromise short of that?"

"None."

"Um-m-m." Mallow lit up very slowly, and inhaled the tip of his cigar into a bright glow. "In Hardin's time, when conquest by missionary was new and radical, men like yourself opposed it. Now it is tried, tested, hallowed,—everything a Jorane Sutt would find well. But, tell me, how would you get us out of our present mess?"

"*Your* present mess. I had nothing to do with it."

"Consider the question suitably modified."

"A strong offensive is indicated. The stalemate you seem to be satisfied with is fatal. It would be a confession of weakness to all the worlds of the Periphery, where the appearance of strength is all-important, and there's not one vulture among them that wouldn't join the assault for its share of the corpse. You ought to understand that. You're from Smyrno, aren't you?"

Mallow passed over the significance of the remark. He said, "And if you beat Korell, what of the Empire? *That* is the real enemy."

Sutt's narrow smile tugged at the corners of his mouth, "Oh, no, your records of your visit to Siwenna were complete. The viceroy of the Normannic Sector is interested in creating dissension in the Periphery for his own benefit, but only as a side issue. He isn't going to stake everything on an expedition to the Galaxy's rim when he has fifty hostile neighbors and an emperor to rebel against. I paraphrase your own words."

"Oh, yes he might, Sutt, if he thinks we're strong enough to be dangerous. And he might think so, if we destroy Korell by the main force of frontal attack. We'd have to be considerably more subtle."

"As for instance—"

Mallow leaned back, "Sutt, I'll give you your chance. I don't need you, but I can use you. So I'll tell you what it's all about, and then you can either join me and receive a place in a coalition cabinet, or you can play the martyr and rot in jail."

"Once before you tried that last trick."

"Not very hard, Sutt. The right time has only just come. Now listen." Mallow's eyes narrowed.

"When I first landed on Korell," he began, "I bribed the

Commdor with the trinkets and gadgets that form the trader's usual stock. At the start, that was meant only to get us entrance into a steel foundry. I had no plan further than that, but in that I succeeded. I got what I wanted. But it was only after my visit to the Empire that I first realized exactly what a weapon I could build that trade into.

"This is a Seldon crisis we're facing, Sutt, and Seldon crises are not solved by individuals but by historic forces. Hari Seldon, when he planned our course of future history, did not count on brilliant heroics but on the broad sweeps of economics and sociology. So the solutions to the various crises must be achieved by the forces that become available to us at the time.

"In this case,—trade!"

Sutt raised his eyebrows skeptically and took advantage of the pause, "I hope I am not of subnormal intelligence, but the fact is that your vague lecture isn't very illuminating."

"It will become so," said Mallow. "Consider that until now the power of trade has been underestimated. It has been thought that it took a priesthood under our control to make it a powerful weapon. That is not so, and *this* is my contribution to the Galactic situation. Trade without priests! Trade alone! It is strong enough. Let us become very simple and specific. Korell is now at war with us. Consequently our trade with her has stopped. *But,*—notice that I am making this as simple as a problem in addition,—in the past three years she has based her economy more and more upon the atomic techniques which we have introduced and which only we can continue to supply. Now what do you suppose will happen once the tiny atomic generators begin failing, and one gadget after another goes out of commission?

"The small household appliances go first. After half a year of this stalemate that you abhor, a woman's atomic knife won't work any more. Her stove begins failing. Her washer doesn't do a good job. The temperature-humidity control in her house dies on a hot summer day. What happens?"

He paused for an answer, and Sutt said calmly, "Nothing. People endure a good deal in war."

"Very true. They do. They'll send their sons out in unlimited numbers to die horribly on broken spaceships. They'll bear up under enemy bombardment, if it means they have to live on stale bread and foul water in caves half a mile deep. But it's very hard to bear up under little things when the patriotic uplift of imminent danger is not present. It's going to be a stalemate. There will be no casualties, no bombardments, no battles.

"There will just be a knife that won't cut, and a stove that won't cook, and a house that freezes in the winter. It will be annoying and people will grumble."

Sutt said slowly, wonderingly, "Is that what you're setting your hopes on, man? What do you expect? A housewives' rebellion? A Jacquerie? A sudden uprising of butchers and grocers with their cleavers and bread-knives shouting 'Give us back our Automatic Super-Kleeno Atomic Washing Machines.'"

"No, sir," said Mallow, impatiently, "I do not. I expect, however, a general background of grumbling and dissatisfaction which will be seized on by more important figures later on."

"And what more important figures are these?"

"The manufacturers, the factory owners, the industrialists of Korell. When two years of the stalemate have gone, the machines in the factories will, one by one, begin to fail. Those industries which we have changed from first to last with our new atomic gadgets will find themselves very suddenly ruined. The heavy industries will find themselves *en masse* and at a stroke the owners of nothing but scrap machinery that won't work."

"The factories ran well enough before you came there, Mallow."

"Yes, Sutt, so they did—at about one-twentieth the profits, even if you leave out of consideration the cost of reconversion to the original pre-atomic state. With the industrialist and financier and the average man all against him, how long will the Commdor hold out?"

"As long as he pleases, as soon as it occurs to him to get new atomic generators from the Empire."

And Mallow laughed joyously, "You've missed, Sutt, missed as badly as the Commdor himself. You've missed everything, and understood nothing. Look, man, the Empire can replace nothing. The Empire has always been a realm of colossal resources. They've calculated everything in planets, in stellar systems, in whole sectors of the Galaxy. Their generators are gigantic because they thought in gigantic fashion.

"But we,—*we*, our little Foundation, our single world almost without metallic resources,—have had to work with brute economy. Our generators have had to be the size of our thumb, because it was all the metal we could afford. We had to develop new techniques and new methods,—techniques and methods the Empire can't follow because they have degenerated past the stage where they can make any really vital scientific advance.

"With all their atomic shields, large enough to protect a ship, a city, an entire world; they could never build one to protect a single man. To supply light and heat to a city, they have motors six stories high,—I saw them—where ours could fit into this room. And when I told one of their atomic specialists that a lead container the size of a walnut contained an atomic generator, he almost choked with indignation on the spot.

"Why, they don't even understand their own colossi any longer. The machines work from generation to generation automatically, and the caretakers are a hereditary caste who would be helpless if a single D-tube in all that vast structure burnt out.

"The whole war is a battle between those two systems; between the Empire and the Foundation; between the big and the little. To seize control of a world, they bribe with immense ships that can make war, but lack all economic significance. We, on the other hand, bribe with little things, useless in war, but vital to prosperity and profits.

"A king, or a Commdor, will take the ships and even make war. Arbitrary rulers throughout history have bartered their subjects' welfare for what they consider honor, and glory, and conquest. But it's still the little things in life that count—and Asper Argo won't stand up against the economic depression that will sweep all Korell in two or three years."

Sutt was at the window, his back to Mallow and Jael. It was early evening now, and the few stars that struggled feebly here at the very rim of the Galaxy sparked against the background of the misty, wispy Lens that included the remnants of that Empire, still vast, that fought against them.

Sutt said, "No. You are not the man."

"You don't believe me?"

"I mean I don't trust you. You're smooth-tongued. You befooled me properly when I thought I had you under proper care on your first trip to Korell. When I thought I had you cornered at the trial, you wormed your way out of it and into the mayor's chair by demagoguery. There is nothing straight about you; no motive that hasn't another behind it; no statement that hasn't three meanings.

"Suppose you were a traitor. Suppose your visit to the Empire had brought you a subsidy and a promise of power. Your actions would be precisely what they are now. You would bring about a war after having strengthened the enemy. You would force the Foundation into inactivity. And you would advance a plausible explanation of everything, one so plausible it would convince everyone."

"You mean there'll be no compromise?" asked Mallow, gently.

"I mean you must get out, by free will or force."

"I warned you of the only alternative to co-operation."

Jorane Sutt's face congested with blood in a sudden access of emotion, "And I warn you, Hober Mallow of Smyrno, that if you arrest me, there will be no quarter. My men will stop nowhere in spreading the truth about you, and the common people of the Foundation will unite against their foreign ruler. They have a consciousness of destiny that a Smyrnian can never understand—and that consciousness will destroy you."

Hober Mallow said quietly to the two guards who had entered, "Take him away. He's under arrest."

Sutt said, "Your last chance."

Mallow stubbed out his cigar and never looked up.

And five minutes later, Jael stirred and said, wearily, "Well, now that you've made a martyr for the cause, what next?"

Mallow stopped playing with the ash tray and looked up, "That's not the Sutt I used to know. He's a blood-blind bull. Galaxy, he hates me."

"All the more dangerous then."

"More dangerous? Nonsense! He's lost all power of judgement."

Jael said grimly, "You're overconfident, Mallow. You're ignoring the possibility of a popular rebellion."

Mallow looked up, grim in his turn, "Once and for all, Jael, there is no possibility of a popular rebellion."

"You're sure of yourself!"

"I'm sure of the Seldon crisis and the historical validity of their solutions, externally *and* internally. There are some things I *didn't* tell Sutt right now. He tried to control the Foundation itself by religious forces as he controlled the outer worlds, and he failed,—which is the surest sign that in the Seldon scheme, religion is played out.

"Economic control worked differently. And to paraphrase that famous Salvor Hardin quotation of yours, it's a poor atom blaster that won't point both ways. If Korell prospered with our trade, so did we. If Korellian factories fail without our trade; and if the prosperity of the outer worlds vanishes with commercial isolation; so will our factories fail and our prosperity vanish.

"And there isn't a factory, not a trading center, not a shipping line that isn't under my control; that I couldn't squeeze to nothing if Sutt attempts revolutionary propaganda. Where his propaganda succeeds, or even looks as though it might succeed, I will make certain that prosperity dies. Where it fails, prosperity will continue, because my factories will remain fully staffed.

"So by the same reasoning which makes me sure that the Korellians will revolt in favor of prosperity, I am sure *we* will not revolt against it. The game will be played out to its end."

"So then," said Jael, "you're establishing a plutocracy. You're making us a land of traders and merchant princes. Then what of the future?"

Mallow lifted his gloomy face, and exclaimed fiercely, "What business of mine is the future? No doubt Seldon has foreseen it and prepared against it. There will be other crises in the time to come when money power has become as dead a force as religion is now. Let my successors solve those new problems, as I have solved the one of today."

KORELL— . . . And so after three years of a war which was certainly the most unfought war on record, the Republic of Korell surrendered unconditionally, and Hober Mallow took his place next to Hari Seldon and Salvor Hardin in the hearts of the people of the Foundation.

ENCYCLOPEDIA GALACTICA

THE END

FOUNDATION
AND EMPIRE

To Mary and Henry
For Patience and Endurance

Prologue

The Galactic Empire Was Falling.

It was a colossal Empire, stretching across millions of worlds from arm-end to arm-end of the mighty double-spiral that was the Milky Way. Its fall was colossal, too—and a long one, for it had a long way to go.

It had been falling for centuries before one man became really aware of that fall. That man was Hari Seldon, the man who represented the one spark of creative effort left among the gathering decay. He developed and brought to its highest pitch the science of psycho-history.

Psycho-history dealt not with man, but with man-masses. It was the science of mobs; mobs in their billions. It could forecast reactions to stimuli with something of the accuracy that a lesser science could bring to the forecast of a rebound of a billiard ball. The reaction of one man could be forecast by no known mathematics; the reaction of a billion is something else again.

Hari Seldon plotted the social and economic trends of the time, sighted along the curves and foresaw the continuing and accelerating fall of civilization and the gap of thirty thousand years that must elapse before a struggling new Empire could emerge from the ruins.

It was too late to stop that fall, but not too late to close the gap of barbarism. Seldon established two Foundations at "opposite ends of the Galaxy" and their location was so designed that in one short millennium events would knit and mesh so as to force out of them a stronger, more permanent, more quickly appearing Second Empire.

Foundation (Gnome Press, 1951) has told the story of one of those Foundations during the first two centuries of life.

It began as a settlement of physical scientists on Terminus, a planet at the extreme end of one of the spiral arms of the Galaxy. Separated from the turmoil of the Empire, they worked as compilers of a universal compendium of knowledge, the Encyclopedia Galactica, unaware of the deeper role planned for them by the already-dead Seldon.

As the Empire rotted, the outer regions fell into the hands of independent "kings." The Foundation was threatened by them. However, by playing one petty ruler against another, under the leadership of their first mayor, Salvor Hardin, they maintained a precarious independence. As sole possessors of atomic power among worlds which were losing their sciences and falling back on coal and oil, they even established an ascendancy. The Foundation became the "religious" center of the neighboring kingdoms.

Slowly, the Foundation developed a trading economy as the Encyclopedia receded into the background. Their Traders, dealing in atomic gadgets which not even the Empire in its heyday could have duplicated for compactness, penetrated hundreds of light-years through the Periphery.

Under Hober Mallow, the first of the Foundation's Merchant Princes, they developed the techniques of economic warfare to the point of defeating the Republic of Korell, even though that world was receiving support from one of the outer provinces of what was left of the Empire.

At the end of two hundred years, the Foundation was the most powerful state in the Galaxy, except for the remains of the Empire, which, concentrated in the central third of the Milky Way, still controlled three quarters of the population and wealth of the Universe.

It seemed inevitable that the next danger the Foundation would have to face was the final lash of the dying Empire.

The way must be cleared for the battle of Foundation and Empire.

Contents

PROLOGUE   v

PART I THE GENERAL

1. SEARCH FOR MAGICIANS   3

2. THE MAGICIANS   12

3. THE DEAD HAND   18

4. THE EMPEROR   24

5. THE WAR BEGINS   30

6. THE FAVORITE   42

7. BRIBERY   46

8. TO TRANTOR   59

9. ON TRANTOR   67

10. THE WAR ENDS   75

PART II THE MULE

11. BRIDE AND GROOM   81

12. CAPTAIN AND MAYOR   93

13. LIEUTENANT AND CLOWN   101

14. THE MUTANT   110

15. THE PSYCHOLOGIST   120

16. CONFERENCE   127

17. THE VISI-SONOR   136

18. FALL OF THE FOUNDATION   145

19. START OF THE SEARCH   152

20. CONSPIRATOR   162

21. INTERLUDE IN SPACE   172

22. DEATH ON NEOTRANTOR   182

23. THE RUINS OF TRANTOR   195

24. CONVERT   199

25. DEATH OF A PSYCHOLOGIST   206

26. END OF THE SEARCH   218

PART I

THE GENERAL

1.

Search for Magicians

BEL RIOSE . . . . *In his relatively short career, Riose earned the title of "The Last of the Imperials" and earned it well. A study of his campaigns reveals him to be the equal of Peurifoy in strategic ability and his superior perhaps in his ability to handle men. That he was born in the days of the decline of Empire made it all but impossible for him to equal Peurifoy's record as a conqueror. Yet he had his chance when, the first of the Empire's generals to do so, he faced the Foundation squarely. . . .* °*

ENCYCLOPEDIA GALACTICA

Bel Riose traveled without escort, which is not what court etiquette prescribes for the head of a fleet stationed in a yet-sullen stellar system on the Marches of the Galactic Empire.

But Bel Riose was young and energetic—energetic enough to be sent as near the end of the universe as possible by an unemotional and calculating court—and curious besides. Strange and improbable tales fancifully-repeated by hundreds and murkily-known to thousands intrigued the last faculty; the possibility of a military venture engaged the other two. The combination was overpowering.

He was out of the dowdy ground-car he had appropriated and at the door of the fading mansion that was his destination. He waited. The photonic eye that spanned the doorway was alive, but when the door opened it was by hand.

Bel Riose smiled at the old man. "I am Riose—"

° All quotations from the Encyclopedia Galactica here reproduced are taken from the 116th Edition published in 1020 F.E. by the Encyclopedia Galactica Publishing Co., Terminus, with permission of the publishers.

"I recognize you." The old man remained stiffly and unsurprised in his place. "Your business?"

Riose withdrew a step in a gesture of submission. "One of peace. If you are Ducem Barr, I ask the favor of conversation."

Ducem Barr stepped aside and in the interior of the house the walls glowed into life. The general entered into daylight.

He touched the wall of the study, then stared at his fingertips. "You have this on Siwenna?"

Barr smiled thinly. "Not elsewhere, I believe. I keep this in repair myself as well as I can. I must apologize for your wait at the door. The automatic device registers the presence of a visitor but will no longer open the door."

"Your repairs fall short?" The general's voice was faintly mocking.

"Parts are no longer available. If you will sit, sir. You drink tea?"

"On Siwenna? My good sir, it is socially impossible not to drink it here."

The old patrician retreated noiselessly with a slow bow that was part of the ceremonious legacy left by a *ci-devant* aristocracy of the last century's better days.

Riose looked after his host's departing figure, and his studied urbanity grew a bit uncertain at the edges. His education had been purely military; his experience likewise. He had, as the cliché has it, faced death many times; but always death of a very familiar and tangible nature. Consequently, there is no inconsistency in the fact that the idolized lion of the Twentieth Fleet felt chilled in the suddenly musty atmosphere of an ancient room.

The general recognized the small black-ivroid boxes that lined the shelves to be books. Their titles were unfamiliar. He guessed that the large structure at one end of the room was the receiver that transmuted the books into sight-and-sound on demand. He had never seen one in operation; but he had heard of them.

Once he had been told that long before, during the golden ages when the Empire had been co-extensive with the entire Galaxy, nine houses out of every ten had such receivers—and such rows of books.

But there were borders to watch now; books were for old men. And half the stories told about the old days were mythical anyway. More than half.

The tea arrived, and Riose seated himself. Ducem Barr lifted his cup. "To your honor."

"Thank you. To yours."

Ducem Barr said deliberately, "You are said to be young. Thirty-five?"

"Near enough. Thirty-four."

"In that case," said Barr, with soft emphasis, "I could not begin better than by informing you regretfully that I am not in the possession of love charms, potions, or philtres. Nor am I in the least capable of influencing the favors of any young lady as may appeal to you."

"I have no need of artificial aids in that respect, sir." The complacency undeniably present in the general's voice was stirred with amusement. "Do you receive many requests for such commodities?"

"Enough. Unfortunately, an uninformed public tends to confuse scholarship with magicianry, and love life seems to be that factor which requires the largest quantity of magical tinkering."

"And so would seem most natural. But I differ. I connect scholarship with nothing but the means of answering difficult questions."

The Siwennian considered somberly, "You may be as wrong as they!"

"That may turn out or not." The young general set down his cup in its flaring sheath and it refilled. He dropped the offered flavor-capsule into it with a small splash. "Tell me then, patrician, who are the magicians? The real ones."

Barr seemed startled at a title long-unused. He said, "There are no magicians."

"But people speak of them. Siwenna crawls with the tales of them. There are cults being built about them. There is some strange connection between it and those groups among your countrymen who dream and drivel of ancient days and what they call liberty and autonomy. Eventually the matter might become a danger to the State."

The old man shook his head. "Why ask me? Do you smell rebellion, with myself at the head?"

Riose shrugged, "Never. Never. Oh, it is not a thought completely ridiculous. Your father was an exile in his day; you yourself a patriot and a chauvinist in yours. It is indelicate in me as a guest to mention it, but my business here requires it. And yet a conspiracy now? I doubt it. Siwenna has had the spirit beat out of it these three generations."

The old man replied with difficulty, "I shall be as indelicate a host as you a guest. I shall remind you that once a viceroy thought as you did of the spiritless Siwennians. By the orders of that viceroy my father became a fugitive pauper, my brothers martyrs, and my sister a suicide. Yet that viceroy died a death sufficiently horrible at the hands of these same slavish Siwennians."

"Ah, yes, and there you touch nearly on something I could wish to say. For three years the mysterious death of that viceroy has been no mystery to me. There was a young soldier of his personal guard whose actions were of interest. You were that soldier, but there is no need of details, I think."

Barr was quiet. "None. What do you propose?"

"That you answer my questions."

"Not under threats. I am old, but not yet so old that life means particularly overmuch."

"My good sir, these are hard times," said Riose, with meaning, "and you have children and friends. You have a country for which you have mouthed phrases of love and folly in the past. Come, if I should decide to use force, my aim would not be so poor as to strike you."

Barr said coldly, "What do you want?"

Riose held the empty cup as he spoke. "Patrician, listen to me. These are days when the most successful soldiers are those whose function is to lead the dress parades that wind through the imperial palace grounds on feast days and to escort the sparkling pleasure ships that carry His Imperial Splendor to the summer planets. I . . . I am a failure. I am a failure at thirty-four, and I shall stay a failure. Because, you see, I like to fight.

"That's why they sent me here. I'm too troublesome at court. I don't fit in with the etiquette. I offend the dandies and the lord admirals, but I'm too good a leader of ships and men to be disposed of shortly by being marooned in space. So Siwenna is the substitute. It's a frontier world; a rebellious and a barren province. It is far away, far enough away to satisfy all.

"And so I moulder. There are no rebellions to stamp down, and the border viceroys do not revolt lately; at least, not since His Imperial Majesty's late father of glorious memory made an example of Mountel of Paramay."

"A strong Emperor," muttered Barr.

"Yes, and we need more of them. He is my master; remember that. These are his interests I guard."

Barr shrugged unconcernedly. "How does all this relate to the subject?"

"I'll show you in two words. The magicians I've mentioned come from beyond—out there beyond the frontier guards, where the stars are scattered thinly—"

"'Where the stars are scattered thinly,'" quoted Barr, "'And the cold of space seeps in'."

"Is that poetry?" Riose frowned. Verse seemed frivolous at the moment. "In any case, they're from the Periphery—from the only quarter where I am free to fight for the glory of the Emperor."

"And thus serve His Imperial Majesty's interests and satisfy your own love of a good fight."

"Exactly. But I must know what I fight; and there you can help."

"How do you know?"

Riose nibbled casually at a cakelet. "Because for three years I have traced every rumor, every myth, every breath concerning the magicians—and of all the library of information I have gathered, only two isolated facts are unanimously agreed upon, and are hence certainly true. The first is that the magicians come from the edge of the Galaxy opposite Siwenna; the second is that your father once met a magician, alive and actual, and spoke with him."

The aged Siwennian stared unblinkingly, and Riose continued, "You had better tell me what you know—"

Barr said thoughtfully, "It would be interesting to tell you certain things. It would be a psycho-historic experiment of my own."

"What kind of experiment?"

"Psycho-historic." The old man had an unpleasant edge to his smile. Then, crisply, "You'd better have more tea. I'm going to make a bit of a speech."

He leaned far back into the soft cushions of his chair. The wall-lights had softened to a pink-ivory glow, which mellowed even the soldier's hard profile.

Ducem Barr began, "My own knowledge is the result of two accidents; the accidents of being born the son of my father, and of being born the native of my country. It begins over forty years ago, shortly after the great Massacre, when my father was a fugitive in the forests of the South, while I was a gunner in the viceroy's personal fleet. This same viceroy, by the way, who had ordered the Massacre, and who died such a cruel death thereafter."

Barr smiled grimly, and continued, "My father was a Patrician of the Empire and a Senator of Siwenna. His name was Onum Barr."

Riose interrupted impatiently, "I know the circumstances of his exile very well. You needn't elaborate upon it."

The Siwennian ignored him and proceeded without deflection. "During his exile a wanderer came upon him; a merchant from the edge of the Galaxy; a young man who spoke a strange accent, knew nothing of recent Imperial history, and who was protected by an individual force-shield."

"An individual force-shield?" Riose glared. "You speak extravagance. What generator could be powerful enough to condense a shield to the size of a single man? By the Great Galaxy, did he carry five thousand myria-tons of atomic power-source about with him on a little wheeled gocart?"

Barr said quietly, "This is the magician of whom you hear whispers, stories and myths. The name 'magician' is not lightly earned. He carried no generator large enough to be seen, but not the heaviest weapon you can carry in your hand would have as much as creased the shield he bore."

"Is this all the story there is? Are the magicians born of maunderings of an old man broken by suffering and exile?"

"The story of the magicians antedated even my father, sir. And the proof is more concrete. After leaving my father, this merchant that men call a magician visited a Tech-man at the city to which my father had guided him, and there he left a shield-generator of the type he wore. That generator was retrieved by my father after his return from exile upon the execution of the bloody viceroy. It took a long time to find—

"The generator hangs on the wall behind you, sir. It does not work. It never worked but for the first two days; but if you'll look at it, you will see that no one in the Empire ever designed it."

Bel Riose reached for the belt of linked metal that clung to the curved wall. It came away with a little sucking noise as the tiny adhesion-field broke at the touch of his hand. The ellipsoid at the apex of the belt held his attention. It was the size of a walnut.

"This—" he said.

"Was the generator," nodded Barr. "But it *was* the generator. The secret of its workings are beyond discovery now. Sub-electronic investigations have shown it to be fused into a single lump of metal and not all the most careful study of the diffraction patterns have sufficed to distinguish the discrete parts that had existed before fusion."

"Then your 'proof' still lingers on the frothy border of words backed by no concrete evidence."

Barr shrugged. "You have demanded my knowledge of me and threatened its extortion by force. If you choose to meet it with skepticism, what is that to me? Do you want me to stop?"

"Go on!" said the general, harshly.

"I continued my father's researches after he died, and then the second accident I mentioned came to help me, for Siwenna was well known to Hari Seldon."

"And who is Hari Seldon?"

"Hari Seldon was a scientist of the reign of the Emperor, Daluben IV. He was a psycho-historian; the last and greatest of them all. He once visited Siwenna, when Siwenna was a great commercial center, rich in the arts and sciences."

"Hmph," muttered Riose, sourly, "where is the stagnant planet that does not claim to have been a land of overflowing wealth in older days?"

"The days I speak of are the days of two centuries ago, when

the Emperor yet ruled to the uttermost star; when Siwenna was
a world of the interior and not a semi-barbarian border province.
In those days, Hari Seldon foresaw the decline of Imperial power
and the eventual barbarization of the entire Galaxy."

Riose laughed suddenly. "He foresaw that? Then he foresaw
wrong, my good scientist. I suppose you call yourself that. Why,
the Empire is more powerful now than it has been in a millennium. Your old eyes are blinded by the cold bleakness of the
border. Come to the inner worlds some day; come to the warmth
and the wealth of the center."

The old man shook his head somberly. "Circulation ceases first
at the outer edges. It will take a while yet for the decay to reach
the heart. That is, the apparent, obvious-to-all decay, as distinct
from the inner decay that is an old story of some fifteen centuries."

"And so this Hari Seldon foresaw a Galaxy of uniform barbarism," said Riose, good-humoredly. "And what then, eh?"

"So he established two foundations at the extreme opposing
ends of the Galaxy—Foundations of the best, and the youngest,
and the strongest, there to breed, grow, and develop. The worlds
on which they were placed were chosen carefully; as were the
times and the surroundings. All was arranged in such a way that
the future as foreseen by the unalterable mathematics of psycho-
history would involve their early isolation from the main body
of Imperial civilization and their gradual growth into the germs
of the Second Galactic Empire—cutting an inevitable barbarian
interregnum from thirty thousand years to scarcely a single thousand."

"And where did you find out all this? You seem to know it in
detail."

"I don't and never did," said the patrician with composure.
"It is the painful result of the piecing together of certain evidence
discovered by my father and a little more found by myself. The
basis is flimsy and the superstructure has been romanticized into
existence to fill the huge gaps. But I am convinced that it is essentially true."

"You are easily convinced."

"Am I? It has taken forty years of research."

"Hmph. Forty years! I could settle the question in forty days. In fact, I believe I ought to. It would be—different."

"And how would you do that?"

"In the obvious way. I could become an explorer. I could find this Foundation you speak of and observe with my eyes. You say there are two?"

"The records speak of two. Supporting evidence has been found only for one, which is understandable, for the other is at the extreme end of the long axis of the Galaxy."

"Well, we'll visit the near one." The general was on his feet, adjusting his belt.

"You know where to go?" asked Barr.

"In a way. In the records of the last viceroy but one, he whom you murdered so effectively, there are suspicious tales of outer barbarians. In fact, one of his daughters was given in marriage to a barbarian prince. I'll find my way."

He held out a hand. "I thank you for your hospitality."

Ducem Barr touched the hand with his fingers and bowed formally. "Your visit was a great honor."

"As for the information you gave me," continued Bel Riose, "I'll know how to thank you for that when I return."

Ducem Barr followed his guest submissibly to the outer door and said quietly to the disappearing ground-car, "And *if* you return."

2.

The Magicians

FOUNDATION   . . . *With forty years of expansion behind them, the Foundation faced the menace of Riose. The epic days of Hardin and Mallow had gone and with them a certain hard daring and resolution.* . . .

ENCYCLOPEDIA GALACTICA

There were four men in the room, and the room was set apart where none could approach. The four men looked at each other quickly, then lengthily at the table that separated them. There were four bottles on the table and as many full glasses, but no one had touched them.

And then the man nearest the door stretched out an arm and drummed a slow, padding rhythm on the table.

He said, "Are you going to sit and wonder forever? Does it matter who speaks first?"

"Speak you first, then," said the big man directly opposite. "You're the one who should be the most worried."

Sennett Forell chuckled with noiseless nonhumor. "Because you think I'm the richest. Well— Or is it that you expect me to continue as I have started. I don't suppose you forget that it was my own Trade Fleet that captured this scout ship of theirs."

"You had the largest fleet," said a third, "and the best pilots; which is another way of saying you are the richest. It was a fearful risk; and would have been greater for one of us."

Sennett Forell chuckled again. "There is a certain facility in risk-taking that I inherit from my father. After all, the essential point in running a risk is that the returns justify it. As to which, witness the fact that the enemy ship was isolated and captured without loss to ourselves or warning to the others."

That Forell was a distant collateral relative of the late great Hober Mallow was recognized openly throughout the Foundation. That he was Mallow's illegitimate son was accepted quietly to just as wide an extent.

The fourth man blinked his little eyes stealthily. Words crept out from between thin lips. "It is nothing to sleep over in fat triumph, this grasping of little ships. Most likely, it will but anger that young man further."

"You think he needs motives?" questioned Forell, scornfully.

"I do, and this might, or will, save him the vexation of having to manufacture one." The fourth man spoke slowly, "Hober Mallow worked otherwise. And Salvor Hardin. They let others take the uncertain paths of force, while they maneuvered surely and quietly."

Forell shrugged. "This ship has proved its value. Motives are cheap and we have sold this one at a profit." There was the satisfaction of the born Trader in that. He continued, "The young man is of the old Empire."

"We knew that," said the second man, the big one, with rumbling discontent.

"We suspected that," corrected Forell, softly. "If a man comes with ships and wealth, with overtures of friendliness, and with offers of trade, it is only sensible to refrain from antagonizing him, until we are certain that the profitable mask is not a face after all. But now—"

There was a faint whining edge to the third man's voice as he spoke. "We might have been even more careful. We might have found out first. We might have found out before allowing him to leave. It would have been the truest wisdom."

"That has been discussed and disposed of," said Forell. He waved the subject aside with a flatly final gesture.

"The government is soft," complained the third man. "The mayor is an idiot."

The fourth man looked at the other three in turn and removed the stub of a cigar from his mouth. He dropped it casually into the slot at his right where it disappeared with a silent flash of disruption.

He said sarcastically, "I trust the gentleman who last spoke is speaking through habit only. We can afford to remember here that *we* are the government."

There was a murmur of agreement.

The fourth man's little eyes were on the table. "Then let us leave government policy alone. This young man . . . this stranger might have been a possible customer. There have been cases. All three of you tried to butter him into an advance contract. We have an agreement—a gentleman's agreement—against it, but you tried."

"So did you," growled the second man.

"I know it," said the fourth, calmly.

"Then let's forget what we should have done earlier," interrupted Forell impatiently, "and continue with what we should do now. In any case, what if we had imprisoned him, or killed him, what then? We are not certain of his intentions even yet, and at the worst, we could not destroy an Empire by snipping short one man's life. There might be navies upon navies waiting just the other side of his nonreturn."

"Exactly," approved the fourth man. "Now what did you get out of your captured ship? I'm too old for all this talking."

"It can be told in a few enough words," said Forell, grimly. "He's an Imperial general or whatever rank corresponds to that over there. He's a young man who has proved his military brilliance—so I am told—and who is the idol of his men. Quite a romantic career. The stories they tell of him are no doubt half lies, but even so it makes him out to be a type of wonder man."

"Who are the 'they'?" demanded the second man.

"The crew of the captured ship. Look, I have all their statements recorded on micro-film, which I have in a secure place. Later on, if you wish, you can see them. You can talk to the men yourselves, if you think it necessary. I've told you the essentials."

"How did you get it out of them? How do you know they're telling the truth?"

Forell frowned. "I wasn't gentle, good sir. I knocked them about, drugged them crazy, and used the Probe unmercifully. They talked. You can believe them."

"In the old days," said the third man, with sudden irrelevance, "they would have used pure psychology. Painless, you know, but very sure. No chance of deceit."

"Well, there is a good deal they had in the old days," said Forell, dryly. "These are the new days."

"But," said the fourth man, "what did he want here, this general, this romantic wonder-man?" There was a dogged, weary persistence about him.

Forell glanced at him sharply. "You think he confides the details of state policy to his crew? They didn't know. There was nothing to get out of them in that respect, and I tried, Galaxy knows."

"Which leaves us—"

"To draw our own conclusions, obviously." Forell's fingers were tapping quietly again. "The young man is a military leader of the Empire, yet he played the pretense of being a minor princeling of some scattered stars in an odd corner of the Periphery. That alone would assure us that his real motives are such as it would not benefit him to have us know. Combine the nature of his profession with the fact that the Empire has already subsidized one attack upon us in my father's time, and the possibilities become ominous. That first attack failed. I doubt that the Empire owes us love for that."

"There is nothing in your findings," questioned the fourth man guardedly, "which makes for certainty? You are withholding nothing?"

Forell answered levelly, "I can't withhold anything. From here on there can be no question of business rivalry. Unity is forced upon us."

"Patriotism?" There was a sneer in the third man's thin voice.

"Patriotism be damned," said Forell quietly. "Do you think I give two puffs of atomic emanation for the future Second Empire? Do you think I'd risk a single Trade mission to smooth its path? But—do you suppose Imperial conquest will help my business or yours? If the Empire wins, there will be a sufficient number of yearning carrion crows to crave the rewards of battle."

"And we're the rewards," added the fourth man, dryly.

The second man broke his silence suddenly, and shifted his bulk angrily, so that the chair creaked under him. "But why talk of that. The Empire can't win, can it? There is Seldon's assurance that we will form the Second Empire in the end. This is only another crisis. There have been three before this."

"Only another crisis, yes!" Forell brooded. "But in the case of the first two, we had Salvor Hardin to guide us; in the third, there was Hober Mallow. Whom have we now?"

He looked at the others somberly and continued, "Seldon's rules of psycho-history on which it is so comforting to rely probably have as one of the contributing variables, a certain normal initiative on the part of the people of the Foundation themselves. Seldon's laws help those who help themselves."

"The times make the man," said the third man. "There's another proverb for you."

"You can't count on that, not with absolute assurance," grunted Forell. "Now the way it seems to me is this. If this is the fourth crisis, then Seldon has foreseen it. If he has, then it can be beaten, and there should be a way of doing it.

"Now the Empire is stronger than we; it always has been. But this is the first time we are in danger of its direct attack, so that strength becomes terribly menacing. Then if it can be beaten, it must be once again as in all past crises by a method other than pure force. We must find the weak side of its enemy and attack it there."

"And what is that weak side?" asked the fourth man. "Do you intend advancing a theory?"

"No. That is the point I'm leading up to. Our great leaders of the past always saw the weak points of their enemies and aimed at that. But now—"

There was a helplessness in his voice, and for a moment none volunteered a comment.

Then the fourth man said, "We need spies."

Forell turned to him eagerly. "Right! I don't know when the Empire will attack. There may be time."

"Hober Mallow himself entered the Imperial dominions," suggested the second man.

But Forell shook his head. "Nothing so direct. None of us are precisely youthful; and all of us are rusty with red-tape and administrative detail. We need young men that are in the field now—"

"The independent traders?" asked the fourth man.

And Forell nodded his head and whispered, "If there is yet time—"

3.

The Dead Hand

Bel Riose interrupted his annoyed stridings to look up hopefully when his aide entered. "Any word of the *Starlet?*"

"None. The scouting party has quartered space, but the instruments have detected nothing. Commander Yume has reported that the Fleet is ready for an immediate attack in retaliation."

The general shook his head. "No, not for a patrol ship. Not yet. Tell him to double— Wait! I'll write out the message. Have it coded and transmitted by tight beam."

He wrote as he talked and thrust the paper at the waiting officer. "Has the Siwennian arrived yet?"

"Not yet."

"Well, see to it that he is brought in here as soon as he does arrive."

The aide saluted crisply and left. Riose resumed his caged stride.

When the door opened a second time, it was Ducem Barr that stood on the threshold. Slowly, in the footsteps of the ushering aide, he stepped into the garish room whose ceiling was an ornamented stereoscopic model of the Galaxy, and in the center of which Bel Riose stood in field uniform.

"Patrician, good day!" The general pushed forward a chair with his foot and gestured the aide away with a "That door is to stay closed till I open it."

He stood before the Siwennian, legs apart, hand grasping wrist behind his back, balancing himself slowly, thoughtfully, on the balls of his feet.

Then, harshly, "Patrician, are you a loyal subject of the Emperor?"

Barr, who had maintained an indifferent silence till then, wrinkled a noncommittal brow. "I have no cause to love Imperial rule."

"Which is a long way from saying that you would be a traitor."

"True. But the mere act of not being a traitor is also a long way from agreeing to be an active helper."

"Ordinarily also true. But to refuse your help at this point," said Riose, deliberately, "will be considered treason and treated as such."

Barr's eyebrows drew together. "Save your verbal cudgels for your subordinates. A simple statement of your needs and wants will suffice me here."

Riose sat down and crossed his legs. "Barr, we had an earlier discussion half a year ago."

"About your magicians?"

"Yes. You remember what I said I would do."

Barr nodded. His arms rested limply in his lap. "You were going to visit them in their haunts, and you've been away these four months. Did you find them?"

"Find them? That I did," cried Riose. His lips were stiff as he spoke. It seemed to require effort to refrain from grinding molars. "Patrician, they are not magicians; they are devils. It is as far from belief as the outer nebulae from here. Conceive it! It is a world the size of a handkerchief, of a fingernail; with resources so petty, power so minute, a population so microscopic as would never suffice the most backward worlds of the dusty prefects of the Dark Stars. Yet with that, a people so proud and ambitious as to dream quietly and methodically of Galactic rule.

"Why, they are so sure of themselves that they do not even hurry. They move slowly, phlegmatically; they speak of necessary centuries. They swallow worlds at leisure; creep through systems with dawdling complacence.

"And they succeed. There is no one to stop them. They have built up a filthy trading community that curls its tentacles about the systems further than their toy ships dare reach. For parsecs, their Traders—which is what their agents call themselves—penetrate."

Ducem Barr interrupted the angry flow. "How much of this information is definite; and how much is simply fury?"

The soldier caught his breath and grew calmer. "My fury does not blind me. I tell you I was in worlds nearer to Siwenna than to the Foundation, where the Empire was a myth of the distance, and where Traders were living truths. We ourselves were mistaken for Traders."

"The Foundation itself told you they aimed at Galactic dominion?"

"Told me!" Riose was violent again. "It was not a matter of telling me. The officials said nothing. They spoke business exclusively. But I spoke to ordinary men. I absorbed the ideas of the common folk; their 'manifest destiny,' their calm acceptance of a great future. It is a thing that can't be hidden; a universal optimism they don't even try to hide."

The Siwennian openly displayed a certain quiet satisfaction. "You will notice that so far it would seem to bear out quite accurately my reconstruction of events from the paltry data on the subject that I have gathered."

"It is no doubt," replied Riose with vexed sarcasm, "a tribute to your analytical powers. It is also a hearty and bumptious commentary on the growing danger to the domains of His Imperial Majesty."

Barr shrugged his unconcern, and Riose leaned forward suddenly, to seize the old man's shoulders and stare with curious gentleness into his eyes.

He said, "Now, patrician, none of that. I have no desire to be barbaric. For my part, the legacy of Siwennian hostility to the Imperium is an odious burden, and one which I would do everything in my power to wipe out. But my province is the military and interference in civil affairs is impossible. It would bring about my recall and ruin my usefulness at once. You see that? I know you see that. Between yourself and myself then, let the atrocity of forty years ago be repaid by your vengeance upon its author and so forgotten. I need your help. I frankly admit it."

There was a world of urgency in the young man's voice, but Ducem Barr's head shook gently and deliberately in a negative gesture.

Riose said pleadingly, "You don't understand, patrician, and I doubt my ability to make you. I can't argue on your ground. You're the scholar, not I. But this I can tell you. Whatever you think of the Empire, you will admit its great services. Its armed forces have committed isolated crimes, but in the main they have been a force for peace and civilization. It was the Imperial navy that created the *Pax Imperium* that ruled over all the Galaxy for two thousand years. Contrast the twelve millennia of peace under the Sun-and-Spaceship of the Empire with the two millennia of interstellar anarchy that preceded it. Consider the wars and devastations of those old days and tell me if, with all its faults, the Empire is not worth preserving.

"Consider," he drove on forcefully, "to what the outer fringe of the Galaxy is reduced in these days of their break-away and independence, and ask yourself if for the sake of a petty revenge you would reduce Siwenna from its position as a province under the protection of a mighty Navy to a barbarian world in a barbarian Galaxy, all immersed in its fragmentary independence and its common degradation and misery."

"Is it so bad—so soon?" murmured the Siwennian.

"No," admitted Riose. "We would be safe ourselves no doubt, were our lifetimes quadrupled. But it is for the Empire I fight; that, and a military tradition which is something for myself alone, and which I can not transfer to you. It is a military tradition built on the Imperial institution which I serve."

"You are getting mystical, and I always find it difficult to penetrate another person's mysticism."

"No matter. You understand the danger of this Foundation."

"It was I who pointed out what you call the danger before ever you headed outward from Siwenna."

"Then you realize that it must be stopped in embryo or perhaps not at all. You have known of this Foundation before anyone had heard of it. You know more about it than anyone else in the Empire. You probably know how it might best be attacked; and you can probably forewarn me of its countermeasures. Come, let us be friends."

Ducem Barr rose. He said flatly, "Such help as I could give you means nothing. So I will make you free of it in the face of your strenuous demand."

"I will be the judge of its meaning."

"No, I am serious. Not all the might of the Empire could avail to crush this pygmy world."

"Why not?" Bel Riose's eyes glistened fiercely. "No, stay where you are. I'll tell you when you may leave. Why not? If you think I underestimate this enemy I have discovered, you are wrong. Patrician," he spoke reluctantly, "I lost a ship on my return. I have no proof that it fell into the hands of the Foundation; but it has not been located since and were it merely an accident, its dead hulk should certainly have been found along the route we took. It is not an important loss—less than the tenth part of a fleabite, but it may mean that the Foundation has already opened hostilities. Such eagerness and such disregard for consequences might mean secret forces of which I know nothing. Can you help me then by answering a specific question? What is their military power?"

"I haven't any notion."

"Then explain yourself on your own terms. Why do you say the Empire can not defeat this small enemy?"

The Siwennian seated himself once more and looked away from Riose's fixed glare. He spoke heavily, "Because I have faith in the principles of psycho-history. It is a strange science. It reached mathematical maturity with one man, Hari Seldon, and died with him, for no man since has been capable of manipulating its intricacies. But in that short period, it proved itself the most powerful instrument ever invented for the study of humanity. Without pretending to predict the actions of individual humans, it formulated definite laws capable of mathematical analysis and extrapolation to govern and predict the mass action of human groups."

"So—"

"It was that psycho-history which Seldon and the group he worked with applied in full force to the establishment of the Foundation. The place, time, and conditions all conspire mathematically and so, inevitably, to the development of Universal Empire."

Riose's voice trembled with indignation. "You mean that this art of his predicts that I would attack the Foundation and lose such and such a battle for such and such a reason? You are trying to say that I am a silly robot following a predetermined course into destruction."

"No," replied the old patrician, sharply. "I have already said that the science had nothing to do with individual actions. It is the vaster background that has been foreseen."

"Then we stand clasped tightly in the forcing hand of the Goddess of Historical Necessity."

"Of *Psycho*-Historical Necessity," prompted Barr, softly.

"And if I exercise my prerogative of freewill? If I choose to attack next year, or not to attack at all? How pliable is the Goddess? How resourceful?"

Barr shrugged. "Attack now or never; with a single ship, or all the force in the Empire; by military force or economic pressure; by candid declaration of war or by treacherous ambush. Do whatever you wish in your fullest exercise of freewill. You will still lose."

"Because of Hari Seldon's dead hand?"

"Because of the dead hand of the mathematics of human behavior that can neither be stopped, swerved, nor delayed."

The two faced each other in deadlock, until the general stepped back.

He said simply, "I'll take that challenge. It's a dead hand against a living will."

4.

The Emperor

CLEON II   *commonly called "The Great." The last strong Emperor of the First Empire, he is important for the political and artistic renaissance that took place during his long reign. He is best known to romance, however, for his connection with Bel Riose, and to the common man, he is simply "Riose's Emperor." It is important not to allow events of the last year of his reign to overshadow forty years of. . . .*

ENCYCLOPEDIA GALACTICA

Cleon II was Lord of the Universe. Cleon II also suffered from a painful and undiagnosed ailment. By the queer twists of human affairs, the two statements are not mutually exclusive, nor even particularly incongruous. There have been a wearisomely large number of precedents in history.

But Cleon II cared nothing for such precedents. To meditate upon a long list of similar cases would not ameliorate personal suffering an electron's worth. It soothed him as little to think that where his great-grandfather had been the pirate ruler of a dust-speck planet, he himself slept in the pleasure palace of Ammenetik the Great, as heir of a line of Galactic rulers stretching backward into a tenuous past. It was at present no source of comfort to him that the efforts of his father had cleansed the realm of its leprous patches of rebellion and restored it to the peace and unity it had enjoyed under Stanel VI; that, as a consequence, in the twenty-five years of his reign, not one cloud of revolt had misted his burnished glory.

The Emperor of the Galaxy and the Lord of All whimpered as he lolled his head backward into the invigorating plane of force about his pillows. It yielded in a softness that did not touch, and

at the pleasant tingle, Cleon relaxed a bit. He sat up with difficulty and stared morosely at the distant walls of the grand chamber. It was a bad room to be alone in. It was too big. All the rooms
were too big.

But better to be alone during these crippling bouts than to endure the prinking of the courtiers, their lavish sympathy, their
soft, condescending dullness. Better to be alone than to watch
those insipid masks behind which spun the tortuous speculations
on the chances of death and the fortunes of the succession.

His thoughts hurried him. There were his three sons; three
straight-backed youths full of promise and virtue. Where did they
disappear on these bad days? Waiting, no doubt. Each watching
the other; and all watching him.

He stirred uneasily. And now Brodrig craved audience. The
low-born, faithful Brodrig; faithful because he was hated with a
unanimous and cordial hatred that was the only point of agreement between the dozen cliques that divided his court.

Brodrig—the faithful favorite, who had to be faithful, since unless he owned the fastest speed-ship in the Galaxy and took to it
the day of the Emperor's death, it would be the atom-chamber
the day after.

Cleon II touched the smooth knob on the arm of his great di-
van, and the huge door at the end of the room dissolved to transparency.

Brodrig advanced along the crimson carpet, and knelt to kiss
the Emperor's limp hand.

"Your health, sire?" asked the Privy Secretary in a low tone of
becoming anxiety.

"I live," snapped the Emperor with exasperation, "if you can
call it life where every scoundrel who can read a book of medicine uses me as a blank and receptive field for his feeble experi-
ments. If there is a conceivable remedy, chemical, physical, or
atomic, which has not yet been tried, why then, some learned
babbler from the far corners of the realm will arrive tomorrow to
try it. And still another newly-discovered book, or forgery more-
like, will be used as authority.

"By my father's memory," he rumbled savagely, "it seems there
is not a biped extant who can study a disease before his eyes with

those same eyes. There is not one who can count a pulse-beat without a book of the ancients before him. I'm sick and they call it 'unknown.' The fools! If in the course of millennia, human bodies learn new methods of falling askew, it remains uncovered by the studies of the ancients and uncurable forevermore. The ancients should be alive now, or I then."

The Emperor ran down to a low-breathed curse while Brodrig waited dutifully. Cleon II said peevishly, "How many are waiting outside?"

He jerked his head in the direction of the door.

Brodrig said patiently, "The Great Hall holds the usual number."

"Well, let them wait. State matters occupy me. Have the Captain of the Guard announce it. Or wait, forget the state matters. Just have it announced I hold no audience, and let the Captain of the Guard look doleful. The jackals among them may betray themselves." The Emperor sneered nastily.

"There is a rumor, sire," said Brodrig, smoothly, "that it is your heart that troubles you."

The Emperor's smile was little removed from the previous sneer. "It will hurt others more than myself if any act prematurely on that rumor. But what is it *you* want. Let's have this over."

Brodrig rose from his kneeling posture at a gesture of permission and said, "It concerns General Bel Riose, the Military Governor of Siwenna."

"Riose?" Cleon II frowned heavily. "I don't place him. Wait, is he the one who sent that quixotic message some months back? Yes, I remember. He panted for permission to enter a career of conquest for the glory of the Empire and Emperor."

"Exactly, sire."

The Emperor laughed shortly. "Did you think I had such generals left me, Brodrig? He seems to be a curious atavism. What was the answer? I believe you took care of it."

"I did, sire. He was instructed to forward additional information and to take no steps involving naval action without further orders from the Imperium."

"Hmp. Safe enough. Who is this Riose? Was he ever at court?"

Brodrig nodded and his mouth twisted ever so little. "He began his career as a cadet in the Guards ten years back. He had part in that affair off the Lemul Cluster."

"The Lemul Cluster? You know, my memory isn't quite— Was that the time a young soldier saved two ships of the line from a head-on collision by . . . uh . . . something or other?" He waved a hand impatiently. "I don't remember the details. It was something heroic."

"Riose was that soldier. He received a promotion for it," Brodrig said dryly, "and an appointment to field duty as captain of a ship."

"And now Military Governor of a border system and still young. Capable man, Brodrig!"

"Unsafe, sire. He lives in the past. He is a dreamer of ancient times, or rather, of the myths of what ancient times used to be. Such men are harmless in themselves, but their queer lack of realism makes them fools for others." He added, "His men, I understand, are completely under his control. He is one of your *popular* generals."

"Is he?" the Emperor mused. "Well, come, Brodrig, I would not wish to be served entirely by incompetents. They certainly set no enviable standard for faithfulness themselves."

"An incompetent traitor is no danger. It is rather the capable men who must be watched."

"You among them, Brodrig?" Cleon II laughed and then grimaced with pain. "Well, then, you may forget the lecture for the while. What new development is there in the matter of this young conqueror? I hope you haven't come merely to reminisce."

"Another message, sire, has been received from General Riose."

"Oh? And to what effect?"

"He has spied out the land of these barbarians and advocates an expedition in force. His arguments are long and fairly tedious. It is not worth annoying Your Imperial Majesty with it at present, during your indisposition. Particularly since it will be discussed at length during the session of the Council of Lords." He glanced sidewise at the Emperor.

Cleon II frowned. "The Lords? Is it a question for them, Brodrig? It will mean further demands for a broader interpretation of the Charter. It always comes to that."

"It can't be avoided, sire. It might have been better if your august father could have beaten down the last rebellion without granting the Charter. But since it is here, we must endure it for the while."

"You're right, I suppose. Then the Lords it must be. But why all this solemnity, man? It is, after all, a minor point. Success on a remote border with limited troops is scarcely a state affair."

Brodrig smiled narrowly. He said coolly, "It is an affair of a romantic idiot; but even a romantic idiot can be a deadly weapon when an unromantic rebel uses him as a tool. Sire, the man was popular here and is popular there. He is young. If he annexes a vagrant barbarian planet or two, he will become a conqueror. Now a young conqueror who has proven his ability to rouse the enthusiasm of pilots, miners, tradesmen and suchlike rabble is dangerous at any time. Even if he lacked the desire to do to you as your august father did to the usurper, Ricker, then one of our loyal Lords of the Domain may decide to use him as his weapon."

Cleon II moved an arm hastily and stiffened with pain. Slowly he relaxed, but his smile was weak, and his voice a whisper. "You are a valuable subject, Brodrig. You always suspect far more than is necessary, and I have but to take half your suggested precautions to be utterly safe. We'll put it up to the Lords. We shall see what they say and take our measures accordingly. The young man, I suppose, has made no hostile moves yet."

"He reports none. But already he asks for reinforcements."

"Reinforcements!" The Emperor's eyes narrowed with wonder. "What force has he?"

"Ten ships of the line, sire, with a full complement of auxiliary vessels. Two of the ships are equipped with motors salvaged from the old Grand Fleet, and one has a battery of power artillery from the same source. The other ships are new ones of the last fifty years, but are serviceable, nevertheless."

"Ten ships would seem adequate for any reasonable undertaking. Why, with less than ten ships my father won his first victories against the usurper. Who *are* these barbarians he's fighting?"

The Privy Secretary raised a pair of supercilious eyebrows. "He refers to them as 'the Foundation.'"

"The Foundation? What is it?"

"There is no record of it, sire. I have searched the archives carefully. The area of the Galaxy indicated falls within the ancient province of Anacreon, which two centuries since gave itself up to brigandage, barbarism, and anarchy. There is no planet known as Foundation in the province, however. There was a vague reference to a group of scientists sent to that province just before its separation from our protection. They were to prepare an Encyclopedia." He smiled thinly. "I believe they called it the Encyclopedia Foundation."

"Well," the Emperor considered it somberly, "that seems a tenuous connection to advance."

"I'm not advancing it, sire. No word was ever received from that expedition after the growth of anarchy in that region. If their descendants still live and retain their name, then they have reverted to barbarism most certainly."

"And so he wants reinforcements." The Emperor bent a fierce glance at his secretary. "This is most peculiar; to propose to fight savages with ten ships and to ask for more before a blow is struck. And yet I begin to remember this Riose; he was a handsome boy of loyal family. Brodrig, there are complications in this that I don't penetrate. There may be more importance in it than would seem."

His fingers played idly with the gleaming sheet that covered his stiffened legs. He said, "I need a man out there; one with eyes, brains and loyalty. Brodrig—"

The secretary bent a submissive head. "And the ships, sire?"

"Not yet!" The Emperor moaned softly as he shifted his position in gentle stages. He pointed a feeble finger, "Not till we know more. Convene the Council of Lords for this day week. It will be a good opportunity for the new appropriation as well. I'll put *that* through or lives will end."

He leaned his aching head into the soothing tingle of the forcefield pillow, "Go now, Brodrig, and send in the doctor. He's the worst bumbler of the lot."

5.

The War Begins

From the radiating point of Siwenna, the forces of the Empire reached out cautiously into the black unknown of the Periphery. Giant ships passed the vast distances that separated the vagrant stars at the Galaxy's rim, and felt their way around the outermost edge of Foundation influence

Worlds isolated in their new barbarism of two centuries felt the sensation once again of Imperial overlords upon their soil. Allegiance was sworn in the face of the massive artillery covering capital cities.

Garrisons were left; garrisons of men in Imperial uniform with the Spaceship-and-Sun insignia upon their shoulders. The old men took notice and remembered once again the forgotten tales of their grandfathers' fathers of the times when the universe was big, and rich, and peaceful and that same Spaceship-and-Sun ruled all.

Then the great ships passed on to weave their line of forward bases further around the Foundation. And as each world was knotted into its proper place in the fabric, the report went back to Bel Riose at the General Headquarters he had established on the rocky barrenness of a wandering sunless planet.

Now Riose relaxed and smiled grimly at Ducem Barr. "Well, what do *you* think, patrician?"

"I? Of what value are my thoughts? I am not a military man." He took in with one wearily distasteful glance the crowded disorder of the rock-bound room which had been carved out of the wall of a cavern of artificial air, light, and heat which marked the single bubble of life in the vastness of a bleak world.

"For the help I could give you," he muttered, "or would want to give you, you might return me to Siwenna."

"Not yet. Not yet." The general turned his chair to the corner which held the huge, brilliantly-transparent sphere that mapped the old Imperial prefect of Anacreon and its neighboring sectors. "Later, when this is over, you will go back to your books and to more. I'll see to it that the estates of your family are restored to you and to your children for the rest of time."

"Thank you," said Barr, with faint irony, "but I lack your faith in the happy outcome of all this."

Riose laughed harshly, "Don't start your prophetic croakings again. This map speaks louder than all your woeful theories." He caressed its curved invisible outline gently. "Can you read a map in radial projection? You can? Well, here, see for yourself. The stars in gold represent the Imperial territories. The red stars are those in subjection to the Foundation and the pink are those which are probably within the economic sphere of influence. Now watch—"

Riose's hand covered a rounded knob, and slowly an area of hard, white pinpoints changed into a deepening blue. Like an inverted cup they folded about the red and the pink.

"Those blue stars have been taken over by my forces," said Riose with quiet satisfaction, "and they still advance. No opposition has appeared anywhere. The barbarians are quiet. And particularly, no opposition has come from Foundation forces. They sleep peacefully and well."

"You spread your force thinly, don't you?" asked Barr.

"As a matter of fact," said Riose, "despite appearances, I don't. The key points which I garrison and fortify are relatively few, but they are carefully chosen. The result is that the force expended is small, but the strategic result great. There are many advantages, more than would ever appear to anyone who hasn't made a careful study of spatial tactics, but it is apparent to anyone, for instance, that I can base an attack from any point in an inclosing sphere, and that when I am finished it will be impossible for the Foundation to attack at flank or rear. I shall have no flank or rear with respect to them.

"This strategy of the Previous Inclosure has been tried before, notably in the campaigns of Loris VI, some two thousand years ago, but always imperfectly; always with the knowledge and attempted interference of the enemy. This is different."

"The ideal textbook case?" Barr's voice was languid and indifferent. Riose was impatient, "You still think my forces will fail?"

"They must."

"You understand that there is no case in military history where an inclosure has been completed that the attacking forces have not eventually won, except where an outside Navy exists in sufficient force to break the Inclosure."

"If you say so."

"And you still adhere to your faith."

"Yes."

Riose shrugged. "Then do so."

Barr allowed the angry silence to continue for a moment, then asked quietly, "Have you received an answer from the Emperor?"

Riose removed a cigarette from a wall container behind his head, placed a filter tip between his lips and puffed it aflame carefully. He said, "You mean my request for reinforcements? It came, but that's all. Just the answer."

"No ships."

"None. I half-expected that. Frankly, patrician, I should never have allowed myself to be stampeded by your theories into requesting them in the first place. It puts me in a false light."

"Does it?"

"Definitely. Ships are at a premium. The civil wars of the last two centuries have smashed up more than half of the Grand Fleet and what's left is in pretty shaky condition. You know it isn't as if the ships we build these days are worth anything. I don't think there's a man in the Galaxy today who can build a first-rate hyperatomic motor."

"I knew that," said the Siwennian. His eyes were thoughtful and introspective. "I didn't know that *you* knew it. So his Imperial Majesty can spare no ships. Psycho-history could have predicted that; in fact, it probably did. I should say that Hari Seldon's dead hand wins the opening round."

Riose answered sharply, "I have enough ships as it is. Your

Seldon wins nothing. Should the situation turn more serious, then more ships *will* be available. As yet, the Emperor does not know all the story."

"Indeed? What haven't you told him?"

"Obviously—your theories." Riose looked sardonic. "The story is, with all respect to you, inherently improbable. If developments warrant; if events supply me with proof, then, but only then, would I make out the case of mortal danger.

"And in addition," Riose drove on, casually, "the story, unbolstered by fact, has a flavor of *lese majeste* that could scarcely be pleasant to His Imperial Majesty."

The old patrician smiled. "You mean that telling him his august throne is in danger of subversion by a parcel of ragged barbarians from the ends of the universe is not a warning to be believed or appreciated. Then you expect nothing from him."

"Unless you count a special envoy as something."

"And why a special envoy?"

"It's an old custom. A direct representative of the crown is present on every military campaign which is under government auspices."

"Really? Why?"

"It's a method of preserving the symbol of personal Imperial leadership in all campaigns. It's gained a secondary function of insuring the fidelity of generals. It doesn't always succeed in that respect."

"You'll find that inconvenient, general. Extraneous authority, I mean."

"I don't doubt that," Riose reddened faintly, "but it can't be helped—"

The receiver at the general's hand glowed warmly, and with an unobtrusive jar, the cylindered communication popped into its slot. Riose unrolled it, "Good! This is it!"

Ducem Barr raised a mildly questioning eyebrow.

Riose said, "You know we've captured one of these Trader people. Alive—and with his ship intact."

"I've heard talk of it."

"Well, they've just brought him in, and we'll have him here in a minute. You keep your seat, patrician. I want you here when

I'm questioning him. It's why I asked you here today in the first place. You may understand him where I might miss important points."

The door signal sounded and a touch of the general's toe swung the door wide. The man who stood on the threshold was tall and bearded, wore a short coat of a soft, leathery plastic, with an attached hood shoved back on his neck. His hands were free, and if he noticed the men about him were armed, he did not trouble to indicate it.

He stepped in casually, and looked about with calculating eyes. He favored the general with a rudimentary wave of the hand and a half nod.

"Your name?" demanded Riose, crisply.

"Lathan Devers." The trader hooked his thumbs into his wide and gaudy belt. "Are you the boss here?"

"You are a trader of the Foundation?"

"That's right. Listen, if you're the boss, you'd better tell your hired men here to lay off my cargo."

The general raised his head and regarded the prisoner coldly. "Answer questions. Do not volunteer orders."

"All right. I'm agreeable. But one of your boys blasted a two-foot hole in his chest already, by sticking his fingers where he wasn't supposed to."

Riose shifted his gaze to the lieutenant in charge. "Is this man telling the truth? Your report, Vrank, had it that no lives were lost."

"None were, sir," the lieutenant spoke stiffly, apprehensively, "at the time. There was later some disposition to search the ship, there having arisen a rumor that a woman was aboard. Instead, sir, many instruments of unknown nature were located, instruments which the prisoner claims to be his stock in trade. One of them flashed on handling, and the soldier holding it died."

The general turned back to the trader. "Does your ship carry atomic explosives?"

"Galaxy, no. What for? That fool grabbed an atomic puncher, wrong end forward and set at maximum dispersion. You're not supposed to do that. Might as well point a neut-gun at your head. I'd have stopped him, if five men weren't sitting on my chest."

Riose gestured at the waiting guard, "You go. The captured ship is to be sealed against all intrusion. Sit down, Devers."

The trader did so, in the spot indicated, and withstood stolidly the hard scrutiny of the Imperial general and the curious glance of the Siwennian patrician.

Riose said, "You're a sensible man, Devers."

"Thank you. Are you impressed by my face, or do you want something? Tell you what, though. I'm a good business man."

"It's about the same thing. You surrendered your ship when you might have decided to waste our ammunition and have yourself blown to electron-dust. It could result in good treatment for you, if you continue that sort of outlook on life."

"Good treatment is what I mostly crave, boss."

"Good, and co-operation is what I mostly crave." Riose smiled, and said in a low aside to Ducem Barr, "I hope the word 'crave' means what I think it does. Did you ever hear such a barbarous jargon?"

Devers said blandly, "Right. I check you. But what kind of co-operation are you talking about, boss? To tell you straight, I don't know where I stand." He looked about him, "Where's this place, for instance, and what's the idea?"

"Ah, I've neglected the other half of the introductions. I apologize." Riose was in good humor. "That gentleman is Ducem Barr, Patrician of the Empire. I am Bel Riose, Peer of the Empire, and General of the Third Class in the armed forces of His Imperial Majesty."

The trader's jaw slackened. Then, "The Empire? I mean the old Empire they taught us about at school? Huh! Funny! I always had the sort of notion that it didn't exist any more."

"Look about you. It does," said Riose grimly.

"Might have known it though," and Lathan Devers pointed his beard at the ceiling. "That was a mightily polished-looking set of craft that took my tub. No kingdom of the Periphery could have turned them out." His brow furrowed. "So what's the game, boss? Or do I call you general?"

"The game is war."

"Empire versus Foundation, that it?"

"Right."

"Why?"

"I think you know why."

The trader stared sharply and shook his head.

Riose let the other deliberate, then said softly, "I'm sure you know why."

Lathan Devers muttered, "Warm here," and stood up to remove his hooded jacket. Then he sat down again and stretched his legs out before him.

"You know," he said, comfortably, "I figure you're thinking I ought to jump up with a whoop and lay about me. I can catch you before you could move if I choose my time, and this old fellow who sits there and doesn't say anything couldn't do much to stop me."

"But you won't," said Riose, confidently.

"I won't," agreed Devers, amiably. "First off, killing you wouldn't stop the war, I suppose. There are more generals where you came from."

"Very accurately calculated."

"Besides which, I'd probably be slammed down about two seconds after I got you, and killed fast, or maybe slow, depending. But I'd be killed, and I never like to count on that when I'm making plans. It doesn't pay off."

"I said you were a sensible man."

"But there's one thing I would like, boss. I'd like you to tell me what you mean when you say I know why you're jumping us. I don't; and guessing games bother me no end."

"Yes? Ever hear of Hari Seldon?"

"No. I *said* I don't like guessing games."

Riose flicked a side glance at Ducem Barr who smiled with a narrow gentleness and resumed his inwardly-dreaming expression.

Riose said with a grimace, "Don't *you* play games, Devers. There is a tradition, or a fable, or sober history—I don't care what—upon your Foundation, that eventually you will found the Second Empire. I know quite a detailed version of Hari Seldon's psycho-historical claptrap, and your eventual plans of aggression against the Empire."

"That so?" Devers nodded thoughtfully. "And who told you all that?"

"Does that matter?" said Riose with dangerous smoothness. "You're here to question nothing. I want what you know about the Seldon Fable."

"But if it's a Fable—"

"Don't play with words, Devers."

"I'm not. In fact, I'll give it to you straight. You know all I know about it. It's silly stuff, half-baked. Every world has its yarns; you can't keep it away from them. Yes, I've heard that sort of talk; Seldon, Second Empire, and so on. They put kids to sleep at night with the stuff. The young squirts curl up in the spare rooms with their pocket projectors and suck up Seldon thrillers. But it's strictly non-adult. Non-intelligent adult, anyway." The trader shook his head.

The Imperial general's eyes were dark. "Is that really so? You waste your lies, man. I've been on the planet, Terminus. I know your Foundation. I've looked it in the face."

"And you ask me? Me, when I haven't kept foot on it for two months at a piece in ten years. You *are* wasting your time. But go ahead with your war, if it's fables you're after."

And Barr spoke for the first time, mildly, "You are so confident then that the Foundation will win?"

The trader turned. He flushed faintly and an old scar on one temple showed whitely, "Hm-m-m, the silent partner. How'd you squeeze *that* out of what I said, doc?"

Riose nodded very slightly at Barr, and the Siwennian continued in a low voice, "Because the notion *would* bother you if you thought your world might lose this war, and suffer the bitter reapings of defeat, I know. *My* world once did, and still does."

Lathan Devers fumbled his beard, looked from one of his opponents to the other, then laughed shortly. "Does he always talk like that, boss. Listen," he grew serious, "what's defeat? I've seen wars and I've seen defeats. What if the winner does take over? Who's bothered? Me? Guys like me?" He shook his head in derision.

"Get this," the trader spoke forcefully and earnestly, "there are five or six fat slobs who usually run an average planet. They get the rabbit punch, but I'm not losing peace of mind over them. See. The people? The ordinary run of guys? Sure, some get killed, and the rest pay extra taxes for a while. But it settles itself out; it runs itself down. And then it's the old situation again with a different five or six."

Ducem Barr's nostrils flared, and the tendons of his old right hand jerked; but he said nothing.

Lathan Devers' eyes were on him. They missed nothing. He said, "Look. I spend my life in space for my five-and-dime gadgets and my beer-and-pretzel kickback from the Combines. There's fat fellows back there," his thumb jerked over his shoulder and back, "that sit home and collect my year's income every minute—out of skimmings from me and more like me. Suppose *you* run the Foundation. You'll still need us. You'll need us more than ever the Combines do—because you'd not know your way around, and we could bring in the hard cash. We'd make a better deal with the Empire. Yes, we would; and I'm a man of business. If it adds up to a plus mark, I'm for it."

And he stared at the two with sardonic belligerence.

The silence remained unbroken for minutes, and then a cylinder rattled into its slot. The general flipped it open, glanced at the neat printing and in-circuited the visuals with a sweep.

"Prepare plan indicating position of each ship in action. Await orders on full-armed defensive."

He reached for his cape. As he fastened it about his shoulders, he whispered in a stiff-lipped monotone to Barr, "I'm leaving this man to you. I'll expect results. This is war and I can be cruel to failures. Remember!" He left, with a salute to both.

Lathan Devers looked after him, "Well, something's hit him where it hurts. What goes on?"

"A battle, obviously," said Barr, gruffly. "The forces of the Foundation are coming out for their first battle. You'd better come along."

There were armed soldiers in the room. Their bearing was respectful and their faces were hard. Devers followed the proud old Siwennian patriarch out of the room.

The room to which they were led was smaller, barer. It contained two beds, a visi-screen, and shower and sanitary facilities. The soldiers marched out, and the thick door boomed hollowly shut.

"*Hmp?*" Devers stared disapprovingly about. "This looks permanent."

"It is," said Barr, shortly. The old Siwennian turned his back.

The trader said irritably, "What's your game, doc?"

"I have no game. You're in my charge, that's all."

The trader rose and advanced. His bulk towered over the unmoving patrician. "Yes? But you're in this cell with me and when you were marched here the guns were pointed just as hard at you as at me. Listen, you were all boiled up about my notions on the subject of war and peace."

He waited fruitlessly, "All right, let me ask you something. You said *your* country was licked once. By whom? Comet people from the outer nebulae?"

Barr looked up. "By the Empire."

"That so? Then what are you doing here?"

Barr maintained an eloquent silence.

The trader thrust out a lower lip and nodded his head slowly. He slipped off the flat-linked bracelet that hugged his right wrist and held it out. "What do you think of that?" He wore the mate to it on his left.

The Siwennian took the ornament. He responded slowly to the trader's gesture and put it on. The odd tingling at the wrist passed away quickly.

Devers' voice changed at once. "Right, doc, you've got the action now. Just speak casually. If this room is wired, they won't get a thing. That's a Field Distorter you've got there; genuine Mallow design. Sells for twenty-five credits on any world from here to the outer rim. You get it free. Hold your lips still when you talk and take it easy. You've got to get the trick of it."

Ducem Barr was suddenly weary. The trader's boring eyes were luminous and urging. He felt unequal to their demands.

Barr said, "What do you want?" The words slurred from between unmoving lips.

"I've told you. You make mouth noises like what we call a

patriot. Yet your own world has been mashed up by the Empire, and here you are playing ball with the Empire's fair-haired general. Doesn't make sense, does it?"

Barr said, "I have done my part. A conquering Imperial viceroy is dead because of me."

"That so? Recently?"

"Forty years ago."

"Forty . . . years . . . ago!" The words seemed to have meaning to the trader. He frowned, "That's a long time to live on memories. Does that young squirt in the general's uniform know about it?"

Barr nodded.

Devers' eyes were dark with thought. "You want the Empire to win?"

And the old Siwennian patrician broke out in sudden deep anger, "May the Empire and all its works perish in universal catastrophe. All Siwenna prays that daily. I had brothers once, a sister, a father. But I have children now, grandchildren. The general knows where to find them."

Devers waited.

Barr continued in a whisper, "But that would not stop me if the results in view warranted the risk. They would know how to die."

The trader said gently, "You killed a viceroy once, huh? You know, I recognize a few things. We once had a mayor, Hober Mallow his name was. He visited Siwenna; that's your world, isn't it? He met a man named Barr."

Ducem Barr stared hard, suspiciously. "What do you know of this?"

"What every trader on the Foundation knows. You might be a smart old fellow put in here to get on my right side. Sure, they'd point guns at you, and you'd hate the Empire and be all-out for its smashing. Then I'd fall all over you and pour out my heart to you, and wouldn't the general be pleased. There's not much chance of that, doc.

"But just the same I'd like to see you prove that you're the son of Onum Barr of Siwenna—the sixth and youngest who escaped the massacre."

Ducem Barr's hand shook as he opened the flat metal box in a wall recess. The metal object he withdrew clanked softly as he thrust it into the trader's hands.

"Look at that," he said.

Devers stared. He held the swollen central link of the chain close to his eyes and swore softly. "That's Mallow's monogram, or I'm a space-struck rookie, and the design is fifty years old if it's a day."

He looked up and smiled.

"Shake, doc. A man-sized atomic shield is all the proof I need," and he held out his large hand.

6.

The Favorite

The tiny ships had appeared out of the vacant depths and darted into the midst of the Armada. Without a shot or a burst of energy, they weaved through the ship-swollen area, then blasted on and out, while the Imperial wagons turned after them like lumbering beasts. There were two noiseless flares that pin-pointed space as two of the tiny gnats shriveled in atomic disintegration, and the rest were gone.

The great ships searched, then returned to their original task, and world by world, the great web of the Inclosure continued.

Brodrig's uniform was stately; carefully tailored and as carefully worn. His walk through the gardens of the obscure planet Wanda, now temporary Imperial headquarters, was leisurely; his expression was somber.

Bel Riose walked with him, his field uniform open at the collar, and doleful in its monotonous gray-black.

Riose indicated the smooth black bench under the fragrant tree-fern whose large spatulate leaves lifted flatly against the white sun. "See that, sir. It is a relic of the Imperium. The ornamented benches, built for lovers, linger on, fresh and useful, while the factories and the palaces collapse into unremembered ruin."

He seated himself, while Cleon II's Privy Secretary stood erect before him and clipped the leaves above neatly with precise swings of his ivory staff.

Riose crossed his legs and offered a cigarette to the other. He fingered one himself as he spoke, "It is what one would expect from the enlightened wisdom of His Imperial Majesty to send so competent an observer as yourself. It relieves any anxiety I might have felt that the press of more important and more immediate business might perhaps force into the shadows a small campaign on the Periphery."

"The eyes of the Emperor are everywhere," said Brodrig, mechanically. "We do not underestimate the importance of the campaign; yet still it would seem that too great an emphasis is being placed upon its difficulty. Surely their little ships are no such barrier that we must move through the intricate preliminary maneuver of an Inclosure."

Riose flushed, but he maintained his equilibrium. "I cannot risk the lives of my men, who are few enough, or the destruction of my ships which are irreplaceable, by a too-rash attack. The establishment of an Inclosure will quarter my casualties in the ultimate attack, howsoever difficult it be. The military reasons for that I took the liberty to explain yesterday."

"Well, well, I am not a military man. In this case, you assure me that what seems patently and obviously right is, in reality, wrong. We will allow that. Yet your caution shoots far beyond that. In your second communication, you requested reinforcements. And these, against an enemy poor, small, and barbarous, with whom you have had no one skirmish at the time. To desire more forces under the circumstances would savor almost of incapacity or worse, had not your earlier career given sufficient proof of your boldness and imagination."

"I thank you," said the general, coldly, "but I would remind you that there is a difference between boldness and blindness. There is a place for a decisive gamble when you know your enemy and can calculate the risks at least roughly; but to move at all against an *unknown* enemy is boldness in itself. You might as well ask why the same man sprints safely across an obstacle course in the day, and falls over the furniture in his room at night."

Brodrig swept away the other's words with a neat flirt of the fingers. "Dramatic, but not satisfactory. You have been to this barbarian world yourself. You have in addition this enemy prisoner you coddle, this trader. Between yourself and the prisoner you are not in a night fog."

"No? I pray you to remember that a world which has developed in isolation for two centuries can not be interpreted to the point of intelligent attack by a month's visit. I am a soldier, not a cleft-chinned, barrel-chested hero of a subetheric trimensional thriller. Nor can a single prisoner, and one who is an obscure member of an economic group which has no close connection with the enemy world introduce me to all the inner secrets of enemy strategy."

"You have questioned him?"

"I have."

"Well?"

"It has been useful, but not vitally so. His ship is tiny, of no account. He sells little toys which are amusing if nothing else. I have a few of the cleverest which I intend sending to the Emperor as curiosities. Naturally, there is a good deal about the ship and its workings which I do not understand, but then I am not a tech-man."

"But you have among you those who are," pointed out Brodrig.

"I, too, am aware of that," replied the general in faintly caustic tones. "But the fools have far to go before they could meet my needs. I have already sent for clever men who can understand the workings of the odd atomic field-circuits the ship contains. I have received no answer."

"Men of that type can not be spared, general. Surely, there must be one man of your vast province who understands atomics."

"Were there such a one, I would have him heal the limping, invalid motors that power two of my small fleet of ships. Two ships of my meager ten that can not fight a major battle for lack of sufficient power supply. One fifth of my force condemned to the carrion activity of consolidating positions behind the lines."

The secretary's fingers fluttered impatiently. "Your position is not unique in that respect, general. The Emperor has similar troubles."

The general threw away his shredded, never-lit cigarette, lit another, and shrugged. "Well, it is beside the immediate point, this lack of first-class tech-men. Except that I might have made more progress with my prisoner were my Psychic Probe in proper order."

The secretary's eyebrows lifted. "You have a Probe?"

"An old one. A superannuated one which fails me the one

time I needed it. I set it up during the prisoner's sleep, and received nothing. So much for the Probe. I have tried it on my own men and the reaction is quite proper, but again there is not one among my staff of tech-men who can tell me why it fails upon the prisoner. Ducem Barr, who is a theoretician of parts, though no mechanic, says the psychic structure of the prisoner may be unaffected by the Probe since from childhood he has been subjected to alien environments and neural stimuli. I don't know. But he may yet be useful. I save him in that hope."

Brodrig leaned on his staff. "I shall see if a specialist is available in the capital. In the meanwhile, what of this other man you just mentioned, this Siwennian? You keep too many enemies in your good graces."

"He knows the enemy. He, too, I keep for future reference and the help he may afford me."

"But he is a Siwennian and the son of a proscribed rebel."

"He is old and powerless, and his family acts as hostage."

"I see. Yet I think that I should speak to this trader myself."

"Certainly."

"Alone," the secretary added coldly, making his point.

"Certainly," repeated Riose, blandly. "As a loyal subject of the Emperor, I accept his personal representative as my superior. However, since the trader is at the permanent base, you will have to leave the front areas at an interesting moment."

"Yes? Interesting in what way?"

"Interesting in that the Inclosure is complete today. Interesting in that within the week, the Twentieth Fleet of the Border advances inward towards the core of resistance." Riose smiled and turned away.

In a vague way, Brodrig felt punctured.

7.

Bribery

Sergeant Mori Luk made an ideal soldier of the ranks. He came from the huge agricultural planets of the Pleiades where only army life could break the bond to the soil and the unavailing life of drudgery; and he was typical of that background. Unimaginative enough to face danger without fear, he was strong and agile enough to face it successfully. He accepted orders instantly, drove the men under him unbendingly and adored his general unswervingly.

And yet with that, he was of a sunny nature. If he killed a man in the line of duty without a scrap of hesitation, it was also without a scrap of animosity.

That Sergeant Luk should signal at the door before entering was further a sign of tact, for he would have been perfectly within his rights to enter without signaling.

The two within looked up from their evening meal and one reached out with his foot to cut off the cracked voice which rattled out of the battered pocket-transmitter with bright liveliness.

"More books?" asked Lathan Devers.

The sergeant held out the tightly-wound cylinder of film and scratched his neck. "It belongs to Engineer Orre, but he'll have to have it back. He's going to send it to his kids, you know, like what you might call a souvenir, you know."

Ducem Barr turned the cylinder in his hands with interest. "And where did the engineer get it? He hasn't a transmitter also, has he?"

The sergeant shook his head emphatically. He pointed to the knocked-about remnant at the foot of the bed. "That's the only one in the place. This fellow, Orre, now, he got that book from one of these pig-pen worlds out here we captured. They had it in a big building by itself and he had to kill a few of the natives that tried to stop him from taking it."

He looked at it appraisingly. "It makes a good souvenir—for kids."

He paused, then said stealthily, "There's big news floating about, by the way. It's only scuttlebutt, but even so, it's too good to keep. The general did it again." And he nodded slowly, gravely.

"That so?" said Devers. "And what did he do?"

"Finished the Inclosure, that's all." The sergeant chuckled with a fatherly pride. "Isn't he the corker, though? Didn't he work it fine? One of the fellows who's strong on fancy talk, says it went as smooth and even as the music of the spheres, whatever they are."

"The big offensive starts now?" asked Barr, mildly.

"Hope so," was the boisterous response. "I want to get back on my ship now that my arm is in one piece again. I'm tired of sitting on my scupper out here."

"So am I," muttered Devers, suddenly and savagely. There was a bit of underlip caught in his teeth, and he worried it.

The sergeant looked at him doubtfully, and said, "I'd better go now. The captain's round is due and I'd just as soon he didn't catch me in here."

He paused at the door. "By the way, sir," he said with sudden, awkward shyness to the trader, "I heard from my wife. She says that little freezer you gave me to send her works fine. It doesn't cost her anything, and she just about keeps a month's supply of food froze up complete. I appreciate it."

"It's all right. Forget it."

The great door moved noiselessly shut behind the grinning sergeant.

Ducem Barr got out of his chair. "Well, he gives us a fair return for the freezer. Let's take a look at this new book. Ahh, the title is gone."

He unrolled a yard or so of the film and looked through at the light. Then he murmured, "Well, skewer me through the scupper, as the sergeant says. This is 'The Garden of Summa,' Devers."

"That so?" said the trader, without interest. He shoved aside what was left of his dinner. "Sit down, Barr. Listening to this old-time literature isn't doing me any good. You heard what the sergeant said?"

"Yes, I did. What of it?"

"The offensive will start. And we sit here!"

"Where do you want to sit?"

"You know what I mean. There's no use just waiting."

"Isn't there?" Barr was carefully removing the old film from the transmitter and installing the new. "You told me a good deal of Foundation history in the last month, and it seems that the great leaders of past crises did precious little more than sit—and wait."

"Ah, Barr, but they knew where they were going."

"Did they? I suppose they said they did when it was over, and for all I know maybe they did. But there's no proof that things would not have worked out as well or better if they had not known where they were going. The deeper economic and socio-logical forces aren't directed by individual men."

Devers sneered. "No way of telling that things wouldn't have worked out worse, either. You're arguing tail-end backwards." His eyes were brooding. "You know, suppose I blasted him?"

"Whom? Riose?"

"Yes."

Barr sighed. His aging eyes were troubled with a reflection of the long past. "Assassination isn't the way out, Devers. I once tried it, under provocation, when I was twenty—but it solved nothing. I removed a villain from Siwenna, but not the Imperial yoke; and it was the Imperial yoke and not the villain that mattered."

"But Riose is not just a villain, doc. He's the whole blamed army. It would fall apart without him. They hang on him like babies. The sergeant out there slobbers every time he mentions him."

"Even so. There are other armies and other leaders. You must go deeper. There is this Brodrig, for instance—no one more than he has the ear of the Emperor. He could demand hundreds of ships where Riose must struggle with ten. I know him by reputation."

"That so? What about him?" The trader's eyes lost in frustration what they gained in sharp interest.

"You want a pocket outline? He's a low-born rascal who has by unfailing flattery tickled the whims of the Emperor. He's well-hated by the court aristocracy, vermin themselves, because he can lay claim to neither family nor humility. He is the Emperor's adviser in all things, and the Emperor's tool in the worst things. He is faithless by choice but loyal by necessity. There is not a man in the Empire as subtle in villainy or as crude in his pleasures. And they say there is no way to the Emperor's favor but through him; and no way to his, but through infamy."

"Wow!" Devers pulled thoughtfully at his neatly trimmed beard. "And he's the old boy the Emperor sent out here to keep an eye on Riose. Do you know I have an idea?"

"I do now."

"Suppose this Brodrig takes a dislike to our young Army's Delight?"

"He probably has already. He's not noted for a capacity for liking."

"Suppose it gets really bad. The Emperor might hear about it, and Riose might be in trouble."

"Uh-huh. Quite likely. But how do you propose to get that to happen?"

"I don't know. I suppose he could be bribed?"

The patrician laughed gently. "Yes, in a way, but not in the manner you bribed the sergeant—not with a pocket freezer. And even if you reach his scale, it wouldn't be worth it. There's probably no one so easily bribed, but he lacks even the fundamental honesty of honorable corruption. He doesn't *stay* bribed; not for any sum. Think of something else."

Devers swung a leg over his knee and his toe nodded quickly and restlessly. "It's the first hint, though—"

He stopped; the door signal was flashing once again, and the sergeant was on the threshold once more. He was excited, and his broad face was red and unsmiling.

"Sir," he began, in an agitated attempt at deference, "I am

very thankful for the freezer, and you have always spoken to me very fine, although I am only the son of a farmer and you are great lords."

His Pleiade accent had grown thick, almost too much so for easy comprehension; and with excitement, his lumpish peasant derivation wiped out completely the soldierly bearing so long and so painfully cultivated.

Barr said softly, "What is it, sergeant?"

"Lord Brodrig is coming to see you. Tomorrow! I know, because the captain told me to have my men ready for dress review tomorrow for . . . for him. I thought—I might warn you."

Barr said, "Thank you, sergeant, we appreciate that. But it's all right, man; no need for—"

But the look on Sergeant Luk's face was now unmistakably one of fear. He spoke in a rough whisper, "You don't hear the stories the men tell about him. He has sold himself to the space fiend. No, don't laugh. There are most terrible tales told about him. They say he has men with blast-guns who follow him everywhere, and when he wants pleasure, he just tells them to blast down anyone they meet. And they do—and he laughs. They say even the Emperor is in terror of him, and that he forces the Emperor to raise taxes and won't let him listen to the complaints of the people.

"And he hates the general, that's what they say. They say he would like to kill the general, because the general is so great and wise. But he can't because our general is a match for anyone and he knows Lord Brodrig is a bad 'un."

The sergeant blinked; smiled in a sudden incongruous shyness at his own outburst; and backed toward the door. He nodded his head, jerkily. "You mind my words. Watch him."

He ducked out.

And Devers looked up, hard-eyed. "This breaks things our way, doesn't it, doc?"

"It depends," said Barr, dryly, "on Brodrig, doesn't it?"

But Devers was thinking, not listening.

He was thinking hard.

Lord Brodrig ducked his head as he stepped into the cramped living quarters of the trading ship, and his two armed guards followed quickly, with bared guns and the professionally hard scowls of the hired bravos.

The Privy Secretary had little of the look of the lost soul about him just then. If the space fiend had bought him, he had left no visible mark of possession. Rather might Brodrig have been considered a breath of court-fashion come to enliven the hard, bare ugliness of an army base.

The stiff, tight lines of his sheened and immaculate costume gave him the illusion of height, from the very top of which his cold, emotionless eyes stared down the declivity of a long nose at the trader. The mother-of-pearl ruches at his wrists fluttered filmily as he brought his ivory stick to the ground before him and leaned upon it daintily.

"No," he said, with a little gesture, "you remain here. Forget your toys; I am not interested in them."

He drew forth a chair, dusted it carefully with the iridescent square of fabric attached to the top of his white stick, and seated himself. Devers glanced towards the mate to the chair, but Brodrig said lazily, "You will stand in the presence of a Peer of the Realm."

He smiled.

Devers shrugged. "If you're not interested in my stock in trade, what am I here for?"

The Privy Secretary waited coldly, and Devers added a slow, "Sir."

"For privacy," said the secretary. "Now is it likely that I would come two hundred parsecs through space to inspect trinkets? It's *you* I want to see." He extracted a small pink tablet from an engraved box and placed it delicately between his teeth. He sucked it slowly and appreciatively.

"For instance," he said, "who are you? Are you really a citizen of this barbarian world that is creating all this fury of military frenzy?"

Devers nodded gravely.

"And you were really captured by him *after* the beginning of this squabble he calls a war. I am referring to our young general."

Devers nodded again.

"So! Very well, my worthy Outlander. I see your fluency of

speech is at a minimum. I shall smooth the way for you. It seems that our general here is fighting an apparently meaningless war with frightful transports of energy—and this over a forsaken flea-bite of a world at the end of nowhere, which to a logical man would not seem worth a single blast of a single gun. Yet the general is not illogical. On the contrary, I would say he was extremely intelligent. Do you follow me?"

"Can't say I do, sir."

The secretary inspected his fingernails and said, "Listen further, then. The general would not waste his men and ships on a sterile feat of glory. I know he *talks* of glory and of Imperial honor, but it is quite obvious that the affectation of being one of the insufferable old demigods of the Heroic Age won't wash. There is something more than glory here—and he does take queer, unnecessary care of you. Now if you were *my* prisoner and told *me* as little of use as you have our general, I would slit open your abdomen and strangle you with your own intestines."

Devers remained wooden. His eyes moved slightly, first to one of the secretary's bully-boys, and then to the other. They were ready; eagerly ready.

The secretary smiled. "Well, now, you're a silent devil. According to the general, even a Psychic Probe made no impression, and that was a mistake on his part, by the way, for it convinced me that our young military whizz-bang was lying." He seemed in high humor.

"My honest tradesman," he said, "I have a Psychic Probe of my own, one that ought to suit you peculiarly well. You see this—"

And between thumb and forefinger, held negligently, were intricately designed, pink-and-yellow rectangles which were most definitely obvious in identity.

Devers said so. "It looks like cash," he said.

"Cash it is—and the best cash of the Empire, for it is backed by my estates, which are more extensive than the Emperor's own. A hundred thousand credits. All here! Between two fingers! Yours!"

"For what, sir? I am a good trader, but all trades go in both directions."

"For what? For the truth! What is the general after? Why is he fighting this war?"

Lathan Devers sighed, and smoothed his beard thoughtfully. "What he's after?" His eyes were following the motions of the secretary's hands as he counted the money slowly, bill by bill. "In a word, the Empire."

"*Hmp.* How ordinary! It always comes to that in the end. But how? What is the road that leads from the Galaxy's edge to the peak of Empire so broadly and invitingly?"

"The Foundation," said Devers, bitterly, "has secrets. They have books, old books—so old that the language they are in is only known to a few of the top men. But the secrets are shrouded in ritual and religion, and none may use them. I tried and now I am here—and there is a death sentence waiting for me, there."

"I see. And these old secrets? Come, for one hundred thousand I deserve the intimate details."

"The transmutation of elements," said Devers, shortly.

The secretary's eyes narrowed and lost some of their detachment. "I have been told that practical transmutation is impossible by the laws of atomics."

"So it is, if atomic forces are used. But the ancients were smart boys. There are sources of power greater than the atoms. If the Foundation used those sources as I suggested—"

Devers felt a soft, creeping sensation in his stomach. The bait was dangling; the fish was nosing it.

The secretary said suddenly, "Continue. The general, I am sure, is aware of all this. But what does he intend doing once he finishes this opera-bouffe affair?"

Devers kept his voice rock-steady. "With transmutation he controls the economy of the whole set-up of your Empire. Mineral holdings won't be worth a sneeze when Riose can make tungsten out of aluminum and iridium out of iron. An entire production system based on the scarcity of certain elements and the abundance of others is thrown completely out of whack. There'll be the greatest disjointment the Empire has ever seen, and only Riose will be able to stop it. *And* there is the question of this new power I mentioned, the use of which won't give Riose religious heebies.

"There's nothing that can stop him now. He's got the Foundation by the back of the neck, and once he's finished with it, he'll be Emperor in two years."

"So." Brodrig laughed lightly. "Iridium out of iron, that's what you said, isn't it? Come, I'll tell you a state secret. Do you know that the Foundation has already been in communication with the general?"

Devers' back stiffened.

"You look surprised. Why not? It seems logical now. They offered him a hundred tons of iridium a year to make peace. A hundred tons of *iron* converted to iridium in violation of their religious principles to save their necks. Fair enough, but no wonder our rigidly incorruptible general refused—when he can have the iridium and the Empire as well. And poor Cleon called him his one honest general. My bewhiskered merchant, you have earned your money."

He tossed it, and Devers scrambled after the flying bills.

Lord Brodrig stopped at the door and turned. "One reminder, trader. My playmates with the guns here have neither middle ears, tongues, education, nor intelligence. They can neither hear, speak, write, nor even make sense to a Psychic Probe. But they are very expert at interesting executions. I have bought you, man, at one hundred thousand credits. You will be good and worthy merchandise. Should you forget that you are bought at any time and attempt to . . . say . . . repeat our conversation to Riose, you will be executed. But executed my way."

And in that delicate face there were sudden hard lines of eager cruelty that changed the studied smile into a red-lipped snarl. For one fleeting second, Devers saw that space fiend who had bought his buyer, look out of his buyer's eyes.

Silently, he preceded the two thrusting blast-guns of Brodrig's "playmates" to his quarters.

And to Ducem Barr's question, he said with brooding satisfaction, "No, that's the queerest part of it. *He* bribed *me*."

Two months of difficult war had left their mark on Bel Riose. There was heavy-handed gravity about him; and he was short-tempered.

It was with impatience that he addressed the worshiping Sergeant Luk. "Wait outside, soldier, and conduct these men back to their quarters when I am through. No one is to enter until I call. No one at all, you understand."

The sergeant saluted himself stiffly out of the room, and Riose with muttered disgust scooped up the waiting papers on his desk, threw them into the top drawer and slammed it shut.

"Take seats," he said shortly, to the waiting two. "I haven't much time. Strictly speaking, I shouldn't be here at all, but it is necessary to see you."

He turned to Ducem Barr, whose long fingers were caressing with interest the crystal cube in which was set the simulacrum of the lined, austere face of His Imperial Majesty, Cleon II.

"In the first place, patrician," said the general, "your Seldon is losing. To be sure, he battles well, for these men of the Foundation swarm like senseless bees and fight like madmen. Every planet is defended viciously, and once taken, every planet heaves so with rebellion it is as much trouble to hold as to conquer. But they are taken, and they are held. Your Seldon is losing."

"But he has not yet lost," murmured Barr politely.

"The Foundation itself retains less optimism. They offer me millions in order that I may not put this Seldon to the final test."

"So rumor goes."

"Ah, is rumor preceding me? Does it prate also of the latest?"

"What is the latest?"

"Why, that Lord Brodrig, the darling of the Emperor, is now second in command at his own request."

Devers spoke for the first time. "At his own request, boss? How come? Or are you growing to like the fellow?" He chuckled.

Riose said, calmly, "No, can't say I do. It's just that he bought the office at what I considered a fair and adequate price."

"Such as?"

"Such as a request to the Emperor for reinforcements."

Devers' contemptuous smile broadened. "He has communicated with the Emperor, huh? And I take it, boss, you're just waiting for these reinforcements, but they'll come any day. Right?"

"Wrong! They have already come. Five ships of the line; smooth and strong, with a personal message of congratulations from the Emperor, and more ships on the way. What's wrong, trader?" he asked, sardonically.

Devers spoke through suddenly frozen lips. "Nothing!"

Riose strode out from behind his desk and faced the trader, hand on the butt of his blast-gun.

"I say, what's wrong, trader? The news would seem to disturb you. Surely, you have no sudden birth of interest in the Foundation."

"I haven't."

"Yes—there are queer points about you."

"That so, boss?" Devers smiled tightly, and balled the fists in his pockets. "Just you line them up and I'll knock them down for you."

"Here they are. You were caught easily. You surrendered at first blow with a burnt-out shield. You're quite ready to desert your world, and that without a price. Interesting, all this, isn't it?"

"I crave to be on the winning side, boss. I'm a sensible man; you called me that yourself."

Riose said with tight throatiness, "Granted! Yet no trader since has been captured. No trade ship but has had the speed to escape at choice. No trade ship but has had a screen that could take all the beating a light cruiser could give it, should it choose to fight. And no trader but has fought to death when occasion warranted. Traders have been traced as the leaders and instigators of the guerilla warfare on occupied planets and of the flying raids in occupied space.

"Are you the *only* sensible man then? You neither fight nor flee, but turn traitor without urging. You are unique, amazingly unique—in fact, suspiciously unique."

Devers said softly, "I take your meaning, but you have nothing on me. I've been here now six months, and I've been a good boy."

"So you have, and I have repaid you by good treatment. I have left your ship undisturbed and treated you with every consideration. Yet you fall short. Freely offered information, for instance, on your gadgets might have been helpful. The atomic principles on which they are built would seem to be used in some of the Foundation's nastiest weapons. Right?"

"I am only a trader," said Devers, "and not one of these big-wig technicians. I sell the stuff; I don't make it."

"Well, that will be seen shortly. It is what I came here for. For instance, your ship will be searched for a personal force-shield. You have never worn one; yet all soldiers of the Foundation do. It will be significant evidence that there is information you do not choose to give me. Right?"

There was no answer. He continued, "And there will be more direct evidence. I have brought with me the Psychic Probe. It failed once before, but contact with the enemy is a liberal education."

His voice was smoothly threatening and Devers felt the gun thrust hard in his midriff—the general's gun, hitherto in its holster.

The general said quietly, "You will remove your wristband and any other metal ornament you wear and give them to me. Slowly! Atomic fields can be distorted, you see, and Psychic Probes might probe only into static. That's right. I'll take it."

The receiver on the general's desk was glowing and a message capsule clicked into the slot, near which Barr stood and still held the trimensional Imperial bust.

Riose stepped behind his desk, with his blast-gun held ready. He said to Barr, "You too, patrician. Your wristband condemns you. You have been helpful earlier, however, and I am not vindictive, but I shall judge the fate of your behostaged family by the results of the Psychic Probe."

And as Riose leaned over to take out the message capsule, Barr lifted the crystal-enveloped bust of Cleon and quietly and methodically brought it down upon the general's head.

It happened too suddenly for Devers to grasp. It was as if a sudden demon had grown into the old man.

"Out!" said Barr, in a tooth-clenched whisper. "Quickly!" He seized Riose's dropped blaster and buried it in his blouse.

Sergeant Luk turned as they emerged from the narrowest possible crack of the door.

Barr said easily, "Lead on, sergeant!"

Devers closed the door behind him.

Sergeant Luk led in silence to their quarters, and then, with the briefest pause, continued onward, for there was the nudge of a blast-gun muzzle in his ribs, and a hard voice in his ears which said, "To the trade ship."

Devers stepped forward to open the air lock, and Barr said, "Stand where you are, Luk. You've been a decent man, and we're not going to kill you."

But the sergeant recognized the monogram on the gun. He cried in choked fury, "You've killed the general."

With a wild, incoherent yell, he charged blindly upon the blasting fury of the gun and collapsed in blasted ruin.

The trade ship was rising above a dead planet before the signal lights began their eerie blink and against the creamy cobweb of the great Lens in the sky which was the Galaxy, other black forms rose.

Devers said grimly, "Hold tight, Barr—and let's see if they've got a ship that can match my speed."

He knew they hadn't!

And once in open space, the trader's voice seemed lost and dead as he said, "The line I fed Brodrig was a little too good. It seems as if he's thrown in with the general."

Swiftly they raced into the depths of the star-mass that was the Galaxy.

8.

To Trantor

Devers bent over the little dead globe, watching for a tiny sign of life. The directional control was slowly and thoroughly sieving space with its jabbing tight sheaf of signals.

Barr watched patiently from his seat on the low cot in the corner. He asked, "No more signs of them?"

"The Empire boys? No." The trader growled the words with evident impatience. "We lost the scuppers long ago. Space! With the blind jumps we took through hyperspace, it's lucky we didn't land up in a sun's belly. They couldn't have followed us even if they outranged us, which they didn't."

He sat back and loosened his collar with a jerk. "I don't know what those Empire boys have done here. I think some of the gaps are out of alignment."

"I take it, then, you're trying to get to the Foundation."

"I'm calling the Association—or trying to."

"The Association? Who are they?"

"Association of Independent Traders. Never heard of it, huh? Well, you're not alone. We haven't made our splash yet!"

For a while there was a silence that centered about the unresponsive Reception Indicator, and Barr said, "Are you within range?"

"I don't know. I haven't but a small notion where we are, going by dead reckoning. That's why I have to use directional control. It could take years, you know."

"Might it?"

Barr pointed; and Devers jumped and adjusted his earphones. Within the little murky sphere there was a tiny glowing whiteness.

For half an hour, Devers nursed the fragile, groping thread of communication that reached through hyperspace to connect two points that laggard light would take five hundred years to bind together.

Then he sat back, hopelessly. He looked up, and shoved the earphones back.

"Let's eat, doc. There's a needle-shower you can use if you want to, but go easy on the hot water."

He squatted before one of the cabinets that lined one wall and felt through the contents. "You're not a vegetarian, I hope?"

Barr said, "I'm omnivorous. But what about the Association. Have you lost them?"

"Looks so. It was extreme range, a little too extreme. Doesn't matter, though. I got all that counted."

He straightened, and placed the two metal containers upon the table. "Just give it five minutes, doc, then slit it open by pushing the contact. It'll be plate, food, and fork—sort of handy for when you're in a hurry, if you're not interested in such incidentals as napkins. I suppose you want to know what I got out of the Association."

"If it isn't a secret."

Devers shook his head. "Not to you. What Riose said was true."

"About the offer of tribute?"

"Uh-huh. They offered it, *and* had it refused. Things are bad. There's fighting in the outer suns of Loris."

"Loris is close to the Foundation?"

"Huh? Oh, you wouldn't know. It's one of the original Four Kingdoms. You might call it part of the inner line of defense. That's not the worst. They've been fighting large ships previously never encountered. Which means Riose wasn't giving us the works. He *has* received more ships. Brodrig *has* switched sides, and I *have* messed things up."

His eyes were bleak as he joined the food-container contact-points and watched it fall open neatly. The stewlike dish steamed its aroma through the room. Ducem Barr was already eating.

"So much," said Barr, "for improvisations, then. We can do nothing here; we can not cut through the Imperial lines to return to the Foundation; we can do nothing but that which is most sensible—to wait patiently. However, if Riose has reached the inner line I trust the wait will not be too long."

And Devers put down his fork. "Wait, is it?" he snarled, glowering. "That's all right for *you*. You've got nothing at stake."

"Haven't I?" Barr smiled thinly.

"No. In fact, I'll tell you." Devers' irritation 'skimmed the surface. "I'm tired of looking at this whole business as if it were an interesting something-or-other on a microscope slide. I've got friends somewhere out there, dying; and a whole world out there, my home, dying also. You're an outsider. You don't know."

"I have seen friends die." The old man's hands were limp in his lap and his eyes were closed. "Are you married?"

Devers said, "Traders don't marry."

"Well, I have two sons and a nephew. They have been warned, but—for reasons—they could take no action. Our escape means their death. My daughter and my two grandchildren have, I hope, left the planet safely before this, but even excluding them, I have already risked and lost more than you."

Devers was morosely savage. "I know. But that was a matter of choice. You might have played ball with Riose. I never asked you to—"

Barr shook his head. "It was not a matter of choice, Devers. Make your conscience free; I didn't risk my sons for you. I cooperated with Riose as long as I dared. But there was the Psychic Probe."

The Siwennian patrician opened his eyes and they were sharp with pain. "Riose came to me once; it was over a year ago. He spoke of a cult centering about the magicians, but missed the truth. It is not quite a cult. You see, it is forty years now that Siwenna has been gripped in the same unbearable vise that threatens your world. Five revolts have been ground out. Then I discovered the ancient records of Hari Seldon—and now this 'cult' waits.

"It waits for the coming of the 'magicians' and for that day it is ready. My sons are leaders of those who wait. It is *that* secret which is in my mind and which the Probe must never touch. And so they must die as hostages; for the alternative is their death as rebels and half of Siwenna with them. You see, I had no choice! And I am no outsider."

Devers' eyes fell, and Barr continued softly, "It is on a Foundation victory that Siwenna's hopes depend. It is for a Foundation victory that my sons are sacrificed. And Hari Seldon does not pre-calculate the inevitable salvation of Siwenna as he does that of the Foundation. I have no certainty for *my* people—only hope."

"But you are still satisfied to wait. Even with the Imperial Navy at Loris."

"I would wait, in perfect confidence," said Barr, simply, "if they had landed on the planet, Terminus, itself."

The trader frowned hopelessly. "I don't know. It can't really work like that; not just like magic. Psycho-history or not, they're terribly strong, and we're weak. What can Seldon do about it?"

"There's nothing to *do*. It's all already *done*. It's proceeding now. Because you don't hear the wheels turning and the gongs beating doesn't mean it's any the less certain."

"Maybe; but I wish you had cracked Riose's skull for keeps. He's more the enemy than all his army."

"Cracked his skull? With Brodrig his second in command?" Barr's face sharpened with hate. "All Siwenna would have been my hostage. Brodrig has proven his worth long since. There exists a world which five years ago lost one male in every ten—and simply for failure to meet outstanding taxes. This same Brodrig was the tax-collector. No, Riose may live. His punishments are mercy in comparison."

"But six months, *six months*, in the enemy Base, with nothing to show for it." Devers' strong hands clasped each other tautly, so that his knuckles cracked. "Nothing to show for it!"

"Well, now, wait. You remind me—" Barr fumbled in his pouch. "You might want to count this." And he tossed the small sphere of metal on the table.

Devers snatched it. "What is it?"

"The message capsule. The one that Riose received just before I jacked him. Does that count as something?"

"I don't know. Depends on what's in it!" Devers sat down and turned it over carefully in his hand.

When Barr stepped from his cold shower and, gratefully, into the mild warm current of the air dryer, he found Devers silent and absorbed at the workbench.

The Siwennian slapped his body with a sharp rhythm and spoke above the punctuating sounds. "What are you doing?"

Devers looked up. Droplets of perspiration glittered in his beard. "I'm going to open this capsule."

"*Can* you open it without Riose's personal characteristic?" There was mild surprise in the Siwennian's voice.

"If I can't, I'll resign from the Association and never skipper a ship for what's left of my life. I've got a three-way electronic analysis of the interior now, and I've got little jiggers that the Empire never heard of, especially made for jimmying capsules. I've been a burglar before this, y'know. A trader has to be something of everything."

He bent low over the little sphere, and a small flat instrument probed delicately and sparked redly at each fleeting contact.

He said, "This capsule is a crude job, anyway. These Imperial boys are no shakes at this small work. I can see that. Ever see a Foundation capsule? It's half the size and impervious to electronic analysis in the first place."

And then he was rigid, the shoulder muscles beneath his tunic tautening visibly. His tiny probe pressed slowly—

It was noiseless when it came, but Devers relaxed and sighed. In his hand was the shining sphere with its message unrolled like a parchment tongue.

"It's from Brodrig," he said. Then, with contempt, "The message medium is permanent. In a Foundation capsule, the message would be oxidized to gas within the minute."

But Ducem Barr waved him silent. He read the message quickly.

FROM: AMMEL BRODRIG, ENVOY EXTRAORDINARY OF HIS IMPE-RIAL MAJESTY, PRIVY SECRETARY OF THE COUNCIL, AND PEER OF THE REALM.

TO: BEL RIOSE, MILITARY GOVERNOR OF SIWENNA, GENERAL OF THE IMPERIAL FORCES, AND PEER OF THE REALM.

I GREET YOU.

PLANET #1120 NO LONGER RESISTS. THE PLANS OF OFFENSE

AS OUTLINED CONTINUE SMOOTHLY. THE ENEMY WEAKENS VISIBLY AND THE ULTIMATE ENDS IN VIEW WILL SURELY BE GAINED.

Barr raised his head from the almost microscopic print and cried bitterly, "The fool! The forsaken blasted fop! *That* a message?"

"Huh?" said Devers. He was vaguely disappointed.

"It says nothing," ground out Barr. "Our lick-spittle courtier is playing at general now. With Riose away, he is the field commander and must sooth his paltry spirit by spewing out his pompous reports concerning military affairs he has nothing to do with. 'So-and-so planet no longer resists.' 'The offensive moves on.' 'The enemy weakens.' The vacuum-headed peacock."

"Well, now, wait a minute. Hold on—"

"Throw it away." The old man turned away in mortification. "The Galaxy knows I never expected it to be world-shakingly important, but in wartime it is reasonable to assume that even the most routine order left undelivered might hamper military movements and lead to complications later. It's why I snatched it. But this! Better to have left it. It would have wasted a minute of Riose's time that will now be put to more constructive use."

But Devers had arisen. "Will you hold on and stop throwing your weight around? For Seldon's sake—"

He held out the sliver of message before Barr's nose, "Now read that again. What does he mean by 'ultimate ends in view'?"

"The conquest of the Foundation. Well?"

"Yes? And maybe he means the conquest of the Empire. You know he *believes* that to be the ultimate end."

"And if he does?"

"If he does!" Devers' one-sided smile was lost in his beard. "Why, watch then, and I'll show you."

With one finger the lavishly monogrammed sheet of message-parchment was thrust back into its slot. With a soft twang, it disappeared and the globe was a smooth, unbroken whole again. Somewhere inside was the tiny oiled whir of the controls as they lost their setting by random movements.

"Now there is no known way of opening this capsule without knowledge of Riose's personal characteristic, is there?"

"To the Empire, no," said Barr.

"Then the evidence it contains is unknown to us and absolutely authentic."

"To the Empire, yes," said Barr.

"And the Emperor can open it, can't he? Personal Characteristics of Government officials must be on file. They are at the Foundation."

"At the Imperial capital as well," agreed Barr.

"Then when you, a Siwennian patrician and Peer of the Realm, tell this Cleon, this Emperor, that his favorite tame-parrot and his shiniest general are getting together to knock him over, and hand him the capsule as evidence, what will *he* think Brodrig's 'ultimate ends' are?"

Barr sat down weakly. "Wait, I don't follow you." He stroked one thin cheek, and said, "You're not really serious, are you?"

"I am." Devers was angrily excited. "Listen, nine out of the last ten Emperors got their throats cut, or their gizzards blasted out by one or another of their generals with big-time notions in their heads. You told me that yourself more than once. Old man Emperor would believe us so fast it would make Riose's head swim."

Barr muttered feebly, "He *is* serious. For the Galaxy's sake, man, you can't beat a Seldon crisis by a far-fetched, impractical, storybook scheme like that. Suppose you had never got hold of the capsule. Suppose Brodrig hadn't used the word 'ultimate.' Seldon doesn't depend on wild luck."

"If wild luck comes our way, there's no law says Seldon can't take advantage of it."

"Certainly. But . . . but," Barr stopped, then spoke calmly but with visible restraint. "Look, in the first place, how will you get to the planet Trantor? You don't know its location in space, and I certainly don't remember the co-ordinates, to say nothing of the ephemerae. You don't even know your own position in space."

"You can't get lost in space," grinned Devers. He was at the controls already. "Down we go to the nearest planet, and back we come with complete bearings and the best navigation charts Brodrig's hundred thousand smackers can buy."

"*And* a blaster in our belly. Our descriptions are probably in every planet in this quarter of the Empire."

"Doc," said Devers, patiently, "don't be a hick from the sticks. Riose said my ship surrendered too easily and, brother, he wasn't kidding. This ship has enough fire-power and enough juice in its shield to hold off anything we're likely to meet this deep inside the frontier. And we have personal shields, too. The Empire boys never found them, you know, but they weren't meant to be found."

"All right," said Barr, "all right. Suppose yourself on Trantor. How do you see the Emperor then? You think he keeps office hours?"

"Suppose we worry about that on Trantor," said Devers.

And Barr muttered helplessly, "All right again. I've wanted to see Trantor before I die for half a century now. Have your way."

The hyperatomic motor was cut in. The lights flickered and there was the slight internal wrench that marked the shift into hyperspace.

9.

On Trantor

The stars were as thick as weeds in an unkempt field, and for the first time, Lathan Devers found the figures to the right of the decimal point of prime importance in calculating the cuts through the hyper-regions. There was a claustrophobic sensation about the necessity for leaps of not more than a light-year. There was a frightening harshness about a sky which glittered unbrokenly in every direction. It was being lost in a sea of radiation.

And in the center of a cluster of ten thousand stars, whose light tore to shreds the feebly encircling darkness, there circled the huge Imperial planet, Trantor.

But it was more than a planet; it was the living pulse beat of an Empire of twenty million stellar systems. It had only one function, administration; one purpose, government; and one manufactured product, law.

The entire world was one functional distortion. There was no living object on its surface but man, his pets, and his parasites. No blade of grass or fragment of uncovered soil could be found outside the hundred square miles of the Imperial Palace. No water outside the Palace grounds existed but in the vast underground cisterns that held the water supply of a world.

The lustrous, indestructible, incorruptible metal that was the unbroken surface of the planet was the foundation of the huge, metal structures that mazed the planet. They were structures connected by causeways; laced by corridors; cubbyholed by offices; basemented by the huge retail centers that covered square miles; penthoused by the glittering amusement world that sparkled into life each night.

One could walk around the world of Trantor and never leave that one conglomerate building, nor see the city.

A fleet of ships greater in number than all the war fleets the

Empire had ever supported landed their cargoes on Trantor each day to feed the forty billions of humans who gave nothing in exchange but the fulfillment of the necessity of untangling the myriads of threads that spiraled into the central administration of the most complex government Humanity had ever known.

Twenty agricultural worlds were the granary of Trantor. A universe was its servant—

Tightly held by the huge metal arms on either side, the trade ship was gently lowered down the huge ramp that led to the hangar. Already Devers had fumed his way through the manifold complications of a world conceived in paper work and dedicated to the principle of the form-in-quadruplicate.

There had been the preliminary halt in space, where the first of what had grown into a hundred questionnaires had been filled out. There were the hundred cross-examinations, the routine administration of a simple Probe, the photographing of the ship, the Characteristic-Analysis of the two men, and the subsequent recording of the same, the search for contraband, the payment of the entry tax—and finally the question of the identity cards and visitor's visa.

Ducem Barr was a Siwennian and subject of the Emperor, but Lathan Devers was an unknown without the requisite documents. The official in charge at the moment was devastated with sorrow, but Devers could not enter. In fact, he would have to be held for official investigation.

From somewhere a hundred credits in crisp, new bills backed by the estates of Lord Brodrig made their appearance, and changed hands quietly. The official hemmed importantly and the devastation of his sorrow was assuaged. A new form made its appearance from the appropriate pigeonhole. It was filled out rapidly and efficiently, with the Devers characteristic thereto formally and properly attached.

The two men, trader and patrician, entered Siwenna.

In the hangar, the trade ship was another vessel to be cached, photographed, recorded, contents noted, identity cards of passengers facsimiled, and for which a suitable fee was paid, recorded, and receipted.

And then Devers was on a huge terrace under the bright white sun, along which women chattered, children shrieked, and men sipped drinks languidly and listened to the huge televisors blaring out the news of the Empire.

Barr paid a requisite number of iridium coins and appropriated the uppermost member of a pile of newspapers. It was the Trantor *Imperial News,* official organ of the government. In the back of the news room, there was the soft clicking noise of additional editions being printed in long-distance sympathy with the busy machines at the *Imperial News* offices ten thousand miles away by corridor—six thousand by air-machine—just as ten million sets of copies were being likewise printed at that moment in ten million other news rooms all over the planet.

Barr glanced at the headlines and said softly, "What shall we do first?"

Devers tried to shake himself out of his depression. He was in a universe far removed from his own, on a world that weighed him down with its intricacy, among people whose doings were incomprehensible and whose language was nearly so. The gleaming metallic towers that surrounded him and continued onwards in never-ending multiplicity to beyond the horizon oppressed him; the whole busy, unheeding life of a world-metropolis cast him into the horrible gloom of isolation and pygmyish unimportance.

He said, "I better leave it to you, doc."

Barr was calm, low-voiced. "I tried to tell you, but it's hard to believe without seeing for yourself, I know that. Do you know how many people want to see the Emperor every day? About one million. Do you know how many he sees? About ten. We'll have to work through the civil service, and that makes it harder. But we can't afford the aristocracy."

"We have almost one hundred thousand."

"A single Peer of the Realm would cost us that, and it would take at least three or four to form an adequate bridge to the Emperor. It may take fifty chief commissioners and senior supervisors to do the same, but they would cost us only a hundred apiece perhaps. I'll do the talking. In the first place, they wouldn't understand your accent, and in the second, you don't know the etiquette of Imperial bribery. It's an art, I assure you. Ah!"

The third page of the *Imperial News* had what he wanted and he passed the paper to Devers.

Devers read slowly. The vocabulary was strange, but he understood. He looked up, and his eyes were dark with concern. He slapped the news sheet angrily with the back of his hand. "You think this can be trusted?"

"Within limits," replied Barr, calmly. "It's highly improbable that the Foundation fleet was wiped out. They've probably reported *that* several times already, if they've gone by the usual war-reporting technique of a world capital far from the actual scene of fighting. What it means, though, is that Riose has won another battle, which would be none-too-unexpected. It says he's captured Loris. Is that the capital planet of the Kingdom of Loris?"

"Yes," brooded Devers, "or of what used to be the Kingdom of Loris. And it's not twenty parsecs from the Foundation. Doc, we've got to work fast."

Barr shrugged. "You can't go fast on Trantor. If you try, you'll end up at the point of an atom-blaster, most likely."

"How long will it take?"

"A month, if we're lucky. A month, and our hundred thousand credits—if even that will suffice. And that is providing the Emperor does not take it into his head in the meantime to travel to the Summer Planets, where he sees no petitioners at all."

"But the Foundation—"

"—Will take care of itself, as heretofore. Come, there's the question of dinner. I'm hungry. And afterwards, the evening is ours and we may as well use it. We shall never see Trantor or any world like it again, you know."

The Home Commissioner of the Outer Provinces spread his pudgy hands helplessly and peered at the petitioners with owlish nearsightedness. "But the Emperor is indisposed, gentlemen. It is really useless to take the matter to my superior. His Imperial Majesty has seen no one in a week."

"He will see us," said Barr, with an affectation of confidence. "It is but a question of seeing a member of the staff of the Privy Secretary."

"Impossible," said the commissioner emphatically. "It would

be the worth of my job to attempt that. Now if you could but be more explicit concerning the nature of your business. I'm willing to help you, understand, but naturally I want something less vague, something I can present to my superior as reason for taking the matter further."

"If my business were such that it could be told to any but the highest," suggested Barr, smoothly, "it would scarcely be important enough to rate audience with His Imperial Majesty. I propose that you take a chance. I might remind you that if His Imperial Majesty attaches the importance to our business which we guarantee that he will, you will stand certain to receive the honors you will deserve for helping us now."

"Yes, but—" and the commissioner shrugged, wordlessly.

"It's a chance," agreed Barr. "Naturally, a risk should have its compensation. It is a rather great favor to ask you, but we have already been greatly obliged with your kindness in offering us this opportunity to explain our problem. But if you would *allow* us to express our gratitude just slightly by—"

Devers scowled. He had heard this speech with its slight variations twenty times in the past month. It ended, as always, in a quick shift of the half-hidden bills. But the epilogue differed here. Usually the bills vanished immediately; here they remained in plain view, while slowly the commissioner counted them, inspecting them front and back as he did so.

There was a subtle change in his voice. "Backed by the Privy Secretary, hey? Good money!"

"To get back to the subject—" urged Barr.

"No, but wait," interrupted the commissioner, "let us go back by easy stages. I really do wish to know what your business can be. This money, it is fresh and new, and you must have a good deal, for it strikes me that you have seen other officials before me. Come, now, what about it?"

Barr said, "I don't see what you are driving at."

"Why, see here, it might be proven that you are upon the planet illegally, since the Identification and Entry Cards of your silent friend are certainly inadequate. He is not a subject of the Emperor."

"I deny that."

"It doesn't matter that you do," said the commissioner, with sudden bluntness. "The official who signed his Cards for the sum of a hundred credits has confessed—under pressure—and we know more of you than you think."

"If you are hinting, sire, that the sum we have asked you to accept is inadequate in view of the risks—"

The commissioner smiled. "On the contrary, it is more than adequate." He tossed the bills aside. "To return to what I was saying, it is the Emperor himself who has become interested in your case. Is it not true, sirs, that you have recently been guests of General Riose? Is it not true that you have escaped from the midst of his army with, to put it mildly, astonishing ease? Is it not true that you possess a small fortune in bills backed by Lord Brodrig's estates? In short, is it not true that you are a pair of spies and assassins sent here to— Well, you shall tell us yourself who paid you and for what!"

"Do you know," said Barr, with silky anger, "I deny the right of a petty commissioner to accuse us of crimes. We will leave."

"You will not leave." The commissioner arose, and his eyes no longer seemed near-sighted. "You need answer no question now; that will be reserved for a later—and more forceful—time. Nor am I a commissioner; I am a Lieutenant of the Imperial Police. You are under arrest."

There was a glitteringly efficient blast-gun in his fist as he smiled. "There are greater men than you under arrest this day. It is a hornet's nest we are cleaning up."

Devers snarled and reached slowly for his own gun. The lieutenant of police smiled more broadly and squeezed the contacts. The blasting line of force struck Devers' chest in an accurate blaze of destruction—that bounced harmlessly off his personal shield in sparkling spicules of light.

Devers shot in turn, and the lieutenant's head fell from off an upper torso that had disappeared. It was still smiling as it lay in the jag of sunshine which entered through the new-made hole in the wall.

It was through the back entrance that they left.

Devers said huskily, "Quickly to the ship. They'll have the alarm out in no time." He cursed in a ferocious whisper. "It's another plan that's backfired. I could swear the space fiend himself is against me."

It was in the open that they became aware of the jabbering crowds that surrounded the huge televisors. They had no time to wait; the disconnected roaring words that reached them, they disregarded. But Barr snatched a copy of the *Imperial News* before diving into the huge barn of the hangar, where the ship lifted hastily through a giant cavity burnt fiercely into the roof.

"Can you get away from them?" asked Barr.

Ten ships of the traffic-police wildly followed the runaway craft that had burst out of the lawful, radio-beamed Path of Leaving, and then broken every speed law in creation. Further behind still, sleek vessels of the Secret Service were lifting in pursuit of a carefully described ship manned by two thoroughly identified murderers.

"Watch me," said Devers, and savagely shifted into hyperspace two thousand miles above the surface of Trantor. The shift, so near a planetary mass, meant unconsciousness for Barr and a fearful haze of pain for Devers, but light-years further, space above them was clear.

Devers' somber pride in his ship burst to the surface. He said, "There's not an Imperial ship that could follow me anywhere."

And then, bitterly, "But there is nowhere left to run to for us, and we can't fight their weight. What's there to do? What can anyone do?"

Barr moved feebly on his cot. The effect of the hyper-shift had not yet worn off, and each of his muscles ached. He said, "No one has to do anything. It's all over. Here!"

He passed the copy of the *Imperial News* that he still clutched, and the headlines were enough for the trader.

"Recalled and arrested—Riose and Brodrig," Devers muttered. He stared blankly at Barr. "Why?"

"The story doesn't say, but what does it matter? The war with the Foundation is over, and at this moment, Siwenna is revolting. Read the story and see." His voice was drifting off. "We'll stop in some of the provinces and find out the later details. If you don't mind, I'll go to sleep now."

And he did.

In grasshopper jumps of increasing magnitude, the trade ship was spanning the Galaxy in its return to the Foundation.

10.

The War Ends

Lathan Devers felt definitely uncomfortable, and vaguely resentful. He had received his own decoration and withstood with mute stoicism the turgid oratory of the mayor which accompanied the slip of crimson ribbon. That had ended his share of the ceremonies, but, naturally, formality forced him to remain. And it was formality, chiefly—the type that couldn't allow him to yawn noisily or to swing a foot comfortably onto a chair seat—that made him long to be in space, where he belonged.

The Siwennese delegation, with Ducem Barr a lionized member, signed the Convention, and Siwenna became the first province to pass directly from the Empire's political rule to the Foundation's economic one.

Five Imperial Ships of the Line—captured when Siwenna rebelled behind the lines of the Empire's Border Fleet—flashed overhead, huge and massive, detonating a roaring salute as they passed over the city.

Nothing but drinking, etiquette, and small talk now—

A voice called him. It was Forell; the man who, Devers realized coldly, could buy twenty of him with a morning's profits—but a Forell who now crooked a finger at him with genial condescension.

He stepped out upon the balcony into the cool night wind, and bowed properly, while scowling into his bristling beard. Barr was there, too; smiling. He said, "Devers, you'll have to come to my rescue. I'm being accused of modesty, a horrible and thoroughly unnatural crime."

"Devers," Forell removed the fat cigar from the side of his mouth when he spoke, "Lord Barr claims that your trip to Cleon's capital had nothing to do with the recall of Riose."

"Nothing at all, sir." Devers was curt. "We never saw the Em-

peror. The reports we picked up on our way back concerning the
trial, showed it up to be the purest frame-up. There was a mess
of rigmarole about the general being tied up with subversive
interests at the court."

"And he was innocent?"

"Riose?" interposed Barr. "Yes! By the Galaxy, yes. Brodrig
was a traitor on general principles but was never guilty of the
specific accusations brought against him. It was a judicial farce;
but a necessary one, a predictable one, an inevitable one."

"By psycho-historical necessity, I presume." Forell rolled the
phrase sonorously with the humorous ease of long familiarity.

"Exactly." Barr grew serious. "It never penetrated earlier, but
once it was over and I could . . . well . . . look at the answers
in the back of the book, the problem became simple. We can see,
now, that the social background of the Empire makes wars of
conquest impossible for it. Under weak Emperors, it is torn apart
by generals competing for a worthless and surely death-bringing
throne. Under strong Emperors, the Empire is frozen into a para-
lytic rigor in which disintegration apparently ceases for the moment, but only at the sacrifice of all possible growth."

Forell growled bluntly through strong puffs, "You're not clear,
Lord Barr."

Barr smiled slowly. "Mm, I suppose so. It's the difficulty of not
being trained in psycho-history. Words are a pretty fuzzy substitute for mathematical equations. But let's see now—"

Barr considered, while Forell relaxed, back to railing, and
Devers looked into the velvet sky and thought wonderingly of
Trantor.

Then Barr said, "You see, sir, you—and Devers—and everyone
no doubt, had the idea that beating the Empire meant first prying apart the Emperor and his general. You, and Devers, and
everyone else were right—right all the time, as far as the principle of internal disunion was concerned.

"You were wrong, however, in thinking that this internal split
was something to be brought about by individual acts, by inspi-
rations of the moment. You tried bribery and lies. You appealed
to ambition and to fear. But you got nothing for all your pains.
In fact, appearances were worse after each attempt.

"And through all this wild threshing up of tiny ripples, the Seldon tidal wave continued onward, quietly—but quite irresistibly."

Ducem Barr turned away, and looked over the railing at the lights of a rejoicing city. He said, "There was a dead hand pushing all of us; the mighty general and the great Emperor; my world and your world—the dead hand of Hari Seldon. He knew that a man like Riose would have to fail, since it was his success that brought failure; and the greater the success, the surer the failure."

Forell said dryly, "I can't say you're getting clearer."

"A moment," continued Barr earnestly. "Look at the situation. A weak general could never have endangered us, obviously. A strong general during the time of a weak Emperor would never have endangered us, either; for he would have turned his arms towards a much more fruitful target. Events have shown that three-fourths of the Emperors of the last two centuries were rebel generals and rebel viceroys before they were Emperors.

"So it is only the combination of strong Emperor *and* strong general that can harm the Foundation; for a strong Emperor can not be dethroned easily, and a strong general is forced to turn outwards, past the frontiers.

"*But,* what keeps the Emperor strong? What kept Cleon strong? It's obvious. He is strong, because he permits no strong subjects. A courtier who becomes too rich, or a general who becomes too popular is dangerous. All the recent history of the Empire proves that to any Emperor intelligent enough to be strong.

"Riose won victories, so the Emperor grew suspicious. All the atmosphere of the times forced him to be suspicious. Did Riose refuse a bribe? Very suspicious; ulterior motives. Did his most trusted courtier suddenly favor Riose? Very suspicious; ulterior motives. It wasn't the individual acts that were suspicious. Anything else would have done—which is why our individual plots were unnecessary and rather futile. It was the *success* of Riose that was suspicious. So he was recalled, and accused, condemned, murdered. The Foundation wins again.

"Why, look, there is not a conceivable combination of events that does not result in the Foundation winning. It was inevitable; whatever Riose did, whatever we did."

The Foundation magnate nodded ponderously. "So! But what if the Emperor and the general had been the same person. Hey? What then? That's a case you didn't cover, so you haven't proved your point yet."

Barr shrugged. "I can't *prove* anything; I haven't the mathematics. But I appeal to your reason. With an Empire in which every aristocrat, every strong man, every pirate can aspire to the Throne—and, as history shows, often successfully—what would happen to even a strong Emperor who preoccupied himself with foreign wars at the extreme end of the Galaxy? How long would he have to remain away from the capital before somebody raised the standards of civil war and forced him home. The social environment of the Empire would make that time short.

"I once told Riose that not all the Empire's strength could swerve the dead hand of Hari Seldon."

"Good! Good!" Forell was expansively pleased. "Then you imply the Empire can never threaten us again."

"It seems to me so," agreed Barr. "Frankly, Cleon may not live out the year, and there's going to be a disputed succession almost as a matter of course, which might mean the *last* civil war for the Empire."

"Then," said Forell, "there are no more enemies."

Barr was thoughtful. "There's a Second Foundation."

"At the other end of the Galaxy? Not for centuries."

Devers turned suddenly at this, and his face was dark as he faced Forell. "There are internal enemies, perhaps."

"Are there?" asked Forell, coolly. "Who, for instance?"

"People, for instance, who might like to spread the wealth a bit, and keep it from concentrating too much *out* of the hands that work for it. See what I mean?"

Slowly, Forell's gaze lost its contempt and grew one with the anger of Devers' own.

PART II

THE MULE

11.

Bride and Groom

THE MULE   *Less is known of "The Mule" than of any character of comparable significance to Galactic history. His real name is unknown; his early life mere conjecture. Even the period of his greatest renown is known to us chiefly through the eyes of his antagonists and, principally, through those of a young bride. . . .*
ENCYCLOPEDIA GALACTICA

Bayta's first sight of Haven was entirely the contrary of spectacular. Her husband pointed it out—a dull star lost in the emptiness of the Galaxy's edge. It was past the last sparse clusters, to where straggling points of light gleamed lonely. And even among these it was poor and inconspicuous.

Toran was quite aware that as the earliest prelude to married life, the Red Dwarf lacked impressiveness and his lips curled self-consciously. "I know, Bay— It isn't exactly a proper change, is it? I mean from the Foundation to this."

"A horrible change, Toran. I should never have married you."

And when his face looked momentarily hurt, before he caught himself, she said with her special "cozy" tone, "All right, silly. Now let your lower lip droop and give me that special dying-duck look—the one just before you're supposed to bury your head on my shoulder, while I stroke your hair full of static electricity. You were fishing for some drivel, weren't you? You were expecting me to say 'I'd be happy anywhere with you, Toran!' or 'The interstellar depths themselves would be home, my sweet, were you but with me!' Now you admit it."

She pointed a finger at him and snatched it away an instant before his teeth closed upon it.

He said, "If I surrender, and admit you're right, will you prepare dinner?"

She nodded contentedly. He smiled, and just looked at her.

She wasn't beautiful on the grand scale to others—he admitted that—even if everybody did look twice. Her hair was dark and glossy, though straight, her mouth a bit wide—but her meticulous, close-textured eyebrows separated a white, unlined forehead from the warmest mahogany eyes ever filled with smiles.

And behind a very sturdily-built and staunchly-defended facade of practical, unromantic, hard-headedness towards life, there was just that little pool of softness that would never show if you poked for it, but could be reached if you knew just how—and never let on that you were looking for it.

Toran adjusted the controls unnecessarily and decided to relax. He was one interstellar jump, and then several milli-microparasecs "on the straight" before manipulation by hand was necessary. He leaned over backwards to look into the storeroom, where Bayta was juggling appropriate containers.

There was quite a bit of smugness about his attitude towards Bayta—the satisfied awe that marks the triumph of someone who has been hovering at the edge of an inferiority complex for three years.

After all he was a provincial—and not merely a provincial, but the son of a renegade Trader. And she was of the Foundation itself—and not merely that, but she could trace her ancestry back to Mallow.

And with all that, a tiny quiver underneath. To take her back to Haven, with its rock-world and cave-cities was bad enough. To have her face the traditional hostility of Trader for Foundation—nomad for city dweller—was worse.

Still— After supper, the last jump!

Haven was an angry crimson blaze, and the second planet was a ruddy patch of light with atmosphere-blurred rim and a half-sphere of darkness. Bayta leaned over the large view-table with its spidering of crisscross lines that centered Haven II neatly.

She said gravely, "I wish I had met your father first. If he takes a dislike to me—"

"Then," said Toran matter-of-factly, "you would be the first pretty girl to inspire *that* in him. Before he lost his arm and stopped roving around the Galaxy, he— Well, if you ask him about it, he'll talk to you about it till your ears wear down to a nubbin. After a while I got to thinking that he was embroidering; because he never told the same story twice the same way—"

Haven II was rushing up at them now. The landlocked sea wheeled ponderously below them, slate-gray in the lowering dimness and lost to sight, here and there, among the wispy clouds. Mountains jutted raggedly along the coast.

The sea became wrinkled with nearness and, as it veered off past the horizon just at the end, there was one vanishing glimpse of shore-hugging ice fields.

Toran grunted under the fierce deceleration, "Is your suit locked?"

Bayta's plump face was round and ruddy in the incasing sponge-foam of the internally-heated, skin-clinging costume.

The ship lowered crunchingly on the open field just short of the lifting of the plateau.

They climbed out awkwardly into the solid darkness of the outer-galactic night, and Bayta gasped as the sudden cold bit, and the thin wind swirled emptily. Toran seized her elbow and nudged her into an awkward run over the smooth, packed ground towards the sparking of artificial light in the distance.

The advancing guards met them halfway, and after a whispered exchange of words, they were taken onward. The wind and the cold disappeared when the gate of rock opened and then closed behind them. The warm interior, white with walllight, was filled with an incongruous humming bustle. Men looked up from their desks, and Toran produced documents.

They were waved onward after a short glance and Toran whispered to his wife, "Dad must have fixed up the preliminaries. The usual lapse here is about five hours."

They burst into the open and Bayta said suddenly, "Oh, *my*—"

The cave city was in daylight—the white daylight of a young sun. Not that there was a sun, of course. What should have been the sky was lost in the unfocused glow of an over-all brilliance. And the warm air was properly thick and fragrant with greenery.

Bayta said, "Why, Toran, it's beautiful."

Toran grinned with anxious delight. "Well, now, Bay, it isn't like anything on the Foundation, of course, but it's the biggest city on Haven II—twenty thousand people, you know—and you'll get to like it. No amusement palaces, I'm afraid, but no secret police either."

"Oh, Torie, it's just like a toy city. It's all white and pink—and so clean."

"Well—" Toran looked at the city with her. The houses were two stories high for the most part, and of the smooth vein rock indigenous to the region. The spires of the Foundation were missing, and the colossal community houses of the Old Kingdoms—but the smallness was there and the individuality; a relic of personal initiative in a Galaxy of mass life.

He snapped to sudden attention. "Bay— There's Dad! Right there—where I'm pointing, silly. Don't you see him?"

She did. It was just the impression of a large man, waving frantically, fingers spread wide as though groping wildly in air. The deep thunder of a drawn-out shout reached them. Bayta trailed her husband, rushing downwards over the close-cropped lawn. She caught sight of a smaller man, white-haired, almost lost to view behind the robust One-arm, who still waved and still shouted.

Toran cried over his shoulder, "It's my father's half brother. The one who's been to the Foundation. You know."

They met in the grass, laughing and incoherent, and Toran's father let out a final whoop for sheer joy. He hitched at his short jacket and adjusted the metal-chased belt that was his one concession to luxury.

His eyes shifted from one of the youngsters to the other, and then he said, a little out of breath, "You picked a rotten day to return home, boy!"

"What? Oh, it *is* Seldon's birthday, isn't it?"

"It is. I had to rent a car to make the trip here, and dragoon Randu to drive it. Not a public vehicle to be had at gun's point."

His eyes were on Bayta now, and didn't leave. He spoke to her more softly, "I have the crystal of you right here—and it's good, but I can see the fellow who took it was an amateur."

He had the small cube of transparency out of his jacket pocket and in the light the laughing little face within sprang to vivid colored life as a miniature Bayta.

"That one!" said Bayta. "Now I wonder why Toran should send that caricature. I'm surprised you let me come near you, sir."

"Are you now? Call me Fran. I'll have none of this fancy mess. For that, I think you can take my arm, and we'll go on to the car. Till now I never did think my boy knew what he was ever up to. I think I'll change that opinion. I think I'll *have* to change that opinion."

Toran said to his half uncle softly, "How is the old man these days? Does he still hound the women?"

Randu puckered up all over his face when he smiled. "When he can, Toran, when he can. There are times when he remembers that his next birthday will be his sixtieth, and that disheartens him. But he shouts it down, this evil thought, and then he is himself. He is a Trader of the ancient type. But you, Toran. Where did you find such a pretty wife?"

The young man chuckled and linked arms. "Do you want a three years' history at a gasp, uncle?"

It was in the small living room of the home that Bayta struggled out of her traveling cloak and hood and shook her hair loose. She sat down, crossing her knees, and returned the appreciative stare of this large, ruddy man.

She said, "I know what you're trying to estimate, and I'll help you; Age, twenty-four, height, five-four, weight, one-ten, educational specialty, history." She noticed that he always crooked his stand so as to hide the missing arm.

But now Fran leaned close and said, "Since you mention it—weight, one-twenty."

He laughed loudly at her flush. Then he said to the company in general, "You can always tell a woman's weight by her upper arm—with due experience, of course. Do you want a drink, Bay?"

"Among other things," she said, and they left together, while Toran busied himself at the book shelves to check for new additions.

Fran returned alone and said, "She'll be down later."

He lowered himself heavily into the large corner chair and

placed his stiff-jointed left leg on the stool before it. The laughter had left his red face, and Toran turned to face him.

Fran said, "Well, you're home, boy, and I'm glad you are. I like your woman. She's no whining ninny."

"I married her," said Toran simply.

"Well, that's another thing altogether, boy." His eyes darkened. "It's a foolish way to tie up the future. In my longer life, and more experienced, I never did such a thing."

Randu interrupted from the corner where he stood quietly. "Now Franssart, what comparisons are you making? Till your crash landing six years ago you were never in one spot long enough to establish residence requirements for marriage. And since then, who would have you?"

The one-armed man jerked erect in his seat and replied hotly, "Many, you snowy dotard—"

Toran said with hasty tact, "It's largely a legal formality, Dad. The situation has its conveniences."

"Mostly for the woman," grumbled Fran.

"And even if so," argued Randu, "it's up to the boy to decide. Marriage is an old custom among the Foundationers."

"The Foundationers are not fit models for an honest Trader," smoldered Fran.

Toran broke in again, "My wife is a Foundationer." He looked from one to the other, and then said quietly, "She's coming."

The conversation took a general turn after the evening meal, which Fran had spiced with three tales of reminiscence composed of equal parts of blood, women, profits, and embroidery. The small televisor was on, and some classic drama was playing itself out in an unregarded whisper. Randu had hitched himself into a more comfortable position on the low couch and gazed past the slow smoke of his long pipe to where Bayta had knelt down upon the softness of the white fur mat brought back once long ago from a trade mission and now spread out only upon the most ceremonious occasions.

"You have studied history, my girl?" he asked, pleasantly.

Bayta nodded. "I was the despair of my teachers, but I learned a bit, eventually."

"A citation for scholarship," put in Toran, smugly, "that's all!"

"And what did you learn?" proceeded Randu, smoothly.

"Everything? Now?" laughed the girl.

The old man smiled gently. "Well then, what do you think of the Galactic situation?"

"I think," said Bayta, concisely, "that a Seldon crisis is pending —and that if it isn't then away with the Seldon plan altogether. It is a failure."

(*"Whew,"* muttered Fran, from his corner. "What a way to speak of Seldon." But he said nothing aloud.)

Randu sucked at his pipe speculatively. "Indeed? Why do you say that? I was to the Foundation, you know, in my younger days, and I, too, once thought great dramatic thoughts. But, now, why do you say that?"

"Well," Bayta's eyes misted with thought as she curled her bare toes into the white softness of the rug and nestled her little chin in one plump hand, "it seems to me that the whole essence of Seldon's plan was to create a world better than the ancient one of the Galactic Empire. It was falling apart, that world, three centuries ago, when Seldon first established the Foundation—and if history speaks truly, it was falling apart of the triple disease of inertia, despotism, and maldistribution of the goods of the universe."

Randu nodded slowly, while Toran gazed with proud, luminous eyes at his wife, and Fran in the corner clucked his tongue and carefully refilled his glass.

Bayta said, "If the story of Seldon is true, he foresaw the complete collapse of the Empire through his laws of psycho-history, and was able to predict the necessary thirty thousand years of barbarism before the establishment of a new Second Empire to restore civilization and culture to humanity. It was the whole aim of his life-work to set up such conditions as would insure a speedier rejuvenation."

The deep voice of Fran burst out, "And that's why he established the two Foundations, honor be to his name."

"And that's why he established the two Foundations," assented Bayta. "Our Foundation was a gathering of the scientists of the dying Empire intended to carry on the science and learning of man to new heights. And the Foundation was so situated in space and the historical environment was such that through the careful calculations of his genius, Seldon foresaw that in one thousand years, it would become a newer, greater Empire."

There was a reverent silence.

The girl said softly, "It's an old story. You all know it. For almost three centuries every human being of the Foundation has known it. But I thought it would be appropriate to go through it—just quickly. Today *is* Seldon's birthday, you know, and even if I *am* of the Foundation, and you are of Haven, we have that in common—"

She lit a cigarette slowly, and watched the glowing tip absently. "The laws of history are as absolute as the laws of physics, and if the probabilities of error are greater, it is only because history does not deal with as many humans as physics does atoms, so that individual variations count for more. Seldon predicted a series of crises through the thousand years of growth, each of which would force a new turning of our history into a pre-calculated path. It is those crises which direct us—and therefore a crisis must come now.

"Now!" she repeated, forcefully. "It's almost a century since the last one, and in that century, every vice of the Empire has been repeated in the Foundation. Inertia! Our ruling class knows one law; no change. Despotism! They know one rule; force. Maldistribution! They know one desire; to hold what is theirs."

"While others starve!" roared Fran suddenly with a mighty blow of his fist upon the arm of his chair. "Girl, your words are pearls. The fat guts on their moneybags ruin the Foundation, while the brave Traders hide their poverty on dregs of worlds like Haven. It's a disgrace to Seldon, a casting of dirt in his face, a spewing in his beard." He raised his arm high, and then his face lengthened. "If I had my other arm! If—once—they had listened to me!"

"Dad," said Toran, "take it easy."

"Take it easy. Take it easy," his father mimicked savagely. "We'll live here and die here forever—and you say, take it easy."

"That's our modern Lathan Devers," said Randu, gesturing with his pipe, "this Fran of ours. Devers died in the slave mines eighty years ago with your husband's great-grandfather, because he lacked wisdom and didn't lack heart—"

"Yes, by the Galaxy, I'd do the same if I were he," swore Fran. "Devers was the greatest Trader in history—greater than the overblown windbag, Mallow, the Foundationers worship. If the cutthroats who lord the Foundation killed him because he loved justice, the greater the blood-debt owed them."

"Go on, girl," said Randu. "Go on, or, surely, he'll talk all the night and rave all the next day."

"There's nothing to go on about," she said, with a sudden gloom. "There must be a crisis, but I don't know how to make one. The progressive forces on the Foundation are oppressed fearfully. You Traders may have the will, but you are hunted and disunited. If all the forces of good will in and out of the Foundation could combine—"

Fran's laugh was a raucous jeer. "Listen to her, Randu, listen to her. In and out of the Foundation, she says. Girl, girl, there's no hope in the flab-sides of the Foundation. Among them some hold the whip and the rest are whipped—dead whipped. Not enough spunk left in the whole rotten world to outface one good Trader."

Bayta's attempted interruptions broke feebly against the overwhelming wind.

Toran leaned over and put a hand over her mouth. "Dad," he said, coldly, "you've never been on the Foundation. You know nothing about it. I tell you that the underground there is brave and daring enough. I could tell you that Bayta was one of them—"

"All right, boy, no offense. Now, where's the cause for anger?" He was genuinely perturbed.

Toran drove on fervently, "The trouble with you, Dad, is that you've got a provincial outlook. You think because some hundred thousand Traders scurry into holes on an unwanted planet at the end of nowhere, that they're a great people. Of course, any tax collector from the Foundation that gets here never leaves again, but that's cheap heroism. What would you do if the Foundation sent a fleet?"

"We'd blast them," said Fran, sharply.

"And get blasted—with the balance in their favor. You're outnumbered, outarmed, outorganized—and as soon as the Foundation thinks it worth its while, you'll realize that. So you had better seek your allies—on the Foundation itself, if you can."

"Randu," said Fran, looking at his brother like a great, helpless bull.

Randu took his pipe away from his lips, "The boy's right, Fran. When you listen to the little thoughts deep inside you, you know he is. But they're uncomfortable thoughts, so you drown them out with that roar of yours. But they're still there. Toran, I'll tell you why I brought all this up."

He puffed thoughtfully awhile, then dipped his pipe into the neck of the tray, waited for the silent flash, and withdrew it clean. Slowly, he filled it again with precise tamps of his little finger.

He said, "Your little suggestion of Foundation's interest in us, Toran, is to the point. There have been two recent visits lately—for tax purposes. The disturbing point is that the second visitor was accompanied by a light patrol ship. They landed in Gleiar City—giving us the miss for a change—and they never lifted off again, naturally. But now they'll surely be back. Your father is aware of all this, Toran, he really is.

"Look at the stubborn rakehell. He knows Haven is in trouble, and he knows we're helpless, but he repeats his formulas. It warms and protects him. But once he's had his say, and roared his defiance, and feels he's discharged his duty as a man and a Bull Trader, why he's as reasonable as any of us."

"Any of who?" asked Bayta.

He smiled at her. "We've formed a little group, Bayta—just in our city. We haven't done anything, yet. We haven't even managed to contact the other cities yet, but it's a start."

"But towards what?"

Randu shook his head. "We don't know—yet. We hope for a miracle. We have decided that, as you say, a Seldon crisis must be at hand." He gestured widely upwards. "The Galaxy is full of the chips and splinters of the broken Empire. The generals swarm. Do you suppose the time may come when one will grow bold?"

Bayta considered, and shook her head decisively, so that the long straight hair with the single inward curl at the end swirled about her ears. "No, not a chance. There's not one of those generals who doesn't know that an attack on the Foundation is suicide. Bel Riose of the old Empire was a better man than any of them, and he attacked with the resources of a galaxy, and couldn't win against the Seldon Plan. Is there one general that doesn't know that?"

"But what if we spur them on?"

"Into where? Into an atomic furnace? With what could you possibly spur them?"

"Well, there is one—a new one. In this past year or two, there has come word of a strange man whom they call the Mule."

"The Mule?" She considered. "Ever hear of him, Torie?"

Toran shook his head. She said, "What about him?"

"I don't know. But he wins victories at, they say, impossible odds. The rumors may be exaggerated, but it would be interesting, in any case, to become acquainted with him. Not every man with sufficient ability and sufficient ambition would believe in Hari Seldon and his laws of psycho-history. We could encourage that disbelief. He might attack."

"And the Foundation would win."

"Yes—but not necessarily easily. It might be a crisis, and we could take advantage of such a crisis to force a compromise with the despots of the Foundation. At the worst, they would forget us long enough to enable us to plan farther."

"What do you think, Torie?"

Toran smiled feebly and pulled at a loose brown curl that fell over one eye. "The way he describes it, it can't hurt; but who is the Mule? What do you know of him, Randu?"

"Nothing yet. For that, we could use you, Toran. And your wife, if she's willing. We've talked of this, your father and I. We've talked of this thoroughly."

"In what way, Randu? What do you want of us?" The young man cast a quick inquisitive look at his wife.

"Have you had a honeymoon?"

"Well . . . yes . . . if you can call the trip from the Foundation a honeymoon."

"How about a better one on Kalgan? It's semitropical—beaches—

water sports—bird hunting—quite the vacation spot. It's about seven thousand parsecs in—not too far."

"What's on Kalgan?"

"The Mule! His men, at least. He took it last month, and without a battle, though Kalgan's warlord broadcast a threat to blow the planet to ionic dust before giving it up."

"Where's the warlord now?"

"He isn't," said Randu, with a shrug. "What do you say?"

"But what are we to do?"

"I don't know. Fran and I are old; we're provincial. The Traders of Haven are all essentially provincial. Even you say so. Our trading is of a very restricted sort, and we're not the Galaxy roamers our ancestors were. Shut up, Fran! But you two know the Galaxy. Bayta, especially, speaks with a nice Foundation accent. We merely wish whatever you can find out. If you can make contact . . . but we wouldn't expect that. Suppose you two think it over. You can meet our entire group if you wish . . . oh, not before next week. You ought to have some time to catch your breath."

There was a pause and then Fran roared, "Who wants another drink? I mean, besides me?"

12.

Captain and Mayor

Captain Han Pritcher was unused to the luxury of his surroundings and by no means impressed. As a general thing, he discouraged self-analysis and all forms of philosophy and metaphysics not directly connected with his work.

It helped.

His work consisted largely of what the War Department called "intelligence," the sophisticates, "espionage," and the romanticists, "spy stuff." And, unfortunately, despite the frothy shrillness of the televisors, "intelligence," "espionage," and "spy stuff" are at best a sordid business of routine betrayed and bad faith. It is excused by society since it is in the "interest of the State," but since philosophy seemed always to lead Captain Pritcher to the conclusion that even in that holy interest, society is much more easily soothed than one's own conscience—he discouraged philosophy.

And now, in the luxury of the mayor's anteroom, his thoughts turned inward despite himself.

Men had been promoted over his head continuously, though of lesser ability—that much was admitted. He had withstood an eternal rain of black marks and official reprimands, and survived it. And stubbornly he had held to his own way in the firm belief that insubordination in that same holy "interest of the State" would yet be recognized for the service it was.

So here he was in the anteroom of the mayor—with five soldiers as a respectful guard, and probably a court-martial awaiting him.

The heavy, marble doors rolled apart smoothly, silently, revealing satiny walls, a red plastic carpeting, and two more marble doors, metal-inlaid, within. Two officials in the straight-lined costume of three centuries back, stepped out, and called:

"An audience to Captain Han Pritcher of Information."

They stepped back with a ceremonious bow as the captain started forward. His escort stopped at the outer door, and he entered the inner alone.

On the other side of the doors, in a large room strangely simple, behind a large desk strangely angular, sat a small man, almost lost in the immensity.

Mayor Indbur—successively the third of that name—was the grandson of the first Indbur, who had been brutal and capable; and who had exhibited the first quality in spectacular fashion by his manner of seizing power, and the latter by the skill with which he put an end to the last farcical remnants of free election and the even greater skill with which he maintained a relatively peaceful rule.

Mayor Indbur was also the son of the second Indbur, who was the first Mayor of the Foundation to succeed to his post by right of birth—and who was only half his father, for he was merely brutal.

So Mayor Indbur was the third of the name and the second to succeed by right of birth, and he was the least of the three, for he was neither brutal nor capable—but merely an excellent bookkeeper born wrong.

Indbur the Third was a peculiar combination of ersatz characteristics to all but himself.

To him, a stilted geometric love of arrangement was "system," an indefatigable and feverish interest in the pettiest facets of day-to-day bureaucracy was "industry," indecision when right was "caution," and blind stubbornness when wrong, "determination."

And withal he wasted no money, killed no man needlessly, and meant extremely well.

If Captain Pritcher's gloomy thoughts ran along these lines as he remained respectfully in place before the large desk, the wooden arrangement of his features yielded no insight into the fact. He neither coughed, shifted weight, nor shuffled his feet until the thin face of the mayor lifted slowly as the busy stylus ceased in its task of marginal notations, and a sheet of close-printed paper was lifted from one neat stack and placed upon another neat stack.

Mayor Indbur clasped his hands carefully before him, deliberately refraining from disturbing the careful arrangement of desk accessories.

He said, in acknowledgment, "Captain Han Pritcher of Information."

And Captain Pritcher in strict obedience to protocol bent one knee nearly to the ground and bowed his head until he heard the words of release.

"Arise, Captain Pritcher!"

The mayor said with an air of warm sympathy, "You are here, Captain Pritcher, because of certain disciplinary action taken against yourself by your superior officer. The papers concerning such action have come, in the ordinary course of events, to my notice, and since no event in the Foundation is of disinterest to me, I took the trouble to ask for further information on your case. You are not, I hope, surprised."

Captain Pritcher said unemotionally, "Excellence, no. Your justice is proverbial."

"Is it? Is it?" His tone was pleased, and the tinted contact lenses he wore caught the light in a manner that imparted a hard, dry gleam to his eyes. Meticulously, he fanned out a series of metal-bound folders before him. The parchment sheets within crackled sharply as he turned them, his long finger following down the line as he spoke.

"I have your record here, captain—complete. You are forty-three and have been an Officer of the Armed Forces for seventeen years. You were born in Loris, of Anacreonian parents, no serious childhood diseases, an attack of myo . . . well, that's of no importance . . . education, pre-military, at the Academy of Sciences, major, hyper-engines, academic standing . . . hm-m-m, very good, you are to be congratulated . . . entered the Army as Under-Officer on the one hundred second day of the 293rd year of the Foundation Era."

He lifted his eyes momentarily as he shifted the first folder, and opened the second.

"You see," he said, "in my administration, nothing is left to chance. Order! System!"

He lifted a pink, scented jelly-globule to his lips. It was his one vice, and but dolingly indulged in. Witness the fact that the mayor's desk lacked that almost-inevitable atom-flash for the disposal of dead tobacco. For the mayor did not smoke.

Nor, as a matter of course, did his visitors.

The mayor's voice droned on, methodically, slurringly, mumblingly—now and then interspersed with whispered comments of equally mild and equally ineffectual commendation or reproof.

Slowly, he replaced the folders as originally, in a single neat pile.

"Well, captain," he said, briskly, "your record is unusual. Your ability is outstanding, it would seem, and your services valuable beyond question. I note that you have been wounded in the line of duty twice, and that you have been awarded the Order of Merit for bravery beyond the call of duty. Those are facts not lightly to be minimized."

Captain Pritcher's expressionless face did not soften. He remained stiffly erect. Protocol required that a subject honored by an audience with the mayor may not sit down—a point perhaps needlessly reinforced by the fact that only one chair existed in the room, the one underneath the mayor. Protocol further required no statements other than those needed to answer a direct question.

The mayor's eyes bore down hard upon the soldier and his voice grew pointed and heavy. "However, you have not been promoted in ten years, and your superiors report, over and over again, of the unbending stubbornness of your character. You are reported to be chronically insubordinate, incapable of maintaining a correct attitude towards superior officers, apparently uninterested in maintaining frictionless relationships with your colleagues, and an incurable troublemaker, besides. How do you explain that, captain?"

"Excellence, I do what seems right to me. My deeds on behalf of the State, and my wounds in that cause bear witness that what seems right to me is also in the interest of the State."

"A soldierly statement, captain, but a dangerous doctrine. More of that, later. Specifically, you are charged with refusing an assignment three times in the face of orders signed by my legal delegates. What have you to say to that?"

"Excellence, the assignment lacks significance in a critical time, where matters of first importance are being ignored."

"Ah, and who tells you these matters you speak of are of the first importance at all, and if they are, who tells you further that they are ignored?"

"Excellence, these things are quite evident to me. My experience and my knowledge of events—the value of neither of which my superiors deny—make it plain."

"But, my good captain, are you blind that you do not see that by arrogating to yourself the right to determine Intelligence policy, you usurp the duties of your superior?"

"Excellence, my duty is primarily to the state, and not to my superior."

"Fallacious, for your superior has his superior, and that superior is myself, and I am the State. But come, you shall have no cause to complain of this justice of mine that you say is proverbial. State in your own words the nature of the breach in discipline that has brought all this on."

"Excellence, my duty is primarily to the State, and not to my living the life of a retired merchant mariner upon the world of Kalgan. My instructions were to direct Foundation activity upon the planet, perfect an organization to act as check upon the warlord of Kalgan, particularly as regards his foreign policy."

"This is known to me. Continue!"

"Excellence, my reports have continually stressed the strategic positions of Kalgan and the systems it controls. I have reported on the ambition of the warlord, his resources, his determination to extend his domain and his essential friendliness—or, perhaps, neutrality—towards the Foundation."

"I have read your reports thoroughly. Continue!"

"Excellence, I returned two months ago. At that time, there was no sign of impending war; no sign of anything but an almost superfluity of ability to repel any conceivable attack. One month ago, an unknown soldier of fortune, took Kalgan without a fight. The man who was once warlord of Kalgan is apparently no longer alive. Men do not speak of treason—they speak only of the power and genius of this strange condottiere—this Mule."

"This who?" the mayor leaned forward, and looked offended.

"Excellence, he is known as the Mule. He is spoken of little, in a factual sense, but I have gathered the scraps and fragments of knowledge and winnowed out the most probable of them. He is apparently a man of neither birth nor standing. His father, unknown. His mother, dead in childbirth. His upbringing, that of a vagabond. His education, that of the tramp worlds, and the backwash alleys of space. He has no name other than that of the Mule, a name reportedly applied by himself to himself, and signifying, by popular explanation, his immense physical strength, and stubbornness of purpose."

"What is his military strength, captain? Never mind his physique."

"Excellence, men speak of huge fleets, but in this they may be influenced by the strange fall of Kalgan. The territory he controls is not large, though its exact limits are not capable of definite determination. Nevertheless, this man must be investigated."

"Hm-m-m. So! So!" The mayor fell into a reverie, and slowly with twenty-four strokes of his stylus drew six squares in hexagonal arrangements upon the blank top sheet of a pad, which he tore off, folded neatly in three parts and slipped into the wastepaper slot at his right hand. It slid towards a clean and silent atomic disintegration.

"Now then, tell me, captain, what is the alternative? You have told me what 'must' be investigated. What have you been *ordered* to investigate?"

"Excellence, there is a rat hole in space that, it seems does not pay its taxes."

"Ah, and is that all? You are not aware, and have not been told that these men who do not pay their taxes, are descendants of the wild Traders of our early days—anarchists, rebels, social maniacs who claim Foundation ancestry and deride Foundation culture. You are not aware, and have not been told, that this rat hole in space, is not one, but many; that these rat holes are in greater number than we know; that these rat holes conspire together, one with the other, and all with the criminal elements that still exist throughout Foundation territory. Even here, captain, even here!"

The mayor's momentary fire subsided quickly. "You are not aware, captain?"

"Excellence, I have been told all this. But as servant of the State, I must serve faithfully—and he serves most faithfully who serves Truth. Whatever the political implications of these dregs of the ancient Traders—the warlords who have inherited the splinters of the old Empire have the power. The Traders have neither arms nor resources. They have not even unity. I am not a tax collector to be sent on a child's errand."

"Captain Pritcher, you are a soldier, and count guns. It is a failing to be allowed you up to the point where it involves disobedience to myself. Take care. My justice is not simply weakness. Captain, it has already been proven that the generals of the Imperial Age and the warlords of the present age are equally impotent against us. Seldon's science which predicts the course of the Foundation is based, not on individual heroism, as you seem to believe, but on the social and economic trends of history. We have passed successfully through four crises already, have we not?"

"Excellence, we have. Yet Seldon's science is known—only to Seldon. We ourselves have but faith. In the first three crises, as I have been carefully taught, the Foundation was led by wise leaders who foresaw the nature of the crises and took the proper precautions. Otherwise—who can say?"

"Yes, captain, but you omit the fourth crisis. Come, captain, we had no leadership worthy of the name then, and we faced the cleverest opponent, the heaviest armor, the strongest force of all. Yet we won by the inevitability of history."

"Excellence, that is true. But this history you mention became inevitable only after we had fought desperately for over a year. The inevitable victory we won cost us half a thousand ships and half a million men. Excellence, Seldon's plan helps those who help themselves."

Mayor Indbur frowned and grew suddenly tired of his patient exposition. It occurred to him that there was a fallacy in condescension, since it was mistaken for permission to argue eternally; to grow contentious; to wallow in dialectic.

He said, stiffly, "Nevertheless, captain, Seldon guarantees victory over the warlords, and I can not, in these busy times, indulge in a dispersal of effort. These Traders you dismiss are Foundation-derived. A war with them would be a civil war. Seldon's plan makes no guarantee there for us—since they *and* we are Foundation. So they must be brought to heel. You have your orders."

"Excellence—"

"You have been asked no question, captain. You have your orders. You will obey those orders. Further argument of any sort with myself or those representing myself will be considered treason. You are excused."

Captain Han Pritcher knelt once more, then left with slow, backward steps.

Mayor Indbur, third of his name, and second mayor of Foundation history to be so by right of birth, recovered his equilibrium, and lifted another sheet of paper from the neat stack at his left. It was a report on the saving of funds due to the reduction of the quantity of metal-foam edging on the uniforms of the police force. Mayor Indbur crossed out a superfluous comma, corrected a misspelling, made three marginal notations, and placed it upon the neat stack at his right. He lifted another sheet of paper from the neat stack at his left—

Captain Han Pritcher of Information found a Personal Capsule waiting for him when he returned to barracks. It contained orders, terse and redly underlined with a stamped "URGENT" across it, and the whole initialed with a precise, capital "I".

Captain Han Pritcher was ordered to the "rebel world called Haven" in the strongest terms.

Captain Han Pritcher, alone in his light one-man speedster, set his course quietly and calmly for Kalgan. He slept that night the sleep of a successfully stubborn man.

13.

Lieutenant and Clown

If, from a distance of seven thousand parsecs, the fall of Kalgan to the armies of the Mule had produced reverberations that had excited the curiosity of an old Trader, the apprehension of a dogged captain, and the annoyance of a meticulous mayor—to those on Kalgan itself, it produced nothing and excited no one. It is the invariable lesson to humanity that distance in time, and in space as well, lends focus. It is not recorded, incidentally, that the lesson has ever been permanently learned.

Kalgan was—Kalgan. It alone of all that quadrant of the Galaxy seemed not to know that the Empire had fallen, that the Stannells no longer ruled, that greatness had departed, and peace had disappeared.

Kalgan was the luxury world. With the edifice of mankind crumbling, it maintained its integrity as a producer of pleasure, a buyer of gold and a seller of leisure.

It escaped the harsher vicissitudes of history, for what conqueror would destroy or even seriously damage a world so full of the ready cash that would buy immunity.

Yet even Kalgan had finally become the headquarters of a warlord and its softness had been tempered to the exigencies of war.

Its tamed jungles, its mildly modeled shores, and its garishly glamorous cities echoed to the march of imported mercenaries and impressed citizens. The worlds of its province had been armed and its money invested in battleships rather than bribes for the first time in its history. Its ruler proved beyond doubt that he was determined to defend what was his and eager to seize what was others.

He was a great one of the Galaxy, a war and peace maker, a builder of Empire, an establisher of dynasty.

And an unknown with a ridiculous nickname had taken him—and his arms—and his budding Empire—and had not even fought a battle.

So Kalgan was as before, and its uniformed citizens hurried back to their older life, while the foreign professionals of war merged easily into the newer bands that descended.

Again as always, there were the elaborate luxury hunts for the cultivated animal life of the jungles that never took human life; and the speedster bird-chases in the air above, that was fatal only to the Great Birds.

In the cities, the escapers of the Galaxy could take their varieties of pleasure to suit their purse, from the ethereal sky-palaces of spectacle and fantasy that opened their doors to the masses at the jingle of half a credit, to the unmarked, unnoted haunts to which only those of great wealth were of the cognoscenti.

To the vast flood, Toran and Bayta added not even a trickle. They registered their ship in the huge common hangar on the East Peninsula, and gravitated to that compromise of the middle-classes, the Inland Sea—where the pleasures were yet legal, and even respectable, and the crowds not yet beyond endurance.

Bayta wore dark glasses against the light, and a thin, white robe against the heat. Warm-tinted arms, scarcely the goldener for the sun, clasped her knees to her, and she stared with firm, abstracted gaze at the length of her husband's outstretched body —almost shimmering in the brilliance of white sun-splendor.

"Don't overdo it," she had said at first, but Toran was of a dying-red star. Despite three years of the Foundation, sunlight was a luxury, and for four days now his skin, treated beforehand for ray resistance, had not felt the harshness of clothing, except for the brief shorts.

Bayta huddled close to him on the sand and they spoke in whispers.

Toran's voice was gloomy, as it drifted upwards from a relaxed face, "No, I admit we're nowhere. But where is he? Who is he? This mad world says nothing of him. Perhaps he doesn't exist."

"He exists," replied Bayta, with lips that didn't move. "He's clever, that's all. And your uncle is right. He's a man we could use—if there's time."

A short pause. Toran whispered, "Know what I've been doing, Bay? I'm just daydreaming myself into a sun-stupor. Things figure themselves out so neatly—so sweetly." His voice nearly trailed off, then returned, "Remember the way Dr. Amann talked back at college, Bay. The Foundation can never lose, but that does not mean the *rulers* of the Foundation can't. Didn't the real history of the Foundation begin when Salvor Hardin kicked out the Encyclopedists and took over the planet Terminus as the first mayor? And then in the next century, didn't Hober Mallow gain power by methods almost as drastic? That's *twice* the rulers were defeated, so it can be done. So why not by us?"

"It's the oldest argument in the books, Torie. What a waste of good reverie."

"Is it? Follow it out. What's Haven? Isn't it part of the Foundation? It's simply part of the external proletariat, so to speak. If we become top dog, it's still the Foundation winning, and only the current rulers losing."

"Lots of difference between 'we can' and 'we will.' You're just jabbering."

Toran squirmed. "Nuts, Bay, you're just in one of your sour, green moods. What do you want to spoil my fun for? I'll just go to sleep if you don't mind."

But Bayta was craning her head, and suddenly—quite a *non sequitur*—she giggled, and removed her glasses to look down the beach with only her palm shading her eyes.

Toran looked up, then lifted and twisted his shoulders to follow her glance.

Apparently, she was watching a spindly figure, feet in air, who teetered on his hands for the amusement of a haphazard crowd. It was one of the swarming acrobatic beggars of the shore, whose supple joints bent and snapped for the sake of the thrown coins.

A beach guard was motioning him on his way and with a surprising one-handed balance, the clown brought a thumb to his nose in an upside-down gesture. The guard advanced threateningly and reeled backward with a foot in his stomach. The clown righted himself without interrupting the motion of the initial kick and was away, while the frothing guard was held off by a thoroughly unsympathetic crowd.

The clown made his way raggedly down the beach. He brushed past many, hesitated often, stopped nowhere. The original crowd had dispersed. The guard had departed.

"He's a queer fellow," said Bayta, with amusement, and Toran agreed indifferently. The clown was close enough now to be seen clearly. His thin face drew together in front into a nose of generous planes and fleshy tip that seemed all but prehensile. His long, lean limbs and spidery body, accentuated by his costume, moved easily and with grace, but with just a suggestion of having been thrown together at random.

To look was to smile.

The clown seemed suddenly aware of their regard, for he stopped after he had passed, and, with a sharp turn, approached. His large, brown eyes fastened upon Bayta.

She found herself disconcerted.

The clown smiled, but it only saddened his beaked face, and when he spoke it was with the soft, elaborate phrasing of the Central Sectors.

"Were I to use the wits the good Spirits gave me," he said, "then I would say this lady can not exist—for what sane man would hold a dream to be reality. Yet rather would I not be sane and lend belief to charmed, enchanted eyes."

Bayta's own eyes opened wide. She said, "Wow!"

Toran laughed, "Oh, you enchantress. Go ahead, Bay, that deserves a five-credit piece. Let him have it."

But the clown was forward with a jump. "No, my lady, mistake me not. I spoke for money not at all, but for bright eyes and sweet face."

"Well, *thanks*," then, to Toran, "Golly, you think the sun's in his eyes?"

"Yet not alone for eyes and face," babbled the clown, as his words hurled past each other in heightened frenzy, "but also for a mind, clear and sturdy—and kind as well."

Toran rose to his feet, reached for the white robe he had crooked his arm about for four days, and slipped into it. "Now, bud," he said, "suppose you tell me what you want, and stop annoying the lady."

The clown fell back a frightened step, his meager body cringing. "Now, sure I meant no harm. I am a stranger here, and it's been said I am of addled wits; yet there is something in a face that I can read. Behind this lady's fairness, there is a heart that's kind, and that would help me in my trouble for all I speak so boldly."

"Will five credits cure your trouble?" said Toran, dryly, and held out the coin.

But the clown did not move to take it, and Bayta said, "Let me talk to him, Torie." She added swiftly, and in an undertone, "There's no use being annoyed at his silly way of talking. That's just his dialect; and our speech is probably as strange to him."

She said, "What is your trouble? You're not worried about the guard, are you? He won't bother you."

"Oh, no, not he. He's but a windlet that blows the dust about my ankles. There is another that I flee, and he is a storm that sweeps the worlds aside and throws them plunging at each other. A week ago, I ran away, have slept in city streets, and hid in city crowds. I've looked in many faces for help in need. I find it here." He repeated the last phrase in softer, anxious tones, and his large eyes were troubled, "I find it here."

"Now," said Bayta, reasonably, "I would like to help, but really, friend, I'm no protection against a world-sweeping storm. To be truthful about it, I could use—"

There was an uplifted, powerful voice that bore down upon them.

"Now, then, you mud-spawned rascal—"

It was the beach guard, with a fire-red face, and snarling mouth, that approached at a run. He pointed with his low-power stun pistol.

"Hold him, you two. Don't let him get away." His heavy hand fell upon the clown's thin shoulder, so that a whimper was squeezed out of him.

Toran said, "What's he done?"

"What's he done? What's he done? Well, now, that's good!" The guard reached inside the dangling pocket attached to his belt, and removed a purple handkerchief, with which he mopped his bare neck. He said with relish, "I'll tell you what he's done. He's run away. The word's all over Kalgan and I would have recognized him before this if he had been on his feet instead of on his hawkface top." And he rattled his prey in a fierce good humor.

Bayta said with a smile, "Now where did he escape from, sir?"

The guard raised his voice. A crowd was gathering, pop-eyed and jabbering, and with the increase of audience, the guard's sense of importance increased in direct ratio.

"Where did he escape from?" he declaimed in high sarcasm. "Why, I suppose you've heard of the Mule, now."

All jabbering stopped, and Bayta felt a sudden iciness trickle down into her stomach. The clown had eyes only for her—he still quivered in the guard's brawny grasp.

"And who," continued the guard heavily, "would this infernal ragged piece be, but his lordship's own court fool who's run away." He jarred his captive with a massive shake, "Do you admit it, fool?"

There was only white fear for answer, and the soundless sibilance of Bayta's voice close to Toran's ear.

Toran stepped forward to the guard in friendly fashion, "Now, my man, suppose you take your hand away for just a while. This entertainer you hold has been dancing for us and has not yet danced out his fee."

"Here!" The guard's voice rose in sudden concern. "There's a reward—"

"You'll have it, if you can prove he's the man you want. Suppose you withdraw till then. You know that you're interfering with a guest, which could be serious for you."

"But you're interfering with his lordship and that *will* be serious for you." He shook the clown once again, "Return the man's fee, carrion."

Toran's hand moved quickly and the guard's stun pistol was wrenched away with half a finger nearly following it. The guard howled his pain and rage. Toran shoved him violently aside, and the clown, unhanded, scuttled behind him.

The crowd, whose fringes were now lost to the eye, paid little attention to the latest development. There was among them a craning of necks, and a centrifugal motion as if many had decided to increase their distance from the center of activity.

Then there was a bustle, and a rough order in the distance. A corridor formed itself and two men strode through, electric whips in careless readiness. Upon each purple blouse was designed an angular shaft of lightning with a splitting planet underneath.

A dark giant, in lieutenant's uniform, followed them; dark of skin, and hair, and scowl.

The dark man spoke with the dangerous softness that meant he had little need of shouting to enforce his whims. He said, "Are you the man who notified us?"

The guard was still holding his wrenched hand, and with a pain-distorted face mumbled, "I claim the reward, your mightiness, and I accuse that man—"

"You'll get your reward," said the lieutenant, without looking at him. He motioned curtly to his men, "Take him."

Toran felt the clown tearing at his robe with a maddened grip. He raised his voice and kept it from shaking, "I'm sorry, lieutenant; this man is mine."

The soldiers took the statement without blinking. One raised his whip casually, but the lieutenant's snapped order brought it down.

His dark mightiness swung forward and planted his square body before Toran, "Who are you?"

And the answer rang out, "A citizen of the Foundation."

It worked—with the crowd, at any rate. The pent-up silence broke into an intense hum. The Mule's name might excite fear, but it was, after all, a new name and scarcely stuck as deeply in the vitals as the old one of the Foundation—that had destroyed the Empire—and the fear of which ruled a quadrant of the Galaxy with ruthless despotism.

The lieutenant kept face. He said, "Are you aware of the identity of the man behind you?"

"I have been told he's a runaway from the court of your leader, but my only sure knowledge is that he is a friend of mine. You'll need firm proof of his identity to take him."

There were high-pitched sighs from the crowd, but the lieutenant let it pass. "Have you your papers of Foundation citizenship with you?"

"At my ship."

"You realize that your actions are illegal? I can have you shot."

"Undoubtedly. But then you would have shot a Foundation citizen and it is quite likely that your body would be sent to the Foundation—quartered—as part compensation. It's been done by other warlords."

The lieutenant wet his lips. The statement was true.

He said, "Your name?"

Toran followed up his advantage, "I will answer further questions at my ship. You can get the cell number at the Hangar; it is registered under the name 'Bayta'."

"You won't give up the runaway?"

"To the Mule, perhaps. Send your master!"

The conversation had degenerated to a whisper and the lieutenant turned sharply away.

"Disperse the crowd!" he said to his men, with suppressed ferocity.

The electric whips rose and fell. There were shrieks and a vast surge of separation and flight.

Toran interrupted his reverie only once on their way back to the Hangar. He said, almost to himself, "Galaxy, Bay, what a time I had! I was so scared—"

"Yes," she said, with a voice that still shook, and eyes that still showed something akin to worship, "it was quite out of character."

"Well, I still don't know what happened. I just got up there with a stun pistol that I wasn't even sure I knew how to use, and talked back to him. I don't know why I did it."

He looked across the aisle of the short-run air vessel that was carrying them out of the beach area, to the seat on which the Mule's clown scrunched up in sleep, and added distastefully, "It was the hardest thing I've ever done."

The lieutenant stood respectfully before the colonel of the garrison, and the colonel looked at him and said, "Well done. Your part's over now."

But the lieutenant did not retire immediately. He said darkly,

"The Mule has lost face before a mob, sir. It will be necessary to undertake disciplinary action to restore proper atmosphere of respect."

"Those measures have already been taken."

The lieutenant half turned, then, almost with resentment, "I'm willing to agree, sir, that orders are orders, but standing before that man with his stun pistol and swallowing his insolence whole, was the hardest thing I've ever done."

14.

The Mutant

The "hangar" on Kalgan is an institution peculiar unto itself, born of the need for the disposition of the vast number of ships brought in by the visitors from abroad, and the simultaneous and consequent vast need for living accommodations for the same. The original bright one who had thought of the obvious solution had quickly become a millionaire. His heirs—by birth or finance—were easily among the richest on Kalgan.

The "hangar" spreads fatly over square miles of territory, and "hangar" does not describe it at all sufficiently. It is essentially a hotel—for ships. The traveler pays in advance and his ship is awarded a berth from which it can take off into space at any desired moment. The visitor then lives in his ship as always. The ordinary hotel services such as the replacement of food and medical supplies at special rates, simple servicing of the ship itself, special intra-Kalgan transportation for a nominal sum are to be had, of course.

As a result, the visitor combines hangar space and hotel bill into one, at a saving. The owners sell temporary use of ground space at ample profits. The government collects huge taxes. Everyone has fun. Nobody loses. Simple!

The man who made his way down the shadow-borders of the wide corridors that connected the multitudinous wings of the "hangar" had in the past speculated on the novelty and usefulness of the system described above, but these were reflections for idle moments—distinctly unsuitable at present.

The ships hulked in their height and breadth down the long lines of carefully aligned cells, and the man discarded line after line. He was an expert at what he was doing now—and if his preliminary study of the hangar registry had failed to give specific information beyond the doubtful indication of a specific wing—

one containing hundreds of ships—his specialized knowledge could winnow those hundreds into one.

There was the ghost of a sigh in the silence, as the man stopped and faded down one of the lines; a crawling insect beneath the notice of the arrogant metal monsters that rested there.

Here and there the sparkling of light from a porthole would indicate the presence of an early returner from the organized pleasures to simpler—or more private—pleasures of his own.

The man halted, and would have smiled if he ever smiled. Certainly the convolutions of his brain performed the mental equivalent of a smile.

The ship he stopped at was sleek and obviously fast. The peculiarity of its design was what he wanted. It was not a usual model—and these days most of the ships of this quadrant of the Galaxy either imitated Foundation design or were built by Foundation technicians. But this was special. This was a Foundation ship—if only because of the tiny bulges in the skin that were the nodes of the protective screen that only a Foundation ship could possess. There were other indications, too.

The man felt no hesitation.

The electronic barrier strung across the line of the ships as a concession to privacy on the part of the management was not at all important to him. It parted easily, and without activating the alarm, at the use of the very special neutralizing force he had at his disposal.

So the first knowledge within the ship of the intruder without was the casual and almost friendly signal of the muted buzzer in the ship's living room that was the result of a palm placed over the little photocell just one side of the main air lock.

And while that successful search went on, Toran and Bayta felt only the most precarious security within the steel walls of the *Bayta*. The Mule's clown who had reported that within his narrow compass of body he held the lordly name of Magnifico Giganticus, sat hunched over the table and gobbled at the food set before him.

His sad, brown eyes lifted from his meal only to follow Bayta's movements in the combined kitchen and larder where she ate.

"The thanks of a weak one are of but little value," he muttered, "but you have them, for truly, in this past week, little but scraps have come my way—and for all my body is small, yet is my appetite unseemly great."

"Well, then, eat!" said Bayta, with a smile. "Don't waste your time on thanks. Isn't there a Central Galaxy proverb about gratitude that I once heard?"

"Truly there is, my lady. For a wise man, I have been told, once said, 'Gratitude is best and most effective when it does not evaporate itself in empty phrases.' But alas, my lady, I am but a mass of empty phrases, it would seem. When my empty phrases pleased the Mule, it brought me a court dress, and a grand name—for, see you, it was originally simply Bobo, one that pleases him not—and then when my empty phrases pleased him not, it would bring upon my poor bones beatings and whippings."

Toran entered from the pilot room, "Nothing to do now but wait, Bay. I hope the Mule is capable of understanding that a Foundation ship is Foundation territory."

Magnifico Giganticus, once Bobo, opened his eyes wide and exclaimed, "How great is the Foundation before which even the cruel servants of the Mule tremble."

"Have you heard of the Foundation, too?" asked Bayta, with a little smile.

"And who has not?" Magnifico's voice was a mysterious whisper. "There are those who say it is a world of great magic, of fires that can consume planets, and secrets of mighty strength. They say that not the highest nobility of the Galaxy could achieve the honor and deference considered only the natural due of a simple man who could say 'I am a citizen of the Foundation,'—were he only a salvage miner of space, or a nothing like myself."

Bayta said, "Now, Magnifico, you'll never finish if you make speeches. Here, I'll get you a little flavored milk. It's good."

She placed a pitcher of it upon the table and motioned Toran out of the room.

"Torie, what are we going to do now—about him?" and she motioned towards the kitchen.

"How do you mean?"

"If the Mule comes, are we going to give him up?"

"Well, what else, Bay?" He sounded harassed, and the gesture

with which he shoved back the moist curl upon his forehead testified to that.

He continued impatiently, "Before I came here I had a sort of
vague idea that all we had to do was to ask for the Mule, and
then get down to business—just business, you know, nothing
definite."

"I know what you mean, Torie. I wasn't much hoping to see the
Mule myself, but I did think we could pick up *some* firsthand
knowledge of the mess, and then pass it over to people who know
a little more about this interstellar intrigue. I'm no storybook
spy."

"You're not behind me, Bay." He folded his arms and frowned.
"What a situation! You'd never know there *was* a person like the
Mule, except for this last queer break. Do you suppose he'll come
for his clown?"

Bayta looked up at him, "I don't know that I want him to. I
don't know what to say or do. Do you?"

The inner buzzer sounded with its intermittent burring noise.
Bayta's lips moved wordlessly, "The Mule!"

Magnifico was in the doorway, eyes wide, his voice a whimper,
"The Mule?"

Toran murmured, "I've got to let them in."

A contact opened the air lock and the outer door closed behind
the newcomer. The scanner showed only a single shadowed
figure.

"It's only one person," said Toran, with open relief, and his
voice was almost shaky as he bent toward the signal tube, "Who
are you?"

"You'd better let me in and find out, hadn't you?" The words
came thinly out the receiver.

"I'll inform you that this is a Foundation ship and consequently
Foundation territory by international treaty."

"I know that."

"Come with your arms free, or I'll shoot. I'm well-armed."

"Done!"

Toran opened the inner door and closed contact on his blast
pistol, thumb hovering over the pressure point. There was the

sound of footsteps and then the door swung open, and Magnifico cried out, "It's not the Mule. It's but a man."

The "man" bowed to the clown somberly, "Very accurate. I'm not the Mule." He held his hands apart, "I'm not armed, and I come on a peaceful errand. You might relax and put the blast pistol away. Your hand isn't steady enough for my peace of mind."

"Who are you?" asked Toran, brusquely.

"I might ask *you* that," said the stranger, coolly, "since you're the one under false pretenses, not I."

"How so?"

"You're the one who claims to be a Foundation citizen when there's not an authorized Trader on the planet."

"That's not so. How would you know?"

"Because I *am* a Foundation citizen, and have my papers to prove it. Where are yours?"

"I think you'd better get out."

"I think not. If you know anything about Foundation methods, and despite your imposture you might, you'd know that if I don't return alive to my ship at a specified time, there'll be a signal at the nearest Foundation headquarters—so I doubt if your weapons will have much effect, practically speaking."

There was an irresolute silence and then Bayta said, calmly, "Put the blaster away, Toran, and take him at face value. He sounds like the real thing."

"Thank you," said the stranger.

Toran put his gun on the chair beside him, "Suppose you explain all this now."

The stranger remained standing. He was long of bone and large of limb. His face consisted of hard flat planes and it was somehow evident that he never smiled. But his eyes lacked hardness.

He said, "News travels quickly, especially when it is apparently beyond belief. I don't suppose there's a person on Kalgan who doesn't know that the Mule's men were kicked in the teeth today by two tourists from the Foundation. I knew of the important details before evening, and, as I said, there are no Foundation tourists aside from myself on the planet. We know about those things."

"Who are the 'we'?"

"'We' are—'we'! Myself for one! I knew you were at the Hangar—you had been overheard to say so. I had my ways of checking the registry, and my ways of finding the ship."

He turned to Bayta suddenly, "You're from the Foundation—by birth, aren't you?"

"Am I?"

"You're a member of the democratic opposition—they call it 'the underground.' I don't remember your name, but I do the face. You got out only recently—and wouldn't have if you were more important."

Bayta shrugged, "You know a lot."

"I do. You escaped with a man. That one?"

"Does it matter what I say?"

"No. I merely want a thorough mutual understanding. I believe that the password during the week you left so hastily was 'Seldon, Hardin, and Freedom.' Porfirat Hart was your section leader."

"Where'd you get that?" Bayta was suddenly fierce. "Did the police get him?" Toran held her back, but she shook herself loose and advanced.

The man from the Foundation said quietly, "Nobody has him. It's just that the underground spreads widely and in queer places. I'm Captain Han Pritcher of Information, and I'm a section leader myself—never mind under what name."

He waited, then said, "No, you don't have to believe me. In our business it is better to overdo suspicion than the opposite. But I'd better get past the preliminaries."

"Yes," said Toran, "suppose you do."

"May I sit down? Thanks." Captain Pritcher swung a long leg across his knee and let an arm swing loose over the back of the chair. "I'll start out by saying that I don't know what all this is about—from your angle. You two aren't from the Foundation, but it's not a hard guess that you're from one of the independent Trading worlds. That doesn't bother me overmuch. But out of curiosity, what do you want with that fellow, that clown you snatched to safety? You're risking your life to hold on to him."

"I can't tell you that."

"Hm-m-m. Well, I didn't think you would. But if you're waiting for the Mule himself to come behind a fanfarade of horns, drums, and electric organs—relax! The Mule doesn't work that way."

"What?" It came from both Toran and Bayta, and in the corner where Magnifico lurked with ears almost visibly expanded, there was a sudden joyful start.

"That's right. I've been trying to contact him myself, and doing a rather more thorough job of it than you two amateurs can. It won't work. The man makes no personal appearance, does not allow himself to be photographed or simulated, and is seen only by his most intimate associates."

"Is that supposed to explain your interest in us, captain?" questioned Toran.

"No. That clown is the key. That clown is one of the very few that *have* seen him. I want him. He may be the proof I need—and I need something. Galaxy knows—to awaken the Foundation."

"It needs awakening?" broke in Bayta with sudden sharpness. "Against what? And in what role do you act as alarm, that of rebel democrat or of secret police and provocateur?"

The captain's face set in its hard lines. "When the entire Foundation is threatened, Madame Revolutionary, both democrats and tyrants perish. Let us save the tyrants from a greater, that we may overthrow them in their turn."

"Who's the greater tyrant you speak of?" flared Bayta.

"The Mule! I know a bit about him, enough to have been my death several times over already, if I had moved less nimbly. Send the clown out of the room. This will require privacy."

"Magnifico," said Bayta, with a gesture, and the clown left without a sound.

The captain's voice was grave and intense, and low enough so that Toran and Bayta drew close.

He said, "The Mule is a shrewd operator—far too shrewd not to realize the advantage of the magnetism and glamour of personal leadership. If he gives that up, it's for a reason. That reason must be the fact that personal contact would reveal something that is of overwhelming importance *not* to reveal."

He waved aside questions, and continued more quickly, "I went back to his birthplace for this, and questioned people who for their knowledge will not live long. Few enough are still alive. They remember the baby born thirty years before—the death of his mother—his strange youth. *The Mule is not a human being!*"

And his two listeners drew back in horror at the misty implications. Neither understood, fully or clearly, but the menace of the phrase was definite.

The captain continued, "He is a mutant, and obviously from his subsequent career, a highly successful one. I don't know his powers or the exact extent to which he is what our thrillers would call a 'superman,' but the rise from nothing to the conqueror of Kalgan's warlord in two years is revealing. You see, don't you, the danger? Can a genetic accident of unpredictable biological properties be taken into account in the Seldon plan?"

Slowly, Bayta spoke, "I don't believe it. This is some sort of complicated trickery. Why didn't the Mule's men kill us when they could have, if he's a superman?"

"I told you that I don't know the extent of his mutation. He may not be ready, yet, for the Foundation, and it would be a sign of the greatest wisdom to resist provocation until ready. Suppose you let me speak to the clown."

The captain faced the trembling Magnifico, who obviously distrusted this huge, hard man who faced him.

The captain began slowly, "Have you seen the Mule with your own eyes?"

"I have but too well, respected sir. And felt the weight of his arm with my own body as well."

"I have no doubt of that. Can you describe him?"

"It is frightening to recall him, respected sir. He is a man of mighty frame. Against him, even you would be but a spindling. His hair is of a burning crimson, and with all my strength and weight I could not pull down his arm, once extended—not a hair's thickness." Magnifico's thinness seemed to collapse upon itself in a huddle of arms and legs. "Often, to amuse his generals or to amuse only himself, he would suspend me by one finger in my belt from a fearful height, while I chattered poetry. It was only after the twentieth verse that I was withdrawn, and each improvised and each a perfect rhyme, or else start over. He is a man of overpowering might, respected sir, and cruel in the use of his power—and his eyes, respected sir, no one sees."

"What? What's that last?"

"He wears spectacles, respected sir, of a curious nature. It is said that they are opaque and that he sees by a powerful magic that far transcends human powers. I have heard," and his voice was small and mysterious, "that to see his eyes is to see death; that he kills with his eyes, respected sir."

Magnifico's eyes wheeled quickly from one watching face to another. He quavered, "It is true. As I live, it is true."

Bayta drew a long breath, "Sounds like you're right, captain. Do you want to take over?"

"Well, let's look at the situation. You don't owe anything here? The hangar's barrier above is free?"

"I can leave any time."

"Then leave. The Mule may not wish to antagonize the Foundation, but he runs a frightful risk in letting Magnifico get away. It probably accounts for the hue and cry after the poor devil in the first place. So there may be ships waiting for you upstairs. If you're lost in space, who's to pin the crime?"

"You're right," agreed Toran, bleakly.

"However, you've got a shield and you're probably speedier than anything they've got, so as soon as you're clear of the atmosphere make the circle in neutral to the other hemisphere, then just cut a track outwards at top acceleration."

"Yes," said Bayta coldly, "and when we are back on the Foundation, what then, captain?"

"Why, you are then co-operative citizens of Kalgan, are you not? I know nothing to the contrary, do I?"

Nothing was said. Toran turned to the controls. There was an imperceptible lurch.

It was when Toran had left Kalgan sufficiently far in the rear to attempt his first interstellar jump, that Captain Pritcher's face first creased slightly—for no ship of the Mule had in any way attempted to bar their leaving.

"Looks like he's letting us carry off Magnifico," said Toran. "Not so good for your story."

"Unless," corrected the captain, "he wants us to carry him off, in which case it's not so good for the Foundation."

It was after the last jump, when within neutral-flight distance of the Foundation, that the first ultra-wave news broadcast reached the ship.

And there was one news item barely mentioned. It seemed that a warlord—unidentified by the bored speaker—had made representations to the Foundation concerning the forceful abduction of a member of his court. The announcer went on to the sports news.

Captain Pritcher said icily, "He's one step ahead of us after all." Thoughtfully, he added, "He's ready for the Foundation, and he uses this as an excuse for action. It makes things more difficult for us. We will have to act before we are really ready."

15.

The Psychologist

There was reason to the fact that the element known as "pure science" was the freest form of life on the Foundation. In a Galaxy where the predominance—and even survival—of the Foundation still rested upon the superiority of its technology—even despite its large access of physical power in the last century and a half—a certain immunity adhered to The Scientist. He was needed, and he knew it.

Likewise, there was reason to the fact that Ebling Mis—only those who did not know him added his titles to his name—was the freest form of life in the "pure science" of the Foundation. In a world where science was respected, he was The Scientist—with capital letters and no smile. He was needed, and he knew it.

And so it happened, that when others bent their knee, he refused and added loudly that his ancestors in their time bowed no knee to any stinking mayor. And in his ancestors' time the mayor was elected anyhow, and kicked out at will, and that the only people that inherited anything by right of birth were the congenital idiots.

So it also happened, that when Ebling Mis decided to allow Indbur to honor him with an audience, he did not wait for the usual rigid line of command to pass his request up and the favored reply down, but, having thrown the less disreputable of his two formal jackets over his shoulders and pounded an odd hat of impossible design on one side of his head, and lit a forbidden cigar into the bargain, he barged past two ineffectually bleating guards and into the mayor's palace.

The first notice his excellence received of the intrusion was when from his garden he heard the gradually nearing uproar of expostulation and the answering bull-roar of inarticulate swearing.

Slowly, Indbur lay down his trowel; slowly, he stood up; and slowly, he frowned. For Indbur allowed himself a daily vacation from work, and for two hours in the early afternoon, weather permitting, he was in his garden. There in his garden, the blooms grew in squares and triangles, interlaced in a severe order of red and yellow, with little dashes of violet at the apices, and greenery bordering the whole in rigid lines. There in his garden no one disturbed him—*no one!*

Indbur peeled off his soil-stained gloves as he advanced toward the little garden door.

Inevitably, he said, "What is the meaning of this?"

It is the precise question and the precise wording thereof that has been put to the atmosphere on such occasions by an incredible variety of men since humanity was invented. It is not recorded that it has ever been asked for any purpose other than dignified effect.

But the answer was literal this time, for Mis's body came plunging through with a bellow, and a shake of a fist at the ones who were still holding tatters of his cloak.

Indbur motioned them away with a solemn, displeased frown, and Mis bent to pick up his ruin of a hat, shake about a quarter of the gathered dirt off it, thrust it under his armpit and say:

"Look here, Indbur, those unprintable minions of yours will be charged for one good cloak. Lots of good wear left in this cloak." He puffed and wiped his forehead with just a trace of theatricality.

The mayor stood stiff with displeasure, and said haughtily from the peak of his five-foot-two, "It has not been brought to my attention, Mis, that you have requested an audience. You have certainly not been assigned one."

Ebling Mis looked down at his mayor with what was apparently shocked disbelief, "Ga-LAX-y, Indbur, didn't you get my note yesterday? I handed it to a flunky in purple uniform day before. I would have handed it to you direct, but I know how you like formality."

"Formality!" Indbur turned up exasperated eyes. Then, strenuously, "Have you ever heard of proper organization? At all future times you are to submit your request for an audience, properly made out in triplicate, at the government office intended for the purpose. You are then to wait until the ordinary course of events brings you notification of the time of audience to be granted. You are then to appear, properly clothed—properly clothed, do you understand—and with proper respect, too. You may leave."

"What's wrong with my clothes?" demanded Mis, hotly. "Best cloak I had till those unprintable fiends got their claws on it. I'll leave just as soon as I deliver what I came to deliver. Ga-LAX-y, if it didn't involve a Seldon Crisis, I would leave right now."

"Seldon crisis!" Indbur exhibited first interest. Mis *was* a great psychologist—a democrat, boor, and rebel certainly, but a psychologist, too. In his uncertainty, the mayor even failed to put into words the inner pang that stabbed suddenly when Mis plucked a casual bloom, held it to his nostrils expectantly, then flipped it away with a wrinkled nose.

Indbur said coldly, "Would you follow me? This garden wasn't made for serious conversation."

He felt better in his built-up chair behind his large desk from which he could look down on the few hairs that quite ineffectually hid Mis's pink scalp-skin. He felt much better when Mis cast a series of automatic glances about him for a non-existent chair and then remained standing in uneasy shifting fashion. He felt best of all when in response to a careful pressure of the correct contact, a liveried underling scurried in, bowed his way to the desk, and laid thereon a bulky, metal-bound volume.

"Now, in order," said Indbur, once more master of the situation, "to make this unauthorized interview as short as possible, make your statement in the fewest possible words."

Ebling Mis said unhurriedly, "You know what I'm doing these days?"

"I have your reports here," replied the mayor, with satisfaction, "together with authorized summaries of them. As I understand it, your investigations into the mathematics of psycho-history have been intended to duplicate Hari Seldon's work and, eventually, trace the projected course of future history, for the use of the Foundation."

"Exactly," said Mis, dryly. "When Seldon first established the Foundation, he was wise enough to include no psychologists among the scientists placed here—so that the Foundation has always worked blindly along the course of historical necessity. In the course of my researches, I have based a good deal upon hints found at the Time Vault."

"I am aware of that, Mis. It is a waste of time to repeat."

"I'm not repeating," blared Mis, "because what I'm going to tell you isn't in any of those reports."

"How do you mean, not in the reports?" said Indbur, stupidly. "How could—"

"Ga-LAX-y! Let me tell this my own way, you offensive little creature. Stop putting words into my mouth and questioning my every statement or I'll tramp out of here and let everything crumble around you. Remember, you unprintable fool, the Foundation will come through because it must, but if I walk out of here now—*you* won't."

Dashing his hat on the floor, so that clods of earth scattered, he sprang up the stairs of the dais on which the wide desk stood and shoving papers violently, sat down upon a corner of it.

Indbur thought frantically of summoning the guard, or using the built-in blasters of his desk. But Mis's face was glaring down upon him and there was nothing to do but cringe the best face upon it.

"Dr. Mis," he began, with weak formality, "you must—"

"Shut up," said Mis, ferociously, "and listen. If this thing here," and his palm came down heavily on the metal of the bound data, "is a mess of my reports—throw it out. Any report I write goes up through some twenty-odd officials, gets to you, and then sort of winds down through twenty more. That's fine if there's nothing you don't want kept secret. Well, I've got something confidential here. It's so confidential, even the boys working for me haven't got wind of it. They did the work, of course, but each just a little unconnected piece—and I put it together. You know what the Time Vault is?"

Indbur nodded his head, but Mis went on with loud enjoyment of the situation, "Well, I'll tell you anyhow because I've been sort of imagining this unprintable situation for a Ga-LAX-y of a long time; I can read your mind, you puny fraud. You've got your hand right near a little knob that'll call in about five hundred or so armed men to finish me off, but you're afraid of what I know —you're afraid of a Seldon Crisis. Besides which, if you touch anything on your desk, I'll knock your unprintable head off before anyone gets here. You and your bandit father and pirate grandfather have been blood-sucking the Foundation long enough anyway."

"This is treason," gabbled Indbur.

"It certainly is," gloated Mis, "but what are you going to do about it? Let me tell you about the Time Vault. That Time Vault is what Hari Seldon placed here at the beginning to help us over the rough spots. For every crisis, Seldon has prepared a personal simulacrum to help—and explain. Four crises so far—four appearances. The first time he appeared at the height of the first crisis. The second time, he appeared at a moment just after the successful evolution of the second crisis. Our ancestors were there to listen to him both times. At the third and fourth crises, he was ignored—probably because he was not needed, but recent investigations—*not* included in those reports you have—indicate that he appeared anyway, and at the proper times. Get it?"

He did not wait for any answer. His cigar, a tattered, dead ruin was finally disposed of, a new cigar groped for, and lit. The smoke puffed out violently.

He said, "Officially I've been trying to rebuild the science of psycho-history. Well, no one man is going to do *that*, and it won't get done in any one century, either. But I've made advances in the more simple elements and I've been able to use it as an excuse to meddle with the Time Vault. What I *have* done, involves the determination, to a pretty fair kind of certainty, of the exact date of the next appearance of Hari Seldon. I can give you the exact day, in other words, that the coming Seldon Crisis, the fifth, will reach its climax."

"How far off?" demanded Indbur, tensely.

And Mis exploded his bomb with cheerful nonchalance, "Four months," he said. "Four unprintable months, less two days."

"Four months," said Indbur, with uncharacteristic vehemence. "Impossible."

"Impossible, my unprintable eye."

"Four months? Do you understand what that means? For a

crisis to come to a head in four months would mean that it has been preparing for years."

"And why not? Is there a law of Nature that requires the process to mature in the full light of day?"

"But nothing impends. Nothing hangs over us." Indbur almost wrung his hands for anxiety. With a sudden spasmodic recrudescence of ferocity, he screamed, "*Will* you get off my desk and let me put it in order? How do you expect me to *think?*"

Mis, startled, lifted heavily and moved aside.

Indbur replaced objects in their appropriate niches with a feverish motion. He was speaking quickly, "You have no right to come here like this. If you had presented your theory—"

"It is not a *theory.*"

"I say it *is* a theory. If you had presented it together with your evidence and arguments, in appropriate fashion, it would have gone to the Bureau of Historical Sciences. There it could have been properly treated, the resulting analyses submitted to me, and then, of course, proper action would have been taken. As it is, you've vexed me to no purpose. Ah, here it is."

He had a sheet of transparent, silvery paper in his hand which he shook at the bulbous psychologist beside him.

"This is a short summary I prepare myself—weekly—of foreign matters in progress. Listen—we have completed negotiations for a commercial treaty with Mores, continue negotiations for one with Lyonesse, sent a delegation to some celebration or other on Bonde, received some complaint or other from Kalgan and we've promised to look into it, protested some sharp trade practices in Asperta and they've promised to look into it—and so on and so on." The mayor's eyes swarmed down the list of coded notations, and then he carefully placed the sheet in its proper place in the proper folder in the proper pigeonhole.

"I tell you, Mis, there's not a thing there that breathes anything but order and peace—"

The door at the far, long end opened, and, in far too dramatically coincident a fashion to suggest anything but real life, a plainly-costumed notable stepped in.

Indbur half-rose. He had the curiously swirling sensation of unreality that comes upon those days when too much happens.

After Mis's intrusion and wild fumings there now came the equally improper, hence disturbing, intrusion unannounced, of his secretary, who at least knew the rules.

The secretary kneeled low.

Indbur said, sharply, "Well!"

The secretary addressed the floor, "Excellence, Captain Han Pritcher of Information, returning from Kalgan, in disobedience to your orders, has according to prior instructions—your order X20-513—been imprisoned, and awaits execution. Those accompanying him are being held for questioning. A full report has been filed."

Indbur, in agony, said, "A full report has been received. *Well!*"

"Excellence, Captain Pritcher has reported, vaguely, dangerous designs on the part of the new warlord of Kalgan. He has been given, according to prior instructions—your order X20-651—no formal hearing, but his remarks have been recorded and a full report filed."

Indbur screamed, "A full report has been received. *Well!*"

"Excellence, reports have within the quarter-hour been received from the Salinnian frontier. Ships identified as Kalganian have been entering Foundation territory, unauthorized. The ships are armed. Fighting has occurred."

The secretary was bent nearly double. Indbur remained standing. Ebling Mis shook himself, clumped up to the secretary, and tapped him sharply on the shoulder.

"Here, you'd better have them release this Captain Pritcher, and have him sent here. Get out."

The secretary left, and Mis turned to the mayor, "Hadn't you better get the machinery moving, Indbur? Four months, you know."

Indbur remained standing, glaze-eyed. Only one finger seemed alive—and it traced rapid jerky triangles on the smooth desk top before him.

16.

Conference

When the twenty-seven independent Trading worlds, united only by their distrust of the mother planet of the Foundation, concert an assembly among themselves, and each is big with a pride grown of its smallness, hardened by its own insularity and embittered by eternal danger—there are preliminary negotiations to be overcome of a pettiness sufficiently staggering to heart-sicken the most persevering.

It is not enough to fix in advance such details as methods of voting, type of representation—whether by world or by population. These are matters of involved political importance. It is not enough to fix matters of priority at the table, both council and dinner, those are matters of involved social importance.

It was the place of meeting—since that was a matter of over-powering provincialism. And in the end the devious routes of diplomacy led to the world of Radole, which some commentators had suggested at the start for logical reason of central position.

Radole was a small world—and, in military potential, perhaps the weakest of the twenty-seven. That, by the way, was another factor in the logic of the choice.

It was a ribbon world—of which the Galaxy boasts sufficient, but among which, the inhabited variety is a rarity. It was a world, in other words, where the two halves face the monotonous extremes of heat and cold, while the region of possible life is the birdling ribbon of the twilight zone.

Such a world invariably sounds uninviting to those who have not tried it, but there exist spots, strategically placed—and Radole City was located in such a one.

It spread along the soft slopes of the foothills before the hacked-out mountains that backed it along the rim of the cold hemisphere and held off the frightful ice. The warm, dry air of the sun-half spilled over, and from the mountains was piped the water—and between the two, Radole City became a continuous garden, swimming in the eternal morning of an eternal June.

Each house nestled among its flower garden, open to the fang-less elements. Each garden was a horticultural forcing ground, where luxury plants grew in fantastic patterns for the sake of the foreign exchange they brought—until Radole had almost become a producing world, rather than a typical Trading world.

So, in its way, Radole City was a little point of softness and luxury on a horrible planet—a tiny scrap of Eden—and that, too, was a factor in the logic of the choice.

The strangers came from each of the twenty-six other Trading worlds: delegates, wives, secretaries, newsmen, ships, and crews —and Radole's population nearly doubled and Radole's resources strained themselves to the limit. One ate at will, and drank at will, and slept not at all.

Yet there were few among the roisterers who were not in-tensely aware that all that volume of the Galaxy burnt slowly in a sort of quiet, slumbrous war. And of those who were aware, there were three classes. First, there were the many who knew little and were very confident—

Such as the young space pilot who wore the Haven cockade on the clasp of his cap, and who managed, in holding his glass before his eyes, to catch those of the faintly smiling Radolian girl op-posite. He was saying:

"We came right through the war-zone to get here—on purpose. We traveled about a light-minute or so, in neutral, right past Horleggor—"

"Horleggor?" broke in a long-legged native, who was playing host to that particular gathering. "That's where the Mule got the guts beat out of him last week, wasn't it?"

"Where'd you hear that the Mule got the guts beat out of him?" demanded the pilot, loftily.

"Foundation radio."

"Yeah? Well, the Mule's *got* Horleggor. We almost ran into a convoy of his ships, and that's where they were coming from. It isn't a gut-beating when you stay where you fought, and the gut-beater leaves in a hurry."

Someone else said in a high, blurred voice, "Don't talk like that. Foundation always takes it on the chin for a while. You watch; just sit tight and watch. Ol' Foundation knows when to come back. And then—*pow!*" The thick voice concluded and was succeeded by a bleary grin.

"Anyway," said the pilot from Haven, after a short pause, "As I say, we saw the Mule's ships, and they looked pretty good, pretty good. I tell you what—they looked new."

"New?" said the native, thoughtfully. "They build them themselves?" He broke a leaf from an overhanging branch, sniffed delicately at it, then crunched it between his teeth, the bruised tissues bleeding greenly and diffusing a minty odor. He said, "You trying to tell me they beat Foundation ships with home-built jobs? Go on."

"We saw them, doc. And I can tell a ship from a comet, too, you know."

The native leaned close. "You know what I think. Listen, don't kid yourself. Wars don't just start by themselves, and we have a bunch of shrewd apples running things. They know what they're doing."

The well-unthirsted one said with sudden loudness, "You watch ol' Foundation. They wait for the last minute, then—*pow!*" He grinned with vacuously open mouth at the girl, who moved away from him.

The Radolian was saying, "For instance, old man, you think maybe that this Mule guy's running things. No-o-o." And he wagged a finger horizontally. "The way I hear it, and from pretty high up, mind you, he's our boy. We're paying him off, and we probably built those ships. Let's be realistic about it—we probably did. Sure, he can't beat the Foundation in the long run, but he can get them shaky, and when he does—*we get in.*"

The girl said, "Is that all you can talk about, Klev? The war? You make me tired."

The pilot from Haven said, in an access of gallantry, "Change the subject. Can't make the girls tired."

The bedewed one took up the refrain and banged a mug to the rhythm. The little groups of two that had formed broke up with giggles and swagger, and a few similar groups of twos emerged from the sun-house in the background.

The conversation became more general, more varied, more meaningless—

Then there were those who knew a little more and were less confident.

Such as the one-armed Fran, whose large bulk represented Haven as official delegated, and who lived high in consequence, and cultivated new friendships—with women when he could and with men when he had to.

It was on the sun platform of the hilltop home, of one of these new friends, that he relaxed for the first of what eventually proved to be a total of two times while on Radole. The new friend was Iwo Lyon, a kindred soul of Radole. Iwo's house was apart from the general cluster, apparently alone in a sea of floral perfume and insect chatter. The sun platform was a grassy strip of lawn set at a forty-five degree angle, and upon it Fran stretched out and fairly sopped up sun.

He said, "Don't have anything like this on Haven."

Iwo replied, sleepily, "Ever seen the cold side. There's a spot twenty miles from here where the oxygen runs like water."

"Go on."

"Fact."

"Well, I'll tell you, Iwo— In the old days before my arm was chewed off I knocked around, see—and you won't believe this, but"— The story that followed lasted considerably, and Iwo didn't believe it.

Iwo said, through yawns, "They don't make them like in the old days, that's the truth."

"No, guess they don't. Well, now," Fran fired up, "don't say that. I told you about my son, didn't I? *He's* one of the old school, if you like. He'll make a great Trader, blast it. He's his old man up and down. Up and down, except that he gets married."

"You mean legal contract? With a girl?"

"That's right. Don't see the sense in it myself. They went to Kalgan for their honeymoon."

"Kalgan? *Kalgan?* When the Galaxy was this?"

Fran smiled broadly, and said with slow meaning, "Just before the Mule declared war on the Foundation."

"That so?"

Fran nodded and motioned Iwo closer with his head. He said, hoarsely, "In fact, I can tell you something, if you don't let it go any further. My boy was sent to Kalgan for a purpose. Now I wouldn't like to let it out, you know, just what the purpose was, naturally, but you look at the situation now, and I suppose you can make a pretty good guess. In any case, my boy was the man for the job. We Traders needed some sort of ruckus." He smiled, craftily. "It's here. I'm not saying how we did it, but—my boy went to Kalgan, and the Mule sent out his ships. My son!"

Iwo was duly impressed. He grew confidential in his turn, "That's good. You know, they say we've got five hundred ships ready to pitch in on our own at the right time."

Fran said authoritatively, "More than that, maybe. This is real strategy. This is the kind I like." He clawed loudly at the skin of his abdomen. "But don't you forget that the Mule is a smart boy, too. What happened at Horleggor worries me."

"I heard he lost about ten ships."

"Sure, but he had a hundred more, and the Foundation had to get out. It's all to the good to have those tyrants beaten, but not as quickly as all that." He shook his head.

"The question I ask is where does the Mule get his ships? There's a widespread rumor we're making them for him."

"We? The Traders? Haven has the biggest ship factories anywhere in the independent worlds, and we haven't made one for anyone but ourselves. Do you suppose any world is building a fleet for the Mule on its own, without taking the precaution of united action? That's a . . . a fairy tale."

"Well, where does he get them?"

And Fran shrugged, "Makes them himself, I suppose. That worries me, too."

Fran blinked at the sun and curled his toes about the smooth wood of the polished foot-rest. Slowly, he fell asleep and the soft burr of his breathing mingled with the insect sibilance.

Lastly, there were the very few who knew considerable and were not confident at all.

Such as Randu, who on the fifth day of the all-Trader convention entered the Central Hall and found the two men he had asked to be there, waiting for him. The five hundred seats were empty—and were going to stay so.

Randu said quickly, almost before he sat down, "We three represent about half the military potential of the Independent Trading Worlds."

"Yes," said Mangin of Iss, "my colleague and I have already commented upon the fact."

"I am ready," said Randu, "to speak quickly and earnestly. I am not interested in bargaining or subtlety. Our position is radically in the worse."

"As a result of—" urged Ovall Gri of Mnemon.

"Of developments of the last hour. Please! From the beginning. First, our position is not of our doing, and but doubtfully of our control. Our original dealings were not with the Mule, but with several others; notably the ex-warlord of Kalgan, whom the Mule defeated at a most inconvenient time for us."

"Yes, but this Mule is a worthy substitute," said Mangin. "I do not cavil at details."

"You may when you know *all* the details." Randu leaned forward and placed his hands upon the table palms-up in an obvious gesture.

He said, "A month ago I sent my nephew and my nephew's wife to Kalgan."

"Your nephew!" cried Ovall Gri, in surprise. "I did not know he was your nephew."

"With what purpose," asked Mangin, dryly. "This?" And his thumb drew an inclusive circle high in the air.

"No. If you mean the Mule's war on the Foundation, no. How could I aim so high. The young man knew nothing—neither of our organization nor of our aims. He was told I was a minor member of an intra-Haven patriotic society, and his function at Kalgan was nothing but that of an amateur observer. My motives were, I must admit, rather obscure. Mainly, I was curious about the Mule. He is a strange phenomenon—but that's a chewed cud; I'll not go into it. Secondly, it would make an interesting and educational training project for a man who had experience with the

Foundation and the Foundation underground and showed promise of future usefulness to us. You see—"

Ovall's long face fell into vertical lines as he showed his large teeth, "You must have been surprised at the outcome, then, since there is not a word among the Traders, I believe, that does not know that this nephew of yours abducted a Mule underling in the name of the Foundation and furnished the Mule with a *casus belli*. Galaxy, Randu, you spin romances. I find it hard to believe you had no hand in that. Come, it was a skillful job."

Randu shook his white head, "Not of my doing. Nor, willfully, of my nephew's, who is now held prisoner at the Foundation, and may not live to see the completion of this so-skillful job. I have just heard from him. The Personal Capsule has been smuggled out somehow, come through the war zone, gone to Haven, and traveled from there to here. It has been a month on its travels."

"And?—"

Randu leaned a heavy hand upon the heel of his palm and said, sadly, "I'm afraid we are cast for the same role that the one-time warlord of Kalgan played. The Mule is a mutant!"

There was a momentary qualm; a faint impression of quickened heartbeats. Randu might easily have imagined it.

When Mangin spoke, the evenness of his voice was unchanged, "How do you know?"

"Only because my nephew says so, but he was on Kalgan."

"What kind of a mutant? There are all kinds, you know."

Randu forced the rising impatience down, "All kinds of mutants, yes, Mangin. All kinds! But only one kind of Mule. What kind of a mutant would start as an unknown, assemble an army, establish, they say, a five-mile asteroid as original base, capture a planet, then a system, then a region—and then attack the Foundation, and *defeat* them at Horleggor. *And all in two or three years!*"

Ovall Gri shrugged, "So you think he'll beat the Foundation?"

"I don't know. Suppose he does?"

"Sorry, I can't go that far. You *don't* beat the Foundation. Look, there's not a new fact we have to go on except for the statements of a . . . well, of an inexperienced boy. Suppose we shelve it for a while. With all the Mule's victories, we weren't worried until now, and unless he goes a good deal further than he has, I see no reason to change that. Yes?"

Randu frowned and despaired at the cobweb texture of his argument. He said to both, "Have we yet made any contact with the Mule?"

"No," both answered.

"It's true, though, that we've tried, isn't it? It's true that there's not much purpose to our meeting unless we do reach him, isn't it? It's true that so far there's been more drinking than thinking, and more wooing than doing—I quote from an editorial in today's Radole Tribune—and all because we can't reach the Mule. Gentlemen, we have nearly a thousand ships waiting to be thrown into the fight at the proper moment to seize control of the Foundation. I say we should change that. I say, throw those thousand onto the board now—*against the Mule.*"

"You mean for the Tyrant Indbur and the bloodsuckers of the Foundation?" demanded Mangin, with quiet venom.

Randu raised a weary hand, "Spare me the adjectives. Against the Mule, I say, and for I-don't-care-who."

Ovall Gri rose, "Randu, I'll have nothing to do with that. You present it to the full council tonight if you particularly hunger for political suicide."

He left without another word and Mangin followed silently, leaving Randu to drag out a lonely hour of endless, insoluble consideration.

At the full council that night, he said nothing.

But it was Ovall Gri who pushed into his room the next morning; an Ovall Gri only sketchily dressed and who had neither shaved nor combed his hair.

Randu stared at him over a yet-uncleared breakfast table with an astonishment sufficiently open and strenuous to cause him to drop his pipe.

Ovall said baldly, harshly. "Mnemon has been bombarded from space by treacherous attack."

Randu's eyes narrowed, "The Foundation?"

"The Mule!" exploded Ovall. "The Mule!" His words raced, "It was unprovoked and deliberate. Most of our fleet had joined the international flotilla. The few left as Home Squadron were insufficient and were blown out of the sky. There have been no landings yet, and there may not be, for half the attackers are reported destroyed—but it is war—and I have come to ask how Haven stands on the matter."

"Haven, I am sure, will adhere to the spirit of the Charter of Federation. But, you see? He attacks us as well."

"This Mule is a madman. Can he defeat the universe?" He faltered and sat down to seize Randu's wrist, "Our few survivors have reported the Mule's poss . . . enemy's possession of a new weapon. An atomic-field depressor."

"A what?"

Ovall said, "Most of our ships were lost because their atomic weapons failed them. It could not have happened by either accident or sabotage. It must have been a weapon of the Mule. It didn't work perfectly; the effect was intermittent; there were ways to neutralize—my dispatches are not detailed. But you see that such a tool would change the nature of war and, possibly, make our entire fleet obsolete."

Randu felt an old, old man. His face sagged hopelessly, "I am afraid a monster is grown that will devour all of us. Yet we must fight him."

17.

The Visi-Sonor

Ebling Mis's house in a not-so-pretentious neighborhood of Terminus City was well known to the intelligentsia, literati, and just-plain-well-read of the Foundation. Its notable characteristics depended, subjectively, upon the source material that was read. To a thoughtful biographer, it was the "symbolization of a retreat from a nonacademic reality," a society columnist gushed silkily at its "frightfully masculine atmosphere of careless disorder," a University Ph.D. called it brusquely, "bookish, but unorganized," a nonuniversity friend said, "good for a drink anytime and you can put your feet on the sofa," and a breezy newsweekly broadcast, that went in for color, spoke of the "rocky, down-to-earth, no-nonsense living quarters of blaspheming, Leftish, balding Ebling Mis."

To Bayta, who thought for no audience but herself at the moment, and who had the advantage of first-hand information, it was merely sloppy.

Except for the first few days, her imprisonment had been a light burden. Far lighter, it seemed, than this half-hour wait in the psychologist's home—under secret observation, perhaps? She had been with Toran then, at least—

Perhaps she might have grown wearier of the strain, had not Magnifico's long nose drooped in a gesture that plainly showed his own far greater tension.

Magnifico's pipe-stem legs were folded up under a pointed, sagging chin, as if he were trying to huddle himself into disappearance, and Bayta's hand went out in a gentle and automatic gesture of reassurance. Magnifico winced, then smiled.

"Surely, my lady, it would seem that even yet my body denies the knowledge of my mind and expects of others' hands a blow."

"There's no need for worry, Magnifico. I'm with you, and I won't let anyone hurt you."

The clown's eyes sidled towards her, then drew away quickly. "But they kept me away from you earlier—and from your kind husband—and, on my word, you may laugh, but I was lonely for missing friendship."

"I wouldn't laugh at that. I was, too."

The clown brightened, and he hugged his knees closer. He said, "You have not met this man who will see us?" It was a cautious question.

"No. But he is a famous man. I have seen him in the newscasts and heard quite a good deal of him. I think he's a good man, Magnifico, who means us no harm."

"Yes?" The clown stirred uneasily. "That may be, my lady, but he has questioned me before, and his manner is of an abruptness and loudness that bequivers me. He is full of strange words, so that the answers to his questions could not worm out of my throat. Almost, I might believe the romancer who once played on my ignorance with a tale that, at such moments, the heart lodged in the windpipe and prevented speech."

"But it's different now. We're two to his one, and he won't be able to frighten the both of us, will he?"

"No, my lady."

A door slammed somewheres, and the roaring of a voice entered the house. Just outside the room, it coagulated into words with a fierce, "Get the Ga-LAX-y out of here!" and two uniformed guards were momentarily visible through the opening door, in quick retreat.

Ebling Mis entered frowning, deposited a carefully wrapped bundle on the floor, and approached to shake Bayta's hand with careless pressure. Bayta returned it vigorously, man-fashion. Mis did a double-take as he turned to the clown, and favored the girl with a longer look.

He said, "Married?"

"Yes. We went through the legal formalities."

Mis paused. Then, "Happy about it?"

"So far."

Mis shrugged, and turned again to Magnifico. He unwrapped the package, "Know what this is, boy?"

Magnifico fairly hurled himself out of his seat and caught the

multi-keyed instrument. He fingered the myriad knobby contacts
and threw a sudden back somersault of joy, to the imminent
destruction of the nearby furniture.

He croaked, "A Visi-Sonor—and of a make to distill joy out of a
dead man's heart." His long fingers caressed softly and slowly,
pressing lightly on contacts with a rippling motion, resting momentarily on one key then another—and in the air before them
there was a soft glowing rosiness, just inside the range of vision.

Ebling Mis said, "All right, boy, you said you could pound on
one of those gadgets, and there's your chance. You'd better tune
it, though. It's out of a museum." Then, in an aside to Bayta,
"Near as I can make it, no one on the Foundation can make it
talk right."

He leaned closer and said quickly, "The clown won't talk without you. Will you help?"

She nodded.

"Good!" he said. "His state of fear is almost fixed, and I doubt
that his mental strength would possibly stand a psychic probe.
If I'm to get anything out of him otherwise, he's got to feel absolutely at ease. You understand?"

She nodded again.

"This Visi-Sonor is the first step in the process. He says he can
play it; and his reaction now makes it pretty certain that it's one
of the great joys of his life. So whether the playing is good or bad,
be interested and appreciative. Then exhibit friendliness and
confidence in me. Above all, follow my lead in everything." There
was a swift glance at Magnifico, huddled in a corner of the sofa,
making rapid adjustments in the interior of the instrument. He
was completely absorbed.

Mis said in a conversational tone to Bayta, "Ever hear a Visi-
Sonor?"

"Once," said Bayta, equally casually, "at a concert of rare instruments. I wasn't impressed."

"Well, I doubt that you came across good playing. There are
very few really good players. It's not so much that it requires
physical co-ordination—a multi-bank piano requires more, for
instance—as a certain type of free-wheeling mentality." In a
lower voice, "That's why our living skeleton there might be better

than we think. More often than not, good players are idiots other-wise. It's one of those queer setups that makes psychology in-teresting."

He added, in a patent effort to manufacture light conversation, "You know how the beblistered thing works? I looked it up for this purpose, and all I've made out so far is that its radiations stimulate the optic center of the brain directly, without ever touching the optic nerve. It's actually the utilization of a sense never met with in ordinary nature. Remarkable, when you come to think of it. What you hear is all right. That's ordinary. Ear-drum, cochlea, all that. But— *Shh!* He's ready. Will you kick that switch. It works better in the dark."

In the darkness, Magnifico was a mere blob, Ebling Mis a heavy-breathing mass. Bayta found herself straining her eyes anxiously, and at first with no effect. There was a thin, reedy quaver in the air, that wavered raggedly up the scale. It hovered, dropped and caught itself, gained in body, and swooped into a booming crash that had the effect of a thunderous split in a veil-ing curtain.

A little globe of pulsing color grew in rhythmic spurts and burst in midair into formless gouts that swirled high and came down as curving streamers in interlacing patterns. They coa-lesced into little spheres, no two alike in color—and Bayta began discovering things.

She noticed that closing her eyes made the color pattern all the clearer; that each little movement of color had its own little pattern of sound; that she could not identify the colors; and, lastly, that the globes were not globes but little figures.

Little figures; little shifting flames, that danced and flickered in their myriads; that dropped out of sight and returned from nowhere; that whipped about one another and coalesced then into a new color.

Incongruously, Bayta thought of the little blobs of color that come at night when you close your eyelids till they hurt, and stare patiently. There was the old familiar effect of the marching polka dots of shifting color, of the contracting concentric circles, of the shapeless masses that quiver momentarily. All that, larger, multivaried—and each little dot of color a tiny figure.

They darted at her in pairs, and she lifted her hands with a sudden gasp, but they tumbled and for an instant she was the center of a brilliant snowstorm, while cold light slipped off her shoulders and down her arm in a luminous ski-slide, shooting off her stiff fingers and meeting slowly in a shining midair focus. Beneath it all, the sound of a hundred instruments flowed in liquid streams until she could not tell it from the light.

She wondered if Ebling Mis were seeing the same thing, and if not, what he did see. The wonder passed, and then—

She was watching again. The little figures—were they little figures?—little tiny women with burning hair that turned and bent too quickly for the mind to focus?—seized one another in star-shaped groups that turned—and the music was faint laughter —girls' laughter that began inside the ear.

The stars drew together, sparked toward one another, grew slowly into structure—and from below, a palace shot upward in rapid evolution. Each brick a tiny color, each color a tiny spark, each spark a stabbing light that shifted patterns and led the eye skyward to twenty jeweled minarets.

A glittering carpet shot out and about, whirling, spinning an insubstantial web that engulfed all space, and from it luminous shoots stabbed upward and branched into trees that sang with a music all their own.

Bayta sat inclosed in it. The music welled about her in rapid, lyrical flights. She reached out to touch a fragile tree and blossoming spicules floated downwards and faded, each with its clear, tiny tinkle.

The music crashed in twenty cymbals, and before her an area flamed up in a spout and cascaded down invisible steps into Bayta's lap, where it spilled over and flowed in rapid current, raising the fiery sparkle to her waist, while across her lap was a rainbow bridge and upon it the little figures—

A place, and a garden, and tiny men and women on a bridge, stretching out as far as she could see, swimming through the stately swells of stringed music converging in upon her—

And then—there seemed a frightened pause, a hesitant, indrawn motion, a swift collapse. The colors fled, spun into a globe that shrank, and rose, and disappeared.

And it was merely dark again.

A heavy foot scratched for the pedal, reached it, and the light flooded in; the flat light of a prosy sun. Bayta blinked until the tears came, as though for the longing of what was gone. Ebling Mis was a podgy inertness with his eyes still round and his mouth still open.

Only Magnifico himself was alive, and he fondled his Visi-Sonor in a crooning ecstasy.

"My lady," he gasped, "it is indeed of an effect the most magical. It is of balance and response almost beyond hope in its delicacy and stability. On this, it would seem I could work wonders. How liked you my composition, my lady?"

"Was it yours?" breathed Bayta. "Your own?"

At her awe, his thin face turned a glowing red to the tip of his mighty nose. "My very own, my lady. The Mule liked it not, but often and often I have played it for my own amusement. It was once, in my youth, that I saw the palace—a gigantic place of jeweled riches that I saw from a distance at a time of high carnival. There were people of a splendor undreamed of—and magnificence more than ever I saw afterwards, even in the Mule's service. It is but a poor makeshift I have created, but my mind's poverty precludes more. I call it, 'The Memory of Heaven.'"

Now through the midst of the chatter, Mis shook himself to active life. "Here," he said, "here, Magnifico, would you like to do that same thing for others?"

For a moment, the clown drew back. "For others?" he quavered.

"For thousands," cried Mis, "in the great Halls of the Foundation. Would you like to be your own master, and honored by all, wealthy, and . . . and—" his imagination failed him. "And all that? Eh? What do you say?"

"But how may I be all that, mighty sir, for indeed I am but a poor clown ungiven to the great things of the world?"

The psychologist puffed out his lips, and passed the back of his hand across his brow. He said, "But your playing, man. The world is yours if you would play so for the mayor and his Trading Trusts. Wouldn't you like that?"

The clown glanced briefly at Bayta, "Would *she* stay with me?"

Bayta laughed, "Of course, silly. Would it be likely that I'd leave you now that you're on the point of becoming rich and famous?"

"It would all be yours," he replied earnestly, "and surely the wealth of Galaxy itself would be yours before I could repay my debt to your kindness."

"But," said Mis, casually, "if you would first help me—"

"What is that?"

The psychologist paused, and smiled, "A little surface probe that doesn't hurt. It wouldn't touch but the peel of your brain."

There was a flare of deadly fear in Magnifico's eyes. "Not a probe. I have seen it used. It drains the mind and leaves an empty skull. The Mule did use it upon traitors and let them wander mindless through the streets, until out of mercy, they were killed." He held up his hand to push Mis away.

"That was a psychic probe," explained Mis, patiently, "and even that would only harm a person when misused. This probe I have is a surface probe and wouldn't hurt a baby."

"That's right, Magnifico," urged Bayta. "It's only to help beat the Mule and keep him far away. Once that's done, you and I will be rich and famous all our lives."

Magnifico held out a trembling hand, "Will you hold my hand, then?"

Bayta took it in both her own, and the clown watched the approach of the burnished terminal plates with large eyes.

Ebling Mis rested carelessly on the too-lavish chair in Mayor Indbur's private quarters, unregenerately unthankful for the condescension shown him and watched the small mayor's fidgeting unsympathetically. He tossed away a cigar stub and spat out a shred of tobacco.

"And, incidentally, if you want something for your next concert at Mallow Hall, Indbur," he said, "you can dump out those electronic gadgeteers into the sewers they came from and have this little freak play the Visi-Sonor for you. Indbur—it's out of this world."

Indbur said peevishly, "I did not call you here to listen to your lectures on music. What of the Mule? Tell me that. What of the Mule?"

"The Mule? Well, I'll tell you—I used a surface probe and got little. Can't use the psychic probe because the freak is scared blind of it, so that his resistance will probably blow his unprintable mental fuses as soon as contact is made. But this is what I've got, if you'll just stop tapping your fingernails—

"First place, de-stress the Mule's physical strength. He's probably strong, but most of the freak's fairy tales about it are probably considerably blown up by his own fearful memory. He wears queer glasses and his eyes kill, he evidently has mental powers."

"So much we had at the start," commented the mayor, sourly.

"Then the probe confirms it, and from there on I've been working mathematically."

"So? And how long will all this take? Your word-rattling will deafen me yet."

"About a month, I should say, and I may have something for you. And I may not, of course. But what of it? If this is all outside Seldon's plans, our chances are precious little, unprintable little."

Indbur whirled on the psychologist fiercely, "Now I have you, traitor. Lie! Say you're not one of these criminal rumor-mongers that are spreading defeatism and panic through the Foundation, and making my work doubly hard."

"I? I?" Mis gathered anger slowly.

Indbur swore at him, "Because by the dust-clouds of space, the Foundation will win—the Foundation *must* win."

"Despite the loss at Horleggor?"

"It was not a loss. You have swallowed that spreading lie, too? We were outnumbered and betreasoned—"

"By whom?" demanded Mis, contemptuously.

"By the lice-ridden democrats of the gutter," shouted Indbur back at him. "I have known for long that the fleet has been riddled by democratic cells. Most have been wiped out, but enough remain for the unexplained surrender of twenty ships in the thickest of the swarming fight. Enough to force an apparent defeat.

"For that matter, my rough-tongued, simple patriot and epitome of the primitive virtues, what are your own connections with the democrats?"

Ebling Mis shrugged it off, "You rave, do you know that? What of the retreat since, and the loss of half of Siwenna? Democrats again?"

"No. Not democrats," the little man smiled sharply. "We retreat —as the Foundation has always retreated under attack, until the inevitable march of history turns with us. Already, I see the outcome. Already, the so-called underground of the democrats has issued manifestoes swearing aid and allegiance to the Government. It could be a feint, a cover for a deeper treachery, but I make good use of it, and the propaganda distilled from it will have its effect, whatever the crawling traitors scheme. And better than that—"

"Even better than that, Indbur?"

"Judge for yourself. Two days ago, the so-called Association of Independent Traders declared war on the Mule, and the Foundation fleet is strengthened, at a stroke, by a thousand ships. You see, this Mule goes too far. He finds us divided and quarreling among ourselves and under the pressure of his attack we unite and grow strong. He *must* lose. It is inevitable—as always."

Mis still exuded skepticism, "Then you tell me that Seldon planned even for the fortuitous occurrence of a mutant."

"A mutant! I can't tell him from a human, nor could you but for the ravings of a rebel captain, some outland youngsters, and an addled juggler and clown. You forget the most conclusive evidence of all—your own."

"My own?" For just a moment, Mis was startled.

"Your own," sneered the mayor. "The Time Vault opens in nine weeks. What of that? It opens for a crisis. If this attack of the Mule is *not* the crisis, where is the 'real' one, the one the Vault is opening for? Answer me, you lardish ball."

The psychologist shrugged, "All right. If it keeps you happy. Do me a favor, though. Just in case . . . just in *case* old Seldon makes his speech and it *does* go sour, suppose you let me attend the Grand Opening."

"All right. Get out of here. And stay out of my sight for nine weeks."

"With unprintable pleasure, you wizened horror," muttered Mis to himself as he left.

18.

Fall of the Foundation

There was an atmosphere about the Time Vault that just missed definition in several directions at once. It was not one of decay, for it was well-lit and well-conditioned, with the color scheme of the walls lively, and the rows of fixed chairs comfortable and apparently designed for eternal use. It was not even ancient, for three centuries had left no obvious mark. There was certainly no effort at the creation of awe or reverence, for the appointments were simple and everyday—next door to bareness, in fact.

Yet after all the negatives were added and the sum disposed of, something was left—and that something centered about the glass cubicle that dominated half the room with its clear emptiness. Four times in three centuries, the living simulacrum of Hari Seldon himself had sat there and spoken. Twice he had spoken to no audience.

Through three centuries and nine generations, the old man who had seen the great days of universal empire projected himself—and still he understood more of the Galaxy of his great-ultra-great-grandchildren, than did those grandchildren themselves.

Patiently that empty cubicle waited.

The first to arrive was Mayor Indbur III, driving his ceremonial ground car through the hushed and anxious streets. Arriving with him was his own chair, higher than those that belonged there, and wider. It was placed before all the others, and Indbur dominated all but the empty glassiness before him.

The solemn official at his left bowed a reverent head. "Excellence, arrangements are completed for the widest possible sub-etheric spread for the official announcement by your excellence tonight."

"Good. Meanwhile, special interplanetary programs concerning the Time Vault are to continue. There will, of course, be no predictions or speculations of any sort on the subject. Does popular reaction continue satisfactory?"

"Excellence, very much so. The vicious rumors prevailing of late have decreased further. Confidence is widespread."

"Good!" He gestured the man away and adjusted his elaborate neckpiece to a nicety.

It was twenty minutes of noon!

A select group of the great props of the mayoralty—the leaders of the great Trading organizations—appeared in ones and twos with the degree of pomp appropriate to their financial status and place in mayoral favor. Each presented himself to the mayor, received a gracious word or two, took an assigned seat.

Somewhere, incongruous among the stilted ceremony of all this, Randu of Haven made his appearance and wormed his way unannounced to the mayor's seat.

"Excellence!" he muttered, and bowed

Indbur frowned. "You have not been granted an audience."

"Excellence, I have requested one for a week."

"I regret that the matters of State involved in the appearance of Seldon have—"

"Excellence, I regret them, too, but I must ask you to rescind your order that the ships of the Independent Traders be distributed among the fleets of the Foundation."

Indbur had flushed red at the interruption. "This is not the time for discussion."

"Excellence, it is the only time," Randu whispered urgently. "As representative of the Independent Trading Worlds, I tell you such a move can not be obeyed. It must be rescinded before Seldon solves our problem for us. Once the emergency is passed, it will be too late to conciliate and our alliance will melt away."

Indbur stared at Randu coldly. "You realize that I am head of the Foundation armed forces? Have I the right to determine military policy or have I not?"

"Excellence, you have, but some things are inexpedient."

"I recognize no inexpediency. It is dangerous to allow your people separate fleets in this emergency. Divided action plays into the hands of the enemy. We must unite, ambassador, militarily as well as politically."

Randu felt his throat muscles tighten. He omitted the courtesy of the opening title. "You feel safe now that Seldon will speak, and you move against us. A month ago you were soft and yielding, when our ships defeated the Mule at Terel. I might remind you, sir, that it is the Foundation Fleet that has been defeated in open battle five times, and that the ships of the Independent Trading Worlds have won your victories for you."

Indbur frowned dangerously, "You are no longer welcome upon Terminus, ambassador. Your return will be requested this evening. Furthermore, your connection with subversive democratic forces on Terminus will be—and has been—investigated."

Randu replied, "When I leave, our ships will go with me. I know nothing of your democrats. I know only that your Foundation's ships have surrendered to the Mule by the treason of their high officers, not their sailors, democratic or otherwise. I tell you that twenty ships of the Foundation surrendered at Horleggor at the orders of their rear admiral, when they were unharmed and unbeaten. The rear admiral was your own close associate—he presided at the trial of my nephew when he first arrived from Kalgan. It is not the only case we know of and our ships and men will not be risked under potential traitors."

Indbur said, "You will be placed under guard upon leaving here."

Randu walked away under the silent stares of the contemptuous coterie of the rulers of Terminus.

It was ten minutes of twelve!

Bayta and Toran had already arrived. They rose in their back seats and beckoned to Randu as he passed.

Randu smiled gently, "You are here after all. How did you work it?"

"Magnifico was our politician," grinned Toran. "Indbur insists upon his Visi-Sonor composition based on the Time Vault, with himself, no doubt, as hero. Magnifico refused to attend without us, and there was no arguing him out of it. Ebling Mis is with us, or was. He's wandering about somewhere." Then, with a sudden access of anxious gravity, "Why, what's wrong, uncle? You don't look well."

Randu nodded, "I suppose not. We're in for bad times, Toran. When the Mule is disposed of, our turn will come, I'm afraid."

A straight solemn figure in white approached, and greeted them with a stiff bow.

Bayta's dark eyes smiled, as she held out her hand, "Captain Pritcher! Are you on space duty then?"

The captain took the hand and bowed lower, "Nothing like it. Dr. Mis, I understand, has been instrumental in bringing me here, but it's only temporary. Back to home guard tomorrow. What time is it?"

It was three minutes of twelve!

Magnifico was the picture of misery and heartsick depression. His body curled up, in his eternal effort at self-effacement. His long nose was pinched at the nostrils and his large, down-slanted eyes darted uneasily about.

He clutched at Bayta's hand, and when she bent down, he whispered, "Do you suppose, my lady, that all these great ones were in the audience, perhaps, when I . . . when I played the Sono-Visor?"

"Everyone, I'm sure," Bayta assured him, and shook him gently. "And I'm sure they all think you're the most wonderful player in the Galaxy and that your concert was the greatest ever seen, so you just straighten yourself and sit correctly. We must have dignity."

He smiled feebly at her mock-frown and unfolded his long-boned limbs slowly.

It was noon—

—and the glass cubicle was no longer empty.

It was doubtful that anyone had witnessed the appearance. It was a clean break; one moment not there and the next moment there.

In the cubicle was a figure in a wheelchair, old and shrunken, from whose wrinkled face bright eyes shone, and whose voice, as it turned out, was the livest thing about him. A book lay face downward in his lap, and the voice came softly.

"I am Hari Seldon!"

He spoke through a silence, thunderous in its intensity.

"I am Hari Seldon! I do not know if anyone is here at all by mere sense-perception but that is unimportant. I have few fears as yet of a breakdown in the Plan. For the first three centuries the percentage probability of nondeviation is nine-four point two."

He paused to smile, and then said genially, "By the way, if any of you are standing, you may sit. If any would like to smoke, please do. I am not here in the flesh. I require no ceremony.

"Let us take up the problem of the moment, then. For the first time, the Foundation has been faced, or perhaps, is in the last stages of facing, civil war. Till now, the attacks from without have been adequately beaten off, and inevitably so, according to the strict laws of psycho-history. The attack at present is that of a too-undisciplined outer group of the Foundation against the too-authoritarian central government. The procedure was necessary, the result obvious."

The dignity of the high-born audience was beginning to break. Indbur was half out of his chair.

Bayta leaned forward with troubled eyes. What was the great Seldon talking about? She had missed a few of the words—

"—that the compromise worked out is necessary in two respects. The revolt of the Independent Traders introduces an element of new uncertainty in a government perhaps grown over-confident. The element of striving is restored. Although beaten, a healthy increase of democracy—"

There were raised voices now. Whispers had ascended the scale of loudness, and the edge of panic was in them.

Bayta said in Toran's ear, "Why doesn't he talk about the Mule? The Traders never revolted."

Toran shrugged his shoulders.

The seated figure spoke cheerfully across and through the increasing disorganization:

"—a new and firmer coalition government was the necessary and beneficial outcome of the logical civil war forced upon the Foundation. And now only the remnants of the old Empire stand in the way of further expansion, and in them, for the next few years, at any rate, is no problem. Of course, I can not reveal the nature of the next prob—"

In the complete uproar, Seldon's lips moved soundlessly.

Ebling Mis was next to Randu, face ruddy. He was shouting. "Seldon is off his rocker. He's got the wrong crisis. Were your Traders ever planning civil war?"

Randu said thinly, "We planned one, yes. We called it off in the face of the Mule."

"Then the Mule is an added feature, unprepared for in Seldon's psycho-history. Now what's happened?"

In the sudden, frozen silence, Bayta found the cubicle once again empty. The atomic glow of the walls was dead, the soft current of conditioned air absent.

Somewhere the sound of a shrill siren was rising and falling in the scale and Randu formed the words with his lips, "Space raid!"

And Ebling Mis held his wrist watch to his ears and shouted suddenly, "Stopped, by the Ga-LAX-y! Is there a watch in the room that is going?" His voice was a roar.

Twenty wrists went to twenty ears. And in far less than twenty seconds, it was quite certain that none were.

"Then," said Mis, with a grim and horrible finality, "something has stopped all atomic power in the Time Vault—and the Mule is attacking."

Indbur's wail rose high above the noise, "Take your seats! The Mule is fifty parsecs distant."

"He was," shouted back Mis, "a week ago. Right now, Terminus is being bombarded."

Bayta felt a deep depression settle softly upon her. She felt its folds tighten close and thick, until her breath forced its way only with pain past her tightened throat.

The outer noise of a gathering crowd was evident. The doors were thrown open and a harried figure entered, and spoke rapidly to Indbur, who had rushed to him.

"Excellence," he whispered, "not a vehicle is running in the city, not a communication line to the outside is open. The Tenth Fleet is reported defeated and the Mule's ships are outside the atmosphere. The general staff—"

Indbur crumpled, and was a collapsed figure of impotence

upon the floor. In all that hall, not a voice was raised now. Even the growing crowd without was fearful, but silent, and the horror of cold panic hovered dangerously.

Indbur was raised. Wine was held to his lips. His lips moved before his eyes opened, and the word they formed was, "Surrender!"

Bayta found herself near to crying—not for sorrow or humiliation, but simply and plainly out of a vast frightened despair. Ebling Mis plucked at her sleeve. "Come, young lady—"

She was pulled out of her chair, bodily.

"We're leaving," he said, "and take your musician with you." The plump scientist's lips were trembling and colorless.

"Magnifico," said Bayta, faintly. The clown shrank in horror. His eyes were glassy.

"The Mule," he shrieked. "The Mule is coming for me."

He thrashed wildly at her touch. Toran leaned over and brought his fist up sharply. Magnifico slumped into unconsciousness and Toran carried him out potato-sack fashion.

The next day, the ugly, battle-black ships of the Mule poured down upon the landing fields of the planet Terminus. The attacking general sped down the empty main street of Terminus City in a foreign-made ground car that ran where a whole city of atomic cars still stood useless.

The proclamation of occupation was made twenty-four hours to the minute after Seldon had appeared before the former mighty of the Foundation.

Of all the Foundation planets, only the Independent Traders still stood, and against them the power of the Mule—conqueror of the Foundation—now turned itself.

19.

Start of the Search

The lonely planet, Haven—only planet of an only sun of a Galactic Sector that trailed raggedly off into intergalactic vacuum—was under siege.

In a strictly military sense, it was certainly under siege, since no area of space on the Galactic side further than twenty parsecs distance was outside range of the Mule's advance bases. In the four months since the shattering fall of the Foundation, Haven's communications had fallen apart like a spiderweb under the razor's edge. The ships of Haven converged inwards upon the home world, and only Haven itself was now a fighting base.

And in other respects, the siege was even closer; for the shrouds of helplessness and doom had already invaded—

Bayta plodded her way down the pink-waved aisle past the rows of milky plastic-topped tables and found her seat by blind reckoning. She eased on to the high, armless chair, answered half-heard greetings mechanically, rubbed a wearily-itching eye with the back of a weary hand, and reached for her menu.

She had time to register a violent mental reaction of distaste to the pronounced presence of various cultured-fungus dishes, which were considered high delicacies at Haven, and which her Foundation taste found highly inedible—and then she was aware of the sobbing near her and looked up.

Until then, her notice of Juddee, the plain, snub-nosed, indifferent blonde at the dining unit diagonally across had been the superficial one of the nonacquaintance. And now Juddee was crying, biting woefully at a moist handkerchief, and choking back sobs until her complexion was blotched with turgid red. Her shapeless radiation-proof costume was thrown back upon her shoulders, and her transparent face shield had tumbled forward into her dessert, and there remained.

Bayta joined the three girls who were taking turns at the eternally applied and eternally inefficacious remedies of shoulder-patting, hair-smoothing, and incoherent murmuring.

"What's the matter?" she whispered.

One turned to her and shrugged a discreet, "I don't know." Then, feeling the inadequacy of the gesture, she pulled Bayta aside.

"She's had a hard day, I guess. And she's worrying about her husband."

"Is he on space patrol?"

"Yes."

Bayta reached a friendly hand out to Juddee.

"Why don't you go home, Juddee?" Her voice was a cheerfully businesslike intrusion on the soft, flabby inanities that had preceded.

Juddee looked up half in resentment. "I've been out once this week already—"

"Then you'll be out twice. If you try to stay on, you know, you'll just be out three days next week—so going home now amounts to patriotism. Any of you girls work in her department? Well, then, suppose you take care of her card. Better go to the washroom first, Juddee, and get the peaches and cream back where it belongs. Go ahead! Shoo!"

Bayta returned to her seat and took up the menu again with a dismal relief. These moods were contagious. One weeping girl would have her entire department in a frenzy these nerve-torn days.

She made a distasteful decision, pressed the correct buttons at her elbow and put the menu back into its niche.

The tall, dark girl opposite her was saying, "Isn't much any of us can do except cry, is there?"

Her amazingly full lips scarcely moved, and Bayta noticed that their ends were carefully touched to exhibit that artificial, just-so half-smile that was the current last word in sophistication.

Bayta investigated the insinuating thrust contained in the words with lashed eyes and welcomed the diversion of the arrival of her lunch, as the tile-top of her unit moved inward and the food lifted. She tore the wrappings carefully off her cutlery and handled them gingerly till they cooled.

She said, "Can't *you* think of anything else to do, Hella?"

"Oh, yes," said Hella. "*I* can!" She flicked her cigarette with a casual and expert finger-motion into the little recess provided and the tiny atom-flash caught it before it hit shallow bottom.

"For instance," and Hella clasped slender, well-kept hands under her chin, "I think we could make a very nice arrangement with the Mule and stop all this nonsense. But then *I* don't have the . . . uh . . . facilities to manage to get out of places quickly when the Mule takes over."

Bayta's clear forehead remained clear. Her voice was light and indifferent. "You don't happen to have a brother or husband in the fighting ships, do you?"

"No. All the more credit that I see no reason for the sacrifice of the brothers and husbands of others."

"The sacrifice will come the more surely for surrender."

"The Foundation surrendered and is at peace. Our men are away and the Galaxy is against us."

Bayta shrugged, and said sweetly, "I'm afraid it is the first of the pair that bothers you." She returned to her vegetable platter and ate it with the clammy realization of the silence about her. No one in ear-shot had cared to answer Hella's cynicism.

She left quickly, after stabbing at the button which cleared her dining unit for the next shift's occupant.

A new girl, three seats away, stage-whispered to Hella, "Who was she?"

Hella's mobile lips curled in indifference. "She's our co-ordinator's niece. Didn't you know that?"

"Yes?" Her eyes sought out the last glimpse of disappearing back. "What's she doing here?"

"Just an assembly girl. Don't you know it's fashionable to be patriotic? It's all so democratic, it makes me retch."

"Now, Hella," said the plump girl to her right. "She's never pulled her uncle on us yet. Why don't you lay off?"

Hella ignored her neighbor with a glazed sweep of eyes and lit another cigarette.

The new girl was listening to the chatter of the bright-eyed accountant opposite. The words were coming quickly, "—and she's supposed to have been in the Vault—actually in the Vault, you know—when Seldon spoke—and they say the mayor was in frothing furies and there were riots, and all of that sort of thing, you know. She got away before the Mule landed, and they say she had the most tha-rilling escape—had to go through the blockade, and all—and I do wonder she doesn't write a book about it, these war books being so popular these days, you know. And she was supposed to be on this world of the Mule's, too—Kalgan, you know—and—"

The time bell shrilled and the dining room emptied slowly. The accountant's voice buzzed on, and the new girl interrupted only with the conventional and wide-eyed, "Really-y-y-y?" at appropriate points.

The huge cave lights were being shielded group-wise in the gradual descent towards the darkness that meant sleep for the righteous and hard-working, when Bayta returned home.

Toran met her at the door, with a slice of buttered bread in his hand.

"Where've you been?" he asked, food-muffled. Then, more clearly, "I've got a dinner of sorts rassled up. If it isn't much, don't blame me."

But she was circling him, wide-eyed. "Torie! Where's your uniform? What are you doing in civvies?"

"Orders, Bay. Randu is holed up with Ebling Mis right now, and what it's all about, I don't know. So there you have everything."

"Am I going?" She moved towards him impulsively.

He kissed her before he answered, "I believe so. It will probably be dangerous."

"What isn't dangerous?"

"Exactly. Oh, yes, and I've already sent for Magnifico, so he's probably coming too."

"You mean his concert at the Engine Factory will have to be cancelled."

"Obviously."

Bayta passed into the next room and sat down to a meal that

definitely bore signs of having been "rassled-up." She cut the sandwiches in two with quick efficiency and said:

"That's too bad about the concert. The girls at the factory were looking forward to it. Magnifico, too, for that matter. Darn it, he's such a queer thing."

"Stirs your mother-complex, Bay, that's what he does. Some day we'll have a baby, and then you'll forget Magnifico."

Bayta answered from the depths of her sandwich, "Strikes me that you're all the stirring my mother-complex can stand."

And then she laid the sandwich down, and was gravely serious in a moment.

"Torie."

"M-m-m?"

"Torie, I was at City Hall today—at the Bureau of Production. That is why I was so late today."

"What were you doing there?"

"Well . . ." she hesitated, uncertainly. "It's been building up. I was getting so I couldn't stand it at the factory. Morale—just doesn't exist. The girls go on crying jags for no particular reason. Those who don't get sick become sullen. Even the little mousie types pout. In my particular section, production isn't a quarter what it was when I came, and there isn't a day that we have a full roster of workers."

"All right," said Toran, "tie in the B. of P. What did you do there?"

"Asked a few questions. And it's so, Torie, it's so all over Haven. Dropping production, increasing sedition and disaffection. The bureau chief just shrugged his shoulders—after I had sat in the anteroom an hour to see him, and only got in because I was the co-ordinator's niece—and said it was beyond him. Frankly, I don't think he cared."

"Now, don't go off base, Bay."

"I don't think he did." She was strenuously fiery. "I tell you there's something wrong. It's that same horrible frustration that hit me in the Time Vault when Seldon deserted us. You felt it yourself."

"Yes, I did."

"Well, it's back," she continued savagely. "And we'll never be able to resist the Mule. Even if we had the material, we lack the heart, the spirit, the will—Torie, there's no use fighting—"

Bayta had never cried in Toran's memory, and she did not cry now. Not really. But Toran laid a light hand on her shoulder and whispered, "Suppose you forget it, baby. I know what you mean. But there's nothing—"

"Yes, there's nothing we can do! Everyone says that—and we just sit and wait for the knife to come down."

She returned to what was left of her sandwich and tea. Quietly, Toran was arranging the beds. It was quite dark outside.

Randu, as newly-appointed co-ordinator—in itself a wartime post—of the confederation of cities on Haven, had been assigned, at his own request, to an upper room, out of the window of which he could brood over the roof tops and greenery of the city. Now, in the fading of the cave lights, the city receded into the level lack of distinction of the shades. Randu did not care to meditate upon the symbolism.

He said to Ebling Mis—whose clear, little eyes seemed to have no further interest than the red-filled goblet in his hand—"There's a saying on Haven that when the cave lights go out, it is time for the righteous and hard-working to sleep."

"Do you sleep much lately?"

"No! Sorry to call you so late, Mis. I like the night better somehow these days. Isn't that strange? The people on Haven condition themselves pretty strictly on the lack of light meaning sleep. Myself, too. But it's different now—"

"You're hiding," said Mis, flatly. "You're surrounded by people in the waking period, and you feel their eyes and their hopes on you. You can't stand up under it. In the sleep period, you're free."

"Do you feel it, too, then? This miserable sense of defeat?"

Ebling Mis nodded slowly, "I do. It's a mass psychosis, an unprintable mob panic. Ga-LAX-y, Randu, what do you expect? Here you have a whole culture brought up to a blind, blubbering belief that a folk hero of the past has everything all planned out and is taking care of every little piece of their unprintable lives. The thought-pattern evoked has characteristics *ad religio*, and you know what that means."

"Not a bit."

Mis was not enthusiastic about the necessity of explanation. He never was. So he growled, stared at the long cigar he rolled thoughtfully between his fingers and said, "Characterized by strong faith reactions. Beliefs can't be shaken short of a major shock, in which case, a fairly complete mental disruption results. Mild cases—hysteria, morbid sense of insecurity. Advanced cases —madness and suicide."

Randu bit at a thumbnail. "When Seldon fails us, in other words, our prop disappears, and we've been leaning upon it so long, our muscles are atrophied to where we can not stand without it."

"That's it. Sort of a clumsy metaphor, but that's it."

"And you, Ebling, what of your own muscles?"

The psychologist filtered a long draught of air through his cigar, and let the smoke laze out. "Rusty, but not atrophied. My profession has resulted in just a bit of independent thinking."

"And you see a way out?"

"No, but there must be one. Maybe Seldon made no provisions for the Mule. Maybe he didn't guarantee our victory. But, then, neither did he guarantee defeat. He's just out of the game and we're on our own. The Mule can be licked."

"How?"

"By the only way anyone can be licked—by attacking in strength at weakness. See here, Randu, the Mule isn't a superman. If he is finally defeated, everyone will see that for himself. It's just that he's an unknown, and the legends cluster quickly. He's supposed to be a mutant. Well, what of that? A mutant means a 'superman' to the ignoramuses of humanity. Nothing of the sort.

"It's been estimated that several million mutants are born in the Galaxy every day. Of the several million, all but one or two percent can be detected only by means of microscopes and chemistry. Of the one or two percent macromutants, that is, those with mutations detectable to the naked eye or naked mind, all but one or two percent are freaks, fit for the amusement centers, the laboratories, and death. Of the few macromutants whose differences are to the good, almost all are harmless curiosities, unusual

in some single respect, normal—and often subnormal—in most
others. You see that, Randu?"

"I do. But what of the Mule?"

"Supposing the Mule to be a mutant then, we can assume that
he has some attribute, undoubtedly mental, which can be used to
conquer worlds. In other respects, he undoubtedly has his shortcomings, which we must locate. He would not be so secretive, so
shy of others' eyes, if these shortcomings were not apparent and
fatal. *If* he's a mutant."

"Is there an alternative?"

"There might be. Evidence for mutation rests on Captain Han
Pritcher of what used to be Foundation's Intelligence. He drew
his conclusions from the feeble memories of those who claimed
to know the Mule—or somebody who might have been the Mule—
in infancy and early childhood. Pritcher worked on slim pickings
there, and what evidence he found might easily have been
planted by the Mule for his own purposes, for it's certain that the
Mule has been vastly aided by his reputation as a mutant-super-
man."

"This is interesting. How long have you thought that?"

"I never thought that, in the sense of believing it. It is merely
an alternative to be considered. For instance, Randu, suppose the
Mule has discovered a form of radiation capable of depressing
mental energy just as he is in possession of one which depresses
atomic reactions. What then, eh? Could that explain what's hitting us now—and what did hit the Foundation?"

Randu seemed immersed in a near-wordless gloom.

He said, "What of your own researches on the Mule's clown."

And now Ebling Mis hesitated. "Useless as yet. I spoke bravely
to the mayor previous to the Foundation's collapse, mainly to
keep his courage up—partly to keep my own up as well. But,
Randu, if my mathematical tools were up to it, then from the
clown alone I could analyze the Mule completely. Then we would
have him. Then we could solve the queer anomalies that have impressed me already."

"Such as?"

"Think, man. The Mule defeated the navies of the Foundation
at will, but he has not once managed to force the much weaker

fleets of the Independent Traders to retreat in open combat. The Foundation fell at a blow; the Independent Traders hold out against all his strength. He first used his Extinguishing Field upon the atomic weapons of the Independent Traders of Mnemon. The element of surprise lost them that battle but they countered the Field. He was never able to use it successfully against the Independents again.

"But over and over again, it worked against Foundation forces. It worked on the Foundation itself. Why? With our present knowledge, it is all illogical. So there must be factors of which we are not aware."

"Treachery?"

"That's rattle-pated nonsense, Randu. Unprintable twaddle. There wasn't a man on the Foundation who wasn't sure of victory. Who would betray a certain-to-win side."

Randu stepped to the curved window and stared unseeingly out into the unseeable. He said, "But we're certain to lose now, if the Mule had a thousand weaknesses; if he were a network of holes—"

He did not turn. It was as if the slump of his back, the nervous groping for one another of the hands behind him that spoke. He said, "We escaped easily after the Time Vault episode, Ebling. Others might have escaped as well. A few did. Most did not. The Extinguishing Field could have been counteracted. It asked ingenuity and a certain amount of labor. All the ships of the Foundation Navy could have flown to Haven or other nearby planets to continue the fight as we did. Not one percent did so. In effect, they deserted to the enemy.

"The Foundation underground, upon which most people here seem to rely so heavily, has thus far done nothing of consequence. The Mule has been politic enough to promise to safeguard the property and profits of the great Traders and they have gone over to him."

Ebling Mis said stubbornly, "The plutocrats have always been against us."

"They always held the power, too. Listen, Ebling. We have reason to believe that the Mule or his tools have already been in contact with powerful men among the Independent Traders. At least ten of the twenty-seven Trading Worlds are known to have gone over to the Mule. Perhaps ten more waver. There are personalities on Haven itself who would not be unhappy over the Mule's domination. It's apparently an insurmountable temptation to give up endangered political power, if that will maintain your hold over economic affairs."

"You don't think Haven can fight the Mule?"

"I don't think Haven will." And now Randu turned his troubled face full upon the psychologist. "I think Haven is waiting to surrender. It's what I called you here to tell you. I want you to leave Haven."

Ebling Mis puffed up his plump cheeks in amazement. "Already?"

Randu felt horribly tired. "Ebling, you are the Foundation's greatest psychologist. The real master-psychologists went out with Seldon, but you're the best we have. You're our only chance of defeating the Mule. You can't do that here; you'll have to go to what's left of the Empire."

"To Trantor?"

"That's right. What was once the Empire is bare bones today, but something must still be at the center. They've got the records there, Ebling. You may learn more of mathematical psychology; perhaps enough to be able to interpret the clown's mind. He will go with you, of course."

Mis responded dryly, "I doubt if he'd be willing to, even for fear of the Mule, unless your niece went with him."

"I know that. Toran and Bayta are leaving with you for that very reason. And, Ebling, there's another, greater purpose. Hari Seldon founded *two* Foundations three centuries ago; one at each end of the Galaxy. *You must find that Second Foundation.*"

20.

Conspirator

The mayor's palace—what was once the mayor's palace—was a looming smudge in the darkness. The city was quiet under its conquest and curfew, and the hazy milk of the great Galactic Lens, with here and there a lonely star, dominated the sky of the Foundation.

In three centuries the Foundation had grown from a private project of a small group of scientists to a tentacular trade empire sprawling deep into the Galaxy and half a year had flung it from its heights to the status of another conquered province.

Captain Han Pritcher refused to grasp that.

The city's sullen nighttime quiet, the darkened palace, intruder-occupied, were symbolic enough, but Captain Han Pritcher, just within the outer gate of the palace, with the tiny atomic bomb under his tongue, refused to understand.

A shape drifted closer—the captain bent his head.

The whisper came deathly low, "The alarm system is as it always was, captain. Proceed! It will register nothing."

Softly, the captain ducked through the low archway, and down the fountain-lined path to what had been Indbur's garden.

Four months ago had been the day in the Time Vault, the fullness of which his memory balked at. Singly and separately the impressions would come back, unwelcome, mostly at night.

Old Seldon speaking his benevolent words that were so shatteringly wrong—the jumbled confusion—Indbur, with his mayoral costume incongruously bright about his pinched, unconscious face —the frightened crowds gathering quickly, waiting noiselessly for the inevitable word of surrender—the young man, Toran, disappearing out of a side door with the Mule's clown dangling over his shoulder.

And himself, somehow out of it all afterward, with his car unworkable.

Shouldering his way along and through the leaderless mob that was already leaving the city—destination unknown.

Making blindly for the various rat holes which were—which had once been—the headquarters for a democratic underground that for eighty years had been failing and dwindling.

And the rat holes were empty.

The next day, black alien ships were momentarily visible in the sky, sinking gently into the clustered buildings of the nearby city. Captain Han Pritcher felt an accumulation of helplessness and despair drown him.

He started his travels in earnest.

In thirty days he had covered nearly two hundred miles on foot, changed to the clothing of a worker in the hydroponic factories whose body he found newly-dead by the side of the road, grown a fierce beard of russet intensity—

And found what was left of the underground.

The city was Newton, the district a residential one of one-time elegance slowly edging towards squalor, the house an undistinguished member of a row, and the man a small-eyed, big-boned whose knotted fists bulged through his pockets and whose wiry body remained unbudgingly in the narrow door opening.

The captain mumbled, "I come from Miran."

The man returned the gambit, grimly. "Miran is early this year."

The captain said, "No earlier than last year."

But the man did not step aside. He said, "Who are you?"

"Aren't you Fox?"

"Do you always answer by asking?"

The captain took an imperceptibly longer breath, and then said calmly, "I am Han Pritcher, Captain of the Fleet, and member of the Democratic Underground Party. Will you let me in?"

The Fox stepped aside. He said, "My real name is Orum Palley."

He held out his hand. The captain took it.

The room was well-kept, but not lavish. In one corner stood a decorative book-film projector, which to the captain's military eyes might easily have been a camouflaged blaster of respectable caliber. The projecting lens covered the doorway, and such could be remotely controlled.

The Fox followed his bearded guest's eyes, and smiled tightly. He said, "Yes! But only in the days of Indbur and his lackey-hearted vampires. It wouldn't do much against the Mule, eh? Nothing would help against the Mule. Are you hungry?"

The captain's jaw muscles tightened beneath his beard, and he nodded.

"It'll take a minute if you don't mind waiting." The Fox removed cans from a cupboard and placed two before Captain Pritcher. "Keep your finger on it, and break them when they're hot enough. My heat-control unit's out of whack. Things like that remind you there's a war on—or was on, eh?"

His quick words had a jovial content, but were said in anything but a jovial tone—and his eyes were coldly thoughtful. He sat down opposite the captain and said, "There'll be nothing but a burn-spot left where you're sitting, if there's anything about you I don't like. Know that?"

The captain did not answer. The cans before him opened at a pressure.

The Fox said, shortly, "Stew! Sorry, but the food situation is short."

"I know," said the captain. He ate quickly; not looking up.

The Fox said, "I once saw you. I'm trying to remember, and the beard is definitely out of the picture."

"I haven't shaved in thirty days." Then, fiercely, "What do you want? I had the correct passwords. I have identification."

The other waved a hand, "Oh, I'll grant you're Pritcher all right. But there are plenty who have the passwords, and the identifications, and the *identities*—who are with the Mule. Ever hear of Levvaw, eh?"

"Yes."

"He's with the Mule."

"What? He—"

"Yes. He was the man they called 'No Surrender.'" The Fox's lips made laughing motions, with neither sound nor humor. "Then

there's Willig. With the Mule! Garre and Noth. With the Mule!
Why not Pritcher as well, eh? How would I know?"

The captain merely shook his head.

"But it doesn't matter," said the Fox, softly. "They must have
my name, if Noth has gone over—so if you're legitimate, you're
in more new danger than I am over our acquaintanceship."

The captain had finished eating. He leaned back, "If you have
no organization here, where can I find one? The Foundation may
have surrendered, but I haven't."

"So! You can't wander forever, captain. Men of the Foundation
must have travel permits to move from town to town these days.
You know that? Also identity cards. You have one? Also, all officers of the old Navy have been requested to report to the nearest
occupation headquarters. That's you, eh?"

"Yes." The captain's voice was hard. "Do you think I run
through fear. I was on Kalgan not long after *its* fall to the Mule.
Within a month, not one of the old warlord's officers was at large,
because they were the natural military leaders of any revolt. It's
always been the underground's knowledge that no revolution can
be successful without the control of at least part of the Navy. The
Mule evidently knows it, too."

The Fox nodded thoughtfully, "Logical enough. The Mule is
thorough."

"I discarded the uniform as soon as I could. I grew the beard.
Afterwards there may be a chance that others have taken the
same action."

"Are you married?"

"My wife is dead. I have no children."

"You're hostage-immune, then."

"Yes."

"You want my advice?"

"If you have any."

"I don't know what the Mule's policy is or what he intends, but
skilled workers have not been harmed so far. Pay rates have gone
up. Production of all sorts of atomic weapons is booming."

"Yes? Sounds like a continuing offensive."

"I don't know. The Mule's a subtle son of a drab, and he may
merely be soothing the workers into submission. If Seldon

couldn't figure him out with all his psycho-history, I'm not going to try. But you're wearing work clothes. That suggests something, eh?"

"I'm not a skilled worker."

"You've had a military course in atomics, haven't you?"

"Certainly."

"That's enough. The Atom-Field Bearings, Inc., is located here in town. Tell them you've had experience. The stinkers who used to run the factory for Indbur are still running it—for the Mule. They won't ask questions, as long as they need more workers to make their fat hunk. They'll give you an identity card and you can apply for a room in the Corporation's housing district. You might start now."

In that manner, Captain Han Pritcher of the National Fleet became Shield-man Lo Moro of the 45 Shop of Atom-Field Bearings, Inc. And from an Intelligence agent, he descended the social scale to "conspirator"—a calling which led him months later to what had been Indbur's private garden.

In the garden, Captain Pritcher consulted the radometer in the palm of his hand. The inner warning field was still in operation, and he waited. Half an hour remained to the life of the atomic bomb in his mouth. He rolled it gingerly with his tongue.

The radometer died into an ominous darkness and the captain advanced quickly.

So far, matters had progressed well.

He reflected objectively that the life of the atomic bomb was his as well; that its death was his death—and the Mule's death.

And the grand climacteric of a four-month's private war would be reached; a war that had passed from flight through a Newton factory—

For two months, Captain Pritcher wore leaden aprons and heavy face shields, till all things military had been frictioned off his outer bearing. He was a laborer, who collected his pay, spent his evenings in town, and never discussed politics.

For two months, he did not see the Fox.

And then, one day, a man stumbled past his bench, and there was a scrap of paper in his pocket. The word "Fox" was on it. He tossed it into the atom chamber, where it vanished in a sightless puff, sending the energy output up a millimicrovolt—and turned back to his work.

That night he was at the Fox's home, and took a hand in a game of cards with two other men he knew by reputation and one by name and face.

Over the cards and the passing and repassing tokens, they spoke.

The captain said, "It's a fundamental error. You live in the exploded past. For eighty years our organization has been waiting for the correct historical moment. We've been blinded by Seldon's psycho-history, one of the first propositions of which is that the individual does not count, does not make history, and that complex social and economic factors override him, make a puppet out of him." He adjusted his cards carefully, appraised their value and said, as he put out a token, "Why not kill the Mule?"

"Well, now, and what good would that do?" demanded the man at his left, fiercely.

"You see," said the captain, discarding two cards, "that's the attitude. What is one man—out of trillions. The Galaxy won't stop rotating because one man dies. But the Mule is not a man, he is a Mutant. Already, he had upset Seldon's plan, and if you'll stop to analyze the implications, it means that he—one man—one mutant —upset all of Seldon's psycho-history. If he had never lived, the Foundation would not have fallen. If he ceased living, it would not remain fallen.

"Come, the democrats have fought the mayors and the traders for eighty years by connivery. Let's try assassination."

"How?" interposed the Fox, with cold common sense.

The captain said, slowly, "I've spent three months of thought on that with no solution. I came here and had it in five minutes." He glanced briefly at the man whose broad, pink melon of a face smiled from the place at his right. "You were once Mayor Indbur's chamberlain. I did not know you were of the underground."

"Nor I, that you were."

"Well, then, in your capacity as chamberlain you periodically checked the working of the alarm system of the palace."

"I did."

"And the Mule occupies the palace now."

"So it has been announced—though he is a modest conqueror who makes no speeches, proclamations nor public appearances of any sort."

"That's an old story, and affects nothing. You, my ex-chamberlain, are all we need."

The cards were shown and the Fox collected the stakes. Slowly, he dealt a new hand.

The man who had once been chamberlain picked up his cards, singly. "Sorry, captain. I checked the alarm system, but it was routine. I know nothing about it."

"I expected that, but your mind carries an eidetic memory of the controls if it can be probed deeply enough—with a psychic probe."

The chamberlain's ruddy face paled suddenly and sagged. The cards in his hand crumpled under sudden fist-pressure, "A psychic probe?"

"You needn't worry," said the captain, sharply. "I know how to use one. It will not harm you past a few days' weakness. And if it did, it is the chance you take and the price you pay. There are some among us, no doubt, who from the controls of the alarm could determine the wave-length combinations. There are some among us who could manufacture a small bomb under time-control and I myself will carry it to the Mule."

The men gathered over the table.

The captain continued, "On a given evening, a riot will start in Terminus City in the neighborhood of the palace. No real fighting. Disturbance—then flight. As long as the palace guard is attracted . . . or, at the very least, distracted—"

From that day for a month the preparations went on, and Captain Han Pritcher of the National Fleet having become conspirator descended further in the social scale and became an "assassin."

Captain Pritcher, assassin, was in the palace itself, and found himself grimly pleased with his psychology. A thorough alarm system outside meant few guards within. In this case, it meant none at all.

The floor plan was clear in his mind. He was a blob moving noiselessly up the well-carpeted ramp. At its head, he flattened against the wall and waited.

The small closed door of a private room was before him. Behind that door must be the mutant who had beaten the unbeatable. He was early—the bomb had ten minutes of life in it.

Five of these passed, and still in all the world there was no sound. The Mule had five minutes to live— So had Captain Pritcher—

He stepped forward on sudden impulse. The plot could no longer fail. When the bomb went, the palace would go with it —all the palace. A door between—ten yards between—was nothing. But he wanted to see the Mule as they died together.

In a last, insolent gesture, he thundered upon the door—

And it opened and let out the blinding light.

Captain Pritcher staggered, then caught himself. The solemn man, standing in the center of the small room before a suspended fish bowl, looked up mildly.

His uniform was a somber black, and as he tapped the bowl in an absent gesture, it bobbed quickly and the feather-finned orange and vermilion fish within darted wildly.

He said, "Come in, captain!"

To the captain's quivering tongue the little metal globe beneath was swelling ominously—a physical impossibility, the captain knew. But it was in its last minute of life.

The uniformed man said, "You had better spit out the foolish pellet and free yourself for speech. It won't blast."

The minute passed and with a slow, sodden motion the captain bent his head and dropped the silvery globe into his palm. With a furious force it was flung against the wall. It rebounded with a tiny, sharp clangor, gleaming harmlessly as it flew.

The uniformed man shrugged. "So much for that, then. It would have done you no good in any case, captain. I am not the Mule. You will have to be satisfied with his viceroy."

"How did you know?" muttered the captain, thickly.

"Blame it on an efficient counter-espionage system. I can name every member of your little gang, every step of their planning—"

"And you let it go this far?"

"Why not? It has been one of my great purposes here to find you and some others. Particularly you. I might have had you some months ago, while you were still a worker at the Newton

Bearings Works, but this is much better. If you hadn't suggested the main outlines of the plot yourself, one of my own men would have advanced something of much the same sort for you. The result is quite dramatic, and rather grimly humorous."

The captain's eyes were hard. "I find it so, too. Is it all over now?"

"Just begun. Come, captain, sit down. Let us leave heroics for the fools who are impressed by it. Captain, you are a capable man. According to the information I have, you were the first on the Foundation to recognize the power of the Mule. Since then you have interested yourself, rather daringly, in the Mule's early life. You have been one of those who carried off his clown, who, incidentally, has not yet been found, and for which there will yet be full payment. Naturally, your ability is recognized and the Mule is not of those who fear the ability of his enemies as long as he can convert it into the ability of a new friend."

"Is that what you're hedging up to? Oh, no!"

"Oh, yes! It was the purpose of tonight's comedy. You are an intelligent man, yet your little conspiracies against the Mule fail humorously. You can scarcely dignify it with the name of conspiracy. Is it part of your military training to waste ships in hopeless actions?"

"One must first admit them to be hopeless."

"One will," the viceroy assured him, gently. "The Mule has conquered the Foundation. It is rapidly being turned into an arsenal for accomplishment of his greater aims."

"What greater aims?"

"The conquest of the entire Galaxy. The reunion of all the torn worlds into a new Empire. The fulfillment, you dull-witted patriot, of your own Seldon's dream seven hundred years before he hoped to see it. And in the fulfillment, you can help us."

"I can, undoubtedly. But I won't, undoubtedly."

"I understand," reasoned the viceroy, "that only three of the Independent Trading Worlds yet resist. They will not last much longer. It will be the last of all Foundation forces. You still hold out."

"Yes."

"Yet you won't. A voluntary recruit is the most efficient. But the other kind will do. Unfortunately, the Mule is absent. He leads the fight, as always, against the resisting Traders. But he is in continual contact with us. You will not have to wait long."

"For what?"

"For your conversion."

"The Mule," said the captain, frigidly, "will find that beyond his ability."

"But he won't. *I* was not beyond it. You don't recognize me? Come, you were on Kalgan, so you have seen me. I wore a monocle, a fur-lined scarlet robe, a high-crowned hat—"

The captain stiffened in dismay. "You were the warlord of Kalgan."

"Yes. And now I am the loyal viceroy of the Mule. You see, he is persuasive."

21.

Interlude in Space

The blockade was run successfully. In the vast volume of space, not all the navies ever in existence could keep their watch in tight proximity. Given a single ship, a skillful pilot, and a moderate degree of luck, and there are holes and to spare.

With cold-eyed calm, Toran drove a protesting vessel from the vicinity of one star to that of another. If the neighborhood of great mass made an interstellar jump erratic and difficult, it also made the enemy detection devices useless or nearly so.

And once the girdle of ships had been passed the inner sphere of dead space, through whose blockaded sub-ether no message could be driven, was passed as well. For the first time in over three months Toran felt unisolated.

A week passed before the enemy news programs dealt with anything more than the dull, self-laudatory details of growing control over the Foundation. It was a week in which Toran's armored trading ship fleeted in from the Periphery with hasty jumps.

Ebling Mis called out to the pilot room and Toran rose blink-eyed from his charts.

"What's the matter?" Toran stepped down into the small central chamber which Bayta had inevitably devised into a living room.

Mis shook his head, "Bescuppered if I know. The Mule's newsmen are announcing a special bulletin. Thought you might want to get in on it."

"Might as well. Where's Bayta?"

"Setting the table in the diner and picking out a menu—or some such frippery."

Toran sat down upon the cot that served as Magnifico's bed, and waited. The propaganda routine of the Mule's "special bulletins" were monotonously similar. First the martial music, and then the buttery slickness of the announcer. The minor news items would come, following one another in patient lock step. Then the pause. Then the trumpets and the rising excitement and the climax.

Toran endured it. Mis muttered to himself.

The newscaster spilled out, in conventional war-correspondent phraseology, the unctuous words that translated into sound the molten metal and blasted flesh of a battle in space.

"Rapid cruiser squadrons under Lieutenant General Sammin hit back hard today at the task force striking out from Iss—" The carefully expressionless face of the speaker upon the screen faded into the blackness of a space cut through by the quick swaths of ships reeling across emptiness in deadly battle. The voice continued through the soundless thunder—

"The most striking action of the battle was the subsidiary combat of the heavy cruiser *Cluster* against three enemy ships of the 'Nova' class—"

The screen's view veered and closed in. A great ship sparked and one of the frantic attackers glowed angrily, twisted out of focus, swung back and rammed. The *Cluster* bowed wildly and survived the glancing blow that drove the attacker off in twisting reflection.

The newsman's smooth unimpassioned delivery continued to the last blow and the last hulk.

Then a pause, and a largely similar voice-and-picture of the fight off Mnemon, to which the novelty was added of a lengthy description of a hit-and-run landing—the picture of a blasted city —huddled and weary prisoners—and off again.

Mnemon had not long to live.

The pause again—and this time the raucous sound of the expected brasses. The screen faded into the long, impressively soldier-lined corridor up which the government spokesman in councilor's uniform strode quickly.

The silence was oppressive.

The voice that came at last was solemn, slow and hard:

"By order of our sovereign, it is announced that the planet, Haven, hitherto in warlike opposition to his will, has submitted to the acceptance of defeat. At this moment, the forces of our sovereign are occupying the planet. Opposition was scattered, unco-ordinated, and speedily crushed."

The scene faded out, the original newsman returned to state importantly that other developments would be transmitted as they occurred.

Then there was dance music, and Ebling Mis threw the shield that cut the power.

Toran rose and walked unsteadily away, without a word. The psychologist made no move to stop him.

When Bayta stepped out of the kitchen, Mis motioned silence. He said, "They've taken Haven."

And Bayta said, "Already?" Her eyes were round, and sick with disbelief.

"Without a fight. Without an unprin–" He stopped and swallowed. "You'd better leave Toran alone. It's not pleasant for him. Suppose we eat without him this once."

Bayta looked once toward the pilot room, then turned hopelessly. "Very well!"

Magnifico sat unnoticed at the table. He neither spoke nor ate but stared ahead with a concentrated fear that seemed to drain all the vitality out of his thread of a body.

Ebling Mis pushed absently at his iced-fruit dessert and said, harshly, "Two Trading worlds fight. They fight, and bleed, and die and don't surrender. Only at Haven– Just as at the Foundation–"

"But why? Why?"

The psychologist shook his head. "It's of a piece with all the problem. Every queer facet is a hint at the nature of the Mule. First, the problem of how he could conquer the Foundation, with little blood, and at a single blow essentially–while the Independent Trading Worlds held out. The blanket on atomic reactions was a puny weapon–we've discussed that back and forth till I'm sick of it–and it did not work on any but the Foundation.

"Randu suggested," and Ebling's grizzly eyebrows pulled together, "it might have been a radiant Will-Depresser. It's what might have done the work on Haven. But then why wasn't it used on Mnemon and Iss–which even now fight with such demonic intensity that it is taking half the Foundation fleet in addition to the Mule's forces to beat them down. Yes, I recognized Foundation ships in the attack."

Bayta whispered, "The Foundation, then Haven. Disaster seems to follow us, without touching. We always seem to get out by a hair. Will it last forever?"

Ebling Mis was not listening. To himself, he was making a point. "But there's another problem—another problem. Bayta, you remember the news item that the Mule's clown was not found on Terminus; that it was suspected he had fled to Haven, or been carried there by his original kidnapers. There is an importance attached to him, Bayta, that doesn't fade, and we have not located it yet. Magnifico must know something that is fatal to the Mule. I'm sure of it."

Magnifico, white and stuttering, protested, "Sire . . . noble lord . . . indeed, I swear it is past my poor reckoning to penetrate your wants. I have told what I know to the utter limits, and with your probe, you have drawn out of my meager wit that which I knew, but knew not that I knew."

"I know . . . I know. It is something small. A hint so small that neither you nor I recognize it for what it is. Yet I must find it— for Mnemon and Iss will go soon, and when they do, we are the last remnants, the last droplets of the independent Foundation."

The stars begin to cluster closely when the core of the Galaxy is penetrated. Gravitational fields begin to overlap at intensities sufficient to introduce perturbations in an interstellar jump that can not be overlooked.

Toran became aware of that when a jump landed their ship in the full glare of a red giant which clutched viciously, and whose grip was loosed, then wrenched apart, only after twelve sleepless, soul-battering hours.

With charts limited in scope, and an experience not at all fully developed, either operationally or mathematically, Toran resigned himself to days of careful plotting between jumps.

It became a community project of a sort. Ebling Mis checked Toran's mathematics and Bayta tested possible routes, by the various generalized methods, for the presence of real solutions. Even Magnifico was put to work on the calculating machine for routine computations, a type of work, which, once explained, was a source of great amusement to him and at which he was surprisingly proficient.

So at the end of a month, or nearly, Bayta was able to survey the red line that wormed its way through the ship's trimensional model of the Galactic Lens halfway to its center, and say with satiric relish, "You know what it looks like. It looks like a ten-foot earth-worm with a terrific case of indigestion. Eventually, you'll land us back in Haven."

"I will," growled Toran, with a fierce rustle of his chart, "if you don't shut up."

"And at that," continued Bayta, "there is probably a route right through, straight as a meridian of longitude."

"Yeah? Well, in the first place, dimwit, it probably took five hundred ships five hundred years to work out that route by hit-and-miss, and my lousy half-credit charts don't give it. Besides, maybe those straight routes are a good thing to avoid. They're probably choked up with ships. And besides—"

"Oh, for Galaxy's sake, stop driveling and slavering so much righteous indignation." Her hands were in his hair.

He yowled, "Ouch! Let go!" seized her wrists and whipped downward, whereupon Toran, Bayta, and chair formed a tangled threesome on the floor. It degenerated into a panting wrestling match, composed mostly of choking laughter and various foul blows.

Toran broke loose at Magnifico's breathless entrance.

"What is it?"

The lines of anxiety puckered the clown's face and tightened the skin whitely over the enormous bridge of his nose. "The instruments are behaving queerly, sir. I have not, in the knowledge of my ignorance, touched anything—"

In two seconds, Toran was in the pilot room. He said quietly to Magnifico, "Wake up Ebling Mis. Have him come down here."

He said to Bayta, who was trying to get a basic order back to her hair by use of her fingers, "We've been detected, Bay."

"Detected?" And Bayta's arms dropped. "By whom?"

"Galaxy knows," muttered Toran, "but I imagine by someone with blasters already ranged and trained."

He sat down and in a low voice was already sending into the sub-ether the ship's identification code.

And when Ebling Mis entered, bathrobed and blear-eyed, Toran said with a desperate calm, "It seems we're inside the borders of a local Inner Kingdom which is called the Autarchy of Filia."

"Never heard of it," said Mis, abruptly.

"Well, neither did I," replied Toran, "but we're being stopped by a Filian ship just the same, and I don't know what it will involve."

The captain-inspector of the Filian ship crowded aboard with six armed men following him. He was short, thin-haired, thin-lipped, and dry-skinned. He coughed a sharp cough as he sat down and threw open the folio under his arm to a blank page.

"Your passports and ship's clearance, please."

"We have none," said Toran.

"None, hey?" he snatched up a microphone suspended from his belt and spoke into it quickly, "Three men and one woman. Papers not in order." He made an accompanying notation in the folio.

He said, "Where are you from?"

"Siwenna," said Toran warily.

"Where is that?"

"A hundred thousand parsecs, eighty degrees west Trantor, forty degrees—"

"Never mind, never mind!" Toran could see that his inquisitor had written down: "Point of origin—Periphery."

The Filian continued, "Where are you going?"

Toran said, "Trantor sector."

"Purpose?"

"Pleasure trip."

"Carrying any cargo?"

"No."

"Hm-m-m. We'll check on that." He nodded and two men jumped to activity. Toran made no move to interfere.

"What brings you into Filian territory?" The Filian's eyes gleamed unamiably.

"We didn't know we were. I lack a proper chart."

"You will be required to pay a hundred credits for that lack—and, of course, the usual fees required for tariff duties, et cetera."

He spoke again into the microphone—but listened more than he spoke. Then, to Toran, "Know anything about atomic technology?"

"A little," replied Toran, guardedly.

"Yes?" The Filian closed his folio, and added, "The men of the Periphery have a knowledgeable reputation that way. Put on a suit and come with me."

Bayta stepped forward. "What are you going to do with him?"

Toran put her aside gently, and asked coldly, "Where do you want me to come?"

"Our power plant needs minor adjustments. He'll come with you." His pointing finger aimed directly at Magnifico, whose brown eyes opened wide in a blubbery dismay.

"What's he got to do with it?" demanded Toran fiercely.

The official looked up coldly. "I am informed of pirate activities in this vicinity. A description of one of the known thugs tallies roughly. It is a purely routine matter of identification."

Toran hesitated, but six men and six blasters are eloquent arguments. He reached into the cupboard for the suits.

An hour later, he rose upright in the bowels of the Filian ship and raged, "There's not a thing wrong with the motors that I can see. The busbars are true, the L-tubes are feeding properly and the reaction analysis checks. Who's in charge here?"

The head engineer said quietly, "I am."

"Well, get me out of here—"

He was led to the officers' level and the small anteroom held only an indifferent ensign.

"Where's the man who came with me?"

"Please wait," said the ensign.

It was fifteen minutes later that Magnifico was brought in.

"What did they do to you?" asked Toran quickly.

"Nothing. Nothing at all." Magnifico's head shook a slow negative.

It took two hundred and fifty credits to fulfill the demands of Filia—fifty credits of it for instant release—and they were in free space again.

Bayta said with a forced laugh, "Don't we rate an escort? Don't we get the usual figurative boot over the border?"

And Toran replied, grimly, "That was no Filian ship—and we're not leaving for a while. Come in here."

They gathered about him.

He said, whitely, "That was a Foundation ship, and those were the Mule's men aboard."

Ebling bent to pick up the cigar he had dropped. He said, "Here? We're thirty thousand parsecs from the Foundation."

"And *we're* here. What's to prevent them from making the same trip. Galaxy, Ebling, don't you think I can tell ships apart? I saw their engines, and that's enough for me. I tell you it was a Foundation engine in a Foundation ship."

"And how did they get here?" asked Bayta, logically. "What are the chances of a random meeting of two given ships in space?"

"What's that to do with it?" demanded Toran, hotly. "It would only show we've been followed."

"Followed?" hooted Bayta. "Through hyperspace?"

Ebling Mis interposed wearily, "That can be done—given a good ship and a great pilot. But the possibility doesn't impress me."

"I haven't been masking my trail," insisted Toran. "I've been building up take-off speed on the straight. A blind man could have calculated our route."

"The blazes he could," cried Bayta. "With the cockeyed jumps you are making, observing our initial direction didn't mean a thing. We came out of the jump wrong-end forwards more than once."

"We're wasting time," blazed Toran, with gritted teeth. "It's a Foundation ship under the Mule. It's stopped us. It's searched us. It's had Magnifico—alone—with me as hostage to keep the rest of you quiet, in case you suspected. And we're going to burn it out of space right now."

"Hold on now," and Ebling Mis clutched at him. "Are you going to destroy us for one ship you think is an enemy? Think, man, would those scuppers chase us over an impossible route half through the bestinkered Galaxy, look us over, and then *let us go?*"

"They're still interested in where we're going."

"Then why stop us and put us on our guard? You can't have it both ways, you know."

"I'll have it my way. Let go of me, Ebling, or I'll knock you down."

Magnifico leaned forward from his balanced perch on his favorite chair back. His long nostrils flared with excitement. "I crave your pardon for my interruption, but my poor mind is of a sudden plagued with a queer thought."

Bayta anticipated Toran's gesture of annoyance, and added her grip to Ebling's. "Go ahead and speak, Magnifico. We will all listen faithfully."

Magnifico said, "In my stay in their ship what addled wits I have were bemazed and bemused by a chattering fear that befell me. Of a truth I have a lack of memory of most that happened. Many men staring at me, and talk I did not understand. But towards the last—as though a beam of sunlight had dashed through a cloud rift—there was a face I knew. A glimpse, the merest glimmer—and yet it glows in my memory ever stronger and brighter."

Toran said, "Who was it?"

"That captain who was with us so long a time ago, when first you saved me from slavery."

It had obviously been Magnifico's intention to create a sensation, and the delighted smile that curled broadly in the shadow of his proboscis, attested to his realization of the intention's success.

"Captain . . . Han . . . Pritcher?" demanded Mis, sternly. "You're sure of that? Certain sure now?"

"Sir, I swear," and he laid a bone-thin hand upon his narrow chest. "I would uphold the truth of it before the Mule and swear it in his teeth, though all his power were behind him to deny it."

Bayta said in pure wonder, "Then what's it all about?"

The clown faced her eagerly, "My lady, I have a theory. It came upon me, ready made, as though the Galactic Spirit had gently laid it in my mind." He actually raised his voice above Toran's interrupting objection.

"My lady," he addressed himself exclusively to Bayta, "if this captain had, like us, escaped with a ship; if he, like us, were on a trip for a purpose of his own devising; if he blundered upon us—

he would suspect us of following and waylaying him, as *we* suspect *him* of the like. What wonder he played this comedy to enter our ship?"

"Why would he want us in *his* ship, then?" demanded Toran. "That doesn't fit."

"Why, yes, it does," clamored the clown, with a flowing inspiration. "He sent an underling who knew us not, but who described us into his microphone. The listening captain would be struck at my own poor likeness—for, of a truth there are not many in this great Galaxy who bear a resemblance to my scantiness. I was the proof of the identity of the rest of you."

"And so he leaves us?"

"What do we know of this mission, and the secrecy thereof? He has spied us out for not an enemy and having it done so, must he needs think it wise to risk his plan by widening the knowledge thereof?"

Bayta said slowly, "Don't be stubborn, Torie. It *does* explain things."

"It could be," agreed Mis.

Toran seemed helpless in the face of united resistance. Something in the clown's fluent explanations bothered him. Something was wrong. Yet he was bewildered and, in spite of himself, his anger ebbed.

"For a while," he whispered, "I thought we might have had *one* of the Mule's ships."

And his eyes were dark with the pain of Haven's loss.

The others understood.

22.

Death on Neotrantor

NEOTRANTOR *The small planet of Delicass, renamed after the Great Sack, was for nearly a century, the seat of the last dynasty of the First Empire. It was a shadow world and a shadow Empire and its existence is only of legalistic importance. Under the first of the Neotrantorian dynasty. . . .*

ENCYCLOPEDIA GALACTICA

Neotrantor was the name! New Trantor! And when you have said the name you have exhausted at a stroke all the resemblances of the new Trantor to the great original. Two parsecs away, the sun of Old Trantor still shone and the Galaxy's Imperial Capital of the previous century still cut through space in the silent and eternal repetition of its orbit.

Men even inhabited Old Trantor. Not many—a hundred million, perhaps, where fifty years before, forty billions had swarmed. The huge, metal world was in jagged splinters. The towering thrusts of the multi-towers from the single world-girdling base were torn and empty—still bearing the original blast-holes and firegut—shards of the Great Sack of forty years earlier.

It was strange that a world which had been the center of a Galaxy for twelve thousand years—that had ruled limitless space and been home to legislators and rulers whose whims spanned the parsecs—could die in a month. It was strange that a world which had been untouched through the vast conquering sweeps and retreats of a millennium, and equally untouched by the civil wars and palace revolutions of another millennium—should lie dead at last. It was strange that the Glory of the Galaxy should be a rotting corpse.

And pathetic!

For centuries would yet pass before the mighty works of fifty generations of humans would decay past use. Only the declining powers of men, themselves, rendered them useless now.

The millions left after the billions had died tore up the gleaming metal base of the planet and exposed soil that had not felt the touch of sun in a thousand years.

Surrounded by the mechanical perfections of human efforts, encircled by the industrial marvels of mankind freed of the tyranny of environment—they returned to the land. In the huge traffic clearings, wheat and corn grew. In the shadow of the towers, sheep grazed.

But Neotrantor existed—an obscure village of a planet drowned in the shadow of mighty Trantor, until a heart-throttled royal family, racing before the fire and flame of the Great Sack sped to it as its last refuge—and held out there, barely, until the roaring wave of rebellion subsided. There it ruled in ghostly splendor over a cadaverous remnant of Imperium.

Twenty agricultural worlds were a Galactic Empire!

Dagobert IX, ruler of twenty worlds of refractory squires and sullen peasants, was Emperor of the Galaxy, Lord of the Universe.

Dagobert IX had been twenty-five on the bloody day he arrived with his father upon Neotrantor. His eyes and mind were still alive with the glory and the power of the Empire that was. But his son, who might one day be Dagobert X, was born on Neotrantor.

Twenty worlds were all he knew.

Jord Commason's open air car was the finest vehicle of its type on all Neotrantor—and, after all, justly so. It did not end with the fact that Commason was the largest landowner on Neotrantor. It began there. For in earlier days he had been the companion and evil genius of a young crown prince, restive in the dominating grip of a middle-aged emperor. And now he was the companion and still the evil genius of a middle-aged crown prince who hated and dominated an old emperor.

So Jord Commason, in his air car, which in mother-of-pearl finish and gold-and-lumetron ornamentation needed no coat of arms as owner's identification, surveyed the lands that were his, and the miles of rolling wheat that were his, and the huge threshers

and harvesters that were his, and the tenant-farmers and ma-
chine-tenders that were his—and considered his problems cautiously.

Beside him, his bent and withered chauffeur, guided the ship
gently through the upper winds and smiled.

Jord Commason spoke to the wind, the air, and the sky, "You
remember what I told you, Inchney?"

Inchney's thin gray hair wisped lightly in the wind. His gap-
toothed smile widened in its thin-lipped fashion and the vertical
wrinkles of his cheeks deepened as though he were keeping an
eternal secret from himself. The whisper of his voice whistled between his teeth.

"I remember, sire, and I have thought."

"And what have you thought, Inchney?" There was an impatience about the question.

Inchney remembered that he had been young and handsome,
and a lord on Old Trantor. Inchney remembered that he was a
disfigured ancient on Neotrantor, who lived by grace of Squire
Jord Commason, and paid for the grace by lending his subtlety
on request. He sighed very softly.

He whispered again, "Visitors from the Foundation, sire, are a
convenient thing to have. Especially, sire, when they come with
but a single ship, and but a single fighting man. How welcome
they might be?"

"Welcome?" said Commason, gloomily. "Perhaps so. But those
men are magicians and may be powerful."

"Pugh," muttered Inchney, "the mistiness of distance hides the
truth. The Foundation is but a world. Its citizens are but men. If
you blast them, they die."

Inchney held the ship on its course. A river was a winding
sparkle below. He whispered, "And is there not a man they speak
of now who stirs the worlds of the Periphery?"

Commason was suddenly suspicious. "What do you know of
this?"

There was no smile on his chauffeur's face. "Nothing, sire. It
was but an idle question."

The squire's hesitation was short. He said, with brutal directness, "Nothing you ask is idle, and your method of acquiring

knowledge will have your scrawny neck in a vise yet. But—have it! This man is called the Mule, and a subject of his had been here some months ago on a . . . matter of business. I await another . . . now . . . for its conclusion."

"And these newcomers? They are not the ones you want, perhaps?"

"They lack the identification they should have."

"It has been reported that the Foundation has been captured—"

"I did not tell you that."

"It has been so reported," continued Inchney, coolly, "and if that is correct, then these may be refugees from the destruction, and may be held for the Mule's man out of honest friendship."

"Yes?" Commason was uncertain.

"And, sire, since it is well-known that the friend of a conqueror is but the last victim, it would be but a measure of honest self-defense. For there are such things as psychic probes, and here we have four Foundation brains. There is much about the Foundation it would be useful to know, much even about the Mule. And then the Mule's friendship would be a trifle the less overpowering."

Commason, in the quiet of the upper air, returned with a shiver to his first thought. "But if the Foundation has not fallen. If the reports are lies. It is said that it has been foretold it can not fall."

"We are past the age of soothsayers, sire."

"And yet if it did not fall, Inchney. Think! If it did not fall. The Mule made me promises, indeed—" He had gone too far, and backtracked. "That is, he made boasts. But boasts are wind and deeds are hard."

Inchney laughed noiselessly. "Deeds are hard indeed, until begun. One could scarcely find a further fear than a Galaxy-end Foundation."

"There is still the prince," murmured Commason, almost to himself.

"He deals with the Mule also, then, sire?"

Commason could not quite choke down the complacent shift of features. "Not entirely. Not as I do. But he grows wilder, more uncontrollable. A demon is upon him. If I seize these people and he takes them away for his own use—for he does not lack a certain shrewdness—I am not yet ready to quarrel with him." He frowned and his heavy cheeks bent downwards with dislike.

"I saw those strangers for a few moments yesterday," said the gray chauffeur, irrelevantly, "and it is a strange woman, that dark one. She walks with the freedom of a man and she is of a startling paleness against the dark luster of hair." There was almost a warmth in the husky whisper of the withered voice, so that Commason turned toward him in sudden surprise.

Inchney continued, "The prince, I think, would not find his shrewdness proof against a reasonable compromise. You could have the rest, if you left him the girl—"

A light broke upon Commason, "A thought! Indeed a thought! Inchney, turn back! And Inchney, if all turns well, we will discuss further this matter of your freedom."

It was with an almost superstitious sense of symbolism that Commason found a Personal Capsule waiting for him in his private study when he returned. It had arrived by a wave length known to few. Commason smiled a fat smile. The Mule's man was coming and the Foundation had indeed fallen.

Bayta's misty visions, when she had them, of an Imperial palace, did not jibe with the reality, and inside her, there was a vague sense of disappointment. The room was small, almost plain, almost ordinary. The palace did not even match the mayor's residence back at the Foundation—and Dagobert IX—

Bayta had *definite* ideas of what an emperor ought to look like. He ought *not* look like somebody's benevolent grandfather. He ought not be thin and white and faded—or serving cups of tea with his own hand in an expressed anxiety for the comfort of his visitors.

But so it was.

Dagobert IX chuckled as he poured tea into her stiffly outheld cup.

"This is a great pleasure for me, my dear. It is a moment away from ceremony and courtiers. I have not had the opportunity for welcoming visitors from my outer provinces for a time now. My son takes care of these details now that I'm older. You haven't met my son? A fine boy. Headstrong, perhaps. But then he's young. Do you care for a flavor capsule? No?"

Toran attempted an interruption, "Your imperial majesty—"

"Yes?"

"Your imperial majesty, it has not been our intention to intrude upon you—"

"Nonsense, there is no intrusion. Tonight there will be the official reception, but until then, we are free. Let's see, where did you say you were from? It seems a long time since we had an official reception. You said you were from the Province of Anacreon?"

"From the Foundation, your imperial majesty!"

"Yes, the Foundation. I remember now. I had it located. It is in the Province of Anacreon. I have never been there. My doctor forbids extensive traveling. I don't recall any recent reports from my viceroy at Anacreon. How are conditions there?" he concluded anxiously.

"Sire," mumbled Toran, "I bring no complaints."

"That is gratifying. I will commend my viceroy."

Toran looked helplessly at Ebling Mis, whose brusque voice rose. "Sire, we have been told that it will require your permission for us to visit the Imperial University Library on Trantor."

"Trantor?" questioned the emperor, mildly, "Trantor?"

Then a look of puzzled pain crossed his thin face. "Trantor?" he whispered. "I remember now. I am making plans now to return there with a flood of ships at my back. You shall come with me. Together we will destroy the rebel, Gilmer. Together we shall restore the empire!"

His bent back had straightened. His voice had strengthened. For a moment his eyes were hard. Then, he blinked and said softly, "But Gilmer is dead. I seem to remember— Yes. Yes! Gilmer is dead! Trantor is dead— For a moment, it seemed— Where was it you said you came from?"

Magnifico whispered to Bayta, "Is this really an emperor? For somehow I thought emperors were greater and wiser than ordinary men."

Bayta motioned him quiet. She said, "If your imperial majesty would but sign an order permitting us to go to Trantor, it would avail greatly the common cause."

"To Trantor?" The emperor was blank and uncomprehending.

"Sire, the Viceroy of Anacreon, in whose name we speak, sends word that Gilmer is yet alive—"

"Alive! Alive!" thundered Dagobert. "Where? It will be war!"

"Your imperial majesty, it must not yet be known. His whereabouts are uncertain. The viceroy sends us to acquaint you of the fact, and it is only on Trantor that we may find his hiding place. Once discovered—"

"Yes, yes— He must be found—" The old emperor doddered to the wall and touched the little photocell with a trembling finger. He muttered, after an ineffectual pause, "My servants do not come. I can not wait for them."

He was scribbling on a blank sheet, and ended with a flourished "D." He said, "Gilmer will yet learn the power of his emperor. Where was it you came from? Anacreon? What are the conditions there? Is the name of the emperor powerful?"

Bayta took the paper from his loose fingers, "Your imperial majesty is beloved by the people. Your love for them is widely known."

"I shall have to visit my good people of Anacreon, but my doctor says . . . I don't remember what he says, but—" He looked up, his old gray eyes sharp, "Were you saying something of Gilmer?"

"No, your imperial majesty."

"He shall not advance further. Go back and tell your people that. Trantor shall hold! My father leads the fleet now, and the rebel vermin Gilmer shall freeze in space with his regicidal rabble."

He staggered into a seat and his eyes were blank once more. "What was I saying?"

Toran rose and bowed low. "Your imperial majesty has been kind to us, but the time allotted us for an audience is over."

For a moment, Dagobert IX looked like an emperor indeed as he rose and stood stiff-backed while, one by one, his visitors retreated backward through the door—

—to where twenty armed men intervened and locked a circle about them.

A hand-weapon flashed—

To Bayta, consciousness returned sluggishly, but without the

"Where am I?" sensation. She remembered clearly the odd old man who called himself emperor, and the other men who waited outside. The arthritic tingle in her finger joints meant a stun pistol.

She kept her eyes closed, and listened with painful attention to the voices.

There were two of them. One was slow and cautious, with a slyness beneath the surface obsequity. The other was hoarse and thick, almost sodden, and blurted out in viscous spurts. Bayta liked neither.

The thick voice was predominant.

Bayta caught the last words, "He will live forever, that old madman. It wearies me. It annoys me. Commason, I will have it. I grow older, too."

"Your highness, let us first see of what use these people are. It may be we shall have sources of strength other than your father still provides."

The thick voice was lost in a bubbling whisper. Bayta caught only the phrase, "—the girl—" but the other, fawning voice was a nasty, low, running chuckle followed by a comradely, near-patronizing, "Dagobert, you do not age. They lie who say you are not a youth of twenty."

They laughed together, and Bayta's blood was an icy trickle. Dagobert—your highness— The old emperor had spoken of a headstrong son, and the implication of the whispers now beat dully upon her. But such things didn't happen to people in real life—

Toran's voice broke upon her in a slow, hard current of cursing.

She opened her eyes, and Toran's, which were upon her, showed open relief. He said, fiercely, "This banditry will be answered by the emperor. Release us."

It dawned upon Bayta that her wrists and ankles were fastened to wall and floor by a tight attraction field.

Thick Voice approached Toran. He was paunchy, his lower eyelids puffed darkly, and his hair was thinning out. There was a gay feather in his peaked hat, and the edging of his doublet was embroidered with silvery metal-foam.

He sneered with a heavy amusement. "The emperor? The poor, mad emperor?"

"I have his pass. No subject may hinder our freedom."

"But I am no subject, space-garbage. I am the regent and crown prince and am to be addressed as such. As for my poor silly father, it amuses him to see visitors occasionally. And we humor him. It tickles his mock-Imperial fancy. But, of course, it has no other meaning."

And then he was before Bayta, and she looked up at him contemptuously. He leaned close and his breath was overpoweringly minted.

He said, "Her eyes suit well, Commason—she is even prettier with them open. I think she'll do. It will be an exotic dish for a jaded taste, eh?"

There was a futile surge upwards on Toran's part, which the crown prince ignored and Bayta felt the iciness travel outward to the skin. Ebling Mis was still out; head lolling weakly upon his chest, but, with a sensation of surprise, Bayta noted that Magnifico's eyes were open, sharply open, as though awake for many minutes. Those large brown eyes swiveled towards Bayta and stared at her out of a doughy face.

He whimpered, and nodded with his head towards the crown prince, "That one has my Visi-Sonor."

The crown prince turned sharply toward the new voice, "This is yours, monster?" He swung the instrument from his shoulder where it had hung, suspended by its green strap, unnoticed by Bayta.

He fingered it clumsily, tried to sound a chord and got nothing for his pains, "Can you play it, monster?"

Magnifico nodded once.

Toran said suddenly, "You've rifled a ship of the Foundation. If the emperor will not avenge, the Foundation will."

It was the other, Commason, who answered slowly, "*What* Foundation? Or is the Mule no longer the Mule?"

There was no answer to that. The prince's grin showed large uneven teeth. The clown's binding field was broken and he was nudged ungently to his feet. The Visi-Sonor was thrust into his hand.

"Play for us, monster," said the prince. "Play us a serenade of love and beauty for our foreign lady here. Tell her that my father's country prison is no palace, but that I can take her to one where she can swim in rose water—and know what a prince's love is. Sing of a prince's love, monster."

He placed one thick thigh upon a marble table and swung a leg idly, while his fatuous smiling stare swept Bayta into a silent rage. Toran's sinews strained against the field, in painful, perspiring effort. Ebling Mis stirred and moaned.

Magnifico gasped, "My fingers are of useless stiffness—"

"Play, monster!" roared the prince. The lights dimmed at a gesture to Commason and in the dimness he crossed his arms and waited.

Magnifico drew his fingers in rapid, rhythmic jumps from end to end of the multikeyed instrument—and a sharp, gliding rainbow of light jumped across the room. A low, soft tone sounded—throbbing, tearful. It lifted in sad laughter, and underneath it there sounded a dull tolling.

The darkness seemed to intensify and grow thick. Music reached Bayta through the muffled folds of invisible blankets. Gleaming light reached her from the depths as though a single candle glowed at the bottom of a pit.

Automatically, her eyes strained. The light brightened, but remained blurred. It moved fuzzily, in confused color, and the music was suddenly brassy, evil—flourishing in high crescendo. The light flickered quickly, in swift motion to the wicked rhythm. Something writhed within the light. Something with poisonous metallic scales writhed and yawned. And the music writhed and yawned with it.

Bayta struggled with a strange emotion and then caught herself in a mental gasp. Almost, it reminded her of the time in the Time Vault, of those last days on Haven. It was that horrible, cloying, clinging spiderweb of horror and despair. She shrunk beneath it oppressed.

The music dinned upon her, laughing horribly, and the writhing terror at the wrong end of the telescope in the small circle of light was lost as she turned feverishly away. Her forehead was wet and cold.

The music died. It must have lasted fifteen minutes, and a vast pleasure at its absence flooded Bayta. Light glared, and Magnifico's face was close to hers, sweaty, wild-eyed, lugubrious.

"My lady," he gasped, "how fare you?"

"Well enough," she whispered, "but why did you play like that?"

She became aware of the others in the room. Toran and Mis were limp and helpless against the wall, but her eyes skimmed over them. There was the prince, lying strangely still at the foot of the table. There was Commason, moaning wildly through an open, drooling mouth.

Commason flinched, and yelled mindlessly, as Magnifico took a step towards him.

Magnifico turned, and with a leap, turned the others loose.

Toran lunged upwards and with eager, taut fists seized the landowner by the neck, "You come with us. We'll want you—to make sure we get to our ship."

Two hours later, in the ship's kitchen, Bayta served a walloping homemade pie, and Magnifico celebrated the return to space by attacking it with a magnificent disregard of table manners.

"Good, Magnifico?"

"Um-m-m-m!"

"Magnifico?"

"Yes, my lady?"

"What was it you played back there?"

The clown writhed, "I . . . I'd rather not say. I learned it once, and the Visi-Sonor is of an effect upon the nervous system most profound. Surely, it was an evil thing, and not for your sweet innocence, my lady."

"Oh, now, come, Magnifico. I'm not as innocent as that. Don't flatter so. Did I see anything like what *they* saw?"

"I hope not. I played it for them only. If you saw, it was but the rim of it—from afar."

"And that was enough. Do you know you knocked the prince out?"

Magnifico spoke grimly through a large, muffling piece of pie. "I *killed* him, my lady."

"What?" She swallowed, painfully.

"He was dead when I stopped, or I would have continued. I cared not for Commason. His greatest threat was death or torture. But, my lady, this prince looked upon you wickedly, and—" he choked in a mixture of indignation and embarrassment.

Bayta felt strange thoughts come and repressed them sternly. "Magnifico, you've got a gallant soul."

"Oh, my lady." He bent a red nose into his pie, but, somehow did not eat.

Ebling Mis stared out the port. Trantor was near—its metallic shine fearfully bright. Toran was standing there, too.

He said with dull bitterness, "We've come for nothing, Ebling. The Mule's man precedes us."

Ebling Mis rubbed his forehead with a hand that seemed shriveled out of its former plumpness. His voice was an abstracted mutter.

Toran was annoyed. "I say those people know the Foundation has fallen. I say—"

"Eh?" Mis looked up, puzzled. Then, he placed a gentle hand upon Toran's wrist, in complete oblivion of any previous conversation, "Toran, I . . . I've been looking at Trantor. Do you know . . . I have the queerest feeling . . . ever since we arrived on Neotrantor. It's an urge, a driving urge that's pushing and pushing inside. Toran, I can do it; I know I can do it. Things are becoming clear in my mind—they have never been so clear."

Toran stared—and shrugged. The words brought him no confidence.

He said, tentatively, "Mis?"

"Yes?"

"You didn't see a ship come down on Neotrantor as we left?" Consideration was brief. "No."

"I did. Imagination, I suppose, but it could have been that Filian ship."

"The one with Captain Han Pritcher on it?"

"The one with space knows who upon it. Magnifico's information— It followed us here, Mis."

Ebling Mis said nothing.

Toran said strenuously, "Is there anything wrong with you? Aren't you well?"

Mis's eyes were thoughtful, luminous, and strange. He did not answer.

23.

The Ruins of Trantor

The location of an objective upon the great world of Trantor presents a problem unique in the Galaxy. There are no continents or oceans to locate from a thousand miles distance. There are no rivers, lakes, and islands to catch sight of through the cloud rifts.

The metal-covered world was—had been—one colossal city, and only the old Imperial palace could be identified readily from outer space by a stranger. The *Bayta* circled the world at almost air-car height in repeated painful search.

From polar regions, where the icy coating of the metal spires were somber evidence of the breakdown or neglect of the weather-conditioning machinery, they worked southwards. Occasionally they could experiment with the correlations—(or presumable correlations)—between what they saw and what the inadequate map obtained at Neotrantor showed.

But it was unmistakable when it came. The gap in the metal coat of the planet was fifty miles. The unusual greenery spread over hundreds of square miles, inclosing the mighty grace of the ancient Imperial residences.

The *Bayta* hovered and slowly oriented itself. There were only the huge supercauseways to guide them. Long straight arrows on the map; smooth, gleaming ribbons there below them.

What the map indicated to be the University area was reached by dead reckoning, and upon the flat area of what once must have been a busy landing-field, the ship lowered itself.

It was only as they submerged into the welter of metal that the smooth beauty apparent from the air dissolved into the broken, twisted near-wreckage that had been left in the wake of the Sack. Spires were truncated, smooth walls gouted and twisted, and just for an instant there was the glimpse of a shaven area of earth—perhaps several hundred acres in extent—dark and plowed.

Lee Senter waited as the ship settled downward cautiously. It was a strange ship, not from Neotrantor, and inwardly he sighed. Strange ships and confused dealings with the men of outer space could mean the end of the short days of peace, a return to the old grandiose times of death and battle. Senter was leader of the group; the old books were in his charge and he had read of those old days. He did not want them.

Perhaps ten minutes spent themselves as the strange ship came down to nestle upon the flatness, but long memories telescoped themselves in that time. There was first the great farm of his childhood—that remained in his mind merely as busy crowds of people. Then there was the trek of the young families to new lands. He was ten, then; an only child, puzzled, and frightened.

Then the new buildings; the great metal slabs to be uprooted and torn aside; the exposed soil to be turned, and freshened, and invigorated; neighboring buildings to be torn down and leveled; others to be transformed to living quarters.

There were crops to be grown and harvested; peaceful relations with neighboring farms to be established—

There was growth and expansion, and the quiet efficiency of self-rule. There was the coming of a new generation of hard, little youngsters born to the soil. There was the great day when he was chosen leader of the Group and for the first time since his eighteenth birthday he did not shave and saw the first stubble of his Leader's Beard appear.

And now the Galaxy might intrude and put an end to the brief idyll of isolation—

The ship landed. He watched wordlessly as the port opened. Four emerged, cautious and watchful. There were three men, varied, old, young, thin and beaked. And a woman striding among them like an equal. His hand left the two glassy black tufts of his beard as he stepped forward.

He gave the universal gesture of peace. Both hands were before him; hard, calloused palms upward.

The young man approached two steps and duplicated the gesture. "I come on peace."

The accent was strange, but the words were understandable, and welcome. He replied, deeply, "In peace be it. You are welcome to the hospitality of the Group. Are you hungry? You shall eat. Are you thirsty? You shall drink."

Slowly, the reply came, "We thank you for your kindness, and shall bear good report of your Group when we return to our world."

A queer answer, but good. Behind him, the men of the Group were smiling, and from the recesses of the surrounding structures, the women emerged.

In his own quarters, he removed the locked, mirror-walled box from its hidden place, and offered each of the guests the long, plump cigars that were reserved for great occasions. Before the woman, he hesitated. She had taken a seat among the men. The strangers evidently allowed, even expected, such effrontery. Stiffly, he offered the box.

She accepted one with a smile, and drew in its aromatic smoke, with all the relish one could expect. Lee Senter repressed a scandalized emotion.

The stiff conversation, in advance of the meal, touched politely upon the subject of farming on Trantor.

It was the old man who asked, "What about hydroponics? Surely, for such a world as Trantor, hydroponics would be the answer."

Senter shook his head slowly. He felt uncertain. His knowledge was the unfamiliar matter of the books he had read, "Artificial farming in chemicals, I think? No, not on Trantor. This hydroponics requires a world of industry—for instance, a great chemical industry. And in war or disaster, when industry breaks down, the people starve. Nor can all foods be grown artificially. Some lose their food value. The soil is still cheaper, still better—always more dependable."

"And your food supply is sufficient?"

"Sufficient; perhaps monotonous. We have fowl that supply eggs, and milk-yielders for our dairy products—but our meat supply rests upon our foreign trade."

"Trade." The young man seemed roused to sudden interest. "You trade then. But what do you export?"

"Metal," was the curt answer. "Look for yourself. We have an infinite supply, ready processed. They come from Neotrantor with

ships, demolish an indicated area—increasing our growing space
—and leave us in exchange meat, canned fruit, food concentrates,
farm machinery and so on. They carry off the metal and both sides
profit."

They feasted on bread and cheese, and a vegetable stew that
was unreservedly delicious. It was over the dessert of frosted
fruit, the only imported item on the menu, that, for the first time,
the Outlanders became other than mere guests. The young man
produced a map of Trantor.

Calmly, Lee Senter studied it. He listened—and said gravely,
"The University Grounds are a static area. We farmers do not
grow crops on it. We do not, by preference, even enter it. It is
one of our few relics of another time we would keep undisturbed."

"We are seekers after knowledge. We would disturb nothing.
Our ship would be our hostage." The old man offered this—eagerly, feverishly.

"I can take you there then," said Senter.

That night the strangers slept, and that night Lee Senter sent a
message to Neotrantor.

24.

Convert

The thin life of Trantor trickled to nothing when they entered among the wide-spaced buildings of the University grounds. There was a solemn and lonely silence over it.

The strangers of the Foundation knew nothing of the swirling days and nights of the bloody Sack that had left the University untouched. They knew nothing of the time after the collapse of the Imperial power, when the students, with their borrowed weapons, and their pale-faced inexperienced bravery, formed a protective volunteer army to protect the central shrine of the science of the Galaxy. They knew nothing of the Seven Days Fight, and the armistice that kept the University free, when even the Imperial palace clanged with the boots of Gilmer and his soldiers, during the short interval of their rule.

Those of the Foundation, approaching for the first time, realized only that in a world of transition from a gutted old to a strenuous new this area was a quiet, graceful museum-piece of ancient greatness.

They were intruders in a sense. The brooding emptiness rejected them. The academic atmosphere seemed still to live and to stir angrily at the disturbance.

The library was a deceptively small building which broadened out vastly underground into a mammoth volume of silence and reverie. Ebling Mis paused before the elaborate murals of the reception room.

He whispered—one had to whisper here: "I think we passed the catalog rooms back a way. I'll stop there."

His forehead was flushed, his hand trembling, "I mustn't be disturbed, Toran. Will you bring my meals down to me?"

"Anything you say. We'll do all we can to help. Do you want us to work under you—"

"No. I must be alone—"

"You think you will get what you want."

And Ebling Mis replied with a soft certainty, "I know I will!"

Toran and Bayta came closer to "setting up housekeeping" in normal fashion than at any time in their year of married life. It was a strange sort of "housekeeping." They lived in the middle of grandeur with an inappropriate simplicity. Their food was drawn largely from Lee Senter's farm and was paid for in the little atomic gadgets that may be found on any Trader's ship.

Magnifico taught himself how to use the projectors in the library reading room, and sat over adventure novels and romances to the point where he was almost as forgetful of meals and sleep as was Ebling Mis.

Ebling himself was completely buried. He had insisted on a hammock being slung up for him in the Psychology Reference Room. His face grew thin and white. His vigor of speech was lost and his favorite curses had died a mild death. There were times when the recognition of either Toran or Bayta seemed a struggle.

He was more himself with Magnifico who brought him his meals and often sat watching him for hours at a time, with a queer, fascinated absorption, as the aging psychologist transcribed endless equations, cross-referred to endless book-films, scurried endlessly about in a wild mental effort towards an end he alone saw.

Toran came upon her in the darkened room, and said sharply, "Bayta!"

Bayta started guiltily. "Yes? You want me, Torie?"

"Sure I want you. What in space are you sitting there for? You've been acting all wrong since we got to Trantor. What's the matter with you?"

"Oh, Torie, stop," she said, wearily.

And "Oh, Torie, stop!" he mimicked impatiently. Then, with sudden softness, "Won't you tell me what's wrong, Bay? something's bothering you."

"No! Nothing is, Torie. If you keep on just nagging and nagging, you'll have me mad. I'm just—thinking."

"Thinking about what?"

"About nothing. Well, about the Mule, and Haven, and the Foundation, and everything. About Ebling Mis and whether he'll find anything about the Second Foundation, and whether it will help us when he does find it—and a million other things. Are you satisfied?" Her voice was agitated.

"If you're just brooding, do you mind stopping? It isn't pleasant and it doesn't help the situation."

Bayta got to her feet and smiled weakly. "All right. I'm happy. See, I'm smiling and jolly."

Magnifico's voice was an agitated cry outside. "My lady—"

"What is it? Come—"

Bayta's voice choked off sharply when the opening door framed the large, hard-faced—

"Pritcher," cried Toran.

Bayta gasped, "Captain! How did you find us?"

Han Pritcher stepped inside. His voice was clear and level, and utterly dead of feeling, "My rank is colonel now—under the Mule."

"Under the . . . Mule!" Toran's voice trailed off. They formed a tableau there, the three.

Magnifico stared wildly and shrank behind Toran. Nobody stopped to notice him.

Bayta said, her hands trembling in each other's tight grasp, "You are arresting us? You have really gone over to them?"

The colonel replied quickly, "I have not come to arrest you. My instructions make no mention of you. With regard to you, I am free, and I choose to exercise our old friendship, if you will let me."

Toran's face was a twisted suppression of fury, "How did you find us? You were in the Filian ship, then? You followed us?"

The wooden lack of expression on Pritcher's face might have flickered in embarrassment. "I *was* on the Filian ship! I met you in the first place . . . well . . . by chance."

"It is a chance that is mathematically impossible."

"No. Simply rather improbable, so my statement will have to stand. In any case, you admitted to the Filians—there is, of course, no such nation as Filia actually—that you were heading for the Trantor sector, and since the Mule already has his contacts upon Neotrantor, it was easy to have you detained there. Unfortunately, you got away before I arrived, but not long before. I had time to have the farms on Trantor ordered to report your arrival. It was done and I am here. May I sit down? I come in friendliness, believe me."

He sat. Toran bent his head and thought futilely. With a numbed lack of emotion, Bayta prepared tea.

Toran looked up harshly. "Well, what are you waiting for—colonel? What's your friendship? If it's not arrest, what is it then? Protective custody? Call in your men and give your orders."

Patiently, Pritcher shook his head. "No, Toran. I come of my own will to speak to you, to persuade you of the uselessness of what you are doing. If I fail I shall leave. That is all."

"That is all? Well, then peddle your propaganda, give us your speech, and leave. I don't want any tea, Bayta."

Pritcher accepted a cup, with a grave word of thanks. He looked at Toran with a clear strength as he sipped lightly. Then he said, "The Mule *is* a mutant. He can not be beaten in the very nature of the mutation—"

"Why? What is the mutation?" asked Toran, with sour humor. "I suppose you'll tell us now, eh?"

"Yes, I will. Your knowledge won't hurt him. You see—he is capable of adjusting the emotional balance of human beings. It sounds like a little trick, but it's quite unbeatable."

Bayta broke in, "The emotional balance?" She frowned, "Won't you explain that? I don't quite understand."

"I mean that it is an easy matter for him to instill into a capable general, say, the emotion of utter loyalty to the Mule and complete belief in the Mule's victory. His generals are emotionally controlled. They can not betray him; they can not weaken—and the control is permanent. His most capable enemies become his most faithful subordinates. The warlord of Kalgan surrenders his planet and becomes his viceroy for the Foundation."

"And you," added Bayta, bitterly, "betray your cause and become Mule's envoy to Trantor. I see!"

"I haven't finished. The Mule's gift works in reverse even more effectively. Despair is an emotion! At the crucial moment, keymen on the Foundation—keymen on Haven—despaired. Their worlds fell without too much struggle."

"Do you mean to say," demanded Bayta, tensely, "that the feeling I had in the Time Vault was the Mule juggling my emotional control."

"Mine, too. Everyone's. How was it on Haven towards the end?"

Bayta turned away.

Colonel Pritcher continued earnestly, "As it works for worlds, so it works for individuals. Can you light a force which can make you surrender willingly when it so desires; can make you a faithful servant when it so desires?"

Toran said slowly, "How do I know this is the truth?"

"Can you explain the fall of the Foundation and of Haven otherwise? Can you explain—my conversion otherwise? Think, man! What have you—or I—or the whole Galaxy accomplished against the Mule in all this time? What one little thing?"

Toran felt the challenge, "By the Galaxy, I can!" With a sudden touch of fierce satisfaction, he shouted, "Your wonderful Mule had contacts with Neotrantor you say that were to have detained us, eh? Those contacts are dead or worse. We killed the crown prince and left the other a whimpering idiot. The Mule did not stop us there, and so much has been undone."

"Why, no, not at all. Those weren't our men. The crown prince was a wine-soaked mediocrity. The other man, Commason, is phenomenally stupid. He was a power on his world but that didn't prevent him from being vicious, evil, and completely incompetent. We had nothing really to do with them. They were, in a sense, merely feints—"

"It was they who detained us, or tried."

"Again, no. Commason had a personal slave—a man called Inchney. Detention was *his* policy. He is old, but will serve our temporary purpose. You would not have killed him, you see."

Bayta whirled on him. She had not touched her own tea. "But, by your very statement, your own emotions have been tampered with. You've got faith and belief in the Mule, an unnatural, a *diseased* faith in the Mule. Of what value are your opinions? You've lost all power of objective thought."

"You are wrong." Slowly, the colonel shook his head. "Only my emotions are fixed. My reason is as it always was. It may be influenced in a certain direction by my conditioned emotions, but it is not *forced.* And there are some things I can see more clearly now that I am freed of my earlier emotional trend.

"I can see that the Mule's program is an intelligent and worthy one. In the time since I have been—converted, I have followed his career from its start seven years ago. With his mutant mental power, he began by winning over a condottiere and his band. With that—and his power—he won a planet. With that—and his power—he extended his grip until he could tackle the warlord of Kalgan. Each step followed the other logically. With Kalgan in his pocket, he had a first-class fleet, and with that—and his power—he could attack the Foundation.

"The Foundation is the key. It is the greatest area of industrial concentration in the Galaxy, and now that the atomic techniques of the Foundation are in his hands, he is the actual master of the Galaxy. With those techniques—and his power—he can force the remnants of the Empire to acknowledge his rule, and eventually—with the death of the old emperor, who is mad and not long for this world—to crown him emperor. He will then have the name as well as the fact. With that—and his power—where is the world in the Galaxy that can oppose him?

"In these last seven years, he has established a new Empire. In seven years, in other words, he will have accomplished what all Seldon's psycho-history could not have done in less than an additional seven hundred. The Galaxy will have peace and order at last.

"And you could not stop it—any more than you could stop a planet's rush with your shoulders."

A long silence followed Pritcher's speech. What remained of his tea had grown cold. He emptied his cup, filled it again, and drained it slowly. Toran bit viciously at a thumbnail. Bayta's face was cold, and distant, and white.

Then Bayta said in a thin voice, "We are not convinced. If the Mule wishes us to be, let him come here and condition us himself. You fought him until the last moment of your conversion, I imagine, didn't you?"

"I did," said Colonel Pritcher, solemnly.

"Then allow us the same privilege."

Colonel Pritcher arose. With a crisp air of finality, he said, "Then I leave. As I said earlier, my mission at present concerns you in no way. Therefore, I don't think it will be necessary to report your presence here. That is not too great a kindness. If the Mule wishes you stopped, he no doubt has other men assigned to the job, and you will be stopped. But, for what it is worth, I shall not contribute more than my requirement."

"Thank you," said Bayta faintly.

"As for Magnifico. Where is he? Come out, Magnifico, I won't hurt you—"

"What about him?" demanded Bayta, with sudden animation.

"Nothing. My instructions make no mention of him, either. I have heard that he is searched for, but the Mule will find him when the time suits him. I shall say nothing. Will you shake hands?"

Bayta shook her head. Toran glared his frustrated contempt.

There was the slightest lowering of the colonel's iron shoulders. He strode to the door, turned and said:

"One last thing. Don't think I am not aware of the source of your stubbornness. It is known that you search for the Second Foundation. The Mule, in his time, will take his measures. Nothing will help you— But I knew you in other times; perhaps there is something in my conscience that urged me to this; at any rate, I tried to help you and remove you from the final danger before it was too late. Good-by."

He saluted sharply—and was gone.

Bayta turned to a silent Toran, and whispered, "They even know about the Second Foundation."

In the recesses of the library, Ebling Mis, unaware of all, crouched under the one spark of light amid the murky spaces and mumbled triumphantly to himself.

25.

Death of a Psychologist

After that there were only two weeks left to the life of Ebling Mis.

And in those two weeks, Bayta was with him three times. The first time was on the night after the evening upon which they saw Colonel Pritcher. The second was one week later. And the third was again a week later—on the last day—the day Mis died.

First, there was the night of Colonel Pritcher's evening, the first hour of which was spent by a stricken pair in a brooding, unmerry merry-go-round.

Bayta said, "Torie, let's tell Ebling."

Toran said dully, "Think he can help?"

"We're only two. We've got to take some of the weight off. Maybe he *can* help."

Toran said, "He's changed. He's lost weight. He's a little feathery; a little woolly." His fingers groped in air, metaphorically. "Sometimes, I don't think he'll help us much—ever. Sometimes, I don't think anything will help."

"Don't!" Bayta's voice caught and escaped a break, "Torie, don't! When you say that, I think the Mule's getting us. Let's tell Ebling, Torie—now!"

Ebling Mis raised his head from the long desk, and bleared at them as they approached. His thinning hair was scuffed up, his lips made sleepy, smacking sounds.

"Eh?" he said. "Someone want me?"

Bayta bent to her knees, "Did we wake you? Shall we leave?"

"Leave? Who is it? Bayta? No, no, stay! Aren't there chairs? I saw them—" His finger pointed vaguely.

Toran pushed two ahead of him. Bayta sat down and took one

of the psychologist's flaccid hands in hers. "May we talk to you, doctor?" She rarely used the title.

"Is something wrong?" A little sparkle returned to his abstracted eyes. His sagging cheeks regained a touch of color. "Is something wrong?"

Bayta said, "Captain Pritcher has been here. Let *me* talk, Torie. You remember Captain Pritcher, doctor?"

"Yes— Yes—" His fingers pinched his lips and released them. "Tall man. Democrat."

"Yes, he. He's discovered the Mule's mutation. He was here, doctor, and told us."

"But that is nothing new. The Mule's mutation is straightened out." In honest astonishment, "Haven't I told you? Have I forgotten to tell you?"

"Forgotten to tell us what?" put in Toran, quickly.

"About the Mule's mutation, of course. He tampers with emotions. Emotional control! I haven't told you? Now what made me forget?" Slowly, he sucked in his under lip and considered.

Then, slowly, life crept into his voice and his eyelids lifted wide, as though his sluggish brain had slid onto a well-greased single track. He spoke in a dream, looking between the two listeners rather than at them. "It is really so simple. It requires no specialized knowledge. In the mathematics of psycho-history, of course, it works out promptly, in a third-level equation involving no more— Never mind that. It can be put into ordinary words —roughly—and have it make sense, which isn't usual with psychohistorical phenomena.

"Ask yourselves— What can upset Hari Seldon's careful scheme of history, eh?" He peered from one to the other with a mild, questioning anxiety. "What were Seldon's original assumptions? First, that there would be no fundamental change in human society over the next thousand years.

"For instance, suppose there were a major change in the Galaxy's technology, such as finding a new principle for the utilization of energy, or perfecting the study of electronic neurobiology. Social changes would render Seldon's original equations obsolete. But that hasn't happened, has it now?

"Or suppose that a new weapon were to be invented by forces

outside the Foundation, capable of withstanding all the Foundation's armaments. *That* might cause a ruinous deviation, though less certainly. But even that hasn't happened. The Mule's Atomic Field-Depressor was a clumsy weapon and could be countered. And that was the only novelty he presented, poor as it was.

"But there was a second assumption, a more subtle one! Seldon assumed that human reaction to stimuli would remain constant. Granted that the first assumption held true, *then the second must have broken down!* Some factor must be twisting and distorting the emotional responses of human beings or Seldon couldn't have failed and the Foundation couldn't have fallen. And what factor but the Mule?

"Am I right? Is there a flaw in the reasoning?"

Bayta's plump hand patted his gently. "No flaw, Ebling."

Mis was joyful, like a child. "This and more comes so easily. I tell you I wonder sometimes what is going on inside me. I seem to recall the time when so much was a mystery to me and now things are so clear. Problems are absent. I come across what might be one, and somehow, inside me, I see and understand. And my guesses, my theories seem always to be borne out. There's a drive in me . . . always onward . . . so that I can't stop . . . and I don't want to eat or sleep . . . but always go on . . . and on . . . and on—"

His voice was a whisper; his wasted, blue-veined hand rested tremblingly upon his forehead. There was a frenzy in his eyes that faded and went out.

He said more quietly, "Then I never told you about the Mule's mutant powers, did I? But then . . . did you say you knew about it?"

"It was Captain Pritcher, Ebling," said Bayta. "Remember?"

"He told you?" There was a tinge of outrage in his tone. "But how did he find out?"

"He's been conditioned by the Mule. He's a colonel now, a Mule's man. He came to advise us to surrender to the Mule, and he told us—what you told us."

"Then the Mule knows we're here? I must hurry— Where's Magnifico? Isn't he with you?"

"Magnifico's sleeping," said Toran, impatiently. "It's past midnight, you know."

"It is? Then— Was I sleeping when you came in?"

"You were," said Bayta decisively, "and you're not going back to work, either. You're getting into bed. Come on, Torie, help me. And you stop pushing at me, Ebling, because it's just your luck I don't shove you under a shower first. Pull off his shoes, Torie, and tomorrow you come down here and drag him out into the open air before he fades completely away. Look at you, Ebling, you'll be growing cobwebs. Are you hungry?"

Ebling Mis shook his head and looked up from his cot in a peevish confusion. "I want you to send Magnifico down tomorrow," he muttered.

Bayta tucked the sheet around his neck. "You'll have *me* down tomorrow, with washed clothes. You're going to take a good bath, and then get out and visit the farm and feel a little sun on you."

"I won't do it," said Mis weakly. "You hear me? I'm too busy."

His sparse hair spread out on the pillow like a silver fringe about his head. His voice was a confidential whisper. "You want that Second Foundation, don't you?"

Toran turned quickly and squatted down on the cot beside him. "What about the Second Foundation, Ebling?"

The psychologist freed an arm from beneath the sheet and his tired fingers clutched at Toran's sleeve. "The Foundations were established at a great Psychological Convention presided over by Hari Seldon. Toran, I have located the published minutes of that Convention. Twenty-five fat films. I have already looked through various summaries."

"Well?"

"Well, do you know that it is very easy to find from them the exact location of the First Foundation, if you know anything at all about psycho-history. It is frequently referred to, when you understand the equations. But Toran, nobody mentions the Second Foundation. There has been no reference to it anywhere."

Toran's eyebrows pulled into a frown. "It doesn't exist?"

"Of course it exists," cried Mis, angrily, "who said it didn't? But there's less talk of it. Its significance—and all about it—are better hidden, better obscured. Don't you see? It's the more important of the two. It's the critical one; *the one that counts!* And I've got the minutes of the Seldon Convention. The Mule hasn't won yet—"

Quietly, Bayta turned the lights down. "Go to sleep!"

Without speaking, Toran and Bayta made their way up to their own quarters.

The next day, Ebling Mis bathed and dressed himself, saw the sun of Trantor and felt the wind of Trantor for the last time. At the end of the day he was once again submerged in the gigantic recesses of the library, and never emerged thereafter.

In the week that followed, life settled again into its groove. The sun of Neotrantor was a calm, bright star in Trantor's night sky. The farm was busy with its spring planting. The University grounds were silent in their desertion. The Galaxy seemed empty. The Mule might never have existed.

Bayta was thinking that as she watched Toran light his cigar carefully and look up at the sections of blue sky visible between the swarming metal spires that encircled the horizon.

"It's a nice day," he said.

"Yes, it is. Have you everything mentioned on the list, Torie?"

"Sure. Half pound butter, dozen eggs, string beans— Got it all down here, Bay. I'll have it right."

"Good. And make sure the vegetables are of the last harvest and not museum relics. Did you see Magnifico anywhere, by the way?"

"Not since breakfast. Guess he's down with Ebling, watching a book-film."

"All right. Don't waste any time, because I'll need the eggs for dinner."

Toran left with a backward smile and a wave of the hand.

Bayta turned away as Toran slid out of sight among the maze of metal. She hesitated before the kitchen door, about-faced slowly, and entered the colonnade leading to the elevator that burrowed down into the recesses.

Ebling Mis was there, head bent down over the eyepieces of the projector, motionless, a frozen, questing body. Near him sat Magnifico, screwed up into a chair, eyes sharp and watching—a bundle of slatty limbs with a nose emphasizing his scrawny face.

Bayta said softly, "Magnifico—"

Magnifico scrambled to his feet. His voice was an eager whisper. "My lady!"

"Magnifico," said Bayta, "Toran has left for the farm and won't be back for a while. Would you be a good boy and go out after him with a message that I'll write for you?"

"Gladly, my lady. My small services are but too eagerly yours, for the tiny uses you can put them to."

She was alone with Ebling Mis, who had not moved. Firmly, she placed her hand upon his shoulder. "Ebling—"

The psychologist started, with a peevish cry, "What is it?" He wrinkled his eyes. "Is it you, Bayta? Where's Magnifico?"

"I sent him away. I want to be alone with you for a while." She enunciated her words with exaggerated distinctness. "I want to talk to you, Ebling."

The psychologist made a move to return to his projector, but her hand on his shoulder was firm. She felt the bone under the sleeve clearly. The flesh seemed to have fairly melted away since their arrival on Trantor. His face was thin, yellowish, and bore a half-week stubble. His shoulders were visibly stooped, even in a sitting position.

Bayta said, "Magnifico isn't bothering you, is he, Ebling? He seems to be down here night and day."

"No, no, no! Not at all. Why, I don't mind him. He is silent and never disturbs me. Sometimes he carries the films back and forth for me; seems to know what I want without my speaking. Just let him be."

"Very well—but, Ebling, doesn't he make you wonder? Do you hear me, Ebling? Doesn't he make you wonder?"

She jerked a chair close to his and stared at him as though to pull the answer out of his eyes.

Ebling Mis shook his head. "No. What do you mean?"

"I mean that Colonel Pritcher and you both say the Mule can condition the emotions of human beings. But are you sure of it? Isn't Magnifico himself a flaw in the theory?"

There was silence.

Bayta repressed a strong desire to shake the psychologist. "What's *wrong* with you, Ebling? Magnifico was the Mule's clown.

Why wasn't he conditioned to love and faith? Why should he, of all those in contact with the Mule, hate him so."

"But . . . but he *was* conditioned. Certainly, Bay!" He seemed to gather certainty as he spoke. "Do you suppose that the Mule treats his clown the way he treats his generals? He needs faith and loyalty in the latter, but in his clown he needs only fear. Didn't you ever notice that Magnifico's continual state of panic is pathological in nature? Do you suppose it is natural for a human being to be as frightened as that all the time? Fear to such an extent becomes comic. It was probably comic to the Mule—and helpful, too, since it obscured what help we might have gotten earlier from Magnifico."

Bayta said, "You mean Magnifico's information about the Mule was false?"

"It was misleading. It was colored by pathological fear. The Mule is not the physical giant Magnifico thinks. He is more probably an ordinary man outside his mental powers. But if it amused him to appear a superman to poor Magnifico—" The psychologist shrugged. "In any case, Magnifico's information is no longer of importance."

"What is, then?"

But Mis shook himself loose and returned to his projector.

"What is, then?" she repeated. "The Second Foundation?"

The psychologist's eyes jerked towards her. "Have I told you anything about that? I don't remember telling you anything. I'm not ready yet. What have I told you?"

"Nothing," said Bayta, intensely. "Oh, Galaxy, you've told me nothing, but I wish you would because I'm deathly tired. When will it be over?"

Ebling Mis peered at her, vaguely rueful, "Well, now, my . . . my dear, I did not mean to hurt you. I forget sometimes . . . who my friends are. Sometimes it seems to me that I must not talk of all this. There's a need for secrecy—but from the Mule, not from you, my dear." He patted her shoulder with a weak amiability.

She said, "What about the Second Foundation?"

His voice was automatically a whisper, thin and sibilant. "Do you know the thoroughness with which Seldon covered his traces? The proceedings of the Seldon Convention would have been of no use to me at all as little as a month ago, before this strange insight came. Even now, it seems—tenuous. The papers put out by the Convention are often apparently unrelated; always obscure. More than once I wondered if the members of the Convention, themselves, knew all that was in Seldon's mind. Sometimes I think he used the Convention only as a gigantic front, and single-handed erected the structure—"

"Of the Foundations?" urged Bayta.

"Of the Second Foundation! Our Foundation was simple. But the Second Foundation was only a name. It was mentioned, but if there was any elaboration, it was hidden deep in the mathematics. There is still much I don't even begin to understand, but for seven days, the bits have been clumping together into a vague picture.

"Foundation Number One was a world of physical scientists. It represented a concentration of the dying science of the Galaxy under the conditions necessary to make it live again. No psychologists were included. It was a peculiar distortion, and must have had a purpose. The usual explanation was that Seldon's psycho-history worked best where the individual working units— human beings—had no knowledge of what was coming, and could therefore react naturally to all situations. Do you follow me, my dear—"

"Yes, doctor."

"Then listen carefully. Foundation Number Two was a world of mental scientists. It was the mirror image of our world. Psychology, not physics, was king." Triumphantly. "You see?"

"I don't."

"But think, Bayta, use your head. Hari Seldon knew that his psycho-history could predict only probabilities, and not certainties. There was always a margin of error, and as time passed that margin increases in geometric progression. Seldon would naturally guard as well as he could against it. Our Foundation was scientifically vigorous. It could conquer armies and weapons. It could pit force against force. But what of the mental attack of a mutant such as the Mule?"

"That would be for the psychologists of the Second Foundation!" Bayta felt excitement rising within her.

"Yes, yes, yes! Certainly!"

"But they have done nothing so far."

"How do you know they haven't?"

Bayta considered that, "I don't. Do you have evidence that they are?"

"No. There are many factors I know nothing of. The Second Foundation could not have been established full-grown, any more than we were. We developed slowly and grew in strength; they must have also. The stars know at what stage their strength is now. Are they strong enough to fight the Mule? Are they aware of the danger in the first place? Have they capable leaders?"

"But if they follow Seldon's plan, then the Mule *must* be beaten by the Second Foundation."

"Ah," and Ebling Mis's thin face wrinkled thoughtfully, "is it that again? But the Second Foundation was a more difficult job than the First. Its complexity is hugely greater; and consequently so is its possibility of error. And if the Second Foundation should not beat the Mule, it is bad—ultimately bad. It is the end, may be, of the human race as we know it."

"No."

"Yes. If the Mule's descendants inherit his mental powers— You see? Homo sapiens could not compete. There would be a new dominant race—a new aristocracy—with homo sapiens demoted to slave labor as an inferior race. Isn't that so?"

"Yes, that is so."

"And even if by some chance the Mule did not establish a dynasty, he would still establish a distorted new Empire upheld by his personal power only. It would die with his death; the Galaxy would be left where it was before he came, except that there would no longer be Foundations around which a real and healthy Second Empire could coalesce. It would mean thousands of years of barbarism. It would mean no end in sight."

"What can we do? Can we warn the Second Foundation?"

"We must, or they may go under through ignorance, which we can not risk. But there is no way of warning them."

"No way?"

"I don't know where they are located. They are 'at the other end of the Galaxy' but that is all, and there are millions of worlds to choose from."

"But, Ebling, don't they say?" She pointed vaguely at the films that covered the table.

"No, they don't. Not where I can find it—yet. The secrecy must mean something. There must be a reason—" A puzzled expression returned to his eyes. "But I wish you'd leave. I have wasted enough time, and it's growing short—it's growing short."

He tore away, petulant and frowning.

Magnifico's soft step approached. "Your husband is home, my lady."

Ebling Mis did not greet the clown. He was back at his projector.

That evening Toran, having listened, spoke, "And you think he's really right, Bay? You think he isn't—" He hesitated.

"He is right, Torie. He's sick, I know that. The change that's come over him, the loss in weight, the way he speaks—he's sick. But as soon as the subject of the Mule or the Second Foundation, or anything he is working on, comes up, listen to him. He is lucid and clear as the sky of outer space. He knows what he's talking about. I believe him."

"Then there's hope." It was half a question.

"I . . . I haven't worked it out. Maybe! Maybe not! I'm carrying a blaster from now on." The shiny-barreled weapon was in her hand as she spoke. "Just in case, Torie, just in case."

"In case what?"

Bayta laughed with a touch of hysteria, "Never mind. Maybe I'm a little crazy, too—like Ebling Mis."

Ebling Mis at that time had seven days to live, and the seven days slipped by, one after the other, quietly.

To Toran, there was a quality of stupor about them. The warming days and the dull silence covered him with lethargy. All life seemed to have lost its quality of action, and changed into an infinite sea of hibernation.

Mis was a hidden entity whose burrowing work produced nothing and did not make itself known. He had barricaded himself. Neither Toran nor Bayta could see him. Only Magnifico's go-between characteristics were evidence of his existence. Magnifico, grown silent and thoughtful, with his tiptoed trays of food and his still, watchful witness in the gloom.

Bayta was more and more a creature of herself. The vivacity died, the self-assured competence wavered. She, too, sought her own worried, absorbed company, and once Toran had come upon her, fingering her blaster. She had put it away quickly, forced a smile.

"What are you doing with it, Bay?"

"Holding it. Is that a crime?"

"You'll blow your fool head off."

"Then I'll blow it off. Small loss!"

Married life had taught Toran the futility of arguing with a female in a dark-brown mood. He shrugged, and left her.

On the last day, Magnifico scampered breathless into their presence. He clutched at them, frightened. "The learned doctor calls for you. He is not well."

And he wasn't well. He was in bed, his eyes unnaturally large, unnaturally bright. He was dirty, unrecognizable.

"Ebling!" cried Bayta.

"Let me speak," croaked the psychologist, lifting his weight to a thin elbow with an effort. "Let me speak. I am finished; the work I pass on to you. I have kept no notes; the scrap-figures I have destroyed. No other must know. All must remain in your minds."

"Magnifico," said Bayta, with rough directness. "Go upstairs!"

Reluctantly, the clown rose and took a backward step. His sad eyes were on Mis.

Mis gestured weakly, "He won't matter; let him stay. Stay, Magnifico."

The clown sat down quickly. Bayta gazed at the floor. Slowly, slowly, her lower lip caught in her teeth.

Mis said, in a hoarse whisper, "I am convinced the Second Foundation can win, if it is not caught prematurely by the Mule. It has kept itself secret; the secrecy must be upheld; it has a purpose. You must go there; your information is vital . . . may make all the difference. Do you hear me?"

Toran cried in near-agony, "Yes, yes! Tell us how to get there, Ebling? Where is it?"

"I can tell you," said the faint voice.

He never did.

Bayta, face frozen white, lifted her blaster and shot, with an echoing clap of noise. From the waist upward, Mis was not, and a ragged hole was in the wall behind. From numb fingers, Bayta's blaster dropped to the floor.

26.

End of the Search

There was not a word to be said. The echoes of the blast rolled away into the outer rooms and rumbled downward into a hoarse, dying whisper. Before its death, it had muffled the sharp clamor of Bayta's falling blaster, smothered Magnifico's high-pitched cry, drowned out Toran's inarticulate roar.

There was a silence of agony.

Bayta's head was bent into obscurity. A droplet caught the light as it fell. Bayta had never wept before.

Toran's muscles almost cracked in their spasm, but he did not relax—he felt as if he would never unclench his teeth again. Magnifico's face was a faded, lifeless mask.

Finally, from between teeth still tight, Toran choked out in an unrecognizable voice, "You're a Mule's woman, then. He got to you!"

Bayta looked up, and her mouth twisted with a painful merriment, "I, a Mule's woman? That's ironic."

She smiled—a brittle effort—and tossed her hair back. Slowly, her voice verged back to the normal, or something near it. "It's over, Toran; I can talk now. How much I will survive, I don't know. But I can start talking—"

Toran's tension had broken of its own weight and faded into a flaccid dullness, "Talk about what, Bay? What's there to talk about?"

"About the calamity that's followed us. We've remarked about it before, Torie. Don't you remember? How defeat has always bitten at our heels and never actually managed to nip us? We were on the Foundation, and it collapsed while the Independent Traders still fought—but we got out in time to go to Haven. We were on Haven, and it collapsed while the others still fought—

and again we got out in time. We went to Neotrantor, and by now it's undoubtedly joined the Mule."

Toran listened and shook his head, "I don't understand."

"Torie, such things don't happen in real life. You and I are insignificant people; we don't fall from one vortex of politics into another continuously for the space of a year—unless we carry the vortex with us. *Unless we carry the source of infection with us!* Now do you see?"

Toran's lips tightened. His glance fixed horribly upon the bloody remnants of what had once been a human, and his eyes sickened.

"Let's get out of here, Bay. Let's get out into the open."

It was cloudy outside. The wind scudded about them in drab spurts and disordered Bayta's hair. Magnifico had crept after them and now he hovered at the edge of their conversation.

Toran said tightly, "You killed Ebling Mis because you believed *him* to be the focus of infection?" Something in her eyes struck him. He whispered, "He was the Mule?" He did not—could not—believe the implications of his own words.

Bayta laughed sharply, "Poor Ebling the Mule? Galaxy, no! I couldn't have killed him if he were the Mule. He would have detected the emotion accompanying the move and changed it for me to love, devotion, adoration, terror, whatever he pleased. No, I killed Ebling because he was *not* the Mule. I killed him because he knew where the Second Foundation was, and in two seconds would have told the Mule the secret."

"Would have told the Mule the secret," Toran repeated stupidly. "Told the Mule—"

And then he emitted a sharp cry, and turned to stare in horror at the clown, who might have been crouching unconscious there for the apparent understanding he had of what he heard.

"Not Magnifico?" Toran whispered the question.

"Listen!" said Bayta. "Do you remember what happened on Neotrantor? Oh, think for yourself, Torie—"

But he shook his head and mumbled at her.

She went on, wearily, "A man died on Neotrantor. A man died with no one touching him. Isn't that true? Magnifico played on his Visi-Sonor and when he was finished, the crown prince was dead. Now isn't that strange? Isn't it queer that a creature afraid of everything, apparently helpless with terror, has the capacity to kill at will."

"The music and the light-effects," said Toran, "have a profound emotional effect—"

"Yes, an *emotional* effect. A pretty big one. Emotional effects happen to be the Mule's specialty. That, I suppose, can be considered a coincidence. And a creature who can kill by suggestion is so full of fright. Well, the Mule tampered with his mind, supposedly, so that can be explained. But, Toran, I caught a little of that Visi-Sonor selection that killed the crown prince. Just a little—but it was enough to give me that same feeling of despair I had in the Time Vault and on Haven. Toran, I can't mistake that particular feeling."

Toran's face was darkening, "I . . . felt it, too. I forgot. I never thought—"

"It was then that it first occurred to me. It was just a vague feeling—intuition, if you like. I had nothing to go on. And then Pritcher told us of the Mule and his mutation, and it was clear in a moment. It was the Mule who had created the despair in the Time Vault; it was Magnifico who had created the despair on Neotrantor. It was the same emotion. Therefore, the Mule and Magnifico were the same person. Doesn't it work out nicely, Torie? Isn't it just like an axiom in geometry—things equal to the same thing are equal to each other?"

She was at the edge of hysteria, but dragged herself back to sobriety by main force. She continued, "The discovery scared me to death. If Magnifico were the Mule, he could know my emotions—and cure them for his own purposes. I dared not let him know. I avoided him. Luckily, he avoided me also; he was too interested in Ebling Mis. I planned killing Mis before he could talk. I planned it secretly—as secretly as I could—so secretly I didn't dare tell it to myself. If I could have killed the Mule himself— But I couldn't take the chance. He would have noticed, and I would have lost everything."

She seemed drained of emotion.

Toran said harshly and with finality, "It's impossible. Look at the miserable creature. *He* the Mule? He doesn't even hear what we're saying."

But when his eyes followed his pointing finger, Magnifico was erect and alert, his eyes sharp and darkly bright. His voice was without a trace of an accent, "I hear her, my friend. It is merely that I have been sitting here and brooding on the fact that with all my cleverness and forethought I could make a mistake, and lose so much."

Toran stumbled backward as if afraid the clown might touch him or that his breath might contaminate him.

Magnifico nodded, and answered the unspoken question. "I am the Mule."

He seemed no longer a grotesque; his pipestem limbs, his beak of a nose lost their humor-compelling qualities. His fear was gone; his bearing was firm.

He was in command of the situation with an ease born of usage.

He said, tolerantly, "Seat yourselves. Go ahead; you might as well sprawl out and make yourselves comfortable. The game's over, and I'd like to tell you a story. It's a weakness of mine—I want people to understand me."

And his eyes as he looked at Bayta were still the old, soft sad brown ones of Magnifico, the clown.

"There is nothing really to my childhood," he began, plunging bodily into quick, impatient speech, "that I care to remember. Perhaps you can understand that. My meagerness is glandular; my nose I was born with. It was not possible for me to lead a normal childhood. My mother died before she saw me. I do not know my father. I grew up haphazard; wounded and tortured in mind, full of self-pity and hatred of others. I was known then as a queer child. All avoided me; most out of dislike; some out of fear. Queer incidents occurred— Well, never mind! Enough happened to enable Captain Pritcher, in his investigation of my childhood to realize that I was a mutant, which was more than *I* ever realized until I was in my twenties."

Toran and Bayta listened distantly. The wash of his voice broke over them, seated on the ground as they were, unheeded almost. The clown—or the Mule—paced before them with little steps, speaking downward to his own folded arms.

"The whole notion of my unusual power seems to have broken on me so slowly, in such sluggish steps. Even toward the end, I couldn't believe it. To me, men's minds are dials, with pointers that indicate the prevailing emotion. It is a poor picture, but how else can I explain it? Slowly, I learned that I could reach into those minds and turn the pointer to the spot I wished, that I could nail it there forever. And then it took even longer to realize that others couldn't.

"But the consciousness of power came, and with it, the desire to make up for the miserable position of my earlier life. Maybe you can understand it. Maybe you can try to understand it. It isn't easy to be a freak—to have a mind and an understanding and be a freak. Laughter and cruelty! To be different! To be an outsider!

"You've never been through it!"

Magnifico looked up to the sky and teetered on the balls of his feet and reminisced stonily, "But I eventually did learn, and I decided that the Galaxy and I could take turns. Come, they had had their innings, and I had been patient about it—for twenty-two years. My turn! It would be up to the rest of you to take it! And the odds would be fair enough for the Galaxy. One of me! Trillions of them!"

He paused to glance at Bayta swiftly. "But I had a weakness. I was nothing in myself. If I could gain power, it could only be by means of others. Success came to me through middlemen. Always! It was as Pritcher said. Through a pirate, I obtained my first asteroidal base of operations. Through an industrialist I got my first foothold on a planet. Through a variety of others ending with the warlord of Kalgan, I won Kalgan itself and got a navy. After that, it was the Foundation—and you two come into the story.

"The Foundation," he said, softly, "was the most difficult task I had met. To beat it, I would have to win over, break down, or render useless an extraordinary proportion of its ruling class. I could have done it from scratch—but a short cut was possible, and I looked for it. After all, if a strong man can lift five hundred pounds, it does not mean that he is eager to do so continuously. My emotional control is not an easy task, I prefer not to use it, where not fully necessary. So I accepted allies in my first attack upon the Foundation.

"As my clown, I looked for the agent, or agents, of the Foundation that must inevitably have been sent to Kalgan to investigate my humble self. I know now it was Han Pritcher I was looking for. By a stroke of fortune, I found you instead. I *am* a telepath, but not a complete one, and, my lady, you were from the Foundation. I was led astray by that. It was not fatal for Pritcher joined us afterward, but it was the starting point of an error which *was* fatal."

Toran stirred for the first time. He spoke in an outraged tone, "Hold on, now. You mean that when I outfaced that lieutenant on Kalgan with only a stun pistol, and rescued you—that you had emotionally-controlled me into it." He was spluttering. "You mean I've been tampered with all along."

A thin smile played on Magnifico's face. "Why not? You don't think it's likely? Ask yourself then— Would you have risked death for a strange grotesque you had never seen before, if you had been in your right mind? I imagine you were surprised at events in cold after-blood."

"Yes," said Bayta, distantly, "he was. It's quite plain."

"As it was," continued the Mule, "Toran was in no danger. The lieutenant had his own strict instructions to let us go. So the three of us and Pritcher went to the Foundation—and see how my campaign shaped itself instantly. When Pritcher was court-martialed and we were present, I was busy. The military judges of that trial later commanded their squadrons in the war. They surrendered rather easily, and my Navy won the battle of Horleggor, and other lesser affairs.

"Through Pritcher, I met Dr. Mis, who brought me a Visi-Sonor, entirely of his own accord, and simplified my task immensely. Only it wasn't *entirely* of his own accord."

Bayta interrupted, "Those concerts! I've been trying to fit them in. Now I see."

"Yes," said Magnifico, "the Visi-Sonor acts as a focusing device. In a way, it is a primitive device for emotional-control in itself. With it, I can handle people in quantity and single people more intensively. The concerts I gave on Terminus before it fell and Haven before *it* fell contributed to the general defeatism. I might have made the crown prince of Neotrantor very sick without the Visi-Sonor, but I could not have killed him. You see?

"But it was Ebling Mis who was my most important find. He might have been—" Magnifico said it with chagrin, then hurried on, "There is a special facet to emotional control you do not know about. Intuition or insight or hunch-tendency, whatever you wish to call it, can be treated as an emotion. At least, I can treat it so. You don't understand it, do you?"

He waited for no negative, "The human mind works at low efficiency. Twenty percent is the figure usually given. When, momentarily, there is a flash of greater power it is termed a hunch, or insight, or intuition. I found early that I could induce a continual use of high brain-efficiency. It is a killing process for the person affected, but it is useful— The atomic field-depressor which I used in the war against the Foundation was the result of high-pressuring a Kalgan technician. Again I work through others.

"Ebling Mis was the bull's-eye. His potentialities were high, and I needed him. Even before my war with the Foundation had opened, I had already sent delegates to negotiate with the Empire. It was at that time I began my search for the Second Foundation. Naturally, I didn't find it. Naturally, I knew that I must find it—and Ebling Mis was the answer. With his mind at high efficiency, he might possibly have duplicated the work of Hari Seldon.

"Partly, he did. I drove him to the utter limit. The process was ruthless, but had to be completed. He was dying at the end, but he lived—" Again, his chagrin interrupted him. "He *would* have lived long enough. Together, we three could have gone onward to the Second Foundation. It would have been the last battle—but for my mistake."

Toran stirred his voice to hardness, "Why do you stretch it out so? What was your mistake, and . . . and have done with your speech."

"Why, your wife was the mistake. Your wife was an unusual person. I had never met her like before in my life. I . . . I—" Quite suddenly, Magnifico's voice broke. He recovered with difficulty. There was a grimness about him as he continued. "She liked me without my having to juggle her emotions. She was neither repelled by me nor amused by me. She pitied me. She *liked* me!

"Don't you understand? Can't you see what that would mean to me? Never before had anyone— Well, I . . . cherished that. My own emotions played me false, though I was master of all others. I stayed out of her mind, you see; I did not tamper with it. I cherished the *natural* feeling too greatly. It was my mistake —the first.

"You, Toran, were under control. You never suspected me; never questioned me; never saw anything peculiar or strange about me. As for instance, when the 'Filian' ship stopped us. They knew our location, by the way, because I was in communication with them, as I've remained in communication with my generals at all times. When they stopped us, I was taken aboard to adjust Han Pritcher, who was on it as a prisoner. When I left, he was a colonel, a Mule's man, and in command. The whole procedure was too open even for you, Toran. Yet you accepted my explanation of the matter, which was full of fallacies. See what I mean?"

Toran grimaced, and challenged him, "How did you retain communications with your generals?"

"There was no difficulty to it. Ultra-wave senders are easy to handle and eminently portable. Nor could I be detected in a real sense! Anyone who did catch me in the act would leave me with a slice gapped out of his memory. It happened, on occasion.

"On Neotrantor, my own foolish emotions betrayed me again. Bayta was not under my control, but even so might never have suspected me if I had kept my head about the crown prince. His intentions towards Bayta—annoyed me. I killed him. It was a foolish gesture. An unobtrusive fight would have served as well.

"And still your suspicions would not have been certainties, if

I had stopped Pritcher in his well-intentioned babbling, or paid less attention to Mis and more to you—" He shrugged.

"That's the end of it?" asked Bayta.

"That's the end."

"What now, then?"

"I'll continue with my program. That I'll find another as adequately brained and trained as Ebling Mis in these degenerate days, I doubt. I shall have to search for the Second Foundation otherwise. In a sense you have defeated me."

And now Bayta was upon her feet, triumphant. "In a sense? Only in a sense? We have defeated you *entirely!* All your victories outside the Foundation count for nothing, since the Galaxy is a barbarian vacuum now. The Foundation itself is only a minor victory, since it wasn't meant to stop *your* variety of crisis. It's the Second Foundation you must beat—*the Second Foundation*—and it's the Second Foundation that will defeat you. Your only chance was to locate it and strike it before it was prepared. You won't do that now. Every minute from now on, they will be readier for you. At this moment, *at this moment,* the machinery may have started. You'll know—when it strikes you, and your short term of power will be over, and you'll be just another strutting conqueror, flashing quickly and meanly across the bloody face of history."

She was breathing hard, nearly gasping in her vehemence, "And we've defeated you, Toran and I. I am satisfied to die."

But the Mule's sad, brown eyes were the sad, brown, loving eyes of Magnifico. "I won't kill you or your husband. It is, after all, impossible for you two to hurt me further; and killing you won't bring back Ebling Mis. My mistakes were my own, and I take responsibility for them. Your husband and yourself may leave! Go in peace, for the sake of what I call—friendship."

Then, with a sudden touch of pride, "And meanwhile I am still the Mule, the most powerful man in the Galaxy. I shall *still* defeat the Second Foundation."

And Bayta shot her last arrow with a firm, calm certitude, "You won't! I have faith in the wisdom of Seldon yet. You shall be the last ruler of your dynasty, as well as the first."

Something caught Magnifico. "Of my dynasty? Yes, I had

thought of that, often. That I might establish a dynasty. That I might have a suitable consort."

Bayta suddenly caught the meaning of the look in his eyes and froze horribly.

Magnifico shook his head. "I sense your revulsion, but that's silly. If things were otherwise, I could make you happy very easily. It would be an artificial ecstasy, but there would be no difference between it and the genuine emotion. But things are not otherwise. I call myself the Mule—but not because of my strength—obviously—"

He left them, never looking back.

SECOND
FOUNDATION

Prologue

The First Galactic Empire had endured for tens of thousands of years. It had included all the planets of the Galaxy in a centralized rule, sometimes tyrannical, sometimes benevolent, always orderly. Human beings had forgotten that any other form of existence could be.

All except Hari Seldon.

Hari Seldon was the last great scientist of the First Empire. It was he who brought the science of psycho-history to its full development. Psycho-history was the quintessence of sociology; it was the science of human behavior reduced to mathematical equations.

The individual human being is unpredictable, but the reactions of human mobs, Seldon found, could be treated statistically. The larger the mob, the greater the accuracy that could be achieved. And the size of the human masses that Seldon worked with was no less than the population of the Galaxy which in his time was numbered in the quintillions.

It was Seldon, then, who foresaw, against all common sense and popular belief, that the brilliant Empire which seemed so strong was in a state of irremediable decay and decline. He foresaw (or he solved his equations and interpreted its symbols, which amounts to the same thing) that left to itself, the Galaxy would pass through a thirty thousand year period of misery and anarchy before a unified government would rise once more.

He set about to remedy the situation, to bring about a state of affairs that would restore peace and civilization in a single thousand of years. Carefully, he set up two colonies of scientists that he called "Foundations." With deliberate intention, he set them up "at opposite ends of the Galaxy." One Foundation was set up in the full daylight of publicity. The existence of the other, the Second Foundation, was drowned in silence.

In *Foundation* (Gnome, 1951) and *Foundation and Empire*

(Gnome, 1952) are told the first three centuries of the history of the First Foundation. It began as a small community of Encyclopedists lost in the emptiness of the outer periphery of the Galaxy. Periodically, it faced a crisis in which the variables of human intercourse, of the social and economic currents of the time constricted about it. Its freedom to move lay along only one certain line and when it moved in that direction, a new horizon of development opened before it. All had been planned by Hari Seldon, long dead now.

The First Foundation, with its superior science, took over the barbarized planets that surrounded it. It faced the anarchic Warlords that broke away from the dying Empire and beat them. It faced the remnant of the Empire itself under its last strong Emperor and its last strong General and beat it.

Then it faced something which Hari Seldon could not foresee, the overwhelming power of a single human being, a Mutant. The creature known as the Mule was born with the ability to mold men's emotions and to shape their minds. His bitterest opponents were made into his devoted servants. Armies could not, *would* not fight him. Before him, the First Foundation fell and Seldon's schemes lay partly in ruins.

There was left the mysterious Second Foundation, the goal of all searches. The Mule must find it to make his conquest of the Galaxy complete. The faithful of what was left of the First Foundation must find it for quite another reason. But where was it? That no one knew.

This, then, is the story of the search for the Second Foundation!

Contents

PROLOGUE   iii

PART I   SEARCH BY THE MULE

1. TWO MEN AND THE MULE   3
First Interlude

2. TWO MEN WITHOUT THE MULE   19
Second Interlude

3. TWO MEN AND A PEASANT   32
Third Interlude

4. TWO MEN AND THE ELDERS   40
Fourth Interlude

5. ONE MAN AND THE MULE   51

6. ONE MAN, THE MULE—AND ANOTHER   63
Last Interlude

PART II   SEARCH BY THE FOUNDATION

7. ARCADIA   79

8. SELDON'S PLAN   93

9. THE CONSPIRATORS   104

10. APPROACHING CRISIS   116

11. STOWAWAY   120

12. LORD   130

13. LADY   136

14. ANXIETY   142

15. THROUGH THE GRID   154

16. BEGINNING OF WAR   166

17. WAR   177

18. GHOST OF A WORLD   181

19. END OF WAR   188

20. "I KNOW . . ."   197

21. THE ANSWER THAT SATISFIED   210

22. THE ANSWER THAT WAS TRUE   220

PART I

SEARCH BY THE MULE

1

Two Men and the Mule

THE MULE *It was after the fall of the First Foundation that the constructive aspects of the Mule's regime took shape. After the definite break-up of the first Galactic Empire, it was he who first presented history with a unified volume of space truly imperial in scope. The earlier commercial empire of the fallen Foundation had been diverse and loosely knit, despite the impalpable backing of the predictions of psycho-history. It was not to be compared with the tightly controlled 'Union of Worlds' under the Mule, comprising as it did, one-tenth the volume of the Galaxy and one-fifteenth of its population. Particularly during the era of the so-called Search. . . .*

ENCYCLOPEDIA GALACTICA*

There is much more that the Encyclopedia has to say on the subject of the Mule and his Empire but almost all of it is not germane to the issue at immediate hand, and most of it is considerably too dry for our purposes in any case. Mainly, the article concerns itself at this point with the economic conditions that led to the rise of the "First Citizen of the Union"—the Mule's official title—and with the economic consequences thereof.

If, at any time, the writer of the article is mildly astonished at the colossal haste with which the Mule rose from nothing to vast dominion in five years, he conceals it. If he is further sur-

* All quotations from the Encyclopedia Galactica here reproduced are taken from the 116th Edition published in 1020 F.E. by the Encyclopedia Galactica Publishing Co., Terminus, with permission of the publishers.

prised at the sudden cessation of expansion in favor of a five-year consolidation of territory, he hides the fact.

We therefore abandon the Encyclopedia and continue on our own path for our own purposes and take up the history of the Great Interregnum—between the First and Second Galactic Empires—at the end of that five years of consolidation.

Politically, the Union is quiet. Economically, it is prosperous. Few would care to exchange the peace of the Mule's steady grip for the chaos that had preceded. On the worlds that five years previously had known the Foundation, there might be a nostalgic regret, but no more. The Foundation's leaders were dead, where useless; and Converted, where useful.

And of the Converted, the most useful was Han Pritcher, now lieutenant general.

In the days of the Foundation, Han Pritcher had been a captain and a member of the underground Democratic Opposition. When the Foundation fell to the Mule without a fight, Pritcher fought the Mule. Until, that is, he was Converted.

The Conversion was not the ordinary one brought on by the power of superior reason. Han Pritcher knew that well enough. He had been changed because the Mule was a mutant with mental powers quite capable of adjusting the conditions of ordinary humans to suit himself. But that satisfied him completely. That was as it should be. The very contentment with the Conversion was a prime symptom of it, but Han Pritcher was no longer even curious about the matter.

And now that he was returning from his fifth major expedition into the boundlessness of the Galaxy outside the Union, it was with something approaching artless joy that the veteran spaceman and Intelligence agent considered his approaching audience with the "First Citizen." His hard face, gouged out of a dark, grainless wood that did not seem to be capable of smiling without cracking, didn't show it—but the outward indications were unnecessary. The Mule could see the emotions within, down to the smallest, much as an ordinary man could see the twitch of an eyebrow.

Pritcher left his air car at the old vice-regal hangars and entered the palace grounds on foot as was required. He walked one mile along the arrowed highway—which was empty and silent. Pritcher knew that over the square miles of palace grounds, there was not one guard, not one soldier, not one armed man.

The Mule had need of no protection.

The Mule was his own best, all-powerful protector.

Pritcher's footsteps beat softly in his own ears, as the palace reared its gleaming, incredibly light and incredibly strong metallic walls before him in the daring, overblown, near-hectic arches that characterized the architecture of the Late Empire. It brooded strongly over the empty grounds, over the crowded city on the horizon.

Within the palace was that one man—by himself—on whose inhuman mental attributes depended the new aristocracy, and the whole structure of the Union.

The huge, smooth door swung massively open at the general's approach, and he entered. He stepped on to the wide, sweeping ramp that moved upward under him. He rose swiftly in the noiseless elevator. He stood before the small plain door of the Mule's own room in the highest glitter of the palace spires.

It opened—

Bail Channis was young, and Bail Channis was Unconverted. That is, in plainer language, his emotional make-up had been unadjusted by the Mule. It remained exactly as it had been formed by the original shape of its heredity and the subsequent modifications of his environment. And that satisfied him, too.

At not quite thirty, he was in marvelously good odor in the capital. He was handsome and quick-witted—therefore successful in society. He was intelligent and self-possessed—therefore successful with the Mule. And he was thoroughly pleased at both successes.

And now, for the first time, the Mule had summoned him to personal audience.

His legs carried him down the long, glittering highway that

led tautly to the sponge-aluminum spires that had been once the
residence of the viceroy of Kalgan, who ruled under the old emperors; and that had been later the residence of the independent
princes of Kalgan, who ruled in their own name; and that was
now the residence of the First Citizen of the Union, who ruled
over an empire of his own.

Channis hummed softly to himself. He did not doubt what
this was all about. The Second Foundation, naturally! That all-
embracing bogey, the mere consideration of which had thrown
the Mule back from his policy of limitless expansion into static
caution. The official term was "consolidation."

Now there were rumors—you couldn't stop rumors. The Mule
was to begin the offensive once more. The Mule had discovered
the whereabouts of the Second Foundation, and would attack.
The Mule had come to an agreement with the Second Foundation and divided the Galaxy. The Mule had decided the Second
Foundation did not exist and would take over all the Galaxy.

No use listing all the varieties one heard in the anterooms. It
was not even the first time such rumors had circulated. But now
they seemed to have more body in them, and all the free, expan-
sive souls who thrived on war, military adventure, and political
chaos and withered in times of stability and stagnant peace were
joyful.

Bail Channis was one of these. He did not fear the mysterious
Second Foundation. For that matter, he did not fear the Mule,
and boasted of it. Some, perhaps, who disapproved of one at
once so young and so well-off, waited darkly for the reckoning
with the gay ladies' man who employed his wit openly at the
expense of the Mule's physical appearance and sequestered life.
None dared join him and few dared laugh, but when nothing
happened to him, his reputation rose accordingly.

Channis was improvising words to the tune he was humming.
Nonsense words with the recurrent refrain: "Second Foundation
threatens the Nation and all of Creation."

He was at the palace.

The huge, smooth door swung massively open at his approach
and he entered. He stepped on to the wide, sweeping ramp

that moved upward under him. He rose swiftly in the noiseless elevator. He stood before the small plain door of the Mule's own room in the highest glitter of the palace spires.

It opened—

The man who had no name other than the Mule, and no title other than First Citizen looked out through the one-way transparency of the wall to the light and lofty city on the horizon.

In the darkening twilight, the stars were emerging, and not one but owed allegiance to him.

He smiled with fleeting bitterness at the thought. The allegiance they owed was to a personality few had ever seen.

He was not a man to look at, the Mule—not a man to look at without derision. Not more than one hundred and twenty pounds was stretched out into his five-foot-eight length. His limbs were bony stalks that jutted out of his scrawniness in graceless angularity. And his thin face was nearly drowned out in the prominence of a fleshy beak that thrust three inches outward.

Only his eyes played false with the general farce that was the Mule. In their softness—a strange softness for the Galaxy's greatest conqueror—sadness was never entirely subdued.

In the city was to be found all the gaiety of a luxurious capital on a luxurious world. He might have established his capital on the Foundation, the strongest of his now-conquered enemies, but it was far out on the very rim of the Galaxy. Kalgan, more centrally located, with a long tradition as aristocracy's playground, suited him better—strategically.

But in its traditional gaiety, enhanced by unheard-of prosperity, he found no peace.

They feared him and obeyed him and, perhaps, even respected him—from a goodly distance. But who could look at him without contempt? Only those he had Converted. And of what value was their artificial loyalty? It lacked flavor. He might have adopted titles, and enforced ritual and invented elaborations, but even that would have changed nothing. Better—or at least, no worse— to be simply the First Citizen—and to hide himself.

There was a sudden surge of rebellion within him—strong and

brutal. Not a portion of the Galaxy must be denied him. For five years he had remained silent and buried here on Kalgan because of the eternal, misty, space-ridden menace of the unseen, unheard, unknown Second Foundation. He was thirty-two. Not old —but he felt old. His body, whatever its mutant mental powers, was physically weak.

Every star! Every star he could see—and every star he couldn't see. It must all be his!

Revenge on all. On a humanity of which he wasn't a part. On a Galaxy in which he didn't fit.

The cool, overhead warning light flickered. He could follow the progress of the man who had entered the palace, and simultaneously, as though his mutant sense had been enhanced and sensitized in the lonely twilight, he felt the wash of emotional content touch the fibers of his brain.

He recognized the identity without an effort. It was Pritcher.

Captain Pritcher of the one-time Foundation. The Captain Pritcher who had been ignored and passed over by the bureaucrats of that decaying government. The Captain Pritcher whose job as petty spy he had wiped out and whom he had lifted from its slime. The Captain Pritcher whom he had made first colonel and then general; whose scope of activity he had made Galaxy-wide.

The now-General Pritcher who was, iron rebel though he began, completely loyal. And yet with all that, not loyal because of benefits gained, not loyal out of gratitude, not loyal as a fair return—but loyal only through the artifice of Conversion.

The Mule was conscious of that strong unalterable surface layer of loyalty and love that colored every swirl and eddy of the emotionality of Han Pritcher—the layer he had himself implanted five years before. Far underneath there were the original traces of stubborn individuality, impatience of rule, idealism—but even he, himself, could scarcely detect them any longer.

The door behind him opened, and he turned. The transparency of the wall faded to opacity, and the purple evening light gave way to the whitely blazing glow of atomic power.

Han Pritcher took the seat indicated. There was neither bowing, nor kneeling nor the use of honorifics in private audiences with the Mule. The Mule was merely "First Citizen." He was addressed as "sir." You sat in his presence, and you could turn your back on him if it so happened that you did.

To Han Pritcher this was all evidence of the sure and confident power of the man. He was warmly satisfied with it.

The Mule said: "Your final report reached me yesterday. I can't deny that I find it somewhat depressing, Pritcher."

The general's eyebrows closed upon each other: "Yes, I imagine so—but I don't see to what other conclusions I could have come. There just isn't any Second Foundation, sir."

And the Mule considered and then slowly shook his head, as he had done many a time before: "There's the evidence of Ebling Mis. There is always the evidence of Ebling Mis."

It was not a new story. Pritcher said without qualification: "Mis may have been the greatest psychologist of the Foundation, but he was a baby compared to Hari Seldon. At the time he was investigating Seldon's works, he was under the artificial stimulation of your own brain control. You may have pushed him too far. He might have been wrong. Sir, he *must* have been wrong."

The Mule sighed, his lugubrious face thrust forward on its thin stalk of a neck. "If only he had lived another minute. He was on the point of telling me where the Second Foundation was. He *knew*, I'm telling you. I need not have retreated. I need not have waited and waited. So much time lost. Five years gone for nothing."

Pritcher could not have been censorious over the weak longing of his ruler; his controlled mental make-up forbade that. He was disturbed instead; vaguely uneasy. He said: "But what alternative explanation can there possibly be, sir? Five times I've gone out. You yourself have plotted the routes. And I've left no asteroid unturned. It was three hundred years ago—that Hari Seldon of the old Empire supposedly established two Foundations to act as nuclei of a new Empire to replace the dying old one. One hundred years after Seldon, the First Foundation—the one we know so well—was known through all the Periphery. One hundred fifty years after Seldon—at the time of the last battle with the old Empire—it was known throughout the Galaxy. And now it's three hundred years—and where should this mysterious Second be? In no eddy of the Galactic stream has it been heard of."

"Ebling Mis said it kept itself secret. Only secrecy can turn its weakness to strength."

"Secrecy as deep as this is past possibility without nonexistence as well."

The Mule looked up, large eyes sharp and wary. "No. It *does* exist." A bony finger pointed sharply. "There is going to be a slight change in tactics."

Pritcher frowned. "You plan to leave yourself? I would scarcely advise it."

"No, of course not. You will have to go out once again—one last time. But with another in joint command."

There was a silence, and Pritcher's voice was hard, "Who, sir?"

"There's a young man here in Kalgan. Bail Channis."

"I've never heard of him, sir."

"No, I imagine not. But he's got an agile mind, he's ambitious —and he's *not* Converted."

Pritcher's long jaw trembled for a bare instant, "I fail to see the advantage in that."

"There is one, Pritcher. You're a resourceful and experienced man. You have given me good service. But you are Converted. Your motivation is simply an enforced and helpless loyalty to myself. When you lost your native motivations, you lost something, some subtle drive, that I cannot possibly replace."

"I don't feel that, sir," said Pritcher, grimly. "I recall myself quite well as I was in the days when I was an enemy of yours. I feel none the inferior."

"Naturally not," and the Mule's mouth twitched into a smile. "Your judgment in this matter is scarcely objective. This Channis, now, is ambitious—for himself. He is completely trustworthy —out of no loyalty but to himself. He knows that it is on my coattails that he rides and he would do anything to increase my power that the ride might be long and far and that the destination might be glorious. If he goes with you, there is just that added push behind *his* seeking—that push for himself."

"Then," said Pritcher, still insistent, "why not remove my own Conversion, if you think that will improve me. I can scarcely be mistrusted, now."

"That never, Pritcher. While you are within arm's reach, or blaster reach, of myself, you will remain firmly held in Conversion. If I were to release you this minute, I would be dead the next."

The general's nostrils flared. "I am hurt that you should think so."

"I don't mean to hurt you, but it is impossible for you to realize what your feelings would be if free to form themselves along the lines of your natural motivation. The human mind resents control. The ordinary human hypnotist cannot hypnotize a person against his will for that reason. I can, because I'm not a hypnotist, and, believe me, Pritcher, the resentment that you cannot show and do not even know you possess is something I wouldn't want to face."

Pritcher's head bowed. Futility wrenched him and left him gray and haggard inside. He said with an effort: "But how can you trust this man. I mean, completely—as you can trust me in my Conversion."

"Well, I suppose I can't entirely. That is why you must go with him. You see, Pritcher," and the Mule buried himself in the large armchair against the soft back of which he looked like an angularly animated toothpick, "if he *should* stumble on the Second Foundation—if it *should* occur to him that an arrangement with them might be more profitable than with me— You understand?"

A profoundly satisfied light blazed in Pritcher's eyes. "That is better, sir."

"Exactly. But remember, he must have a free rein as far as possible."

"Certainly."

"And . . . uh . . . Pritcher. The young man is handsome, pleasant, and extremely charming. Don't let him fool you. He's a dangerous and unscrupulous character. Don't get in his way un-less you're prepared to meet him properly. That's all."

The Mule was alone again. He let the lights die and the wall before him kicked to transparency again. The sky was purple now, and the city was a smudge of light on the horizon.

What was it all for? And if he *were* the master of all there was —what then? Would it really stop men like Pritcher from being straight and tall, self-confident, strong? Would Bail Channis lose his looks? Would he himself be other than he was?

He cursed his doubts. What was he really after?

The cool, overhead warning light flickered. He could follow the progress of the man who had entered the palace and, almost against his will, he felt the soft wash of emotional content touch the fibers of his brain.

He recognized the identity without an effort. It was Channis. Here the Mule saw no uniformity, but the primitive diversity of a strong mind, untouched and unmolded except by the manifold disorganizations of the Universe. It writhed in floods and waves. There was caution on the surface, a thin, smoothing effect, but with touches of cynical ribaldry in the hidden eddies of it. And underneath there was the strong flow of self-interest and self-love, with a gush of cruel humor here and there, and a deep, still pool of ambition underlying all.

The Mule felt that he could reach out and dam the current, wrench the pool from its basin and turn it in another course, dry up one flow and begin another. But what of it? If he could bend Channis' curly head in the profoundest adoration, would that change his own grotesquerie that made him shun the day and love the night, that made him a recluse inside an empire that was unconditionally his?

The door behind him opened, and he turned. The transparency of the wall faded to opacity, and the darkness gave way to the whitely blazing artifice of atomic power.

Bail Channis sat down lightly and said: "This is a not-quite-unexpected honor, sir."

The Mule rubbed his proboscis with all four fingers at once and sounded a bit irritable in his response. "Why so, young man?"

"A hunch, I suppose. Unless I want to admit that I've been listening to rumors."

"Rumors? Which one of the several dozen varieties are you referring to?"

"Those that say a renewal of the Galactic Offensive is being planned. It is a hope with me that such is true and that I might play an appropriate part."

"Then you think there *is* a Second Foundation?"

"Why not? It would make things so much more interesting."

"And you find interest in it as well?"

"Certainly. In the very mystery of it! What better subject could you find for conjecture? The newspaper supplements are full of nothing else lately—which is probably significant. The *Cosmos* had one of its feature writers compose a weirdie about a world consisting of beings of pure mind—the Second Foundation, you see—who had developed mental force to energies large enough to compete with any known to physical science. Spaceships could be blasted light-years away, planets could be turned out of their orbits—"

"Interesting. Yes. But do *you* have any notions on the subject? Do you subscribe to this mind-power notion?"

"Galaxy, no! Do you think creatures like that would stay on their own planet? No, sir. I think the Second Foundation remains hidden because it is weaker than we think."

"In that case, I can explain myself very easily. How would you like to head an expedition to locate the Second Foundation?"

For a moment Channis seemed caught up by the sudden rush of events at just a little greater speed than he was prepared for. His tongue had apparently skidded to a halt in a lengthening silence.

The Mule said dryly: "Well?"

Channis corrugated his forehead. "Certainly. But where am I to go? Have you any information available?"

"General Pritcher will be with you—"

"Then I'm *not* to head it?"

"Judge for yourself when I'm done. Listen, you're not of the Foundation. You're a native of Kalgan, aren't you? Yes. Well, then, your knowledge of the Seldon plan may be vague. When the first Galactic Empire was falling, Hari Seldon and a group of psychohistorians, analyzing the future course of history by mathematical tools no longer available in these degenerate times, set up two Foundations, one at each end of the Galaxy, in such a way that the economic and sociological forces that were slowly evolving, would make them serve as foci for the Second Empire. Hari Seldon planned on a thousand years to accomplish that—and it would have taken thirty thousand without the Foundations. But he couldn't count on *me*. I am a mutant and I am unpredictable by psychohistory which can only deal with the average reactions of numbers. Do you understand?"

"Perfectly, sir. But how does that involve me?"

"You'll understand shortly. I intend to unite the Galaxy now—and reach Seldon's thousand-year goal in three hundred. One Foundation—the world of physical scientists—is still flourishing, under *me*. Under the prosperity and order of the Union, the atomic weapons they have developed are capable of dealing with anything in the Galaxy—except perhaps the Second Foundation. So I must know more about it. General Pritcher is of the definite opinion that it does not exist at all. I know otherwise."

Channis said delicately: "How do you know, sir?"

And the Mule's words were suddenly liquid indignation: "Because minds under my control have been interfered with. Delicately! Subtly! But not so subtly that I couldn't notice. And these interferences are increasing, and hitting valuable men at important times. Do you wonder now that a certain discretion has kept me motionless these years?

"That is your importance. General Pritcher is the best man left me, so he is no longer safe. Of course, he does not know that. But *you* are Unconverted and therefore not instantly detectable as a Mule's man. You may fool the Second Foundation longer than one of my own men would—perhaps just sufficiently longer. Do you understand?"

"Um-m-m. Yes. But pardon me, sir, if I question you. How are these men of yours disturbed, so that I might detect change in General Pritcher, in case any occurs. Are they Unconverted again? Do they become disloyal?"

"No. I told you it was subtle. It's more disturbing than that, because it's harder to detect and sometimes I have to wait before acting, uncertain whether a key man is being normally erratic or has been tampered with. Their loyalty is left intact, but initiative and ingenuity are rubbed out. I'm left with a perfectly normal person, apparently, but one completely useless. In the last year, six have been so treated. Six of my best." A corner of his mouth lifted. "They're in charge of training bases now—and my most earnest wishes go with them that no emergencies come up for them to decide upon."

"Suppose, sir . . . suppose it were not the Second Foundation. What if it were another, such as yourself—another mutant?"

"The planning is too careful, too long range. A single man would be in a greater hurry. No, it is a world, and you are to be my weapon against it."

Channis' eyes shone as he said: "I'm delighted at the chance."

But the Mule caught the sudden emotional upwelling. He said: "Yes, apparently it occurs to you, that you will perform a unique service, worthy of a unique reward—perhaps even that of being my successor. Quite so. But there are unique punishments, too, you know. My emotional gymnastics are not confined to the creation of loyalty alone."

And the little smile on his thin lips was grim, as Channis leaped out of his seat in horror.

For just an instant, just one, flashing instant, Channis had felt the pang of an overwhelming grief close over him. It had slammed down with a physical pain that had blackened his mind unbearably, and then lifted. Now nothing was left but the strong wash of anger.

The Mule said: "Anger won't help . . . yes, you're covering it up now, aren't you? But I can see it. So just remember—*that* sort of business can be made more intense and kept up. I've killed men by emotional control, and there's no death crueler."

He paused: "That's all!"

The Mule was alone again. He let the lights die and the wall before him kicked to transparency again. The sky was black, and the rising body of the Galactic Lens was spreading its bespanglement across the velvet depths of space.

All that haze of nebula was a mass of stars so numerous that they melted one into the other and left nothing but a cloud of light.

And all to be his—

And now but one last arrangement to make, and he could sleep.

FIRST INTERLUDE

The Executive Council of the Second Foundation was in session. To us they are merely voices. Neither the exact scene of the meeting nor the identity of those present are essential at the point.

Nor, strictly speaking, can we even consider an exact reproduction of any part of the session—unless we wish to sacrifice completely even the minimum comprehensibility we have a right to expect.

We deal here with psychologists—and not merely psychologists. Let us say, rather, scientists with a psychological orientation. That is, men whose fundamental conception of scientific philosophy is pointed in an entirely different direction from all of the orientations we know. The "psychology" of scientists brought up among the axioms deduced from the observational habits of physical science has only the vaguest relationship to PSYCHOLOGY.

Which is about as far as I can go in explaining color to a blind man—with myself as blind as the audience.

The point being made is that the minds assembled understood thoroughly the workings of each other, not only by general theory but by the specific application over a long period of these theories to particular individuals. Speech as known to us was unnecessary. A fragment of a sentence amounted almost to long-winded redundancy. A gesture, a grunt, the curve of a facial line—even a significantly timed pause yielded informational juice.

The liberty is taken, therefore, of freely translating a small portion of the conference into the extremely specific word-combinations necessary to minds oriented from childhood to a physical science philosophy, even at the risk of losing the more delicate nuances.

There was one "voice" predominant, and that belonged to the individual known simply as the First Speaker.

He said: "It is apparently quite definite now as to what stopped the Mule in his first mad rush. I can't say that the matter reflects credit upon . . . well, upon the organization of the situation. Apparently, he almost located us, by means of the artificially heightened brain-energy of what they call a 'psychologist' on the First Foundation. This psychologist was killed just before he could communicate his discovery to the Mule. The events leading to that killing were completely fortuitous for all calculations below Phase Three. Suppose you take over."

It was the Fifth Speaker who was indicated by an inflection of the voice. He said, in grim nuances: "It is certain that the situation was mishandled. We are, of course, highly vulnerable under mass attack, particularly an attack led by such a mental phenomenon as the Mule. Shortly after he first achieved Galactic eminence with the conquest of the First Foundation, half a year after to be exact, he was on Trantor. Within another half year he would have been here and the odds would have been stupendously against us—96.3 plus or minus 0.05% to be exact. We have spent considerable time analyzing the forces that stopped him. We know, of course, what was driving him on so in the first place. The internal ramifications of his physical deformity and mental uniqueness are obvious to all of us. However, it was only through penetration to Phase Three that we could determine—*after the fact*—the possibility of his anomalous action in the presence of another human being who had an honest affection for him.

"And since such an anomalous action would depend upon the presence of such another human being at the appropriate time, to that extent the whole affair was fortuitous. Our agents are certain that it was a girl that killed the Mule's psychologist—a girl for whom the Mule felt trust out of sentiment, and whom he, therefore, did not control mentally—simply because she liked him.

"Since that event—and for those who want the details, a mathematical treatment of the subject has been drawn up for the Central Library—which warned us, we have held the Mule off by unorthodox methods with which we daily risk Seldon's entire scheme of history. That is all."

The First Speaker paused an instant to allow the individuals assembled to absorb the full implications. He said: "The situation is then highly unstable. With Seldon's original scheme bent to the fracture point—and I must emphasize that we have blundered badly in this whole matter, in our horrible lack of foresight —we are faced with an irreversible breakdown of the Plan. Time is passing us by. I think there is only one solution left us—and even that is risky.

"We must allow the Mule to find us—in a sense."

Another pause, in which he gathered the reactions, then: "I repeat—in a sense!"

2

Two Men without the Mule

The ship was in near-readiness. Nothing lacked, but the destination. The Mule had suggested a return to Trantor—the world that was the hulk of an incomparable Galactic metropolis of the hugest Empire mankind had ever known—the dead world that had been capital of all the stars.

Pritcher disapproved. It was an old path—sucked dry.

He found Bail Channis in the ship's navigation room. The young man's curly hair was just sufficiently disheveled to allow a single curl to droop over the forehead—as if it had been carefully placed there—and even teeth showed in a smile that matched it. Vaguely, the stiff officer felt himself harden against the other.

Channis' excitement was evident, "Pritcher, it's too far a coincidence."

The general said coldly: "I'm not aware of the subject of conversation."

"Oh— Well, then drag up a chair, old man, and let's get into it. I've been going over your notes. I find them excellent."

"How . . . pleasant that you do."

"But I'm wondering if you've come to the conclusions I have. Have you ever tried analyzing the problem deductively? I mean, it's all very well to comb the stars at random, and to have done all you did in five expeditions is quite a bit of star-hopping. That's obvious. But have you calculated how long it would take to go through every known world at this rate?"

"Yes. Several times." Pritcher felt no urge to meet the young man halfway, but there was the importance of filching the other's mind—the other's uncontrolled, and hence, unpredictable, mind.

"Well, then, suppose we're analytical about it and try to decide just what we're looking for?"

"The Second Foundation," said Pritcher, grimly.

"A Foundation of psychologists," corrected Channis, "who are as weak in physical science as the First Foundation was weak in psychology. Well, you're from the First Foundation, which I'm not. The implications are probably obvious to you. We must find a world which rules by virtue of mental skills, and yet which is very backwards scientifically."

"Is that necessarily so?" questioned Pritcher, quietly. "Our own 'Union of Worlds' isn't backwards scientifically, even though our ruler owes his strength to his mental powers."

"Because he has the skills of the First Foundation to draw upon," came the slightly impatient answer, "and that is the only such reservoir of knowledge in the Galaxy. The Second Foundation must live among the dry crumbs of the broken Galactic Empire. There are no pickings there."

"So then you postulate mental power sufficient to establish their rule over a group of worlds and physical helplessness as well?"

"*Comparative* physical helplessness. Against the decadent neighboring areas, they are competent to defend themselves. Against the resurgent forces of the Mule, with his background of a mature atomic economy, they cannot stand. Else, why is their location so well-hidden, both at the start by the founder, Hari Seldon, and now by themselves. Your own First Foundation made no secret of its existence and did not have it made for them, when they were an undefended single city on a lonely planet three hundred years ago."

The smooth lines of Pritcher's dark face twitched sardonically. "And now that you've finished your deep analysis, would you like a list of all the kingdoms, republics, planet states and dictatorships of one sort or another in that political wilderness out there that correspond to your description and to several factors besides?"

"All this has been considered then?" Channis lost none of his brashness.

"You won't find it here, naturally, but we have a completely worked out guide to the political units of the Opposing Periphery. Really, did you suppose the Mule would work entirely hit-and-miss?"

"Well, then," and the young man's voice rose in a burst of energy, "what of the Oligarchy of Tazenda?"

Pritcher touched his ear thoughtfully, "Tazenda? Oh, I think I know it. They're not in the Periphery, are they? It seems to me they're fully a third of the way towards the center of the Galaxy."

"Yes. What of that?"

"The records we have place the Second Foundation at the other end of the Galaxy. Space knows it's the only thing we have to go on. Why talk of Tazenda anyway? Its angular deviation from the First Foundation radian is only about one hundred ten to one hundred twenty degrees anyway. Nowhere near one hundred eighty."

"There's another point in the records. The Second Foundation was established at 'Star's End.'"

"No such region in the Galaxy has ever been located."

"Because it was a local name, suppressed later for greater secrecy. Or maybe one invented for the purpose by Seldon and his group. Yet there's some relationship between 'Star's End' and 'Tazenda,' don't you think?"

"A vague similarity in sound? Insufficient."

"Have you ever been there?"

"No."

"Yet it is mentioned in your records."

"Where? Oh, yes, but that was merely to take on food and water. There was certainly nothing remarkable about the world."

"Did you land at the ruling planet? The center of government?"

"I couldn't possibly say."

Channis brooded about it under the other's cold gaze. Then, "Would you look at the Lens with me for a moment?"

"Certainly."

The Lens was perhaps the newest feature of the interstellar cruisers of the day. Actually, it was a complicated calculating machine which could throw on a screen a reproduction of the night sky as seen from any given point of the Galaxy.

Channis adjusted the co-ordinate points and the wall lights of the pilot room were extinguished. In the dim red light at the control board of the Lens, Channis' face glowed ruddily. Pritcher sat in the pilot seat, long legs crossed, face lost in the gloom.

Slowly, as the induction period passed, the points of light brightened on the screen. And then they were thick and bright with the generously populated star-groupings of the Galaxy's center.

"This," explained Channis, "is the winter night-sky as seen from Trantor. That is the important point that, as far as I know, has been neglected so far in your search. All intelligent orientation must start from Trantor as zero point. Trantor was the capital of the Galactic Empire. Even more so scientifically and culturally, than politically. And, therefore, the significance of any descriptive name should stem, nine times out of ten, from a Trantorian orientation. You'll remember in this connection that, although Seldon was from Helicon, towards the Periphery, his group worked on Trantor itself."

"What is it you're trying to show me?" Pritcher's level voice plunged icily into the gathering enthusiasm of the other.

"The map will explain it. Do you see the dark nebula?" The shadow of his arm fell upon the screen, which took on the bespanglement of the Galaxy. The pointing finger ended on a tiny patch of black that seemed a hole in the speckled fabric of light. "The stellagraphical records call it Pelot's Nebula. Watch it. I'm going to expand the image."

Pritcher had watched the phenomenon of Lens Image expansion before but he still caught his breath. It was like being at the visiplate of a spaceship storming through a horribly crowded Galaxy without entering hyperspace. The stars diverged towards them from a common center, flared outwards and tumbled off the edge of the screen. Single points became double, then globular. Hazy patches dissolved into myriad points. And always that illusion of motion.

Channis spoke through it all, "You'll notice that we are moving along the direct line from Trantor to Pellot's Nebula, so that in effect we are still looking at a stellar orientation equivalent to that of Trantor. There is probably a slight error because of the gravitic deviation of light that I haven't the math to calculate for, but I'm sure it can't be significant."

The darkness was spreading over the screen. As the rate of magnification slowed, the stars slipped off the four ends of the screen in a regretful leave-taking. At the rims of the growing nebula, the brilliant universe of stars shone abruptly in token for that light which was merely hidden behind the swirling unradiating atom fragments of sodium and calcium that filled cubic parsecs of space.

And Channis pointed again, "This has been called 'The Mouth' by the inhabitants of that region of space. And that is significant because it is only from the Trantorian orientation that it looks like a mouth." What he indicated was a rift in the body of the Nebula, shaped like a ragged, grinning mouth in profile, outlined by the glazing glory of the starlight with which it was filled.

"Follow 'The Mouth.'" said Channis. "Follow 'The Mouth' towards the gullet as it narrows down to a thin, splintering line of light."

Again the screen expanded a trifle, until the Nebula stretched away from "The Mouth" to block off all the screen but that narrow trickle and Channis' finger silently followed it down, to where it straggled to a halt, and then, as his finger continued moving onward, to a spot where one single star sparked lonesomely; and there his finger halted, for beyond that was blackness, unrelieved.

"'Star's End,'" said the young man, simply. "The fabric of the Nebula is thin there and the light of that one star finds its way through in just that one direction—to shine on Trantor."

"You're trying to tell me that—" the voice of the Mule's general died in suspicion.

"I'm not trying. That *is* Tazenda—Star's End."

The lights went on. The Lens flicked off. Pritcher reached Channis in three long strides, "What made you think of this?"

And Channis leaned back in his chair with a queerly puzzled

expression on his face. "It was accidental. I'd like to take intellectual credit for this, but it was only accidental. In any case, however it happens, it fits. According to our references, Tazenda is an oligarchy. It rules twenty-seven inhabited planets. It is not advanced scientifically. And most of all, it is an obscure world that has adhered to a strict neutrality in the local politics of that stellar region, and is not expansionist. I think we ought to see it."

"Have you informed the Mule of this?"

"No. Nor shall we. We're in space now, about to make the first hop."

Pritcher, in sudden horror, sprang to the visiplate. Cold space met his eyes when he adjusted it. He gazed fixedly at the view, then turned. Automatically, his hand reached for the hard, comfortable curve of the butt of his blaster.

"By whose order?"

"By my order, general"—it was the first time Channis had ever used the other's title—"while I was engaging you here. You probably felt no acceleration, because it came at the moment I was expanding the field of the Lens and you undoubtedly imagined it to be an illusion of the apparent star motion."

"Why? Just what are you doing? What was the point of your nonsense about Tazenda, then?"

"That was no nonsense. I was completely serious. We're going there. We left today because we were scheduled to leave three days from now. General, you don't believe there is a Second Foundation, and I do. *You* are merely following the Mule's orders without faith; *I* recognize a serious danger. The Second Foundation has now had five years to prepare. How they've prepared, I don't know, but what if they have agents on Kalgan. If I carry about in my mind the knowledge of the whereabouts of the Second Foundation, they may discover that. My life might be no longer safe, and I have a great affection for my life. Even on a thin and remote possibility such as that, I would rather play safe. So no one knows of Tazenda but you, and you found out only after we were out in space. And even so, there is the question of the crew." Channis was smiling again, ironically, in obviously complete control of the situation.

Pritcher's hand fell away from his blaster, and for a moment a vague discomfort pierced him. What kept *him* from action? What deadened *him?* There was a time when he was a rebellious and unpromoted captain of the First Foundation's commercial empire, when it would have been *himself* rather than Channis who would have taken prompt and daring action such as that. Was the Mule right? Was his controlled mind so concerned with obedience as to lose initiative? He felt a thickening despondency drive him down into a strange lassitude.

He said, "Well done! However, you will consult me in the future before making decisions of this nature."

The flickering signal caught his attention.

"That's the engine room," said Channis, casually. "They warmed up on five minutes' notice and I asked them to let me know if there was any trouble. Want to hold the fort?"

Pritcher nodded mutely, and cogitated in the sudden loneliness on the evils of approaching fifty. The visiplate was sparsely starred. The main body of the Galaxy misted one end. What if he were free of the Mule's influence—

But he recoiled in horror at the thought.

Chief Engineer Huxlani looked sharply at the young, ununiformed man who carried himself with the assurance of a Fleet officer and seemed to be in a position of authority. Huxlani, as a regular Fleet man from the days his chin had dripped milk, generally confused authority with specific insignia.

But the Mule had appointed this man, and the Mule was, of course, the last word. The only word for that matter. Not even subconsciously did he question that. Emotional control went deep.

He handed Channis the little oval object without a word.

Channis hefted it, and smiled engagingly.

"You're a Foundation man, aren't you, chief?"

"Yes, sir. I served in the Foundation Fleet eighteen years before the First Citizen took over."

"Foundation training in engineering?"

"Qualified Technician, First Class—Central School on Anac-reon."

"Good enough. And you found this on the communication circuit, where I asked you to look?"

"Yes, sir."

"Does it belong there?"

"No, sir."

"Then what is it?"

"A hypertracer, sir."

"That's not enough. I'm not a Foundation man. What is it?"

"It's a device to allow the ship to be traced through hyperspace."

"In other words we can be followed anywhere."

"Yes, sir."

"All right. It's a recent invention, isn't it? It was developed by one of the Research Institutes set up by the First Citizen, wasn't it?"

"I believe so, sir."

"And its workings are a government secret. Right?"

"I believe so, sir."

"Yet here it is. Intriguing."

Channis tossed the hypertracer methodically from hand to hand for a few seconds. Then, sharply, he held it out, "Take it, then, and put it back exactly where you found it and exactly how you found it. Understand? And then forget this incident. Entirely!"

The chief choked down his near-automatic salute, turned sharply and left.

The ship bounded through the Galaxy, its path a wide-spaced dotted line through the stars. The dots, referred to, were the scant stretches of ten to sixty light-seconds spent in normal space and between them stretched the hundred-and-up light-year gaps that represented the "hops" through hyperspace.

Bail Channis sat at the control panel of the Lens and felt again the involuntary surge of near-worship at the contemplation of it.

He was not a Foundation man and the interplay of forces at the twist of a knob or the breaking of a contact was not second nature to him.

Not that the Lens ought quite to bore even a Foundation man. Within its unbelievably compact body were enough electronic circuits to pin point accurately a hundred million separate stars in exact relationship to each other. And as if that were not a feat in itself, it was further capable of translating any given portion of the Galactic Field along any of the three spatial axes or to rotate any portion of the Field about a center.

It was because of that, that the Lens had performed a near-revolution in interstellar travel. In the younger days of interstellar travel, the calculation of each "hop" through hyperspace meant any amount of work from a day to a week—and the larger portion of such work was the more or less precise calculation of "Ship's Position" on the Galactic scale of reference. Essentially that meant the accurate observation of at least three widely-spaced stars, the position of which, with reference to the arbitrary Galactic triple-zero, were known.

And it is the word "known," that is the catch. To any who know the star field well from one certain reference point, stars are as individual as people. Jump ten parsecs, however, and not even your own sun is recognizable. It may not even be visible.

The answer was, of course, spectroscopic analysis. For centuries, the main object of interstellar engineering was the analysis of the "light signature" of more and more stars in greater and greater detail. With this, and the growing precision of the "hop" itself, standard routes of travel through the Galaxy were adopted and interstellar travel became less of an art and more of a science.

And yet, even under the Foundation with improved calculating machines and a new method of mechanically scanning the star field for a known "light signature," it sometimes took days to locate three stars and then calculate position in regions not previously familiar to the pilot.

It was the Lens that changed all that. For one thing it required only a single known star. For another, even a space tyro such as Channis could operate it.

The nearest sizable star at the moment was Vincetori, according to "hop" calculations, and on the visiplate now, a bright star was centered. Channis hoped that it was Vincetori.

The field screen of the Lens was thrown directly next that of the visiplate and with careful fingers, Channis punched out the co-ordinates of Vincetori. He closed a relay, and the star field sprang to bright view. In it, too, a bright star was centered, but otherwise there seemed no relationship. He adjusted the Lens along the Z-Axis and expanded the Field to where the photometer showed both centered stars to be of equal brightness.

Channis looked for a second star, sizably bright, on the visiplate and found one on the field screen to correspond. Slowly, he rotated the screen to similar angular deflection. He twisted his mouth and rejected the result with a grimace. Again he rotated and another bright star was brought into position, and a third. And then he grinned. That did it. Perhaps a specialist with trained relationship perception might have clicked first try, but he'd settle for three.

That was the adjustment. In the final step, the two fields overlapped and merged into a sea of not-quite-rightness. Most of the stars were close doubles. But the fine adjustment did not take long. The double stars melted together, one field remained, and the "Ship's Position" could now be read directly off the dials. The entire procedure had taken less than half an hour.

Channis found Han Pritcher in his private quarters. The general was quite apparently preparing for bed. He looked up.

"News?"

"Not particularly. We'll be at Tazenda in another hop."

"I know."

"I don't want to bother you if you're turning in, but have you looked through the film we picked up in Cil?"

Han Pritcher cast a disparaging look at the article in question, where it lay in its black case upon his low bookshelf, "Yes."

"And what do you think?"

"I think that if there was ever any science to History, it has been quite lost in this region of the Galaxy."

Channis grinned broadly, "I know what you mean. Rather barren, isn't it?"

"Not if you enjoy personal chronicles of rulers. Probably unreliable, I should say, in both directions. Where history concerns mainly personalities, the drawings become either black or white according to the interests of the writer. I find it all remarkably useless."

"But there is talk about Tazenda. That's the point I tried to make when I gave you the film. It's the only one I could find that even mentioned them."

"All right. They have good rulers and bad. They've conquered a few planets, won some battles, lost a few. There is nothing distinctive about them. I don't think much of your theory, Channis."

"But you've missed a few points. Didn't you notice that they never formed coalitions? They always remained completely outside the politics of this corner of the star swarm. As you say, they conquered a few planets, but then they stopped—and that without any startling defeat of consequence. It's just as if they spread out enough to protect themselves, but not enough to attract attention."

"Very well," came the unemotional response. "I have no objection to landing. At the worst—a little lost time."

"Oh, no. At the worst—complete defeat. If it *is* the Second Foundation. Remember it would be a world of space-knows-how-many Mules."

"What do you plan to do?"

"Land on some minor subject planet. Find out as much as we can about Tazenda first, then improvise from that."

"All right. No objection. If you don't mind now, I *would* like the light out."

Channis left with a wave of his hand.

And in the darkness of a tiny room in an island of driving metal lost in the vastness of space, General Han Pritcher remained awake, following the thoughts that led him through such fantastic reaches.

If everything he had so painfully decided were true—and how

all the facts were beginning to fit—then Tazenda *was* the Second Foundation. There was no way out. But how? How?

Could it be Tazenda? An ordinary world? One without distinction? A slum lost amid the wreckage of an Empire? A splinter among the fragments? He remembered, as from a distance, the Mule's shriveled face and his thin voice as he used to speak of the old Foundation psychologist, Ebling Mis, the one man who had —maybe—learned the secret of the Second Foundation.

Pritcher recalled the tension of the Mule's words: "It was as if astonishment had overwhelmed Mis. It was as though something about the Second Foundation had surpassed all his expectations, had driven in a direction completely different from what he might have assumed. If I could only have read his thoughts rather than his emotions. Yet the emotions were plain—and above everything else was this vast surprise."

Surprise was the keynote. Something supremely astonishing! And now came this boy, this grinning youngster, glibly joyful about Tazenda and its undistinguished subnormality. And he had to be right. He *had* to. Otherwise, nothing made sense.

Pritcher's last conscious thought had a touch of grimness. That hypertracer along the Etheric tube was still there. He had checked it one hour back, with Channis well out of the way.

SECOND INTERLUDE

It was a casual meeting in the anteroom of the Council Chamber—just a few moments before passing into the Chamber to take up the business of the day—and the few thoughts flashed back and forth quickly.

"So the Mule is on his way."

"That's what I hear, too. Risky! Mighty risky!"

"Not if affairs adhere to the functions set up."

"The Mule is not an ordinary man—and it is difficult to manipulate his chosen instruments without detection by him. The controlled minds are difficult to touch. They say he's caught on to a few cases."

"Yes, I don't see how that can be avoided."

"Uncontrolled minds are easier. But so few are in positions of authority under him—"

They entered the Chamber. Others of the Second Foundation followed them.

Two Men and a Peasant

Rossem is one of those marginal worlds usually neglected in Galactic history and scarcely ever obtruding itself upon the notice of men of the myriad happier planets.

In the latter days of the Galactic Empire, a few political prisoners had inhabited its wastes, while an observatory and a small Naval garrison served to keep it from complete desertion. Later, in the evil days of strife, even before the time of Hari Seldon, the weaker sort of men, tired of the periodic decades of insecurity and danger; weary of sacked planets and a ghostly succession of ephemeral emperors making their way to the Purple for a few wicked, fruitless years—these men fled the populated centers and sought shelter in the barren nooks of the Galaxy.

Along the chilly wastes of Rossem, villages huddled. Its sun was a small ruddy niggard that clutched its dribble of heat to itself, while snow beat thinly down for nine months of the year. The tough native grain lay dormant in the soil those snow-filled months, then grew and ripened in almost panic speed, when the sun's reluctant radiation brought the temperature to nearly fifty.

Small, goatlike animals cropped the grasslands, kicking the thin snow aside with tiny, tri-hooved feet.

The men of Rossem had, thus, their bread and their milk—and when they could spare an animal—even their meat. The darkly ominous forests that gnarled their way over half of the equatorial region of the planet supplied a tough, fine-grained wood for housing. This wood, together with certain furs and minerals, was even worth exporting, and the ships of the Empire came at times and brought in exchange farm machinery, atomic heaters, even televisor sets. The last was not really incongruous, for the long winter imposed a lonely hibernation upon the peasant.

Imperial history flowed past the peasants of Rossem. The trading ships might bring news in impatient spurts; occasionally new fugitives would arrive—at one time, a relatively large group arrived in a body and remained—and these usually had news of the Galaxy.

It was then that the Rossemites learned of sweeping battles and decimated populations or of tyrannical emperors and rebellious viceroys. And they would sigh and shake their heads, and draw their fur collars closer about their bearded faces as they sat about the village square in the weak sun and philosophized on the evil of men.

Then after a while, no trading ships arrived at all, and life grew harder. Supplies of foreign, soft food, of tobacco, of machinery stopped. Vague word from scraps gathered on the televisor brought increasingly disturbing news. And finally it spread that Trantor had been sacked. The great capital world of all the Galaxy, the splendid, storied, unapproachable and incomparable home of the emperors had been despoiled and ruined and brought to utter destruction.

It was something inconceivable, and to many of the peasants of Rossem, scratching away at their fields, it might well seem that the end of the Galaxy was at hand.

And then one day not unlike other days a ship arrived again. The old men of each village nodded wisely and lifted their old eyelids to whisper that thus it had been in their father's time—but it wasn't, quite.

This ship was not an Imperial ship. The glowing Spaceship-and-Sun of the Empire was missing from its prow. It was a stubby affair made of scraps of older ships—and the men within called themselves soldiers of Tazenda.

The peasants were confused. They had not heard of Tazenda, but they greeted the soldiers nevertheless in the traditional fashion of hospitality. The newcomers inquired closely as to the nature of the planet, the number of its inhabitants, the number of its cities—a word mistaken by the peasants to mean "villages" to the confusion of all concerned—its type of economy and so on.

Other ships came and proclamations were issued all over the world that Tazenda was now the ruling world, that tax-collecting stations would be established girdling the equator—the inhabited region—that percentages of grain and furs according to certain numerical formulae would be collected annually.

The Rossemites had blinked solemnly, uncertain of the word "taxes." When collection time came, many had paid, or had stood by in confusion while the uniformed, other-wordlings loaded the harvested corn and the pelts on to the broad ground-cars.

Here and there indignant peasants banded together and brought out ancient hunting weapons—but of this nothing ever came. Grumblingly they had disbanded when the men of Tazenda came and with dismay watched their hard struggle for existence become harder.

But a new equilibrium was reached. The Tazendian governor lived dourly in the village of Gentri, from which all Rossemites were barred. He and the officials under him were dim other-world beings that rarely impinged on the Rossemite ken. The tax-farmers, Rossemites in the employ of Tazenda, came periodically, but they were creatures of custom now—and the peasant had learned how to hide his grain and drive his cattle into the forest, and refrain from having his hut appear too ostentatiously prosperous. Then with a dull, uncomprehending expression he would greet all sharp questioning as to his assets by merely pointing at what they could see.

Even that grew less, and taxes decreased, almost as if Tazenda wearied of extorting pennies from such a world.

Trading sprang up and perhaps Tazenda found that more profitable. The men of Rossem no longer received in exchange the polished creations of the Empire, but even Tazendian machines and Tazendian food was better than the native stuff. And there were clothes for the women of other than gray home-spun, which was a very important thing.

So once again, Galactic history glided past peacefully enough, and the peasants scrabbled life out of the hard soil.

Narovi blew into his beard as he stepped out of his cottage.

The first snows were sifting across the hard ground and the sky was a dull, overcast pink. He squinted carefully upward and decided that no real storm was in sight. He could travel to Gentri without much trouble and get rid of his surplus grain in return for enough canned foods to last the winter.

He roared back through the door, which he opened a crack for the purpose: "Has the car been fed its fuel, yunker?"

A voice shouted from within, and then Narovi's oldest son, his short, red beard not yet completely outgrown its boyish sparseness, joined him.

"The car," he said, sullenly, "is fueled and rides well, but for the bad condition of the axles. For that I am of no blame. I have told you it needs expert repairs."

The old man stepped back and surveyed his son through lowering eyebrows, then thrust his hairy chin outward: "And is the fault mine? Where and in what manner may I achieve expert repairs? Has the harvest then been anything but scanty for five years? Have my herds escaped the pest? Have the pelts climbed of themselves—"

"*Narovi!*" The well-known voice from within stopped him in mid-word. He grumbled, "Well, well—and now your mother must insert herself into the affairs of a father and his son. Bring out the car, and see to it that the storage trailers are securely attached."

He pounded his gloved hands together, and looked upward again. The dimly-ruddy clouds were gathering and the gray sky that showed in the rifts bore no warmth. The sun was hidden.

He was at the point of looking away, when his dropping eyes caught and his finger almost automatically rose on high while his mouth fell open in a shout, in complete disregard of the cold air.

"Wife," he called vigorously, "Old woman—come here."

An indignant head appeared at a window. The woman's eyes followed his finger, gaped. With a cry, she dashed down the wooden stairs, snatching up an old wrap and a square of linen as she went. She emerged with the linen wrapped insecurely over her head and ears, and the wrap dangling from her shoulders.

She snuffled: "It is a ship from outer space."

And Narovi remarked impatiently: "And what else could it be? We have visitors, old woman, visitors!"

The ship was sinking slowly to a landing on the bare frozen field in the northern portions of Narovi's farm.

"But what shall we do?" gasped the woman. "Can we offer these people hospitality? Is the dirt floor of our hovel to be theirs and the pickings of last week's hoecake?"

"Shall they then go to our neighbors?" Narovi purpled past the crimson induced by the cold and his arms in their sleek fur covering lunged out and seized the woman's brawny shoulders.

"Wife of my soul," he purred, "you will take the two chairs from our room downstairs; you will see that a fat youngling is slaughtered and roasted with tubers; you will bake a fresh hoecake. I go now to greet these men of power from outer space . . . and . . . and—" He paused, placed his great cap awry, and scratched hesitantly. "Yes, I shall bring my jug of brewed grain as well. Hearty drink is pleasant."

The woman's mouth had flapped idly during this speech. Nothing came out. And when that stage passed, it was only a discordant screech that issued.

Narovi lifted a finger, "Old woman, what was it the village Elders said a se'nnight since? Eh? Stir your memory. The Elders went from farm to farm—themselves! Imagine the importance of it!—to ask us that should any ships from outer space land, they were to be informed immediately *on the orders of the governor.*

"And now shall I not seize the opportunity to win into the good graces of those in power? Regard that ship. Have you ever seen its like? These men from the outer worlds are rich, great. The governor himself sends such urgent messages concerning them that the Elders walk from farm to farm in the cooling weather. Perhaps the message is sent throughout all Rossem that these men are greatly desired by the Lords of Tazenda—and it is on *my* farm that they are landing."

He fairly hopped for anxiety, "The proper hospitality now—the mention of my name to the governor—and what may not be ours?"

His wife was suddenly aware of the cold biting through her

thin house-clothing. She leaped towards the door, shouting over her shoulders, "Leave then quickly."

But she was speaking to a man who was even then racing towards the segment of the horizon against which the ship sank.

Neither the cold of the world, nor its bleak, empty spaces worried General Han Pritcher. Nor the poverty of their surroundings, nor the perspiring peasant himself.

What did bother him was the question of the wisdom of their tactics? He and Channis were alone here.

The ship, left in space, could take care of itself in ordinary circumstances, but still, he felt unsafe. It was Channis, of course, who was responsible for this move. He looked across at the young man and caught him winking cheerfully at the gap in the furred partition, in which a woman's peeping eyes and gaping mouth momentarily appeared.

Channis, at least, seemed completely at ease. That fact Pritcher savored with a vinegary satisfaction. His game had not much longer to proceed exactly as he wished it. Yet, meanwhile their wrist ultrawave sender-receivers were their only connection with the ship.

And then the peasant host smiled enormously and bobbed his head several times and said in a voice oily with respect, "Noble Lords, I crave leave to tell you that my eldest son—a good, worthy lad whom my poverty prevents from educating as his wisdom deserves—has informed me that the Elders will arrive soon. I trust your stay here has been as pleasant as my humble means—for I am poverty-stricken, though a hard-working, honest, and humble farmer, as anyone here will tell you—could afford."

"Elders?" said Channis, lightly. "The chief men of the region here?"

"So they are, Noble Lords, and honest, worthy men all of them, for our entire village is known throughout Rossem as a just and righteous spot—though living is hard and the returns of the fields and forests meager. Perhaps you will mention to the Elders, Noble Lords, of my respect and honor for travelers and it may happen that they will request a new motor wagon for our household as the old one can scarcely creep and upon the remnant of it depends our livelihood."

He looked humbly eager and Han Pritcher nodded with the properly aloof condescension required of the role of "Noble Lords" bestowed upon them.

"A report of your hospitality shall reach the ears of your Elders."

Pritcher seized the next moments of isolation to speak to the apparently half-sleeping Channis.

"I am not particularly fond of this meeting of the Elders," he said. "Have you any thoughts on the subject?"

Channis seemed surprised. "No. What worries you?"

"It seems we have better things to do than to become conspicuous here."

Channis spoke hastily, in a low monotoned voice: "It may be necessary to risk becoming conspicuous in our next moves. We won't find the type of men we want, Pritcher, by simply reaching out a hand into a dark bag and groping. Men who rule by tricks of the mind need not necessarily be men in obvious power. In the first place, the psychologists of the Second Foundation are probably a very small minority of the total population, just as on your own First Foundation, the technicians and scientists formed a minority. The ordinary inhabitants are probably just that—very ordinary. The psychologists may even be well hidden, and the men in the apparently ruling position, may honestly think they are the true masters. Our solution to that problem may be found here on this frozen lump of a planet."

"I don't follow that at all."

"Why, see here, it's obvious enough. Tazenda is probably a huge world of millions or hundreds of millions. How could we identify the psychologists among them and be able to report truly to the Mule that we have located the Second Foundation? But here, on this tiny peasant world and subject planet, all the Tazendian rulers, our host informs us, are concentrated in their chief village of Gentri. There may be only a few hundred of them there, Pritcher, and among them *must* be one or more of the men of the Second Foundation. We will go there eventually, but let us see the Elders first—it's a logical step on the way."

They drew apart easily, as their black-bearded host tumbled into the room again, obviously agitated.

"Noble Lords, the Elders are arriving. I crave leave to beg you once more to mention a word, perhaps, on my behalf—" He almost bent double in a paroxysm of fawning.

"We shall certainly remember you," said Channis. "Are these your Elders?"

They apparently were. There were three.

One approached. He bowed with a dignified respect and said: "We are honored. Transportation has been provided, Respected sirs, and we hope for the pleasure of your company at our Meeting Hall."

THIRD INTERLUDE

The First Speaker gazed wistfully at the night sky. Wispy clouds scudded across the faint stargleams. Space looked actively hostile. It was cold and awful at best but now it contained that strange creature, the Mule, and the very content seemed to darken and thicken it into ominous threat.

The meeting was over. It had not been long. There had been the doubts and questionings inspired by the difficult mathematical problem of dealing with a mental mutant of uncertain makeup. All the extreme permutations had had to be considered.

Were they even yet certain? Somewhere in this region of space —within reaching distance as Galactic spaces go—was the Mule. What would he do?

It was easy enough to handle his men. They reacted—and were reacting—according to plan.

But what of the Mule himself?

4

Two Men and the Elders

The Elders of this particular region of Rossem were not exactly what one might have expected. They were not a mere extrapolation of the peasantry; older, more authoritative, less friendly.

Not at all.

The dignity that had marked them at first meeting had grown in impression till it had reached the mark of being their predominant characteristic.

They sat about their oval table like so many grave and slow-moving thinkers. Most were a trifle past their physical prime, though the few who possessed beards wore them short and neatly arranged. Still, enough appeared younger than forty to make it quite obvious that "Elders" was a term of respect rather than entirely a literal description of age.

The two from outer space were at the head of the table and in the solemn silence that accompanied a rather frugal meal that seemed ceremonious rather than nourishing, absorbed the new, contrasting atmosphere.

After the meal and after one or two respectful remarks—too short and simple to be called speeches—had been made by those of the Elders apparently held most in esteem, an informality forced itself upon the assembly.

It was as if the dignity of greeting foreign personages had finally given way to the amiable rustic qualities of curiosity and friendliness.

They crowded around the two strangers and the flood of questions came.

They asked if it were difficult to handle a spaceship, how many men were required for the job, if better motors could be made for their ground-cars, if it was true that it rarely snowed on other worlds as was said to be the case with Tazenda, how many people lived on their world, if it was as large as Tazenda, if it was far away, how their clothes were woven and what gave them the metallic shimmer, why they did not wear furs, if they shaved every day, what sort of stone that was in Pritcher's ring— The list stretched out.

And almost always the questions were addressed to Pritcher as though, as the elder, they automatically invested him with the greater authority. Pritcher found himself forced to answer at greater and greater length. It was like an immersion in a crowd of children. Their questions were those of utter and disarming wonder. Their eagerness to know was completely irresistible and would not be denied.

Pritcher explained that spaceships were not difficult to handle and that crews varied with the size, from one to many, that the motors of their ground-cars were unknown in detail to him but could doubtless be improved, that the climates of worlds varied almost infinitely, that many hundreds of millions lived on his world but that it was far smaller and more insignificant than the great empire of Tazenda, that their clothes were woven of silicone plastics in which metallic luster was artificially produced by proper orientation of the surface molecules, and that they could be artificially heated so that furs were unnecessary, that they shaved every day, that the stone in his ring was an amethyst. The list stretched out. He found himself thawing to these naive provincials against his will.

And always as he answered there was a rapid chatter among the Elders, as though they debated the information gained. It was difficult to follow these inner discussions of theirs for they lapsed into their own accented version of the universal Galactic language that, through long separation from the currents of living speech, had become archaic.

Almost, one might say, their curt comments among themselves hovered on the edge of understanding, but just managed to elude the clutching tendrils of comprehension.

Until finally Channis interrupted to say, "Good sirs, you must answer us for a while, for we are strangers and would be very much interested to know all we can of Tazenda."

And what happened then was that a great silence fell and each of the hitherto voluble Elders grew silent. Their hands, which had been moving in such rapid and delicate accompaniment to their words as though to give them greater scope and varied shades of meaning, fell suddenly limp. They stared furtively at one another, apparently quite willing each to let the other have all the floor.

Pritcher interposed quickly, "My companion asks this in friendliness, for the fame of Tazenda fills the Galaxy and we, of course, shall inform the governor of the loyalty and love of the Elders of Rossem."

No sigh of relief was heard but faces brightened. An Elder stroked his beard with thumb and forefinger, straightening its slight curl with a gentle pressure, and said: "We are faithful servants of the Lords of Tazenda."

Pritcher's annoyance at Channis' bald question subsided. It was apparent, at least, that the age that he had felt creeping over him of late had not yet deprived him of his own capacity for making smooth the blunders of others.

He continued: "We do not know, in our far part of the universe, much of the past history of the Lords of Tazenda. We presume they have ruled benevolently here for a long time."

The same Elder who spoke before, answered. In a soft, automatic way he had become spokesman. He said: "Not the grandfather of the oldest can recall a time in which the Lords were absent."

"It has been a time of peace?"

"It has been a time of peace!" He hesitated. "The governor is a strong and powerful Lord who would not hesitate to punish traitors. None of us are traitors, of course."

"He has punished some in the past, I imagine, as they deserve."

Again hesitation, "None here have ever been traitors, or our fathers or our fathers' fathers. But on other worlds, there have been such, and death followed for them quickly. It is not good to think of for we are humble men who are poor farmers and not concerned with matters of politics."

The anxiety in his voice, the universal concern in the eyes of all of them was obvious.

Pritcher said smoothly: "Could you inform us as to how we can arrange an audience with your governor."

And instantly an element of sudden bewilderment entered the situation.

For after a long moment, the elder said: "Why, did you not know? The governor will be here tomorrow. He has expected you. It has been a great honor for us. We . . . we hope earnestly that you will report to him satisfactorily as to our loyalty to him."

Pritcher's smile scarcely twitched. "Expected us?"

The Elder looked wonderingly from one to the other. "Why . . . it is now a week since we have been waiting for you."

Their quarters were undoubtedly luxurious for the world. Pritcher had lived in worse. Channis showed nothing but indifference to externals.

But there was an element of tension between them of a different nature than hitherto. Pritcher felt the time approaching for a definite decision and yet there was still the desirability of additional waiting. To see the governor first would be to increase the gamble to dangerous dimensions and yet to win that gamble might multi-double the winnings. He felt a surge of anger at the slight crease between Channis' eyebrows, the delicate uncertainty with which the young man's lower lip presented itself to an upper tooth. He detested the useless play-acting and yearned for an end to it.

He said: "We seem to be anticipated."

"Yes," said Channis, simply.

"Just that? You have no contribution of greater pith to make. We come here and find that the governor expects us. Presumably we shall find from the governor that Tazenda itself expects us. Of what value then is our entire mission?"

Channis looked up, without endeavoring to conceal the weary

note in his voice: "To expect us is one thing; to know who we are and what we came for, is another."

"Do you expect to conceal these things from men of the Second Foundation?"

"Perhaps. Why not? Are you ready to throw your hand in? Suppose our ship was detected in space. Is it unusual for a realm to maintain frontier observation posts? Even if we were ordinary strangers, we would be of interest."

"Sufficient interest for a governor to come to us rather than the reverse?"

Channis shrugged: "We'll have to meet that problem later. Let us see what this governor is like."

Pritcher bared his teeth in a bloodless kind of scowl. The situation was becoming ridiculous.

Channis proceeded with an artificial animation: "At least we know one thing. Tazenda is the Second Foundation or a million shreds of evidence are unanimously pointing the wrong way. How do you interpret the obvious terror in which these natives hold Tazenda? I see no signs of political domination. Their groups of Elders apparently meet freely and without interference of any sort. The taxation they speak of doesn't seem at all extensive to me or efficiently carried through. The natives speak much of poverty but seem sturdy and well-fed. The houses are uncouth and their villages rude, but are obviously adequate for the purpose.

"In fact, the world fascinates me. I have never seen a more forbidding one, yet I am convinced there is no suffering among the population and that their uncomplicated lives manage to contain a well-balanced happiness lacking in the sophisticated populations of the advanced centers."

"Are you an admirer of peasant virtues, then?"

"The stars forbid." Channis seemed amused at the idea. "I merely point out the significance of all this. Apparently, Tazenda is an efficient administrator—efficient in a sense far different from the efficiency of the old Empire or of the First Foundation, or even of our own Union. All these have brought mechanical efficiency to their subjects at the cost of more intangible values. Tazenda brings happiness and sufficiency. Don't you see that the whole orientation of their domination is different? It is not physical, but psychological."

"Really?" Pritcher allowed himself irony. "And the terror with which the Elders spoke of the punishment of treason by these kind hearted psychologist administrators? How does that suit your thesis?"

"Were they the objects of the punishment? They speak of punishment only of others. It is as if knowledge of punishment has been so well implanted in them that punishment itself need never be used. The proper mental attitudes are so inserted into their minds that I am certain that not a Tazendian soldier exists on the planet. Don't you *see* all this?"

"I'll see perhaps," said Pritcher, coldly, "when I see the governor. And what, by the way, if *our* mentalities are handled?"

Channis replied with brutal contempt: "*You* should be accustomed to *that*."

Pritcher whitened perceptibly, and, with an effort, turned away. They spoke to one another no more that day.

It was in the silent windlessness of the frigid night, as he listened to the soft, sleeping motions of the other, that Pritcher silently adjusted his wrist-transmitter to the ultrawave region for which Channis' was unadjustable and, with noiseless touches of his fingernail, contacted the ship.

The answer came in little periods of noiseless vibration that barely lifted themselves above the sensory threshold.

Twice Pritcher asked: "Any communications at all yet?"

Twice the answer came: "None. We wait always."

He got out of bed. It was cold in the room and he pulled the furry blanket around him as he sat in the chair and stared out at the crowding stars so different in the brightness and complexity of their arrangement from the even fog of the Galactic Lens that dominated the night sky of his native Periphery.

Somewhere there between the stars was the answer to the complications that overwhelmed him, and he felt the yearning for that solution to arrive and end things.

For a moment he wondered again if the Mule were right—if

Conversion had robbed him of the firm sharp edge of self-reliance. Or was it simply age and the fluctuations of these last years?

He didn't really care.

He was tired.

The governor of Rossem arrived with minor ostentation. His only companion was the uniformed man at the controls of the ground-car.

The ground-car itself was of lush design but to Pritcher it appeared inefficient. It turned clumsily; more than once it apparently balked at what might have been a too-rapid change of gears. It was obvious at once from its design that it ran on chemical, and not on atomic, fuel.

The Tazendian governor stepped softly on to the thin layer of snow and advanced between two lines of respectful Elders. He did not look at them but entered quickly. They followed after him.

From the quarters assigned to them, the two men of the Mule's Union watched. He—the governor—was thickset, rather stocky, short, unimpressive.

But what of that?

Pritcher cursed himself for a failure of nerve. His face, to be sure, remained icily calm. There was no humiliation before Channis—but he knew very well that his blood pressure had heightened and his throat had become dry.

It was not a case of physical fear. He was not one of those dull-witted, unimaginative men of nerveless meat who were too stupid ever to be afraid—but physical fear he could account for and discount.

But this was different. It was the other fear.

He glanced quickly at Channis. The young man glanced idly at the nails of one hand and poked leisurely at some trifling unevenness.

Something inside Pritcher became vastly indignant. What had Channis to fear of mental handling?

Pritcher caught a mental breath and tried to think back. How had he been before the Mule had Converted him from the die-hard Democrat that he was. It was hard to remember. He could not place himself mentally. He could not break the clinging wires that bound him emotionally to the Mule. Intellectually, he could remember that he had once tried to assassinate the Mule but not for all the straining he could endure, could he remember his emotions at the time. That might be the self-defense of his own mind, however, for at the intuitive thought of what those emotions might have been—not realizing the details, but merely comprehending the drift of it—his stomach grew queasy.

What if the governor tampered with his mind?

What if the insubstantial mental tendrils of a Second Foundationer insinuated itself down the emotional crevices of his makeup and pulled them apart and rejoined them—

There had been no sensation the first time. There had been no pain, no mental jar—not even a feeling of discontinuity. He had always loved the Mule. If there had ever been a time long before—as long before as five short years—when he had thought he hadn't loved him, that he had hated him—that was just a horrid illusion. The thought of that illusion embarrassed him.

But there had been no pain.

Would meeting the governor duplicate that? Would all that had gone before—all his service for the Mule—all his life's orientation—join the hazy, other-life dream that held the word, Democracy. The Mule also a dream, and only to Tazenda, his loyalty—

Sharply, he turned away.

There was that strong desire to retch.

And then Channis' voice clashed on his ear, "I think this is it, general."

Pritcher turned again. An Elder had opened the door silently and stood with a dignified and calm respect upon the threshold.

He said, "His Excellency, Governor of Rossem, in the name of the Lords of Tazenda, is pleased to present his permission for an audience and request your appearance before him."

"Sure thing," and Channis tightened his belt with a jerk and adjusted a Rossemian hood over his head.

Pritcher's jaw set. *This* was the beginning of the real gamble.

The governor of Rossem was not of formidable appearance. For one thing, he was bareheaded, and his thinning hair, light brown, tending to gray, lent him mildness. His bony eye-ridges lowered at them, and his eyes, set in a fine network of surrounding wrinkles, seemed calculating, but his fresh-cropped chin was soft and small and, by the universal convention of followers of the pseudoscience of reading character by facial bony structure, seemed "weak."

Pritcher avoided the eyes and watched the chin. He didn't know whether that would be effective—if anything would be.

The governor's voice was high-pitched, indifferent: "Welcome to Tazenda. We greet you in peace. You have eaten?"

His hand—long fingers, gnarled veins—waved almost regally at the U-shaped table.

They bowed and sat down. The governor sat at the outer side of the base of the U, they on the inner; along both arms sat the double row of silent Elders.

The governor spoke in short, abrupt sentences—praising the food as Tazendian importations—and it had indeed a quality different if, somehow, not so much better, than the rougher food of the Elders—disparaging Rossemian weather, referring with an attempt at casualness to the intricacies of space travel.

Channis talked little. Pritcher not at all.

Then it was over. The small, stewed fruits were finished; the napkins used and discarded, and the governor leaned back.

His small eyes sparkled.

"I have inquired as to your ship. Naturally, I would like to see that it receives due care and overhaul. I am told its whereabouts are unknown."

"True," Channis replied lightly. "We have left it in space. It is a large ship, suitable for long journeys in sometimes hostile regions, and we felt that landing it here might give rise to doubts as to our peaceful intentions. We preferred to land alone, unarmed."

"A friendly act," commented the governor, without conviction. "A large ship, you say?"

"Not a vessel of war, excellency."

"Ha, hum. Where is it you come from?"

"A small world of the Santanni sector, your excellency. It may be you are not aware of its existence for it lacks importance. We are interested in establishing trade relationships."

"Trade, eh? And what have you to sell?"

"Machines of all sorts, excellency. In return, food, wood, ores—"

"Ha, hum." The governor seemed doubtful. "I know little of these matters. Perhaps mutual profit may be arranged. Perhaps, after I have examined your credentials at length—for much information will be required by my government before matters may proceed, you understand—and after I have looked over your ship, it would be advisable for you to proceed to Tazenda."

There was no answer to that, and the governor's attitude iced perceptibly.

"It is necessary that I see your ship, however."

Channis said distantly: "The ship, unfortunately, is undergoing repairs at the moment. If your excellency would not object to giving us forty-eight hours, it will be at your service."

"I am not accustomed to waiting."

For the first time, Pritcher met the glare of the other, eye to eye, and his breath exploded softly inside him. For a moment, he had the sensation of drowning, but then his eyes tore away.

Channis did not waver. He said: "The ship cannot be landed for forty-eight hours, excellency. We are here and unarmed. Can you doubt our honest intentions?"

There was a long silence, and then the governor said gruffly: "Tell me of the world from which you come."

That was all. It passed with that. There was no more unpleasantness. The governor, having fulfilled his official duty, apparently lost interest and the audience died a dull death.

And when it was *all* over, Pritcher found himself back in their quarters and took stock of himself.

Carefully—holding his breath—he "felt" his emotions. Certainly he seemed no different to himself, but *would* he feel any difference? Had he felt different after the Mule's Conversion? Had not everything seemed natural? As it should have been?

He experimented.

With cold purpose, he shouted inside the silent caverns of his mind, and the shout was, "The Second Foundation must be discovered and destroyed."

And the emotion that accompanied it was honest hate. There was not as much as a hesitation involved in it.

And then it was in his mind to substitute the word "Mule" for the phrase "Second Foundation" and his breath caught at the mere emotion and his tongue clogged.

So far, good.

But had he been handled otherwise—more subtly? Had tiny changes been made? Changes that he couldn't detect because their very existence warped his judgment.

There was no way to tell.

But he still felt absolute loyalty to the Mule! If that were unchanged, nothing else really mattered.

He turned his mind to action again. Channis was busy at his end of the room. Pritcher's thumbnail idled at his wrist communicator.

And then at the response that came he felt a wave of relief surge over him and leave him weak.

The quiet muscles of his face did not betray him, but inside he was shouting with joy—and when Channis turned to face him, he knew that the farce was about over.

FOURTH INTERLUDE

The two Speakers passed each other on the road and one stopped the other.

"I have word from the First Speaker."

There was a half-apprehensive flicker in the other's eyes. "Intersection point?"

"Yes! May we live to see the dawn!"

5

One Man and the Mule

There was no sign in any of Channis' actions that he was aware of any subtle change in the attitude of Pritcher and in their relations to each other. He leaned back on the hard wooden bench and spread-eagled his feet out in front of him.

"What did you make of the governor?"

Pritcher shrugged: "Nothing at all. He certainly seemed no mental genius to me. A very poor specimen of the Second Foundation, if that's what he was supposed to be."

"I don't think he was, you know. I'm not sure what to make of it. Suppose you were a Second Foundationer," Channis grew thoughtful, "what would *you* do? Suppose you had an idea of our purpose here. How would you handle us?"

"Conversion, of course."

"Like the Mule?" Channis looked up, sharply. "Would we know if they *had* converted us? I wonder— And what if they were simply psychologists, but very clever ones."

"In that case, I'd have us killed rather quickly."

"And our ship? No." Channis wagged a forefinger. "We're playing a bluff, Pritcher, old man. It can only be a bluff. Even if they have emotional control down pat, we—you and I—are only fronts. It's the Mule they must fight, and they're being just as careful of us as we are of them. I'm assuming that they know who we are."

Pritcher stared coldly: "What do you intend doing?"

"Wait." The word was bitten off. "Let them come to us. They're worried, maybe about the ship, but probably about the Mule. They bluffed with the governor. It didn't work. We stayed pat. The next person they'll send *will* be a Second Foundationer, and he'll propose a deal of some sort."

"And then?"

"And then we make the deal."

"I don't think so."

"Because you think it will double-cross the Mule? It won't."

"No, the Mule could handle your double-crosses, any you could invent. But I still don't think so."

"Because you think then we couldn't double-cross the Foundationers?"

"Perhaps not. But that's not the reason."

Channis let his glance drop to what the other held in his fist, and said grimly: "You mean *that's* the reason."

Pritcher cradled his blaster, "That's right. You are under arrest."

"Why?"

"For treason to the First Citizen of the Union."

Channis' lips hardened upon one another: "What's going on?"

"Treason! As I said. And correction of the matter, on my part."

"Your proof? Or evidence, assumptions, daydreams? Are you mad?"

"No. Are you? Do you think the Mule sends out unweaned youngsters on ridiculous swashbuckling missions for nothing? It was queer to me at the time. But I wasted time in doubting myself. Why should he send *you*? Because you smile and dress well? Because you're twenty-eight."

"Perhaps because I can be trusted. Or aren't you in the market for logical reasons?"

"Or perhaps because you can't be trusted. Which is logical enough, as it turns out."

"Are we matching paradoxes, or is this all a word game to see who can say the least in the most words?"

And the blaster advanced, with Pritcher after it. He stood erect before the younger man: "Stand up!"

Channis did so, in no particular hurry, and felt the muzzle of the blaster touch his belt with no shrinking of the stomach muscles.

Pritcher said: "What the Mule wanted was to find the Second Foundation. He had failed and I had failed, and the secret that neither of us can find is a well-hidden one. So there was one out-standing possibility left—and that was to find a seeker who already knew the hiding-place."

"Is that I?"

"Apparently it was. I didn't know then, of course, but though my mind must be slowing, it still points in the right direction. How easily we found Star's End! How miraculously you examined the correct Field Region of the Lens from among an infinite number of possibilities! And having done so, how nicely we observe just the correct point for observation! You clumsy fool! Did you so underestimate me that no combination of impossible fortuities struck you as being too much for me to swallow?"

"You mean I've been too successful?"

"Too successful by half for any loyal man."

"Because the standards of success you set me were so low?"

And the blaster prodded, though in the face that confronted Channis only the cold glitter of the eyes betrayed the growing anger: "Because you are in the pay of the Second Foundation."

"Pay?"—infinite contempt. "Prove that."

"Or under the mental influence."

"Without the Mule's knowledge? Ridiculous."

"*With* the Mule's knowledge. Exactly my point, my young dullard. *With* the Mule's knowledge. Do you suppose else that you would be given a ship to play with? You led us to the Second Foundation as you were supposed to do."

"I thresh a kernel of something or other out of this immensity of chaff. May I ask why I'm supposed to be doing all this? If I were a traitor, why should I lead you to the Second Foundation? Why not hither and yon through the Galaxy, skipping gaily, finding no more than you ever did?"

"For the sake of the ship. And because the men of the Second Foundation quite obviously need atomic warfare for self-defense."

"You'll have to do better than that. One ship won't mean anything to them, and if they think they'll learn science from it and build atomic power plants next year, they are very, very simple

Second Foundationers, indeed. On the order of simplicity as yourself, I should say."

"You will have the opportunity to explain that to the Mule."

"We're going back to Kalgan?"

"On the contrary. We're staying here. And the Mule will join us in fifteen minutes—more or less. Do you think he hasn't followed us, my sharp-witted, nimble-minded lump of self-admiration? You have played the decoy well in reverse. You may not have led our victims to us, but you have certainly led us to our victims."

"May I sit down," said Channis, "and explain something to you in picture drawings? Please."

"You will remain standing."

"At that, I can say it as well standing. You think the Mule followed us because of the hypertracer on the communication circuit?"

The blaster might have wavered. Channis wouldn't have sworn to it. He said: "You don't look surprised. But I don't waste time doubting that you feel surprised. Yes, I knew about it. And now, having shown you that I knew of something you didn't think I did, I'll tell you something *you* don't know, that I know you don't."

"You allow yourself too many preliminaries, Channis. I should think your sense of invention was more smoothly greased.

"There's on invention to this. There *have* been traitors, of course, or enemy agents, if you prefer that term. But the Mule knew of that in a rather curious way. It seems, you see, that some of his Converted men had been tampered with."

The blaster did waver that time. Unmistakably.

"I emphasize that, Pritcher. It was why he needed me. I was an Unconverted man. Didn't he emphasize to you that he needed an Unconverted? Whether he gave you the real reason or not?"

"Try something else, Channis. If I were against the Mule, I'd know it." Quietly, rapidly, Pritcher was feeling his mind. It felt the same. It felt the same. Obviously the man was lying.

"You mean you feel loyal to the Mule. Perhaps. Loyalty wasn't tampered with. Too easily detectable, the Mule said. But how do you feel mentally? Sluggish? Since you started this trip, have you always felt normal? Or have you felt strange sometimes, as though you weren't quite yourself? What are you trying to do, bore a hole through me without touching the trigger?"

Pritcher withdrew his blaster half an inch, "What are you trying to say?"

"I say that you've been tampered with. You've been handled. You didn't see the Mule install that hypertracer. You didn't see anyone do it. You just found it there, and assumed it was the Mule, and ever since you've been assuming he was following us. Sure, the wrist receiver you're wearing contacts the ship on a wave length mine isn't good for. Do you think I didn't know that?" He was speaking quickly now, angrily. His cloak of indifference had dissolved into savagery. "But it's not the Mule that's coming toward us from out there. It's not the Mule."

"Who, if not?"

"Well, who do you suppose? I found that hypertracer, the day we left. But I didn't think it was the Mule. *He* had no reason for indirection at that point. Don't you see the nonsense of it? If I were a traitor and he knew that, I could be Converted as easily as you were, and he would have the secret of the location of the Second Foundation out of my mind without sending me half across the Galaxy. Can *you* keep a secret from the Mule? And if I *didn't* know, then I couldn't lead him to it. So why send me in either case?

"Obviously, that hypertracer must have been put there by an agent of the Second Foundation. *That's* who's coming towards us now. And would you have been fooled if your precious mind hadn't been tampered with? What kind of normality have you that you imagine immense folly to be wisdom? *Me* bring a ship to the Second Foundation? What would they do with a ship?

"It's *you* they want, Pritcher. You know more about the Union than anyone but the Mule, and you're not dangerous to them while he is. That's why they put the direction of search into my mind. Of course, it was completely impossible for me to find

Tazenda by random searchings of the Lens. I knew that. But I knew there was the Second Foundation after us, and I knew they engineered it. Why not play their game? It was a battle of bluffs. They wanted us and I wanted their location—and space take the one that couldn't outbluff the other.

"But it's we that will lose as long as you hold that blaster on me. And it obviously isn't your idea. It's theirs. Give me the blaster, Pritcher. I know it seems wrong to you, but it isn't your mind speaking, it's the Second Foundation within you. Give me the blaster, Pritcher, and we'll face what's coming now, together."

Pritcher faced a growing confusion in horror. Plausibility! Could he be so wrong? Why this eternal doubt of himself? Why wasn't he sure? What made Channis sound so plausible?

Plausibility!

Or was it his own tortured mind fighting the invasion of the alien.

Was he split in two?

Hazily, he saw Channis standing before him, hand outstretched —and suddenly, he knew he was going to give him the blaster.

And as the muscles of his arm were on the point of contracting in the proper manner to do so, the door opened, not hastily, behind him—and he turned.

There are perhaps men in the Galaxy who can be confused for one another even by men at their peaceful leisure. Correspondingly, there may be conditions of mind when even unlikely pairs may be mis-recognized. But the Mule rises above any combination of the two factors.

Not all Pritcher's agony of mind prevented the instantaneous mental flood of cool vigor that engulfed him.

Physically, the Mule could not dominate any situation. Nor did he dominate this one.

He was rather a ridiculous figure in his layers of clothing that thickened him past his normality without allowing him to reach normal dimensions even so. His face was muffled and the usually dominant beak covered what was left in a cold-red prominence.

Probably as a vision of rescue, no greater incongruity could exist.

He said: "Keep your blaster, Pritcher."

Then he turned to Channis, who had shrugged and seated himself: "The emotional context here seems rather confusing and considerably in conflict. What's this about someone other than myself following you?"

Pritcher intervened sharply: "Was a hypertracer placed upon our ship by your orders, sir?"

The Mule turned cool eyes upon him, "Certainly. Is it very likely that any organization in the Galaxy other than the Union of Worlds would have access to it?"

"He said—"

"Well, he's here, general. Indirect quotation is not necessary. Have you been saying anything, Channis?"

"Yes. But mistakes apparently, sir. It has been my opinion that the tracer was put there by someone in the pay of the Second Foundation and that we had been led here for some purpose of theirs, which I was prepared to counter. I was under the further impression that the general was more or less in their hands."

"You sound as if you think so no longer."

"I'm afraid not. Or it would not have been you at the door."

"Well, then, let us thresh this out." The Mule peeled off the outer layers of padded, and electrically heated clothing. "Do you mind if I sit down as well? Now—we are safe here and perfectly free of any danger of intrusion. No native of this lump of ice will have any desire to approach this place. I assure you of that," and there was a grim earnestness about his insistence upon his powers.

Channis showed his disgust. "Why privacy? Is someone going to serve tea and bring out the dancing girls?"

"Scarcely. What was this theory of yours, young man? A Second Foundationer was tracing you with a device which no one but I have and—how did you say you found this place?"

"Apparently, sir, it seems obvious, in order to account for known facts, that certain notions have been put into my head—"

"By these same Second Foundationers?"

"No one else, I imagine."

"Then it did not occur to you that if a Second Foundationer could force, or entice, or inveigle you into going to the Second Foundation for purposes of his own—and I assume you imagined he used methods similar to mine, though, mind you, I can implant only emotions, not ideas—it did not occur to you that if he could do that there was little necessity to put a hypertracer on you."

And Channis looked up sharply and met his sovereign's large eyes with sudden startle. Pritcher grunted and a visible relaxation showed itself in his shoulders.

"No," said Channis, "that hadn't occurred to me."

"Or that if they were obliged to trace you, they couldn't feel capable of directing you, and that, undirected, you could have precious little chance of finding your way here as you did. Did *that* occur to you?"

"That, neither."

"Why not? Has your intellectual level receded to a so-much-greater-than-probable degree?"

"The only answer is a question, sir. Are you joining General Pritcher in accusing me of being a traitor?"

"You have a defense in case I am?"

"Only the one I presented to the general. If I were a traitor and knew the whereabouts of the Second Foundation, you could Convert me and learn the knowledge directly. If you felt it necessary to trace me, then I hadn't the knowledge beforehand and wasn't a traitor. So I answer your paradox with another."

"Then your conclusion?"

"That I am not a traitor."

"To which I must agree, since your argument is irrefutable."

"Then may I ask you why you had us secretly followed?"

"Because to all the facts there is a third explanation. Both you and Pritcher explained some facts in your own individual ways, but not all. I—if you can spare me the time—will explain all. And in a rather short time, so there is little danger of boredom. Sit down, Pritcher, and give me your blaster. There is no danger of attack on us any longer. None from in here and none from out there. None in fact even from the Second Foundation. Thanks to you, Channis."

The room was lit in the usual Rossemian fashion of electrically heated wire. A single bulb was suspended from the ceiling and in its dim yellow glow, the three cast their individual shadows.

The Mule said: "Since I felt it necessary to trace Channis, it was obvious I expect to gain something thereby. Since he went to the Second Foundation with a startling speed and directness, we can reasonably assume that that was what I was expecting to happen. Since I did not gain the knowledge from him directly, something must have been preventing me. Those are the facts. Channis, of course, knows the answer. So do I. Do you see it, Pritcher?"

And Pritcher said doggedly: "No, sir."

"Then I'll explain. Only one kind of man can both know the location of the Second Foundation and prevent me from learning it. Channis, I'm afraid you're a Second Foundationer yourself."

And Channis' elbows rested on his knees as he leaned forward, and through stiff and angry lips said: "What is your direct evidence? Deduction has proven wrong twice today."

"There is direct evidence, too, Channis. It was easy enough. I told you that my men had been tampered with. The tamperer must have been, obviously, someone who was a) Unconverted, and b) fairly close to the center of things. The field was large but not entirely unlimited. You were too successful, Channis. People liked you too much. You got along too well. I wondered—

"And then I summoned you to take over this expedition and it didn't set you back. I watched your emotions. It didn't bother you. You overplayed the confidence there, Channis. No man of real competence could have avoided a dash of uncertainty at a job like that. Since your mind did avoid it, it was either a foolish one or a controlled one.

"It was easy to test the alternatives. I seized your mind at a moment of relaxation and filled it with grief for an instant and then removed it. You were angry afterwards with such accomplished art that I could have sworn it was a natural reaction, but for that which went first. For when I wrenched at your emotions, for just one instant, for one tiny instant before you could catch yourself, your mind resisted. It was all I needed to know.

"No one could have resisted me, even for that tiny instant, without control similar to mine."

Channis' voice was low and bitter: "Well, then? Now what?"

"And now you die—as a Second Foundationer. Quite necessary, as I believe you realize."

And once again Channis stared into the muzzle of a blaster. A muzzle guided this time by a mind, not like Pritcher's capable of offhand twisting to suit himself, but by one as mature as his own and as resistant to force as his own.

And the period of time allotted him for a correction of events was small.

What followed thereafter is difficult to describe by one with the normal complement of senses and the normal incapacity for emotional control.

Essentially, this is what Channis realized in the tiny space of time involved in the pushing of the Mule's thumb upon the trigger contact.

The Mule's current emotional makeup was one of a hard and polished determination, unmisted by hesitation in the least. Had Channis been sufficiently interested afterward to calculate the time involved from the determination to shoot to the arrival of the disintegrating energies, he might have realized that his leeway was about one-fifth of a second.

That was barely time.

What the Mule realized in that same tiny space of time was that the emotional potential of Channis' brain had surged suddenly upwards without his own mind feeling any impact and that, simultaneously, a flood of pure, thrilling hatred cascaded upon him from an unexpected direction.

It was that new emotional element that jerked his thumb off the contact. Nothing else could have done it, and almost together with his change of action, came complete realization of the new situation.

It was a tableau that endured far less than the significance adhering to it should require from a dramatic standpoint. There was the Mule, thumb off the blaster, staring intently upon Channis. There was Channis, taut, not quite daring to breathe yet. And there was Pritcher, convulsed in his chair; every muscle at a spasmodic breaking point; every tendon writhing in an effort to hurl forward; his face twisted at last out of schooled woodenness into an unrecognizable death mask of horrid hate; and his eyes only and entirely and supremely upon the Mule.

Only a word or two passed between Channis and the Mule—only a word or two and that utterly revealing stream of emotional consciousness that remains forever the true interplay of understanding between such as they. For the sake of our own limits, it is necessary to translate into words what went on, then, and thenceforward.

Channis said, tensely: "You're between two fires, First Citizen. You can't control two minds simultaneously, not when one of them is mine—so you have your choice. Pritcher is free of your Conversion now. I've snapped the bonds. He's the old Pritcher; the one who tried to kill you once; the one who thinks you're the enemy of all that is free and right and holy; and he's the one besides who knows that you've debased him to helpless adulation for five years. I'm holding him back now by suppressing his will, but if you kill me, that ends, and in considerably less time than you could shift your blaster or even your will—he will kill you."

The Mule quite plainly realized that. He did not move.

Channis continued: "If you turn to place him under control, to kill him, to do anything, you won't ever be quick enough to turn again to stop me."

The Mule still did not move. Only a soft sigh of realization.

"So," said Channis, "throw down the blaster, and let us be on even terms again, and you can have Pritcher back."

"I made a mistake," said the Mule, finally. "It was wrong to have a third party present when I confronted you. It introduced one variable too many. It is a mistake that must be paid for, I suppose."

He dropped the blaster carelessly, and kicked it to the other end of the room. Simultaneously, Pritcher crumpled into profound sleep.

"He'll be normal when he awakes," said the Mule, indifferently.

The entire exchange from the time the Mule's thumb had begun pressing the trigger-contact to the time he dropped the blaster had occupied just under a second and a half of time.

But just beneath the borders of consciousness, for a time just above the borders of detection, Channis caught a fugitive emotional gleam in the Mule's mind. And it was still one of sure and confident triumph.

6

One Man, the Mule—and Another

Two men, apparently relaxed and entirely at ease, poles apart physically—with every nerve that served as emotional detector quivering tensely.

The Mule, for the first time in long years, had insufficient surety of his own way. Channis knew that, though he could protect himself for the moment, it was an effort—and that the attack upon him was none such for his opponent. In a test of endurance, Channis knew he would lose.

But it was deadly to think of that. To give away to the Mule an emotional weakness would be to hand him a weapon. There was already that glimpse of something—a winner's something— in the Mule's mind.

To gain time—

Why did the others delay? Was that the source of the Mule's confidence? What did his opponent know that he didn't? The mind he watched told nothing. If only he could read ideas. And yet—

Channis braked his own mental whirling roughly. There was only that; to gain time—

Channis said: "Since it is decided, and not denied by myself after our little duel over Pritcher, that I am a Second Foundationer, suppose you tell me why I came to Tazenda."

"Oh, no," and the Mule laughed, with high-pitched confidence, "I am not Pritcher. I need make no explanations to you. You had what you thought were reasons. Whatever they were, your actions suited me, and so I inquire no further."

"Yet there must be such gaps in your conception of the story. Is Tazenda the Second Foundation you expected to find? Pritcher spoke much of your other attempt at finding it, and of your psy-

chologist tool, Ebling Mis. He babbled a bit sometimes under my
. . . uh . . . slight encouragement. Think back on Ebling Mis,
First Citizen."

"Why should I?" Confidence!

Channis felt that confidence edge out into the open, as if with
the passage of time, any anxiety the Mule might be having was
increasingly vanishing.

He said, firmly restraining the rush of desperation: "You lack
curiosity, then? Pritcher told me of Mis' vast surprise at *something*. There was his terribly drastic urging for speed, for a rapid
warning of the Second Foundation? Why? Why? Ebling Mis died.
The Second Foundation was not warned. And yet the Second
Foundation exists."

The Mule smiled in real pleasure, and with a sudden and surprising dash of cruelty that Channis felt advance and suddenly
withdraw: "But apparently the Second Foundation *was* warned.
Else how and why did one Bail Channis arrive on Kalgan to
handle my men and to assume the rather thankless task of out-
witting me. The warning came too late, that is all."

"Then," and Channis allowed pity to drench outward from
him, "you don't even know what the Second Foundation is, or
anything of the deeper meaning of all that has been going on."

To gain time!

The Mule felt the other's pity, and his eyes narrowed with
instant hostility. He rubbed his nose in his familiar four-fingered
gesture, and snapped: "Amuse yourself, then. What *of* the Second Foundation?"

Channis spoke deliberately, in words rather than in emotional
symbology. He said: "From what I have heard, it was the mystery
that surrounded the Second Foundation that most puzzled Mis.
Hari Seldon founded his two units so differently. The First Foundation was a splurge that in two centuries dazzled half the Galaxy. And the Second was an abyss that was dark.

"You won't understand why that was, unless you can once
again feel the intellectual atmosphere of the days of the dying
Empire. It was a time of absolutes, of the great final generalities,
at least in thought. It was a sign of decaying culture, of course,

that dams had been built against the further development of ideas. It was his revolt against these dams that made Seldon famous. It was that one last spark of youthful creation in him that lit the Empire in a sunset glow and dimly foreshadowed the rising sun of the Second Empire."

"Very dramatic. So what?"

"So he created his Foundations according to the laws of psychohistory, but who knew better than he that even those laws were relative. *He* never created a finished product. Finished products are for decadent minds. His was an evolving mechanism and the Second Foundation was the instrument of that evolution. *We*, First Citizen of your Temporary Union of Worlds, *we* are the guardians of Seldon's Plan. Only we!"

"Are you trying to talk yourself into courage," inquired the Mule, contemptuously, "or are you trying to impress me? For the Second Foundation, Seldon's Plan, the Second Empire all impresses me not the least, nor touches any spring of compassion, sympathy, responsibility, nor any other source of emotional aid you may be trying to tap in me. And in any case, poor fool, speak of the Second Foundation in the past tense, for it is destroyed."

Channis felt the emotional potential that pressed upon his mind rise in intensity as the Mule rose from his chair and approached. He fought back furiously, but something crept relentlessly on within him, battering and bending his mind back—and back.

He felt the wall behind him, and the Mule faced him, skinny arms akimbo, lips smiling terribly beneath that mountain of nose.

The Mule said: "Your game is through, Channis. The game of all of you—of all the men of what used to be the Second Foundation. Used to be! *Used to be!*

"What were you sitting here waiting for all this time, with your babble to Pritcher, when you might have struck him down and taken the blaster from him without the least effort of physical force? You were waiting for me, weren't you, waiting to greet me in a situation that would not too arouse my suspicions.

"Too bad for you that I needed no arousal. I knew you. I knew you well, Channis of the Second Foundation.

"But what are you waiting for now? You still throw words at me desperately, as though the mere sound of your voice would freeze me to my seat. And all the while you speak, something in your mind is waiting and waiting and is still waiting. But no one is coming. None of those you expect—none of your allies. You are alone here, Channis, and you will remain alone. Do you know why?

"It is because your Second Foundation miscalculated me to the very dregs of the end. I knew their plan early. They thought I would follow you here and be proper meat for their cooking. You were to be a decoy indeed—a decoy for a poor, foolish weakling mutant, so hot on the trail of Empire that he would fall blindly into an obvious pit. But am I their prisoner?

"I wonder if it occurred to them that I'd scarcely be here without my fleet—against the artillery of any unit of which they are entirely and pitifully helpless? Did it occur to them that I would not pause for discussion or wait for events?

"My ships were launched against Tazenda twelve hours ago and they are quite, quite through with their mission. Tazenda is laid in ruins; its centers of population are wiped out. There was no resistance. The Second Foundation no longer exists, Channis —and I, the queer, ugly weakling, am the ruler of the Galaxy."

Channis could do nothing but shake his head feebly. "No— No—"

"Yes— Yes—" mimicked the Mule. "And if you are the last one alive, and you may be, that will not be for long either."

And then there followed a short, pregnant pause, and Channis almost howled with the sudden pain of that tearing penetration of the innermost tissues of his mind.

The Mule drew back and muttered: "Not enough. You do not pass the test after all. Your despair is pretense. Your fear is not the broad overwhelming that adheres to the destruction of an ideal, but the puny seeping fear of personal destruction."

And the Mule's weak hand seized Channis by the throat in a puny grip that Channis was somehow unable to break.

"You are my insurance, Channis. You are my director and safeguard against any underestimation I may make." The Mule's eyes bore down upon him. Insistent— Demanding—

"Have I calculated rightly, Channis? Have I outwitted your men of the Second Foundation? Tazenda *is* destroyed, Channis, tremendously destroyed; so why is your despair pretense? Where is the reality? I must have reality and truth! Talk, Channis, talk. Have I penetrated then, not deeply enough? Does the danger still exist? *Talk, Channis.* Where have I done wrong?"

Channis felt the words drag out of his mouth. They did not come willingly. He clenched his teeth against them. He bit his tongue. He tensed every muscle of his throat.

And they came out—gasping—pulled out by force and tearing his throat and tongue and teeth on the way.

"Truth," he squeaked, "truth—"

"Yes, truth. What is left to be done?"

"Seldon founded Second Foundation here. Here, as I said. I told no lie. The psychologists arrived and took control of the native population."

"Of Tazenda?" The Mule plunged deeply into the flooding torture of the other's emotional upwellings—tearing at them brutally. "It is Tazenda I have destroyed. You know what I want. Give it to me."

"*Not* Tazenda. I *said* Second Foundationers might not be those apparently in power; Tazenda is the figurehead—" The words were almost unrecognizable, forming themselves against every atom of will of the Second Foundationer, "Rossem— Rossem— *Rossem is the world—*"

The Mule loosed his grip and Channis dropped into a huddle of pain and torture.

"And you thought to fool me?" said the Mule, softly.

"You *were* fooled." It was the last dying shred of resistance in Channis.

"But not long enough for you and yours. I am in communication with my Fleet. And after Tazenda can come Rossem. But first—"

Channis felt the excruciating darkness rise against him, and the automatic lift of his arm to his tortured eyes could not ward it off. It was a darkness that throttled, and as he felt his torn, wounded mind reeling backwards, backwards into the everlasting black—there was that final picture of the triumphant Mule —laughing matchstick—that long, fleshy nose quivering with laughter.

The sound faded away. The darkness embraced him lovingly.

It ended with a cracking sensation that was like the jagged glare of a lightning flash, and Channis came slowly to earth while sight returned painfully in blurry transmission through tear-drenched eyes.

His head ached unbearably, and it was only with a stab of agony that he could bring up a hand to it.

Obviously, he was alive. Softly, like feathers caught up in an eddy of air that had passed, his thoughts steadied and drifted to rest. He felt comfort suck in—from outside. Slowly, torturedly, he bent his neck—and relief was a sharp pang.

For the door was open; and the First Speaker stood just inside the threshold. He tried to speak, to shout, to warn—but his tongue froze and he knew that a part of the Mule's mighty mind still held him and clamped all speech within him.

He bent his neck once more. The Mule was still in the room. He was angry and hot-eyed. He laughed no longer, but his teeth were bared in a ferocious smile.

Channis felt the First Speaker's mental influence moving gently over his mind with a healing touch and then there was the numbing sensation as it came into contact with the Mule's defense for an instant of struggle and withdrew.

The Mule said gratingly, with a fury that was grotesque in his meagre body: "Then another comes to greet me." His agile mind reached its tendrils out of the room—out—out—

"You are alone," he said.

And the First Speaker interrupted with an acquiescence: "I am thoroughly alone. It is necessary that I be alone, since it was I who miscalculated your future five years ago. There would be a certain satisfaction to me in correcting that matter without aid. Unfortunately, I did not count on the strength of your Field of Emotional Repulsion that surrounded this place. It took me long to penetrate. I congratulate you upon the skill with which it was constructed."

"Thank you for nothing," came the hostile rejoinder. "Bandy no compliments with me. Have you come to add your brain splinter to that of yonder cracked pillar of your realm?"

The First Speaker smiled: "Why, the man you call Bail Channis performed his mission well, the more so since he was not your mental equal by far. I can see, of course, that you have mistreated him, yet it may be that we may restore him fully even yet. He is a brave man, sir. He volunteered for this mission although we were able to predict mathematically the huge chance of damage to his mind—a more fearful alternative than that of mere physical crippling."

Channis' mind pulsed futilely with what he wanted to say and couldn't; the warning he wished to shout and was unable to. He could only emit that continuous stream of fear—fear—

The Mule was calm. "You know, of course, of the destruction of Tazenda."

"I do. The assault by your fleet was foreseen."

Grimly: "Yes, so I suppose. But not prevented, eh?"

"No, not prevented." The First Speaker's emotional symbology was plain. It was almost a self-horror; a complete self-disgust: "And the fault is much more mine than yours. Who could have imagined your powers five years ago. We suspected from the start—from the moment you captured Kalgan—that you had the powers of emotional control. That was not too surprising, First Citizen, as I can explain to you.

"Emotional contact such as you and I possess is not a very new development. Actually it is implicit in the human brain. Most humans can read emotion in a primitive manner by associating it pragmatically with facial expression, tone of voice and so on. A good many animals possess the faculty to a higher degree; they use the sense of smell to a good extent, and the emotions involved are, of course, less complex.

"Actually, humans are capable of much more, but the faculty of direct emotional contact tended to atrophy with the development of speech a million years back. It has been the great advance of our Second Foundation that this forgotten sense has been restored to at least some of its potentialities.

"But we are not born with its full use. A million years of decay is a formidable obstacle, and we must educate the sense, exercise it as we exercise our muscles. And there you have the main difference. *You* were born with it.

"So much we could calculate. We could also calculate the effect of such a sense upon a person in a world of men who did not possess it. The seeing man in the kingdom of the blind—We calculated the extent to which a megalomania would take control of you and we thought we were prepared. But for two factors we were not prepared.

"The first was the great extent of your sense. *We* can induce emotional contact only when in eyeshot, which is why we are more helpless against physical weapons than you might think. Sight plays such an enormous part. Not so with you. You are definitely known to have had men under control, and, further, to have had intimate emotional contact with them when out of sight and out of earshot. That was discovered too late.

"Secondly, we did not know of your physical shortcomings, particularly the one that seemed so important to you, that you adopted the name of the Mule. We didn't foresee that you were not merely a mutant, but a sterile mutant and the added psychic distortion due to your inferiority complex passed us by. We allowed only for a megalomania—not for an intensely psychopathic paranoia as well.

"It is myself that bears the responsibility for having missed all that, for I was the leader of the Second Foundation when you captured Kalgan. When you destroyed the First Foundation, we found out—but too late—and for that fault millions have died on Tazenda."

"And you will correct things now?" The Mule's thin lips curled, his mind pulsing with hate: "What will you do? Fatten me? Restore me to a masculine vigor? Take away from my past the long childhood in an alien environment. Do you regret *my* sufferings? Do you regret *my* unhappiness? I have no sorrow for what I did in my necessity. Let the Galaxy protect itself as best it can, since it stirred not a whit for my protection when I needed it."

"Your emotions are, of course," said the First Speaker, "only the children of your background and are not to be condemned— merely changed. The destruction of Tazenda was unavoidable. The alternative would have been a much greater destruction generally throughout the Galaxy over a period of centuries. We did our best in our limited way. We withdrew as many men from Tazenda as we could. We decentralized the rest of the world. Unfortunately, our measures were of necessity far from adequate. It left many millions to die—do you not regret that?"

"Not at all—any more than I regret the hundred thousand that must die on Rossem in not more than six hours."

"On Rossem?" said the First Speaker, quickly.

He turned to Channis who had forced himself into a half-sitting posture, and his mind exerted its force. Channis felt the duel of minds strain over him, and then there was a short snapping of the bond and the words came tumbling out of his mouth: "Sir, I have failed completely. He forced it from me not ten minutes before your arrival. I could not resist him and I offer no excuses. He knows Tazenda is not the Second Foundation. He knows that Rossem is."

And the bonds closed down upon him again.

The First Speaker frowned: "I see. What is it you are planning to do?"

"Do you really wonder? Do you really find it difficult to penetrate the obvious? All this time that you have preached to me of the nature of emotional contact—all this time that you have been throwing words such as megalomania and paranoia at me, I have been working. I have been in contact with my Fleet and it has its orders. In six hours, unless I should for some reason counteract my orders, they are to bombard all of Rossem except this lone village and an area of a hundred square miles about it. They are to do a thorough job and are then to land here.

"You have six hours, and in six hours, you cannot beat down my mind, nor can you save the rest of Rossem."

The Mule spread his hands and laughed again while the First Speaker seemed to find difficulty in absorbing this new state of affairs.

He said: "The alternative?"

"Why should there even be an alternative? I can stand to gain no more by any alternative. Is it the lives of those on Rossem I'm to be chary of? Perhaps if you allow my ships to land and submit, all of you—all the men on the Second Foundation—to mental control sufficient to suit myself, I may countermand the bombardment orders. It may be worthwhile to put so many men of high intelligence under my control. But then again it would be a considerable effort and perhaps not worth it after all, so I'm not particularly eager to have you agree to it. What do you say, Second Foundationer? What weapon have you against my mind which is as strong as yours at least and against my ships which are stronger than' anything you have ever dreamed of possessing?"

"What have I?" repeated the First Speaker, slowly: "Why nothing—except a little grain—such a little grain of knowledge that even yet you do not possess."

"Speak quickly," laughed the Mule, "speak inventively. For squirm as you might, you won't squirm out of this."

"Poor mutant," said the First Speaker, "I have nothing to squirm out of. Ask yourself—why was Bail Channis sent to Kalgan as a decoy—Bail Channis, who though young and brave is almost as much your mental inferior as is this sleeping officer of yours, this Han Pritcher. Why did not I go, or another of our leaders, who would be more your match?"

"Perhaps," came the supremely confident reply, "you were not sufficiently foolish, since perhaps none of you are my match."

"The true reason is more logical. You knew Channis to be a Second Foundationer. He lacked the capacity to hide that from you. And you knew, too, that you were his superior, so you were not afraid to play his game and follow him as he wished you to in order to outwit him later. Had I gone to Kalgan, you would have killed me for I would have been a real danger, or had I avoided death by concealing my identity, I would yet have failed in persuading you to follow me into space. It was only known inferiority that lured you on. And had you remained on Kalgan, not all the force of the Second Foundation could have harmed you, surrounded as you were by your men, your machines, and your mental power."

"My mental power is yet with me, squirmer," said the Mule, "and my men and machines are not far off."

"Truly so, but you are not on Kalgan. You are here in the Kingdom of Tazenda, logically presented to you as the Second Foundation—very logically presented. It had to be so presented, for you are a wise man, First Citizen, and would follow only logic."

"Correct, and it was a momentary victory for your side, but there was still time for me to worm the truth from your man, Channis, and still wisdom in me to realize that such a truth might exist."

"And on our side, oh, not-quite-sufficiently-subtle one, was the realization that you might go that one step further and so Bail Channis was prepared for you."

"That he most certainly was not, for I stripped his brain clean as any plucked chicken. It quivered bare and open before me and when he said Rossem was the Second Foundation, it was basic truth for I had ground him so flat and smooth that not the smidgeon of a deceit could have found refuge in any microscopic crevice."

"True enough. So much the better for our foresight. For I have told you already that Bail Channis was a volunteer. Do you know what sort of a volunteer? Before he left our Foundation for Kalgan and you, he submitted to emotional surgery of a drastic nature. Do you think it was sufficient to deceive you? Do you think Bail Channis, mentally untouched, could possibly deceive you? No, Bail Channis was himself deceived, of necessity and voluntarily. Down to the inmost core of his mind, Bail Channis honestly believes that Rossem is the Second Foundation.

"And for three years now, we of the Second Foundation have built up the appearance of that here in the Kingdom of Tazenda, in preparation and waiting for you. And we have succeeded, have we not? You penetrated to Tazenda, and beyond that, to Rossem —but past that, you could not go."

The Mule was upon his feet: "You dare tell me that Rossem also, is not the Second Foundation?"

Channis, from the floor, felt his bonds burst for good, under a stream of mental force on the part of the First Speaker and strained upright. He let out one long, incredulous cry: "You mean Rossem is *not* the Second Foundation?"

The memories of life, the knowledge of his mind—everything —whirled mistily about him in confusion.

The First Speaker smiled: "You see, First Citizen, Channis is as upset as you are. Of course, Rossem is not the Second Foundation. Are we madmen then, to lead you, our greatest, most powerful, most dangerous enemy to our own world? Oh, no!

"Let your Fleet bombard Rossem, First Citizen, if you must have it so. Let them destroy all they can. For at most they can kill only Channis and myself—and that will leave you in a situation improved not in the least.

"For the Second Foundation's Expedition to Rossem which has been here for three years and has functioned, temporarily, as Elders in this village, embarked yesterday and are returning to Kalgan. They will evade your Fleet, of course, and they will arrive in Kalgan at least a day before you can, which is why I tell you all this. Unless I countermand my orders, when you return, you will find a revolting Empire, a disintegrated realm, and only the men with you in your Fleet here will be loyal to you. They will be hopelessly outnumbered. And moreover, the men of the Second Foundation will be with your Home Fleet and will see to it that you reconvert no one. Your Empire is done, mutant."

Slowly, the Mule bowed his head, as anger and despair cornered his mind completely, "Yes. Too late— Too late— Now I see it."

"Now you see it," agreed the First Speaker, "and now you don't."

In the despair of that moment, when the Mule's mind lay open, the First Speaker—ready for that moment and pre-sure of its nature—entered quickly. It required a rather insignificant fraction of a second to consummate the change completely.

The Mule looked up and said: "Then I shall return to Kalgan?"

"Certainly. How do you feel?"

"Excellently well." His brow puckered: "Who are you?"

"Does it matter?"

"Of course not." He dismissed the matter, and touched Pritcher's shoulder: "Wake up, Pritcher, we're going home."

It was two hours later that Bail Channis felt strong enough to walk by himself. He said: "He won't ever remember?"

"Never. He retains his mental powers and his Empire—but his motivations are now entirely different. The notion of a Second Foundation is a blank to him, and he is a man of peace. He will be a far happier man henceforward, too, for the few years of life left him by his maladjusted physique. And then, after he is dead, Seldon's Plan will go on—somehow."

"And it is true," urged Channis, "it is true that Rossem is not the Second Foundation? I could swear—I tell you I *know* it is. I am not mad."

"You are not mad, Channis, merely, as I have said, changed. Rossem is *not* the Second Foundation. Come! We, too, will return home."

LAST INTERLUDE

Bail Channis sat in the small white-tiled room and allowed his mind to relax. He was content to live in the present. There were the walls and the window and the grass outside. They had no names. They were just things. There was a bed and a chair and books that developed themselves idly on the screen at the foot of his bed. There was the nurse who brought him his food.

At first he had made efforts to piece together the scraps of things he had heard. Such as those two men talking together.

One had said: "Complete aphasia now. It's cleaned out, and I think without damage. It will only be necessary to return the re-cording of his original brain-wave makeup."

He remembered the sounds by rote, and for some reason they seemed peculiar sounds—as if they meant something. But why bother.

Better to watch the pretty changing colors on the screen at the foot of the thing he lay on.

And then someone entered and did things to him and for a long time, he slept.

And when that had passed, the bed was suddenly a bed and he knew he was in a hospital, and the words he remembered made sense.

He sat up: "What's happening?"

The First Speaker was beside him, "You're on the Second Foun-dation, and you have your mind back—your original mind."

"Yes! *Yes!*" Channis came to the realization that he was *himself*, and there was incredible triumph and joy in that.

"And now tell me," said the First Speaker, "do you know where the Second Foundation is now?"

And the truth came flooding down in one enormous wave and Channis did not answer. Like Ebling Mis before him, he was con-scious of only one vast, numbing surprise.

Until he finally nodded, and said: "By the Stars of the Galaxy —now, I know."

PART II

SEARCH BY THE FOUNDATION

7

Arcadia

DARELL, ARKADY   *novelist, born 11, 5, 362 F.E., died 1, 7, 443 F.E. Although primarily a writer of fiction, Arkady Darell is best known for her biography of her grandmother, Bayta Darell. Based on first-hand information, it has for centuries served as a primary source of information concerning the Mule and his times. . . . Like "Unkeyed Memories", her novel "Time and Time and Over" is a stirring reflection of the brilliant Kalganian society of the early Interregnum, based, it is said, on a visit to Kalgan in her youth. . . .*

ENCYCLOPEDIA GALACTICA

Arcadia Darell declaimed firmly into the mouthpiece of her transcriber:
"The Future of Seldon's Plan, by A. Darell"
and then thought darkly that some day when she was a great writer, she would write all her masterpieces under the pseudonym of Arkady. Just Arkady. No last name at all.

"A. Darell" *would* be just the sort of thing that she would have to put on all her themes for her class in Composition and Rhetoric —so tasteless. All the other kids had to do it, too, except for Olynthus Dam, because the class laughed so when he did it the first time. And "Arcadia" was a little girl's name, wished on her because her great-grandmother had been called that; her parents just had no imagination *at all*.

Now that she was two days past fourteen, you'd think they'd recognize the simple fact of adulthood and call her Arkady. Her lips tightened as she thought of her father looking up from his book-viewer just long enough to say, "But if you're going to pretend you're nineteen, Arcadia, what will you do when you're twenty-five and all the boys think you're thirty?"

From where she sprawled across the arms and into the hollow of her own special armchair, she could see the mirror on her dresser. Her foot was a little in the way because her house slipper kept twirling about her big toe, so she pulled it in and sat up with an unnatural straightness to her neck that she felt sure, somehow, lengthened it a full two inches into slim regality.

For a moment, she considered her face thoughtfully—too fat. She opened her jaws half an inch behind closed lips, and caught the resultant trace of unnatural gauntness at every angle. She licked her lips with a quick touch of tongue and let them pout a bit in moist softness. Then she let her eyelids droop in a weary, worldly way— Oh, golly if only her cheeks weren't that silly *pink*.

She tried putting her fingers to the outer corners of her eye and tilting the lids a bit to get that mysterious exotic languor of the women of the inner star systems, but her hands were in the way and she couldn't see her face very well.

Then she lifted her chin, caught herself at a half-profile, and with her eyes a little strained from looking out the corner and her neck muscles faintly aching, she said, in a voice one octave below its natural pitch, "Really, father, if you think it makes a *particle* of difference to me what some silly old *boys* think, you just—"

And then she remembered that she still had the transmitter open in her hand and said, drearily, "Oh, golly," and shut it off.

The faintly violet paper with the peach margin line on the left had upon it the following:

"THE FUTURE OF SELDON'S PLAN

"Really, father, if you think it makes a particle of difference to me what some silly old boys think, you just
"Oh, golly."

She pulled the sheet out of the machine with annoyance and another clicked neatly into place.

But her face smoothed out of its vexation, nevertheless, and her wide, little mouth stretched into a self-satisfied smile. She sniffed at the paper delicately. Just right. Just that proper touch of elegance and charm. And the penmanship was just the last word.

The machine had been delivered two days ago on her first adult birthday. She had said, "But father, everybody—just *everybody* in the class who has the slightest pretensions to *being* anybody has one. Nobody but some old drips would use hand machines—"

The salesman had said, "There is no other model as compact on the one hand and as adaptable on the other. It will spell and punctuate correctly according to the sense of the sentence. Naturally, it is a great aid to education since it encourages the user to employ careful enunciation and breathing in order to make sure of the correct spelling, to say nothing of demanding a proper and elegant delivery for correct punctuation."

Even then her father had tried to get one geared for type-print as if she were some dried-up, old-maid teacher.

But when it was delivered, it was the model she wanted—obtained perhaps with a little more wail and sniffle than quite went with the adulthood of fourteen—and copy was turned out in a charming and entirely feminine handwriting, with the most beautifully graceful capitals anyone ever saw.

Even the phrase, "Oh, golly," somehow breathed glamour when the Transcriber was done with it.

But just the same she had to get it right, so she sat up straight in her chair, placed her first draft before her in businesslike fashion, and began again, crisply and clearly; her abdomen flat, her chest lifted, and her breathing carefully controlled. She intoned, with dramatic fervor:

"The Future of Seldon's Plan.

"The Foundation's past history is, I am sure, well-known to all of us who have had the good fortune to be educated in our planet's efficient and well-staffed school system.

(There! That would start things off right with Miss Erlking, that mean old hag.)

That past history is largely the past history of the great Plan of Hari Seldon. The two are one. But the question in the mind of most people today is whether this Plan will continue in all its great wisdom, or whether it will be foully destroyed, or, perhaps, has been so destroyed already.

"To understand this, it may be best to pass quickly over some of the highlights of the Plan as it has been revealed to humanity thus far.

(This part was easy because she had taken Modern History the semester before.)

"In the days, nearly four centuries ago, when the First Galactic Empire was decaying into the paralysis that preceded final death, one man—the great Hari Seldon—foresaw the approaching end. Through the science of psychohistory, the intrissacies of whose mathematics has long since been forgotten,

(She paused in a trifle of doubt. She was sure that "intricacies" was pronounced with soft *c*'s but the spelling didn't look right. Oh, well, the machine couldn't very well be wrong—)

he and the men who worked with him are able to foretell the course of the great social and economic currents sweeping the Galaxy at the time. It was possible for them to realize that, left to itself, the Empire would break up, and that thereafter there would be at least thirty thousand years of anarchic chaos prior to the establishment of a new Empire.

"It was too late to prevent the great Fall, but it was still possible, at least, to cut short the intermediate period of chaos. The Plan was, therefore, evolved whereby only a single millennium would separate the Second Empire from the First. We are completing the fourth century of that millennium, and many generations of men have lived and died while the Plan has continued its inexorable workings.

"Hari Seldon established two Foundations at the opposite ends of the Galaxy, in a manner and under such circumstances as would yield the best mathematical solution for his psychohistorical problem. In one of these, *our* Foundation, established here on Terminus, there was concentrated the physical science of the Empire, and through the possession of that science, the Foundation was able to withstand the attacks of the barbarous kingdoms

which had broken away and become independent, out at the
fringe of the Empire.

"The Foundation, indeed, was able to conquer in its turn these
short-lived kingdoms by means of the leadership of a series of
wise and heroic men like Salvor Hardin and Hober Mallow who
were able to interpret the Plan intelligently and to guide our
land through its

(She had written "intricacies" here also, but decided not to risk
it a second time.)

                                                    complica-
tions. All our planets still revere their memories although centuries have passed.

"Eventually, the Foundation established a commercial system
which controlled a large portion of the Siwennian and Anacreonian sectors of the Galaxy, and even defeated the remnants of the
old Empire under its last great general, Bel Riose. It seemed that
nothing could now stop the workings of Seldon's plan. Every crisis
that Seldon had planned had come at its appropriate time and
had been solved, and with each solution the Foundation had
taken another giant stride toward Second Empire and peace.

"And then,

(Her breath came short at this point, and she hissed the words
between her teeth, but the Transmitter simply wrote them,
calmly and gracefully.)

                                                    with the last rem-
nants of the dead First Empire gone and with only ineffectual
warlords ruling over the splinters and remnants of the decayed
colossus,

(She got *that* phrase out of a thriller on the video last week,
but old Miss Erlking never listened to anything but symphonies
and lectures, so *she'd* never know.)
there came the Mule.

"This strange man was not allowed for in the Plan. He was a
mutant, whose birth could not have been predicted. He had the
strange and mysterious power of controlling and manipulating
human emotions and in this manner could bend all men to his
will. With breath-taking swiftness, he became a conqueror and

Empire-builder, until, finally, he even defeated the Foundation itself.

"Yet he never obtained universal dominion, since in his first overpowering lunge he was stopped by the wisdom and daring of a great woman

(Now there was that old problem again. Father *would* insist that she never bring up the fact that she was the grandchild of Bayta Darell. Everyone knew it and Bayta was just about the greatest woman there ever was and she *had* stopped the Mule singlehanded.)

in a manner the true story of which is known in its entirety to very few.

(There! If she had to read it to the class, that last could be said in a dark voice, and someone would be sure to ask what the true story was, and then—well, and then she couldn't *help* tell the truth if they asked her, could she? In her mind, she was already wordlessly whizzing through a hurt and eloquent explanation to a stern and questioning paternal parent.)

"After five years of restricted rule, another change took place, the reasons for which are not known, and the Mule abandoned all plans for further conquest. His last five years were those of an enlightened despot.

"It is said by some that the change in the Mule was brought about by the intervention of the Second Foundation. However, no man has ever discovered the exact location of this other Foundation, nor knows its exact function, so that theory remains unproven.

"A whole generation has passed since the death of the Mule. What of the future, then, now that he has come and gone? He interrupted Seldon's Plan and seemed to have burst it to fragments, yet as soon as he died, the Foundation rose again, like a nova from the dead ashes of a dying star.

(She had made that up herself.)

Once again, the planet Terminus houses the center of a commercial federation almost as great and as rich as before the conquest, and even more peaceful and democratic.

"Is this planned? Is Seldon's great dream still alive, and will a Second Galactic Empire yet be formed six hundred years from now? I, myself, believe so, because

(This was the important part. Miss Erlking always had those large, ugly red-pencil scrawls that went: 'But this is only descriptive. What are your personal reactions? Think! Express yourself! Penetrate your own soul!' Penetrate your own soul. A lot *she* knew about souls, with her lemon face that never smiled in its life—)

never at any time has the political situation been so favorable. The old Empire is completely dead and the period of the Mule's rule put an end to the era of warlords that preceded him. Most of the surrounding portions of the Galaxy are civilized and peaceful.

"Moreover the internal health of the Foundation is better than ever before. The despotic times of the pre-Conquest hereditary mayors have given way to the democratic elections of early times. There are no longer dissident worlds of independent Traders; no longer the injustices and dislocations that accompanied accumulations of great wealth in the hands of a few.

"There is no reason, therefore, to fear failure, unless it is true that the Second Foundation itself presents a danger. Those who think so have no evidence to back their claim, but merely vague fears and superstitions. I think that our confidence in ourselves, in our nation, and in Hari Seldon's great Plan should drive from our hearts and minds all uncertainties and

(Hm-m-m. This was awfully corny, but something like this was expected at the end.)

so I say—"

That is as far as "The Future of Seldon's Plan" got, at that moment, because there was the gentlest little tap on the window, and when Arcadia shot up to a balance on one arm of the chair, she found herself confronted by a smiling face beyond the glass, its even symmetry of feature interestingly accentuated by the short, vertical line of a finger before its lips.

With the slight pause necessary to assume an attitude of bepuzzlement, Arcadia dismounted from the armchair, walked to the couch that fronted the wide window that held the apparition and, kneeling upon it, stared out thoughtfully.

The smile upon the man's face faded quickly. While the fingers of one hand tightened whitely upon the sill, the other made a quick gesture. Arcadia obeyed calmly, and closed the latch that moved the lower third of the window smoothly into its socket in the wall, allowing the warm spring air to interfere with the conditioning within.

"You can't get in," she said, with comfortable smugness. "The windows are all screened, and keyed only to people who belong here. If you come in, all sorts of alarms will break loose." A pause, then she added, "You look sort of silly balancing on that ledge underneath the window. If you're not careful, you'll fall and break your neck and a lot of valuable flowers."

"In that case," said the man at the window, who had been thinking that very thing—with a slightly different arrangement of adjectives— "will you shut off the screen and let me in?"

"No use in doing that," said Arcadia. "You're probably thinking of a different house, because I'm not the kind of girl who lets strange men into their . . . her bedroom this time of night." Her eyes, as she said it, took on a heavy-lidded sultriness—or an unreasonable facsimile thereof.

All traces of humor whatever had disappeared from the young stranger's face. He muttered, "This is Dr. Darell's house, isn't it?"

"Why should I tell you?"

"Oh, Galaxy— Good-by—"

"If you jump off, young man, I will personally give the alarm." (This was intended as a refined and sophisticated thrust of irony, since to Arcadia's enlightened eyes, the intruder was an obviously mature thirty, at least—quite elderly, in fact.)

Quite a pause. Then, tightly, he said, "Well, now, look here, girlie, if you don't want me to stay, and don't want me to go, what *do* you want me to do?"

"You can come in, I suppose. Dr. Darell *does* live here. I'll shut off the screen now."

Warily, after a searching look, the young man poked his hand through the window, then hunched himself up and through it. He brushed at his knees with an angry, slapping gesture, and lifted a reddened face at her.

"You're quite sure that your character and reputation won't suffer when they find me here, are you?"

"Not as much as yours would, because just as soon as I hear footsteps outside, I'll just shout and yell and say you forced your way in here."

"Yes?" he replied with heavy courtesy, "And how do you intend to explain the shut-off protective screen?"

"Poof! That would be easy. There wasn't any there in the first place."

The man's eyes were wide with chagrin. "That was a bluff? How old are you, kid?"

"I consider that a very impertinent question, young man. And I am not accustomed to being addressed as 'kid.'"

"I don't wonder. You're probably the Mule's grandmother in disguise. Do you mind if I leave now before you arrange a lynching party with myself as star performer?"

"You had better not leave—because my father's expecting you."

The man's look became a wary one, again. An eyebrow shot up as he said, lightly, "Oh? Anyone with your father?"

"No."

"Anyone called on him lately?"

"Only tradespeople—and you."

"Anything unusual happen at all?"

"Only you."

"Forget me, will you? No, don't forget me. Tell me, how did you know your father was expecting me?"

"Oh, that was easy. Last week, he received a Personal Capsule, keyed to him personally, with a self-oxidizing message, you know. He threw the capsule shell into the Trash Disinto, and yesterday, he gave Poli—that's our maid, you see—a month's vacation so she could visit her sister in Terminus City, and this afternoon, he made up the bed in the spare room. So I knew he expected somebody that I wasn't supposed to know anything about. Usually, he tells me everything."

"Really! I'm surprised he has to. I should think you'd know everything before he tells you."

"I usually do." Then she laughed. She was beginning to feel very much at ease. The visitor was elderly, but very distinguished-looking with curly brown hair and very blue eyes. Maybe she could meet somebody like that again, sometimes, when she was old herself.

"And just how," he asked, "did you know it was *I* he expected."

"Well, who else *could* it be? He was expecting somebody in so secrety a way, if you know what I mean—and then you come gumping around trying to sneak through windows, instead of walking through the front door, the way you would if you had any sense." She remembered a favorite line, and used it promptly. "Men are so stupid!"

"Pretty stuck on yourself, aren't you, kid? I mean, Miss. You could be wrong, you know. What if I told you that all this is a mystery to me and that as far as I know, your father is expecting someone else, not me."

"Oh, I don't think so. I didn't ask you to come in, until after I saw you drop your briefcase."

"My what?"

"Your briefcase, young man. I'm not blind. You didn't drop it by accident, because you looked down *first*, so as to make sure it would land right. Then you must have realized it would land just under the hedges and wouldn't be seen, so you dropped it and *didn't* look down afterwards. Now since you came to the window instead of the front door, it must mean that you were a little afraid to trust yourself in the house before investigating the place. And after you had a little trouble with me, you took care of your briefcase before taking care of yourself, which means that you consider whatever your briefcase has in it to be more valuable than your own safety, and *that* means that as long as you're in here and the briefcase is out there and we know that it's out there, you're probably pretty helpless."

She paused for a much-needed breath, and the man said, grittily, "Except that I think I'll choke you just about medium dead and get out of here, *with* the briefcase."

"Except, young man, that I happen to have a baseball bat under my bed, which I can reach in two seconds from where I'm sitting, and I'm very strong for a girl."

Impasse. Finally, with a strained courtesy, the "young man" said, "Shall I introduce myself, since we're being so chummy. I'm Pelleas Anthor. And your name?"

"I'm Arca— Arkady Darell. Pleased to meet you."

"And now Arkady, would you be a good little girl and call your father?"

Arcadia bridled. "I'm not a little girl. I think you're very rude—especially when you're asking a favor."

Pelleas Anthor sighed. "Very well. Would you be a good, kind, dear, little old lady, just chock full of lavender, and call your father?"

"That's not what I meant either, but I'll call him. Only not so I'll take my eyes off *you*, young man." And she stamped on the floor.

There came the sound of hurrying footsteps in the hall, and the door was flung open.

"Arcadia—" There was a tiny explosion of exhaled air, and Dr. Darell said, "Who are you, sir?"

Pelleas sprang to his feet in what was quite obviously relief. "Dr. Toran Darell? I am Pelleas Anthor. You've received word about me, I think. At least, your daughter says you have."

"My *daughter* says I have?" He bent a frowning glance at her which caromed harmlessly off the wide-eyed and impenetrable web of innocence with which she met the accusation.

Dr. Darell said, finally: "I *have* been expecting you. Would you mind coming down with me, please?" And he stopped as his eye caught a flicker of motion, which Arcadia caught simultaneously.

She scrambled toward her Transcriber, but it was quite useless, since her father was standing right next to it. He said, sweetly, "You've left it going all this time, Arcadia."

"Father," she squeaked, in real anguish, "it is very ungentlemanly to read another person's private correspondence, especially when it's talking correspondence."

"Ah," said her father, "but 'talking correspondence' with a strange man in your bedroom! As a father, Arcadia, I must protect you against evil."

"Oh, golly—it was nothing like *that.*"

Pelleas laughed suddenly, "Oh, but it was, Dr. Darell. The young lady was going to accuse me of all sorts of things, and I must insist that you read it, if only to clear *my* name."

"Oh—" Arcadia held back her tears with an effort. Her own father didn't even trust her. And that darned Transcriber— If that silly fool hadn't come gooping at the window, and making her forget to turn it off. And now her father would be making long, gentle speeches about what young ladies aren't supposed to do. There just wasn't anything they *were* supposed to do, it looked like, except choke and die, maybe.

"Arcadia," said her father, gently, "it strikes me that a young lady—"

She knew it. She knew it.

"—should not be quite so impertinent to men older than she is."

"Well, what did he want to come peeping around my window for? A young lady has a right to privacy— Now I'll have to do my whole darned composition over."

"It's not up to you to question his propriety in coming to your window. You should simply not have let him in. You should have called me instantly—especially if you thought I was expecting him."

She said, peevishly, "It's just as well if you didn't see him— stupid thing. He'll give the whole thing away if he keeps on going to windows, instead of doors."

"Arcadia, nobody wants your opinion on matters you know nothing of."

"I do, too. It's the Second Foundation, that's what it is."

There was a silence. Even Arcadia felt a little nervous stirring in her abdomen.

Dr. Darell said, softly, "Where have you heard this?"

"Nowheres, but what else is there to be so secret about? And you don't have to worry that I'll tell anyone."

"Mr. Anthor," said Dr. Darell, "I must apologize for all this."

"Oh, that's all right," came Anthor's rather hollow response. "It's not your fault if she's sold herself to the forces of darkness. But do you mind if I ask her a question before we go. Miss Arcadia—"

"What do you want?"

"Why do you think it is stupid to go to windows instead of to doors?"

"Because you advertise what you're trying to hide, silly. If I have a secret, I don't put tape over my mouth and let everyone *know* I have a secret. I talk just as much as usual, only about something else. Didn't you ever read any of the sayings of Salvor Hardin? He was our first Mayor, you know."

"Yes, I know."

"Well, he used to say that only a lie that wasn't ashamed of itself could possibly succeed. He also said that nothing had to *be* true, but everything had to *sound* true. Well, when you come in through a window, it's a lie that's ashamed of itself and it doesn't sound true."

"Then what would you have done?"

"If I had wanted to see my father on top secret business, I would have made his acquaintance openly and seen him about all sorts of strictly legitimate things. And then when everyone knew all about you and connected you with my father as a matter of course, you could be as top secret as you want and nobody would ever think of questioning it."

Anthor looked at the girl strangely, then at Dr. Darell. He said, "Let's go. I have a briefcase I want to pick up in the garden. Wait! Just one last question. Arcadia, you don't really have a baseball bat under your bed, do you?"

"No! I don't."

"Hah. I didn't think so."

Dr. Darell stopped at the door. "Arcadia," he said, "when you rewrite your composition on the Seldon Plan, don't be unnecessarily mysterious about your grandmother. There is no necessity to mention that part at all."

He and Pelleas descended the stairs in silence. Then the visitor asked in a strained voice, "Do you mind, sir? How old is she?"

"Fourteen, day before yesterday."

"*Fourteen?* Great Galaxy— Tell me, has she ever said she expects to marry some day?"

"No, she hasn't. Not to me."

"Well, if she ever does, shoot him. The one she's going to marry, I mean." He stared earnestly into the older man's eyes. "I'm serious. Life could hold no greater horror than living with what she'll be like when she's twenty. I don't mean to offend you, of course."

"You don't offend me. I think I know what you mean."

Upstairs, the object of their tender analyses faced the Transcriber with revolted weariness and said, dully: "Thefutureofseldonsplan." The Transcriber with infinite aplomb, translated that into elegantly, complicated script capitals as:

"The Future of Seldon's Plan."

8

Seldon's Plan

MATHEMATICS   *The synthesis of the calculus of n-variables
and of n-dimensional geometry is the basis of what Seldon once
called "my little algebra of humanity".* . . .

ENCYCLOPEDIA GALACTICA

Consider a room!

The location of the room is not in question at the moment. It
is merely sufficient to say that in that room, more than anywhere,
the Second Foundation existed.

It was a room which, through the centuries, had been the
abode of pure science—yet it had none of the gadgets with which,
through millennia of association, science has come to be considered equivalent. It was a science, instead, which dealt with
mathematical concepts only, in a manner similar to the speculation of ancient, ancient races in the primitive, prehistoric days
before technology had come to be; before Man had spread beyond a single, now-unknown world.

For one thing, there was in that room—protected by a mental
science as yet unassailable by the combined physical might of
the rest of the Galaxy—the Prime Radiant, which held in its vitals
the Seldon Plan—complete.

For another, there was a man, too, in that room— The First
Speaker.

He was the twelfth in the line of chief guardians of the Plan,
and his title bore no deeper significance than the fact that at the
gatherings of the leaders of the Second Foundation, he spoke first.

His predecessor had beaten the Mule, but the wreckage of
that gigantic struggle still littered the path of the Plan— For

twenty-five years, he, and his administration, had been trying to force a Galaxy of stubborn and stupid human beings back to the path— It was a terrible task.

The First Speaker looked up at the opening door. Even while, in the loneliness of the room, he considered his quarter century of effort, which now so slowly and inevitably approached its climax; even while he had been so engaged, his mind had been considering the newcomer with a gentle expectation. A youth, a student, one of those who might take over, eventually.

The young man stood uncertainly at the door, so that the First Speaker had to walk to him and lead him in, with a friendly hand upon the shoulder.

The Student smiled shyly, and the First Speaker responded by saying, "First, I must tell you why you are here."

They faced each other now, across the desk. Neither was speaking in any way that could be recognized as such by any man in the Galaxy who was not himself a member of the Second Foundation.

Speech, originally, was the device whereby Man learned, imperfectly, to transmit the thoughts and emotions of his mind. By setting up arbitrary sounds and combinations of sounds to represent certain mental nuances, he developed a method of communication—but one which in its clumsiness and thick-thumbed inadequacy degenerated all the delicacy of the mind into gross and guttural signaling.

Down—down—the results can be followed; and all the suffering that humanity ever knew can be traced to the one fact that no man in the history of the Galaxy, until Hari Seldon, and very few men thereafter, could really understand one another. Every human being lived behind an impenetrable wall of choking mist within which no other but he existed. Occasionally there were the dim signals from deep within the cavern in which another man was located—so that each might grope toward the other. Yet because they did not know one another, and could not understand one another, and dared not trust one another, and felt from infancy the terrors and insecurity of that ultimate isolation

—there was the hunted fear of man for man, the savage rapacity of man toward man.

Feet, for tens of thousands of years, had clogged and shuffled in the mud—and held down the minds which, for an equal time, had been fit for the companionship of the stars.

Grimly, Man had instinctively sought to circumvent the prison bars of ordinary speech. Semantics, symbolic logic, psychoanalysis —they had all been devices whereby speech could either be refined or by-passed.

Psychohistory had been the development of mental science, the final mathematicization thereof, rather, which had finally succeeded. Through the development of the mathematics necessary to understand the facts of neural physiology and the electrochemistry of the nervous system, which themselves had to be, *had* to be, traced down to nuclear forces, it first became possible to truly develop psychology. And through the generalization of psychological knowledge from the individual to the group, sociology was also mathematicized.

The larger groups; the billions that occupied planets; the trillions that occupied Sectors; the quadrillions that occupied the whole Galaxy, became, not simply human beings, but gigantic forces amenable to statistical treatment—so that to Hari Seldon, the future became clear and inevitable, and the Plan could be set up.

The same basic developments of mental science that had brought about the development of the Seldon Plan, thus made it also unnecessary for the First Speaker to use words in addressing the Student.

Every reaction to a stimulus, however slight, was completely indicative of all the trifling changes, of all the flickering currents that went on in another's mind. The First Speaker could not sense the emotional content of the Student's instinctively, as the Mule would have been able to do—since the Mule was a mutant with powers not ever likely to become completely comprehensible to any ordinary man, even a Second Foundationer—rather he deduced them, as the result of intensive training.

Since, however, it is inherently impossible in a society based on speech to indicate truly the method of communication of Second Foundationers among themselves, the whole matter will be hereafter ignored. The First Speaker will be represented as speaking in ordinary fashion, and if the translation is not always entirely valid, it is at least the best that can be done under the circumstances.

It will be pretended therefore, that the First Speaker *did* actually say, "First, I must tell you why you are here," instead of smiling *just* so and lifting a finger *exactly* thus.

The First Speaker said, "You have studied mental science hard and well for most of your life. You have absorbed all your teachers could give you. It is time for you and a few others like yourself to begin your apprenticeship for Speakerhood."

Agitation from the other side of the desk.

"No—now you must take this phlegmatically. You had hoped you would qualify. You had feared you would not. Actually, both hope and fear are weaknesses. You *knew* you would qualify and you hesitate to admit the fact because such knowledge might stamp you as cocksure and therefore unfit. Nonsense! The most hopelessly stupid man is he who is not aware that he is wise. It is part of your qualification that you *knew* you would qualify."

Relaxation on the other side of the desk.

"Exactly. Now you feel better and your guard is down. You are fitter to concentrate and fitter to understand. Remember, to be truly effective, it is not necessary to hold the mind under a tight, controlling barrier which to the intelligent probe is as informative as a naked mentality. Rather, one should cultivate an innocence, an awareness of self, and an unself-consciousness of self which leaves one nothing to hide. My mind is open to you. Let this be so for both of us."

He went on. "It is not an easy thing to be a Speaker. It is not an easy thing to be a Psychohistorian in the first place; and not even the best Psychohistorian need necessarily qualify to be a Speaker. There is a distinction here. A Speaker must not only be aware of the mathematical intricacies of the Seldon Plan; he must have a sympathy for it and for its ends. He must *love* the Plan; to him it must be life and breath. More than that, it must even be as a living friend.

"Do you know what this is?"

The First Speaker's hand hovered gently over the black, shining cube in the middle of the desk. It was featureless.

"No, Speaker, I do not."

"You have heard of the Prime Radiant?"

"This?" —Astonishment.

"You expected something more noble and awe-inspiring? Well, that is natural. It was created in the days of the Empire, by men of Seldon's time. For nearly four hundred years, it has served our needs perfectly, without requiring repairs or adjustment. And fortunately so, since none of the Second Foundation is qualified to handle it in any technical fashion." He smiled gently. "Those of the First Foundation might be able to duplicate this, but they must never know, of course."

He depressed a lever on his side of the desk and the room was in darkness. But only for a moment, since with a gradually livening flush, the two long walls of the room glowed to life. First, a pearly white, unrelieved, then a trace of faint darkness here and there, and finally, the fine neatly printed equations in black, with an occasional red hairline that wavered through the darker forest like a staggering rillet.

"Come, my boy, step here before the wall. You will not cast a shadow. This light does not radiate from the Radiant in an ordinary manner. To tell you the truth, I do not know even faintly by what medium this effect is produced, but you will not cast a shadow. I know that."

They stood together in the light. Each wall was thirty feet long, and ten high. The writing was small and covered every inch.

"This is not the whole Plan," said the First Speaker. "To get it all upon both walls, the individual equations would have to be reduced to microscopic size—but that is not necessary. What you now see represents the main portions of the Plan till now. You have learned about this, have you not?"

"Yes, Speaker, I have."

"Do you recognize any portion."

A slow silence. The student pointed a finger and as he did so, the line of equations marched down the wall, until the single series of functions he had thought of—one could scarcely consider the quick, generalized gesture of the finger to have been sufficiently precise—was at eye-level.

The First Speaker laughed softly, "You will find the Prime Radiant to be attuned to your mind. You may expect more surprises from the little gadget. What were you about to say about the equation you have chosen?"

"It," faltered the Student, "is a Rigellian integral, using a planetary distribution of a bias indicating the presence of two chief economic classes on the planet, or maybe a Sector, plus an unstable emotional pattern."

"And what does it signify?"

"It represents the limit of tension, since we have here"—he pointed, and again the equations veered—"a converging series."

"Good," said the First Speaker. "And tell me, what do you think of all this. A finished work of art, is it not?"

"Definitely!"

"Wrong! It is not." This, with sharpness. "It is the first lesson you must unlearn. The Seldon Plan is neither complete nor correct. Instead, it is merely the best that could be done at the time. Over a dozen generations of men have pored over these equations, worked at them, taken them apart to the last decimal place, and put them together again. They've done more than that. They've watched nearly four hundred years pass and against the predictions and equations, they've checked reality, and they have learned.

"They have learned more than Seldon ever knew, and if with the accumulated knowledge of the centuries we could repeat Seldon's work, we could do a better job. Is that perfectly clear to you?"

The Student appeared a little shocked.

"Before you obtain your Speakerhood," continued the First Speaker, "you yourself will have to make an original contribution to the Plan. It is not such great blasphemy. Every red mark you see on the wall is the contribution of a man among us who lived since Seldon. Why . . . why—" He looked upward, "There!"

The whole wall seemed to whirl down upon him.

"This," he said, "is mine." A fine red line encircled two forking arrows and included six square feet of deductions along each path. Between the two were a series of equations in red.

"It does not," said the Speaker, "seem to be much. It is at a point in the Plan which we will not reach yet for a time as long as that which has already passed. It is at the period of coalescence, when the Second Empire that is to be is in the grip of rival personalities who will threaten to pull it apart if the fight is too even, or clamp it into rigidity, if the fight is too uneven. Both possibilities are considered here, followed, and the method of avoiding either indicated.

"Yet it is all a matter of probabilities and a third course can exist. It is one of comparatively low likelihood—twelve point six four percent, to be exact—but even smaller chances have *already* come to pass and the Plan is only forty percent complete. This third probability consists of a possible compromise between two or more of the conflicting personalities being considered. This, I showed, would first freeze the Second Empire into an unprofitable mold, and then, eventually, inflict more damage through civil wars than would have taken place had a compromise never been made in the first place. Fortunately, that could be prevented, too. And that was my contribution."

"If I may interrupt, Speaker— How is a change made?"

"Through the agency of the Radiant. You will find in your own case, for instance, that your mathematics will be checked rigorously by five different boards; and that you will be required to defend it against a concerted and merciless attack. Two years will then pass, and your development will be reviewed again. It has happened more than once that a seemingly perfect piece of work has uncovered its fallacies only after an induction period of months or years. Sometimes, the contributor himself discovers the flaw.

"If, after two years, another examination, not less detailed than the first, still passes it, and—better still—if in the interim the young scientist has brought to light additional details, subsidiary evidence, the contribution will be added to the Plan. It was the climax of my career; it will be the climax of yours.

"The Prime Radiant can be adjusted to your mind, and all corrections and additions can be made through mental rapport. There will be nothing to indicate that the correction or addition is yours. In all the history of the Plan there has been no personalization. It is rather a creation of all of us together. Do you understand?"

"Yes, Speaker!"

"Then, enough of that." A stride to the Prime Radiant, and the walls were blank again save for the ordinary room-lighting region along the upper borders. "Sit down here at my desk, and let me talk to you. It is enough for a Psychohistorian, as such, to know his Biostatistics and his Neurochemical Electromathematics. Some know nothing else and are fit only to be statistical technicians. But a Speaker must be able to discuss the Plan without mathematics. If not the Plan itself, at least its philosophy and its aims.

"First of all, what is the aim of the Plan? Please tell me in your own words—and don't grope for fine sentiment. You won't be judged on polish and suavity, I assure you."

It was the Student's first chance at more than a bisyllable, and he hesitated before plunging into the expectant space cleared away for him. He said, diffidently: "As a result of what I have learned, I believe that it is the intention of the Plan to establish a human civilization based on an orientation entirely different from anything that ever before existed. An orientation which, according to the findings of Psychohistory, could never *spontaneously* come into being—"

"Stop!" The First Speaker was insistent. "You must not say 'never.' That is a lazy slurring over of the facts. Actually, Psychohistory predicts only probabilities. A particular event may be infinitesimally probable, but the probability is always greater than zero."

"Yes, Speaker. The orientation desired, if I may correct myself, then, is well known to possess no significant probability of spontaneously coming to pass."

"Better. What is the orientation?"

"It is that of a civilization based on mental science. In all the known history of Mankind, advances have been made primarily in physical technology; in the capacity of handling the inanimate world about Man. Control of self and society has been left to chance or to the vague gropings of intuitive ethical systems based on inspiration and emotion. As a result, no culture of greater stability than about fifty-five percent has ever existed, and these only as the result of great human misery."

"And why is the orientation we speak of a nonspontaneous one?"

"Because a large minority of human beings are mentally equipped to take part in the advance of physical science, and all receive the crude and visible benefits thereof. Only an insignificant minority, however, are inherently able to lead Man through the greater involvements of Mental Science; and the benefits derived therefrom, while longer lasting, are more subtle and less apparent. Furthermore, since such an orientation would lead to the development of a benevolent dictatorship of the mentally best—virtually a higher subdivision of Man—it would be resented and could not be stable without the application of a force which would depress the rest of Mankind to brute level. Such a development is repugnant to us and must be avoided."

"What, then, is the solution?"

"The solution is the Seldon Plan. Conditions have been so arranged and so maintained that in a millennium from its beginnings—six hundred years from now, a Second Galactic Empire will have been established in which Mankind will be ready for the leadership of Mental Science. In that same interval, the Second Foundation in *its* development, will have brought forth a group of Psychologists ready to assume leadership. Or, as I have myself often thought, the First Foundation supplies the physical framework of a single political unit, and the Second Foundation supplies the mental framework of a ready-made ruling class."

"I see. Fairly adequate. Do you think that *any* Second Empire,

even if formed in the time set by Seldon, would do as a fulfillment of his Plan?"

"No, Speaker, I do not. There are several possible Second Empires that may be formed in the period of time stretching from
nine hundred to seventeen hundred years after the inception of
the Plan, but only one of these is *the* Second Empire."

"And in view of all this, why is it necessary that the existence
of the Second Foundation be hidden—above all, from the First
Foundation?"

The Student probed for a hidden meaning to the question and
failed to find it. He was troubled in his answer, "For the same
reason that the details of the Plan as a whole must be hidden
from Mankind in general. The laws of Psychohistory are statistical in nature and are rendered invalid if the actions of individual men are not random in nature. If a sizable group of human
beings learned of key details of the Plan, their actions would be
governed by that knowledge and would no longer be random in
the meaning of the axioms of Psychohistory. In other words, they
would no longer be perfectly predictable. Your pardon, Speaker,
but I feel that the answer is not satisfactory."

"It is well that you do. Your answer is quite incomplete. It is
the Second Foundation itself which must be hidden, not simply
the Plan. The Second Empire is not yet formed. We have still a
society which would resent a ruling class of psychologists, and
which would fear its development and fight against it. Do you
understand that?"

"Yes, Speaker, I do. The point has never been stressed—"

"Don't minimize. It has never been made—in the classroom,
though you should be capable of deducing it yourself. This and
many other points we will make now and in the near future during your apprenticeship. You will see me again in a week. By
that time, I would like to have comments from you as to a certain
problem which I now set before you. I don't want complete and
rigorous mathematical treatment. That would take a year for an
expert, and not a week for you. But I do want an indication as to
trends and directions—

"You have here a fork in the Plan at a period in time of about half a century ago. The necessary details are included. You will note that the path followed by the assumed reality diverges from all the plotted predictions; its probability being under one percent. You will estimate for how long the divergence may continue before it becomes uncorrectable. Estimate also the probable end if uncorrected, and a reasonable method of correction."

The Student flipped the Viewer at random and looked stonily at the passages presented on the tiny, built-in screen.

He said: "Why this particular problem, Speaker? It obviously has significance other than purely academic."

"Thank you, my boy. You are as quick as I had expected. The problem is not supposititious. Nearly half a century ago, the Mule burst into Galactic history and for ten years was the largest single fact in the universe. He was unprovided for; uncalculated for. He bent the Plan seriously, but not fatally.

"To stop him before he *did* become fatal, however, we were forced to take active part against him. We revealed our existence, and infinitely worse, a portion of our power. The First Foundation has learned of us, and their actions are now predicated on that knowledge. Observe in the problem presented. Here. And here.

"Naturally, you will not speak of this to anyone."

There was an appalled pause, as realization seeped into the Student. He said: "Then the Seldon Plan has failed!"

"Not yet. It merely *may* have failed. The probabilities of success are *still* twenty-one point four percent, as of the last assessment."

9

The Conspirators

For Dr. Darell and Pelleas Anthor, the evenings passed in friendly intercourse; the days in pleasant unimportance. It might have been an ordinary visit. Dr. Darell introduced the young man as a cousin from across space, and interest was dulled by the cliché.

Somehow, however, among the small talk, a name might be mentioned. There would be an easy thoughtfulness. Dr. Darell might say, "No," or he might say, "Yes." A call on the open Communi-wave issued a casual invitation, "Want you to meet my cousin."

And Arcadia's preparations proceeded in their own manner. In fact, her actions might be considered the least straightforward of all.

For instance, she induced Olynthus Dam at school to donate to her a home-built, self-contained sound-receiver by methods which indicated a future for her that promised peril to all males with whom she might come into contact. To avoid details, she merely exhibited such an interest in Olynthus' self-publicized hobby—he had a home workshop—combined with such a well-modulated transfer of this interest to Olynthus' own pudgy features, that the unfortunate youth found himself: 1) discoursing at great and animated length upon the principles of the hyperwave motor; 2) becoming dizzyingly aware of the great, absorbed eyes that rested so lightly upon his; and 3) forcing into her willing hands his own greatest creation, the aforesaid sound-receiver.

Arcadia cultivated Olynthus in diminishing degree thereafter for just long enough to remove all suspicion that the sound-receiver had been the cause of the friendship. For months afterwards, Olynthus felt the memory of that short period in his life over and over again with the tendrils of his mind; until finally, for lack of further addition, he gave up and let it slip away.

When the seventh evening came, and five men sat in the Darell living room with food within and tobacco without, Arcadia's desk upstairs was occupied by this quite unrecognizable home-product of Olynthus' ingenuity.

Five men then. Dr. Darell, of course, with graying hair and meticulous clothing, looking somewhat older than his forty-two years. Pelleas Anthor, serious and quick-eyed at the moment, looking young and unsure of himself. And the three new men: Jole Turbor, visicastor, bulky and plump-lipped; Dr. Elvett Semic, professor-emeritus of physics at the University, scrawny and wrinkled, his clothes only half-filled; Homir Munn, librarian, lanky and terribly ill-at-ease.

Dr. Darell spoke easily, in a normal, matter-of-fact tone: "This gathering has been arranged, gentlemen, for a trifle more than merely social reasons. You may have guessed this. Since you have been deliberately chosen because of your backgrounds, you may also guess the danger involved. I won't minimize it, but I will point out that we are all condemned men, in any case.

"You will notice that none of you have been invited with any attempt at secrecy. None of you have been asked to come here unseen. The windows are not adjusted to non-insight. No screen of any sort is about the room. We have only to attract the attention of the enemy to be ruined; and the best way to attract that attention is to assume a false and theatrical secrecy.

(*Hah*, thought Arcadia, bending over the voices coming—a bit screechily—out of the little box.)

"Do you understand that?"

Elvett Semic twitched his lower lip and bared his teeth in the screwup, wrinkled gesture that preceded his every sentence. "Oh, get on with it. Tell us about the youngster."

Dr. Darell said, "Pelleas Anthor is his name. He was a student of my old colleague, Kleise, who died last year. Kleise sent me his brain-pattern to the fifth sublevel, before he died, which pattern has been now checked against that of the man before you. You know, of course, that a brain-pattern cannot be duplicated that far, even by men of the Science of Psychology. If you don't know that, you'll have to take my word for it."

Turbor said, purse-lipped, "We might as well make a beginning somewheres. We'll take your word for it, especially since you're the greatest electroneurologist in the Galaxy now that Kleise is dead. At least, that is the way I've described you in my visicast comment, and I even believe it myself. How old are you, Anthor?"

"Twenty-nine, Mr. Turbor."

"Hm-m-m. And are you an electroneurologist, too? A great one?"

"Just a student of the science. But I work hard, and I've had the benefit of Kleise's training."

Munn broke in. He had a slight stammer at periods of tension. "I . . . I wish you'd g . . . get started. I think everyone's t . . . talking too much."

Dr. Darell lifted an eyebrow in Munn's direction. "You're right, Homir. Take over, Pelleas."

"Not for a while," said Pelleas Anthor, slowly, "because before we can get started—although I appreciate Mr. Munn's sentiment —I must request brain-wave data."

Darell frowned. "What is this, Anthor? What brain-wave data do you refer to?"

"The patterns of all of you. You have taken mine, Dr. Darell. I must take yours and those of the rest of you. And I must take the measurements myself."

Turbor said, "There's no reason for him to trust us, Darell. The young man is within his rights."

"Thank you," said Anthor. "If you'll lead the way to your laboratory then, Dr. Darell, we'll proceed. I took the liberty this morning of checking your apparatus."

The science of electroencephalography was at once new and old. It was old in the sense that the knowledge of the microcurrents generated by nerve cells of living beings belonged to that immense category of human knowledge whose origin was completely lost. It was knowledge that stretched back as far as the earliest remnants of human history—

And yet it was new, too. The fact of the existence of microcurrents slumbered through the tens of thousands of years of Galactic Empire as one of those vivid and whimsical, but quite useless, items of human knowledge. Some had attempted to form classifications of waves into waking and sleeping, calm and excited, well and ill—but even the broadest conceptions had had their hordes of vitiating exceptions.

Others had tried to show the existence of brain-wave groups, analogous to the well-known blood groups, and to show that external environment was the defining factor. These were the race-minded people who claimed that Man could be divided into subspecies. But such a philosophy could make no headway against the overwhelming ecumenical drive involved in the fact of Galactic Empire—one political unit covering twenty million stellar systems, involving all of Man from the central world of Trantor—now a gorgeous and impossible memory of the great past —to the loneliest asteroid on the periphery.

And then again, in a society given over, as that of the First Empire was, to the physical sciences and inanimate technology, there was a vague but mighty sociological *push* away from the study of the mind. It was less respectable because less immediately useful; and it was poorly financed since it was less profitable.

After the disintegration of the First Empire, there came the fragmentation of organized science, back, back—past even the fundamentals of atomic power into the chemical power of coal and oil. The one exception to this, of course, was the First Foundation where the spark of science, revitalized and grown more intense was maintained and fed to flame. Yet there, too, it was the physical that ruled, and the brain, except for surgery, was neglected ground.

Hari Seldon was the first to express what afterwards came to be accepted as truth.

"Neural microcurrents," he once said, "carry within them the spark of every varying impulse and response, conscious and unconscious. The brain-waves recorded on neatly squared paper in trembling peaks and troughs are the mirrors of the combined thought-pulses of billions of cells. Theoretically, analysis should reveal the thoughts and emotions of the subject, to the last and least. Differences should be detected that are due not only to gross physical defects, inherited or acquired, but also to shifting states of emotion, to advancing education and experience, even to something as subtle as a change in the subject's philosophy of life."

But even Seldon could approach no further than speculation.

And now for fifty years, the men of the First Foundation had been tearing at that incredibly vast and complicated storehouse of new knowledge. The approach, naturally, was made through new techniques—as, for example, the use of electrodes at skull sutures by a newly-developed means which enabled contact to be made directly with the gray cells, without even the necessity of shaving a patch of skull. And then there was a recording device which automatically recorded the brain-wave data as an overall total, and as separate functions of six independent variables.

What was most significant, perhaps, was the growing respect in which encephalography and the encephalographer was held. Kleise, the greatest of them, sat at scientific conventions on an equal basis with the physicist. Dr. Darell, though no longer active in the science, was known for his brilliant advances in encephalographic analysis almost as much as for the fact that he was the son of Bayta Darell, the great heroine of the past generation.

And so now, Dr. Darell sat in his own chair, with the delicate touch of the feathery electrodes scarcely hinting at pressure upon his skull, while the vacuum-incased needles wavered to and fro. His back was to the recorder—otherwise, as was well known, the sight of the moving curves induced an unconscious effort to control them, with noticeable results—but he knew that the central dial was expressing the strongly rhythmic and little-varying Sigma curve, which was to be expected of his own powerful and disciplined mind. It would be strengthened and purified in the subsidiary dial dealing with the Cerebellar wave. There would be the sharp, near-discontinuous leaps from the frontal lobe, and the subdued shakiness from the subsurface regions with its narrow range of frequencies—

He knew his own brain-wave pattern much as an artist might be perfectly aware of the color of his eyes.

Pelleas Anthor made no comment when Darell rose from the reclining chair. The young man abstracted the seven recordings, glanced at them with the quick, all-embracing eyes of one who knows exactly what tiny facet of near-nothingness is being looked for.

"If you don't mind, Dr. Semic."

Semic's age-yellowed face was serious. Electroencephalography was a science of his old age of which he knew little; an upstart that he faintly resented. He knew that he was old and that his wave-pattern would show it. The wrinkles on his face showed it, the stoop in his walk, the shaking of his hand—but *they* spoke only of his body. The brain-wave patterns might show that his mind was old, too. An embarrassing and unwarranted invasion of a man's last protecting stronghold, his own mind.

The electrodes were adjusted. The process did not hurt, of course, from beginning to end. There was just that tiny tingle, far below the threshold of sensation.

And then came Turbor, who sat quietly and unemotionally through the fifteen minute process, and Munn, who jerked at the first touch of the electrodes and then spent the session rolling his eyes as though he wished he could turn them backwards and watch through a hole in his occiput.

"And now—" said Darell, when all was done.

"And now," said Anthor, apologetically, "there is one more person in the house."

Darell, frowning, said: "My daughter?"

"Yes. I suggested that she stay home tonight, if you'll remember."

"For encephalographical analysis? What in the Galaxy for?"

"I cannot proceed without it."

Darell shrugged and climbed the stairs. Arcadia, amply warned, had the sound-receiver off when he entered; then followed him down with mild obedience. It was the first time in her life—except for the taking of her basic mind pattern as an infant, for identification and registration purposes—that she found herself under the electrodes.

"May I see," she asked, when it was over, holding out her hand.

Dr. Darell said, "You would not understand, Arcadia. Isn't it time for you to go to bed?"

"Yes, father," she said, demurely. "Good night, all."

She ran up the stairs and plumped into bed with a minimum of basic preparation. With Olynthus' sound-receiver propped beside her pillow, she felt like a character out of a book-film, and hugged every moment of it close to her chest in an ecstasy of "spy-stuff."

The first words she heard were Anthor's and they were: "The analyses, gentlemen, are all satisfactory. The child's as well."

Child, she thought disgustedly, and bristled at Anthor in the darkness.

Anthor had opened his briefcase now, and out of it, he took several dozen brain-wave records. They were not originals. Nor had the briefcase been fitted with an ordinary lock. Had the key been held in any hand other than his own, the contents thereof would have silently and instantly oxidized to an indecipherable ash. Once removed from the briefcase, the records did so anyway after half an hour.

But during their short lifetime, Anthor spoke quickly. "I have the records here of several minor government officials at Anacreon. This is a psychologist at Locris University; this an industrialist at Siwenna. The rest are as you see."

They crowded closely. To all but Darell, they were so many quivers on parchment. To Darell, they shouted with a million tongues.

Anthor pointed lightly, "I call your attention, Dr. Darell, to the plateau region among the secondary Tauian waves in the frontal lobe, which is what all these records have in common. Would you use my Analytical Rule, sir, to check my statement?"

The Analytical Rule might be considered a distant relation—as

a skyscraper is to a shack—of that kindergarten toy, the loga-
rithmic Slide Rule. Darell used it with the wristflip of long prac-
tice. He made freehand drawings of the result and, as Anthor
stated, there were featureless plateaus in frontal lobe regions
where strong swings should have been expected.

"How would you interpret that, Dr. Darell?" asked Anthor.

"I'm not sure. Offhand, I don't see how it's possible. Even in
cases of amnesia, there is suppression, but not removal. Drastic
brain surgery, perhaps?"

"Oh, something's been cut out," cried Anthor, impatiently,
"yes! Not in the physical sense, however. You know, the Mule
could have done just that. He could have suppressed completely
all capacity for a certain emotion or attitude of mind, and leave
nothing but just such a flatness. Or else—"

"Or else the Second Foundation could have done it. Is that it?"
asked Turbor, with a slow smile.

There was no real need to answer that thoroughly rhetorical
question.

"What made you suspicious, Mr. Anthor?" asked Munn.

"It wasn't I. It was Dr. Kleise. He collected brain-wave patterns, much as the Planetary Police do, but along different lines.
He specialized in intellectuals, government officials and business
leaders. You see, it's quite obvious that if the Second Foundation
is directing the historical course of the Galaxy—of us—that they
must do it subtly and in as minimal a fashion as possible. If they
work through minds, as they must, it is the minds of people with
influence; culturally, industrially, or politically. And with those
he concerned himself."

"Yes," objected Munn, "but is there corroboration? How do
these people act—I mean the ones with the plateau. Maybe it's
all a perfectly normal phenomenon." He looked hopelessly at
the others out of his, somehow, childlike blue eyes, but met no
encouraging return.

"I leave that to Dr. Darell," said Anthor. "Ask him how many
times he's seen this phenomenon in his general studies, or in reported cases in the literature over the past generation. Then ask

him the chances of it being discovered in almost one out of every thousand cases among the categories Dr. Kleise studied."

"I suppose that there is no doubt," said Darell, thoughtfully, "that these are artificial mentalities. They have been tampered with. In a way, I have suspected this—"

"I know that, Dr. Darell," said Anthor. "I also know you once worked with Dr. Kleise. I would like to know why you stopped."

There wasn't actually hostility in his question. Perhaps nothing more than caution; but, at any rate, it resulted in a long pause. Darell looked from one to another of his guests, then said brusquely, "Because there was no point to Kleise's battle. He was competing with an adversary too strong for him. He was detecting what we—he and I—knew he would detect—that we were not our own masters. *And I didn't want to know!* I had my self-respect. I liked to think that our Foundation was captain of its collective soul; that our forefathers had not quite fought and died for nothing. I thought it would be most simple to turn my face away as long as I was not quite sure. I didn't need my position since the Government pension awarded to my mother's family in perpetuity would take care of my uncomplicated needs. My home laboratory would suffice to keep boredom away, and life would some day end— Then Kleise died—"

Semic showed his teeth and said: "This fellow Kleise; I don't know him. How did he die?"

Anthor cut in: "He *died*. He thought he would. He told me half a year before that he was getting too close—"

"Now *we're* too c . . . close, too, aren't we?" suggested Munn, dry-mouthed, as his Adam's apple jiggled.

"Yes," said Anthor, flatly, "but we were, anyway—all of us. It's why you've all been chosen. I'm Kleise's student. Dr. Darell was his colleague. Jole Turbor has been denouncing our blind faith in the saving hand of the Second Foundation on the air, until the government shut him off—through the agency, I might mention, of a powerful financier whose brain shows what Kleise used to call the Tamper Plateau. Homir Munn has the largest home collection of Muliana—if I may use the phrase to signify collected data concerning the Mule—in existence, and has published some papers containing speculation on the nature and function of the Second Foundation. Dr. Semic has contributed as much as anyone to the mathematics of encephalographic analysis, though I don't believe he realized that his mathematics could be so applied."

Semic opened his eyes wide and chuckled gaspingly, "No, young fellow. I was analyzing intranuclear motions—the n-body problem, you know. I'm lost in encephalography."

"Then we know where we stand. The government can, of course, do nothing about the matter. Whether the mayor or anyone in his administration is aware of the seriousness of the situation, I don't know. But this I do know—we five have nothing to lose and stand to gain much. With every increase in our knowledge, we can widen ourselves in safe directions. We are but a beginning, you understand."

"How widespread," put in Turbor, "is this Second Foundation infiltration?"

"I don't know. There's a flat answer. All the infiltrations we have discovered were on the outer fringes of the nation. The capital world may yet be clean, though even that is not certain—else I would not have tested you. You were particularly suspicious, Dr. Darell, since you abandoned research with Kleise. Kleise never forgave you, you know. I thought that perhaps the Second Foundation had corrupted you, but Kleise always insisted that you were a coward. You'll forgive me, Dr. Darell, if I explain this to make my own position clear. I, personally, think I understand your attitude, and, if it was cowardice, I consider it venial."

Darell drew a breath before replying. "I ran away! Call it what you wish. I tried to maintain our friendship, however, yet he never wrote nor called me until the day he sent me your brainwave data, and that was scarcely a week before he died—"

"If you don't mind," interrupted Homir Munn, with a flash of nervous eloquence, "I d . . . don't see what you think you're doing. We're a p . . . poor bunch of conspirators, if we're just going to talk and talk and t . . . talk. And I don't see what else we can do, anyway. This is v . . . very childish. B . . . brain-waves and mumbo jumbo and all that. Is there just one thing you intend to *do?*"

Pelleas Anthor's eyes were bright, "Yes, there is. We need more information on the Second Foundation. It's the prime necessity. The Mule spent the first five years of his rule in just that quest for information and failed—or so we have all been led to believe. But then he stopped looking. Why? Because he failed? Or because he succeeded?"

"M . . . more talk," said Munn, bitterly. "How are we ever to know?"

"If you'll listen to me— The Mule's capital was on Kalgan. Kalgan was not part of the Foundation's commercial sphere of influence before the Mule and it is not part of it now. Kalgan is ruled, at the moment, by the man, Stettin, unless there's another palace revolution by tomorrow. Stettin calls himself First Citizen and considers himself the successor of the Mule. If there is any tradition in that world, it rests with the super-humanity and greatness of the Mule—a tradition almost superstitious in intensity. As a result, the Mule's old palace is maintained as a shrine. No unauthorized person may enter; nothing within has ever been touched."

"Well?"

"Well, why is that so? At times like these, nothing happens without a reason. What if it is not superstition only that makes the Mule's palace inviolate? What if the Second Foundation has so arranged matters? In short what if the results of the Mule's five-year search are within—"

"Oh, p . . . poppycock."

"Why not?" demanded Anthor. "Throughout its history the Second Foundation has hidden itself and interfered in Galactic affairs in minimal fashion only. I know that to us it would seem more logical to destroy the Palace or, at the least, to remove the data. But you must consider the psychology of these master psychologists. They are Seldons; they are Mules and they work by indirection, through the mind. They would never destroy or remove when they could achieve their ends by creating a state of mind. Eh?"

No immediate answer, and Anthor continued, "And you, Munn, are just the one to get the information we need."

"I?" It was an astounded yell. Munn looked from one to the other rapidly, "I can't do such a thing. I'm no man of action; no hero of any teleview. I'm a librarian. If I can help you that way, all right, and I'll risk the Second Foundation, but I'm not going out into space on any qu . . . quixotic thing like that."

"Now, look," said Anthor, patiently, "Dr. Darell and I have both agreed that you're the man. It's the only way to do it naturally. You say you're a librarian. Fine! What is your main field of interest? Muliana! You already have the greatest collection of material on the Mule in the Galaxy. It is natural for you to want more; more natural for you than for anyone else. You could request entrance to the Kalgan Palace without arousing suspicion of ulterior motives. You might be refused but you would not be suspected. What's more, you have a one-man cruiser. You're known to have visited foreign planets during your annual vacation. You've even been on Kalgan before. Don't you understand that you need only act as you always have?"

"But I can't just say, 'W . . . won't you kindly let me in to your most sacred shrine, M . . . Mr. First Citizen?'"

"Why not?"

"Because, by the Galaxy, he won't let me!"

"All right, then. So he won't. Then you'll come home and we'll think of something else."

Munn looked about in helpless rebellion. He felt himself being talked into something he hated. No one offered to help him extricate himself.

So in the end two decisions were made in Dr. Darell's house. The first was a reluctant one of agreement on the part of Munn to take off into space as soon as his summer vacation began.

The other was a highly unauthorized decision on the part of a thoroughly unofficial member of the gathering, made as she clicked off a sound-receiver and composed herself for a belated sleep. This second decision does not concern us just yet.

10

Approaching Crisis

A week had passed on the Second Foundation, and the First Speaker was smiling once again upon the Student.

"You must have brought me interesting results, or you would not be so filled with anger."

The Student put his hand upon the sheaf of calculating paper he had brought with him and said, "Are you sure that the problem is a factual one?"

"The premises are true. I have distorted nothing."

"Then I *must* accept the results, and I do not want to."

"Naturally. But what have your wants to do with it? Well, tell me what disturbs you so. No, no, put your derivations to one side. I will subject them to analysis afterward. Meanwhile, *talk* to me. Let me judge your understanding."

"Well, then, Speaker— It becomes very apparent that a gross overall change in the basic psychology of the First Foundation has taken place. As long as they knew of the existence of a Seldon Plan, without knowing any of the details thereof, they were confident but uncertain. They knew they would succeed, but they didn't know when or how. There was, therefore, a continuous atmosphere of tension and strain—which was what Seldon desired. The First Foundation, in other words, could be counted upon to work at maximum potential."

"A doubtful metaphor," said the First Speaker, "but I understand you."

"But now, Speaker, they know of the existence of a Second Foundation in what amounts to detail, rather merely than as an ancient and vague statement of Seldon's. They have an inkling as to its function as the guardian of the Plan. They know that an agency exists which watches their every step and will not let them fall. So they abandon their purposeful stride and allow themselves to be carried upon a litter. Another metaphor, I'm afraid."

"Nevertheless, go on."

"And that very abandonment of effort; that growing inertia; that lapse into softness and into a decadent and hedonistic culture, means the ruin of the Plan. They *must* be self-propelled."

"Is that all?"

"No, there is more. The majority reaction is as described. But a great probability exists for a minority reaction. Knowledge of our guardianship and our control will rouse among a few, not complacence, but hostility. This follows from Korillov's Theorem—"

"Yes, yes. I know the theorem."

"I'm sorry, Speaker. It is difficult to avoid mathematics. In any case, the effect is that not only is the Foundation's effort diluted, but part of it is turned against us, actively against us."

"And is *that* all?"

"There remains one other factor of which the probability is moderately low—"

"Very good. What is that?"

"While the energies of the First Foundation were directed only to Empire; while their only enemies were huge and outmoded hulks that remained from the shambles of the past, they were obviously concerned only with the physical sciences. With *us* forming a new, large part of their environment, a change in view may well be imposed on them. They may try to become psychologists—"

"That change," said the First Speaker, coolly, "*has* already taken place."

The Student's lips compressed themselves into a pale line. "Then all is over. It is the basic incompatibility with the Plan. Speaker, would I have known of this if I had lived—outside?"

The First Speaker spoke seriously, "You feel humiliated, my young man, because, thinking you understood so much so well, you suddenly find that many very apparent things were unknown to you. Thinking you were one of the Lords of the Galaxy; you suddenly find that you stand near to destruction. Naturally, you will resent the ivory tower in which you lived; the seclusion in which you were educated; the theories on which you were reared.

"I once had that feeling. It is normal. Yet it was necessary that in your formative years you have no direct contact with the Galaxy; that you remain *here*, where all knowledge is filtered to you, and your mind carefully sharpened. We could have shown you this . . . this part-failure of the Plan earlier and spared you the shock now, but you would not have understood the significance properly, as you now will. Then you find no solution at all to the problem?"

The Student shook his head and said hopelessly, "None!"

"Well, it is not surprising. Listen to me, young man. A course of action exists and has been followed for over a decade. It is not a usual course, but one that we have been forced into against our will. It involves low probabilities, dangerous assumptions— We have even been forced to deal with individual reactions at times, because that was the only possible way, and you know that Psychostatistics by its very nature has no meaning when applied to less than planetary numbers."

"Are we succeeding?" gasped the Student.

"There's no way of telling yet. We have kept the situation stable so far—but for the first time in the history of the Plan, it is possible for the unexpected actions of a single individual to destroy it. We have adjusted a minimum number of outsiders to a needful state of mind; we have our agents—but their paths are planned. They dare not improvise. That should be obvious to you. And I will not conceal the worst—if we are discovered, here, on this world, it will not only be the Plan that is destroyed, but ourselves, our physical selves. So you see, our solution is not very good."

"But the little you have described does not sound like a solution at all, but like a desperate guess."

"No. Let us say, an intelligent guess."

"When is the crisis, Speaker? When will we know whether we have succeeded or not?"

"Well within the year, no doubt."

The Student considered that, then nodded his head. He shook hands with the Speaker. "Well, it's good to know."

He turned on his heel and left.

The first Speaker looked out silently as the window gained transparency. Past the giant structures to the quiet, crowding stars.

A year would pass quickly. Would any of them, any of Seldon's heritage, be alive at its end?

11

Stowaway

It was a little over a month before the summer could be said to have started. Started, that is, to the extent that Homir Munn had written his final financial report of the fiscal year, seen to it that the substitute librarian supplied by the Government was sufficiently aware of the subtleties of the post—last year's man had been quite unsatisfactory—and arranged to have his little cruiser the *Unimara*—named after a tender and mysterious episode of twenty years past—taken out of its winter cobwebbery.

He left Terminus in a sullen distemper. No one was at the port to see him off. That would not have been natural since no one ever had in the past. He knew very well that it was important to have this trip in no way different from any he had made in the past, yet he felt drenched in a vague resentment. He, Homir Munn, was risking his neck in derring-doery of the most outrageous sort, and yet he left alone.

At least, so he thought.

And it was because he thought wrongly, that the following day was one of confusion, both on the *Unimara* and in Dr. Darell's suburban home.

It hit Dr. Darell's home first, in point of time, through the medium of Poli, the maid, whose month's vacation was now quite a thing of the past. She flew down the stairs in a flurry and stutter.

The good doctor met her and she tried vainly to put emotion into words but ended by thrusting a sheet of paper and a cubical object at him.

He took them unwillingly and said: "What's wrong, Poli?"

"She's *gone*, doctor."

"Who's gone?"

"Arcadia!"

"What do you mean, gone? Gone where? What are you talking about?"

And she stamped her foot: "*I* don't know. She's gone, and there's a suitcase and some clothes gone with her and there's that letter. Why don't you read it, instead of just standing there? Oh, you *men!*"

Dr. Darell shrugged and opened the envelope. The letter was not long, and except for the angular signature, "Arkady," was in the ornate and flowing handwriting of Arcadia's transcriber.

Dear Father:

It would have been simply too heartbreaking to say good-by to you in person. I might have cried like a little girl and you would have been ashamed of me. So I'm writing a letter instead to tell you how much I'll miss you, even while I'm having this perfectly wonderful summer vacation with Uncle Homir. I'll take good care of myself and it won't be long before I'm home again. Meanwhile, I'm leaving you something that's all my own. You can have it now.

Your loving daughter,

Arkady.

He read it through several times with an expression that grew blanker each time. He said stiffly, "Have you read this, Poli?"

Poli was instantly on the defensive. "I certainly can't be blamed for that, doctor. The envelope has 'Poli' written on the outside, and I had no way of telling there was a letter for you on the inside. I'm no snoop, doctor, and in the years I've been with—"

Darell held up a placating hand, "Very well, Poli. It's not important. I just wanted to make sure you understood what had happened."

He was considering rapidly. It was no use telling her to forget the matter. With regard to the enemy, "forget" was a meaningless word; and the advice, insofar as it made the matter more important, would have had an opposite effect.

He said instead, "She's a queer little girl, you know. Very romantic. Ever since we arranged to have her go off on a space trip this summer, she's been quite excited."

"And just why has no one told *me* about this space trip?"

"It was arranged while you were away, and we forgot. It's nothing more complicated than that."

Poli's original emotions now concentrated themselves into a single, overwhelming indignation, "Simple, is it? The poor chick has gone off with one suitcase, without a decent stitch of clothes to her, and alone at that. How long will she be away?"

"Now I won't have you worrying about it, Poli. There will be plenty of clothes for her on the ship. It's been all arranged. Will you tell Mr. Anthor that I want to see him? Oh, and first—is this the object that Arcadia has left for me?" He turned it over in his hand.

Poli tossed her head. "I'm sure I don't know. The letter was on top of it and that's every bit I can tell you. Forget to tell me, indeed. If her mother were alive—"

Darell waved her away. "Please call Mr. Anthor."

Anthor's viewpoint on the matter differed radically from that of Arcadia's father. He punctuated his initial remarks with clenched fists and torn hair, and from there, passed on to bitterness.

"Great Space, what are you waiting for? What are we both waiting for? Get the spaceport on the viewer and have them contact the *Unimara*."

"Softly, Pelleas, she's *my* daughter."

"But it's not your Galaxy."

"Now, wait. She's an intelligent girl, Pelleas, and she's thought this thing out carefully. We had better follow her thoughts while this thing is fresh. Do you know what this thing is?"

"No. Why should it matter what it is?"

"Because it's a sound-receiver."

"That thing?"

"It's homemade, but it will work. I've tested it. Don't you see? It's her way of telling us that she's been a party to our conversations of policy. She knows where Homir Munn is going and why. She's decided it would be exciting to go along."

"Oh, Great Space," groaned the younger man. "Another mind for the Second Foundation to pick."

"Except that there's no reason why the Second Foundation should, *a priori*, suspect a fourteen-year-old girl of being a danger—*unless* we do anything to attract attention to her, such as calling back a ship out of space for no reason other than to take her off. Do you forget with whom we're dealing? How narrow the margin is that separates us from discovery? How helpless we are thereafter?"

"But we can't have everything depend on an insane child."

"She's not insane, and we have no choice. She need not have written the letter, but she did it to keep us from going to the police after a lost child. Her letter suggests that we convert the entire matter into a friendly offer on the part of Munn to take an old friend's daughter off for a short vacation. And why not? He's been my friend for nearly twenty years. He's known her since she was three, when I brought her back from Trantor. It's a perfectly natural thing, and, in fact, ought to decrease suspicion. A spy does not carry a fourteen-year-old niece about with him."

"So. And what will Munn do when he finds her?"

Dr. Darell heaved his eyebrows once. "I can't say—but I presume she'll handle him."

But the house was somehow very lonely at night and Dr. Darell found that the fate of the Galaxy made remarkably little difference while his daughter's mad little life was in danger.

The excitement on the *Unimara*, if involving fewer people, was considerably more intense.

In the luggage compartment, Arcadia found herself, in the first place, aided by experience, and in the second, hampered by the reverse.

Thus, she met the initial acceleration with equanimity and the more subtle nausea that accompanied the inside-outness of the first jump through hyperspace with stoicism. Both had been experienced on space hops before, and she was tensed for them. She knew also that luggage compartments were included in the ship's ventilation-system and that they could even be bathed in wall-light. This last, however, she excluded as being too unconscionably unromantic. She remained in the dark, as a conspirator should, breathing very softly, and listening to the little miscellany of noises that surrounded Homir Munn.

They were undistinguished noises, the kind made by a man alone. The shuffling of shoes, the rustle of fabric against metal, the soughing of an upholstered chair seat retreating under weight, the sharp click of a control unit, or the soft slap of a palm over a photoelectric cell.

Yet, eventually, it was the lack of experience that caught up with Arcadia. In the book films and on the videos, the stowaway seemed to have such an infinite capacity for obscurity. Of course, there was always the danger of dislodging something which would fall with a crash, or of sneezing—in videos you were almost sure to sneeze; it was an accepted matter. She knew all this, and was careful. There was also the realization that thirst and hunger might be encountered. For this, she was prepared with ration cans out of the pantry. But yet things remained that the films never mentioned, and it dawned upon Arcadia with a shock that, despite the best intentions in the world, she could stay hidden in the closet for only a limited time.

And on a one-man sports-cruiser, such as the *Unimara*, living space consisted, essentially, of a single room, so that there wasn't even the risky possibility of sneaking out of the compartment while Munn was engaged elsewhere.

She waited frantically for the sounds of sleep to arise. If only she knew whether he snored. At least she knew where the bunk was and she could recognize the rolling protest of one when she heard it. There was a long breath and then a yawn. She waited through a gathering silence, punctuated by the bunk's soft protest against a changed position or a shifted leg.

The door of the luggage compartment opened easily at the pressure of her finger, and her craning neck—

There was a definite human sound that broke off sharply.

Arcadia solidified. Silence! Still silence!

She tried to poke her eyes outside the door without moving her head and failed. The head followed the eyes.

Homir Munn was awake, of course—reading in bed, bathed in the soft, unspreading bed light, staring into the darkness with wide eyes, and groping one hand stealthily under the pillow.

Arcadia's head moved sharply back of itself. Then, the light went out entirely and Munn's voice said with shaky sharpness, "I've got a blaster, and I'm shooting, by the Galaxy—"

And Arcadia wailed, "It's only me. Don't shoot."

Remarkable what a fragile flower romance is. A gun with a nervous operator behind it can spoil the whole thing.

The light was back on—all over the ship—and Munn was sitting up in bed. The somewhat grizzled hair on his thin chest and the sparse one-day growth on his chin lent him an entirely fallacious appearance of disreputability.

Arcadia stepped out, yanking at her metallene jacket which was supposed to be guaranteed wrinkleproof.

After a wild moment in which he almost jumped out of bed, but remembered, and instead yanked the sheet up to his shoulders, Munn gargled, "W . . . wha . . . what—"

He was completely incomprehensible.

Arcadia said meekly, "Would you excuse me for a minute? I've got to wash my hands." She knew the geography of the vessel, and slipped away quickly. When she returned, with her courage oozing back, Homir Munn was standing before her with a faded bathrobe on the outside and a brilliant fury on the inside.

"What the black holes of Space are you d . . . doing aboard this ship? H . . . how did you get on here? What do you th . . . think I'm supposed to do with you? What's going *on* here?"

He might have asked questions indefinitely, but Arcadia interrupted sweetly, "I just wanted to come along, Uncle Homir."

"*Why?* I'm not going anywhere?"

"You're going to Kalgan for information about the Second Foundation."

And Munn let out a wild howl and collapsed completely. For one horrified moment, Arcadia thought he would have hysterics or beat his head against the wall. He was still holding the blaster and her stomach grew ice-cold as she watched it.

"Watch out— Take it easy—" was all she could think of to say.

But he struggled back to relative normality and threw the blaster on to the bunk with a force that should have set it off and blown a hole through the ship's hull.

"How did you get on?" he asked slowly, as though gripping each word with his teeth very carefully to prevent it from trembling before letting it out.

"It was easy. I just came into the hangar with my suitcase, and said, 'Mr. Munn's baggage!' and the man in charge just waved his thumb without even looking up."

"I'll have to take you back, you know," said Homir, and there was a sudden wild glee within him at the thought. By Space, this wasn't his fault.

"You can't," said Arcadia, calmly, "it would attract attention."

"What?"

"*You* know. The whole purpose of *your* going to Kalgan was because it was natural for you to go and ask for permission to look into the Mule's records. And you've got to be so natural that you're to attract no attention at all. If you go back with a girl stowaway, it might even get into the tele-news reports."

"Where did you g . . . get those notions about Kalgan? These . . . uh . . . childish—" He was far too flippant for conviction, of course, even to one who knew less than did Arcadia.

"I heard," she couldn't avoid pride completely, "with a sound-recorder. I know all about it—so you've *got* to let me come along."

"What about your father?" He played a quick trump. "For all he knows, you're kidnaped . . . dead."

"I left a note," she said, overtrumping, "and he probably knows he mustn't make a fuss, or anything. You'll probably get a space-gram from him."

To Munn the only explanation was sorcery, because the receiving signal sounded wildly two seconds after she finished.

She said: "That's my father, I bet," and it was.

The message wasn't long and it was addressed to Arcadia. It

said: "Thank you for your lovely present, which I'm sure you put to good use. Have a good time."

"You see," she said, "that's instructions."

Homir grew used to her. After a while, he was glad she was there. Eventually, he wondered how he would have made it without her. She prattled! She was excited! Most of all, she was completely unconcerned. She knew the Second Foundation was the enemy, yet it didn't bother her. She knew that on Kalgan, he was to deal with a hostile officialdom, but she could hardly wait.

Maybe it came of being fourteen.

At any rate, the week-long trip now meant conversation rather than introspection. To be sure, it wasn't a very enlightening conversation, since it concerned, almost entirely, the girl's notions on the subject of how best to treat the Lord of Kalgan. Amusing and nonsensical, and yet delivered with weighty deliberation.

Homir found himself actually capable of smiling as he listened and wondered out of just which gem of historical fiction she got her twisted notion of the great universe.

It was the evening before the last jump. Kalgan was a bright star in the scarcely-twinkling emptiness of the outer reaches of the Galaxy. The ship's telescope made it a sparkling blob of barely-perceptible diameter.

Arcadia sat cross-legged in the good chair. She was wearing a pair of slacks and a none-too-roomy shirt that belonged to Homir. Her own more feminine wardrobe had been washed and ironed for the landing.

She said, "I'm going to write historical novels, you know." She was quite happy about the trip. Uncle Homir didn't the least mind listening to her and it made conversation so much more pleasant when you could talk to a really intelligent person who was serious about what you said.

She continued: "I've read books and books about all the great men of Foundation history. You know, like Seldon, Hardin, Mallow, Devers and all the rest. I've even read most of what you've written about the Mule, except that it isn't much fun to read those parts where the Foundation loses. Wouldn't you rather read a history where they skipped the silly, tragic parts?"

"Yes, I would," Munn assured her, gravely. "But it wouldn't be a fair history, would it, Arkady? You'd never get academic respect, unless you give the whole story."

"Oh, poof. Who cares about academic respect?" She found him delightful. He hadn't missed calling her Arkady for days. "My novels are going to be interesting and are going to sell and be famous. What's the use of writing books unless you sell them and become well-known? I don't want just some old professors to know me. It's got to be everybody."

Her eyes darkened with pleasure at the thought and she wriggled into a more comfortable position. "In fact, as soon as I can get father to let me, I'm going to visit Trantor, so's I can get background material on the First Empire, you know. I was born on Trantor; did you know that?"

He did, but he said, "You were?" and put just the right amount of amazement into his voice. He was rewarded with something between a beam and a simper.

"Uh-huh. My grandmother . . . you know, Bayta Darell, you've heard of *her* . . . was on Trantor once with my grandfather. In fact, that's where they stopped the Mule, when all the Galaxy was at his feet; and my father and mother went there also when they were first married. I was born there. I even lived there till mother died, only I was just three then, and I don't remember much about it. Were you ever on Trantor, Uncle Homir?"

"No, can't say I was." He leaned back against the cold bulkhead and listened idly. Kalgan was very close, and he felt his uneasiness flooding back.

"Isn't it just the most *romantic* world? My father says that under Stannel V, it had more people than any *ten* worlds nowadays. He says it was just one big world of metals—one big city—that was the capital of all the Galaxy. He's shown me pictures that he took on Trantor. It's all in ruins now, but it's still stu*pen*dous. I'd just *love* to see it again. In fact . . . Homir!"

"Yes?"

"Why don't we go there, when we're finished with Kalgan?"

Some of the fright hurtled back into his face. "What? Now don't start on that. This is business, not pleasure. Remember that."

"But it *is* business," she squeaked. "There might be incredible amounts of information on Trantor. Don't you think so?"

"No, I don't." He scrambled to his feet. "Now untangle yourself from the computer. We've got to make the last jump, and then you turn in." One good thing about landing, anyway; he was about fed up with trying to sleep on an overcoat on the metal floor.

The calculations were not difficult. The "Space Route Handbook" was quite explicit on the Foundation-Kalgan route. There was the momentary twitch of the timeless passage through hyperspace and the final light-year dropped away.

The sun of Kalgan was a sun now—large, bright, and yellow-white; invisible behind the portholes that had automatically closed on the sun-lit side.

Kalgan was only a night's sleep away.

12

Lord

Of all the worlds of the Galaxy, Kalgan undoubtedly had the
most unique history. That of the planet Terminus, for instance,
was that of an almost uninterrupted rise. That of Trantor, once
capital of the Galaxy, was that of an almost uninterrupted fall.
But Kalgan—

Kalgan first gained fame as the pleasure world of the Galaxy
two centuries before the birth of Hari Seldon. It was a pleasure
world in the sense that it made an industry—and an immensely
profitable one, at that—out of amusement.

And it was a stable industry. It was the most stable industry in
the Galaxy. When all the Galaxy perished as a civilization, little
by little, scarcely a feather's weight of catastrophe fell upon Kalgan. No matter how the economy and sociology of the neighboring sectors of the Galaxy changed, there was always an elite; and
it is always the characteristic of an elite that it possesses leisure
as *the* great reward of its elite-hood.

Kalgan was at the service, therefore, successively—and successfully—of the effete and perfumed dandies of the Imperial Court
with their sparkling and libidinous ladies; of the rough and raucous warlords who ruled in iron the worlds they had gained in
blood, with their unbridled and lascivious wenches; of the plump
and luxurious businessmen of the Foundation, with their lush and
flagitious mistresses.

It was quite undiscriminating, since they all had money. And
since Kalgan serviced all and barred none; since its commodity
was in unfailing demand; since it had the wisdom to interfere
in no world's politics, to stand on no one's legitimacy, it prospered
when nothing else did, and remained fat when all grew thin.

That is, until the Mule. Then, somehow, it fell, too, before a conqueror who was impervious to amusement, or to anything but conquest. To him all planets were alike, even Kalgan.

So for a decade, Kalgan found itself in the strange role of Galactic metropolis; mistress of the greatest Empire since the end of the Galactic Empire itself.

And then, with the death of the Mule, as sudden as the zoom, came the drop. The Foundation broke away. With it and after it, much of the rest of the Mule's dominions. Fifty years later there was left only the bewildering memory of that short space of power, like an opium dream. Kalgan never quite recovered. It could never return to the unconcerned pleasure world it had been, for the spell of power never quite releases its hold. It lived instead under a succession of men whom the Foundation called the Lords of Kalgan, but who styled themselves First Citizen of the Galaxy, in imitation of the Mule's only title, and who maintained the fiction that they were conquerors too.

The current Lord of Kalgan had held that position for five months. He had gained it originally by virtue of his position at the head of the Kalganian navy, and through a lamentable lack of caution on the part of the previous lord. Yet no one on Kalgan was quite stupid enough to go into the question of legitimacy too long or too closely. These things happened, and are best accepted.

Yet that sort of survival of the fittest in addition to putting a premium on bloodiness and evil, occasionally allowed capability to come to the fore as well. Lord Stettin was competent enough and not easy to manage.

Not easy for his eminence, the First Minister, who, with fine impartiality, had served the last lord as well as the present; and who would, if he lived long enough, serve the next as honestly.

Nor easy for the Lady Callia, who was Stettin's more than friend, yet less than wife.

In Lord Stettin's private apartments the three were alone that evening. The First Citizen, bulky and glistening in the admiral's uniform that he affected, scowled from out the unupholstered chair in which he sat as stiffly as the plastic of which it was composed. His First Minister Lev Meirus, faced him with a far-off unconcern, his long, nervous fingers stroking absently and rhythmically the deep line that curved from hooked nose along gaunt and sunken cheek to the point, nearly, of the gray-bearded chin. The Lady Callia disposed of herself gracefully on the deeply furred covering of a foamite couch, her full lips trembling a bit in an unheeded pout.

"Sir," said Meirus—it was the only title adhering to a lord who was styled only First Citizen, "you lack a certain view of the continuity of history. Your own life, with its tremendous revolutions, leads you to think of the course of civilization as something equally amenable to sudden change. But it is not."

"The Mule showed otherwise."

"But who can follow in his footsteps. He was more than man, remember. And he, too, was not entirely successful."

"Poochie," whimpered the Lady Callia, suddenly, and then shrank into herself at the furious gesture from the First Citizen.

Lord Stettin said, harshly, "Do not interrupt, Callia. Meirus, I am tired of inaction. My predecessor spent his life polishing the navy into a finely-turned instrument that has not its equal in the Galaxy. And he died with the magnificent machine lying idle. Am I to continue that? I, an Admiral of the Navy?

"How long before the machine rusts? At present, it is a drain on the Treasury and returns nothing. Its officers long for dominion, its men for loot. All Kalgan desires the return of Empire and glory. Are you capable of understanding that?"

"These are but words that you use, but I grasp your meaning. Dominion, loot, glory—pleasant when they are obtained, but the process of obtaining them is often risky and always unpleasant. The first fine flush may not last. And in all history, it has never been wise to attack the Foundation. Even the Mule would have been wiser to refrain—"

There were tears in the Lady Callia's blue, empty eyes. Of late, Poochie scarcely saw her, and now, when he had promised the evening to her, this horrible, thin, gray man, who always looked through her rather than at her, had forced his way in. And Poochie *let* him. She dared not say anything; was frightened even of the sob that forced its way out.

But Stettin was speaking now in the voice she hated, hard and impatient. He was saying: "You're a slave to the far past. The Foundation is greater in volume and population, but they are loosely knit and will fall apart at a blow. What holds them together these days is merely inertia; an inertia I am strong enough to smash. You are hypnotized by the old days when only the Foundation had atomic power. They were able to dodge the last hammer blows of the dying Empire and then faced only the unbrained anarchy of the warlords who would counter the Foundation's atomic vessels only with hulks and relics.

"But the Mule, my dear Meirus, has changed that. He spread the knowledge, that the Foundation had hoarded to 'itself, through half the Galaxy and the monopoly in science is gone forever. We can match them."

"And the Second Foundation?" questioned Meirus, coolly.

"And the Second Foundation?" repeated Stettin as coolly. "Do *you* know its intentions? It took ten years to stop the Mule, if, indeed, it was the factor, which some doubt. Are you unaware that a good many of the Foundation's psychologists and sociologists are of the opinion that the Seldon Plan has been completely disrupted since the days of the Mule? If the Plan has gone, then a vacuum exists which I may fill as well as the next man."

"Our knowledge of these matters is not great enough to warrant the gamble."

"*Our* knowledge, perhaps, but we have a Foundation visitor on the planet. Did you know that? A Homir Munn—who, I understand, has written articles on the Mule, and has expressed exactly that opinion, that the Seldon Plan no longer exists."

The First Minister nodded, "I have heard of him, or at least of his writings. What does he desire?"

"He asks permission to enter the Mule's palace."

"Indeed? It would be wise to refuse. It is never advisable to disturb the superstitions with which a planet is held."

"I will consider that—and we will speak again."

Meirus bowed himself out.

Lady Callia said tearfully, "Are you angry with me, Poochie?"

Stettin turned on her savagely. "Have I not told you before never to call me by that ridiculous name in the presence of others?"

"You *used* to like it."

"Well, I don't any more, and it is not to happen again."

He stared at her darkly. It was a mystery to him that he tolerated her these days. She was a soft, empty-headed thing, comfortable to the touch, with a pliable affection that was a convenient facet to a hard life. Yet, even that affection was becoming wearisome. She dreamed of marriage, of being First Lady.

Ridiculous!

She was all very well when he had been an admiral only—but now as First Citizen and future conqueror, he needed more. He needed heirs who could unite his future dominions, something the Mule had never had, which was why his Empire did not survive his strange nonhuman life. He, Stettin, needed someone of the great historic families of the Foundation with whom he could fuse dynasties.

He wondered testily why he did not rid himself of Callia now. It would be no trouble. She would whine a bit— He dismissed the thought. She had her points, occasionally.

Callia was cheering up now. The influence of Graybeard was gone and her Poochie's granite face was softening now. She lifted herself in a single, fluid motion and melted toward him.

"You're not going to scold me, are you?"

"No." He patted her absently. "Now just sit quietly for a while, will you? I want to think."

"About the man from the Foundation?"

"Yes."

"Poochie?" This was a pause.

"What?"

"Poochie, the man has a little girl with him, you said. Remember? Could I see her when she comes? I never—"

"Now what do you think I want him to bring his brat with him for? Is my audience room to be a grammar school? Enough of your nonsense, Callia."

"But I'll take care of her, Poochie. You won't even have to bother with her. It's just that I hardly ever see children, and you know how I love them."

He looked at her sardonically. She never tired of this approach. She loved children; i.e. *his* children; i.e. his *legitimate* children; i.e. marriage. He laughed.

"This particular little piece," he said, "is a great girl of fourteen or fifteen. She's probably as tall as you are."

Callia looked crushed. "Well, could I, anyway? She could tell me about the Foundation? I've always wanted to go there, you know. My grandfather was a Foundation man. Won't you take me there, sometime, Poochie?"

Stettin smiled at the thought. Perhaps he would, as conqueror. The good nature that the thought supplied him with made itself felt in his words, "I will, I will. And you can see the girl and talk Foundation to her all you want. But not near me, understand."

"I won't bother you, honestly. I'll have her in my own rooms." She was happy again. It was not very often these days that she was allowed to have her way. She put her arms about his neck and after the slightest hesitation, she felt its tendons relax and the large head come softly down upon her shoulder.

13

Lady

Arcadia felt triumphant. How life had changed since Pelleas Anthor had stuck his silly face up against her window—and all because she had the vision and courage to do what needed to be done.

Here she was on Kalgan. She had been to the great Central Theater—the largest in the Galaxy—and seen *in person* some of the singing stars who were famous even in the distant Foundation. She had shopped all on her own along the Flowered Path, fashion center of the gayest world in Space. And she had made her own selections because Homir just didn't know anything about it at all. The saleswomen raised no objections at all to long, shiny dresses with those vertical sweeps that made her look so tall—and Foundation money went a long, long way. Homir had given her a ten-credit bill and when she changed it to Kalganian "Kalganids," it made a terribly thick sheaf.

She had even had her hair redone—sort of half-short in back, with two glistening curls over each temple. And it was treated so that it looked goldier than ever; it just *shone*.

But *this*; this was best of all. To be sure, the Palace of Lord Stettin wasn't as grand and lavish as the theaters, or as mysterious and historical as the old palace of the Mule—of which, so far they had only glimpsed the lonely towers in their air flight across the planet—but, imagine, a real Lord. She was rapt in the glory of it.

And not only that. She was actually face to face with his Mistress. Arcadia capitalized the word in her mind, because she knew the role such women had played in history; knew their glamour and power. In fact, she had often thought of being an all-powerful and glittering creature, herself, but somehow mis-

tresses weren't in fashion at the Foundation just then and besides, her father probably wouldn't let her, if it came to that.

Of course, the Lady Callia didn't quite come up to Arcadia's
notion of the part. For one thing, she was rather plump, and
didn't look at all wicked and dangerous. Just sort of faded and
near-sighted. Her voice was high, too, instead of throaty, and—

Callia said, "Would you like more tea, child?"

"I'll have another cup, thank you, your grace,"—or was it your
highness?

Arcadia continued with a connoisseur's condescension, "Those
are lovely pearls you are wearing, my lady." (On the whole,
"my lady" seemed best.)

"Oh? Do you think so?" Callia seemed vaguely pleased. She
removed them and let them swing milkily to and fro. "Would
you like them? You can have them, if you like."

"Oh, my— You really mean—" She found them in her hand,
then, repelling them mournfully, she said, "Father wouldn't like
it."

"He wouldn't like the pearls? But they're quite nice pearls."

"He wouldn't like my taking them, I mean. You're not supposed to take expensive presents from other people, he says."

"You aren't? But . . . I mean, this was a present to me from
Poo . . . from the First Citizen. Was that wrong, do you suppose?"

Arcadia reddened. "I didn't mean—"

But Callia had tired of the subject. She let the pearls slide to
the ground and said, "You were going to tell me about the Foundation. Please do so right now."

And Arcadia was suddenly at a loss. What does one say about
a world dull to tears. To her, the Foundation was a suburban
town, a comfortable house, the annoying necessities of education,
the uninteresting eternities of a quiet life. She said, uncertainly,
"It's just like you view in the book-films, I suppose."

"Oh, do you view book-films? They give me such a headache
when I try. But do you know I always love video stories about
your Traders—such big, savage men. It's always so exciting. Is
your friend, Mr. Munn, one of them? He doesn't seem nearly

savage enough. Most of the Traders had beards and big bass voices, and were so domineering with women—don't you think so?"

Arcadia smiled, glassily. "That's just part of history, my lady. I mean, when the Foundation was young, the Traders were the pioneers pushing back the frontiers and bringing civilization to the rest of the Galaxy. We learned all about that in school. But that time has passed. We don't have Traders any more; just corporations and things."

"Really? What a shame. Then what does Mr. Munn do? I mean, if he's not a Trader."

"Uncle Homir's a librarian."

Callia put a hand to her lips and tittered. "You mean he takes care of book-films. Oh, my! It seems like such a silly thing for a grown man to do."

"He's a very good librarian, my lady. It is an occupation that is very highly regarded at the Foundation." She put down the little, iridescent teacup upon the milky-metaled table surface.

Her hostess was all concern. "But my dear child. I'm sure I didn't mean to offend you. He must be a very *intelligent* man. I could see it in his eyes as soon as I looked at him. They were so . . . so *intelligent*. And he must be brave, too, to want to see the Mule's palace."

"Brave?" Arcadia's internal awareness twitched. This was what she was waiting for. Intrigue! Intrigue! With great indifference, she asked, staring idly at her thumbtip: "Why must one be brave to wish to see the Mule's palace?"

"Didn't you know?" Her eyes were round, and her voice sank. "There's a curse on it. When he died, the Mule directed that no one ever enter it until the Empire of the Galaxy is established. Nobody on Kalgan would dare even to enter the grounds."

Arcadia absorbed that. "But that's superstition—"

"Don't say that," Callia was distressed. "Poochie always says that. He says it's useful to say it isn't though, in order to maintain his hold over the people. But I notice he's never gone in himself. And neither did Thallos, who was First Citizen before

Poochie." A thought struck her and she was all curiosity again: "But why does Mr. Munn want to see the Palace?"

And it was here that Arcadia's careful plan could be put into action. She knew well from the books she had read that a ruler's mistress was the real power behind the throne, that she was the very well-spring of influence. Therefore, if Uncle Homir failed with Lord Stettin—and she was sure he would—she must retrieve that failure with Lady Callia. To be sure, Lady Callia was something of a puzzle. She didn't seem at *all* bright. But, well, all history proved—

She said, "There's a reason, my lady—but will you keep it in confidence?"

"Cross my heart," said Callia, making the appropriate gesture on the soft, billowing whiteness of her breast.

Arcadia's thoughts kept a sentence ahead of her words. "Uncle Homir is a great authority on the Mule, you know. He's written books and books about it, and he thinks that all of Galactic history has been changed since the Mule conquered the Foundation."

"Oh, my."

"He thinks the Seldon Plan—"

Callia clapped her hands. "I know about the Seldon Plan. The videos about the Traders were always all about the Seldon Plan. It was supposed to arrange to have the Foundation win all the time. Science had something to do with it, though I could never quite see how. I always get so restless when I have to listen to explanations. But you go right ahead, my dear. It's different when you explain. You make everything seem so clear."

Arcadia continued, "Well, don't you see then that when the Foundation was defeated by the Mule, the Seldon Plan didn't work and it hasn't worked since. So who will form the Second Empire?"

"The Second Empire?"

"Yes, one must be formed some day, but how? That's the problem, you see. And there's the Second Foundation."

"The *Second* Foundation?" She was quite completely lost.

"Yes, they're the planners of history that are following in the

footsteps of Seldon. They stopped the Mule because he was premature, but now, they may be supporting Kalgan."

"Why?"

"Because Kalgan may now offer the best chance of being the
nucleus for a new Empire."

Dimly, Lady Callia seemed to grasp that. "You mean *Poochie*
is going to make a new Empire."

"We can't tell for sure. Uncle Homir thinks so, but he'll have
to see the Mule's records to find out."

"It's all very complicated," said Lady Callia, doubtfully.

Arcadia gave up. She had done her best.

Lord Stettin was in a more-or-less savage humor. The session
with the milksop from the Foundation had been quite unreward-
ing. It had been worse; it had been embarrassing. To be absolute
ruler of twenty-seven worlds, master of the Galaxy's greatest
military machine, owner of the universe's most vaulting ambition—and left to argue nonsense with an antiquarian.

Damnation!

He was to violate the customs of Kalgan, was he? To allow the
Mule's palace to be ransacked so that a fool could write another
book? The cause of science! The sacredness of knowledge! Great
Galaxy! Were these catchwords to be thrown in his face in all
seriousness? Besides—and his flesh prickled slightly—there was
the matter of the curse. He didn't believe in it; no intelligent
man could. But if he was going to defy it, it would have to be for
a better reason than any the fool had advanced.

"What do *you* want?" he snapped, and Lady Callia cringed
visibly in the doorway.

"Are you busy?"

"Yes. I am busy."

"But there's nobody here, Poochie. Couldn't I even speak to
you for a minute?"

"Oh, Galaxy! What do you want? Now hurry."

Her words stumbled. "The little girl told me they were going
into the Mule's palace. I thought we could go with her. It must
be gorgeous inside."

"She told you that, did she? Well, she isn't and we aren't. Now go tend your own business. I've had about enough of you."

"But, Poochie, why not? Aren't you going to let them? The little girl said that you were going to make an Empire!"

"I don't care what she said— What was that?" He strode to Callia and caught her firmly above the elbow, so that his fingers sank deeply into the soft flesh, "What did she tell you?"

"You're hurting me. I can't remember what she said, if you're going to look at me like that."

He released her, and she stood there for a moment, rubbing vainly at the red marks. She whimpered, "The little girl made me promise not to tell."

"That's too bad. Tell me! *Now!*"

"Well, she said the Seldon Plan was changed and that there was another Foundation somewheres that was arranging to have you make an Empire. That's all. She said Mr. Munn was a very important scientist and that the Mule's palace would have proof of all that. That's every bit of what she said. Are you angry?"

But Stettin did not answer. He left the room, hurriedly, with Callia's cowlike eyes staring mournfully after him. Two orders were sent out over the official seal of the First Citizen before the hour was up. One had the effect of sending five hundred ships of the line into space on what were officially to be termed as "war games." The other had the effect of throwing a single man into confusion.

Homir Munn ceased his preparations to leave when that second order reached him. It was, of course, official permission to enter the palace of the Mule. He read and reread it, with anything but joy.

But Arcadia was delighted. She knew what had happened.

Or, at any rate, she thought she did.

Anxiety

Poli placed the breakfast on the table, keeping one eye on the table news-recorder which quietly disgorged the bulletins of the day. It could be done easily enough without loss of efficiency, this one-eye-absent business. Since all items of food were sterilely packed in containers which served as discardable cooking units, her duties vis-a-vis breakfast consisted of nothing more than choosing the menu, placing the items on the table, and removing the residue thereafter.

She clacked her tongue at what she saw and moaned softly in retrospect.

"Oh, people are so wicked," she said, and Darell merely hemmed in reply.

Her voice took on the high-pitched rasp which she automatically assumed when about to bewail the evil of the world. "Now why do these terrible Kalganese"—she accented the second syllable and gave it a long "a"—"do like that? You'd think they'd give a body peace. But no, it's just trouble, trouble, all the time.

"Now look at that headline: 'Mobs Riot Before Foundation Consulate.' Oh, would I like to give them a piece of my mind, if I could. That's the trouble with people; they just don't remember. They just *don't* remember, Dr. Darell—got no memory at all. Look at the last war after the Mule died—of course I was just a little girl then—and oh, the fuss and trouble. My own uncle was killed, him being just in his twenties and only two years married, with a baby girl. I remember him even yet—blond hair he had, and a dimple in his chin. I have a trimensional cube of him somewheres—

"And now his baby girl has a son of her own in the navy and most like if anything happens—

"And we had the bombardment patrols, and all the old men

taking turns in the stratospheric defense—I could imagine what they would have been able to do if the Kalganese had come that far. My mother used to tell us children about the food rationing and the prices and taxes. A body could hardly make ends meet—

"You'd think if they had sense people would just never want to start it again; just have nothing to do with it. And I suppose it's not people that do it, either; I suppose even Kalganese would rather sit at home with their families and not go fooling around in ships and getting killed. It's that awful man, Stettin. It's a wonder people like that are let live. He kills the old man—what's his name—Thallos, and now he's just spoiling to be boss of everything.

"And why he wants to fight us, I don't know. He's bound to lose—like they always do. Maybe it's all in the Plan, but sometimes I'm sure it must be a wicked plan to have so much fighting and killing in it, though to be sure I haven't a word to say about Hari Seldon, who I'm sure knows much more about that than I do and perhaps I'm a fool to question him. And the *other* Foundation is as much to blame. *They* could stop Kalgan *now* and make everything fine. They'll do it anyway in the end, and you'd think they'd do it before there's any damage done."

Dr. Darell looked up. "Did you say something, Poli?"

Poli's eyes opened wide, then narrowed angrily. "Nothing, doctor, nothing at all. I haven't got a word to say. A body could as soon choke to death as say a word in this house. It's jump here, and jump there, but just try to say a word—" and she went off simmering.

Her leaving made as little impression on Darell as did her speaking.

Kalgan! Nonsense! A merely physical enemy! Those had always been beaten!

Yet he could not divorce himself of the current foolish crisis. Seven days earlier, the mayor had asked him to be Administrator of Research and Development. He had promised an answer today.

Well—

He stirred uneasily. Why, himself! Yet could he refuse? It would seem strange, and he dared not seem strange. After all, what did he care about Kalgan. To him there was only one enemy. Always had been.

While his wife had lived, he was only too glad to shirk the task; to hide. Those long, quiet days on Trantor, with the ruins of the past about them! The silence of a wrecked world and the forgetfulness of it all!

But she had died. Less than five years, all told, it had been; and after that he knew that he could live only by fighting that vague and fearful enemy that deprived him of the dignity of manhood by controlling his destiny; that made life a miserable struggle against a foreordained end; that made all the universe a hateful and deadly chess game.

Call it sublimation; he, himself did call it that—but the fight gave meaning to his life.

First to the University of Santanni, where he had joined Dr. Kleise. It had been five years well-spent.

And yet Kleise was merely a gatherer of data. He could not succeed in the real task—and when Darell had felt that as certainty, he knew it was time to leave.

Kleise may have worked in secret, yet he had to have men working for him and with him. He had subjects whose brains he probed. He had a University that backed him. All these were weaknesses.

Kleise could not understand that; and he, Darell, could not explain that. They parted enemies. It was well; they had to. He *had* to leave in surrender—in case someone watched.

Where Kleise worked with charts; Darell worked with mathematical concepts in the recesses of his mind. Kleise worked with many; Darell with none. Kleise in a University; Darell in the quiet of a suburban house.

And he was almost there.

A Second Foundationer is not human as far as his cerebrum is concerned. The cleverest physiologist, the most subtle neurochemist might detect nothing—yet the difference must be there.

And since the difference was one of the mind, it was *there* that it must be detectable.

Given a man like the Mule—and there was no doubt that the Second Foundationers had the Mule's powers, whether inborn or acquired—with the power of detecting and controlling human emotions, deduce from that the electronic circuit required, and deduce from that the last details of the encephalograph on which it could not help but be betrayed.

And now Kleise had returned into his life, in the person of his ardent young pupil, Anthor.

Folly! Folly! With his graphs and charts of people who had been tampered with. He had learned to detect that years ago, but of what use was it. He wanted the arm; not the tool. Yet he had to agree to join Anthor, since it was the quieter course.

Just as now he would become Administrator of Research and Development. It was the quieter course! And so he remained a conspiracy within a conspiracy.

The thought of Arcadia teased him for a moment, and he shuddered away from it. Left to himself, it would never have happened. Left to himself, no one would ever have been endangered but himself. Left to himself—

He felt the anger rising—against the dead Kleise, the living Anthor, all the well-meaning fools—

Well, she could take care of herself. She was a very mature little girl.

She could take care of herself!

It was a whisper in his mind—

Yet could she?

At the moment, that Dr. Darell told himself mournfully that she could, she was sitting in the coldly austere anteroom of the Executive Offices of the First Citizen of the Galaxy. For half an hour she had been sitting there, her eyes sliding slowly about the walls. There had been two armed guards at the door when she had entered with Homir Munn. They hadn't been there the other times.

She was alone, now, yet she sensed the unfriendliness of the very furnishings of the room. And for the first time.

Now, why should that be?

Homir was with Lord Stettin. Well, was that wrong?

It made her furious. In similar situations in the book-films and the videos, the hero foresaw the conclusion, was prepared for it when it came, and she—she just sat there. *Anything* could happen. *Anything!* And she just sat there.

Well, back again. Think it back. Maybe something would come.

For two weeks, Homir had nearly lived inside the Mule's palace. He had taken her once, with Stettin's permission. It was large and gloomily massive, shrinking from the touch of life to lie sleeping within its ringing memories, answering the footsteps with a hollow boom or a savage clatter. She hadn't liked it.

Better the great, gay highways of the capital city; the theaters and spectacles of a world essentially poorer than the Foundation, yet spending more of its wealth on display.

Homir would return in the evening, awed—

"It's a dream-world for me," he would whisper. "If I could only chip the palace down stone by stone, layer by layer of the aluminum sponge. If I could carry it back to Terminus— What a museum it would make."

He seemed to have lost that early reluctance. He was eager, instead; glowing. Arcadia knew that by the one sure sign; he practically never stuttered throughout that period.

One time, he said, "There are abstracts of the records of General Pritcher—"

"I know him. He was the Foundation renegade, who combed the Galaxy for the Second Foundation, wasn't he?"

"Not exactly a renegade, Arkady. The Mule had Converted him."

"Oh, it's the same thing."

"Galaxy, that combing you speak of was a hopeless task. The original records of the Seldon Convention that established both Foundations five hundred years ago, make only one reference to the Second Foundation. They say it's located 'at the other end of the Galaxy at Star's End.' That's all the Mule and Pritcher had to go on. They had no method of recognizing the Second Foundation even if they found it. What madness!

"They have records"—he was speaking to himself, but Arcadia listened eagerly—"which must cover nearly a thousand worlds, yet the number of worlds available for study must have been closer to a million. And we are no better off—"

Arcadia broke in anxiously, "*Shhh-h*" in a tight hiss.

Homir froze, and slowly recovered. "Let's not talk," he mumbled.

And now Homir was with Lord Stettin and Arcadia waited outside alone and felt the blood squeezing out of her heart for no reason at all. That was more frightening than anything else. That there seemed no reason.

On the other side of the door, Homir, too, was living in a sea of gelatin. He was fighting, with furious intensity, to keep from stuttering and, of course, could scarcely speak two consecutive words clearly as a result.

Lord Stettin was in full uniform, six-feet-six, large-jawed, and hard-mouthed. His balled, arrogant fists kept a powerful time to his sentences.

"Well, you have had two weeks, and you come to me with tales of nothing. Come, sir, tell me the worst. Is my Navy to be cut to ribbons? Am I to fight the ghosts of the Second Foundation as well as the men of the First?"

"I . . . I repeat, my lord, I am no p . . . pre . . . predictor. I . . . I am at a complete . . . loss."

"Or do you wish to go back to warn your countrymen? To deep Space with your play-acting. I want the truth or I'll have it out of you along with half your guts."

"I'm t . . . telling only the truth, and I'll have you re . . . remember, my l . . . lord, that I am a citizen of the Foundation. Y . . . you cannot touch me without harvesting m . . . m . . . more than you count on."

The Lord of Kalgan laughed uproariously. "A threat to frighten children. A horror with which to beat back an idiot. Come, Mr.

Munn, I have been patient with you. I have listened to you for twenty minutes while you detailed wearisome nonsense to me which must have cost you sleepless nights to compose. It was wasted effort. I know you are here not merely to rake through the Mule's dead ashes and to warm over the cinders you find— you come here for more than you have admitted. Is that not true?"

Homir Munn could no more have quenched the burning horror that grew in his eyes than, at that moment, he could have breathed. Lord Stettin saw that, and clapped the Foundation man upon his shoulder so that he and the chair he sat on reeled under the impact.

"Good. Now let us be frank. You are investigating the Seldon Plan. You know that it no longer holds. You know, perhaps, that *I* am the inevitable winner now; I and my heirs. Well, man, what matters it who established the Second Empire, so long as it is established. History plays no favorites, eh? Are you afraid to tell me? You see that I know your mission."

Munn said thickly, "What is it y . . . you w . . . want?"

"Your presence. I would not wish the Plan spoiled through overconfidence. You understand more of these things than I do; you can detect small flaws that I might miss. Come, you will be rewarded in the end; you will have your fair glut of the loot. What can you expect at the Foundation? To turn the tide of a perhaps inevitable defeat? To lengthen the war? Or is it merely a patriotic desire to die for your country?"

"I . . . I—" He finally spluttered into silence. Not a word would come.

"You will stay," said the Lord of Kalgan, confidently. "You have no choice. Wait"—an almost forgotten afterthought—"I have information to the effect that your niece is of the family of Bayta Darell."

Homir uttered a startled: "Yes." He could not trust himself at this point to be capable of weaving anything but cold truth.

"It is a family of note on the Foundation?"

Homir nodded, "To whom they would certainly b . . . brook no harm."

"Harm! Don't be a fool, man; I am meditating the reverse. How old is she?"

"Fourteen."

"So! Well, not even the Second Foundation, or Hari Seldon, himself, could stop time from passing or girls from becoming women."

With that, he turned on his heel and strode to a draped door which he threw open violently.

He thundered, "What in Space have you dragged your shivering carcass here for?"

The Lady Callia blinked at him, and said in a small voice, "I didn't know anyone was with you."

"Well, there is. I'll speak to you later of this, but now I want to see your back, and quickly."

Her footsteps were a fading scurry in the corridor.

Stettin returned, "She is a remnant of an interlude that has lasted too long. It will end soon. Fourteen, you say?"

Homir stared at him with a brand-new horror!

Arcadia started at the noiseless opening of a door—jumping at the jangling sliver of movement it made in the corner of her eye. The finger that crooked frantically at her met no response for long moments, and then, as if in response to the cautions enforced by the very sight of that white, trembling figure, she tiptoed her way across the floor.

Their footsteps were a taut whisper in the corridor. It was the Lady Callia, of course, who held her hand so tightly that it hurt, and for some reason, she did not mind following her. Of the Lady Callia, at least, she was not afraid.

Now, why was that?

They were in a boudoir now, all pink fluff and spun sugar. Lady Callia stood with her back against the door.

She said, "This was our private way to me . . . to my room, you know, from his office. His, you know." And she pointed with a thumb, as though even the thought of him were grinding her soul to death with fear.

"It's so lucky . . . it's so lucky—" Her pupils had blackened out the blue with their size.

"Can you tell me—" began Arcadia timidly.

And Callia was in frantic motion. "No, child, no. There is no time. Take off your clothes. Please. Please. I'll get you more, and they won't recognize you."

She was in the closet, throwing useless bits of flummery in reckless heaps upon the ground, looking madly for something a girl could wear without becoming a living invitation to dalliance.

"Here, this will do. It will have to. Do you have money? Here, take it all—and this." She was stripping her ears and fingers. "Just go home—go home to your Foundation."

"But Homir . . . my uncle." She protested vainly through the muffling folds of the sweet-smelling and luxurious spun-metal being forced over her head.

"He won't leave. Poochie will hold him forever, but *you* mustn't stay. Oh, dear, don't you understand?"

"No." Arcadia forced a standstill, "I *don't* understand."

Lady Callia squeezed her hands tightly together. "You must go back to warn your people there will be war. Isn't that clear?" Absolute terror seemed paradoxically to have lent a lucidity to her thoughts and words that was entirely out of character. "Now come!"

Out another way! Past officials who stared after them, but saw no reason to stop one whom only the Lord of Kalgan could stop with impunity. Guards clicked heels and presented arms when they went through doors.

Arcadia breathed only on occasion through the years the trip seemed to take—yet from the first crooking of the white finger to the time she stood at the outer gate, with people and noise and traffic in the distance was only twenty-five minutes.

She looked back, with a sudden frightened pity. "I . . . I . . . don't know why you're doing this, my lady, but thanks— What's going to happen to Uncle Homir?"

"I don't know," wailed the other. "Can't you leave? Go straight to the spaceport. Don't wait. He may be looking for you this very minute."

And still Arcadia lingered. She would be leaving Homir; and, belatedly, now that she felt the free air about her, she was suspicious. "But what do you care if he does?"

Lady Callia bit her lower lip and muttered, "I can't explain to a little girl like you. It would be improper. Well, you'll be growing up and I . . . I met Poochie when I was sixteen. I can't have you about, you know." There was a half-ashamed hostility in her eyes.

The implications froze Arcadia. She whispered: "What will he do to you when he finds out?"

And she whimpered back: "I don't know," and threw her arm to her head as she left at a half-run, back along the wide way to the mansion of the Lord of Kalgan.

But for one eternal second, Arcadia *still* did not move, for in that last moment before Lady Callia left, Arcadia had seen something. Those frightened, frantic eyes had momentarily—flashingly —lit up with a cold amusement.

A vast, inhuman amusement.

It was much to see in such a quick flicker of a pair of eyes, but Arcadia had no doubt of what she saw.

She was running now—running wildly—searching madly for an unoccupied public booth at which one could press a button for public conveyance.

She was not running from Lord Stettin; not from him or from all the human hounds he could place at her heels—not from all his twenty-seven worlds rolled into a single gigantic phenomenon, hallooing at her shadow.

She was running from a single, frail woman who had helped her escape. From a creature who had loaded her with money and jewels; who had risked her own life to save her. From an entity she knew, certainly and finally, to be a woman of the Second Foundation.

An air-taxi came to a soft clicking halt in the cradle. The wind of its coming brushed against Arcadia's face and stirred at the hair beneath the softly-furred hood Callia had given her.

"Where'll it be, lady?"

She fought desperately to low-pitch her voice to make it not that of a child. "How many spaceports in the city?"

"Two. Which one ya want?"

"Which is closer?"

He stared at her: "Kalgan Central, lady."

"The other one, please. I've got the money." She had a twenty-Kalganid note in her hand. The denomination of the note made little difference to her, but the taxi-man grinned appreciatively.

"Anything ya say, lady. Sky-line cabs take ya anywhere."

She cooled her cheek against the slightly musty upholstery. The lights of the city moved leisurely below her.

What should she do? *What should she do?*

It was in that moment that she knew she was a stupid, *stupid* little girl, away from her father, and frightened. Her eyes were full of tears, and deep down in her throat, there was a small, soundless cry that hurt her insides.

She wasn't afraid that Lord Stettin would catch her. Lady Callia would see to that. Lady Callia! Old, fat, stupid, but she held on to her lord, somehow. Oh, it was clear enough, now. *Everything* was clear.

That tea with Callia at which she had been so smart. Clever little Arcadia! Something inside Arcadia choked and hated itself. That tea had been maneuvered, and then Stettin had probably been maneuvered so that Homir was allowed to inspect the Palace after all. *She,* the foolish Callia, has wanted it so, and arranged to have smart little Arcadia supply a foolproof excuse, one which would arouse no suspicions in the minds of the victims, and yet involve a minimum of interference on her part.

Then why was she free? Homir was a prisoner, of course—Unless—

Unless she went back to the Foundation as a decoy—a decoy to lead others into the hands of . . . of *them.*

So she couldn't return to the Foundation—

"Spaceport, lady." The air-taxi had come to a halt. Strange! She hadn't even noticed.

What a dream-world it was.

"Thanks," she pushed the bill at him without seeing anything and was stumbling out the door, then running across the springy pavement.

Lights. Unconcerned men and women. Large gleaming bulletin boards, with the moving figures that followed every single spaceship that arrived and departed.

Where was she going? She didn't care. She only knew that she wasn't going to the Foundation! Anywhere else at all would suit.

Oh, thank Seldon, for that forgetful moment—that last split-second when Callia wearied of her act because she had to do only with a child and had let her amusement spring through.

And then something else occurred to Arcadia, something that had been stirring and moving at the base of her brain ever since the flight began—something that forever killed the fourteen in her.

And she knew that she *must* escape.

That above all. Though they located every conspirator on the Foundation; though they caught her own father; she could not, dared not, risk a warning. She could not risk her own life—not in the slightest—for the entire realm of Terminus. She was the most important person in the Galaxy. She was the *only* important person in the Galaxy.

She knew that even as she stood before the ticket-machine and wondered where to go.

Because in all the Galaxy, she and she alone, except for *they*, themselves, knew the location of the Second Foundation.

15

Through the Grid

TRANTOR *By the middle of the Interregnum, Trantor was a shadow. In the midst of the colossal ruins, there lived a small community of farmers. . . .*

ENCYCLOPEDIA GALACTICA

There is nothing, never has been anything, quite like a busy spaceport on the outskirts of a capital city of a populous planet. There are the huge machines resting mightily in their cradles. If you choose your time properly, there is the impressive sight of the sinking giant dropping to rest or, more hair-raising still, the swiftening departure of a bubble of steel. All processes involved are nearly noiseless. The motive power is the silent surge of nucleons shifting into more compact arrangements—

In terms of area, ninety-five percent of the port has just been referred to. Square miles are reserved for the machines, and for the men who serve them and for the calculators that serve both.

Only five percent of the port is given over to the floods of humanity to whom it is the way station to all the stars of the Galaxy. It is certain that very few of the anonymous many-headed stop to consider the technological mesh that knits the spaceways. Perhaps some of them might itch occasionally at the thought of the thousands of tons represented by the sinking steel that looks so small off in the distance. One of those cyclopean cylinders could, conceivably, miss the guiding beam and crash half a mile from its expected landing point—through the glassite roof of the immense waiting room perhaps—so that only a thin organic vapor and some powdered phosphates would be left behind to mark the passing of a thousand men.

It could never happen, however, with the safety devices in

use; and only the badly neurotic would consider the possibility for more than a moment.

Then what *do* they think about? It is not just a crowd, you see. It is a crowd with a purpose. That purpose hovers over the field and thickens the atmosphere. Lines queue up; parents herd their children; baggage is maneuvered in precise masses—people are *going* somewheres.

Consider then the complete psychic isolation of a single unit of this terribly intent mob that does not know where to go; yet at the same time feels more intensely than any of the others possibly can, the necessity of going somewheres; anywhere! Or almost anywhere!

Even lacking telepathy or any of the crudely definite methods of mind touching mind, there is a sufficient clash in atmosphere, in intangible mood, to suffice for despair.

To suffice? To overflow, and drench, and drown.

Arcadia Darell, dressed in borrowed clothes, standing on a borrowed planet in a borrowed situation of what seemed even to be a borrowed life, wanted earnestly the safety of the womb. She didn't know that was what she wanted. She only knew that the very openness of the open world was a great danger. She wanted a closed spot somewhere—somewhere far—somewhere in an unexplored nook of the universe—where no one would ever look.

And there she was, age fourteen plus, weary enough for eighty plus, frightened enough for five minus.

What stranger of the hundreds that brushed past her—actually brushed past her, so that she could feel their touch—was a Second Foundationer? What stranger could not help but instantly destroy her for her guilty knowledge—her unique knowledge—of knowing where the Second Foundation was?

And the voice that cut in on her was a thunderclap that iced the scream in her throat into a voiceless slash.

"Look, miss," it said, irritably, "are you using the ticket machine or are you just standing there?"

It was the first she realized that she was standing in front of a ticket machine. You put a high denomination bill into the clipper which sank out of sight. You pressed the button below your destination and a ticket came out together with the correct change as determined by an electronic scanning device that never made a mistake. It was a very ordinary thing and there is no cause for anyone to stand before it for five minutes.

Arcadia plunged a two-hundred credit into the clipper, and was suddenly aware of the button labeled "Trantor." Trantor, dead capital of the dead Empire—the planet on which she was born. She pressed it in a dream. Nothing happened, except that the red letters flicked on and off, reading 172.18—172.18—172.18—

It was the amount she was short. Another two-hundred credit. The ticket was spit out towards her. It came loose when she touched it, and the change tumbled out afterward.

She seized it and ran. She felt the man behind her pressing close, anxious for his own chance at the machine, but she twisted out from before him and did not look behind.

Yet there was nowhere to run. They were all her enemies.

Without quite realizing it, she was watching the gigantic, glowing signs that puffed into the air: *Steffani, Anacreon, Fermus*— There was even one that ballooned, *Terminus,* and she longed for it, but did not dare—

For a trifling sum, she could have hired a notifier which could have been set for any destination she cared and which would, when placed in her purse, make itself heard only to her, fifteen minutes before take-off time. But such devices are for people who are reasonably secure, however; who can pause to think of them.

And then, attempting to look both ways simultaneously, she ran head-on into a soft abdomen. She felt the startled outbreath and grunt, and a hand come down on her arm. She writhed desperately but lacked breath to do more than mew a bit in the back of her throat.

Her captor held her firmly and waited. Slowly, he came into focus for her and she managed to look at him. He was rather plump and rather short. His hair was white and copious, being brushed back to give a pompadour effect that looked strangely incongruous above a round and ruddy face that shrieked its peasant origin.

"What's the matter?" he said finally, with a frank and twinkling curiosity. "You look scared."

"Sorry," muttered Arcadia in a frenzy. "I've got to go. Pardon me."

But he disregarded that entirely, and said, "Watch out, little girl. You'll drop your ticket." And he lifted it from her resistless white fingers and looked at it with every evidence of satisfaction.

"I thought so," he said, and then bawled in bull-like tones, "*Mommuh!*"

A woman was instantly at his side, somewhat more short, somewhat more round, somewhat more ruddy. She wound a finger about a stray gray lock to shove it beneath a well-outmoded hat.

"Pappa," she said, reprovingly, "why do you shout in a crowd like that? People look at you like you were crazy. Do you think you are on the farm?"

And she smiled sunnily at the unresponsive Arcadia, and added, "He has manners like a bear." Then, sharply, "Pappa, let go the little girl. What are you doing?"

But Pappa simply waved the ticket at her. "Look," he said, "she's going to Trantor."

Mamma's face was a sudden beam, "You're from Trantor? Let go her arm, I say, Pappa." She turned the overstuffed valise she was carrying onto its side and forced Arcadia to sit down with a gentle but unrelenting pressure. "Sit down," she said, "and rest your little feet. It will be no ship yet for an hour and the benches are crowded with sleeping loafers. You are from Trantor?"

Arcadia drew a deep breath and gave in. Huskily, she said, "I was born there."

And Mamma clapped her hands gleefully, "One month we've been here and till now we met nobody from home. This is very nice. Your parents—" she looked about vaguely.

"I'm not with my parents," Arcadia said, carefully.

"All alone? A little girl like you?" Mamma was at once a blend of indignation and sympathy, "How does that come to be?"

"Mamma," Pappa plucked at her sleeve, "let me tell you.

There's something wrong. I think she's frightened." His voice, though obviously intended for a whisper was quite plainly audible to Arcadia. "She was running—I was watching her—and not looking where she was going. Before I could step out of the way, she bumped into me. And you know what? I think she's in trouble."

"So shut your mouth, Pappa. Into you, anybody could bump." But she joined Arcadia on the valise, which creaked wearily under the added weight and put an arm about the girl's trembling shoulder. "You're running away from somebody, sweetheart? Don't be afraid to tell me. I'll help you."

Arcadia looked across at the kind gray eyes of the woman and felt her lips quivering. One part of her brain was telling her that here were people from Trantor, with whom she could go, who could help her remain on that planet until she could decide what next to do, where next to go. And another part of her brain, much the louder, was telling her in jumbled incoherence that she did not remember her mother, that she was weary to death of fighting the universe, that she wanted only to curl into a little ball with strong, gentle arms about her, that if her mother had lived, she might . . . she might—

And for the first time that night, she was crying; crying like a little baby, and glad of it; clutching tightly at the old-fashioned dress and dampening a corner of it thoroughly, while soft arms held her closely and a gentle hand stroked her curls.

Pappa stood helplessly looking at the pair, fumbling futilely for a handkerchief which, when produced, was snatched from his hand. Mamma glared an admonition of quietness at him. The crowds surged about the little group with the true indifference of disconnected crowds everywhere. They were effectively alone.

Finally, the weeping trickled to a halt, and Arcadia smiled weakly as she dabbed at red eyes with the borrowed handkerchief. "Golly," she whispered, "I—"

"Shh. Shh. Don't talk," said Mamma, fussily, "just sit and rest for a while. Catch your breath. Then tell us what's wrong, and you'll see, we'll fix it up, and everything will be all right."

Arcadia scrabbled what remained of her wits together. She could not tell them the truth. She could tell nobody the truth— And yet she was too worn to invent a useful lie.

She said, whisperingly, "I'm better, now."

"Good," said Mamma. "Now tell me why you're in trouble. You did nothing wrong? Of course, whatever you did, we'll help you; but tell us the truth."

"For a friend from Trantor, anything," added Pappa, expansively, "eh, Mamma?"

"Shut your mouth, Pappa," was the response, without rancor.

Arcadia was groping in her purse. That, at least, was still hers, despite the rapid clothes-changing forced upon her in Lady Callia's apartments. She found what she was looking for and handed it to Mamma.

"These are my papers," she said, diffidently. It was shiny, synthetic parchment which had been issued her by the Foundation's ambassador on the day of her arrival and which had been countersigned by the appropriate Kalganian official. It was large, florid, and impressive. Mamma looked at it helplessly, and passed it to Pappa who absorbed its contents with an impressive pursing of the lips.

He said, "You're from the Foundation?"

"Yes. But I was born in Trantor. See it says that—"

"Ah-hah. It looks all right to me. You're named Arcadia, eh? That's a good Trantorian name. But where's your uncle? It says here you came in the company of Homir Munn, uncle."

"He's been arrested," said Arcadia, drearily.

"Arrested!"—from the two of them at once. "What for?" asked Mamma. "He did something?"

She shook her head. "I don't know. We were just on a visit. Uncle Homir had business with Lord Stettin but—" She needed no effort to act a shudder. It was there.

Pappa was impressed. "With Lord Stettin. Mm-m-m, your uncle must be a big man."

"I don't know what it was all about, but Lord Stettin wanted *me* to stay—" She was recalling the last words of Lady Callia, which had been acted out for her benefit. Since Callia, as she now knew, was an expert, the story could do for a second time.

She paused, and Mamma said interestedly, "And why you?"

"I'm not sure. He . . . he wanted to have dinner with me all alone, but I said no, because I wanted Uncle Homir along. He looked at me funny and kept holding my shoulder."

Pappa's mouth was a little open, but Mamma was suddenly red and angry. "How old are you, Arcadia?"

"Fourteen and a half, almost."

Mamma drew a sharp breath and said, "That such people should be let live. The dogs in the streets are better. You're running from him, dear, is not?"

Arcadia nodded.

Mamma said, "Pappa, go right to Information and find out exactly when the ship to Trantor comes to berth. Hurry!"

But Pappa took one step and stopped. Loud metallic words were booming overhead, and five thousand pairs of eyes looked startledly upwards.

"Men and women," it said, with sharp force. "The airport is being searched for a dangerous fugitive, and it is now surrounded. No one can enter and no one can leave. The search will, however, be conducted with great speed and no ships will reach or leave berth during the interval, so you will not miss your ship. I repeat, no one will miss his ship. The grid will descend. None of you will move outside your square until the grid is removed, as otherwise we will be forced to use our neuronic whips."

During the minute or less in which the voice dominated the vast dome of the spaceport's waiting room, Arcadia could not have moved if all the evil in the Galaxy had concentrated itself into a ball and hurled itself at her.

They could mean only her. It was not even necessary to formulate that idea as a specific thought. But why—

Callia had engineered her escape. And Callia was of the Second Foundation. Why, then, the search now? Had Callia failed? *Could* Callia fail? Or was this part of the plan, the intricacies of which escaped her?

For a vertiginous moment, she wanted to jump up and shout that she gave up, that she would go with them, that . . . that—

But Mamma's hand was on her wrist. "Quick! Quick! We'll go to the lady's room before they start."

Arcadia did not understand. She merely followed blindly. They oozed through the crowd, frozen as it was into clumps, with the voice still booming through its last words.

The grid was descending now, and Pappa, openmouthed, watched it come down. He had heard of it and read of it, but had never actually been the object of it. It glimmered in the air, simply a series of cross-hatched and tight radiation-beams that set the air aglow in a harmless network of flashing light.

It always was so arranged as to descend slowly from above in order that it might represent a falling net with all the terrific psychological implications of entrapment.

It was at waist-level now, ten feet between glowing lines in each direction. In his own hundred square feet, Pappa found himself alone, yet the adjoining squares were crowded. He felt himself conspicuously isolated but knew that to move into the greater anonymity of a group would have meant crossing one of those glowing lines, stirring an alarm, and bringing down the neuronic whip.

He waited.

He could make out over the heads of the eerily quiet and waiting mob, the far-off stir that was the line of policemen covering the vast floor area, lighted square by lighted square.

It was a long time before a uniform stepped into his square and carefully noted its co-ordinates into an official notebook.

"Papers!"

Pappa handed them over, and they were flipped through in expert fashion.

"You're Preem Palver, native of Trantor, on Kalgan for a month, returning to Trantor. Answer, yes or no."

"Yes, yes."

"What's your business on Kalgan?"

"I'm trading representative of our farm co-operative. I've been negotiating terms with the Department of Agriculture on Kal-gan."

"Um-m-m. Your wife is with you? Where is she? She is men-tioned in your papers."

"Please. My wife is in the—" He pointed.

"Hanto," roared the policeman. Another uniform joined him.

The first one said, dryly, "Another dame in the can, by the Galaxy. The place must be busting with them. Write down her name." He indicated the entry in the papers which gave it.

"Anyone else with you?"

"My niece."

"She's not mentioned in the papers."

"She came separately."

"Where is she? Never mind, I know. Write down the niece's name, too, Hanto. What's her name? Write down Arcadia Palver. You stay right here, Palver. We'll take care of the women before we leave."

Pappa waited interminably. And then, long, long after, Mamma was marching toward him, Arcadia's hand firmly in hers, the two policemen trailing behind her.

They entered Pappa's square, and one said, "Is this noisy old woman your wife?"

"Yes, sir," said Pappa, placatingly.

"Then you'd better tell her she's liable to get into trouble if she talks the way she does to the First Citizen's police." He straightened his shoulders angrily. "Is this your niece?"

"Yes, sir."

"I want her papers."

Looking straight at her husband, Mamma slightly, but no less firmly, shook her head.

A short pause, and Pappa said with a weak smile, "I don't think I can do that."

"What do you mean you can't do that?" The policeman thrust out a hard palm. "Hand it over."

"Diplomatic immunity," said Pappa, softly.

"What do you mean?"

"I said I was trading representative of my farm co-operative.

I'm accredited to the Kalganian government as an official foreign representative and my papers prove it. I showed them to you and now I don't want to be bothered any more."

For a moment, the policeman was taken aback. "I've got to see your papers. It's orders."

"You go away," broke in Mamma, suddenly. "When we want you, we'll send for you, you . . . you *bum*."

The policeman's lips tightened. "Keep your eye on them, Hanto. I'll get the lieutenant."

"Break a leg!" called Mamma after him. Someone laughed, and then choked it off suddenly.

The search was approaching its end. The crowd was growing dangerously restless. Forty-five minutes had elapsed since the grid had started falling and that is too long for best effects. Lieutenant Dirige threaded his way hastily, therefore, toward the dense center of the mob.

"Is this the girl?" he asked wearily. He looked at her and she obviously fitted the description. All this for a child.

He said, "Her papers, if you please?"

Pappa began, "I have already explained—"

"I know what you have explained, and I'm sorry," said the lieutenant, "but I have my orders, and I can't help them. If you care to make a protest later, you may. Meanwhile, if necessary, I must use force."

There was a pause, and the lieutenant waited patiently.

Then Pappa said, huskily, "Give me your papers, Arcadia."

Arcadia shook her head in panic, but Pappa nodded his head. "Don't be afraid. Give them to me."

Helplessly she reached out and let the documents change hands. Pappa fumbled them open and looked carefully through them, then handed them over. The lieutenant in his turn looked through them carefully. For a long moment, he raised his eyes to rest them on Arcadia, and then he closed the booklet with a sharp snap.

"All in order," he said. "All right, men."

He left, and in two minutes, scarcely more, the grid was gone,

and the voice above signified a back-to-normal. The noise of
the crowd, suddenly released, rose high.

Arcadia said: "How . . . how—"

Pappa said, "Sh-h. Don't say a word. Let's better go to the
ship. It should be in the berth soon."

They were on the ship. They had a private stateroom and a
table to themselves in the dining room. Two light-years already
separated them from Kalgan, and Arcadia finally dared to broach
the subject again.

She said, "But they *were* after me, Mr. Palver, and they must
have had my description and all the details. Why did he let
me go?"

And Pappa smiled broadly over his roast beef. "Well, Arcadia,
child, it was easy. When you've been dealing with agents and
buyers and competing co-operatives, you learn some of the tricks.
I've had twenty years or more to learn them in. You see, child,
when the lieutenant opened your papers, he found a five hundred credit bill inside, folded up small. Simple, no?"

"I'll pay you back— Honest, I've got lots of money."

"Well," Pappa's broad face broke into an embarrassed smile,
as he waved it away. "For a country-woman—"

Arcadia desisted. "But what if he'd taken the money and
turned me in anyway. And accused me of bribery."

"And give up five hundred credits? I know these people better
than you do, girl."

But Arcadia knew that he did *not* know people better. Not
these people. In her bed that night, she considered carefully,
and *knew* that no bribe would have stopped a police lieutenant
in the matter of catching her unless that had been planned.
They *didn't* want to catch her, yet had made every motion of
doing so, nevertheless.

Why? To make sure she left? And for Trantor? Were the ob-
tuse and soft-hearted couple she was with now only a pair of
tools in the hands of the Second Foundation, as helpless as she
herself?

They must be!

Or were they?

It was all so useless. How could she fight them. Whatever she did, it might only be what those terrible omnipotents wanted her to do.

Yet she had to outwit them. *Had* to. *Had* to! *Had* to!!

16

Beginning of War

For reason or reasons unknown to members of the Galaxy at the time of the era under discussion, Intergalactic Standard Time defines its fundamental unit, the second, as the time in which light travels 299,776 kilometers. 86,400 seconds are arbitrarily set equal to one Intergalactic Standard Day; and 365 of these days to one Intergalactic Standard Year.

Why 299,776?— Or 86,400?— Or 365?

Tradition, says the historian, begging the question. Because of certain and various mysterious numerical relationships, say the mystics, cultists, numerologists, metaphysicists. Because the original home-planet of humanity had certain natural periods of rotation and revolution from which those relationships could be derived, say a very few.

No one really knew.

Nevertheless, the date on which the Foundation cruiser, the *Hober Mallow* met the Kalganian squadron, headed by the *Fearless*, and, upon refusing to allow a search party to board, was blasted into smoldering wreckage was 185; 11692 G.E. That is, it was the 185th day of the 11,692nd year of the Galactic Era which dated from the accession of the first Emperor of the traditional Kamble dynasty. It was also 185; 419 A.S.—dating from the birth of Seldon—or 185; 348 Y.F.—dating from the establishment of the Foundation. On Kalgan it was 185; 56 F.C.—dating from the establishment of the First Citizenship by the Mule. In each case, of course, for convenience, the year was so arranged as to yield the same day number regardless of the actual day upon which the era began.

And, in addition, to all the millions of worlds of the Galaxy, there were millions of local times, based on the motions of their own particular heavenly neighbors.

But whichever you choose: 185; 11692-419-348-56—or anything —it was this day which historians later pointed to when they spoke of the start of the Stettinian war.

Yet to Dr. Darell, it was none of these at all. It was simply and quite precisely the thirty-second day since Arcadia had left Terminus.

What it cost Darell to maintain stolidity through these days was not obvious to everyone.

But Elvett Semic thought he could guess. He was an old man and fond of saying that his neuronic sheaths had calcified to the point where his thinking processes were stiff and unwieldy. He invited and almost welcomed the universal underestimation of his decaying powers by being the first to laugh at them. But his eyes were none the less seeing for being faded; his mind none the less experienced and wise, for being no longer agile.

He merely twisted his pinched lips and said, "Why don't you do something about it?"

The sound was a physical jar to Darell, under which he winced. He said, gruffly, "Where were we?"

Semic regarded him with grave eyes. "You'd better do something about the girl." His sparse, yellow teeth showed in a mouth that was open in inquiry.

But Darell replied coldly, "The question is: Can you get a Symes-Molff Resonator in the range required?"

"Well, I said I could and you weren't listening—"

"I'm sorry, Elvett. It's like this. What we're doing now can be more important to everyone in the Galaxy than the question of whether Arcadia is safe. At least, to everyone but Arcadia and myself, and I'm willing to go along with the majority. How big would the Resonator be?"

Semic looked doubtful, "I don't know. You can find it somewheres in the catalogues."

"About how big. A ton? A pound? A block long?"

"Oh, I thought you meant exactly. It's a little jigger." He indicated the first joint of his thumb. "About that."

"All right, can you do something like this?" He sketched rapidly on the pad he held in his lap, then passed it over to the old physicist, who peered at it doubtfully, then chuckled.

"Y'know, the brain gets calcified when you get as old as I am. What are you trying to do?"

Darell hesitated. He longed desperately, at the moment, for the physical knowledge locked in the other's brain, so that he need not put his thought into words. But the longing was useless, and he explained.

Semic was shaking his head. "You'd need hyper-relays. The only things that would work fast enough. A thundering lot of them."

"But it can be built?"

"Well, sure."

"Can you get all the parts? I mean, without causing comment? In line with your general work."

Semic lifted his upper lip. "Can't get fifty hyper-relays? I wouldn't use that many in my whole life."

"We're on a defense project, now. Can't you think of something harmless that would use them? We've got the money."

"Hm-m-m. Maybe I can think of something."

"How small can you make the whole gadget?"

"Hyper-relays can be had micro-size . . . wiring . . . tubes—Space, you've got a few hundred circuits there."

"I know. How big?"

Semic indicated with his hands.

"Too big," said Darell. "I've got to swing it from my belt."

Slowly, he was crumpling his sketch into a tight ball. When it was a hard, yellow grape, he dropped it into the ash tray and it was gone with the tiny white flare of molecular decomposition.

He said, "Who's at your door?"

Semic leaned over his desk to the little milky screen above the door signal. He said, "The young fellow, Anthor. Someone with him, too."

Darell scraped his chair back. "Nothing about this, Semic, to the others yet. It's deadly knowledge, if *they* find out, and two lives are enough to risk."

Pelleas Anthor was a pulsing vortex of activity in Semic's office, which, somehow, managed to partake of the age of its occupant. In the slow turgor of the quiet room, the loose, summery sleeves of Anthor's tunic seemed still a-quiver with the outer breezes.

He said, "Dr. Darell, Dr. Semic—Orum Dirige."

The other man was tall. A long straight nose that lent his thin face a saturnine appearance. Dr. Darell held out a hand.

Anthor smiled slightly. "Police Lieutenant Dirige," he amplified. Then, significantly, "Of Kalgan."

And Darell turned to stare with force at the young man. "Police Lieutenant Dirige of Kalgan," he repeated, distinctly. "And you bring him here. Why?"

"Because he was the last man on Kalgan to see your daughter. Hold, man."

Anthor's look of triumph was suddenly one of concern, and he was between the two, struggling violently with Darell. Slowly, and not gently, he forced the older man back into the chair.

"What are you trying to do?" Anthor brushed a lock of brown hair from his forehead, tossed a hip lightly upon the desk, and swung a leg, thoughtfully. "I thought I was bringing you good news."

Darell addressed the policeman directly, "What does he mean by calling you the last man to see my daughter? Is my daughter dead? Please tell me without preliminary." His face was white with apprehension.

Lieutenant Dirige said expressionlessly, "'Last man on Kalgan' was the phrase. She's not on Kalgan now. I have no knowledge past that."

"Here," broke in Anthor, "let me put it straight. Sorry if I overplayed the drama a bit, Doc. You're so inhuman about this, I forget you have feelings. In the first place, Lieutenant Dirige is one of us. He was born on Kalgan, but his father was a Foundation man brought to that planet in the service of the Mule. I answer for the lieutenant's loyalty to the Foundation.

"Now I was in touch with him the day after we stopped getting the daily report from Munn—"

"Why?" broke in Darell, fiercely. "I thought it was quite decided that we were not to make a move in the matter. You were risking their lives and ours."

"Because," was the equally fierce retort, "I've been involved in this game for longer than you. Because I know of certain contacts on Kalgan of which you know nothing. Because I act from deeper knowledge, do you understand?"

"I think you're completely mad."

"Will you listen?"

A pause, and Darell's eyes dropped.

Anthor's lips quirked into a half smile, "All right, Doc. Give me a few minutes. Tell him, Dirige."

Dirige spoke easily: "As far as I know, Dr. Darell, your daughter is at Trantor. At least, she had a ticket to Trantor at the Eastern Spaceport. She was with a Trading Representative from that planet who claimed she was his niece. Your daughter seems to have a queer collection of relatives, doctor. That was the second uncle she had in a period of two weeks, eh? The Trantorian even tried to bribe me—probably thinks that's why they got away." He smiled grimly at the thought.

"How was she?"

"Unharmed, as far as I could see. Frightened. I don't blame her for that. The whole department was after her. I still don't know why."

Darell drew a breath for what seemed the first time in several minutes. He was conscious of the trembling of his hands and controlled them with an effort. "Then she's all right. This Trading Representative, who was he? Go back to him. What part does he play in it?"

"I don't know. Do you know anything about Trantor?"

"I lived there once."

"It's an agricultural world, now. Exports animal fodder and grains, mostly. High quality! They sell them all over the Galaxy. There are a dozen or two farm co-operatives on the planet and each has its representatives overseas. Shrewd sons of guns, too—

I knew this one's record. He'd been on Kalgan before, usually with his wife. Perfectly honest. Perfectly harmless."

"Um-m-m," said Anthor. "Arcadia was born in Trantor, wasn't she, Doc?"

Darell nodded.

"It hangs together, you see. She wanted to go away—quickly and far—and Trantor would suggest itself. Don't *you* think so?"

Darell said: "Why not back here?"

"Perhaps she was being pursued and felt that she had to double off in a new angle, eh?"

Dr. Darell lacked the heart to question further. Well, then, let her be safe on Trantor, or as safe as one could be anywhere in this dark and horrible Galaxy. He groped toward the door, felt Anthor's light touch on his sleeve, and stopped, but did not turn.

"Mind if I go home with you, Doc?"

"You're welcome," was the automatic response.

By evening, the exteriormost reaches of Dr. Darell's personality, the ones that made immediate contact with other people had solidified once more. He had refused to eat his evening meal and had, instead, with feverish insistence, returned to the inchwise advance into the intricate mathematics of encephalographic analysis.

It was not till nearly midnight, that he entered the living room again.

Pelleas Anthor was still there, twiddling at the controls of the video. The footsteps behind him caused him to glance over his shoulder.

"Hi. Aren't you in bed yet? I've been spending hours on the video, trying to get something other than bulletins. It seems the F.S. *Hober Mallow* is delayed in course and hasn't been heard from."

"Really? What do they suspect?"

"What do you think? Kalganian skulduggery. There are reports that Kalganian vessels were sighted in the general space sector in which the *Hober Mallow* was last heard from?"

Darell shrugged, and Anthor rubbed his forehead doubtfully.

"Look, doc," he said, "why don't you go to Trantor?"

"Why should I?"

"Because you're no good to us here. You're not yourself. You can't be. And you could accomplish a purpose by going to Trantor, too. The old Imperial Library with the complete records of the Proceedings of the Seldon Commission are there—"

"No! The Library has been picked clean and it hasn't helped anyone."

"It helped Ebling Mis once."

"How do you know? Yes, he *said* he found the Second Foundation, and my mother killed him five seconds later as the only way to keep him from unwittingly revealing its location to the Mule. But in doing so, she also, you realize, made it impossible ever to tell whether Mis *really* did know the location. After all, no one else has ever been able to deduce the truth from those records."

"Ebling Mis, if you'll remember, was working under the driving impetus of the Mule's mind."

"I know that, too, but Mis' mind was, by that very token, in an abnormal state. Do you and I know anything about the properties of a mind under the emotional control of another; about its abilities and shortcomings? In any case, I will not go to Trantor."

Anthor frowned, "Well, why the vehemence? I merely suggested it as—well, by Space, I don't understand you. You look ten years older. You're obviously having a hellish time of it. You're not doing anything of value here. If I were you, I'd go and get the girl."

"Exactly! It's what I want to do, too. *That's why I won't do it.* Look, Anthor, and try to understand. You're playing—we're both playing—with something completely beyond our powers to fight. In cold blood, if you have any, you know that, whatever you may think in your moments of quixoticism.

"For fifty years, we've known that the Second Foundation is the real descendent and pupil of Seldonian mathematics. What that means, and you know that, too, is that nothing in the Galaxy happens which does not play a part in their reckoning. To us, all life is a series of accidents, to be met with by improvisations. To them, all life is purposive and should be met by pre-calculation.

"But they have their weakness. Their work is statistical and only the mass action of humanity is truly inevitable. Now how *I* play a part, as an individual, in the foreseen course of history, I don't know. Perhaps I have no definite part, since the Plan leaves individuals to indeterminacy and free will. But I am important and they—*they*, you understand—may at least have calculated my probable reaction. So I distrust, my impulses, my desires, my probable reactions.

"I would rather present them with an *im*probable reaction. I will stay here, despite the fact that I yearn very desperately to leave. No! *Because* I yearn very desperately to leave."

The younger man smiled sourly. "You don't know your own mind as well as *they* might. Suppose that—knowing you—they might count on what you think, merely *think*, is the improbable reaction, simply by knowing in advance what your line of reasoning would be."

"In that case, there is no escape. For if I follow the reasoning you have just outlined and go to Trantor, they may have foreseen that, too. There is an endless cycle of double-double-double-doublecrosses. No matter how far I follow that cycle, I can only either go or stay. The intricate act of luring my daughter halfway across the Galaxy cannot be meant to make me stay where I am, since I would most certainly have stayed if they had done nothing. It can only be to make me move, and so I will stay.

"And besides, Anthor, not everything bears the breath of the Second Foundation; not all events are the results of their puppeting. They may have had nothing to do with Arcadia's leave-taking, and she may be safe on Trantor when all the rest of us are dead."

"No," said Anthor, sharply, "now you are off the track."

"You have an alternative interpretation?"

"I have—if you'll listen."

"Oh, go ahead. I don't lack patience."

"Well, then—how well do you know your own daughter?"

"How well can any individual know any other? Obviously, my knowledge is inadequate."

"So is mine on that basis, perhaps even more so—but at least, I viewed her with fresh eyes. Item one: She is a ferocious little romantic, the only child of an ivory-tower academician, growing up in an unreal world of video and book-film adventure. She lives in a weird self-constructed fantasy of espionage and intrigue. Item two: She's intelligent about it; intelligent enough to outwit us, at any rate. She planned carefully to overhear our first conference and succeeded. She planned carefully to go to Kalgan with Munn and succeeded. Item three: She has an unholy hero-worship of her grandmother—your mother—who defeated the Mule.

"I'm right so far, I think? All right, then. Now, unlike you, I've received a complete report from Lieutenant Dirige and, in addition, my sources of information on Kalgan are rather complete, and all sources check. We know, for instance, that Homir Munn, in conference with the Lord of Kalgan was refused admission to the Mule's Palace, and that this refusal was suddenly abrogated after Arcadia had spoken to Lady Callia, the First Citizen's very good friend."

Darell interrupted. "And how do you know all this?"

"For one thing, Munn was interviewed by Dirige as part of the police campaign to locate Arcadia. Naturally, we have a complete transcript of the questions and answers.

"And take Lady Callia herself. It is rumored that she has lost Stettin's interest, but the rumor isn't borne out by facts. She not only remains unreplaced; is not only able to mediate the lord's refusal to Munn into an acceptance; but can even engineer Arcadia's escape openly. Why, a dozen of the soldiers about Stettin's executive mansion testified that they were seen together on the last evening. Yet she remains unpunished. This despite the fact that Arcadia was searched for with every appearance of diligence."

"But what is your conclusion from all this torrent of ill-connection?"

"That Arcadia's escape was arranged."

"As I said."

"With this addition. That Arcadia must have known it was arranged; that Arcadia, the bright little girl who saw cabals everywhere, saw this one and followed your own type of reasoning. They wanted her to return to the Foundation, and so she went to Trantor, instead. But why Trantor?"

"Well, why?"

"Because that is where Bayta, her idolized grandmother, escaped when *she* was in flight. Consciously or unconsciously, Arcadia imitated that. I wonder, then, if Arcadia was fleeing the same enemy."

"The Mule?" asked Darell with polite sarcasm.

"Of course not. I mean, by the enemy, a mentality that she could not fight. She was running from the Second Foundation, or such influence thereof as could be found on Kalgan."

"What influence is this you speak of?"

"Do you expect Kalgan to be immune from that ubiquitous menace? We both have come to the conclusion, somehow, that Arcadia's escape was arranged. Right? She was searched for and found, but deliberately allowed to slip away by Dirige. By Dirige, do you understand? But how was that? Because he was our man. But how did they know that? Were they counting on him to be a traitor? Eh, doc?"

"Now you're saying that they honestly meant to recapture her. Frankly, you're tiring me a bit, Anthor. Finish your say; I want to go to bed."

"My say is quickly finished." Anthor reached for a small group of photo-records in his inner pocket. It was the familiar wigglings of the encephalograph. "Dirige's brainwaves," Anthor said, casually, "taken since he returned."

It was quite visible to Darell's naked eye, and his face was gray when he looked up. "He is Controlled."

"Exactly. He allowed Arcadia to escape not because he was our man but because he was the Second Foundation's."

"Even after he knew she was going to Trantor, and not to Terminus."

Anthor shrugged. "He had been geared to let her go. There was no way *he* could modify that. He was only a tool, you see. It was just that Arcadia followed the least probable course, and is probably safe. Or at least safe until such time as the Second Foundation can modify the plans to take into account this changed state of affairs—"

He paused. The little signal light on the video set was flashing. On an independent circuit, it signified the presence of emergency news. Darell saw it, too, and with the mechanical movement of long habit turned on the video. They broke in upon the middle of a sentence but before its completion, they knew that the *Hober Mallow,* or the wreck thereof, had been found and that, for the first time in nearly half a century, the Foundation was again at war.

Anthor's jaw was set in a hard line. "All right, doc, you heard that. Kalgan has attacked; and Kalgan is under the control of the Second Foundation. Will you follow your daughter's lead and move to Trantor?"

"No. I will risk it. Here."

"Dr. Darell. You are not as intelligent as your daughter. I wonder how far you can be trusted." His long level stare held Darell for a moment, and then without a word, he left.

And Darell was left in uncertainty and—almost—despair.

Unheeded, the video was a medley of excited sight-sound, as it described in nervous detail the first hour of the war between Kalgan and the Foundation.

17

War

The mayor of the Foundation brushed futilely at the picket fence of hair that rimmed his skull. He sighed. "The years that we have wasted; the chances we have thrown away. I make no recriminations, Dr. Darell, but we deserve defeat."

Darell said, quietly, "I see no reason for lack of confidence in events, sir."

"Lack of confidence! Lack of confidence! By the Galaxy, Dr. Darell, on what would you base any other attitude? Come here—"

He half-led half-forced Darell toward the limpid ovoid cradled gracefully on its tiny force-field support. At a touch of the mayor's hand, it glowed within—an accurate three-dimensional model of the Galactic double-spiral.

"In yellow," said the mayor, excitedly, "we have that region of Space under Foundation control; in red, that under Kalgan."

What Darell saw was a crimson sphere resting within a stretching yellow fist that surrounded it on all sides but that toward the center of the Galaxy.

"Galactography," said the mayor, "is our greatest enemy. Our admirals make no secret of our almost hopeless, strategic position. Observe. The enemy has inner lines of communication. He is concentrated; can meet us on all sides with equal ease. He can defend himself with minimum force.

"We are expanded. The average distance between inhabited systems within the Foundation is nearly three times that within Kalgan. To go from Santanni to Locris, for instance, is a voyage of twenty-five hundred parsecs for us, but only eight hundred parsecs for them, if we remain within our respective territories—"

Darell said, "I understand all that, sir."

"And you do not understand that it may mean defeat."

"There is more than distance to war. I say we cannot lose. It is quite impossible."

"And why do you say that?"

"Because of my own interpretation of the Seldon Plan."

"Oh," the mayor's lips twisted, and the hands behind his back flapped one within the other, "then you rely, too, on the mystical help of the Second Foundation."

"No. Merely on the help of inevitability—and of courage and persistence."

And yet behind his easy confidence, he wondered—

What if—

Well— What if Anthor were right, and Kalgan were a direct tool of the mental wizards. What if it was their purpose to defeat and destroy the Foundation. No! It made no sense!

And yet—

He smiled bitterly. Always the same. Always that peering and peering through the opaque granite which, to the enemy, was so transparent.

Nor were the galactographic verities of the situation lost upon Stettin.

The Lord of Kalgan stood before a twin of the Galactic model which the mayor and Darell had inspected. Except that where the mayor frowned, Stettin smiled.

His admiral's uniform glistered imposingly upon his massive figure. The crimson sash of the Order of the Mule awarded him by the former First Citizen whom six months later he had replaced somewhat forcefully, spanned his chest diagonally from right shoulder to waist. The Silver Star with Double Comets and Swords sparkled brilliantly upon his left shoulder.

He addressed the six men of his general staff whose uniforms were only less grandiloquent than his own, and his First Minister as well, thin and gray—a darkling cobweb, lost in the brightness.

Stettin said, "I think the decisions are clear. We can afford to wait. To them, every day of delay will be another blow at their morale. If they attempt to defend all portions of their realm, they will be spread thin and we can strike through in two simultaneous thrusts here and here." He indicated the directions on the Galactic model—two lances of pure white shooting through the yellow fist from the red ball it inclosed, cutting Terminus off on either side in a tight arc. "In such a manner, we cut their fleet into three parts which can be defeated in detail. If they concentrate, they give up two-thirds of their dominions voluntarily and will probably risk rebellion."

The First Minister's thin voice alone seeped through the hush that followed. "In six months," he said, "the Foundation will grow six months stronger. Their resources are greater, as we all know; their navy is numerically stronger; their manpower is virtually inexhaustible. Perhaps a quick thrust would be safer."

His was easily the least influential voice in the room. Lord Stettin smiled and made a flat gesture with his hand. "The six months—or a year, if necessary—will cost us nothing. The men of the Foundation cannot prepare; they are ideologically incapable of it. It is in their very philosophy to believe that the Second Foundation will save them. But not this time, eh?"

The men in the room stirred uneasily.

"You lack confidence, I believe," said Stettin, frigidly. "Is it necessary once again to describe the reports of our agents in Foundation territory, or to repeat the findings of Mr. Homir Munn, the Foundation agent now in our . . . uh . . . service? Let us adjourn, gentlemen."

Stettin returned to his private chambers with a fixed smile still on his face. He sometimes wondered about this Homir Munn. A queer water-spined fellow who certainly did not bear out his early promise. And yet he crawled with interesting information that carried conviction with it—particularly when Callia was present.

His smile broadened. That fat fool had her uses, after all. At least, she got more with her wheedling out of Munn than he could, and with less trouble. Why not give her to Munn? He frowned. Callia. She and her stupid jealousy. Space! If he still had the Darell girl— Why hadn't he ground her skull to powder for that?

He couldn't quite put his finger on the reason.

Maybe because she got along with Munn. And he needed Munn. It was Munn, for instance, who had demonstrated that, at least in the belief of the Mule, there was no Second Foundation. His admirals needed that assurance.

He would have liked to make the proofs public, but it was better to let the Foundation believe in their nonexistent help. Was it actually Callia who had pointed that out? That's right. She had said—

Oh, nonsense! She couldn't have said anything.

And yet—

He shook his head to clear it and passed on.

18

Ghost of a World

Trantor was a world in dregs and rebirth. Set like a faded jewel in the midst of the bewildering crowd of suns at the center of the Galaxy—in the heaps and clusters of stars piled high with aimless prodigality—it alternately dreamed of past and future.

Time had been when the insubstantial ribbons of control had stretched out from its metal coating to the very edges of stardom. It had been a single city, housing four hundred billion administrators; the mightiest capital that had ever been.

Until the decay of the Empire eventually reached it and in the Great Sack of a century ago, its drooping powers had been bent back upon themselves and broken forever. In the blasting ruin of death, the metal shell that circled the planet wrinkled and crumpled into an aching mock of its own grandeur.

The survivors tore up the metal plating and sold it to other planets for seed and cattle. The soil was uncovered once more and the planet returned to its beginnings. In the spreading areas of primitive agriculture, it forgot its intricate and colossal past.

Or would have but for the still mighty shards that heaped their massive ruins toward the sky in bitter and dignified silence.

Arcadia watched the metal rim of the horizon with a stirring of the heart. The village in which the Palvers lived was but a huddle of houses to her—small and primitive. The fields that surrounded it were golden-yellow, wheat-clogged tracts.

But there, just past the reaching point was the memory of the past, still glowing in unrusted splendor, and burning with fire where the sun of Trantor caught it in gleaming highlights. She had been there once during the months since she had arrived at Trantor. She had climbed onto the smooth, unjointed pavement and ventured into the silent dust-streaked structures, where the light entered through the jags of broken walls and partitions.

It had been solidified heartache. It had been blasphemy.

She had left, clangingly—running until her feet pounded softly on earth once more.

And then she could only look back longingly. She dared not disturb that mighty brooding once more.

Somewhere on this world, she knew, she had been born— near the old Imperial Library, which was the veriest Trantor of Trantor. It was the sacred of the sacred; the holy of holies! Of all the world, it alone had survived the Great Sack and for a century it had remained complete and untouched; defiant of the universe.

There Hari Seldon and his group had woven their unimaginable web. There Ebling Mis pierced the secret, and sat numbed in his vast surprise, until he was killed to prevent the secret from going further.

There at the Imperial Library, her grandparents had lived for ten years, until the Mule died, and they could return to the re-born Foundation.

There at the Imperial Library, her own father returned with his bride to find the Second Foundation once again, but failed. There, she had been born and there her mother had died.

She would have liked to visit the Library, but Preem Palver shook his round head. "It's thousands of miles, Arkady, and there's so much to do here. Besides, it's not good to bother there. You know; it's a shrine—"

But Arcadia knew that he had no desire to visit the Library; that it was a case of the Mule's Palace over again. There was this superstitious fear on the part of the pygmies of the present for the relics of the giants of the past.

Yet it would have been horrible to feel a grudge against the funny little man for that. She had been on Trantor now for nearly three months and in all that time, he and she—Pappa and Mamma—had been wonderful to her—

And what was her return? Why, to involve them in the common ruin. Had she warned them that she was marked for destruction, perhaps? No! She let them assume the deadly role of protectors.

Her conscience panged unbearably—yet what choice had she? She stepped reluctantly down the stairs to breakfast. The voices reached her.

Preem Palver had tucked the napkin down his shirt collar with a twist of his plump neck and had reached for his poached eggs with an uninhibited satisfaction.

"I was down in the city yesterday, Mamma," he said, wielding his fork and nearly drowning the words with a capacious mouthful.

"And what is down in the city, Pappa?" asked Mamma indifferently, sitting down, looking sharply about the table, and rising again for the salt.

"Ah, not so good. A ship came in from out Kalgan-way with newspapers from there. It's war there."

"War! So! Well, let them break their heads, if they have no more sense inside. Did your pay check come yet? Pappa, I'm telling you again. You warn old man Cosker this isn't the only cooperative in the world. It's bad enough they pay you what I'm ashamed to tell my friends, but at least on time they could be!"

"Time; shmime," said Pappa, irritably. "Look, don't make me silly talk at breakfast, it should choke me each bite in the throat," and he wreaked havoc among the buttered toast as he said it. He added, somewhat more moderately, "The fighting is between Kalgan and the Foundation, and for two months, they've been at it."

His hands lunged at one another in mock-representation of a space fight.

"Um-m-m. And what's doing?"

"Bad for the Foundation. Well, you saw Kalgan; all soldiers. They were ready. The Foundation was not, and so—*poof!*"

And suddenly, Mamma laid down her fork and hissed, "Fool!"

"Huh?"

"Dumb-head! Your big mouth is always moving and wagging."

She was pointing quickly and when Pappa looked over his shoulder, there was Arcadia, frozen in the doorway.

She said, "The Foundation is at war?"

Pappa looked helplessly at Mamma, then nodded.

"And they're losing?"

Again the nod.

Arcadia felt the unbearable catch in her throat, and slowly approached the table. "Is it over?" she whispered.

"Over?" repeated Pappa, with false heartiness. "Who said it was over? In war, lots of things can happen. And . . . and—"

"Sit down, darling," said Mamma, soothingly. "No one should talk before breakfast. You're not in a healthy condition with no food in the stomach."

But Arcadia ignored her. "Are the Kalganians on Terminus?"

"No," said Pappa, seriously. "The news is from last week, and Terminus is still fighting. This is honest. I'm telling the truth. And the Foundation is still strong. Do you want me to get you the newspapers?"

"Yes!"

She read them over what she could eat of her breakfast and her eyes blurred as she read. Santanni and Korell were gone—without a fight. A squadron of the Foundation's navy had been trapped in the sparsely-sunned Ifni sector and wiped out to almost the last ship.

And now the Foundation was back to the Four-Kingdom core—the original Realm which had been built up under Salvor Hardin, the first mayor. But still it fought—and still there might be a chance—and whatever happened, she must inform her father. She must somehow reach his ear. She *must!*

But how? With a war in the way.

She asked Pappa after breakfast, "Are you going out on a new mission soon, Mr. Palver?"

Pappa was on the large chair on the front lawn, sunning himself. A fat cigar smoldered between his plump fingers and he looked like a beatific pug-dog.

"A mission?" he repeated, lazily. "Who knows? It's a nice vacation and my leave isn't up. Why talk about new missions? You're restless, Arkady?"

"Me? No, I like it here. You're very good to me, you and Mrs. Palver."

He waved his hand at her, brushing away her words.

Arcadia said, "I was thinking about the war."

"But don't think about it. What can *you* do? If it's something you can't help, why hurt yourself over it?"

"But I was thinking that the Foundation has lost most of its farming worlds. They're probably rationing food there."

Pappa looked uncomfortable. "Don't worry. It'll be all right."

She scarcely listened. "I wish I could carry food to them, that's what. You know after the Mule died, and the Foundation rebelled, Terminus was just about isolated for a time and General Han Pritcher, who succeeded the Mule for a while was laying siege to it. Food was running awfully low and my father says that *his* father told him that they only had dry amino-acid concentrates that tasted terrible. Why, one egg cost two hundred credits. And then they broke the siege just in time and food ships came through from Santanni. It must have been an awful time. Probably it's happening all over, now."

There was a pause, and then Arcadia said, "You know, I'll bet the Foundation would be willing to pay smuggler's prices for food now. Double and triple and more. Gee, if any co-operative, f'r instance, here on Trantor took over the job, they might lose some ships, but, I'll bet they'd be war millionaires before it was over. The Foundation Traders in the old days used to do that all the time. There'd be a war, so they'd sell whatever was needed bad and take their chances. Golly, they used to make as much as two million dollars out of one trip—*profit*. That was just out of what they could carry on one ship, too."

Pappa stirred. His cigar had gone out, unnoticed. "A deal for food, huh? Hm-m-m— But the Foundation is so far away."

"Oh, I know. I guess you couldn't do it from here. If you took a regular liner you probably couldn't get closer than Massena or Smushyk, and after that you'd have to hire a small scoutship or something to slip you through the lines."

Pappa's hand brushed at his hair, as he calculated.

Two weeks later, arrangements for the mission were completed. Mamma railed for most of the time— First, at the incurable obstinacy with which he courted suicide. Then, at the incredible obstinacy with which he refused to allow her to accompany him.

Pappa said, "Mamma, why do you act like an old lady. I can't take you. It's a man's work. What do you think a war is? Fun? Child's play?"

"Then why do *you* go? Are *you* a man, you old fool—with a leg and half an arm in the grave. Let some of the young ones go— not a fat bald-head like you?"

"I'm not a bald-head," retorted Pappa, with dignity. "I got yet lots of hair. And why should it not be me that gets the commission? Why, a young fellow? Listen, this could mean millions?"

She knew that and she subsided.

Arcadia saw him once before he left.

She said, "Are you going to Terminus?"

"Why not? You say yourself they need bread and rice and potatoes. Well, I'll make a deal with them, and they'll get it."

"Well, then—just one thing: If you're going to Terminus, could you . . . would you see my father?"

And Pappa's face crinkled and seemed to melt into sympathy, "Oh—and I have to wait for you to tell me. Sure, I'll see him. I'll tell him you're safe and everything's O.K., and when the war is over, I'll bring you back."

"Thanks. I'll tell you how to find him. His name is Dr. Toran Darell and he lives in Stanmark. That's just outside Terminus City, and you can get a little commuting plane that goes there. We're at 55 Channel Drive."

"Wait, and I'll write it down."

"No, no," Arcadia's arm shot out. "You mustn't write anything down. You must remember—and find him without anybody's help."

Pappa looked puzzled. Then he shrugged his shoulders. "All right, then. It's 55 Channel Drive in Stanmark, outside Terminus City, and you commute there by plane. All right?"

"One other thing."

"Yes?"

"Would you tell him something from me?"

"Sure."

"I want to whisper it to you."

He leaned his plump cheek toward her, and the little whispered sound passed from one to the other.

Pappa's eyes were round. "That's what you want me to say? But it doesn't make sense."

"He'll know what you mean. Just say I sent it and that I said he would know what it means. And you say it exactly the way I told you. No different. You won't forget it?"

"How can I forget it? Five little words. Look—"

"No, no." She hopped up and down in the intensity of her feelings. "Don't repeat it. Don't ever repeat it to anyone. Forget all about it except to my father. Promise me."

Pappa shrugged again. "I promise! All right!"

"All right," she said, mournfully, and as he passed down the drive to where the air taxi waited to take him to the spaceport, she wondered if she had signed his death warrant. She wondered if she would ever see him again.

She scarcely dared to walk into the house again to face the good, kind Mamma. Maybe when it was all over, she had better kill herself for what she had done to them.

19

End of War

QUORISTON, BATTLE OF *Fought on 9, 17, 377 F.E. between the forces of the Foundation and those of Lord Stettin of Kalgan, it was the last battle of consequence during the Interregnum....*

ENCYCLOPEDIA GALACTICA

Jole Turbor, in his new role of war correspondent, found his bulk incased in a naval uniform, and rather liked it. He enjoyed being back on the air, and some of the fierce helplessness of the futile fight against the Second Foundation left him in the excitement of another sort of fight with substantial ships and ordinary men.

To be sure, the Foundation's fight had not been remarkable for victories, but it was still possible to be philosophic about the matter. After six months, the hard core of the Foundation was untouched, and the hard core of the Fleet was still in being. With the new additions since the start of the war, it was almost as strong numerically, and stronger technically, than before the defeat at Ifni.

And meanwhile, planetary defenses were being strengthened; the armed forces better trained; administrative efficiency was having some of the water squeezed out of it—and much of the Kalganian's conquering fleet was being wallowed down through the necessity of occupying the "conquered" territory.

At the moment, Turbor was with the Third Fleet in the outer reaches of the Anacreonian sector. In line with his policy of making this a "little man's war," he was interviewing Fennel Leemor, Engineer Third Class, volunteer.

"Tell us a little about yourself, sailor," said Turbor.

"Ain't much to tell," Leemor shuffled his feet and allowed a faint, bashful smile to cover his face, as though he could see all the millions that undoubtedly could see him at the moment. "I'm a Locrian. Got a job in an air-car factory; section head and good pay. I'm married; got two kids, both girls. Say, I couldn't say hello to them, could I—in case they're listening."

"Go ahead, sailor. The video is all yours."

"Gosh, thanks." He burbled, "Hello, Milla, in case you're listening, I'm fine. Is Sunni all right? And Tomma? I think of you all the time and maybe I'll be back on furlough after we get back to port. I got your food parcel but I'm sending it back. We get our regular mess, but they say the civilians are a little tight. I guess that's all."

"I'll look her up next time I'm on Locris, sailor, and make sure she's not short of food. O.K.?"

The young man smiled broadly and nodded his head. "Thank you, Mr. Turbor. I'd appreciate that."

"All right. Suppose you tell us, then— You're a volunteer, aren't you?"

"Sure am. If anyone picks a fight with me, I don't have to wait for anyone to drag me in. I joined up the day I heard about the *Hober Mallow.*"

"That's a fine spirit. Have you seen much action? I notice you're wearing two battle stars."

"*Ptah.*" The sailor spat. "Those weren't battles, they were chases. The Kalganians don't fight, unless they have odds of five to one or better in their favor. Even then they just edge in and try to cut us up ship by ship. Cousin of mine was at Ifni and he was on a ship that got away, the old *Ebling Mis.* He says it was the same there. They had their Main Fleet against just a wing division of ours, and down to where we only had five ships left, they kept stalking instead of fighting. We got twice as many of their ships at *that* fight."

"Then you think we're going to win the war?"

"Sure bet; now that we aren't retreating. Even if things got too bad, that's when I'd expect the Second Foundation to step in. We still got the Seldon Plan—and *they* know it, too."

Turbor's lips curled a bit. "You're counting on the Second Foundation, then?"

The answer came with honest surprise. "Well, doesn't everyone?"

Junior Officer Tippellum stepped into Turbor's room after the visicast. He shoved a cigarette at the correspondent and knocked his cap back to a perilous balance on the occiput.

"We picked up a prisoner," he said.

"Yes?"

"Little crazy fellow. Claims to be a neutral—diplomatic immunity, no less. I don't think they know what to do with him. His name's Palvro, Palver, something like that, and he says he's from Trantor. Don't know what in space he's doing in a war zone."

But Turbor had swung to a sitting position on his bunk and the nap he had been about to take was forgotten. He remembered quite well his last interview with Darell, the day after war had been declared and he was shoving off.

"Preem Palver," he said. It was a statement.

Tippellum paused and let the smoke trickle out the sides of his mouth. "Yeah," he said, "how in space did you know?"

"Never mind. Can I see him?"

"Space, *I* can't say. The old man has him in his own room for questioning. Everyone figures he's a spy."

"You tell the old man that I know him, if he's who he claims he is. I'll take the responsibility."

Captain Dixyl on the flagship of the Third Fleet watched unremittingly at the Grand Detector. No ship could avoid being a source of subatomic radiation—not even if it were lying an inert mass—and each focal point of such radiation was a little sparkle in the three-dimensional field.

Each one of the Foundation's ships were accounted for and no sparkle was left over, now that the little spy who claimed to be a neutral had been picked up. For a while, that outside ship had created a stir in the captain's quarters. The tactics might have needed changing on short notice. As it was—

"Are you sure you have it?" he asked.

Commander Cenn nodded. "I will take my squadron through hyperspace: radius, 10.00 parsecs; theta, 268.52 degrees; phi, 84.15 degrees. Return to origin at 1330. Total absence 11.83 hours."

"Right. Now we are going to count on pin-point return as regards both space and time. Understand?"

"Yes, captain." He looked at his wrist watch, "My ships will be ready by 0140."

"Good," said Captain Dixyl.

The Kalganian squadron was not within detector range now, but they would be soon. There was independent information to that effect. Without Cenn's squadron the Foundation forces would be badly outnumbered, but the captain was quite confident. *Quite* confident.

Preem Palver looked sadly about him. First at the tall, skinny admiral; then at the others, everyone in uniform; and now at this last one, big and stout, with his collar open and no tie—not like the rest—who said he wanted to speak to him.

Jole Turbor was saying: "I am perfectly aware, admiral, of the serious possibilities involved here, but I tell you that if I can be allowed to speak to him for a few minutes, I may be able to settle the current uncertainty."

"Is there any reason why you can't question him before me?"

Turbor pursed his lips and looked stubborn. "Admiral," he said, "while I have been attached to your ships, the Third Fleet has received an excellent press. You may station men outside the door, if you like, and you may return in five minutes. But, meanwhile, humor me a bit, and your public relations will not suffer. Do you understand me?"

He did.

Then Turbor in the isolation that followed, turned to Palver, and said, "Quickly—what is the name of the girl you abducted."

And Palver could simply stare round-eyed, and shake his head.

"No nonsense," said Turbor. "If you do not answer, you will be a spy and spies are blasted without trial in war time."

"Arcadia Darell!" gasped Palver.

"*Well!* All right, then. Is she safe?"

Palver nodded.

"You had better be sure of that, or it won't be well for you."

"She is in good health, perfectly safe," said Palver, palely.

The admiral returned, "Well?"

"The man, sir, is not a spy. You may believe what he tells you. I vouch for him."

"That so?" The admiral frowned. "Then he represents an agricultural co-operative on Trantor that wants to make a trade treaty with Terminus for the delivery of grains and potatoes. Well, all right, but he can't leave now."

"Why not?" asked Palver, quickly.

"Because we're in the middle of a battle. After it is over—assuming we're still alive—we'll take you to Terminus."

The Kalganian fleet that spanned through space detected the Foundation ships from an incredible distance and were themselves detected. Like little fireflies in each other's Grand Detectors, they closed in across the emptiness.

And the Foundation's admiral frowned and said, "This must be their main push. Look at the numbers." Then, "They won't stand up before us, though; not if Cenn's detachment can be counted on."

Commander Cenn had left hours before—at the first detection of the coming enemy. There was no way of altering the plan now. It worked or it didn't, but the admiral felt quite comfortable. As did the officers. As did the men.

Again watch the fireflies.

Like a deadly ballet dance, in precise formations, they sparked.

The Foundation fleet edged slowly backwards. Hours passed and the fleet veered slowly off, teasing the advancing enemy slightly off course, then more so.

In the minds of the dictators of the battle plan, there was a certain volume of space that must be occupied by the Kalganian ships. Out from that volume crept the Foundationers; into it slipped the Kalganians. Those that passed out again were attacked, suddenly and fiercely. Those that stayed within were not touched.

It all depended on the reluctance of the ships of Lord Stettin to take the initiative themselves—on their willingness to remain where none attacked.

Captain Dixyl stared frigidly at his wrist watch. It was 1310. "We've got twenty minutes," he said.

The lieutenant at his side nodded tensely, "It looks all right so far, captain. We've got more than ninety percent of them boxed. If we can keep them that way—"

"Yes! If—"

The Foundation ships were drifting forward again—very slowly. Not quick enough to urge a Kalganian retreat and just quickly enough to discourage a Kalganian advance. They preferred to wait.

And the minutes passed.

At 1325, the admiral's buzzer sounded in seventy-five ships of the Foundation's line, and they built up to a maximum acceleration towards the front-plane of the Kalganian fleet, itself three hundred strong. Kalganian shields flared into action, and the vast energy beams flicked out. Every one of the three hundred concentrated in the same direction, towards their mad attackers who bore down relentlessly, uncaringly and—

At 1330, fifty ships under Commander Cenn appeared from nowhere, in one single bound through hyperspace to a calculated spot at a calculated time—and were spaced in tearing fury at the unprepared Kalganian rear.

The trap worked perfectly.

The Kalganians still had numbers on their side, but they were in no mood to count. Their first effort was to escape and the formation once broken was only the more vulnerable, as the enemy ships bumbled into one another's path.

After a while, it took on the proportions of a rat hunt.

Of three hundred Kalganian ships, the core and pride of their

fleet, some sixty or less, many in a state of near-hopeless disre-
pair, reached Kalgan once more. The Foundation loss was eight
ships out of a total of one hundred twenty-five.

Preem Palver landed on Terminus at the height of the celebration. He found the furore distracting, but before he left the
planet, he had accomplished two things, and received one request.

The two things accomplished were: 1) the conclusion of an
agreement whereby Palver's co-operative was to deliver twenty
shiploads of certain foodstuffs per month for the next year at a
war price, without, thanks to the recent battle, a corresponding
war risk, and 2) the transfer to Dr. Darell of Arcadia's five short
words.

For a startled moment, Darell had stared wide-eyed at him,
and then he had made his request. It was to carry an answer
back to Arcadia. Palver liked it; it was a simple answer and made
sense. It was: "Come back now. There won't be any danger."

Lord Stettin was in raging frustration. To watch his every
weapon break in his hands; to feel the firm fabric of his military
might part like the rotten thread it suddenly turned out to be—
would have turned phlegmaticism itself into flowing lava. And
yet he was helpless, and knew it.

He hadn't really slept well in weeks. He hadn't shaved in three
days. He had canceled all audiences. His admirals were left to
themselves and none knew better than the Lord of Kalgan that
very little time and no further defeats need elapse before he
would have to contend with internal rebellion.

Lev Meirus, First Minister, was no help. He stood there, calm
and indecently old, with his thin, nervous finger stroking, as always, the wrinkled line from nose to chin.

"Well," shouted Stettin at him, "contribute something. We
stand here defeated, do you understand? *Defeated!* And why? I
don't know why. There you have it. I don't know why. Do *you*
know why?"

"I think so," said Meirus, calmly.

"Treason!" The word came out softly, and other words followed as softly. "You've known of treason, and you've kept quiet. You served the fool I ejected from the First Citizenship and you think you can serve whatever foul rat replaces me. If you have acted so, I will extract your entrails for it and burn them before your living eyes."

Meirus was unmoved. "I have tried to fill you with my own doubts, not once, but many times. I have dinned it in your ears and you have preferred the advice of others because it stuffed your ego better. Matters have turned out not as I feared, but even worse. If you do not care to listen now, say so, sir, and I shall leave, and, in due course, deal with your successor, whose first act, no doubt, will be to sign a treaty of peace."

Stettin stared at him red-eyed, enormous fists slowly clenching and unclenching. "Speak, you gray slug. *Speak!*"

"I have told you often, sir, that you are not the Mule. You may control ships and guns but you cannot control the minds of your subjects. Are you aware, sir, of who it is you are fighting? You fight the Foundation, which is never defeated—the Foundation, which is protected by the Seldon Plan—the Foundation, which is destined to form a new Empire."

"There is no Plan. No longer. Munn has said so."

"Then Munn is wrong. And if he were right, what then? You and I, sir, are not the people. The men and women of Kalgan and its subject worlds believe utterly and deeply in the Seldon Plan as do all the inhabitants of this end of the Galaxy. Nearly four hundred years of history teach the fact that the Foundation cannot be beaten. Neither the kingdoms nor the warlords nor the old Galactic Empire itself could do it."

"The Mule did it."

"Exactly, and he was beyond calculation—and you are not. What is worse, the people know that you are not. So your ships go into battle fearing defeat in some unknown way. The insubstantial fabric of the Plan hangs over them so that they are cautious and look before they attack and wonder a little too much. While on the other side, that same insubstantial fabric fills the enemy with confidence, removes fear, maintains morale in the face of early defeats. Why not? The Foundation has always been defeated at first and has always won in the end.

"And your own morale, sir? You stand everywhere on enemy territory. Your own dominions have not been invaded; are still not in danger of invasion—yet you are defeated. You don't believe in the possibility, even, of victory, because you know there is none.

"Stoop, then, or you will be beaten to your knees. Stoop voluntarily, and you may save a remnant. You have depended on metal and power and they have sustained you as far as they could. You have ignored mind and morale and they have failed you. Now, take my advice. You have the Foundation man, Homir Munn. Release him. Send him back to Terminus and he will carry your peace offers."

Stettin's teeth ground behind his pale, set lips. But what choice had he?

On the first day of the new year, Homir Munn left Kalgan again. More than six months had passed since he had left Terminus and in the interim, a war had raged and faded.

He had come alone, but he left escorted. He had come a simple man of private life; he left the unappointed but nevertheless, actual, ambassador of peace.

And what had most changed was his early concern over the Second Foundation. He laughed at the thought of that: and pictured in luxuriant detail the final revelation to Dr. Darell, to that energetic, young competent, Anthor, to all of them—

He knew. He, Homir Munn, finally knew the truth.

20

"I Know . . ."

The last two months of the Stettinian war did not lag for Homir. In his unusual office as Mediator Extraordinary, he found himself the center of interstellar affairs, a role he could not help but find pleasing.

There were no further major battles—a few accidental skirmishes that could scarcely count—and the terms of the treaty were hammered out with little necessity for concessions on the part of the Foundation. Stettin retained his office, but scarcely anything else. His navy was dismantled; his possessions outside the home system itself made autonomous and allowed to vote for return to previous status, full independence or confederation within the Foundation, as they chose.

The war was formally ended on an asteroid in Terminus' own stellar system; site of the Foundation's oldest naval base. Lev Meirus signed for Kalgan, and Homir was an interested spectator.

Throughout all that period he did not see Dr. Darell, nor any of the others. But it scarcely mattered. His news would keep—and, as always, he smiled at the thought.

Dr. Darell returned to Terminus some weeks after VK day, and that same evening, his house served as the meeting place for the five men who, ten months earlier, had laid their first plans.

They lingered over dinner and then over wine as though hesitating to return again to the old subject.

It was Jole Turbor, who, peering steadily into the purple depths of the wineglass with one eye, muttered, rather than said, "Well, Homir, you are a man of affairs now, I see. You handled matters well."

"I?" Munn laughed loudly and joyously. For some reason, he had not stuttered in months. "I hadn't a thing to do with it. It was Arcadia. By the by, Darell, how is she? She's coming back from Trantor, I heard?"

"You heard correctly," said Darell, quietly. "Her ship should dock within the week." He looked, with veiled eyes, at the others, but there were only confused, amorphous exclamations of pleasure. Nothing else.

Turbor said, "Then it's over, really. Who would have predicted all this ten months ago. Munn's been to Kalgan and back. Arcadia's been to Kalgan and Trantor and is coming back. We've had a war and won it, by Space. They tell you that the vast sweeps of history can be predicted, but doesn't it seem conceivable that all that has just happened, with its absolute confusion to those of us who lived through it, couldn't possibly have been predicted."

"Nonsense," said Anthor, acidly. "What makes you so triumphant, anyway? You talk as though we have really won a war, when actually we have won nothing but a petty brawl which has served only to distract our minds from the real enemy."

There was an uncomfortable silence, in which only Homir Munn's slight smile struck a discordant note.

And Anthor struck the arm of his chair with a balled and fury-filled fist, "Yes, I refer to the Second Foundation. There is no mention of it and, if I judge correctly, every effort to have no thought of it. Is it because this fallacious atmosphere of victory that palls over this world of idiots is so attractive that you feel you must participate? Turn somersaults then, handspring your way into a wall, pound one another's back and throw confetti out the window. Do whatever you please, only get it out of your system—and when you are quite done and you are yourselves again, return and let us discuss that problem which exists now precisely as it did ten months ago when you sat here with eyes cocked over your shoulders for fear of you knew not what. Do you really think that the Mind-masters of the Second Foundation are less to be feared because you have beat down a foolish wielder of spaceships."

He paused, red-faced and panting.

Munn said quietly, "Will you hear *me* speak now, Anthor? Or do you prefer to continue your role as ranting conspirator?"

"Have your say, Homir," said Darell, "but let's all of us refrain from over-picturesqueness of language. It's a very good thing in its place, but at present, it bores me."

Homir Munn leaned back in his armchair and carefully refilled his glass from the decanter at his elbow.

"I was sent to Kalgan," he said, "to find out what I could from the records contained in the Mule's Palace. I spent several months doing so. I seek no credit for that accomplishment. As I have indicated, it was Arcadia whose ingenuous intermeddling obtained the entry for me. Nevertheless, the fact remains that to my original knowledge of the Mule's life and times, which, I submit, was not small, I have added the fruits of much labor among primary evidence which has been available to no one else.

"I am, therefore, in a unique position to estimate the true danger of the Second Foundation; much more so than is our excitable friend here."

"And," grated Anthor, "what is your estimate of that danger?"

"Why, zero."

A short pause, and Elvett Semic asked with an air of surprised disbelief, "You mean zero danger?"

"Certainly. Friends, *there is no Second Foundation!*"

Anthor's eyelids closed slowly and he sat there, face pale and expressionless.

Munn continued, attention-centering and loving it, "And what is more, there was never one."

"On what," asked Darell, "do you base this surprising conclusion?"

"I deny," said Munn, "that it is surprising. You all know the story of the Mule's search for the Second Foundation. But what do you know of the intensity of that search—of the single-mindedness of it. He had tremendous resources at his disposal and he spared none of it. He was single-minded—and yet he failed. No Second Foundation was found."

"One could scarcely expect it to be found," pointed out Turbor, restlessly. "It had means of protecting itself against inquiring minds."

"Even when the mind that is inquiring is the Mule's mutant mentality? I think not. But come, you do not expect me to give you the gist of fifty volumes of reports in five minutes. All of it, by the terms of the peace treaty will be part of the Seldon Historical Museum eventually, and you will all be free to be as leisurely in your analysis as I have been. You will find his conclusion plainly stated, however, and that I have already expressed. There is not, and has never been, any Second Foundation."

Semic interposed, "Well, what stopped the Mule, then?"

"Great Galaxy, what *do* you suppose stopped him? Death did; as it will stop all of us. The greatest superstition of the age is that the Mule was somehow stopped in an all-conquering career by some mysterious entities superior even to himself. It is the result of looking at everything in wrong focus.

"Certainly no one in the Galaxy can help knowing that the Mule was a freak, physical as well as mental. He died in his thirties because his ill-adjusted body could no longer struggle its creaking machinery along. For several years before his death he was an invalid. His best health was never more than an ordinary man's feebleness. All right, then. He conquered the Galaxy and, in the ordinary course of nature, proceeded to die. It's a wonder he proceeded as long and as well as he did. Friends, it's down in the very clearest print. You have only to have patience. You have only to try to look at all facts in new focus."

Darell said, thoughtfully, "Good, let us try that, Munn. It would be an interesting attempt and, if nothing else, would help oil our thoughts. These tampered men—the records of which Anthor brought to us nearly a year ago, what of them? Help us to see them in focus."

"Easily. How old a science is encephalographic analysis? Or, put it another way, how well-developed is the study of neuronic pathways."

"We are at the beginning in this respect. Granted," said Darell.

"Right. How certain can we be then as to the interpretation of what I've heard Anthor and yourself call the Tamper Plateau. You have your theories, but how certain can you be. Certain enough to consider it a firm basis for the existence of a mighty force for which all other evidence is negative? It's always easy to explain the unknown by postulating a superhuman and arbitrary will.

"It's a very human phenomenon. There have been cases all through Galactic history where isolated planetary systems have reverted to savagery, and what have we learned there? In every case, such savages attribute the to-them-incomprehensible forces of Nature—storms, pestilences, droughts—to sentient beings more powerful and more arbitrary than men.

"It is called anthropomorphism, I believe, and in this respect, we are savages and indulge in it. Knowing little of mental science, we blame anything we don't know on supermen—those of the Second Foundation in this case, based on the hint thrown us by Seldon."

"Oh," broke in Anthor, "then you *do* remember Seldon. I thought you had forgotten. Seldon did say there was a Second Foundation. Get *that* in focus."

"And are *you* aware then of all Seldon's purposes. Do you know what necessities were involved in his calculations? The Second Foundation may have been a very necessary scarecrow, with a highly specific end in view. How did we defeat Kalgan, for instance? What were you saying in your last series of articles, Turbor?"

Turbor stirred his bulk. "Yes, I see what you're driving at. I was on Kalgan towards the end, Darell, and it was quite obvious that morale on the planet was incredibly bad. I looked through their news-records and—well, they expected to be beaten. Actually, they were completely unmanned by the thought that eventually the Second Foundation would take a hand, on the side of the First, naturally."

"Quite right," said Munn. "I was there all through the war. I told Stettin there was no Second Foundation and he believed me. *He* felt safe. But there was no way of making the people suddenly disbelieve what they had believed all their lives, so that the myth eventually served a very useful purpose in Seldon's cosmic chess game."

But Anthor's eyes opened, quite suddenly, and fixed themselves sardonically on Munn's countenance. "*I say you lie.*"

Homir turned pale, "I don't see that I have to accept, much less answer, an accusation of that nature."

"I say it without any intention of personal offense. You cannot help lying; you don't realize that you are. But you lie just the same."

Semic laid his withered hand on the young man's sleeve. "Take a breath, young fella."

Anthor shook him off, none too gently, and said, "I'm out of patience with all of you. I haven't seen this man more than half a dozen times in my life, yet I find the change in him unbelievable. The rest of you have known him for years, yet pass it by. It is enough to drive one mad. Do you call this man you've been listening to Homir Munn? He is not the Homir Munn *I* knew."

A medley of shock; above which Munn's voice cried, "You claim me to be an impostor?"

"Perhaps not in the ordinary sense," shouted Anthor above the din, "but an impostor nonetheless. Quiet, everyone! I demand to be heard."

He frowned them ferociously into obedience. "Do any of you remember Homir Munn as I do—the introverted librarian who never talked without obvious embarrassment; the man of tense and nervous voice, who stuttered out his uncertain sentences? Does *this* man sound like him? He's fluent, he's confident, he's full of theories, and, by Space, he doesn't stutter. *Is* he the same person?"

Even Munn looked confused, and Pelleas Anthor drove on. "Well, shall we test him?"

"How?" asked Darell.

"*You* ask how? There is the obvious way. You have his encephalographic record of ten months ago, haven't you? Run one again, and compare."

He pointed at the frowning librarian, and said violently, "I dare him to refuse to subject himself to analysis."

"I don't object," said Munn, defiantly. "I am the man I always was."

"Can *you* know?" said Anthor with contempt. "I'll go further. I trust no one here. I want everyone to undergo analysis. There has been a war. Munn has been on Kalgan; Turbor has been on board ship and all over the war areas. Darell and Semic have been absent, too— I have no idea where. Only I have remained here in seclusion and safety, and I no longer trust any of the rest of you. And to play fair, I'll submit to testing as well. Are we agreed then? Or do I leave now and go my own way?"

Turbor shrugged and said, "I have no objection."

"I have already said I don't," said Munn.

Semic moved a hand in silent assent, and Anthor waited for Darell. Finally, Darell nodded his head.

"Take me first," said Anthor.

The needles traced their delicate way across the cross-hatchings as the young neurologist sat frozen in the reclining seat, with lidded eyes brooding heavily. From the files, Darell removed the folder containing Anthor's old encephalographic record. He showed them to Anthor.

"That's your own signature, isn't it?"

"Yes, yes. It's my record. Make the comparison."

The scanner threw old and new on to the screen. All six curves in each recording were there, and in the darkness, Munn's voice sounded in harsh clarity. "Well, now, look there. There's a change."

"Those are the primary waves of the frontal lobe. It doesn't mean a thing, Homir. Those additional jags you're pointing to are just anger. It's the others that count."

He touched a control knob and the six pairs melted into one another and coincided. The deeper amplitude of primaries alone introduced doubling.

"Satisfied?" asked Anthor.

Darell nodded curtly and took the seat himself. Semic followed him and Turbor followed him. Silently the curves were collected; silently they were compared.

Munn was the last to take his seat. For a moment, he hesitated, then, with a touch of desperation in his voice, he said, "Well now, look, I'm coming in last and I'm under tension. I expect due allowance to be made for that."

"There will be," Darell assured him. "No conscious emotion of yours will affect more than the primaries and they are not important."

It might have been hours, in the utter silence that followed—

And then in the darkness of the comparison, Anthor said huskily: "Sure, sure, it's only the onset of a complex. Isn't that what he told us? No such thing as tampering; it's all a silly anthropomorphic notion—but look at it! A coincidence I suppose."

"What's the matter?" shrieked Munn.

Darell's hand was tight on the librarian's shoulder. "Quiet, Munn—you've been handled; you've been adjusted by *them*."

Then the light went on, and Munn was looking about him with broken eyes, making a horrible attempt to smile.

"You can't be serious, surely. There is a purpose to this. You're testing me."

But Darell only shook his head. "No, no, Homir. It's true."

The librarian's eyes were filled with tears, suddenly. "I don't feel any different. I can't believe it." With sudden conviction: "You are all in this. It's a conspiracy."

Darell attempted a soothing gesture, and his hand was struck aside. Munn snarled, "You're planning to kill me. By Space, you're planning to kill me."

With a lunge, Anthor was upon him. There was the sharp crack of bone against bone, and Homir was limp and flaccid with that look of fear frozen on his face.

Anthor rose shakily, and said, "We'd better tie and gag him. Later, we can decide what to do." He brushed his long hair back.

Turbor said, "How did you guess there was something wrong with him?"

Anthor turned sardonically upon him. "It wasn't difficult. You see, *I happen to know where the Second Foundation really is*."

Successive shocks have a decreasing effect—

It was with actual mildness that Semic asked, "Are you sure? I mean we've just gone through this sort of business with Munn—"

"This isn't quite the same," returned Anthor. "Darell, the day the war started, I spoke to you most seriously. I tried to have you leave Terminus. I would have told you then what I will tell you now, if I had been able to trust you."

"You mean you have known the answer for half a year?" smiled Darell.

"I have known it from the time I learned that Arcadia had left for Trantor."

And Darell started to his feet in sudden consternation. "What had Arcadia to do with it? What are you implying?"

"Absolutely nothing that is not plain on the face of all the events we know so well. Arcadia goes to Kalgan and flees in terror to the *very* center of the Galaxy, rather than return home. Lieutenant Dirige, our best agent on Kalgan is tampered with. Homir Munn goes to Kalgan and *he* is tampered with. The Mule conquered the Galaxy, but, queerly enough, he made Kalgan his headquarters, and it occurs to me to wonder if he was conqueror or, perhaps, tool. At every turn, we meet with Kalgan, Kalgan— nothing but Kalgan, the world that somehow survived untouched all the struggles of the warlords for over a century."

"Your conclusion, then."

"Is obvious," Anthor's eyes were intense. "The Second Foundation is on Kalgan."

Turbor interrupted. "I was on Kalgan, Anthor. I was there last week. If there was any Second Foundation on it, I'm mad. Personally, I think you're mad."

The young man whirled on him savagely. "Then you're a fat fool. What do you expect the Second Foundation to be? A grammar school? Do you think that Radiant Fields in tight beams spell out 'Second Foundation' in green and purple along the incoming spaceship routes? Listen to *me*, Turbor. Wherever they are, they form a tight oligarchy. They must be as well hidden on the world on which they exist, as the world itself is in the Galaxy as a whole."

Turbor's jaw muscles writhed. "I don't like your attitude, Anthor."

"That certainly disturbs me," was the sarcastic response. "Take a look about you here on Terminus. We're at the center—the core —the origin of the First Foundation with all its knowledge of physical science. Well, how many of the population are physical scientists? Can *you* operate an Energy Transmitting Station? What do *you* know of the operation of a hyperatomic motor? Eh? The number of real scientists on Terminus—even on Terminus —can be numbered at less than one percent of the population.

"And what then of the Second Foundation where secrecy must be preserved. There will still be less of the cognoscenti, and these will be hidden even from their own world."

"Say," said Semic, carefully. "We just licked Kalgan—"

"So we did. So we did," said Anthor, sardonically. "Oh, we celebrate that victory. The cities are still illuminated; they are still shooting off fireworks; they are still shouting over the televisors. But now, *now*, when the search is on once more for the Second Foundation, where is the last place we'll look; where is the last place anyone will look? Right! Kalgan!

"We haven't hurt them, you know; not really. We've destroyed some ships, killed a few thousands, torn away their Empire, taken over some of their commercial and economic power—but that all means nothing. I'll wager that not one member of the real ruling class of Kalgan is in the least discomfited. On the contrary, they are now safe from curiosity. But not from *my* curiosity. What do you say, Darell?"

Darell shrugged his shoulders. "Interesting. I'm trying to fit it in with a message I received from Arcadia a few months since."

"Oh, a message?" asked Anthor. "And what was it?"

"Well, I'm not certain. Five short words. But it's interesting."

"Look," broke in Semic, with a worried interest, "there's something *I* don't understand."

"What's that?"

Semic chose his words carefully, his old upper lip lifting with each word as if to let them out singly and reluctantly. "Well, now, Homir Munn was saying just a while ago that Hari Seldon was faking when he said that he had established a Second Foundation. Now you're saying that it's not so; that Seldon wasn't faking, eh?"

"Right, he wasn't faking. Seldon said he had established a Second Foundation and so he had."

"All right, then, but he said something else, too. He said he established the two Foundations at opposite ends of the Galaxy. Now, young man, was *that* a fake—because Kalgan isn't at the opposite end of the Galaxy."

Anthor seemed annoyed, "That's a minor point. That part may well have been a cover up to protect them. But after all, think— What real use would it serve to have the Mind-masters at the opposite end of the Galaxy? What is their function? To help preserve the Plan. Who are the main card players of the Plan? We, the First Foundation. Where can they best observe us, then, and serve their own ends? At the opposite end of the Galaxy? Ridiculous! They're within fifty parsecs, actually, which is much more sensible."

"I like that argument," said Darell. "It makes sense. Look here, Munn's been conscious for some time and I propose we loose him. He can't do any harm, really."

Anthor looked rebellious, but Homir was nodding vigorously. Five seconds later he was rubbing his wrists just as vigorously.

"How do you feel?" asked Darell.

"Rotten," said Munn, sulkily, "but never mind. There's something I want to ask this bright young thing here. I've heard what he's had to say, and I'd just like permission to wonder what we do next."

There was a queer and incongruous silence.

Munn smiled bitterly. "Well, suppose Kalgan *is* the Second Foundation. *Who* on Kalgan are they? How are you going to find them? How are you going to tackle them *if* you find them, eh?"

"Ah," said Darell, "I can answer that, strangely enough. Shall I tell you what Semic and I have been doing this past half-year? It may give you another reason, Anthor, why I was anxious to remain on Terminus all this time."

"In the first place," he went on, "I've been working on encephalographic analysis with more purpose than any of you may suspect. Detecting Second Foundation minds is a little more subtle than simply finding a Tamper Plateau—and I did not actually succeed. But I came close enough.

"Do you know, any of you, how emotional control works? It's been a popular subject with fiction writers since the time of the Mule and much nonsense has been written, spoken, and recorded about it. For the most part, it has been treated as something mysterious and occult. Of course, it isn't. That the brain is the source of a myriad, tiny electromagnetic fields, everyone knows. Every fleeting emotion varies those fields in more or less intricate fashion, and everyone should know that, too.

"Now it is possible to conceive a mind which can sense these changing fields and even resonate with them. That is, a special organ of the cerebrum can exist which can take on whatever field-pattern it may detect. Exactly how it would do this, I have no idea, but that doesn't matter. If I were blind, for instance, I could still learn the significance of photons and energy quanta and it could be reasonable to me that the absorption of a photon of such energy could create chemical changes in some organ of the body such that its presence would be detectable. But, of course, I would not be able, thereby, to understand color.

"Do all of you follow?"

There was a firm nod from Anthor; a doubtful nod from the others.

"Such a hypothetical Mind Resonating Organ, by adjusting itself to the Fields emitted by other minds could perform what is popularly known as 'reading emotion,' or even 'reading minds,' which is actually something even more subtle. It is but an easy step from that to imagining a similar organ which could actually force an adjustment on another mind. It could orient with its stronger Field the weaker one of another mind—much as a strong magnet will orient the atomic dipoles in a bar of steel and leave it magnetized thereafter.

"I solved the mathematics of Second Foundationism in the sense that I evolved a function that would predict the necessary combination of neuronic paths that would allow for the formation of an organ such as I have just described—but, unfortunately, the function is too complicated to solve by any of the mathematical tools at present known. That is too bad, because it means that I can never detect a Mind-worker by his encephalographic pattern alone.

"But I could do something else. I could, with Semic's help, construct what I shall describe as a Mental Static device. It is not beyond the ability of modern science to create an energy source that will duplicate an encephalograph-type pattern of electromagnetic field. Moreover, it can be made to shift at complete random, creating, as far as this particular mind-sense is concerned, a sort of 'noise' or 'static' which masks other minds with which it may be in contact.

"Do you still follow?"

Semic chuckled. He had helped create blindly, but he had guessed, and guessed correctly. The old man had a trick or two left—

Anthor said, "I think I do."

"The device," continued Darell, "is a fairly easy one to produce, and I had all the resources of the Foundation under my control as it came under the heading of war research. And now the mayor's offices and the Legislative assemblies are surrounded with Mental Static. So are most of our key factories. So is this building. Eventually, any place we wish can be made absolutely safe from the Second Foundation or from any future Mule. And that's it."

He ended quite simply with a flat-palmed gesture of the hand.

Turbor seemed stunned. "Then it's all over. Great Seldon, it's all over."

"Well," said Darell, "not exactly."

"How, not exactly? Is there something more?"

"Yes, we haven't located the Second Foundation yet!"

"What," roared Anthor, "are you trying to say—"

"Yes, I am. Kalgan is not the Second Foundation."

"How do *you* know?"

"It's easy," grunted Darell. "You see *I happen to know where the Second Foundation really is.*"

21

The Answer That Satisfied

Turbor laughed suddenly—laughed in huge, windy gusts that bounced ringingly off the walls and died in gasps. He shook his head, weakly, and said, "Great Galaxy, this goes on all night. One after another, we put up our straw men to be knocked down. We have fun, but we don't get anywhere. Space! Maybe all planets are the Second Foundation. Maybe they have no planet, just key men spread on all the planets. And what does it matter, since Darell says we have the perfect defense?"

Darell smiled without humor. "The perfect defense is not enough, Turbor. Even my Mental Static device is only something that keeps us in the same place. We cannot remain forever with our fists doubled, frantically staring in all directions for the unknown enemy. We must know not only *how* to win, but whom to defeat. And there *is* a specific world on which the enemy exists."

"Get to the point," said Anthor, wearily. "What's your information?"

"Arcadia," said Darell, "sent me a message, and until I got it, I never saw the obvious. I probably would never have seen the obvious. Yet it was a simple message that went: 'A circle has no end.' Do you see?"

"No," said Anthor, stubbornly, and he spoke, quite obviously, for the others.

"A circle has no end," repeated Munn, thoughtfully, and his forehead furrowed.

"Well," said Darell, impatiently, "it was clear to me— What is the one absolute fact we know about the Second Foundation, eh? I'll tell you! We know that Hari Seldon located it at the opposite end of the Galaxy. Homir Munn theorized that Seldon lied about the existence of the Foundation. Pelleas Anthor theorized that Seldon had told the truth that far, but lied about the location of the Foundation. But I tell you that Hari Seldon lied in no particular; that he told the absolute truth.

"*But*, what is the other end? The Galaxy is a flat, lens-shaped object. A cross section along the flatness of it is a circle, and a circle had no end—as Arcadia realized. We—*we*, the First Foundation—are located on Terminus at the rim of that circle. We are at an end of the Galaxy, by definition. Now follow the rim of that circle and find the other end. Follow it, follow it, follow it, and you will find no other end. You will merely come back to your starting point—

"And *there* you will find the Second Foundation."

"There?" repeated Anthor. "Do you mean *here*?"

"Yes, I mean here!" cried Darell, energetically. "Why, where else could it possibly be? You said yourself that if the Second Foundationers were the guardians of the Seldon Plan, it was unlikely that they could be located at the so-called other end of the Galaxy, where they would be as isolated as they could conceivably be. You thought that fifty parsecs distance was more sensible. I tell you that that is also too far. That no distance at all is more sensible. And where would they be safest? Who would look for them here? Oh, it's the old principle of the most obvious place being the least suspicious.

"Why was poor Ebling Mis so surprised and unmanned by his discovery of the location of the Second Foundation? There he was, looking for·it desperately in order to warn it of the coming of the Mule, only to find that the Mule had already captured both Foundations at a stroke. And why did the Mule himself fail in his search? Why not? If one is searching for an unconquerable menace, one would scarcely look among the enemies already conquered. So the Mind-masters, in their own leisurely time, could lay their plans to stop the Mule, and succeeded in stopping him.

"Oh, it is maddeningly simple. For here *we* are with our plots and our schemes, thinking that we are keeping our secrecy— when all the time we are in the very heart and core of our enemy's stronghold. It's humorous."

Anthor did not remove the skepticism from his face, "You honestly believe this theory, Dr. Darell?"

"I honestly believe it."

"Then any of our neighbors, any man we pass in the street, might be a Second Foundation superman, with his mind watching yours and feeling the pulse of its thoughts."

"Exactly."

"And we have been permitted to proceed all this time, without molestation?"

"Without molestation? Who told you we were not molested? You, yourself, showed that Munn has been tampered with. What makes you think that we sent him to Kalgan in the first place entirely of our own volition—or that Arcadia overheard us and followed him on her own volition? Hah! We have been molested without pause, probably. And after all, why should they do more than they have? It is far more to their benefit to mislead us, than merely to stop us."

Anthor buried himself in meditation and emerged therefrom with a dissatisfied expression. "Well, then, I don't like it. Your Mental Static isn't worth a thought. We can't stay in the house forever and as soon as we leave, we're lost, with what we now think we know. Unless you can build a little machine for every inhabitant in the Galaxy."

"Yes, but we're not quite helpless, Anthor. These men of the Second Foundation have a special sense which we lack. It is their strength and also their weakness. For instance, is there any weapon of attack that will be effective against a normal, sighted man which is useless against a blind man?"

"Sure," said Munn, promptly. "A light in the eyes."

"Exactly," said Darell. "A good, strong blinding light."

"Well, what of it?" asked Turbor.

"But the analogy is clear. I have a Mind Static device. It sets up an artificial electromagnetic pattern, which to the mind of a man of the Second Foundation would be like a beam of light to us. But the Mind Static device is kaleidoscopic. It shifts quickly and continuously, faster than the receiving mind can follow. All right, then, consider it a flickering light; the kind that would give you a headache, if continued long enough. Now intensify that light or that electromagnetic field until it is blinding—and it will become a pain, an unendurable pain. But only to those with the proper sense; *not* to the unsensed."

"Really?" said Anthor, with the beginnings of enthusiasm. "Have you tried this?"

"On whom? Of course, I haven't tried it. But it will work."

"Well, where do you have the controls for the Field that surrounds the house? I'd like to see this thing."

"Here." Darell reached into his jacket pocket. It was a small thing, scarcely bulging his pocket. He tossed the black, knob-studded cylinder to the other.

Anthor inspected it carefully and shrugged his shoulders. "It doesn't make me any smarter to look at it. Look Darell, what mustn't I touch? I don't want to turn off the house defense by accident, you know."

"You won't," said Darell, indifferently. "That control is locked in place." He flicked at a toggle switch that didn't move.

"And what's this knob?"

"That one varies rate of shift of pattern. Here—this one varies the intensity. It's that which I've been referring to."

"May I—" asked Anthor, with his finger on the intensity knob. The others were crowding close.

"Why not?" shrugged Darell. "It won't affect us."

Slowly, almost wincingly, Anthor turned the knob, first in one direction, then in another. Turbor was gritting his teeth, while Munn blinked his eyes rapidly. It was as though they were keening their inadequate sensory equipment to locate this impulse which could not affect them.

Finally, Anthor shrugged and tossed the control box back into Darell's lap. "Well, I suppose we can take your word for it. But it's certainly hard to imagine that anything was happening when I turned the knob."

"But naturally, Pelleas Anthor," said Darell, with a tight smile. "The one I gave you was a dummy. You see I have another." He tossed his jacket aside and seized a duplicate of the control box that Anthor had been investigating, which swung from his belt.

"You see," said Darell, and in one gesture turned the intensity knob to maximum.

And with an unearthly shriek, Pelleas Anthor sank to the floor. He rolled in his agony; whitened, gripping fingers clutching and tearing futilely at his hair.

Munn lifted his feet hastily to prevent contact with the squirming body, and his eyes were twin depths of horror. Semic and Turbor were a pair of plaster casts; stiff and white.

Darell, somber, turned the knob back once more. And Anthor twitched feebly once or twice and lay still. He was alive, his breath racking his body.

"Lift him on to the couch," said Darell, grasping the young man's head. "Help me here."

Turbor reached for the feet. They might have been lifting a sack of flour. Then, after long minutes, the breathing grew quieter, and Anthor's eyelids fluttered and lifted. His face was a horrid yellow; his hair and body was soaked in perspiration, and his voice, when he spoke, was cracked and unrecognizable.

"Don't," he muttered, "don't! Don't do that again! You don't know— You don't know— Oh-h-h." It was a long, trembling moan.

"We won't do it again," said Darell, "if you will tell us the truth. You are a member of the Second Foundation?"

"Let me have some water," pleaded Anthor.

"Get some, Turbor," said Darell, "and bring the whiskey bottle."

He repeated the question after pouring a jigger of whiskey and two glasses of water into Anthor. Something seemed to relax in the young man—

"Yes," he said, wearily. "I am a member of the Second Foundation."

"Which," continued Darell, "is located on Terminus—here?"

"Yes, yes. You are right in every particular, Dr. Darell."

"Good! Now explain what's been happening this past half year. Tell us!"

"I would like to sleep," whispered Anthor.

"Later! Speak now!"

A tremulous sigh. Then words, low and hurried. The others

bent over him to catch the sound, "The situation was growing dangerous. We knew that Terminus and its physical scientists were becoming interested in brain-wave patterns and that the times were ripe for the development of something like the Mind Static device. And there was growing enmity toward the Second Foundation. We had to stop it without ruining Seldon's Plan.

"We . . . we tried to control the movement. We tried to join it. It would turn suspicion and efforts away from us. We saw to it that Kalgan declared war as a further distraction. That's why I sent Munn to Kalgan. Stettin's supposed mistress was one of us. She saw to it that Munn made the proper moves—"

"Callia is—" cried Munn, but Darell waved him silent.

Anthor continued, unaware of any interruption, "Arcadia followed. We hadn't counted on that—can't foresee everything—so Callia maneuvered her to Trantor to prevent interference. That's all. Except that we lost."

"You tried to get me to go to Trantor, didn't you?" asked Darell.

Anthor nodded, "Had to get you out of the way. The growing triumph in your mind was clear enough. You were solving the problems of the Mind Static device."

"Why didn't you put me under control?"

"Couldn't . . . couldn't. Had my orders. We were working according to a Plan. If I improvised, I would have thrown everything off. Plan only predicts probabilities . . . you know that . . . like Seldon's Plan." He was talking in anguished pants, and almost incoherently. His head twisted from side to side in a restless fever. "We worked with individuals . . . not groups . . . very low probabilities involved . . . lost out. Besides . . . if control you . . . someone else invent device . . . no use . . . had to control *times* . . . more subtle . . . First Speaker's own plan . . . don't know all angles . . . except . . . didn't work a-a-a—" He ran down.

Darell shook him roughly, "You can't sleep yet. How many of you are there?"

"Huh? Whatjasay . . . oh . . . not many . . . be surprised . . . fifty . . . don't need more."

"All here on Terminus?"

"Five . . . six out in Space . . . like Callia . . . got to sleep."

He stirred himself suddenly as though to one giant effort, and his expressions gained in clarity. It was a last attempt at self-justification, at moderating his defeat.

"Almost got you at the end. Would have turned off defenses and seized you. Would have seen who was master. But you gave me dummy controls . . . suspected me all along—"

And finally he was asleep.

Turbor said, in awed tones, "How long did you suspect him, Darell?"

"Ever since he first came here," was the quiet response. "He came from Kleise, he said. But I knew Kleise; and I knew on what terms we parted. He was a fanatic on the subject of the Second Foundation and I had deserted him. My own purposes were reasonable, since I thought it best and safest to pursue my own notions by myself. But I couldn't tell Kleise that; and he wouldn't have listened if I had. To him, I was a coward and a traitor, perhaps even an agent of the Second Foundation. He was an unforgiving man and from that time almost to the day of his death he had no dealings with me. Then, suddenly, in his last few weeks of life, he writes me—as an old friend—to greet his best and most promising pupil as a co-worker and begin again the old investigation.

"It was out of character. How could he possibly do such a thing without being under outside influence, and I began to wonder if the only purpose might not be to introduce into my confidence a real agent of the Second Foundation. Well, it was so—"

He sighed and closed his own eyes for a moment.

Semic put in hesitantly, "What will we do with all of them . . . these Second Foundation fellas?"

"I don't know," said Darell, sadly. "We could exile them, I suppose. There's Zoranel, for instance. They can be placed there and the planet saturated with Mind Static. The sexes can be separated, or, better still, they can be sterilized—and in fifty years, the Second Foundation will be a thing of the past. Or perhaps a quiet death for all of them would be kinder."

"Do you suppose," said Turbor, "we could learn the use of this sense of theirs. Or are they born with it, like the Mule."

"I don't know. I think it is developed through long training, since there are indications from encephalography that the potentialities of it are latent in the human mind. But what do you want that sense for? It hasn't helped *them*."

He frowned.

Though he said nothing, his thoughts were shouting.

It had been too easy—too easy. They had fallen, these invincibles, fallen like book-villains, and he didn't like it.

Galaxy! When can a man know he is not a puppet? *How* can a man know he is not a puppet?

Arcadia was coming home, and his thoughts shuddered away from that which he must face in the end.

She was home for a week, then two, and he could not loose the tight check upon those thoughts. How could he? She had changed from child to young woman in her absence, by some strange alchemy. She was his link to life; his link to a bittersweet marriage that scarcely outlasted his honeymoon.

And then, late one evening, he said as casually as he could, "Arcadia, what made you decide that Terminus contained both Foundations?"

They had been to the theater; in the best seats with private trimensional viewers for each; her dress was new for the occasion, and she was happy.

She stared at him for a moment, then tossed it off. "Oh, I don't know, Father. It just came to me."

A layer of ice thickened about Dr. Darell's heart.

"Think," he said, intensely. "This is important. What made you decide both Foundations were on Terminus."

She frowned slightly. "Well, there was Lady Callia. I knew *she* was a Second Foundationer. Anthor said so, too."

"But she was on Kalgan," insisted Darell. "*What made you decide on Terminus?*"

And now Arcadia waited for several minutes before she answered. What *had* made her decide? What had made her decide?

She had the horrible sensation of something slipping just beyond her grasp.

She said, "She knew about things—Lady Callia did—and must have had her information from Terminus. Doesn't that sound right, Father?"

But he just shook his head at her.

"Father," she cried, "I *knew*. The more I thought, the surer I was. It just made *sense*."

There was that lost look in her father's eyes, "It's no good, Arcadia. It's no good. Intuition is suspicious when concerned with the Second Foundation. You see that, don't you? It *might* have been intuition—and it might have been control!"

"Control! You mean they changed me? Oh, no. No, they couldn't." She was backing away from him. "But didn't Anthor say I was right? He admitted it. He admitted everything. And you've found the whole bunch right here on Terminus? Didn't you? Didn't you?" She was breathing quickly.

"I know, but— Arcadia, will you let me make an encephalographic analysis of your brain?"

She shook her head violently, "No, no! I'm too scared."

"Of me, Arcadia? There's nothing to be afraid of. But we must know. You see that, don't you?"

She interrupted him only once, after that. She clutched at his arm just before the last switch was thrown. "What if I *am* different, Father? What will you have to do?"

"I won't have to do anything, Arcadia. If you're different, we'll leave. We'll go back to Trantor, you and I, and . . . and we won't care about anything else in the Galaxy."

Never in Darell's life had an analysis proceeded so slowly, cost him so much, and when it was over, Arcadia huddled down and dared not look. Then she heard him laugh and that was information enough. She jumped up and threw herself into his opened arms.

He was babbling wildly as they squeezed one another, "The house is under maximum Mind Static and your brain-waves are normal. We really have trapped them, Arcadia, and we can go back to living."

"Father," she gasped, "can we let them give us medals now?"

"How did you know I'd asked to be left out of it?" He held her at arm's length for a moment, then laughed again. "Never mind; you know everything. All right, you can have your medal on a platform, with speeches."

"And Father?"

"Yes?"

"Can you call me Arkady from now on."

"But— Very well, Arkady."

Slowly the magnitude of the victory was soaking into him and saturating him. The Foundation—the First Foundation—now the only Foundation—was absolute master of the Galaxy. No further barrier stood between themselves and the Second Empire—the final fulfillment of Seldon's Plan.

They had only to reach for it—

Thanks to—

22

The Answer That Was True

An unlocated room on an unlocated world!

And a man whose plan had worked.

The First Speaker looked up at the Student, "Fifty men and women," he said. "Fifty martyrs! They knew it meant death or permanent imprisonment and they could not even be oriented to prevent weakening—since orientation might have been detected. Yet they did not weaken. They brought the plan through, because they loved the greater Plan."

"Might they have been fewer?" asked the Student, doubtfully.

The First Speaker slowly shook his head, "It was the lower limit. Less could not possibly have carried conviction. In fact, pure objectivism would have demanded seventy-five to leave margin for error. Never mind. Have you studied the course of action as worked out by the Speakers' Council fifteen years ago?"

"Yes, Speaker."

"And compared it with actual developments?"

"Yes, Speaker." Then, after a pause—

"I was quite amazed, Speaker."

"I know. There is always amazement. If you knew how many men labored for how many months—years, in fact—to bring about the polish of perfection, you would be less amazed. Now tell me what happened—in words. I want your translation of the mathematics."

"Yes, Speaker." The young man marshaled his thoughts. "Essentially, it was necessary for the men of the First Foundation to be thoroughly convinced that they had located *and destroyed* the Second Foundation. In that way, there would be reversion to the intended original. To all intents, Terminus would once again know nothing about us; include us in none of their calculations. We are hidden once more, and safe—at the cost of fifty men."

"And the purpose of the Kalganian war?"

"To show the Foundation that they could beat a physical enemy—to wipe out the damage done to their self-esteem and self-assuredness by the Mule."

"There you are insufficient in your analysis. Remember, the population of Terminus regarded us with distinct ambivalence. They hated and envied our supposed superiority; yet they relied on us implicitly for protection. If we had been 'destroyed' before the Kalganian war, it would have meant panic throughout the Foundation. They would then never have had the courage to stand up against Stettin, when he *then* attacked; and he would have. Only in the full flush of victory could the 'destruction' have taken place with minimum ill-effects. Even waiting a year, thereafter, might have meant a too-great cooling off spirit for success."

The Student nodded. "I see. Then the course of history will proceed without deviation in the direction indicated by the Plan."

"Unless," pointed out the First Speaker, "further accidents, unforeseen and individual, occur."

"And for that," said the Student, "*we* still exist. Except— Except— One facet of the present state of affairs worries me, Speaker. The First Foundation is left with the Mind Static device—a powerful weapon against us. That, at least, is not as it was before."

"A good point. But they have no one to use it against. It has become a sterile device; just as without the spur of our own menace against them, encephalographic analysis will become a sterile science. Other varieties of knowledge will once again bring more important and immediate returns. So this first generation of mental scientists among the First Foundation will also be the last —and, in a century, Mind Static will be a nearly forgotten item of the past."

"Well—" The Student was calculating mentally. "I suppose you're right."

"But what I want you most to realize, young man, for the sake of your future in the Council is the consideration given to the tiny intermeshings that were forced into our plan of the last decade and a half simply because we dealt with individuals. There was the manner in which Anthor had to create suspicion against himself in such a way that it would mature at the right time, but that was relatively simple.

"There was the manner in which the atmosphere was so manipulated that to no one on Terminus would it occur, prematurely, that Terminus itself might be the center they were seeking. That knowledge had to be supplied to the young girl, Arcadia, who would be heeded by no one but her own father. She had to be sent to Trantor, thereafter, to make certain that there would be no premature contact with her father. Those two were the two poles of a hyperatomic motor; each being inactive without the other. And the switch had to be thrown—contact had to be made—at just the right moment. I saw to that!

"And the final battle had to be handled properly. The Foundation's fleet had to be soaked in self-confidence, while the fleet of Kalgan made ready to run. I saw to that, also!"

Said the Student, "It seems to me, Speaker, that you . . . I mean, all of us . . . were counting on Dr. Darell not suspecting that Arcadia was our tool. According to *my* check on the calculations, there was something like a thirty percent probability that he *would* so suspect. What would have happened then?"

"We had taken care of that. What have you been taught about Tamper Plateaus? What are they? Certainly not evidence of the introduction of an emotional bias. That can be done without any chance of possible detection by the most refined conceivable encephalographic analysis. A consequence of Leffert's Theorem, you know. It is the removal, the cutting-out, of previous emotional bias, that shows. It *must* show.

"And, of course, Anthor made certain that Darell knew all about Tamper Plateaus.

"However— When can an individual be placed under Control without showing it? Where there is no previous emotional bias to remove. In other words, when the individual is a new-born infant with a blank slate of a mind. Arcadia Darell was such an infant here on Trantor fifteen years ago, when the first line was drawn into the structure of the plan. She will never know that she has been Controlled, and will be all the better for it, since her Control involved the development of a precocious and intelligent personality."

The First Speaker laughed shortly, "In a sense, it is the irony of it all that is most amazing. For four hundred years, so many men have been blinded by Seldon's words 'the other end of the Galaxy.' They have brought their own peculiar, physical-science thought to the problem, measuring off the other end with protractors and rulers, ending up eventually either at a point in the periphery one hundred eighty degrees around the rim of the Galaxy, or back at the original point.

"Yet our very greatest danger lay in the fact that there *was* a possible solution based on physical modes of thought. The Galaxy, you know, is not simply a flat ovoid of any sort; nor is the periphery a closed curve. Actually, it is a double spiral, with at least eighty percent of the inhabited planets on the Main Arm. Terminus is the extreme outer end of the spiral arm, and we are at the other—since, what is the opposite end of a spiral? Why, the center.

"But that is trifling. It is an accidental and irrelevant solution. The solution could have been reached immediately, if the questioners had but remembered that Hari Seldon was a *social* scientist, not a physical scientist and adjusted their thought processes accordingly. What *could* 'opposite ends' mean to a social scientist? Opposite ends on the map? Of course not. That's the mechanical interpretation only.

"The First Foundation was at the periphery, where the original Empire was weakest, where its civilizing influence was least, where its wealth and culture were most nearly absent. And where is the *social opposite end of the Galaxy?* Why, at the place where the original Empire was strongest, where its civilizing influence was most, where its wealth and culture were most strongly present.

"Here! At the center! At Trantor, capital of the Empire of Seldon's time.

"And it is so inevitable. Hari Seldon left the Second Foundation behind him to maintain, improve, and extend his work. That has been known, or guessed at, for fifty years. But where could that best be done? At Trantor, where Seldon's group had worked, and where the data of decades had been accumulated. And it was the purpose of the Second Foundation to protect the Plan against enemies. That, too, was known! And where was the source of greatest danger to Terminus and the Plan?

"Here! Here at Trantor, where the Empire dying though it was, could, for three centuries, still destroy the Foundation, if it could only have decided to do so.

"Then when Trantor fell and was sacked and utterly destroyed, a short century ago, *we* were naturally able to protect our headquarters, and, on all the planet, the Imperial Library and the grounds about it remained untouched. This was well-known to the Galaxy, but even that apparently overwhelming hint passed them by.

"It was here at Trantor that Ebling Mis discovered us; and here that we saw to it that he did not survive the discovery. To do so, it was necessary to arrange to have a normal Foundation girl defeat the tremendous mutant powers of the Mule. Surely, such a phenomenon might have attracted suspicion to the planet on which it happened— It was here that we first studied the Mule and planned his ultimate defeat. It was here that Arcadia was born and the train of events begun that led to the great return to the Seldon Plan.

"And all those flaws in our secrecy; those gaping holes; remained unnoticed because Seldon had spoken of 'the other end' in his way, and they had interpreted it in their way."

The First Speaker had long since stopped speaking to the Student. It was an exposition to himself, really, as he stood before the window, looking up at the incredible blaze of the firmament; at the huge Galaxy that was now safe forever.

"Hari Seldon called Trantor, 'Star's End,'" he whispered, "and why not that bit of poetic imagery. All the universe was once guided from this rock; all the apron strings of the stars led here.

'All roads lead to Trantor,' says the old proverb, and that is where all stars end.'"

Ten months earlier, the First Speaker had viewed those same crowding stars—nowhere as crowded as at the center of that huge cluster of matter Man calls the Galaxy—with misgivings; but now there was a somber satisfaction on the round and ruddy face of Preem Palver—First Speaker.